CRADLES OF THE NEW

Writings on Music 1951–1991

DONALD MITCHELL

Selected by
Christopher Palmer

Edited by
Mervyn Cooke

ff
faber and faber
LONDON · BOSTON

First published in 1995
by Faber and Faber Limited
3 Queen Square London WC1N 3AU

Typography by Agnesi Text Hadleigh
Typeset by Halcyon Type & Design Ipswich
Music examples typeset by Michael Durnin
Printed in England by Clays Ltd, St Ives plc

A CIP record for this book is available from the British Library.

ISBN 0-571-17424-8

2 4 6 8 10 9 7 5 3 1

To Edward W. Said

So here I am, in the middle way, having had twenty years –
Twenty years largely wasted, the years of *l'entre deux guerres* –
Trying to learn to use words, and every attempt
Is a wholly new start, and a different kind of failure
Because one has only learnt to get the better of words
For the thing one no longer has to say, or the way in which
One is no longer disposed to say it. And so each venture
Is a new beginning, a raid on the inarticulate
With shabby equipment always deteriorating
In the general mess of imprecision of feeling,
Undisciplined squads of emotion. And what there is to conquer
By strength and submission, has already been discovered
Once or twice, or several times, by men whom one cannot hope
To emulate – but there is no competition –
There is only the fight to recover what has been lost
And found and lost again and again: and now, under conditions
That seem unpropitious. But perhaps neither gain nor loss.
For us, there is only the trying.

T. S. Eliot
from *East Coker* (1940)

Contents

List of Illustrations

Part-titles

Plate sections

Thinking Like a Composer

Christopher Palmer

It must be some thirty years since I made my initial contact with Donald Mitchell. I was a schoolboy of sixteen or seventeen years of age, and I had just discovered Mahler – the First Symphony, to be precise. I shall never forget my first hearing of that dazzling moment in the first movement when, at the height of the development, the whole world of Nature seems to explode and blaze with trumpet and horn fanfares and trills (in that most brilliant of bright keys, A major); and I thrilled as never before to the sound of the great horn unison in the coda, so daringly naked, with the heavy brass chorale etched all round it ('alle Hörner stehen auf' – what a sense of theatre!).

I had to find out more about Mahler and his music. Now this was in the days quite a long time before the great Mahler boom, when he was regarded as very much a minority interest. In a provincial town like Norwich recordings of his music were very difficult to obtain. True, certain works (the First and Fourth Symphonies, primarily) were in the catalogue and could be ordered from reluctant assistants in music shops; but they often took weeks to arrive, if they ever did. As for the *really* obscure works – Symphonies Nos. 3, 6, 7, 8 – one had to resort to advertising in the back of the *Gramophone*. That was how I first got to know the Eighth – on a disc cut from a live performance at the 1954 Holland Festival, conducted by Eduard Flipse. Curiously, I was to discover years later that DM had been at that performance and had reviewed it, somewhat tepidly, for *Tempo*.[1] No matter: to me at the time it was manna from heaven.

The other thing was to find out as much as I could about Mahler, the man and his life. I could find only two books in the local library: H. F. Redlich's *Bruckner and Mahler* (1955, in the Dent *Master Musicians* series) and Donald Mitchell's *Gustav Mahler: The Early Years* (1958). Both seemed admirable as far as they went, which wasn't far enough. I knew that Mitchell worked for Faber and Faber in London, whereas Redlich was Austrian and Lecturer in Music at Edinburgh. Mitchell seemed the more accessible, so off to him I wrote, not really expecting much, if anything, of a response. To my surprise I received a letter couched in the warmest terms, deploring the state of present-day Mahler scholarship, but ending with the words, 'I want to express my real pleasure in your interest in Mahler's music.'

In later Cambridge and post-Cambridge days I got to know DM much better, not only in person – and, again, I was always very cordially received – but also through his books, broadcasts, lectures, *Daily Telegraph* reviews and sleeve-notes for LPs. Our principal areas of mutual interest were Mahler and Britten (to whom I also wrote, several times, and always received the friendliest of letters back). DM's writings had what I can best describe as a 'kindling' quality – *they made you want to hear the music.* I aspired to write like that. By way of illustration I'm going to quote a number of passages from reviews and articles, most of which DM has probably forgotten long since, but to me they are significant. (Unless otherwise noted, none appears elsewhere in this collection.) The first comes from one of his earliest broadcast talks – on Max Reger, one of his earliest enthusiasms. He delivered it on 7 July 1946, at the age of twenty-one:[2]

> During his short life, Reger was faced with the most bitter criticism and opposition, condemned for being both revolutionary and eclectic. But Reger was wholly a musician, a music-maker in the most literal meaning of that expression, and he confounded the angry scholars and pedants by continuing to compose with all the energy of which he was capable.
>
> He was once asked to write a monograph on 'The Chamber

> Music of the Future' but refused curtly, replying that 'aesthetic word-play' was nonsense and that the future of chamber music 'rests solely on the leading spirits who *create*'. Reger was a man to whom the creation of music was life and no external or part-time occupation.

Next, an undated typescript, perhaps a response to an invitation to contribute to the compilation of a 'short list of marvellous moments in music'. He replied:

> I suppose everyone possesses their own short list of marvellous moments in music that have knocked them for six. On mine, well up among the Top Ten, would certainly be the very opening of Bruckner's Seventh Symphony. The first time I heard this great work, many years ago now, I had no idea what to expect; and I was simply stunned by the wonderful, vaulting arch of melody with which the first movement begins. It is the kind of major inspiration that makes musical life worth living, and in fact one lives on through this first movement of the Seventh in the happy, confident knowledge that Bruckner is bound to restate his noble melody in the recapitulation. And so he does; but this time, as the tune steals back in the cellos, it is combined with a counter-melody in the violins: it is, indeed, not so much a counterpoint as a counterpart, a reflection of the cello melody. This fresh, radiant texture, familiar yet surprising, was another moment that, on first acquaintance, left me breathless; and I still react to it with a special intensity. There's some sense in that, because the point of recapitulation is a critical stage in the structure of a symphonic movement. One expects it to make an impact.[3]

Here now is the 'coda' of a book review of Franz Grasberger's documentary study of Brahms:

> We do not need to be told that the music is the vital aspect of Brahms the man; we know already. But reading these biographical pages, pondering over the bibliographies, gazing at the photographs, all helps to remind us of the splendour of Brahms's genius, and the ultimate mystery and wonder of musical creation surrounded by, and emerging from, the business of everyday life.[4]

And finally, briefly, this, on Britten's *Saint Nicolas*:

> A distinguished contemporary composer's [Lennox Berkeley's] comment: 'Britten has an extraordinary sense of beauty,' is relevant. I don't know that I fully understood what was meant at the time: but his opinion was confirmed for me by my first hearing of *Nicolas*, when I was so confused by its progressively overwhelming impact that all I could find to say was: 'This is too beautiful.' My apprehension was considerable and amounted almost to physical fear at being unable to bear the burden of further listening. I record this 'subjective' opinion unashamedly: it may tell you as much about me as about Britten. But I have yet to be convinced that a strong musical response, in its context, is of no value.[5]

What do all these quoted excerpts from DM's writings have in common? Surely that they all reveal an essentially, primarily *musical* response to music. Of course, enthusiasm or declaration of emotion unsupported by technical knowledge is of no real value; conversely, analytical dissection of music without reference to its nature and meaning leads nowhere too. We need a blend, a balance, of the two qualities – imagination and intellect – to produce a valid critique or interpretation of any musical phenomenon; and it seems to me that everywhere in his writing (e.g. in that first Bruckner excerpt) DM achieves precisely that. After reading his third Mahler volume (1985, primarily concerned with the songs, *Das Lied von der Erde*, and the Eighth), and in particular after reading and absorbing his exhaustive commentaries on *Das Lied*, we can never think of, or listen to, that work in quite the same way again. Our perception of it is permanently enriched and enhanced. DM's is a mode of writing that bears out what Oliver Knussen – who can always be relied on to talk sound musical common sense – once said to him: 'You may not be a composer, but you think like one.'

I'd like to return to those early Reger broadcasts and articles, for it seems to me they open up interesting avenues of exploration and discussion. First, how typical it is of those of DM's outlook and background that they will instinctively take up the cause of interesting composers either unknown to, or derided by, or decently coffined and buried by, the Establishment. Reger probably falls into the latter two categories, but at least as far as the BBC was concerned, he *was* decently dead and buried, he *was* a name in the history books, so they might with impunity permit young Mitchell to work off some energy on *him*. But Benjamin Britten, now! He was an altogether different proposition. Homosexual, a conscientious objector, far more precociously successful than he had any business to be. And here was this young upstart critic in 1952 not only assertively promoting his cause but telling those of his elders and betters who had the temerity to disagree with him to stick their contrary opinions where the proverbial monkey stuck his nuts. No. Wouldn't do. Mitchell must be put in his place. So the BBC's then Director of Music Talks fired a broadside:[6]

> You also ask if the Third Programme is still interested in ideas for brilliant talks. The answer, you will be astonished to hear, is yes, but the difficulty is to find enough. I think it is only fair to tell you that, when I came into this job, I was given the opinion of various people in the Third Programme on music speakers generally, and a strong hope was expressed that the standard might improve! But I am afraid you were one of a number of the people I was 'warned about', and it's because I think you will do good talks later on that I'm prepared to incur your anger and go into this at a bit more length.
>
> I think it was your talk on Britten that was the trouble. I didn't hear it myself, and I'm not even quite sure if Britten really was the subject. I gather that complaints centred on much the same points as those taken up by adverse critics of your Britten book: that you seemed altogether too self-confident, over-assertive and indeed over-aggressive, giving the impression that anyone who held contrary views to your own was not worth serious consideration. This may well be your own view, but the fact remains that a number of listeners, as well as a number of people on the BBC staff, found the way you did this talk irritating.
>
> There is, of course, an audience for criticism of this kind, and the *Evening Standard* for one exploits it to the full. Most of the *Standard* critics (e.g. films, plays, radio) write like omniscient sages castigating the prattling futilities of the very young. They are readable

but infuriating, and these, of course, were the two characteristics of your *Music Survey*. But I don't think the Third Programme is really the place for aggressive criticism. I feel something mellower is required, and it is because I am sure that you yourself are capable of 'mellowing' that I am taking the trouble to write all this. The letter will no doubt confirm you in all your worst opinions of the BBC, but you may, I hope, come to feel there is some sense in what I am writing . . .

Not to be so easily worsted, DM replied as follows:[7]

Your letter of the 1st July has been forwarded on to me here [The Hague; he was attending the Holland Festival]. As you can imagine, I don't care all that much about the Third Programme's bad opinion of me, even though it does mean the loss of a potential source of income.

What I do care about is a bad opinion based on rumour or prejudice and not on facts. Since it is the Britten talk that has mysteriously stuck in somebody's throat I feel – if only in friendly fairness to myself – that you might at least have read the script and seen how far what I actually said coincided with these theories of self-confidence (is this, indeed, a sin?), over-assertiveness and over-aggressiveness, etc. Please do let me have your opinion on this script. If you can honestly write to me (after reading it) that you found it in the style of the *Evening Standard*, i.e. an omniscient sage castigating the prattling futilities of the very young, then I shall give up music criticism the day after. How was it that Alec Robertson (who was never much of an enthusiast for any of my work, broadcast or otherwise) was, on this solitary occasion, memorably complimentary? Or is he yet another person who doesn't mean what he says? Why if listeners protested (and I have plenty of listeners' letters received after this broadcast which were congratulatory not condemnatory) and the BBC rocked with indignation was the talk rebroadcast in a recording a few weeks later – the only time (ironically enough) this has ever happened to a talk of mine! You will realize how hopelessly confusing it all is. At this distance I can't properly answer your letter and all its points. When I'm back in London (about July 16th) I'll ring you and perhaps we can have lunch and an extended conversation. Since you've been 'warned' about me I'll wear spectacles and a beard. But be a good fellow and read that script and see if, in fact, what irritated the BBC's cultural policemen was not me but simply an enthusiastic talk on Britten respectably delivered by someone who knew what he was talking about – this latter item people are never willing to forgive.

Of the reply DM received to *that*, only the first astounding paragraph is worth reproducing:[8]

You quite missed the point of my letter. Nothing would induce me to read your Britten broadcast! I am sure it is excellent in many ways. The point is that it is not me that is objecting. I am on your side and I think, as I said before, that next year would be soon enough to have another go.

One wonders why, if the writer were indeed 'on DM's side', nothing would induce him to read the Britten broadcast! Inevitably, however, in the fullness of time the breach was healed, and DM became one of the BBC's most regular and valued contributors.

I'd like to digress at this point in order to clear up any possible misunderstandings regarding DM's part in the notorious 'Zak' affair of 1961 [see pp. 472–3]. It all began with a BBC internal memo (undated but annotated 'PLEASE DO NOT PUBLISH') which read in part as follows:

On Monday, June 5 the Third Programme will broadcast a concert which includes two performances of *Mobile for tape and percussion* by Piotr Zak, a composer who refuses to allow his music to be published . . .

Piotr Zak is one of the youngest and most controversial figures in contemporary music. He is of Polish extraction, and now lives in Germany. The strong influence of Kagel, Stockhausen and John Cage can be felt in his music, which he will not allow to be published, because he considers his scores as private instructions to the professional performer, which has certain renaissance parallels.

Mobile takes its name from the aerial sculptures of the American John Calder [*recte* Alexander]. It consists of an electronic tape, against which two percussion-players play music written down, but giving scope for improvisation. The tape exploits the full range of the aural spectrum, controlled by strictly measurable quantities – frequency ratios, velocity graphs and decibel indexes.

Mobile will be performed twice in succession; this was also done with Stockhausen's *Zyklus* for solo percussion, and more recently with Stravinsky's *Movements*. The soloists Claude Tessier and Anton Schmidt are coming to this country specially for the performance: they have already given the work in Europe.

Mr Zak would indeed have experienced considerable difficulties in trying to publish his music, since neither composer nor music existed. It was all an elaborate hoax, perpetrated by Hans Keller and Susan Bradshaw, who set the tape running in a BBC studio and then barged about, hitting at random whatever came to hand in the way of percussion instruments or could be pressed into percussive service, *without* of course the participation or knowledge of DM, whose notice in the *Daily Telegraph*, notwithstanding, was unequivocally negative:

The first performance in this country of a *Mobile* (ominous title) for tape and percussion by Piotr Zak, a Polish composer, proved wholly unrewarding. He exploited the percussion with only limited enterprise and his tape emitted a succession of whistles, rattles and punctured sighs that proclaimed, all too shamelessly, their non-musical origins.

There was nothing, one felt, to 'understand' here. It was only the composer's ingenuousness that was mysterious.[9]

Once the affair was revealed as a hoax, and despite the fact that one of its perpetrators, Susan Bradshaw, reported to the *Telegraph* (1 August), 'I must say [your] critic was very clever, writing almost as if he was in on the deception', DM received a considerable amount of stick from people who thought he should have instantaneously recognized it as such on first hearing the 'music'. But how could he have? It was presented with all the trappings of authenticity, having apparently received a Royal Third Programme Imprimatur. After all, composers did, and do, produce 'music' like Zak's. One of the letters the *Telegraph* received was so ludicrously and gratuitously offensive it is worth quoting for the sake of comic relief. Its author (signature illegible) writes from the Isle of Wight (what the 'Lutyens affair' was, we have not been able to identify):

> Time was when a critic in any of the arts once caught out and having had his bluff called would have retired in decent obscurity. But with you THIS HAS OCCURRED TWICE *within the space of a couple of months* (1st time of course the Lutyens affair) and this afternoon you have the face to come to the microphone [i.e. to take part in a discussion of the hoax on the Third Programme] and just waffle . . .
>
> In particular the argument that because a work was presented to the public under BBC auspices, therefore it exonerates a critic from assessing its value is just an insult to the intelligence of listeners.
>
> What really is implied in such a plea is that to the gleeful, fatuous applause of idiot critics creative art in the department of music has been in this century getting nearer and nearer the borders of aural doodling so what more natural than, having dug your grave, you should one day with a little push from the BBC (whom God preserve!) fall into it?
>
> Religious apologetics have nothing on your performance this afternoon. This was a welter of waffling, jesuitical sophistry. Miserable and feeble indeed.
>
> OF COURSE no such thing as Piotr Zak would have been possible in former times. Audiences were not conditioned, crazed and blinded by critical pseudo-science then . . .
>
> The really fatuous thing, the root evil and the fundamental trouble is, given the level of critical intelligence and integrity to-day, ANY kind of bizarre *tohu-bohu* PROVIDED IT IS PRESENTED UNDER THE 'RIGHT' i.e. Left AUSPICES is assured of serious critical appraisal, which *bien entendu* always means cautious equivocal approval–disapproval. GOD what an oily band of humbugs and hypocrites! The function you perform in the intellectual life of society is definitely pestilential. Tennyson dubbed a certain don a louse in the locks of literature. You (who have been made a fool of TWICE and should definitely offer the editor your resignation . . . and take up market-gardening as a career) are the weevil in the piano woodwork.

Is that invective not worthy of Reger or Sorabji or Josef Holbrooke (see some of the latter's correspondence with Leslie

Boosey of Boosey & Hawkes)? Denis Stevens, in a letter (18 August) addressed to the editor of the *Telegraph*, steered clear of invective but remarked with caustic wit at its end, 'If the offender has not the courage to resign, then the BBC should give him the zak.'

DM himself summed up as follows in a letter drafted as an answer to two *Daily Telegraph* correspondents whose letters had appeared in the paper on 12 August:

> In so far as Zak's *Mobile* was intended to fool the critics, which was certainly part, if only a subsidiary part, of the BBC's intention, the hoax was a flop.
>
> Not one of the three critics who wrote about the piece was deceived . . . Yet the BBC seems to claim that the justification for its 'experiment' rested in the critics' inability to distinguish between 'music' and 'non-music'. It is a strange state of affairs when the written fact of *not* taking a work seriously is subsequently used to support an opinion that one did exactly the opposite!
>
> The BBC is right to assume that one did not question the genuineness of the event. But is there anything surprising about that? When one thinks of the steps the BBC took to guarantee the 'authenticity' of the hoax, it would have been astonishing indeed if any listener had heard the *Mobile* as anything else but a *bona fide* première. It is just this element of intensive 'pre-conditioning' that makes the enterprise finally worthless. One cannot take seriously the findings of an experiment in which one set of participants has been subjected to influences that wellnigh determine the outcome.

And herewith let us lay the ghost of this unfortunate non-existent Polish composer to rest, hopefully once and for all.

Alas, I could never persuade DM to share my enthusiasm for our home-grown composers such as Vaughan Williams, Butterworth, Bax, Moeran, *et al.* He was always uneasy with music that failed to reflect a strong awareness of Continental trends, for he saw in it an incorrigible tendency to 'provincialism' and 'insularity'. The fierce tone of the broadcast on Vaughan Williams[10] (see pp. 87–96) reflects this very clearly. On the other hand, Delius, as his early and unusual article on the composer suggests (see pp. 297–301), he heard as far more European than English in his 'language', which provided the basis for an immediately sympathetic response. (*Sea Drift*, *Brigg Fair*, the Violin Concerto and orchestral miniatures, and the songs, enjoy to this day his abiding admiration.) Bridge passed muster because he cast his net more widely; and Britten's 'Englishry', of course, had little if anything to do with any English composer except Purcell. In a broadcast talk on Holst[11] DM makes salient points about *his* cosmopolitanism, and in particular Stravinsky's influence on *The Planets*, 'a major document in the history of modern English music':

> It was modern, indeed, in a specific sense. Here was an English composer reacting positively to the new music that was just beginning to take Europe by storm. Holst was impressed, above all, by Stravinsky; and we can clearly hear the influence Stravinsky had on him in *Mercury*, where a snatch of tune revolves round and round in the authentic Stravinskian manner.
>
> This response to Stravinsky was a remarkable thing in itself, especially when we consider that at the time English music was necessarily turning *away* from Europe and asserting its independence by exploring its own past. This was how Holst's development differed substantially and importantly from his great contemporary, Vaughan Williams. Holst, as deeply involved as he was in the English tradition, and affected by it, kept an amazingly open mind – a European mind, one might say. And it was perhaps the conflict between these two regions of interest, both of which mattered to him profoundly – the English and the European – that lends his music its peculiar historical significance and its sometimes disconcertingly, if fascinatingly, 'mixed' style.

In the same talk he went on to identify the spoken chorus in the *Sanctus* of Britten's *War Requiem* as a development of a similar device in Holst's *Hymn of Jesus* and sees an anticipation of Walton's *Belshazzar's Feast* in the jazzy 5/4 dance in the same work ('Ye who dance not, know not what we are knowing'). Why, then, has DM written widely and sympathetically on Elgar, whose 'Englishry' many regard as archetypal? Precisely because he is so vividly aware of Elgar's Continental affiliations:

> The welcome *Gerontius* received in Germany and Strauss's praise make their own comment on the wholesale cosmopolitanism of Elgar's mature style. A derivative composer he was not – on the contrary, the flavour of his personality is strong and pervasive – but it would be perverse to deny his indebtedness to Wagner and many another European master. Would *Gerontius* have been possible without *Parsifal* as a dramatic precedent? The European climate that *Gerontius* inhabits lifts the work out of its English context and places it where it belongs (and where, incidentally, Elgar belongs) – in the great Continental tradition from which, *nota bene*, emerged oratorios as diverse as Berlioz's *L'enfance du Christ*, Franck's *Les béatitudes*, Liszt's *St Elisabeth* and *Christus*, and even Brahms's *Requiem*). It is when seen 'away' rather than 'at home' that Elgar appears in the round as a major European figure.[12]

The writings on Elgar, however, are more significant than, merely, the chance they give DM to ride one of his favourite hobby-horses. They reveal his intense and abiding interest in *people* – which is another reason why his musical commentaries are so rewarding and insightful. He wants to know, to understand, not only how *compositions* are com-posed, but also how their *composers* are com-posed. He thinks enormously long and hard about creative personalities; why they act as they do, create as they do, are what they are. He finds a biography of Rakhmaninov by Victor Seroff wanting precisely because the author, having marshalled a number of salient facts, completely fails to employ them in the further illumination of the composer and his works. DM does it for him:

> The years of severe mental depression and creative impotence which intervened after the unhappy first performance (1897) of Rachmaninoff's First Symphony have, in Mr Seroff's words, 'been kept shrouded in mystery, and Rachmaninoff himself always avoided speaking of them. They remain as though they had never existed.' As far as Mr Seroff's book is concerned they don't exist either. While all the world is aware of Dr Dahl's successful therapeutic—hypnotic séances, which resulted in the freeing of Rachmaninoff's

> creative ability and the composition of the Second Piano Concerto, the cause and nature of the initial depression itself has been kept top secret. The mystery would hardly matter were it not for the fact that all the musical evidence implies that this spiritual breakdown acted (of course *after* it had been overcome) as Rachmaninoff's chief creative stimulant. It was Rachmaninoff's fear of his depressive mania that drove him to compose – to keep his mania at arm's length so to speak; and at the same time it was in his music that his mania found an outlet and was able to flower. Hence, no doubt, the extremely narrow range of Rachmaninoff's moods, the family (wellnigh incestuous) relationship of his themes, and, in his large-scale pieces, the many beautiful lyrical ideas that are never developed, it seems almost through sheer fatigue and inertia. Yet this very fatigued aspect of Rachmaninoff's music has a striking fascination of its own. One might say with justice that Rachmaninoff cashed in on his neurosis and made something vital out of it; no mean achievement, since it's not every composer who knows what to do with his neurosis. But one day, for the better understanding of his music, we ought to have more detailed information about the depression which was the cradle of Rachmaninoff's creativity.[13]

It follows that DM must make an admirable obituarist: not a calling he has pursued (as far as I am aware) with any particular application. But I never hear the name of the legendary hornplayer Dennis Brain, or hear his matchless playing in the first recording of Britten's *Serenade* for tenor, horn and strings, without their bringing to mind DM's obituary tribute in *Tempo*,[14] in which he wrote that 'Brain's virtuosity was of that rare quality which places the executant in a direct relation to the art of composing – the composer's imagination is stimulated by the potentialities which the instrumental virtuoso unfolds'. This was certainly true of Britten's creative association with Brain; whereas, DM remarks, in the case of Mozart, of whose horn concertos Brain was a 'superb exponent', 'one feels Mozart might have written them for Brain to play'. He continues:

> We witness many a like occasion in which Brain was the very life and soul of the act of creation. The works written for him to play –

> to which his virtuosity gave birth – are too numerous to list in full; but mention of Britten's *Serenade*, of the concertos by, among others, Elisabeth Lutyens, Hindemith, Gordon Jacob and, most recently [i.e. in 1956], Malcolm Arnold, is testament to the *fertility* of his musicianship. He was, moreover, the kind of virtuoso whose virtuosity challenged the composer not only to match it but exceed it; yet whatever the test, Brain imperturbably blew his way through it, taming the composer's imagination, while most scrupulously revealing its very singularity.

'*Brain imperturbably blew his way through it*' – the essence of a musician summed up in one simple phrase.

The essays on Elgar, though confined by space, show the same heroic attempt to come to grips with a complex and fractious personality. The acme of DM's achievement in this respect is undoubtedly the magnificent 67-page introduction to *Benjamin Britten: Letters from a Life*,[15] which is the fruit of long years of personally knowing, thinking about and trying to understand a musical personality no less 'complex and fractious' than Elgar's. It's amazing how many people who write and pontificate about music never seem to take the remotest interest in composers' personalities – almost as if some computer produced the music and all one had to do to find its essential being was to submit it to a laboratory-style dissection. DM, mercifully, has always had better sense.

Having, almost inadvertently as it were, drawn the three names of Elgar, Britten and Mitchell together, I am tempted to speculate on what may be an altogether deeper dimension to the Mitchell–Elgar relationship. It is not something that DM himself, for reasons of modesty, would ever spell out himself; so I hope I may be permitted to spell it out for him. We find a clue, I think, in the sudden increased sharpness of tone in 'The Composer Among the Monuments' (see pp. 269–78 of this volume):

> But what makes one hang one's head in shame, even at this late stage, is the awful tale of Elgar's treatment at the hands of his publisher. The amazing Jaeger, of course, is exempt from these strictures;

> but he was an editor and not part of the business, which seems to have been conducted with a repellent combination of meanness and timidity. Moore lays out for our inspection much of the correspondence between Elgar and Novello & Co. – it is undeniably one of the most interesting narrative threads running through his book – and thoroughly disagreeable it is to read of the financial humiliations to which the composer was subjected, at a time, incidentally, when the concept of the performing right, and the revenue flowing from it, had not been established. Elgar lived long enough to benefit from the starting up of the Performing Right Society and indeed was an early advocate of the cause. Composers may still have their proper grievances but to see how far we have travelled in recognizing the right of the musical creator to be rewarded – no, *paid* – for performances of his works, we only need to remind ourselves of Elgar's miserable haggling over shillings and pence. His 'God help him!' comment on Bax's ambition, read in this perspective, sounds more like compassion than disgruntlement.

Note the following: (a) Elgar's publishers being mercilessly berated by DM; (b) the references to the PRS, which has been one of his major interests for many years; and (c) 'the amazing Jaeger'. Augustus Johannes Jaeger (= 'hunter': his name was later to be immortalized in the *Nimrod* variation in *Enigma*) was a German-born naturalized Englishman employed as an editor by Novello. In 1896 he was assigned to Elgar and quickly became one of his most fervent admirers. Elgar, for his part, came to regard him as his guru, and conceded him an astonishing, unparalleled amount of input into his creative work. How many people realize, for instance, that the grandly spacious coda of the *Enigma Variations* came about as a result of Jaeger's intervention (originally it was much shorter)? And it was Jaeger who persuaded Elgar to paint in orchestrally the stunning moment of the Soul's vision of the Almighty in *Gerontius*.

There is some reason for thinking of DM in the same relation to Britten as Jaeger to Elgar. I doubt, though, if he ever presumed to advise Britten as to the nature and direction of what he was composing, and of course there was one vital difference – Jaeger was an *employee* of the publisher (and had to spend a fair amount of time keeping the peace between the hypersensitive composer and the firm's then managing director), whereas DM *was* (or eventually became) Britten's exclusive publisher after he had parted company, in 1965, with Boosey & Hawkes. Faber Music was actually created in the first instance to publish Britten (though it eventually spread its wings to cover major new talents such as George Benjamin, Jonathan Harvey, Oliver Knussen, Colin Matthews, David Matthews and Peter Sculthorpe) and quickly established an innovating and rarely surpassed standard of music production. And no composer could have enjoyed the services of so steadfast a friend, colleague and skilful negotiator, attributes and skills brought into play when clearing the rights for *Death in Venice*, Britten's last opera:

> One morning, quite out of the blue, Britten had telephoned me at Faber's and asked me to make a few tentative inquiries of Thomas Mann's publishers in London about whom should be approached if he decided to go ahead with the idea [*Death in Venice*]. I made the initial inquiries and reported back. But in fact it was not until the autumn of 1970, when walking round a bleak and muddy Suffolk field that Britten told me he now wanted to undertake the project. I can't honestly say that that wet and soggy Horham field was transformed into a vision of watery Venice; but I was certainly greatly excited by the news, and not long after was off on a mission to yet another watery location, the lake of Zurich, to seek the consent of the Mann family.[16]

The years following Britten's death saw the disinterment and publication of a large number of hitherto unpublished manuscripts, many of them vintage Britten – early chamber and choral works, the *Quatre Chansons Françaises*, the *Cabaret Songs*, *Temporal Variations*, *Young Apollo*, the *Occasional* and *American Overtures*, *Johnson over Jordan*, and most recently *The Rescue of Penelope*. (*Paul Bunyan* had been rescued just before Britten died.) No bottom-of-the-barrel-scraping here; these are all vital works and our perspective on Britten is enhanced through knowing them. And the flood of essays and articles continues, all motivated – thence validated – by love and understanding. What better could any composer, alive or dead, expect? Alas, this particular type of composer–publisher relationship is almost a thing of the past now. But what might have become of Walton without the foresight and fidelity of OUP's Hubert Foss? Or of the younger Britten without the vision of Ralph Hawkes and, later, the skills of Erwin Stein?

There are of course many DMs, and I can't pretend to know them all – scholar; journalist; lecturer (visiting professor at both Sussex and York); broadcaster (radio and TV); prolific writer of programme notes and notes for recordings; standard-bearer; editor; publisher; administrator; trustee (the Britten–Pears Foundation); committee man (Royal Academy of Music and PRS); pacifist; orientalist; democratic socialist (almost an extinct species says DM); tireless globe-trotter in the discharge of both duties and pleasures – he must be one of the most influential, indeed powerful, figures in post-war musical life. (I *do* know, rather better, DM the warm-hearted friend, family man and generous host, along with his wife, Kathleen, who for so long has not only been fundamental to his life but also to his work.) May he enjoy optimum health and strength to continue with and complete his major illuminations of Britten and Mahler. But it's no good suggesting that he drop some of his other time-consuming activities to facilitate this. He wouldn't, couldn't, do that. He's one of those hyperactive people who actually thrive on being stretched to capacity. If he weren't, his work in every sphere would almost certainly suffer. So: the best we can do is to wish him a happy *ad multos annos* and look forward to the *Festschrift* for his eightieth!

London, 1994

NOTES

1 *Tempo* 33 (1954), p. 7.

2 BBC Home Service, *Music Lovers' Diary*; speaker and scriptwriter: DM; pianist: Harold Truscott; producer: Alec Robertson. The music examples were taken from Reger's famous *Mozart Variations* for orchestra, Op. 132; his *Konzert im alten Stil*, Op. 123; E♭ String Quartet, Op. 109; a song – from *Schlichte Weisen*, Op. 76 – and a gavotte from Reger's 'diary' for solo piano, *Aus meinem Tagebuch*, Op. 82. Truscott (1914–1992), an old friend and valued colleague of DM's – he was a frequent contributor to *Music Survey* – was both composer and prodigious pianist (his sight-reading was a phenomenon in its own right). From 1957 he taught at Huddersfield Polytechnic (from 1970 as Principal Lecturer), retiring in 1979. See also the programme book for *Harold Truscott: 75th Birthday Celebration*, Havergal Brian Society, 1989, with a tribute by Robert Simpson.

3 DM remembers nothing about this, and I have not been able to locate its publication (if indeed it were published). It was almost certainly a spin-off from his life as a Fleet Street critic.

4 *Music Review* 15 (1954), pp. 83–4.

5 *Music Survey* 2/4 (spring 1950), p. 221.

6 Roger Fiske to DM, 1 July 1953. The 'talk on Britten' to which Fiske refers had been given by DM on the Third Programme on 17 July 1952. It was entitled 'Benjamin Britten and the English Tradition' and produced by Alec Robertson (1892–1982).

MC: With the help of the BBC Written Archives Centre, we have retrieved a copy of the script. What, on reacquaintance with it, was all the fuss about? Here are three sample paragraphs, chosen virtually at random:

> Perhaps one of the most paradoxical aspects of Britten's music is its popularity both at home and abroad. *Peter Grimes*, so very English in so many vital ways, wasn't out of place in opera houses as far removed as Helsinki and Budapest. As this exportable character of *Peter Grimes* suggests, Britten's Englishness is based on a very broad Europeanism; and it is, in my opinion, his successful fusion of English and European styles that makes his relation to the English tradition such a singular one. Britten's later style where this fusion is most evident – say from 1942 onwards – I should like to call his English synthesis, and it is the achievement of this synthesis that I want to talk about . . .
>
> . . . It was, I believe, in the *Michelangelo Sonnets* that Britten really achieved a consummately flexible style that he could put to any purpose he chose. His Continental stylizations had given him a freedom of style, a freedom of musical movement, a profoundly European musical education, as it were, that enabled him to approach the English language with renewed and absolute confidence. Thus the *Michelangelo Sonnets*, composed in America in 1940, were both a terminus and a transition. Britten, apart from a volume of French folk songs, has set no Continental texts since. He returned to

England in 1942, bringing with him the *Hymn to St Cecilia*, and in the same year produced the enchanting *Ceremony of Carols*. The English synthesis had begun . . .

> . . . It is the compound of Europeanism and Englishness – an amalgamation of cultures – which is so remarkable a feature of Britten's style. That he has, I believe, returned English music to the main flow of European music, and yet developed a European heritage within an instinctively English framework, seems to me to be an achievement without precedent. He came to the English tradition via Europe, and brought Europe with him: an inheritance that makes his Englishness of European validity. Hence the historic importance of Britten's English synthesis is not for ourselves alone.

The conclusion has to follow that, as Fiske himself suggested, there was a backlash from DM's and Hans Keller's pungent commentaries in *Music Survey*; and, perhaps no less significant, a profound resistance to a positive appraisal of Britten, politely couched throughout though it was on this occasion, with scarcely an adverse reflection on anything or anybody. It was antipathy to – perhaps envy of – Britten's 'success' that gave rise to the views that Fiske's letters mirror. A pity, DM still thinks, that he could not bring himself to read a script, the character of which bears no relation at all to his assumptions about it, which in fact had their origins in other people's – in influential people's – prejudices.

7 DM to Roger Fiske, 6 July 1953.

8 Roger Fiske to DM, 13 July 1953. [See also pp. 390–91, note 1.]

9 *Daily Telegraph*, 6 June 1961. Once the hoax had been revealed, there followed a flurry of comment in the press. The *Telegraph* itself devoted a leader to the topic ('Unrelated Noises', 2 August): 'The hoax, in fact, did not really come off. Intended no doubt to prove that there were critics so impressed by novelty or terrorized by fashion that they could no longer tell the difference between sense and nonsense, it proved instead that there are still three critics who can tell and are not afraid to say so.' (The three critics cited were Rollo H. Myers of the *Listener*, the (then) anonymous music critic of *The Times* (was it on this occasion William Mann?), and 'our own' DM.) See also Rene MacColl, 'Now that the BBC has begun pulling our legs . . .', *Daily Express*, 2 August, and 'Acid on the Pen', *The Sunday Times*, 6 August, a reference to the forthcoming Third Programme debate on 13 August. The whole affair calls to mind another and earlier literary hoax, the publication of poems by 'Ern Malley' in 1944 in a Sydney magazine, *Angry Penguins*. The revelation that the poems were a fabrication gave rise to a storm of comment and controversy by no means confined to Australia.

10 There are, however, a number of links between Vaughan Williams and Britten, one of the most interesting of which is the beautiful folksong variously entitled 'The Lynn Apprentice' or 'The Captain's Apprentice' which Vaughan Williams himself collected at King's Lynn in Norfolk in 1907, and incorporated into his orchestral *Norfolk Rhapsody* No. 1. The folk song tells of a seafaring captain who treats his apprentice so badly that the boy dies. Now, how far removed *thematically* is this from Crabbe's sadistic fisherman, Grimes? Surely no further

than the coastal town of King's Lynn is removed *geographically* from Crabbe's Aldeburgh.

11 'Holst Today', in an issue of the BBC's Sunday morning *Music Magazine*, edited by Julian Herbage and Anna Instone. The script is undated. See also 'Vaughan Williams' in the series of 'Revaluations' DM contributed to *Musical Opinion* (May 1955, p. 471), which includes a more elaborate statement of his assessment of Holst. [For further discussion of DM's criticism of Vaughan Williams, see Mervyn Cooke's remarks on pp. XLIII–XLIV below.]

12 *Listener*, 28 February 1957. [See p. 253.]

13 *Tempo* 24 (1952), p. 36.

14 *Tempo* 45 (1957), p. 16.

15 DM and Philip Reed (eds.), *Letters from a Life: Selected Letters and Diaries of Benjamin Britten*, vols. 1 and 2 (Faber and Faber, London, 1991).

16 'Britten's Concerto for Tenor and Opera', programme book for the production of *Death in Venice* at the Royal Opera House, Covent Garden, March–April 1992.

Cradles *in Context*

Mervyn Cooke

I The Critic Among the Monuments

> **Mitchell, Donald.** Died in Binghamton, N.Y., Aug. 17, 1971. Add to books: *Gustav Mahler: The Early Years* (N.Y., 1958); *The Language of Modern Music* (London, 1963).[1]

> Dear (or rather today, not so dear) Nicolas: Donald Mitchell just stormed into my office to tell me that on page 163 of the new *Baker's* supplement you murdered him in August of 1971 in Binghamton, New York, where he has never been in his life and never hopes to be particularly.[2]

So wrote Hans W. Heinsheimer to Nicolas Slonimsky in 1971, protesting on behalf of G. Schirmer Inc. at Slonimsky's inadvertent confusion of DM with his American namesake William John Mitchell (who really *had* died on 17 August). A publisher's *erratum* subsequently attempted to 'exhume Donald Mitchell from his unhallowed grave', and the unwitting deceased wrote to Slonimsky to assert it was worth being 'placed temporarily underground' to have received such a 'charming letter' of apology from his executioner.

An amusing incident, no doubt, but the phenomenon of what Slonimsky terms the 'misplaced tombstone' can raise more serious concerns: there is always a very real danger, for instance, that a *Festschrift* or retrospective collection of an author's writings can unintentionally signal a terminal appreciation for an output once distinguished but now extinct. Why else, one might ask, should we assemble miscellaneous past achievements instead of promoting the new?

In the case of the present volume, there exist at least three distinct answers to this question. In the first place, this selection will coincidentally appear exactly in time to mark the occasion of DM's seventieth birthday in 1995. But this is an anniversary that heralds a new surge in DM's musical and scholarly activities; in fact, he has probably never been busier. The year 1995 will see him bring to fruition in Amsterdam the international symposium *Mahler: The World Listens* for the Concertgebouw's Mahler Festival, after several years in the planning stages. The fourth and final volume of his acclaimed study of Mahler is well under way, and there remain at least two further volumes selected from Britten's copious correspondence to appear under his editorship. His devotion to the music of the Far East, which figures as a prominent influence in the work of both Mahler and Britten, has continued to flourish since he first brought Thai musicians to Aldeburgh in October 1977, and in 1994 it resulted in a series of radio broadcasts devoted to Thai classical music. In DM's case, then, the present retrospective seems more in the nature of a modest prelude to future achievements than merely a resurrection of the past.

An anniversary celebration and the provision of a supplement to ongoing musicological projects: both justifications in their own right for the appearance of *Cradles of the New*. Yet the third and final motivation behind the preparation of this book is much more compelling. Although the writings represented here span a period of some forty years, many date from the 1950s when DM was making a formidable name for himself as a critic who had something to say and would not shrink from saying it. It almost defies belief (and scarcely pays any compliment to the progress of music criticism in the intervening period) to note the disconcerting fact that the opinions he expressed over thirty years ago remain as topical and provocative today as they seemed at the time they were first aired.

His distinctive voice initially developed through a highly active career in music journalism, which included editorships of *Music*

Survey (1947–52) and *Tempo* (1958–62), and posts with the *Musical Times* (1953–7), the *Daily Telegraph* (1959–64) and the *Listener* (1964). When his attention began to turn to musicological projects of considerable substance (notably in Mahler and Britten studies, in both of which fields he was a crusading pioneer), his expertise reflected his unusually broad experience of critical writing. Given his characteristic blend of critical journalism and musicological research, it is fitting that this anthology should commence with his outspoken complaint against what he perceived to be the serious critical malaise prevalent in this country in the mid-1950s ('Criticism: A State of Emergency', pp. 3–12). DM lays the blame partly at the feet of the post-war expansion of historical musicology, which offered in its quest for irrefutable facts a substitute for critical assessment.

At first glance, it is tempting (and perhaps complacent) to regard DM's provocative outcry against the barrenness of music criticism as something of a period piece. Indeed, the publication just one year before his article appeared of Thurston Dart's *The Interpretation of Music* (Hutchinson, London, 1954), a volume that has much to say about notation and performance practice but virtually nothing on questions of musical or critical interpretation, is likely to have been significant. Yet, as Joseph Kerman more recently concluded, 'In Britain, it seems, the reaction against criticism that worried Donald Mitchell in 1955 has in thirty years simply deepened.'[3] DM's central thesis that the growing ascendancy of positivistic musicology offers a convenient escape from the need for musical value judgements (a trend signifying a 'retreat from contemporary culture', as he puts it) is shown by Kerman to have been closely paralleled by developments in American musicology. Kerman made his own complaints known in his paper 'A Profile for American Musicology'[4] which sparked off controversy on his side of the Atlantic. Somewhat later, the rise of analytical studies in the States was seen by Kerman to have had 'the effect of deepening some musicologists' commitment to actual music'.[5] The emergence of serious analysis in Britain has, however, been a comparatively recent phenomenon.

In another area, too, DM's piece on criticism has remained strikingly topical. He laments

> one of the most painful paradoxes of our time that we live in a society whose widespread literacy runs only skin-deep. Despite the all-round increase in education, which one would have presumed to generate and expand [F. R. Leavis's] 'intelligently responsive' public, the composer has still tended to lose the ear of his contemporaries. [p. 5.]

John Carey has recently taken a provocatively penetrating look at the nature of this phenomenon among the literary intelligentsia, and has shown the problems identified by DM in the sphere of music criticism to be depressingly universal.[6]

DM's own ability to demolish specific examples of critical ineptitude is brilliantly demonstrated in his notorious 'More Off than On *Billy Budd*' (1951), a *tour de force* of critical penetration which ranks as an early landmark in Britten criticism. Here DM discusses an important distinction (he was to make it again in his 'State of Emergency' article) between a 'wrong opinion' and a 'wrong judgement':

> I don't care if *The Times* thinks that Captain Vere's musical characterization is all wrong . . . What I do care about is the expression of dogmatic judgements, seemingly based on ascertainable evidence, which, on examination, prove to derive from the purest realms of speculation. Speculators should stick to speculating. [p. 387.]

Earlier he had written that Ernest Newman 'is, of course, quite entitled to his wrong opinion' (p. 373). In his much later tribute to Hans Keller (co-editor of *Music Survey* from 1949 to 1952), DM singled out Keller's remark on the importance of knowing when to withhold ill-informed opinions:

> Every single reader, one or two soft-boiled critics apart, will be able to think of at least one distinguished critic who would have deserved a top salary, and a relaxing pension, for remaining silent all his life. Once again, I speak with the corroboration of personal

> experience: the noblest critical achievements of my life were the moments when I decided to shut up, temporarily or, as in the case of most of the music of Debussy, Delius and Sibelius, for ever. The amount of nonsense I have thus not committed to print, the violence and posthumous torture that has remained unpractised, would have made me a serious rival of the most highly esteemed members of the profession if all those pseudo-thoughts, those thin rationalizations of incomprehension, had been allowed an outlet. [p. 475.]

DM has, in fact, a quality very rare among critics: he is the first person to admit when he himself has been culpable of the 'wrong opinion' syndrome. When confronted by the present author with a 1957 review of Britten's ballet *The Prince of the Pagodas* in which he had dismissed the composer's Balinese borrowings as 'an indiscretion not only inappropriate but boring' (and demonstrating a 'motivic stagnation' which became 'painfully tedious'),[7] DM was quick to quote the offending passage in print and concluded that 'The culture shock that the gamelan music in the *Pagodas* presented was altogether too much for me, which may explain, though not excuse, my inept response to it.'[8] More strikingly still, he now takes a self-deprecating delight in drawing attention to one of the very first issues of *Music Survey* in which, as founding editor at the age of only twenty-two, he declared of the 'Four Sea Interludes' from Britten's opera *Peter Grimes*:

> These extracts are not Britten at his best and they are not improved by their divorce from the opera itself. The third, with its slowly rising figures in the brass, has moments of power; the fourth degenerates into mere sound and fury, signifying nothing. A platitudinous piece of programme music. The one consolation in these rather commonplace canvases is Britten's wonderful sense of the orchestra. He certainly knows how to make exciting and unusual noises.[9]

Earlier in the same editorial he had written: 'The stimulating *Fanfare* that opens *Les Illuminations* is worth a dozen pages of *Peter Grimes* or the derivative *Sinfonia da Requiem*.'

II The Quiet (and Not-So-Quiet) Innovator

> Late one afternoon Giles came into the library. Helen had taken over the 'Returned Books' counter temporarily from one of the juniors and looked up to find him standing in front of her, smiling.
>
> He held up empty hands. 'I'm not a customer. Nothing to declare. But I did have something in mind – a biography of Mahler.'
>
> 'We have Donald Mitchell. I'm not sure if it's on the shelf. You'll find it in . . . '
>
> 'I'd hoped for personal service,' said Giles.

Giles, a character in Penelope Lively's 1989 novel *Passing On*, was to be disappointed: DM's study of Mahler had already been borrowed. He might not have been surprised at this, since *Gustav Mahler: The Early Years* had been something of a bestseller since its first publication in 1958, and Edward R. Reilly noted in 1981 that 'Copies of the volume have long been virtually impossible to obtain.' Reilly welcomed the appearance of the new 1978 edition (revised by Paul Banks and David Matthews), and noted that

> The book holds a special place in the Mahler literature, marking the beginning of the critical re-examination of the earlier biographical material and – more important – a newer and fuller exploration of the compositions. The study served as a powerful and healthy stimulus to a whole new generation of serious younger Mahler scholars.[10]

DM's study had indeed constituted the first 'scientific' (i.e. document-based) examination of the composer's biography and creative achievements to appear in any language. He was also the first scholar to scrutinize Mahler's autograph manuscripts in depth: the article righting a wrong note in *Das Lied von der Erde* reprinted here (pp. 181–6) is typical of his illuminating discoveries. With Britten, too, DM's manuscript detective work set a trend that was to prove inspirational to many younger scholars. In addition, his account of 'Britten's Revisionary Practice' in *Billy Budd* and *The Turn of the Screw* (pp. 393–405) is notable as much for its interpretation of early printed sources as of the manuscripts themselves.

DM's work on Mahler and Britten is today so universally familiar that the revival in the present volume of several of his lesser-known articles on these two composers requires little further comment by way of introduction, beyond perhaps pausing to note how (especially in the case of Britten) he has since the 1960s elevated the formerly impoverished genres of the record sleeve-note and opera-house programme book to the status of scholarly articles (see '*Owen Wingrave* and the Sense of the Past' (1971) and '*Our Hunting Fathers*' (1981) in the first category, 'The Serious Comedy of *Albert Herring*' (1986) and 'Britten and the Ballet' (1989) in the second). A more personal view of Britten and Pears is provided by a timely reprint of DM's affectionate 'Double Portrait', first published in Ronald Blythe's *Aldeburgh Anthology* (Snape Maltings Foundation, Aldeburgh, 1972) and long since unobtainable.

It had, of course, been DM's and Hans Keller's 1952 symposium on Britten,[11] arising naturally from the various spotlights they had focused on the composer in the pages of *Music Survey*, that constituted the initial landmark in Britten studies. Although in later years Britten and DM were to become closely associated (DM going on to found Faber Music Ltd in 1965 with Britten's works taking pride of place in the new catalogue),[12] the 1952 enterprise had in fact been prepared before the two men met for the first time. On 5 January 1953 DM had dinner with Paul Hamburger (a noted contributor to *Music Survey*) and was introduced to Peter Pears. Pears wrote to Britten (who was then staying at Harewood House) on the following day to say: 'Keller should have come but has 'flu or something, so Donald Mitchell came instead – very sweet, young, dotty & enthusiastic – you were of course the main topic of con.'[13] A fortnight later Britten wrote a formal letter to DM and Keller jointly, thanking them for their symposium and concluding:

> [. . .] what I *am* delighted with is the seriousness of it, the thoroughness of its planning & editing, its excellent get-up, & the admirable quality of a good deal of the contents, in which I would like to

include both of your contributions. I haven't time to write fully about it, but I don't see why we should continue to please our detractors by remaining strangers – can't we *really* meet & have a good talk, someday when this opera [*Gloriana*] is finished & we can all be in London?[14]

Apart from his vital work as Britten's publisher from 1965 onwards, DM has in more recent years maintained a lively involvement with musical activities at Aldeburgh, both as an imaginative Guest Artistic Director of the Festival (the cross-cultural theme of the 1991 Festival, for instance, had his hallmark liberally stamped on it) and as a sometime Director of Academic Studies at the Britten–Pears School – a role initiated when Britten himself asked DM to stand in for an indisposed Pears and guide aspiring singers through the composer's song-cycles.

His work as Director of Academic Studies was by no means his only significant educational achievement: in the midst of all his other responsibilities, he found time to serve as the first Professor of Music at the University of Sussex (1971–6). As Professor Boris Ford has recently commented [private communication]:

> Donald was an ideal person to start Music at Sussex. He was already well known for his work on Mahler and Britten, as a critic and broadcaster, and as head of Faber Music. And he proved a stimulating and infectious teacher, so that Music quickly flourished at Sussex. But in addition to having Music as a Major subject, Donald took a leading part in setting up one of the School's Contextual Courses, which were obligatory courses of an inter-disciplinary character for all students in the School. This course was entitled 'Artist and Public in Contemporary Society' and included one-term courses in music, literature and art themes. Donald offered a course on individual Britten operas, and I personally attended the seminars on *The Turn of the Screw*. They were a revelation of meaningful analysis and explication, meaningful above all to students many of whom were not Music majors. He is a superb teacher, at once scholarly and enthusiastic . . .

DM's 1972 inaugural lecture as professor is published for the first time in the present volume ('What is Expressionism?', pp. 203–26).

DM's writings on other British composers are far less familiar than his Britten scholarship, but the present volume reprints a number of his more significant articles on Elgar, Delius, Vaughan Williams and Malcolm Arnold (the last, who dedicated his *Four Irish Dances*, Op. 126, to DM, discussed in a triptych of essays offering a positive critical assessment of a hitherto neglected and sometimes misunderstood musical personality). DM's critique of Vaughan Williams, a contemporaneous review of Michael Kennedy's *The Works of Ralph Vaughan Williams* (Oxford University Press, Oxford, 1964) in which he expanded his critical opinion of the composer's achievements first expressed in print in the shape of a 'Revaluation' some nine years before,[15] is likely still to raise the reader's eyebrow. To dare to criticize Britain's musical patriarch was little short of heresy in those days, and Kennedy's subsequent riposte appeared in a retaliatory preface to the second edition of his book in 1980:

> Although in the years just before and after his death there was a critical reaction against him, this seems to have levelled out and, since 1972, the centenary of his birth, he has been recognized as a great composer of strong individuality, with more emphasis placed on the remarkable variety and power of his music than on the nationalist aspects of his style . . . I have, however, decided not to alter any of the views I expressed when I first wrote this book . . . I said then that I held to the faith that Vaughan Williams was a very great composer. I am unshaken in that faith.

DM had at least spared Kennedy the embarrassment of citing the composer's own notorious comment on his Fourth Symphony: 'I wish I didn't dislike my own stuff so much when I hear it – it all sounds so *incompetent*.'[16]

DM's review was valuable in drawing serious attention to the appalling insularity of the artistic climate in Britain by which Vaughan Williams was bound between the wars. This 'exclusive self-regarding musical culture' (p. 95) may be vividly demonstrated by a cursory glance through almost any copy of the *Musical Times* from this period. In September 1938, for instance, the first European performance of Stravinsky's *Dumbarton Oaks* concerto was relegated to two column inches of incomprehension (the reviewer wrote that the score 'lacks both invention and force', demonstrates an 'arid quality' and marked Stravinsky's 'abdication as a leader of modern music').[17] In contrast, George Dyson's Symphony in G (premièred at that year's Three Choirs Festival) had been accorded no fewer than five pages of detailed discussion with seventeen musical examples in the January issue.[18] Small wonder in this context, therefore, that Vaughan Williams's Fourth Symphony was hailed as 'modern'. It was only during the period of DM's involvement with *Musical Times* (1953–7) that the journal began significantly to expand its critical horizons.

In his substantial considerations of Elgar (singled out by *New Grove* as one of his most neglected achievements), DM rescues the composer from potential exile in 'English Squire's Corner' and, in contrast to Vaughan Williams, sees him as a thoroughly European composer with a style firmly rooted in Germanic models. Elgar, more so than Vaughan Williams, felt trapped by the musical claustrophobia he experienced in England and wrote to A. J. Jaeger in 1902 to declare, 'The horrible musical atmosphere I plunged into at once in this benighted country nearly suffocated me – I wish it had completely' (p. 292). DM in 'Unwritten Music of the Heart' alludes to Elgar's objection to the 1929 Musical Copyright Bill (see p. 290), and thereby draws attention to issues that have been close to his heart over the last twenty years. Since becoming a Director of the Performing Right Society in 1971, he has campaigned tirelessly for parity in international copyright legislation, going on to be appointed to the board of Music Copyright (Overseas) Services in 1977 and Chairman of the PRS in 1989. At the time of writing, he remains a Consultant Director and Honorary Member of the PRS General Council and continues to promote the interests of composers and publishers overseas through his work as Vice-President of the International Confederation of Societies of Authors and Composers (CISAC).

Apart from Mahler, Austrian and German composers are also well represented in the present collection. Berg's second opera *Lulu* has excited so much public and critical interest since the first performance of the complete, three-act version at the Paris Opéra in 1979 that it may come as something of a surprise to discover that DM's 1954 article on Berg's characterization of the opera's eponymous anti-heroine constitutes the only critical assessment dating from the long period between Berg's death in 1935 and the appearance of two authoritative books on the opera within the last ten years.[19] As George Perle notes, 'Between 1937 and 1949 there is no bibliographical reference whatever to *Lulu*, and between 1949 and 1954, when Mitchell's important if mistaken dramatic study of the work was published, there are only paraphrased repetitions of Reich's "analysis" and reviews of the first post-war revivals of the work (1949, 1953).'[20] DM's article grew out of three reviews he wrote of the second of those productions of the (incomplete) two-act version at Essen in 1953, a high-profile staging that (as Jarman points out)[21] did much to stimulate interest in securing a long-overdue completion of the score. Perle, who thought DM's views on the problematic nature of Lulu's character 'mistaken', refuted them in his article 'The Character of Lulu: A Sequel',[22] but Jarman has more recently shown that other commentators have shared DM's original unease. Mosco Carner, too, suggested that Berg would undoubtedly have revised some less-than-satisfactory aspects of his score if he had lived to see the opera into production.[23]

While still a young journalist in his twenties, DM made a spirited attempt to revive interest in the music of Max Reger. In his otherwise comprehensive bibliography compiled for the entry on Reger in *New Grove*, Helmut Wirth lists no items in English before the appearance of two modest and widely spaced articles in 1957 and 1975, the earlier of which was confined to a German journal.[24] The three essays on Reger by DM reprinted in the present volume (and inexplicably omitted by *New Grove*) originated in 1951 and 1953, and in them he made a concerted attempt to rescue this important figure from the undeserved oblivion ('ambiguous obscurity', as he terms it) into which he had fallen in Britain, and which is vividly shown by the thinness of the other British scholastic efforts represented in Wirth's bibliography. In fact, back in 1946 DM's very first appearance in print had taken the form of an appreciation of Reger which coincided with his early broadcast introduction to the composer's work.[25]

Even notable performers had shown a cavalier attitude to Reger's compositions: the pianist Gina Bachauer was seriously taken to task by E. H. W. Meyerstein (the poet and Thomas Chatterton's biographer) in a *Music Survey* review for presenting the *Variations and Fugue on a Theme of Bach*, Op. 81, in truncated form at the Wigmore Hall: 'People who do these atrocious things, by some curious law of nature, generally betray their insensitivity in other ways also.'[26] DM takes issue with the oft-repeated 'textbook characterization' of Reger as a dull conservative whose idiom had little to offer to younger generations of twentieth-century musicians, and concentrates on parallels with the achievements of Schoenberg and Hindemith in order to demonstrate the composer's stature as a transitional genius who successfully combined techniques both traditional and revolutionary. The Schoenberg connection had been noted some years earlier by Constant Lambert, who had commented that most of Schoenberg's imitators 'belong to the type who, in an earlier generation, would have been followers of Max Reger'.[27] Lambert's observation had not been intended as a compliment, however (neither had Irving Kolodin's infamous remark that 'Reger's name is the same either forward or backward, and . . . his music displays the same characteristic'),[28] and it was left to DM to explore the positive side of the parallel.

The background to the first essay ('An introductory musical portrait', here reproduced in shortened form) was a pioneering series of broadcasts devised by DM for the BBC Third Programme in 1951 in an attempt to place Reger's music squarely before British radio listeners. As Harold Rutland noted in his regular

'Music Diary' in the 19 January 1951 issue of the *Radio Times*, the ten programmes formed a 'welcome opportunity to make the acquaintance of [Reger's] work . . . Donald Mitchell, who has arranged the programmes, is editor of *Music Survey* and has an intimate knowledge of Reger's music; his mother was a pupil of Reger at Leipzig. On Monday he is to give a talk on the composer.' DM's mother had indeed studied singing at the Leipzig conservatory both before and during the First World War, although she was never a pupil of Reger himself, and it was from her domestic airings of Reger's *Lieder* that DM first became interested in the composer's work.

DM's introductory talk was broadcast on 22 January under the title 'Max Reger: The Man and his Music' and the first programme of the Reger cycle went on air three days later. The complete cycle of broadcasts was ambitious in scope by any standards, and with a composer as severely neglected in the UK as Reger it constituted by far the most substantial offering of his compositions yet to be made available to the British public.[29]

Although not all critical carping was silenced by this impressive venture (the conservative Dyneley Hussey restricting his comment in the *Listener* to a culinary metaphor comparing the soufflé of works by Lord Berners cooked up by Constant Lambert in the same period to the 'solid dish of not too tender meat with plenty of dumplings and rich gravy' represented by Reger),[30] the general awareness of Reger's achievements undoubtedly increased. The composer and critic Kaikhosru Sorabji, noted for his perceptive comments on other neglected figures, wrote to DM on 23 January 1951 (the day after his introductory talk), responding enthusiastically to his discussion of the significance of Reger's Catholicism in shaping his ecclesiastical output and urging him to proceed to write a full-length study of the composer. Sorabji wrote again on 17 February and laid the blame for Reger's neglect at the door of unadventurous English organists who had failed to appreciate his genius, and who played with a style of *legato* suggesting their fingers had been dipped in glue, cow dung and treacle. Earlier in the month, Reger's widow had written to DM to thank him for the sympathy and comprehension of Reger's achievements he had displayed in his BBC talk.

In November 1952, Sorabji wrote to *Musical Opinion* to reopen the Reger debate with specific reference to Reger's organ music, lamenting the dearth of broadcasts of his music and commenting

> when the BBC *did* broadcast one of the Master's greatest and most powerful creations for the instrument, whom did they get to do it? . . . a performer was chosen who could scarcely cope with the mere notes at more than about quarter-speed . . . The same sort of indiscrimination and utterly inept choice of performer was on another occasion shown in the case of Reger's greatest piano works . . . of any artistic or intellectual grasp of the music [the pianist] showed no signs at all.[31]

In reply, John Holmes took Sorabji to task for presuming to label Reger a 'master', and pointed out that several French organist–composers (Franck, Widor, Vierne, Dupré and Messiaen) might equally deserve the accolade 'greatest master of the organ in modern times'. Holmes declared that the organist referred to by Sorabji was 'far from incompetent' and fired a broadside attacking Reger's style:

> Dr Thalben-Ball said in his presidential address to the RCO [Royal College of Organists] in January, 1949: 'Alfred Einstein, writing of Reger's music, says "harmony and the disease of modulation was heightened to monstrous proportions, while the rhythm was so devitalized as to become amorphous"!'[32]

Incensed by this reiteration of a conventional condemnation of Reger's compositional idiom, DM re-entered the fray by publishing the two further essays on Reger reprinted in the present volume ('The Case of Max Reger', Parts I and II). Beginning with a summary of Reger performances over the preceding years, the articles go on to discuss the composer's fluctuating critical reception in more detail than in DM's earlier Reger publication.

In 1957 DM again organized a Reger cycle for the BBC Third Programme, this time consisting entirely of the composer's organ works and comprising a comparatively modest four programmes.[33] In his introductory remarks to each broadcast, DM highlighted the significance of Reger's adoption of the instrument and noted that he had been successful both in creating a domestic repertoire for it in addition to fostering its potential as a vehicle for quasi-symphonic musical developments. Sorabji sprang to DM's support one more time, writing to him on 6 February 1957 to rebuff roundly the short-sightedness of English critics ('those noxious and obscene parasites on the body of Art!') and quoting with evident glee Reger's own celebrated response to a contemporary critic: 'I am at present seated in the smallest apartment of my house with your criticism before me; presently it will be behind me.'

Reger, quite clearly, would have relished the intellectual jousting and critic-baiting that had launched DM's career so spectacularly with *Music Survey*. If the journal's distinctive character derived from what Arnold Whittall has termed 'the tension between the scholarly and the journalistic, the high ideals of the spiritual aristocrats and the verbal pugilism of the hacks',[34] then this lively tension shines through in all the writings assembled in the present collection. As Edward W. Said recently declared in his introduction to the latest reprinting of DM's influential study *The Language of Modern Music*,[35] the best of his output is distinguished by 'its passionate unflagging energies, its unshakeable faith in communication and community, its deep love of and concern for music as an aesthetic and social practice'. Whether one is delving into the reprinted articles on Mahler and Britten gathered here or is discovering for the first time areas of expertise that have receded into the mists of the last forty years, one finds DM's critical voice speaking to the reader as forthrightly and pertinently today as it always has.

Nottingham, 1994

NOTES

1 Nicolas Slonimsky, *Baker's Biographical Dictionary of Musicians*, 1971 supplement (Schirmer, New York, 1971), p. 163.
2 Quoted in Nicolas Slonimsky, *Perfect Pitch: A Life Story* (Oxford University Press, Oxford, 1988), p. 214.
3 Joseph Kerman, *Musicology* (Fontana, London, 1985), pp. 119–20.
4 *Journal of the American Musicological Society* 18 (spring 1965), pp. 61–9.
5 Kerman, op. cit., p. 120.
6 John Carey, *The Intellectuals and the Masses* (Faber and Faber, London, 1992).
7 *Musical Times* 98 (February 1957), p. 91.
8 DM (ed.), *Benjamin Britten: 'Death in Venice'* (Cambridge University Press (Cambridge Opera Handbook), Cambridge, 1987), p. 207 n. 16.
9 'Editorial: The Edinburgh Festival', *Music Journal* (the original title of what later became *Music Survey*), 1947, p. 2.
10 *MLA Notes*, December 1981, p. 304. See also the same author's *Gustav Mahler and Guido Adler: Records of a Friendship* (Cambridge University Press, Cambridge, 1982), pp. 2–3.
11 DM and Hans Keller (eds.), *Benjamin Britten: A Commentary on his Works by a Group of Specialists* (Rockliff, London, 1952).
12 For a full survey of the innovative work of Faber Music under DM's helmsmanship, see David Wright, *Faber Music: The First 25 Years, 1965–1990* (Faber Music, London, 1990) and, author uncredited, *Faber Books, 1925–1975, & Faber Music: Notes of a Decade* (Faber and Faber, London, 1975). See also Christopher Palmer's remarks on p. xxx. Among the more important tasks DM undertook at Faber's was his editing of the series of conversation books by Igor Stravinsky and Robert Craft: see Craft, *Stravinsky: Glimpses of a Life* (Lime Tree, New York and London, 1993), p. 61. After Stravinsky's (self-confessed) emulation of Brittenesque titles in his later works, it is perhaps only fitting that Craft now appears to be adopting titles redolent of DM's Britten projects (cf. *Pictures from a Life*, *Letters from a Life*, etc.)!
13 Unpublished letter from Peter Pears to Benjamin Britten, 6 January 1953. Quoted by kind permission of the Trustees of the Britten–Pears Foundation and not to be further reproduced without written permission.
14 Unpublished letter from Benjamin Britten to DM and Hans Keller, 21 January 1953. Quoted by kind permission of the Trustees of the Britten–Pears Foundation and not to be further reproduced without written permission.
15 *Musical Opinion* 78 (1954–5), pp. 409, 471. DM had described Vaughan Williams's *Hodie* as 'grossly under-composed. If this is the kind of music that rouses cries of exaltation, then our musical culture is in a worse condition than I thought possible . . . [It is] crudely written, thrown together rather than organized, dreadfully thick in its textures, and second-rate in musical invention.'
16 Michael Kennedy, *The Works of Ralph Vaughan Williams* (Oxford University Press, Oxford, 1964; second edition, 1980), pp. 246–7.
17 Review by Arno Huth, *Musical Times* 79 (September 1938), p. 707.
18 William McNaught, 'Dr George Dyson's Symphony', *Musical Times* 79 (January 1938), pp. 13–17.

19 George Perle, *The Operas of Alban Berg II: 'Lulu'* (University of California Press, California, 1985) and Douglas Jarman, *Alban Berg: 'Lulu'* (Cambridge University Press (Cambridge Opera Handbook), Cambridge, 1991).

20 Perle, op. cit., p. 274.

21 Jarman, op. cit., p. 45.

22 *Music Review* 25/4 (November 1964), p. 311.

23 Mosco Carner, 'Berg and the Reconsideration of *Lulu*', *Musical Times* 124 (August 1983), pp. 477–9.

24 W. Strecker, 'Max Reger in London', *Mitteilung des Max-Reger-Instituts* (1957); P. Prince, 'Reger and the Organ', *Diapason* 64/4 (1973).

25 The article appeared (under the editorship of John Wain) in the Oxford student magazine *Mandrake* 2 (February 1946), pp. 25–33. For further information on DM's 1946 Reger broadcast with Harold Truscott, see Christopher Palmer's remarks on pp. xvi–xvii and p. xxxi, note 2.

26 *Music Survey* 2/4 (spring 1950), pp. 273–4. The recital in question took place on 18 March 1950. Hans Redlich wrote a lengthy letter to the journal on the subject of this truncation, which was published in the October 1951 issue (4/1, pp. 379–80). Redlich argued that the cuts had been sanctioned by Reger himself, but DM riposted by pointing out that 'Composers often have to agree to undesirable compromises in order to achieve a performance. We should not turn their own excusable willingness to negotiate deletions into an excuse for lazy listeners and lazy executants. Mr Frank Merrick was able to play the work in its entirety, and with considerable success, at the Bechstein Hall on April 18th 1910 . . . I am unable to understand why we should lag behind forty years after.' Merrick repeated his performance of the complete set of variations as the third concert in DM's BBC Reger cycle in 1951: see p. 58.

27 Constant Lambert, *Music Ho!: A Study of Music in Decline* (Hogarth Press, London, 1934; revised edition, 1966), p. 251.

28 Quoted in Gervase Hughes, *Sidelights on a Century of Music* (Macdonald, London, 1969), p. 188. Hughes is, nevertheless, a sympathetic writer on Reger who comments that 'The comparative neglect into which even the very best of his music has recently fallen is largely undeserved.'

29 For a complete listing of the programmes' contents, see pp. 57–9, note 2.

30 *Listener* 45 (22 February 1951), p. 315.

31 'The Organ World: Letters to the Editor', *Musical Opinion* 76/902 (November 1952), pp. 117–19.

32 'The Organ World: Letters to the Editor', *Musical Opinion* 76/905 (February 1953), pp. 307–9.

33 The programmes are listed in full on pp. 59–60, note 3.

34 Arnold Whittall, review of the collected single-volume reprint of *Music Survey* (Faber Music, London, 1981) in *Music and Letters* 58/2 (July–October 1982), pp. 288–92.

35 DM, *The Language of Modern Music* (Faber and Faber, London, 1963; revised editions, 1966, 1976; new introduction by Edward W. Said, 1993), p. 12.

ACKNOWLEDGEMENTS

The following articles and talks appear in print for the first time in the present collection: 'Bangkok Diary II: January 1978'; 'Cradles of the New'; 'Mahler's Hungarian Glissando'; a note on the 'Peace' chord in *Owen Wingrave* (see pp. 335–7); and 'What is Expressionism?'. The original source for reprinted material is given at the foot of the first page of each text; where talks or broadcasts were delivered with musical illustrations, this is duly noted or the relevant musical examples incorporated. All additional editorial annotations are preceded by the editor's initials. A complete list of the sources in alphabetical order will be found on p. 490. Without the generous collaboration of all those involved in the original publication of the texts, in whatever medium, this volume would not have been possible.

The author wants to express his particular thanks to Valerie Eliot (Mrs T. S. Eliot) and Faber and Faber for permission to quote the lines from Eliot's *East Coker* which introduce the volume; these have always had a special significance for him. He is also most grateful to the artist Milein Cosman (Mrs Hans Keller) for allowing him the use of some of her drawings. He is further indebted to his fellow Trustees of the Britten–Pears Foundation for permission to quote from the letters of Benjamin Britten. These and all other such writings by Britten are © The Britten–Pears Foundation and their further use or quotation requires written permission.

The compiler and editor are greatly indebted to the following: Jill Burrows, whose skills, enthusiasm and mastery of the technologies involved have made a massive contribution to the production of this book; Eileen Bell, who patiently and expertly transcribed the majority of the texts; friends and colleagues at Faber and Faber who have shown an unfailing interest in and support of the project: Belinda Matthews, Charles Boyle, Ron Costley, Jane Feaver, Sarah Theodosiou. Other friends and colleagues must also be gratefully acknowledged for their assistance in a variety of ways: Sir Malcolm Arnold, Patrick Carnegy, Anthony Day, David Drew, Michael Durnin (responsible for the music examples), John Evans, Boris Ford, Toby Glanville, David Harman, Bruce Hunter, Julian Kershaw, Emma Lake, Mimi Loustas-Cooke, Colin Matthews, Kathleen Mitchell, Andrew Porter, Andrew Potter, Peter Righton, Philip Reed, Judy Young, and, of course, DM himself.

Thanks too must go to the following institutions and individuals for many kindnesses and the provision of much indispensable information: BBC Written Archives Centre (Christina Harris); British Library (Chris Banks); Britten–Pears Library (Paul Banks and his staff, who gave freely of their time and specialized knowledge); Hartley Library, University of Southampton (Janet Pearson).

C.P., M.C.

I

Criticism

DM and Hans Keller editing *Music Survey*:
drawing by Milein Cosman, *c.* 1950

A State of Emergency

'Do learn to discriminate.'
D. H. Lawrence

'Edward figures in her drawing room as one of those queer extinguishers of fire in the corridors of hotels. He's just a bucket on a peg.'
Henry James

My second quotation, that superbly cutting account of a husband, occurs in *The Awkward Age*. The imagery might, under only a little pressure, be made to serve as a description of the present-day music critic, an odd accessory to the world of music who is only rarely (like the fire extinguisher) of practical use: a bucket on a peg, indeed, and all too often an empty one.

It is bad journalism to start off an article with a dead end, by leading it into an immediate cul-de-sac. My views of music criticism are conditioned by the charitable assumption that the buckets, though empty, might be filled to the brim, or persuaded to contain even a half-measure of a critique composed of something other than pure water. In my more desperate moments, I fear that the buckets are no more than colanders through which music effortlessly strains, leaving no trace of a visitation. But it is hard, almost impossible, to write about criticism as it is practised,

---

Tempo 37 (autumn 1955), pp. 6–11

if what one really has in mind as a remedy is a complete change of occupation for most of the practitioners. One must assume, or pretend, that the position can be altered through, as it were, the existing channels. The restricted range of this discussion, an appreciation of my own failings, and, above all, considerations of sheer self-survival, restrain me from tackling the problem of criticism from its most personal, yet probably most acute, angle. I have no wish to suffer compulsory retirement.

If my article must neglect the alarming fact of the probable unmusicality of many a music critic, it must also reduce the sphere of criticism upon which it intends to comment to a very confined space. It is with the functions of the daily (weekly, monthly) critic that I wish strictly to concern myself. It is his activities I have in mind whenever I talk about 'criticism' without additional qualification. It is, I believe, in his field that most may be done to re-create an informed public opinion, to remove 'taste' from the mouths of the dilettantes and re-establish it as the exercise of vital discrimination. The renewal of an educated public opinion should, in my view, be one of criticism's main tasks. The proposition has been well argued across the years by Dr F. R. Leavis, whose topic is literature but whose comments apply to music with equal force. The relevance of these passages is plain enough:

> The *utile* of criticism is to see that the created work fulfils its *raison d'être*; that is, that it is read, understood and duly valued, and has the influence it should have in the contemporary sensibility. The critic who relates his business to a full conception of criticism conceives of himself as helping, in a collaborative process, to define – that is, to form – the contemporary sensibility. What it should be possible to say of 'the skilled reader of literature' is that he 'will tend, by the nature of his skill', to understand and appreciate contemporary *literature* better than his neighbours. The serious critic's concern with the literature of the past is with its life in the present; it will be informed by the kind of perception that can distinguish intelligently and sensitively the significant new life in contemporary literature.

These reminders of the conception of the critical function that

> the editor of a literary review ought to have are enough to enforce my point. If literature, as the critic is committed to supposing it does, matters, then what in relation to it matters above all is that it should be what it ought to be in contemporary life; that is, that there should be such a public as the conception I have pointed to implies: a public intelligently responsive and decisively influential. It is through such a public, and through the conditions of general education implied in the existence of such a public, that literature, as the critic is concerned with it, can reasonably be thought of as influencing contemporary affairs and telling in realms in which literary critics are not commonly supposed to count for much.
>
> That is the faith of the critic.[1]

By and large, that is my 'faith' too, and I would that more of my colleagues might seriously bother themselves with this question of ensuring that music 'should be what it ought to be in contemporary life'. Music, too, of course, 'matters' in just Dr Leavis's subtle sense, and criticism *makes* sense only if the critic realizes that he carries a heavy social responsibility, that he has a responsible role to play in the relation between the artist and his audience. Indeed, the relation between the critic and his public shares many features with that between the composer and his audience; both relationships are (or should be) creative, 'collaborative' as Dr Leavis puts it, and both depend upon the necessity or desire to communicate meaningful statements to an 'intelligently responsive' public. Where we have a public to whom music 'matters', the task of both composer and critic is simplified; a body of responsive opinion exists to which something may be communicated. It is one of the most painful paradoxes of our time that we live in a society whose widespread literacy runs only skin-deep. Despite the all-round increase in education, which one would have presumed to generate and expand that 'intelligently responsive' public, the composer has still tended to lose the ear of his contemporaries, and the critic, likewise, has ceased to function as a creative influence, ceased to tell in even those realms where he should count for something.

It is almost a vicious circle, with the composer often composing *in vacuo*, the public generally unresponsive, the critic sandwiched between the two, often derided by both parties, and often as much at sea with his own culture as those whom he addresses. The composer, mercifully, every now and again breaks out of the circle and the public, surprisingly, rises to the occasion. The critic, however, upon whom such a weighty responsibility devolves, only rarely breaks out of the ineffectual cage to which, in part, his recent history has condemned him. All too frequently, he fails to intervene at just that juncture where a positive judgement is most urgently required of him, where, in fact, a composer has succeeded in creating a work of art that needs intelligent appreciation or, at the least, serious consideration. The critic's business is to see to it that such a work is 'understood and duly valued' by the 'contemporary sensibility', yet how often do we find that he shirks his responsibility by failing to make the necessary evaluation, by not risking an opinion ('objectivity'), by treating all artistic events as if they were of equal importance ('impartiality') – in short, by offering a remarkable incapacity to discriminate, to distinguish the valuable from the worthless and to dismiss the trite, trivial and merely fashionable which threaten to overwhelm our culture?

If the situation is to be saved, and it is dangerous enough in the present enfeebled state of the cultivated minority in *all* social strata, then the critic must, at some stage or other, abandon the evasive tactics in which he has taken refuge for so long.

Nothing will be achieved by the present policy of non-commitment, deceptive neutrality, and bogus waiting upon posterity, which are some of the main symptoms of our critical malaise. Critical standards, in the widest sense – I have in mind a responsive public stimulated by responsible criticism – will never flourish in an absence of positive discriminations. The extraordinary ineffectuality and timidity of our day-to-day musical journalism is almost its most depressing feature. Critics have simply given up criticizing.[2]

If I harp on the problem of contemporary music, it is not at all because I think the past is securely estimated or not a fruitful source of further study. On the contrary, I believe with Dr Leavis that the serious critic must concern himself with the past, 'with its life in the present' – standards of performance of our musical heritage are a most pressing issue – and, of course, the critic's awareness of the past should aid him in his perception of the 'significant new life' in contemporary music. The critic of today who discusses the past can scarcely claim much credit for getting his basic judgements right – the discriminations have been done for him. On the other hand, his views of interpretation (to which quarters, as it were, he allots his praise) are often so grotesque that they suggest a disagreeably incomplete comprehension of the masterpiece in question. All too casual an acceptance of deformations of the past undermines confidence in the critic's evaluation of the music itself. Perhaps those who are in a muddle about their own culture are in a weak position to judge the achievement of another. If we do not understand our present, it is hard, to say the least, to ensure that the past's 'life in the present' fulfils its proper function, either in what is performed or in the quality of the performance.

The present, then, must claim our closest attention, the critical condition of whose culture infects our attitudes to the past: indeed, in one department it has created a whole new field of musical activity which progressively engages more and more of our musical literary talents. No one, I trust, will imagine that I bear an ignorant hostility towards the practice of musicology – history, textual criticism, the exploration and resuscitation of the pre-classics; but can there be any doubt that this often vital study substantially reflects what one might call *the retreat from contemporary culture*, which is so peculiar to our own time? It is not that one does not wholly approve a proper and scrupulous care for the past. One does not so much complain of the care (one *complains* of nothing, perhaps) as remark upon the singular concentration – the exclusiveness – with which musicology is pursued. It is an odd fact that almost every new, young literary talent in music now makes a name for himself in some musicological sphere; or, to put it another way, the kind of serious critical talent that one would like to see working in daily criticism is employed, so to speak, in other centuries; the degree of seriousness with which the musicologist approaches his labour is rarely met with in the round of daily criticism. Indeed, the startling ascendancy of musicology in our time, its virtues apart, is very closely related to the decline of significant criticism. It is not mere coincidence that the prestige, techniques and public recognition of the one have soared, while those of the other have become progressively more and more bankrupt, both in themselves and in the estimation of the musician and the music-lover. The public rightly values, if it somewhat over-estimates, the musicologist's concrete and verifiable achievements in the field of textual 'authenticity', 'genuine' historical discoveries, and so forth. My quotation marks are not ironic but merely spotlight musicology's essential *positivity*; limited though it may be, it makes a wide appeal when contrasted with music criticism's essentially negative character. When one realizes that the 'authenticity' of musicology functions as a kind of substitute for the value judgements that critics have given up making, it is easy to see why so many talents who might have become critics turn instead to historical, textual or pre-classical studies. Musicology offers, by way of relief, a potential series of positives (accuracy, authenticity, and the like) while at the same time not requiring of the practitioner the exercise of that very discrimination which is, or should be, the critic's *raison d'être*; 'authenticity' (of text or work) replaces evaluation. Small wonder, then, that so many minds are attracted to musicology: it is the *vacancy* of present-day criticism that has contributed to its massive *extent* and still extending influence. Only a revival of positive critical judgements can redress the ill-balance of a situation where we permit our own culture to rattle itself to pieces while we impeccably reassemble fragments of the past.

There are, of course, many other smoke-screens behind which the critic retires. Since we live in a time when value judgements themselves have become suspect, it is not surprising perhaps that they have gone out of critical fashion – with disastrous results, I suggest. Yet there is little reason for a critic to sit back and wonder whether he is making a meaningful statement every time he uses 'good', 'bad', or like adjectives which express a qualitative judgement. There is less reason for him to cloud his mind with anxiety about absolutes, musical or otherwise, or to torment himself with reflections upon the eternal wrangle between objectivity and subjectivity. He has all history to learn from, and principles of what constitutes 'good' composition (or great art) may be deduced from past practice; great music of whatever period, from the past to the living present (perhaps the pre-classics must be excepted), shares much more in common than is popularly supposed. The critic of today stands in a more enviable position than his colleague of former times. The potential scope and experience of his musical understanding have been so widened both by the excavations of the historians and by the simple fact that we have a lot of musical history behind us that there is precious little excuse for not bringing our accumulated knowledge of the past successfully to bear upon the problems of the present. When one thinks, moreover, of associated studies, such as sociology and psychology, both of which are of the utmost relevance to the critic of the arts, there seems no real obstacle to the utterance of positive judgements on contemporary topics, judgements that, if the critic has made full use of all the available critical tools, have more than just a 'chance' of being right. The critic of today is in possession of sufficient evidence, of sufficient means of analysis, to enable him to arrive at considered conclusions about his own culture, to understand its failures, to understand, if needs be, his own misunderstanding of its achievements. His predecessors, far less 'knowledgeable', were almost without exception far more positive, and often startlingly right in snap judgements, which could take no account of an unexplored, unknown history – has any culture but ours been so obsessed with the past? – and emerged rather from the exercise of a valid contemporary discrimination. The 'intelligently responsive' public, the liaison between that public and the artist, doubtless benefited the earlier critics, as historical experience, sociology and psychology could benefit ours. It is an ironic fact that while the possibility of making positive judgements – of being 'right' – has substantially increased in our time, the actual practice of criticism – in the sense of exercising discrimination – has diminished. We are now in the ridiculous condition where we cannot even make up our minds about two composers as relatively unproblematical at this stage of our culture as Bruckner and Mahler. How debasingly *absurd* it is that these musicians should be treated as objects of vulgar controversy. It is only a reflection upon the miserably trivial state of criticism that a serious evaluation of the two composers – it would represent, in fact, a large measure of common agreement between those who sympathize and those who do *not*[3] – has not been achieved. Instead, we have 'controversy', which is not, I may add, a true conflict between validly based judgements, but a shameful concentration on irrelevancies, empty of musical significance.

The reluctance of the critic to shoulder the responsibility of value judgements has been assisted, as I have suggested, by our time's scepticism and its persistent assaults upon the value of discrimination. The critic, if pricked by conscience, has been able to justify his timidity in terms of the climate of thought of his own day; he has convinced himself, or allowed himself to be convinced of the ineffectuality of his role; and, at the same time, he may safely blame the general collapse of standards for having none of his own. He takes refuge, in short, in the contemporary malaise. (One might add, in passing, that the blank left in the absence of value judgements has been filled in by all manner of crankiness and deformed prejudice; anything is possible where everything is 'personal opinion'. The rot is notoriously evident even in a standard work of reference.)[4]

If the critic has been swift to use his age and its deficiencies as sop to his conscience, he has been as swift to point to a future age – to posterity – as final arbiter, as Critic-in-Chief, whose inevitable value judgements (the march of time) would render his own superfluous, even if he made them. Contemporary music, the critic seems to argue, is beyond the reach of critical decision; value judgements are in any case suspect; and why worry, when the verdict of posterity is waiting round the corner? Posterity, however, is no more than a convenient exit for the critic who will not venture a positive judgement; and if we look back at the history of posterity, we shall find few examples of its having conferred a valuation upon a composer that was altogether withheld by his own society. Posterity may confirm opinion, and certainly revise it; no less certainly it allows many reputations to die. Contemporary opinion, for its part, is often too broad in its enthusiasms (a fault on the right side). Yet it makes (or has, in the past, made) its essential discriminations, though it would be difficult to assign a method to the process, and it is upon those discriminations that posterity's 'verdict' is based. Posterity, indeed, depends upon a continuity of positive judgements; it can have only hard words for our time's spectacle of critical paralysis, of its prodigious loss of cultural nerve. Posterity's attitude is largely predetermined by the positive assertions of the society that precedes it.[5] A society that cannot value its own culture goes abysmally wrong in taking it for granted that posterity will step in later and distribute the prizes.

No article of this scope and size can hope to deal with all the problems of the critical scene, some of which are directly related to those organizations which play so important a part in our society's cultural life. In our time, for instance, in the absence of public standards and the presence of an enfeebled independent criticism – we must beware of 'public' institutions whose imprimatur in itself seems to constitute a value judgement – one that may be very widely disseminated. The BBC is an example. The very *fact* that a work enjoys a broadcast performance tends to be accepted as established approbation. Without care, without the reinvigoration of an influential criticism and a discriminating public, we shall find our cultural standards imposed by the unchecked taste of a tiny minority which has the means to transmit its discriminations to an immense audience in institutional, and thus quasi-authoritative, guise. The anonymous cultural organization, the BBC, or arts 'council' (at any level, local or national), can all too easily assume the functions of cultural arbiter. Criticism is by-passed, and the act of dissemination accrues to itself the character of a discrimination, regardless of the actual value of the commodity. The better the institution's intentions, the more 'authoritative' and 'impartial' its reputation, the greater is the danger of passive acceptance of its arbitrary standards. Or, to return to the practice of the individual critic, we must beware that a valuable development in the history of criticism – the expectation or demand of the critic that he should be technically explicit when required – is not abused.

What must be insisted upon, as foil to all the evasions, deceits, substitutes and downright cowardice of criticism in our day, is what I have called above 'a continuity of positive judgements'. The question of *wrong* judgements is, of course, bound to be raised, and let me say at once that wrong judgements are not only inevitable but much to be preferred to non-judgements. On the other hand it is vitally important to distinguish the wrong *opinion*, which fails to recognize a composer's genius and rejects him, from the wrong *judgement*, which recognizes a composer's genius and yet resists him. The wrong opinion can only be wrong. The wrong judgement could be right, and in any event represents a serious, even positive estimate of the composer (Hanslick on Wagner is an instance). Criticism today, however, declines to make positive discriminations, and indulges, by way of contrast, only in wrong opinions; even the compensation of wrong judgements is denied us. The case of Schoenberg is almost the perfect example – he is, in a sense, the victim of our day's unforgivably wrong opinions, opinions that reached their giddy zenith in *The Times*'s discovery that he was 'not a composer at all'[6] (I quote from memory). It will be readily understood in the light of what I have written above that a wrong *judgement* could never have promoted a statement so farcical and yet so frightening. The very wrongness of its wrong opinions is a symptom of the disturbing condition of criticism in our time. We should proclaim a state of emergency.

NOTES

1 F. R. Leavis, 'The Responsible Critic: or the Future of Criticism at any Time', *Scrutiny* 19/3 (spring 1953), pp. 162–83.

2 This statement is refreshingly contradicted by a notice in the *Manchester Guardian* of 9 September 1955 (Neville Cardus) in which an admirably outspoken corrective is administered to the popular conception of a much overpraised conductor's maltreatment of the classics. For the importance of this task, see my next paragraph.

MC: Cardus had written of a concert at the 1955 Edinburgh Festival:

> The New York Philharmonic Orchestra, superb under Mitropoulos, suffered a terrible transformation conducted by Cantelli. Now we listened to a monstrous tone machine, music out of the deep freeze, disembowelled and embalmed (but too noisy for that); insensitive, unsubtle, no light or shade, rhythmical as a steelyard, and, for all its exhilarating dynamics, boring in the end. Cantelli, whose repertory is apparently not extensive, gave us a travesty of the C minor Symphony of Brahms.

3 After the completion of this article an example of the very synthesis I have in mind appeared in the shape of Martin Cooper's review of Dr H. F. Redlich's new book on Bruckner and Mahler (cf. 'Two Giants Compared', *Daily Telegraph*, 10 September 1955).

4 MC: DM here refers to the fifth edition of *Grove's Dictionary of Music and Musicians*, which had appeared under the editorship of Eric Blom in 1954.

5 Or as Proust puts it in *Remembrance of Things Past*, 'What artists call posterity is the posterity of the work of art. It is essential that the work . . . shall create its own posterity. For if the work were held in reserve, were revealed only to posterity, that audience, for that particular work, would be not posterity but a group of contemporaries who were merely living half-a-century later in time.' Earlier in the same passage Proust has remarked that 'It was Beethoven's [late] quartets themselves . . . that devoted half-a-century to forming, fashioning and enlarging a public for Beethoven's quartets . . . ' [Volume 3, *Within a Budding Grove*, Part I, translated by C. K. Scott Moncrieff (Chatto and Windus, London, 1924), pp. 146–7.]

6 MC: A notorious remark made in print by Frank Howes (1891–1974), Chief Music Critic of *The Times* from 1943 until 1960. He had first joined the staff of the newspaper in 1925. In the preface to the one-volume reprint of the New Series of *Music Survey* (Faber Music, London, 1981), Hans Keller cited Howes's comment on Schoenberg as an example of an 'official statement' requiring a polemical critical response: see the present volume, pp. 19–20.

A Colloquy

with Hans Keller and Patrick Carnegy

PC: Why was your magazine necessary? What did you want to do that you felt was missing from the tone or style of the other musical journalism published at the time?

HK: Everything was missing at the time; perhaps with the single exception of the *Music Review*, which was open-minded and even allowed itself to publish articles by musicians, there was hardly a musical journal around which published articles of interest to musicians. Up to a point this is still true today. There is hardly a practising musician who reads journals like the *Musical Times*, or even the *Musical Quarterly*, unless he is being reviewed there. So what one was aiming at was a *musical* music journal which – with the partial exception of the *Music Review* – did not exist. Would you agree?

DM: I think the musicality of the responses in *Music Survey* was a central point of the intention of the journal, in so far as it could be said to have a consistent intention. The other day I was re-reading the issue[1] that contained a symposium of reactions to Schoenberg's death. Do you remember, Hans, we published a whole series, a whole sequence of obituaries! What I liked about re-reading them was the warmth and musicality of the responses that came from exceptionally diverse quarters. In short, we chose our writers –

Preface to *Music Survey: New Series 1949–52* (Faber Music, London, 1981)[2]

HK: Wisely . . .

DM: – with care; and I think on looking through the journal as a whole, it is that extraordinarily positive, *musical* response to music that emerges as an outstanding feature. That was genuinely part of the style of running the journal. However, *Music Survey* did not start out quite as it developed to be, after you joined me as co-editor, Hans. That was obviously a crucial moment in the history of the periodical. For six issues I edited *Music Survey* alone, and I should be nonplussed if anybody asked me why in fact I started the paper.

HK: That is interesting.

PC: It is. Can I help by putting this question into perspective? Was it something in particular that you were angry about? Or was it simply that there was a huge blank which you wanted to attempt to fill?

DM: The anger, I think, came in later, though I don't know whether 'anger' is the right word; 'righteous indignation', rather. The polemical character of the paper belonged to the New Series – was a manifestation, if you like, of the new editorial set-up.

PC: You embarked, you said, on your own in the first place?

DM: I think my policy in the early issues was not uninteresting and indeed sat very comfortably alongside the new ideas that Hans brought to the paper when he joined me as co-editor. What really worried me as a young man was the awful parochialism of English musical life, the complacent provinciality of the opinion-makers. I wanted to oppose all that; and if you look at the first six issues of *Music Survey*, you'll find there, for example, two really admirable articles on Pfitzner by Harold Truscott, still a highly interesting and important contribution to a very small literature in English. There were unpublished letters of Max Reger, and two very important articles by Dika Newlin about Schoenberg's compositions from his American period.

HK: Actually, I think these were important articles because, if I'm not mistaken, this was the first time Dika Newlin introduced the concepts of 'progressive' and 'concentric tonality', which meanwhile have become classical terms.

DM: I think that's correct. There were other flags run up too – for example, Mahler was a distinct presence. I'm mentioning these signals because they suggest that whereas I may not have developed an identifiable platform or programme, none the less those early issues of *Music Survey* bear witness to my attempt to bring to the notice of readers those composers whom I felt were neglected or cold-shouldered in England, or to whom the English were indifferent. I had already a sense of certain causes that I was anxious to try to fight, and saw no prospect of winning those battles in established periodicals, at least not in the late 1940s. The solution was to start a periodical of my own which could put forward reasoned arguments for those composers about whom I felt passionately at the time. It was a pretty catholic list when you look at it: Pfitzner, Reger, Schoenberg, Mahler – and, alongside them, Roussel, Sibelius, Mendelssohn, Searle, Haydn . . . Perhaps an indiscriminate taste in some ways, but also unconventional.

PC: They were your enthusiasms at the time?

DM: As a young man; and for some of those composers my enthusiasm has in no way diminished – for Mahler, above all.

PC: How old were you?

DM: Twenty-two. And I think that unorthodox choice of topics was one of the things about those early issues that may have encouraged Hans's interest in the proposal that we should jointly edit *Music Survey*.

PC: Were you in fact writing music articles, criticism, call it what you like, elsewhere before you published the journal?

DM: I think we both were, before, during and after. I wrote everywhere – in places probable and improbable, wherever I could get an opening.

PC: Did you feel a sense of constraint from the editors of those journals in whose pages you then wrote, or would have liked to write?

DM: I certainly felt that many – most – journals and newspapers took up aesthetic attitudes, or showed attitudes to certain composers, with which I was totally out of sympathy. Therefore I didn't expect to find much of a market for my particular interests. As it happens, though, the very first broadcast I ever made for the BBC was on Max Reger with illustrations at the piano by Harold Truscott, who was later to contribute to *Music Survey*, as I've already mentioned. That was a pioneering event when you think of the date – 1945 or 1946, very early days.

But I want to round off this bit of our conversation with an account of how it was that I encountered Hans. It wasn't initially through a meeting but through reading his reviews in the *Music Review*, a quarterly review, still appearing intermittently today but then edited by the late Geoffrey Sharp. There were two things about his reviews that caught my attention at the time: first of all the combative manner of the criticism, and then the detailed information that backed it up, which often included an array of footnotes. I thought that anybody who could mount a serious critical assault, or for that matter a serious critical appraisal, on a given work or composer and reinforce it with a bibliography – this was something I found entirely gripping. Then – a curious coincidence – we found that we both were living in South London, only a mile or two apart. I think it was out of my response to something very special embodied in Hans's critical work that a meeting finally emerged; and out of that meeting developed our partnership as editors of *Music Survey*.

PC: Launching a magazine is a difficult and expensive operation.

How did you set about funding the journal and distributing it?

DM: I was working as a schoolmaster in a prep school in South London, and we were very fortunate in persuading the headmaster of the school to be a generous patron. He put up the money for our enterprise and I am glad to have the chance of warmly acknowledging W. W. Livingston's support. Whether he realized altogether what precisely he was supporting, or whether he always approved of what the editors did with his money, I'm not sure, but he paid the printer's bills, and without that help we would have found it very hard – indeed, impossible – to keep going. As for distribution, it was all done by ourselves. I can remember addressing envelopes, sticking on stamps and delivering the new issue to the local post office. That, I think, was entirely done with some help from outside – friends, relatives, and so on.

PC: Did you rely on subscriptions, or was it possible to get the thing through the conventional distributors?

DM: On the contrary. In those days you could buy *Music Survey* on W. H. Smith's railway-station bookstalls and some people did so. There was in fact a rather rough-and-ready distribution system, but our main support came from our regular subscribers – including some libraries at home and overseas. However, I doubt if there were more than about a hundred or a hundred and fifty subscribers altogether.

PC: What was the print run?

HK: I seem to remember that the maximum was a thousand and the minimum around five hundred.

DM: I think that the paper's reputation was out of all proportion to the actual number of copies sold. There was always a certain number of people eagerly awaiting the appearance of a new issue, who would be first out on the streets to try to secure a copy. Among them, inevitably, were some upon whom we had launched our latest critical attack. I remember hearing about one senior critic, seen walking down the Charing Cross Road with his face buried in the current issue – and I dare say emerging, metaphorically speaking, with a black eye.

PC: Were you actually reviewed by the music critics?

DM: Before we go on to that, may we look at this moment of change when we began editing in harness? I've said how it was that it came about, and I'd been very much gripped by what I'd read of Hans's criticism and then found that we were neighbours in South London. As a result of Hans's coming in as joint editor I think *Music Survey* did develop a policy, with rather more definition and edge to it than has been the case before. Perhaps Hans might have something to say about that?

HK: Well, first of all, I think I ought to answer your question about the constraint which we might have felt in other journals and which might have prompted us to do that in *Music Survey* which we couldn't do elsewhere. As far as I'm concerned, I can't agree that I felt under constraint at the time. As Donald said, I chiefly wrote for the *Music Review*, where I had total freedom, though it must be admitted that there were certain issues, above all that of Britten, where this freedom was not altogether total – so that my essay on 'Britten and Mozart' was refused by the *Music Review* and subsequently accepted by *Music and Letters*; but this was an exceptional instance. On the whole I should say that I did not feel frustrated, and that no such negative feeling was responsible for my enthusiasm for *Music Survey*. In spite of the polemical nature of the journal, the aims I had in mind were entirely positive, and they were closely related to Donald's, except that they were not conceived of in national terms. They were, simply, defence of great or substantial composers whom our musical world neglected. Such defence, of course, inevitably took polemical shape, since one fought people who said that those composers were no good or were not composers at all. Don't forget that this was the time when *the* Music Critic of *The Times*, Frank Howes, published an extended article in which he demonstrated that Schoenberg wasn't a composer at all. Ineluctably, therefore, when one wrote about Schoenberg one's tone was slightly polemical, in view of such official statements.

But behind all such polemics was something which had nothing to do with aggression, which was sheer enthusiasm, musical enthusiasm for great composers who were not yet recognized as being great. And our range was trans-school, which is to say that since there was Schoenberg on the one hand and, shall we say, Britten on the other, there could not have been the slightest suspicion that we subscribed to any current school of compositorial thought. I think we rather commendably concentrated on musical substance – even if it did not betray downright genius, so that composers like Benjamin Frankel and quite a few others were taken up again and again for this simple reason, that there was a great deal of under-estimation; I mention Frankel because, at the moment, his music is suffering a parallel stretch of under-estimation. If I may summarize at this stage, then, it's important to realize that much of the aggression which shows in *Music Survey* is positive; that is to say, it sprang from the spirit of defence of great music. In fact, come to think of it, there was no other aggression. All those who felt attacked had attacked in the first place: we only attacked attackers. It's my recollection that we did not devote much energy to the destruction of rubbish.

DM: There was the *occasional* review which did just that: an act of demolition, very often achieved in one sentence. We aimed in particular to deflate the bogus and pretentious. Proper targets, surely?

HK: The bogus, I quite agree.

DM: For the rest, Hans is absolutely right. Our attacks were born out of our commitment to the composers in whom we believed. Also, I think, they were generated by a belief I still hold to this day that the best criticism is founded in an enthusiasm for –

and thereby, in my view, a comprehension of – the music, or the artist about whom one is writing. We were very much against the philosophy which teaches that criticism means being sceptical or negative, a view which is disseminated still in all too many academic institutions. Many of our colleagues seemed surprised to discover that this was a view we did not share. And, if I can add one further thing to what Hans has said so interestingly and return for a moment to Schoenberg, only the other day I was reading an article by Arnold Whittall about Schoenberg in England, where he happened to make a very revealing comment: that if somebody wanted to find out – from a historical point of view – how the English regarded Schoenberg, and that person read the obituary summings-up published in *Music and Letters* – I don't know if you recall them, but I do very well – then the unavoidable conclusion would be that attitudes to Schoenberg in England in the 1950s were almost exclusively unsympathetic, hostile or negative in tone. But, as Whittall says, that would be a misleading impression because, if your hypothetical researcher then turned to *Music Survey* – Whittall kindly describes us as a 'short-lived but stimulating periodical', or something of the sort – and read *our* anthology of Schoenberg's obituaries, he or she would find radically different attitudes, radically contrasting points of view. In that particular context, I think *Music Survey* can be said to have stood for something that was historically very important, something which went against the tide of received opinion.

If I can just make one other point, I think that while it's absolutely true that neither of us felt, as a critic or writer, under any particular constraint, and contributed widely to a whole range of specialist and minority publications, both good and bad, I doubt if we should have found it easy – in any case, we weren't asked – to have joined the music staff of, say, *The Times* or the *Daily Telegraph*. In other words, the mass media, including the BBC of course, did not hasten to open their doors to us during those years. I'm not suggesting that one was suppressed or censored; but one was not encouraged.

PC: May I remind you, Donald, of one instance indicative of the strange cultural climate of thirty years ago? You had begun to write as a freelance critic for *The Times*, and were just off to review a concert including the Schoenberg First Chamber Symphony, when Frank Howes, 'Our Music Critic', took you on one side to say, 'Well, you know, we have a policy about him', as if the paper had made up its mind about the composer – as indeed it had about its attitude to Europe, Iceland, or whatever – and was going to stick to it.

DM: That is correct. I don't want to criticize Frank Howes so long after his death; he was, in fact, very kind to me as a young man. But certainly, although not saying, 'You've got to write *x*, *y* or *z* about Schoenberg, about the Chamber Symphony', he *did* make it perfectly clear that *The Times* had pronounced its verdict and therefore what *I* should write should not in any way contradict 'official' opinion. *The Times* had spoken. It was not for me to *un*speak it. I think I got round it by talking about the performance, and I'm sure that anybody who read my notice would certainly have got the message that I thought the First Chamber Symphony was a pretty good piece. But I couldn't have written, 'This great work by Schoenberg'; and that in turn reminds me of that extraordinary remark Eric Blom once made to me, when he said, 'Mitchell,' – or 'Donald', or whatever he called me at the time – 'the fact of the matter is we just don't want Mahler here', which is yet further evidence of that continuity of negative opinion to which you referred in connection with *The Times*. 'We just don't want him here': Blom said that without qualification or reservation and in absolute confidence of the rightness of his judgement. Well, that's a view that has experienced a singular reversal.

PC: To what extent did you yourselves revalue your opinions even as you wrote them?

HK: I've got three answers to your question. First, so far as -

revaluation is concerned – and I'm speaking for myself now – I don't think that any revaluation took place at any stage, because when there was music that I hated, disliked and therefore probably did not understand, I hadn't written about it in the first place: I kept off such music, so any revaluation that may have taken place had taken place in private and not in public. Now comes answer number two. So far as one's attitude to tradition was concerned – again I can only speak for myself for the moment – I did not think in terms of tradition, ever – so that, when I was confronted with a traditional attitude, an attitude that insisted on a certain tradition (as indeed Frank Howes did, within the context of Vaughan Williams, for instance), what took place was what Donald calls 'demolition': I tried to demolish all *evaluation in terms of style* in favour of *evaluation in terms of substance*. This brings me to my third answer: the problem which I think you want to raise did not exist at all so far as my own mind was concerned. There was no problem. There was great music which I understood: that I wrote about. There was lousy music which I thought I understood: that I sometimes wrote about too. There was a lot of great music I did not understand, which I never touched upon, and still don't. And there was even lousy music which I could not trust myself to understand – which, likewise, I did not touch upon. In terms of tradition, I reiterate, I never did think, and still do not, with the sole and well-definable exception of the development of composition: if you are saying that there is a tradition of twelve-note technique, inasmuch as this technique has developed within its life-span, yes, that I was interested in – the history of the technique. But my concern with tradition never went beyond such technical aspects. I trust these three answers satisfy your question.

PC: You printed articles; you printed correspondence. Did you also print concert reviews?

HK: Indeed. We wrote them, yes.

PC: How did you choose your writers?

HK: We chose people whose musicality we trusted, and whose understanding of that particular music we trusted.

DM: Yes, we certainly tried to match our reviews to musical events with which we knew they would be sympathetic and about which they would be knowledgeable and thus competent.

HK: We were never scared of over-estimation. We were only scared of under-estimation. After all, from a certain level upwards, there is no such thing as over-estimation, and I'm sure that even now there might be plenty of people who would regard some of the reviews in *Music Survey* as overrating the composer or performers in question. I don't think that problem ever bothered us. On the contrary, other things being equal, we always picked the deepest enthusiasts.

PC: How did you work with your contributors? Did you edit them? And, if so, was this largely a matter of cutting?

HK: *Edit* them? To put it mildly. God!

DM: We worked immensely hard at editing our contributors, a major consequence, I'm sure, of Hans's joining the paper; he introduced an entirely new set of standards into the editorial process. This was not solely a consequence, in my view, of Hans's personality and idiosyncratic editorial techniques. I think there was more to it than that. I don't at all apologize for the Old Series of *Music Survey* which, as I've said, broke quite a lot of new ground in a quiet way – even in a discernibly un-English way in choice of topic. On the other hand, given my own education and a tradition of writing about music in English – elegant, bland, complacent and above all *empty* – which was the only tradition I was familiar with, I doubt if I should have arrived on my own account at the editorial style that came to characterize *Music Survey*. Hans, remember, came from another culture and quite another intellectual tradition. His astonishing linguistic ability enabled him to look at English from the outside and perceive potentialities not immediately apparent to those whose mother tongue English was. It was a linguistic confrontation I found entirely fascinating. Then there were two other rather un-English qualities I believe Hans brought to our editing – discipline and rigour. This meant that everything had to be considered at the deepest level, from the content of a contribution to the distinction between commas roman and italicized, a fine typographical point I've worried about ever since. It almost constituted a symbolic embodiment of the passion we brought to our editing.

PC: Karl Kraus said that if all the commas were in the right place there'd be no more wars.

DM: I learned an enormous amount from the methodology I've just outlined. I believe those were qualities that we tried to make characteristic of the paper as a whole and which we also tried to encourage our contributors to develop in or for themselves. When they were absent, I suppose we tried to write them in.

HK: Indeed, and joyfully so. Since you ask this question about editing, we spent immeasurably more time – correct me if I'm wrong – on editing other people's pieces than on our own writing. In fact, quite often we virtually had to rewrite entire pieces. That was the hardest part of the job, I should think.

PC: You sent them proofs, obviously?

DM: Oh yes, certainly. But the editing was a tremendous chore, an enormous job. So too was the proof-reading. Of course, in those days one was much younger and much less busy, so one had the energy and the time. When the weather allowed, we sat on the terrace at 50 Willow Road, Hampstead, outside the kitchen, with Milein feeding us coffee and other things, and corrected the proofs. I remember that very vividly.

PC: Did your contributors go along with your editing? Were there any protests?

DM: I think the contributors who felt closely allied to the policy of the paper sustained their loyalty through thick and thin, though I don't doubt they had misgivings from time to time. On the other hand, the changing composition of the editorial boards tells its own story. We did bring in various friends and acquaintances to function as a kind of consultative body, even if our consultative process never went very far. But every so often one or other member of the board would send us a letter of resignation. Either we'd trodden on a particularly sensitive toe, or, more likely, written something rude about the institution where the board member worked, or wanted to work. People kept on retiring or retreating, so you find the editorial board – which we finally gave up altogether, I think, because it was impossible to keep a coherent body of people with us – in a constant state of flux. Some toes we trod on emitted a sharp cry of protest. I still recall Ernest Chapman's postcard, in which he threatened to appear with a loaded revolver and shoot the editors if we printed one further review with a qualifying editorial footnote attached to it. The correspondence section, indeed, includes cries from those whose toes had been trodden on by others than ourselves. There's Peter Pears's postcard, for example – do you remember? – from Germany. In it, the music critic of *The Times* was assured that, although he'd buried both Schoenberg and Stravinsky in a recent article, Stravinsky in fact was alive and well – and rehearsing *Oedipus Rex* with Pears in Cologne. The hapless Howes received his own funeral tribute from the great singer: 'Grand Undertaker of Music', or something of the sort.[3]

PC: You've put a lot of stress on passionate advocacy of things you believed in, and yet you also offended and insulted people.

HK: The 'and yet' is wrong. One flowed from the other. The insults flowed from the passion. The insults were confined to attacks on attacks, and the attacks which we attacked were attacks on great music we felt passionate about.

DM: I think, Hans, that there were two crucial, one might almost say classic, examples of this particular aspect of the paper's work. One was your famous article, 'Schoenberg and the Men of the Press', and the other, my piece on *Billy Budd* – 'More Off than On *Billy Budd*'.[4] I think each in its own way admirably documents this particular mode of attacking the attackers.

HK: They are perfect illustrations, I quite agree, of the attackers attacking attacks. Nor did we, as could be seen from those two pieces, attack people as people. We attacked their attacks, directly, and confined ourselves to their attacks when we attacked, though it is true to say that in the case of critics who habitually manifested their non-understanding aggression towards certain great composers, we allowed ourselves to talk about their work as a whole as being destructive of music. But, in principle, the attacks were always confined to the things which most clearly show up in the two pieces Donald mentions: there it can be seen that we concentrated on the actual music, showed where these people failed when they talked about the music, showed what the music meant in reality, how it worked technically. The best and most factual proof of the success of our venture was the spontaneous gratitude of the composers. Schoenberg's gratitude for my strictly musical assault was explosive.

DM: And in the case of Britten it was almost the only article of mine I wrote about him that he actually admitted to having read. I was much moved, years after – it must have been at least twenty years after the event – when he told me how much it had meant to him at the time, reading that particular piece on *Budd*.

HK: At the same time one accumulated so much goodwill amongst composers that way that when it came to rather critical stages such as the publication of Schoenberg's last piece against Thomas Mann, one was treated with friendly understanding. On that occasion, I was really frightened to begin with. Schoenberg had written the article in German, and I translated it. Some of it, however, was clearly libellous. So I had to rewrite little bits in order to keep just within the law of libel and, knowing of Schoenberg's personality, I expected an outburst. But no, he was so happy about us by that stage that when I sent him this rewritten piece he immediately returned it with a postcard which said, 'OK, fine' – an unusual reaction from Schoenberg, which showed the amount of goodwill in our credit account. Briefly, we were liked by composers and hated by critics.

DM: Schoenberg's article on Thomas Mann's *Dr Faustus*:[5] I can very vividly remember its arriving and our looking at it together and coming across Schoenberg's description of Mann as *Tagschreiber* ['hack']; and I remember thinking somewhat uneasily that, although one had a lot of sympathy with what Schoenberg was saying, that show of contempt was carrying it a shade too far – an unease that was intensified when 'tapeworms' were introduced as an image of Mann's sentence structure. I think you had to find some way round of dropping those particular gems.

HK: Precisely, yes.

DM: One of the few reviews the periodical got was from Frank Howes. He wrote that the editors of *Music Survey* may have had interesting ideas, though less than elegantly expressed, but that the important lesson they had not yet learned was that dog does not eat dog. Do you remember that?

HK: Ah yes, indeed I do.

DM: And of course *Music Survey* in this particular area took the contrary view: that dog – when necessary – should eat dog. We didn't accept that unwritten but widely observed code of behaviour, and in so far as we felt we succeeded in demonstrating how much of the dismissal of what we considered to be great music was based, at best on defective, and, at worst, on incompetent reviewing, we felt wholly justified in attacking much of the criticism that was manifest in the 1940s and 1950s. We probably did make quite a dent in how people regarded critics and criticism and perhaps the standard may have risen a bit as a result.

PC: Apart from the dogs wanting to get back at you, presumably there must have been some colleagues who saw the point of what you were doing, and when there was a new number of *Music Survey* went out of their way to draw their readers' attention to it?

HK: On one or two occasions.

DM: You're quite right. Desmond Shawe-Taylor, for example, although I don't think one could describe him as having been an enthusiastic *Music Survey* reader, none the less seemed to see that we were serious and had an intelligent and intelligible point of view. For the rest, I don't think people fell over themselves to try to acquaint a wider public with an influence that they thought to be subversive and with opinions with which they were out of sympathy.

HK: There were quarter-hearted, silent supporters, such as William Mann. And there were, of course, Deryck Cooke and H. C. Robbins Landon. For the rest, you are really implying that there were such people as musical music critics or musical musicologists – whereas what we did, I think, was to offer a lonely platform for musical music criticism and musical musicology. It virtually did not exist elsewhere.

PC: Can I now take you quite a long way back, because you said that the existing so-called music journals didn't get through to the musicians, i.e. the musical musicians, the musical musicologists? Was *Music Survey* read by people who spent their lives thinking about music, and perhaps writing music? Did you get through to lots of conductors and performers?

HK: I would say very occasionally, and the reason why it was only occasionally was that so far as the negative part of our activities was concerned, we concentrated a great deal on the mutilation of great music by performers: long pieces on performances were usually blacklists, very detailed and concrete, specifying lists of what people had done wrong, thus preventing the music from getting across. There were also highly positive pieces on people like Furtwängler; but, of necessity, they were in the minority, because there aren't all that many great performances in the world and, in any case, we did not, as a journal, concentrate on performance. So I would say the answer to your question is, very occasionally: we certainly didn't 'get through to lots'!

PC: As a result of your endeavours, do you think you managed to get more of the music you were interested in published and performed?

HK: In the long run, yes. In the short run, no. Only now perhaps can the effect of our then endeavours be felt. You can't overestimate the degree to which we were regarded as outcasts. Early on, there was no question of any publisher being stimulated by us towards printing something he had not wanted to print. That happened very, very gradually, and I should say the chief effect of *Music Survey* in this respect really manifested itself after its own demise.

PC: In that sense, 'O brave pioneers'!

HK: 'Brave' I'm not sure . . . Pioneers, yes, but courage? What did we risk? Courage you can measure only in terms of risk.

PC: But neither of you was earning your living from journalism?

HK: When I started with Donald, I think that was almost precisely the point at which I had switched over, as far as my living was concerned, from playing to writing – when I earned my living through writing. Mind you, you can't imagine what I wrote. I mean, my chief living came from contributions to *National Entertainment Monthly*, the *Stage* – to twenty-odd awful publications.

PC: Donald, I believe you were a prep-school master when you began *Music Survey*. At what point did you join the *Daily Telegraph*?

DM: Oh, my *Telegraph* job was later, years later. When I was asked to join the *Telegraph* music staff [in 1959] there had been a long enough passage of time for the memory of *Music Survey* to have faded from the scene – I doubt if my association with *Music Survey* would have been thought to have been a recommendation.

PC: Can I ask a word or two about the contributors? How did you choose them?

DM: I don't think we went searching, because that implies we had a map, which we didn't have. I think we just used our noses, our hunches . . .

PC: What about contributors from abroad?

HK: Dika Newlin, she's the only foreigner I can remember.

DM: But there were Schoenberg and Dallapiccola; and perhaps one or two others. René Leibowitz, for example. However, most of the contributors and the contributions – there were many reviews as well as articles, and also a lively correspondence section – most of them came from a fairly small band of friends and acquaintances. I don't think there was ever a coterie: it was a small circle of people sympathetic with what the paper stood for. And often people like Robert Simpson and Harold Truscott –

HK: Two very good examples . . .

DM: – both of whom were very old friends of mine from my youth, would offer – or be conscripted – to write for us.

HK: And they show that one went for musicians in the first place. Robert Simpson is, of course, a marvellous writer, but quite often we had to rewrite things, when they came from sheer musicians.

DM: And a frequent contributor like Paul Hamburger, I'm sure,

Hans, came through your friendship with him. Hans Redlich, I can't quite remember.

HK: I had played with them – in chamber music recitals.

DM: He contributed very substantially, as did Denis Stevens. I was surprised, indeed, on looking through the issues to see how many contributions there were from Denis. It shows that the historical scope of *Music Survey* was broader than I had remembered it to be.

HK: Our contributors certainly didn't choose themselves. We were the choosers, and our criteria were pretty rigid: in the first place, we absolutely insisted on total musical competence. Our literary requirements we sometimes had to postpone until – and meet at – the editing stage.

PC: What kind of relationship, if any, did you have with the so-called academic world – people like Professor [Sir Jack] Westrup and others?

DM: We had very few contacts, I think, in or with the academic world . . .

HK: Redlich.

DM: Yes, there was Redlich. In those days, if I remember correctly, he was an extra-mural-studies man, somewhere in the home counties. I don't think the academic world impinged on us much, and I'm not sure whether we impinged on it. There was, of course, our notorious confrontation with Professor Westrup, which is immortalized in the pages of *Music Survey*. Denis Stevens had jokingly – though, it turned out to be, imprudently – remarked that if Westrup's ambitions as conductor of the University Opera Club continued, then he would have to consider closing down the University Music Faculty altogether. The professor didn't take at all kindly to this suggestion. We received a very stiff letter from his lawyers and had to publish a retraction and an apology – and pay the professor's costs, which we could ill afford.[6] This was about the only crossing of paths with academia that occurred to my knowledge during the life of the paper – more of a collision than a colloquy.

HK: We regarded the academic world, quite rightly, as pretty sterile. So we showed proportionately little interest; after all, this is still true to a considerable extent, though far less so.

PC: Did you have any fellow spirits among BBC producers?

HK: Bob Simpson was the only one. Had he joined . . . ?

DM: I don't think Bob was yet with the BBC. Moreover, our feelings about the BBC were not all that positive at the time.

HK: There was that editorial I wrote, 'A Bedside Editorial for the BBC' . . .

DM: That was about Schoenberg – a pretty sharp editorial.

HK: At the appointments board for my first BBC job, although I was chosen, I was reliably informed that the then Head of Music, Maurice Johnstone, was the first to speak after I had left the room: 'In view of what *Music Survey* has done to us, only over my dead body.'

PC: But it *was* over him, if not over his dead body?

HK: Indeed, and later on we became friends: after a few months, having written an enthusiastic report about me, he took me to lunch in order to tell me that he had been mistaken.

DM: I think it's rather difficult in the 1980s to realize quite what musical opinions were current in the BBC in the late 1940s and early 1950s. I know from my own experience that, despite my early and unusual start at the BBC with a programme about Reger, it was by no means easy to champion musicians to whom the BBC in those days – the musical bureaucrats, I suspect, rather than the producers – had developed a resistance, to put it as politely and as mildly as possible. I can recall a programme I did on Britten in the early years of the Third Programme, not what I said so much as the awful atmosphere that surrounded the talk and its aftermath – a mixture of disbelief and disapprobation, a dislike, certainly, for my particular views which was intensified by distrust of their enthusiastic expression and doubt about the value of the composer's work. In short, taking Britten with such a degree of seriousness gave offence.

I had the same sort of experience in quite another field of study – Furtwängler as a Beethoven interpreter ['Furtwängler and the Art of Conducting', Third Programme, 24 January 1952]. Here the anti-Britten complex was perversely transformed into an anti-Continental complex. Thus the odours were various but mostly ill, and when allied with the famous bad taste and uncouth manners of *Music Survey*, small wonder that, though not exactly proscribed, one was all the same not invited to broadcast, which is how the system worked in those days. I'm not, by the way, making myself out to be a martyr in any sense, but there is no doubt that the kind of opinions we advanced and stood for didn't make us much loved by the BBC of more than twenty-five years ago.

PC: Subsequently, both of you and many of your contributors actually went on to exercise great influence on the BBC and on other institutions, did you not?

HK: Decades later.

DM: When William Glock arrived at the BBC, it was entirely different. But I think many of the views and attitudes that we launched in *Music Survey* took a good ten or fifteen years before they started to be influential.

HK: I would say between ten and twenty years.

DM: I can still remember – which now may seem very extraordinary – I can remember Britten's publishers in the 1950s, Boosey & Hawkes, actually telling me what harm we'd done to

Britten by putting together the symposium[7] and compiling the Britten issue of *Music Survey* – harm, because our enthusiasm for his music had aroused –

HK: . . . had brought him into ill-repute . . .

DM: – had aroused feelings of envy, or whatever the feelings were supposed to be which would have remained benignly dormant if it hadn't been for our passionate advocacy's upsetting the apple cart. That was the kind of *Alice in Wonderland* world in which one lived at that time. However, it was all enormous fun, quite apart from everything one learned from it as an experience. I certainly learned an immense amount from it, and from working with Hans during those years.

HK: Through the development of that collaboration such things as our Britten symposium happened: it was really an extension of *Music Survey*, and wouldn't have happened without it. One need, I think, we were always conscious of – not to be exclusively topical. If and when the occasion on or for which we wrote seemed topical, we were anxious to say things which would be of interest in future years. That purpose one was always acutely conscious of in the case of a musical quarterly: both of us were alive to it in both *Music Survey* and the *Music Review*, which we thus regard as a bit of a sister journal.

DM: That's right, yes.

PC: You came out more often . . . ?

DM: No, we came out quarterly, and in rather irregular quarters, I fear. The journal was printed by a very small firm in the south of London, a family business I'd known since my childhood. I think the type was virtually set by hand on antiquated machinery, while the average age of the printers must have been well over seventy – it wasn't, of course, but so it seemed to me. Somehow, however, we got our issues out.

If you note the topics we chose to have articles written about, the composers we championed, bear in mind our concept of attacking the attacks, our policy of striving for alternative critical standards, of trying to achieve improved critical competence, our emphasis on musicality – then it seems to me that whatever demerits the journal may be said to have had fade away into relative insignificance. And there's still one quality I haven't mentioned – a certain prescience, an instinct not only for what was topical but what would become so. I still cannot help feeling a certain sense of gratification after all these years when I read Redlich's admirable obituary of Kurt Weill.[8] It must have been, in those days, probably the only journal in the English-speaking world that took the opportunity seriously to assess Weill's importance as a composer. In that kind of editorial act I think the value of *Music Survey* resided and continues to reside.

PC: Why did this wonderful enterprise come to an end?

HK: It was purely external, extraneous, incidental circumstances.

DM: I think the patterns of our lives changed radically, though in different ways.

HK: Did it not have to do with money, in other words that for some reason or other the flow of money ceased? I'm not sure, but I have some such vague recollection.

PC: But you couldn't possibly have had any sense that you had accomplished your purpose?

DM: I don't think it was that. We both started to be even busier, and you must remember too that this was an unpaid job.

PC: The contributors weren't paid either?

DM: We did pay our contributors, notional sums, I dare say, but at least something. We didn't pay ourselves anything. It was entirely unpaid, the editorial part of it.

HK: One practical, factual criterion it is interesting to apply: this morning I had an extended look at *Music Survey* and found absolutely nothing in it that's out of date, with the sole exception of things having been positively revalued meanwhile, so that it's no longer necessary to fight for them. But that revaluation in itself shows how relevant the original articles were. There's nothing that gives you the feeling of out-of-dateness from the point of view of today's cultured musician. Would you not agree?

DM: Yes, I think *Music Survey* wears well. Some things are still uproariously funny. For example, I think the exchange of letters about our use of the umlaut, in which Bill Mann sought to give you lessons in German,[9] remains a uniquely comic contribution which I hope will find, like much else in the journal, a whole generation of new readers.

NOTES

1 *Music Survey* 4/1 (October 1951).

2 MC: This conversation, in which DM and Hans Keller were interviewed by Patrick Carnegy about the aims of their journal *Music Survey*, took place in London in December 1980. The periodical was founded by DM in 1947 under the title *Music Journal* but changed its name after its first issue at the request of the Incorporated Society of Musicians, which already published a *Music Journal* of its own. *Music Survey*, as it thus became, was jointly edited by DM and Keller in a New Series from 1949 until it ceased publication in 1952.

3 MC: *Music Survey* 4/2 (February 1952), p. 437. Pears's postcard was sent from Cologne and dated 6 October 1951. He pointed out that Howes had buried both Schoenberg and Stravinsky,

> . . . (prematurely in the latter case, as I, writing from lively rehearsals of *Oedipus Rex* with the composer, can happily testify). This is the second major interment conducted recently by [Howes]; he can now have no serious rivals for the title of Grand Undertaker of Music.

4 MC: DM's 'More Off than On *Billy Budd*' is reprinted in the present volume, pp. 365–92.

5 MC: Arnold Schoenberg, 'Further to the Schoenberg–Mann Controversy', *Music Survey* 2/2 (autumn 1949), pp. 77–80: see also Hans Keller's 'Schoenberg and the Men of the Press', *Music Survey* 3/3 (March 1951), pp. 160–68.

6 MC: Stevens's review appeared in *Music Survey* 3/3 (March 1951), p. 213, and

the obligatory editorial apology followed immediately in *Music Survey* 3/4 (June 1951), p. 232.

7 DM and Hans Keller (eds.), *Benjamin Britten: A Commentary on his Works by a Group of Specialists* (Rockliff, London, 1952).

8 *Music Survey* 3/1 (summer 1950), pp. 4–5.

9 MC: William S. Mann's letter appeared in *Music Survey* 4/1 (October 1951), p. 381:

> . . . The *ummlaut* [*sic* – *Eds.*] is an honoured member of the German vocabularic family. Its ancestry, like that of the French circumflex accent, is irreproachable and its use invaluable. Sirs, you are now making away with it . . . This ugly typographical periphrasis cannot be caused by the want, in your typesetter's armoury, of a's and o's with ummlauts [*sic* – *Eds.*] on top. In your last issue but two, Schütz was spelt as I write him here, in one notice, and, in another, according to your own quaint prejudice – Schuetz . . . Your magazine is designed to be *read*; let it not be an offence to the eye.

Mann added by way of postscript: 'What do you do about *Haüser*?' Keller's response was printed immediately below:

> Our respected contributor's attempt to write more than 250 words about nothing is completely successful; less so his touching endeavour to teach me my mother tongue . . .

Keller then proceeded to add more than 400 words seeking to clarify Mann's observations, concluding with his own biting postscript:

> Previously we should have printed *Haeuser*; nowadays we put your two dots in the right place [i.e. *Häuser*].

II

Contrasts

Max Reger: caricature, Wiesbaden, 1891/92

Max Reger (1873–1916): An Introductory Musical Portrait

I The Problem of the Conservative Revolutionary

'Every composer must start from the beginning.'
Max Reger

History has an odd way of dealing with certain composers, and Reger's fate has been odder than most. That the verdict of his contemporaries was a more discriminating and just appraisal of his talent than that offered by ourselves – and we must count ourselves, even at this short distance, as posterity – would seem to disprove the rule that most contemporary judgements are wrong if and when they come into conflict with posterity's. 'Time alone will tell' is a sound enough proposition until it doesn't; and the rather ambiguous obscurity that envelops Reger (at least as far as this country is concerned) makes one suspect that Time doesn't know quite what to do with him.

What then was the judgement of his contemporaries? That he was a great composer? Undoubtedly a band of devoted disciples thought he was, and during the latter part of his life, and certainly after his death, he was crowned *Meister*. It was not without significance that the traditional laurel wreath encircled Reger's deathbed brow; or that his spectacles, symbol of professorial respectability, were left gracing his nose. In those two scenic details is revealed an essential part of the judgement of Reger's

---

Music Review 12 (1951), pp. 279–88

contemporaries – essential, but by no means the most interesting, since it so very much lends support to today's view of him as the conscientious German academic whose exercises were so convincing that everyone mistook them for the genuine article. Hence the laurel wreath and the fulsome graveside speeches.

While we can always spare a sympathetic smile for the mistaken beliefs of a just-previous generation, this somewhat condescending and superficial attitude completely overlooks the more interesting aspect of the verdict of Reger's contemporaries. To put it in brief, if oversimplified, form, he was considered a 'revolutionary', even a ruthless and dangerous one. So much so that his C major Sonata for violin and piano, Op. 72, received no end of a noisy and outraged press, and his Piano Concerto, Op. 114, was estimated by his countrymen to be 'the most unpopular composition that has appeared for years'. As the late W. J. Turner shrewdly (and wittily) observed, this was 'of itself an achievement in Germany and prejudices one in its favour'. Possibly after all the laurel wreath was more hardly earned than we at first imagined, and from contemporary accounts and from Reger's own voluminous correspondence it would seem that opposition to his music was continuous and often intensely bitter.

Now Reger as 'revolutionary' is an altogether more lively proposition than Reger as 'reactionary' and deserves our closest attention. It may be that the contemporary verdict of him, intended though it was as criticism and not as praise, is altogether nearer the truth than posterity's contrary assumption that he was an arch-conservative of little or no relevance to the music of our own time. Of course it's downright bad-mannered for a musical hangover to persist, and Reger, according to all the illogical, quasi-historical rules, should have been dispelled long ago by draughts of Parisian Alka Seltzer, vintage 1920. Yet his personality remains, if not very substantially for the English-speaking world, then more strongly in Germany and the Low Countries where he made his reputation. But neither Reger's personality, nor his ideals and ambitions, fit very neatly into a conception of 'for home consumption only', and a better appreciation of his music might do something to deflate his textbook characterization as a purely Teutonic composer and enable us to view him as the major figure he undeniably was.

Revolutionary or extreme conservative? The problem can be rewardingly discussed only in the light of Reger's own musical environment and the changed musical landscape that succeeded it – one, indeed, that he helped to change. That he was a conservative composer is, of course, partly true, and more especially true of our own judgement of him. In fact it is only the conservative part of him that we really understand and that we ultimately reject as needless duplication of past centuries. On the other hand, the majority of his contemporaries, far from understanding his conservatism, misunderstood only his rebelliousness – which they in their turn rejected, not for its derivativeness, but for what they thought was an unnecessary upheaval of the academic proprieties of nineteenth-century German music. Their understanding, therefore, of the relatively new aspects of Reger's art was, paradoxically enough, cast in the form of opposition – but at least it was a response on the whole more sensitive and alert than that of succeeding decades.

II The Music-Maker

> '[My pupils] forget that Art [*Kunst*] comes from being able [*können*].'
>
> Max Reger

'But my dear fellow, you're still making music!' Such was the remark made to Reger after a concert of his orchestral works by the eminent, worldly, prosperous and acute Richard Strauss, whose rather clumsy irony does not conceal what was fundamentally a very perceptive appraisal of Reger's music. A comment perhaps tinged with regret, since Strauss was never quite sure how far his colleague approved of what he was doing to further the cause of the 'New' German school. Reger's late excursions into programme music, the *Romantic*, *Böcklin* and *Ballet* suites for orchestra – respectively Opp. 125, 128 and 130 – must have struck Strauss as very half-hearted affairs compared with his own sometimes minute domestic pictorialism. 'Another few jumps and you'll be on our side,' he added hopefully on another occasion. But Strauss was to be disappointed. Reger returned to his old loves, variations and fugues and the restrained proportions of the late chamber works. The Hero's life was not for him; and if Strauss was capable of perceptive irony, so too was Reger. When he came to dedicate a piece to Strauss (the Fantasia and Fugue in D minor, Op. 135b) it was not one that employed the orchestral apparatus, as might reasonably have been imagined, but the organ – the instrument nearest Reger's heart and perhaps farthest removed from Strauss's.

'Still making music!' Probably Reger would not have been displeased with Strauss's phrase as an epitaph. The actual physical business of setting down notes on paper was half the secret of Reger's creativity. His indefatigable *industry* was in itself a continual stimulant to his imagination and explains why he so rarely felt the need of an extra-musical association to induce him to compose (his *Lieder*, of course, excepted). Nothing is more characteristic than his virtual obsession with variation form, either varying his own or others' themes. There are the Hiller and Mozart sets for orchestra (Opp. 100 and 132), the Bach and Telemann for piano solo (Opp. 81 and 134), the Beethoven for two pianos (Op. 86), and the Op. 73 Variations on an Original Theme for organ. Variation procedure haunts his big organ chorale-fantasias, and often his slow movements (particularly in the chamber music) are cast in the form of an *adagio* or an *andante, con variazioni*. Putting a theme through its musical paces, so to speak, was one of his chief delights; hence Reger's reputation as an 'absolute' musician in contra-distinction to Strauss, or even Mahler. His output was fabulously extensive – a fact likely to be looked upon with suspicion today when fertility has become confused with facility.

But this continuous process of writing music, the manual labour of it, was an indispensable element in Reger's attitude to the act of creation. If he had written less he would not have written so much so well. He was first and foremost a 'music-maker', a plain and sober description which fits his biography.

He was born in a prim *Schulhaus* in the small Bavarian village of Brand on 19 March 1873. As a young boy he had a *Hausorgel* built for him by his father, and a more prophetic gift could hardly have been devised. Music was not his parents' profession – they were both schoolteachers, and determined, moreover, that their son should follow in their footsteps – but they were both musical. The father was an accomplished instrumental player and the mother, a more sensitive soul with pronounced artistic leanings rather diffidently expressed, taught her talented son the rudiments of the piano: he repaid the compliment later by writing songs for her to sing. Reger's life at home cannot have been especially eventful but it appears to have been tolerably happy, in spite of his father's chronic asthma and prolonged drinking bouts (a diversion carried by his son to legendary – indeed almost mythical – heights of excess).

A major turn in the young Reger's musical fortunes occurred when he began his musical studies with Adalbert Lindner, the church organist at the nearby town of Weiden. Lindner was a musician of more than local culture and almost at once perceived the latent possibilities of his gifted pupil. In conditions approaching secrecy, the boy's first composition – an Overture in B minor for flute, clarinet, string quintet and piano – was dispatched to the celebrated Hugo Riemann[1] who replied in encouraging terms, taking the opportunity to enclose a copy of one of his own primers.

Nevertheless, Reger, regardless of this pat on the back from a distinguished musical personality, was still uncertain of his musical ambitions. The event that established his determination to compose was a visit to Bayreuth in 1888 when he was fifteen. Hearing both *Parsifal* and *Die Meistersinger*, he decided that music too should be his profession. After a struggle with his cautious parents he entered Sondershausen Conservatory where Riemann, on the strength of Reger's juvenile compositions, had accepted him as a pupil.

He flourished under Riemann, who may have been at times an exacting and exasperatingly doctrinaire teacher but who possessed a mind with which Reger was in immediate sympathy. It was Riemann who introduced Reger to the musical potentialities of the Protestant chorale which was to prove such a dominant influence in much of his work. That he was a devout Catholic did not prevent him from writing extensively for the Protestant church; his four chorale cantatas, which celebrate the main Evangelical festivals, are expert examples of their kind by a composer who was able to embrace the best of both denominational worlds: the communal, universal aspect of the chorale and the opportunities it provided for individual ornamentation and decoration, almost baroque in their richness and complexity. This stylistic characteristic of Reger's is nowhere more evident than in the chorale-fantasias for organ with their endless invention and free variation so often approximating to the lost art of inspired extemporization. Indeed, this use of variation was to become a fundamental constant of Reger's music, and the debt to Riemann is obvious. If Reger was in harmony with the professor, he found his wife of a less enlightened musical disposition than her revered husband. Reger's Op. 2, a Trio for piano, violin and viola, already showing the cloven hoof in the shape of its finale (an *adagio con variazioni*) and its unorthodox instrumentation, failed to meet with the Frau Professor's approval. 'Ah well,' was her gloomy comment, 'if one *must* go one better than Beethoven or Brahms . . .'

Riemann moved to Wiesbaden with Reger on his heels; and it was at Wiesbaden that Reger met not only his future wife but also his first publisher – Herr Augener, head of the London music house. It seems almost quixotically improbable that Reger's early chamber music, songs, piano and organ pieces should have been issued under this familiar English imprint: but the improbable happened, although sales were small, reviews few, and recognition slow.

When Riemann left Wiesbaden for Leipzig, Reger, still only twenty, took over Riemann's Wiesbaden theory class, an appointment that he held until he was called up for his year's military service. The strain of army life proved too much for him, he was invalided out, and shortly after his return to Wiesbaden he suffered a severe nervous collapse and was obliged to seek rest at his home, which, meanwhile, had shifted from Brand to Weiden. For three years Reger dwelt there in comparative retirement – years among the most prolific in his career, when he concentrated with maximum energy on chamber music and music for the organ. Some of his most virile organ chorale-fantasias date from this period. The set of three, Op. 52, are outstanding technical achievements, and the last of the trilogy, *Hallelujah! Gott zu loben, bleibe meine Seelenfreud*, almost overwhelms with its resourcefulness and exuberant vitality; its concluding fugue – an extraordinary gesture of confidence and faith in a time of transition – is proof of Reger's prevailing mood of self-assurance, and an optimism backed by a glorious tradition of which he felt himself to be part. Karl Straube,[2] the eminent organist of Wesel, did much to publicize Reger's organ works and, heartened by growing successes, Reger was able to move to Munich and launch out into wider circles and projects.

Although to the end of his life Reger was never free from controversy, his Munich period (from 1901 to 1907) was the most controversial of his career – for the very good reason that the music he wrote there confounded even his most fanatical adherents. The C major Sonata for piano and violin, Op. 72 – the 'complete lunacy, incurable morbidity and nerve-racking perversity' of which bemused the critics – the F♯ minor Variations and Fugue for organ, Op. 73, and the D minor String Quartet, Op. 74, were a hat trick of musical scandals. Riemann, perhaps a trifle dismayed on discovering that his most brilliant pupil was turning out to be a shade less respectable than he had anticipated, designated the

Munich years Reger's 'wild' period. However wildness brought its own reward, for in 1902 Reger was able to marry, and in 1904 joined the staff of the Munich Academy. But for all his geniality as a man – and Reger never lost his peasant sense of humour either verbally or musically – he was not in the least successful at coming to terms with academic institutions, and what occurred later at Leipzig occurred first at Munich. He fell out with his colleagues, quarrelled with the influential Munich choir of which he was principal conductor, and felt compelled to resign. This might have been an economic disaster had it not been for his prowess as an executant – a fruit of Riemann's insistence on his perfecting his piano technique. From Munich onwards, Reger was continually travelling about Germany, Switzerland and the Low Countries, as an exponent of his own and others' works.

The year 1907 brought with it the offer of a post at the Leipzig Conservatory – then the musical Mecca of middle Europe – which carried with it joint responsibility for musical studies at the University. Reger accepted at once, but, in spite of his high hopes, Leipzig followed a very similar pattern to Munich. Ceaseless concert touring (which included London: Reger gave two successful concerts at the Bechstein Hall and was feasted at the Royal Academy of Music), endless teaching at the Conservatory, unlimited squabbling with his colleagues, furious rows with the students of the University Choir, and, of course, unceasing composition. Towards the end of his Munich years he had more seriously considered the orchestra as a compositional medium and written both a *Sinfonietta*, Op. 90, and a *Serenade*, Op. 95. In Leipzig he continued this association: the *Hiller Variations*, Op. 100, the Violin and Piano Concertos, Opp. 101 and 114, the massive choral and orchestral setting of the 100th Psalm, Op. 106, and the *Symphonic Prologue to a Tragedy*, Op. 108, all date from this period.

If Reger's reputation had increased in stature, his opponents' abuse had decreased in quality. The University Choir insulted him at rehearsals, the press (as he put it) were 'shouting' against him, and Leipzig began to assume as hostile an air as Munich. Once again Reger expressed his dissatisfaction and resigned from the University although he agreed to continue at the Conservatory – a position he filled until his death.

Reger was enabled to turn his back on Leipzig as on Munich by accepting with alacrity new musical employment – on this occasion as *Kapellmeister* to the Grand Duke of Meiningen's famous orchestra. On 1 October 1911, Reger moved to Meiningen, and for the next two years was entirely absorbed in directing his orchestra in concerts over all Germany. 'They say, "The swine composes, plays the piano – now he even tries to conduct,"' Reger reported humorously of himself; his attempts were successful and his programmes enterprising. Debussy's *L'après-midi d'un faune* (1892) found its way into his concerts, an item worth special note since Debussy's influence was to show up in the sensitive scoring of Reger's late orchestral works.[3] He was one of the very few German composers who responded positively and immediately to the then 'new' French school.[4] Naturally, the Meiningen orchestra was a stimulus to Reger's ever active imagination, and a flood of orchestral pieces resulted, three of them with a distinct programmatic bias – a new departure for Reger. The *Romantic Suite*, Op. 125, the four *Böcklin* tone-poems, Op. 128, and the relatively lightly built *Ballet Suite*, Op. 130, less intended for dancing than as a series of evocative musical pantomimes. But Reger, as he wrote on one occasion, was 'pursued by misfortune'; the strain of his combined duties at Meiningen and Leipzig told on his health, and early in 1914 he collapsed and entered a sanatorium in the southern Tyrol. He never returned as *Kapellmeister* to Meiningen – his doctors would not permit it – but nothing was able to stop him writing music; and from this time date the *Mozart Variations and Fugue*, Op. 132, his best-known and probably best-loved orchestral work. Very appropriately, it was dedicated to the members of his own orchestra.

Even Meiningen was not to pass without its share of quarrelling, and during his last months there Reger was involved in his customary routine of petty insults, slander and back-biting, a social game at which the officials at a small European court were past masters. This parochial bickering was terminated in August 1914 by the declaration of war. Reger was called up for service in the *Landsturm*, but his poor physique ensured his rejection and he was able to proceed with his plans for moving to a new house in Jena. He accepted the war with naïve enthusiasm, and his *Fatherland Overture*, Op. 140, represents his mood of 'my country right or wrong'. Soon, however, his martial spirits were to crumble, and he was writing a *Requiem*, Op. 144b, for the German dead. Ensconced at Jena in his spacious villa, he commented morosely on rationing, food queues and postal censorship; the war was not what he had expected it to be, nor was it the 'social revolution' he had hoped for as an apprentice social democrat in Munich.

Removed from his orchestra, he returned once more to chamber music, to the piano and the organ. 'I shall stay in Jena as long as I live,' he wrote. But he was not to live long. On 10 May 1916 he left for Leipzig, suffered a sudden and unexpected stroke, and in the Hotel Hentschel, during the early hours of 11 May, died peacefully in his sleep, spectacles on his nose. The laurel wreath was to follow.

NOTES

1 MC: Hugo Riemann (1849–1919): German theorist whose complex system for labelling functional harmony, although little known in the UK, is still widely taught in his native country.

2 MC: Karl Straube (1873–1950): Leipzig organist and exact contemporary of Reger's.

3 MC: A clear example of Debussy's impact on Reger may be found in the prominent use of the whole-tone scale at the beginning of the *Romantic Suite*, Op. 125 (1912), though this is an instance of an influence that has not been wholly absorbed.

4 MC: If Reger was aware of French musical trends, the French do not appear to have been aware of his own work. Honegger commented in his autobiography *I am a Composer* (Faber and Faber, London, 1966), p. 91, that Reger was unheard of in the French capital in 1911. Reger's concert tours had conspicuously

avoided France and concentrated instead on the Netherlands, England, Austria, Belgium, Hungary and Russia. In Hungary, Bartók was responsible for staging several Reger premières in Budapest in the period 1907–10: see Malcolm Gillies (ed.), *The Bartók Companion* (Faber and Faber, London, 1993), p. 73. The influence of Reger's advanced harmonic language is undoubtedly felt in Bartók's posthumously revived Violin Concerto No. 1, which dates from 1908.

The Case of Max Reger I

Max Reger has never had much of a hearing in this country, although he and his music were both well received when he visited London in 1907.[1] However, from January to March 1951, the BBC Third Programme gave us something like a 'Max Reger Festival' – in all, eleven programmes were devoted to his music[2] – and more recently there have been performances of the *Bach Variations*, Op. 81 (Iso Elinson, Third Programme); the *Telemann Variations*, Op. 134 (Erik Then-Bergh, Wigmore Hall) – both large-scale works for large-scale pianists – and the *Hiller Variations*, Op. 100, which were offered by Karl Rankl and the BBC Symphony Orchestra, once again through the enterprising good offices of the Third Programme. (The *Hiller Variations*, by the way, were first performed in 1907; this performance on the Third Programme – on 2 May 1953 – was, it is believed, their first live presentation in England.) To be sure, this slender account does not represent the sum total of Reger performances during, say, the last quarter. His name crops up now and again on many a concert programme – a song here, a piano piece there – and, this very last April, the valiant Mr Herbert Downes has been playing through the three suites for viola solo (Op. 131d) in regular succession – another item for which we must thank the Third once more. However, when one considers Reger's enormous output, the harvest of performances remains on the small side. Perhaps he is most generously dealt with by the many organists who, more frequently

Musical Opinion 76/909 (June 1953), pp. 539–41

than is generally recognized, include examples of Reger's organ music in their recitals.[3] Mr Frederick Geoghegan, the organist of All Souls, Langham Place, has taken a spirited interest in Reger's organ works, and a visitor to All Souls from the Glaubenskirche, Berlin – Herr Helmut Höing – proved to us, at the end of last year, that Reger is by no means a dead letter as far as German organists are concerned.

All in all, then, Reger survives – if somewhat spasmodically – and he survives not only through the occasional performance, but also in the correspondence columns of this journal, where Mr John Holmes and Mr Kaikhosru Sorabji have been discussing the probable value, and potential fate, of Reger's art. It is, no doubt, indecorous of me to intervene in a dispute in which, strictly speaking, I am not personally involved, but I cannot resist the temptation to make a comment or two on Mr Holmes's latest letter. All those musicians 'far greater' than Mr Sorabji, 'whose names are known and respected throughout the free world', and who, Mr Holmes seems to suggest, are all at one with him in thinking not so very highly of Reger's music – well, who are they? This is not a controversial question designed to provoke. Sir Donald Tovey, surely a 'known and respected' musician, was a respectful, serious and often favourable critic of Reger, if not a wild enthusiast. Or there is Mr Eric Blom, who, I know, dislikes Reger. Yet Mr Blom very properly and justly keeps his private feelings for his autobiography and when writing 'Of Organ Recitals' in the popular *Musical Companion*[4] points out that such recitals would not much attract the musician were it not for Bach 'and for a few composers of genius like César Franck and Max Reger' – a remark, incidentally, that should satisfy both our contestants, since Mr Holmes promotes Franck as a certain candidate for immortality while Mr Sorabji's choice is Reger. And here is Mr Blom spoiling the fun by attributing genius to both composers! Or there is Mr Martin Cooper – a Francophile rather than a Germanophile – who welcomed the performance of the *Telemann Variations* mentioned above, and wrote (in the *Daily Telegraph* of

11 March) that they had proved well worth reviving. Moreover, while turning over this Reger article in my mind I happened to glance at the *Manchester Guardian* of 8 May and there found a warm greeting extended to that belated first English performance of the *Hiller Variations* – 'this mighty work', writes the *Guardian*'s Broadcast Music critic. Or – a final topical quotation – there is Mr W. R. Anderson in the May issue of the *Musical Times*: 'Though Reger is by some sniffed at, I am always glad to hear more of him, for we are given very little of his large – probably too large – output.' I hope Mr Holmes's attention will not need drawing to the fact that I have quoted from sources not usually devoted to lavish Regerian praise. It would be all too easy to play the renowned critical game of countering one adverse and eminent criticism by another – equally eminent, but wholly favourable. Egon Wellesz's is, I believe, a name that commands universal admiration. His last paragraph, in his article dealing with Reger's chamber music in Cobbett's *Cyclopedic Survey of Chamber Music* (Oxford University Press, London, 1930), seems to me to state with admirable precision the truth about Reger as a composer: '. . . a total output of a magnitude without parallel at the present time. A life's work which can be measured only by the standard of the old masters, is in keeping with the age and yet not of it, ever on a high level, ever commanding respect by its sincerity, and – in individual instances – of a truly classical greatness.' Or are we to believe Paul Henry Lang when he writes in *Music in Western Civilization*:

> There is no compelling artistic creative urge in most of this music; the great technical skill of the plodding fugues, the various shades of grey in the slow movements, and the nervously excited *allegros* that he wrote in profusion differ in mood only, not in ideas.[5]

I have been to some pains to collect an anthology of opinions of today and yesterday about Reger, not because I wish flatly to contradict Mr Holmes, but because he seems to be so confident that Reger, one day, will be 'forgotten'. Nobody, of course, can prevent Mr Holmes from burying Reger if he so desires, though not all of us will feel able to participate in the funeral. Has it struck Mr Holmes that if Reger were indeed a musical corpse his music would hardly be capable of arousing – still – such exceptional antagonism and such exceptional praise? If Mr Holmes disbelieves me, he only has to re-read his own letters and those of Mr Sorabji. And what is Mr Holmes's answer to Tovey, to Mr Blom, to Mr Cooper, to Mr Anderson? No, the case of Max Reger is, as yet, far from being decisively settled; nothing like the major part of the evidence for the defence – i.e. the music itself – has been heard by the prosecution, and the verdict, when it comes, and whether it distresses Mr Holmes or not, will, I think, bear some resemblance to Dr Wellesz's scholarly judgement. For the moment, I shall be satisfied if Mr Holmes accepts the fact that not every good musician's opinion of Reger is a bad one.

What is the position of the musical public in relation to Reger and his works? One, maybe, of sheer bewilderment or indifference. There is a great deal of *pro*-ing and *contra*-ing by the specialists, but little opportunity to hear the works the specialists are busy denouncing or expostulating. It may be argued that the comparative neglect by performers of Reger's music makes its own effective comment, but, as I have shown, that neglect is by no means as complete as perhaps the opposition would have it, and, when we examine certain important aspects of Reger's list of works, the fact of his music's seeming neglect becomes progressively less surprising. His works, very roughly, can be divided into four categories: organ music, chamber music, *Lieder* and works for orchestra. It would be stupid to overlook Reger's orchestral music (which embraces a *Sinfonietta*, a Piano Concerto, a Violin Concerto, the celebrated *Mozart Variations*, overtures, suites, etc.), but his organ and chamber music are of equal, if not greater, substance, while his very numerous *Lieder* are, along with Hugo Wolf's, without doubt the most important contributions to the song literature after Brahms's. Here, it is not irrelevant to glance at the nature of Richard Strauss's output. Whereas with Strauss, the orchestra – even when he confined it to the orchestra pit of an opera house – reigned supreme, it was Reger's insistence on chamber music and works for the organ that exposed most clearly those lines of conduct and musical character which not only marked him off from his most distinguished German contemporary, but also decisively separated him from his nineteenth-century predecessors. It would be difficult – probably impossible – to write a representative history of nineteenth-century music in terms of its chamber music alone. The result, inevitably, would be a partial view of the period and of the composers surveyed. But a thorough acquaintance with Reger's organ music, his string quartets and many sonata combinations would present us with a pretty comprehensive account of his accomplishments and with some important information too about the leading characteristics of the music of his time; a music as we shall see that he himself helped to create.

The organ and chamber music: their appeal must be to minority audiences, even in our enlightened age. Hence one good and valid reason for the comparative infrequency of performances of Reger's music is that so much of it is cast in relatively esoteric and intimate musical forms. There is, notwithstanding, no good reason at all for the shameful neglect of his songs. *Lieder* singers are notoriously conservative; they stick with a painful persistence to a famous and 'safe' handful of Brahms, Schubert and Schumann – as if each of those composers wrote no more than half-a-dozen songs worth our attention! – and are content to ignore Reger altogether. This noxious orthodoxy plays its part in keeping Reger's music hidden from its potential public. Good music is not so plentiful that we can afford to leave a single note of any example of it gathering dust in obscurity. No singer, pianist, organist or chamber musician worth their several salts should standardize their repertoires before making a discriminating appraisal of what Reger has to offer in these various fields.

Controversy is nothing new where Reger is concerned. Into a very short lifespan, he packed four hectic careers – composer, conductor, virtuoso pianist, and university teacher – and controversy pursued him in whatever department he engaged his outstanding talents. As a composer he met with particularly virulent abuse, and his 'gross modernism' and 'wildly revolutionary and anarchical techniques' aroused the most fierce opposition. But even by his enemies he was regarded with Strauss as a prominent leader of modern German musical thought. The influence that Reger has had upon the music of our own time – its topical significance, so to speak – are questions I shall touch upon in my next article. Meanwhile, we may take note of the conflicting opinions as to the value of his art and draw comfort from them: for it is surely only genius that gives rise to manifestations of love and hate by friends and foes.

NOTES

1 MC: See 'Max Reger (1873–1916): An Introductory Musical Portrait', p. 48.

2 MC: The BBC's Reger series comprised a broadcast talk by DM, followed by ten varied programmes of Reger's music performed by many noted musicians of the day. The concerts, produced by Denis Stevens, were constituted as follows:

25 January
Mary Jarred *alto*
BBC Symphony Orchestra
Conducted by Walter Goehr
Symphonic Prologue to a Tragedy, Op. 108 (1908)
An die Hoffnung, Op. 124 (1912)
Four Tone Poems on Pictures by Böcklin, Op. 128 (1913)
'Der geigende Eremit'
'Im Spiel der Wellen'
'Die Toteninsel'
'Bacchanal'

28 January
Nora Gruhn *soprano*
Gareth Morris *flute*
Suzanne Rosza and Marie Lidka *violins*
Watson Forbes *viola*
Paul Hamburger and Josephine Lee *pianos*
Violin Sonata No. 4 in C, Op. 72 (1903)

Lieder (composed between 1901 and 1907)
'Warnung'
'Ein Paar'
'Kinder Geschichte'
'Aeolsharfe'
'Hat gesagt' bleibt's nicht dabei'
'Das Dorf'
Serenade in G for flute, violin and viola, Op. 141a (1915)

9 February
Frank Merrick *piano*
Variations and Fugue on a Theme by J. S. Bach, Op. 81 (1904)

12 February
Marjorie Thomas *alto*
Terence MacDonagh *oboe*
BBC Singers
Erich Ackermann and George Thalben-Ball *organs*
Conducted by Leslie Woodgate
Chorale Prelude: *Straf' mich nicht in deinem Zorn*, Op. 67 No. 37 (1903)
Chorale-Cantata: *O Haupt voll Blut und Wunden* (1904)
Chorale-Fantasia: *Hallelujah! Gott zu loben, bleibe meine Seelenfreud*, Op. 52 No. 3 (1900)

21 February
Margaret Ritchie *soprano*
Gervase de Peyer *clarinet*
Franz Reizenstein, Ernest Lush and Gerald Gover *pianos*
Con moto; *Allegretto grazioso*
(*Träume am Kamin*, Op. 143; 1915)
Sostenuto
(*Aus meinem Tagebuch*, Op. 82; 1912)
Schlichte Weisen, Op. 76 (1903–12)
'Wenn die Linde blüht'
'Waldeinsamkeit'
'Mein Schätzlein ist ein gar köstliches Ding'
'In einem Rosengärtlein'
'Einen Brief soll ich schreiben'
'Du meines Herzens Krönelein'
Sonata in B♭ for clarinet and piano, Op. 107 (1908–9)
Prelude and Fugue in G, Op. 99 No. 5 (1906–7)
Prelude and Fugue in D minor, Op. 99 No. 6 (1906–7)

2 March
William Pleeth *cello*
Suite No. 1 in G, Op. 131c (1915)

4 March
Dorian Singers
Ralph Downes *organ*
Conducted by Mátyás Seiber
Chorale Preludes, Op. 135a (1914)
Liebster Jesu
O Haupt voll Blut
Prelude and Fugue in F, Op. 85 No. 3 (1904)
Geistliche Gesänge, Op. 138 (1914)
'Der Mensch lebt und bestehet nur eine kleine Zeit'
'Das Agnus Dei'
'Schlachtgesang'
Variations and Fugue on an Original Theme, Op. 73 (1903)

13 March
Harry Isaacs and York Bowen *pianos*
Variations and Fugue on a Theme by Beethoven, Op. 86 (1904)

21 March
Frederick Thurston *clarinet*
New London String Quartet:
Erich Gruenberg *violin*
Lionel Bentley *violin*
Keith Cummings *viola*
Douglas Cameron *cello*
Quintet in A, Op. 146 (1915)

31 March
Strub String Quartet
Quartet in E♭, Op. 109 (1909)
(gramophone records)

For further discussion of the background to these pioneering broadcasts, see Mervyn Cooke's introduction, '*Cradles* in Context', pp. XLV–XLVIII.

3 MC: In 1957 DM went on to organize a series of four broadcast recitals of Reger's organ music with the following programmes:

25 January
Philip Dore *organ*
Kyrie eleison, Op. 59 No. 7 (1901)
Gloria in excelsis, Op. 59 No. 8 (1901)
Symphonic Fantasia and Fugue, Op. 57 (1901)
Recorded at the Royal Albert Hall, London

30 January
Arnold Richardson *organ*
Toccata and Fugue in D, Op. 59 Nos. 5 and 6 (1901)
Two Easy Chorale Preludes, Op. 67 (1902)
Fantasia and Fugue on BACH, Op. 46 (1900)
Recorded at the Civic Hall, Wolverhampton

4 February
Reginald Moore *organ*
Scherzo, Op. 80 No. 7 (1904)
Intermezzo, Op. 80 No. 10 (1904)
Weihnachten, Op. 145 No. 3 (1916)
Chorale-Fantasia: *Wie schön leucht't uns der Morgenstern*, Op. 40 No. 1 (1899)
Recorded in Exeter Cathedral

10 February
Ralph Downes *organ*
Variations and Fugue on an Original Theme, Op. 73 (1903)
Recorded at the Royal Festival Hall

See '*Cradles* in Context', p. XLIX.

4 Eric Blom, 'An Essay on Performance and Listening' in A. L. Bacharach (ed.), *The Musical Companion* (Gollancz, London, 1940 (8th impression)), p. 669.

5 P. H. Lang, *Music in Western Civilization* (W. W. Norton, New York, 1941), p. 996.

The Case of Max Reger II

A conservative or a revolutionary composer? In the answer to that brief question lies, I believe, the solution to the controversy that still rages over Reger's personality. And like every other question one puts about this remarkable composer, it is capable of being answered in more than one way. There are those who think of him as a conservative; those who think of him as a revolutionary; and perhaps a few (myself amongst them) who think of him as a revolutionary conservative. Mr Eric Blom, despite his attribution of genius to Reger in *The Musical Companion*, declares in his very own *Everyman's Dictionary of Music* that Reger posed 'as a progressive' but was 'in reality a conservative'. That is one critical view.[1] For another, we may turn to one of Reger's contemporary critics who found the famous C major Sonata for piano and violin, Op. 72, replete with 'complete lunacy, incurable morbidity and nerve-racking perversity' – a statement that suggests that somehow, somewhere, this gentleman must have failed to recognize the conservatism uncovered by Mr Blom. With these critical collisions, however, we are already familiar – we may be even a little sceptical about them. How about composers? Have they anything to contribute to the discussion?

Here, it must be admitted, the discussion both deepens and widens and, vacating the windy spaces of critical fancies, we breathe the purer air of musical facts. When the composer who is one of the two central figures of the musical revolution of our time

---

Musical Opinion 76/911 (August 1953), pp. 659–61

indicates that Reger was part of that revolution, then we must listen with respect. What Schoenberg wrote was plain enough and, in his collection of essays *Style and Idea*, it is in (English) print and easily accessible. It reads thus: 'A new technique had to be created and in this development Max Reger, Gustav Mahler, and also I myself played a role'.[2] The 'new technique' to which Schoenberg refers was the art of *developing variation*, i.e. the repetition of 'phrases, motifs and other structural ingredients of themes only *in varied forms*' (my italics), which represents a decisive turning away from the (in Schoenberg's opinion) more 'primitive technique' of themes extended through the use of 'sequences and semi-sequences, that is, unvaried or slightly varied repetitions differing in nothing essential from first appearances, except that they are exactly transposed to other degrees' – and at this juncture Schoenberg cites examples from Schubert, Schumann and Wagner. Elsewhere, moreover, Schoenberg mentions Reger's 'more remote dissonances', which seems to show that he had taken note not only of Reger's novel thematic structures but also of his harmonic adventures – those harmonic 'audacities' which had so distressed the ears of Reger's audiences. In conclusion, it is worth quoting a passage from Dika Newlin's study of Schoenberg.[3] Miss Newlin – an American student and pupil of Schoenberg's – writes: 'One looks at the movements of . . . [Schoenberg's] Suite for String Orchestra . . . and thinks of Reger. Schoenberg had always been interested in the music of Reger and had admired many things in it . . . Certain phases of Reger's style are recalled by the music of the Suite, with its busily moving counterpoint and its strongly chromaticized harmony based on traditional foundations.' She also tells us that it was Schoenberg who inspired Adolf Busch 'to complete his long-contemplated revision of Reger's Violin Concerto, a version which he first performed in New York on January 29th, 1942'.

Schoenberg's tributes to Reger and the fact that Reger turns up as an influence (albeit a slight one) in his String Suite[4] strongly support my contention that Reger's significance has a very real topical validity; after all, no one can deny Schoenberg's profound comprehension of musical history, or his contemporaneity as a composer. In addition, this Schoenbergian evidence tends to favour the 'revolutionary' side to Reger's character. Can Reger have so exclusively belonged to the dead past when he is able to capture the attention of Schoenberg, so pronouncedly a composer of and for the future? Surely, if Reger were an orthodox and even a 'reactionary' composer, we should not be successful in linking him in any manner whatsoever with so radical a figure as Schoenberg?[5] My choice of Schoenberg was, of course, deliberate – for, whatever we may think of the value of his music, we should *least* expect to find a connection with Reger therein, were the latter composer indeed a dull academic of no contemporary interest.

As I have pointed out above, nothing one writes about Reger can remain unqualified. Simple statements do not fit his complex personality. He was neither revolutionary nor conservative, but, like a good many important composers, a combination of both. His revolutionary side was itself substantially qualified by his conservatism; and yet, paradoxically enough, what we now hear as Reger's 'clinging to the past' was, in his own day and historical situation, a revolutionary rather than an orthodox aspect of his art. We have been able to trace certain of Reger's forward-looking innovations through to, and with the help of, Schoenberg; for an estimation of the topical significance of Reger's conservative tendencies we must turn to a composer who is, I think, the leading conservative amongst contemporary composers – Hindemith. This judgement may surprise some readers who recall Hindemith's jazzy experiments of the 1920s; but in recent years he has rejected the thumb-to-nose attitude of his early period and I believe it is fair to say that now he creates within well-defined and often specifically traditional limits. Hindemith is, of course, a most imposing composer, with a genuinely contemporary idiom; but it is an idiom that has more and more disclosed roots based securely in the past – hence the label 'neo-classicist', which was applied to much of Hindemith's music written after 1925. 'Neo-classicism' is excellently described in the *Harvard Dictionary of Music* as

> a movement of twentieth-century music which is characterized by the inclusion into contemporary style of features derived from the music of the Bach era and of still earlier periods. It represents the latest and strongest expression of the general reaction against the unrestrained emotionalism of the late Romanticism. Particularly distinct is the influence of Bach, which makes itself felt in the emphasis on contrapuntal texture; in the revival of early forms such as the suite (not the ballet-suite of the late nineteenth century), toccata, passacaglia, ricercare, concerto grosso, ground; in the reduction of orchestral resources and colours; in the abandoning of programme music, and in a general tendency towards an objective and detached style.[6]

Now, odd though it may seem, this detailed account of a major twentieth-century movement in music (of which Hindemith was such a vital exponent) could stand, with very few alterations and amendments, as a highly condensed summing-up of Reger's position in the history of European music. All those who contemptuously consigned him to oblivion as an 'imitation Bach' were displaying a lamentable lack of historical insight. Reger was not a dead-end composer who happened to alight upon a Bach revival as the best means of achieving a quick and transient notoriety. He was, in reality, the very beginning of this vast 'neo-classical' tidal wave which engulfed European music during the first third of the twentieth century and which, even today, has not fully receded.

Anybody, I think, who examines a handful of Reger's and Hindemith's works with unprejudiced ears will be struck by the many extraordinary similarities of character and genre. Above all, the inquiring musician will be impressed by Reger's and Hindemith's joint devotion to – 'obsession with' might be the better term – contrapuntal devices. Hindemith's *Ludus Tonalis* (1943) – that astonishing compilation of fugues and interludes for piano – is proof, if proof were needed, of his preoccupation with counterpoint, while the massive fugues which inevitably cap

Reger's innumerable sets of variations speak for themselves. It is true that Reger's counterpoint is frequently vertical (harmonic) rather than horizontal. Hindemith's 'linear' counterpoint, i.e. 'the modern type of counterpoint which pays little attention to harmonic combination and euphony' (*Harvard Dictionary*), is, nevertheless, not without its precedents in Reger, who often indulges in a very free part-writing unmistakably prophetic of the younger composer's style. Play one of Reger's late string quartets alongside one of Hindemith's and, I think, the stylistic parallel becomes obvious. It is, perhaps, of interest to learn that when Hindemith founded the famous Amar–Hindemith string quartet (in 1924) he took part in many a performance of Reger's chamber music – actions that speak as loudly as Schoenberg's perceptive words quoted above.

Hindemith is credited with being one of the founders of the 'New Music'. Professor P. H. Lang has judicious things to say about new musical ideas in his *Music in Western Civilization.* He writes: 'One of the most pregnant lessons of history is that the kernel of the new ideas that seem to arise with each succeeding epoch may always be found in previous times. This is also true with regard to styles.' Hindemith, in fact, would not have been what he is, or where he is, without the example of Reger; and the new and enlightened histories of music for which we are all waiting will be severely deficient in their appraisal of contemporary movements if they neglect Reger's substantial contribution to the twentieth-century scene. The succession Brahms–Hindemith makes a good deal of historical and musical sense when Reger is placed between them – an altogether exceptional composer acting as a bridge from the old to the new.

For reasons of space I have been obliged to concentrate on Schoenberg and, more particularly, Hindemith; and it may be that those listeners who find the music of these two composers forbidding and aloof will wonder where, if anywhere, Reger's famous geniality and good humour – both of which are such marked characteristics of some of his music – had an influence on a composer of a generation later than Reger's own. How many people realize that the Czech composer of that cheerful opera *Švanda the Bagpiper* – Jaromír Weinberger – was one of Reger's pupils? And that *Švanda*'s justly celebrated Polka and Fugue – which every Prom audience must be able to whistle from first note to last – are heavily indebted, in form, style and high spirits, to like examples from Reger's output? A clear case, if there ever were one, of the 'copies' being popular while the original 'models' are virtually unknown – their existence unsuspected, even. Some day, perhaps, we shall be able to appreciate both.

NOTES

1 DM (1994): I found, while looking at this article forty years on, a note from Blom among my papers, dated 22 July 1957: 'Don't laugh', he wrote. 'I am an hon. member of the Max Reger Institute, believe it or not! I don't know why, perhaps because I put a full catalogue of his works into *Grove*. If they only knew!'

2 MC: Arnold Schoenberg, 'Criteria for the Evaluation of Music' (1946) in Leonard Stein (ed.), *Style and Idea* (Faber and Faber, London, 1975), pp. 129–30. An excerpt from Reger's Violin Concerto displaying five-bar phrases was quoted by Schoenberg in 'Brahms the Progressive' (ibid., p. 427).

DM: Schoenberg's specific mention of Reger and Mahler – could one think of two composers more sharply contrasted? – reminds me of a singular fact: that Reger contributed, in the shape of a manuscript facsimile of the opening bars of his *Serenade*, Op. 77a, for flute, violin and viola, to the remarkable *Festschrift* in Mahler's honour, put together by Paul Stefan and published by R. Piper and Co., Munich, in 1910.

3 Dika Newlin, *Bruckner, Mahler, Schoenberg* (King's Crown Press, New York, 1947), p. 275.

4 But not only in the Suite for string orchestra. I have no doubt that Schoenberg's late *Variations and Fugue on a Recitative* for organ, Op. 40, composed in 1941, owes a great deal to Reger's F♯ minor *Variations and Fugue on an Original Theme* for organ, Op. 73 – one of his most 'advanced' works, as I have already pointed out.

5 DM (1994): In the jettisoned Part III of 'Max Reger: An Introductory Musical Portrait' I drew attention to 'a strange song' of Reger's – 'Ein Paar', Op. 55 No. 9 – which, I suggested, 'is peculiarly akin, not only in mood, but in melodic and harmonic style, to songs in Schoenberg's half-Impressionist, half-Expressionist manner', i.e. before the evolution of the twelve-note method; and continued –

Herrn kgl. bayer. Kammersänger EUGEN GURA in besonderer Verehrung zugeeignet.

FÜNFZEHN LIEDER

für eine Singstimme mit Begleitung des PIANOFORTE von

MAX REGER.

Op. 55.

Für hohe Stimme.

Verl. Nº 3004 a Nº 1. **Hymnus des Hasses.** „Heil dir der du hassen kannst." (Christian Morgenstern) M 1,–
Verl. Nº 3004 b. Nº 2. **Traum.** „Nun du wie Licht." (Franz Evers.) „ 1,–
Verl. Nº 3004 c. Nº 3. **Der tapfere Schneider.** „Ich wollt', ich wär ein Held." (Gust. Falke.) „ 1,–
Verl. Nº 3004 d Nº 4. **Rosen.** „Eine Schale blühender Rosen." (Marie Itzerott.) „ 1,50.
Verl. Nº 3004 e Nº 5. **Der Narr.** „Keinen Vater, der das Kinn." (L. Jacobowsky.) „ 1,–
Verl. Nº 3004 f Nº 6. **Verklärung.** „Leise deinen Namen flüstern." (Marie Itzerott.) „ 1,–

Für mittlere Stimme

Verl. Nº 3004 g Nº 7 **Sterne.** „Die ihr den Äther mit." (Anna Ritter.) 1,–
Verl. Nº 3004 h Nº 8. **Zwei Gänse** (De Capitolio) „Zur weißen Gans sprach" (Julius Sturm) „ 1,–
Verl. Nº 3004 i Nº 9. **Ein Paar.** „Schweigend geht die." (Richard Braungart.) „ 1,–
Verl. Nº 3004 k Nº 10. **Wären wir zwei kleine Vögel.** „Wären wir zwei kleine Vögel" (Aus dem Rumänischen von Leo Greiner.) „ 1,–
Verl. Nº 3004 l Nº 11. **Viola d'amour.** „Holde Königin der Geigen." (Gust. Falke.) „ 1,–
Verl. Nº 3004 m Nº 12. **Nachtsegen.** „Die Lande durchträumt." (Franz Evers.) „ 1,–
Verl. Nº 3004 n Nº 13. **Gute Nacht.** „Das war der Junker Übermut." (Gust. Falke.) „ 1,–
Verl. Nº 3004 o Nº 14. **Allen Welten abgewandt.** „An den Mondesstrahlen gleiten." (Marie Stona) „ 1,–
Verl. Nº 3004 p Nº 15. **Der Alte.** „Nun steh ich über Grat." (Gust. Falke.) „ 1,–

Eigenthum des Verlegers.
Eingetragen in das Vereinsarchiv.

LEIPZIG, JOS. AIBL VERLAG G.m.b.H.

Copyright 1901 by Jos. Aibl Verlag.
Aufführungsrecht vorbehalten.

France et Belgique et leurs Colonies
Louis Gregh
78 Rue d'Anjou, Paris.

Copyright for the United Kingdom owned by
Breitkopf & Härtel
London W. 54, Great Marlborough Street.

In die „UNIVERSAL-EDITION" aufgenommen.

Title-page of Reger's *Fünfzehn Lieder*, Op. 55 (Universal Edition)

Above and facing: The opening of Max Reger's 'Ein Paar', Op. 55 No. 9

. . . from one aspect Reger's harmony at its most adventurous might be viewed as a kind of limited, though quite unmethodical and probably unconscious, harmonic 'Expressionism'; his complicated chord structures must often be considered as vertical sonorities existing in their own right, although Reger never abandoned key relationships systematically, as did Schoenberg. The sensation of insecurity experienced by so many listeners to Reger's music, ascribed by them to his intense, 'wandering', 'homeless' chromaticism, is really based on their inability to perceive the autonomous nature of the isolated chord or chordal sequence . . . Frequently, the effect of his cadences is as much due to what was harmonically left out as to what, harmonically, was left in – examples abound in the superb B♭ Clarinet Sonata, Op. 107. The resulting ellipsis is liable to sound awkward or unconvincing where the listener's harmonic sensibility is lacking or where

the listener simply cannot keep pace with 'a harmonic style that moves as rapidly as very often Reger's does'.

MC: The song 'Ein Paar' had been broadcast on 28 January 1951 by Nora Gruhn as part of DM's BBC Reger series: see pp. 57–8, note 2.

6 Willi Apel (ed.), *Harvard Dictionary of Music* (Harvard University Press, London, 1951).

The World of Paul Hindemith

For an amusing start, Hindemith's book, *A Composer's World: Horizons and Limitations* (Oxford University Press, Oxford, 1952), puts quite a few of our musical lexicographers in the wrong. Hindemith, it seems, would have none of Mr Eric Blom, who writes in his indispensable *Everyman's Dictionary* that *Gebrauchsmusik* was 'a term invented by Hindemith'; and he would surely scorn Mr Willi Apel who, in the *Harvard Dictionary of Music*, states that the *Gebrauchsmusik* movement 'started under Hindemith'. Hindemith, in his Preface, tells us how mistaken all those are who think he favours the term. He used it, once, to point out 'the danger of an esoteric isolationism in music', and since that occasion the 'slogan' has grown to be 'as abundant, useless, and disturbing as thousands of dandelions in a lawn . . . Up to this day it has been impossible to kill the silly term and the unscrupulous classification that goes with it.' One doubts, however, whether at this late stage, and even with the best will in the world, it is possible to give practical effect to Hindemith's renunciation. The term, 'ugly' or no, has proved its worth simply by reason of its vigorous survival, and in much of Hindemith's early music the *Gebrauch*, despite the composer's disclaimer, is more to the fore than the *Musik*. Hindemith, in an entertaining sentence, writes that the slogan's popularity made him feel 'like the sorcerer's apprentice who had become the victim of his own conjurations'. But was he not, in fact, not so much the victim of his verbal

---

Chesterian 28 (1953–4), pp. 35ff.

conjurations, but of his own singular type of creative character?

So much for the Preface. The remainder of the book, which first took shape as the Charles Eliot Norton Lectures for 1949–50, surveys the composer's technique and environment, performers, musical education, instruments, business matters, musical philosophy, and the important questions of thought and feeling in music. While a composer, of course, most fully reveals himself in his music, what he writes apart from notes is also bound to reflect his personality. Thus *A Composer's World: Horizons and Limitations* offers us, more often than not, a verbal equivalent, as it were, of Hindemith's music. Much of the book, like much of Hindemith's music, is very clearly thought through; it is couched in trenchant language, is direct in expression, is extremely earnest and yet does not fail to invigorate. On the other hand, the first reading is more impressive than the second; as with certain of Hindemith's compositions, the quality of the ideas do not stand up to repeated examination.

The best chapters of Hindemith's book prove to be what he, without doubt, would consider the least weighty. A few brief quotations from the chapters that succeed his opening discussion of musical philosophy, thought and feeling, will serve to illustrate the exceptional pungency of his comments. On arrangers, for example: 'An arrangement is artistically justified only when the arranger's artistic effort is greater than the original composer's.' On arrangements of the *Art of Fugue*, which attempt to convert the work into a concert piece suitable for large halls and large audiences, Hindemith questions the 'democratic' motive that prompts such performances:

> Why should everyone have everything? Even with the most liberal and most democratic distribution of goods there will be many things that the average citizen will hardly ever have in sufficient quantities . . . Should we not be glad to have certain pieces of music similarly kept away from the ordinary musical goings-on, if for no other reason than to give the ambitious seeker of higher musical truths an opportunity to grow?

He later concludes: 'You are not permitted to sell unsanitary macaroni or mustard, but nobody objects to your undermining the public's mental health by feeding it musical forgeries.'

On performers, Hindemith acutely underlines 'the essential tragedy in the performer's existence':

> When the artist succeeds in bringing the listener to his moral goal [i.e., perfectly realizing for the listener the composer's intentions], he himself loses all importance . . . [The listener's] moment of highest satisfaction was the moment of [the artist's] greatest loss.

On education, Hindemith lists the danger of 'teaching teachers who in turn teach teachers', and the defects of trying to teach composition. 'Don't teach composition the way it is usually done,' he writes. 'Teach musicians. If once in a long while one of your students shows creative talent, let nature have its course.' Hindemith wants a return to the days when

> composing was not a special branch of knowledge that had to be taught to those gifted or interested enough. It simply was the logical outgrowth of a healthy and stable system of education, the ideal of which was not an instrumental, vocal, or tone-arranging specialist, but a musician with a universal musical knowledge – a knowledge which, if necessary, could easily be used as a basis for a more specialized development of peculiar talents.

This view of the essential 'practical' composer is closely related to Hindemith's pessimistic opinion of present-day musical culture. He is much alarmed by the domination of the loudspeaker which, he says, 'has become the standard sounding instrument, towards which the sounds of most of our musical instruments are aimed'; he is suspicious of the radio and gramophone; and the decline of the amateur music-maker fills him with despondency. One can appreciate the reasons for Hindemith's particular gloom when one reads his claim that 'The quality of a society's art of ensemble singing and the value of the compositions written to satisfy the demands of the group singers is quite likely the best gauge of a period's musical culture.' It was ensemble singing in the sixteenth and seventeenth centuries, by both amateurs and professionals, that created a literature containing 'the most remarkable pieces ever written by musicians'. 'Our own time,' he continues,

> with its overweening estimation of instrumental music . . . will perhaps, in a later evaluation of music history, count as a period of lowest artistic culture, compared with those epochs in which the art of ensemble activity with the emphasis on vocal participation flourished most noticeably.

In a sense, the whole of this latter part of Hindemith's book urges a regeneration of the practising amateur musician who would become

> a member of a great fraternity, whose purpose is the most dignified one you can imagine: to inspire one another and unite in building up a creation that is greater than one's individual needs. Amateurs of this kind, when listening to music, will not be the stupid receivers, the ideal gourmands of which our audiences predominantly consist.

The composer, moreover,

> would have to provide the music needed and appreciated by the amateur . . . He would have to search for a new technical and stylistic approach, too! . . . Could not the detour through the amateur's musical domain reopen another source of musical regeneration which today is entirely dried up? . . . The musical life of the family . . . as a singing and playing community – could it not be revived?

All these matters lie very close to Hindemith's heart, and he expounds his various theses strenuously and with overwhelming sincerity. It must be admitted, however, that none of the ideas is of immense originality, and some of the more striking one would dispute. To mention only the few that have been mentioned here, one is not certain, for instance, that all arrangements can be condemned wholesale, especially those that do not attempt to supplant the original, but aim at making particular stylistic, textural or formal features more intelligible; the original may then be returned to, our ears literally opened and more responsive than heretofore. With performers, too, has not Hindemith overlooked the fundamental pleasure principle of giving? Does not the performer find satisfaction – a probably masochistic, but common enough satisfaction – in the very act of his 'loss'? On instruments, their development and history, Hindemith stresses 'the struggle to attain a greater efficiency', and is inclined to neglect the continuous historical process of instruments keeping pace with the ever increasing demands of the composer. It is true, perhaps, that Hindemith's educational reforms might reduce the number of bad composers; would they, significantly, multiply the number of good ones? If a flourishing vocal tradition is necessary for a healthy musical culture, why, in the nineteenth century, when England was chorally strong, did we have so few composers of genius? Why, now, when our amateur and vocal traditions are – so the prophets of woe inform us – at a lower ebb, have we relatively so many active and vitally creative artistic figures? And while Hindemith has every right to dislike our kind of culture, it is really not very meaningful to compare it to a culture of quite another kind – his introduction to the sixteenth and seventeenth centuries is a historical red herring. One is not convinced that the nature of music and its social function has not entirely changed – it may be for the worse, but it has changed nevertheless; and to try to put the clock back to madrigals and a revival of the enlightened amateur (vocal or instrumental) seems to be meeting a challenging new cultural situation with inadequate and dated notions. The amateur, of course, has his function – and it should be a livelier function than is widespread today – but whether or not that function will ever again be as creatively influential as it was, or as Hindemith hopes it will be once more, seems to me to be debatable. We must, I think, search for new and more topical remedies.

In his chapter on 'Technique and Style', Hindemith very properly observes that 'The evolutionist theory of music's unceasing development towards higher goals is untenable.' His 'disbelief in a continuous advancement of music' leads him to remark that 'the principles of technical construction . . . do not permit any further advancement once they are thoroughly investigated', and by means of this dubious and highly suspect reasoning he is able to dismiss 'allegedly "modern" achievements' which, as it were, purport to be 'new'. This long argument ends in a severe anticlimax, since Hindemith chooses as his target the 'so-called twelve-note technique', his basic ignorance of which he exposes in a few paragraphs of painful misinformation. While one may excuse Hindemith his factual lapses, quite inexcusable is his thinly disguised attack on Schoenberg's personality, an assault as undignified as it is unworthy of a composer of Hindemith's reputation. His irresponsibility in this sphere, however, knows no bounds, and to his lapses in hard facts and good taste he adds an astonishing blunder when he confidently predicts that dodecaphony has no future. One glance at the number of leading contemporary composers who are, in fact, dodecaphonists proves Hindemith's calculations to be hopelessly awry. In our time indeed, there is a chance that dodecaphony may at last be removed from the field of fruitless partisan warfare, and it is a pity that Hindemith should see fit to perpetuate the wearisome ideological conflict on its lowest level. To declare that dodecaphony – music 'degraded to a game of double-crostic' – must inevitably vanish, 'like epidemics of measles', is as stupid as the statements of those few dodecaphonists (of whom, by the way, Schoenberg was not one) who predicted the total disappearance of tonal music. It is undesirable that one should be obliged to defend dodecaphony and Schoenberg as intensely as Hindemith abuses them – one is, in the eyes of opponents, automatically a 'partisan'; but this crude aspect of Hindemith's book has been unquestioned by most critics, and musical fallacies, wheresoever they appear, must not be left unchallenged for eventual digestion by the gullible. In view of his strictures on sects and systems, it is all the more entertaining when, in the chapter 'Means of Production', which discusses at length intervals pure and tempered, Hindemith discloses that in his bonnet, too, buzzes a substantial and systematic bee (e.g. 'Melodies can, in our time, be constructed rationally').

The first four chapters remain to be considered. They contain the kernel of Hindemith's thought, and have attracted the widest attention. Their respective titles indicate their seriousness – 'The Philosophical Approach', 'Perceiving Music Intellectually', 'Perceiving Music Emotionally', and 'Musical Inspiration'. From the first chapter of all, 'The Philosophical Approach', it is Hindemith's utter seriousness that most strongly emerges, and in so far as philosophy makes an appearance at all, it is but to underline the author's central doctrine which he shares with St Augustine:

> The tenor of that doctrine is: music has to be converted into moral power. We receive its sounds and forms, but they remain meaningless unless we include them in our own mental activity and use their fermenting quality to turn our soul towards everything noble, superhuman, and ideal.

These exalted inclinations, one might say, form the principal motifs of Hindemith's book; as late as his chapter on instruments he writes, 'It is not what we actually achieve that is accounted valuable, but the lofty endeavours which marked our progress toward the goal.' Music, for Hindemith, is inextricably tangled up with morality; he believes, with Boethius, that music 'has the power either to improve or to debase our character'. He would, one may safely presume, along with Augustine, like to see music reinstated 'in an elevated community of sciences, a position it had enjoyed in the times of ancient philosophy'. Most importantly – and here Hindemith develops Augustine's analysis of musical perception in his own second and third chapters – the listener's response to music must be active not passive. Active perception, however, which brings its own satisfaction is not enough; we must put our satisfaction (our enjoyment) 'into the side of the balance that tends towards the order of the heavens and towards the unification of our soul with the divine principle'. Hence Hindemith's distaste for music that merely entertains; music must have a moral 'goal'.

Based upon Augustine's theories are Hindemith's explanations of how the listener perceives music intellectually:

> While listening to the musical structure, as it unfolds before his ears, he is mentally constructing parallel to it and simultaneously with it a mirrored image. Registering the composition's components as they reach him he tries to match them with their corresponding parts of his mental construction. Or he merely surmises the composition's presumable course and compares it with the image of a musical structure which after a former experience he had stored away in his memory . . . Seen from this angle, our way of listening to music or imagining music is based on previous audibly-musical or imaginary-musical experiences.

Certain of Hindemith's opinions in this paragraph are plain sailing and may be confirmed by experience or observation. One is forced to ask, however, (a) how anything 'new' may be introduced in music, and (b) how one makes sense of one's first musical impressions when one's store of musical memories is non-existent. To (a) Hindemith replies that 'There is . . . in principle never anything new in the general order, shape and mutual relationship of musical successions. We may even go so far as to say that basically nothing new can ever be introduced into such successions' [because the listener will be unable to construct an 'image' and the new structure will, therefore, be meaningless].[1] To (b) he replies that we must assume that 'There exists a primordial musical experience of a very primitive nature' which 'comes into existence in the undeveloped being's mind by perceiving a fact of life that is common both to him and to music, namely motion.' The fact is, however, that (b) is no more than a vague surmise upon which the logic of the reply to (a) depends. The reply to (a) moreover, presupposes that the stock of potential musical structures is limited – another assumption which is not susceptible of proof and which, indeed, seems to be contradicted by all the available musical evidence. Most significant of all, the theory, fundamentally, would appear to be no more than a rationalization of Hindemith's own artistic orthodoxy, disguised in a cloak of philosophical objectivity.

These same simple faults in logical thinking (which, incidentally, have been dealt with in greater detail and with more convincing authority by a professional philosopher, Mr Stuart Hampshire, in *The Score*, December 1952) mar Hindemith's chapter on musical feeling. Music, says Hindemith, can express neither the performer's nor the composer's feelings. Perhaps the latter is writing 'an extremely funereal piece', which may require three months of intensive work.

> Is he, during this three-months period, thinking of nothing but funerals? . . . If he really expressed his feelings accurately as they occur during the time of composing and writing, we would be presented with a horrid motley of expressions, among which the grievous part would necessarily occupy but a small place.

No, writes Hindemith, what really happens is this:

> he knows by experience that certain patterns of tone-setting correspond with certain emotional reactions on the listener's part. Writing these patterns frequently and finding his observations confirmed, in anticipating the listener's reaction he believes himself to be in the same mental situation. From here it is a very small step to the further conviction that he himself is not only reproducing the feelings of other individuals, but is actually having these same feelings . . . He believes that he feels what he believes the listener feels . . .

In this paragraph, Hindemith seems to suggest that certain tone-patterns (musical symbols) result in 'emotional reactions', although a few pages earlier he has announced that a fixed language of musical symbolism is an impossibility and a few pages later discusses 'the fact that one given piece of music may cause remarkably diversified reactions with different listeners'; nowhere is this seeming contradiction resolved. As for the feelings of the listeners:

> Their chain of reasoning is: (1) the composer expresses his feelings in his music – which opinion, although wrong, is excusable, since the listener is unaware of the composer's previous miscalculations. (2) The performer expresses the composer's or his own feelings

> (equally wrong, as we have seen) [i.e., because 'the ideal performer will never try to express his own feelings' but the composer's – and the composer, according to Hindemith, has none]. (3) The composer's and performer's feelings, expressed in their musical production, prompt me [the listener] to have the same feelings.

The composer is barred from expressing his 'real' feelings, and his music evokes in the listener not 'real' feelings but 'the images, memories of feelings': 'We cannot have any musical reactions of emotional significance, unless we have once had real feelings the memory of which is revived by the musical impression.'

We can only (musically) experience 'musical grief' if we have suffered 'real' grief, and experience 'musical gaiety' if we have once been really gay. A storehouse of 'real' feelings (similar to the storehouse of musical structures) provides the parallels to the 'musical' feelings.

The whole of Hindemith's complex proposition topples to the ground when we realize that his distinction between 'real' and 'musical' feelings is in itself wholly unreal. Musical feeling is a feeling in its own right; as Mr Hampshire usefully points out:

> It is a primitive psychology which supposes that all feelings must originally arise from 'experience' . . . Why should it be assumed that 'experience' excludes musical experience, and that only events in a man's biography can originally evoke his feelings? . . . The full enjoyment of the music constitutes in itself a feeling or emotions, and there is no need to look further to 'explain' this fact; that people are musical is a fact about them as primitive as the fact that they like to live in families . . . there is no need to derive musical feeling from the feelings of active life.

That we may use the same word 'gay' to describe both a biographical and musical experience does not mean that one feeling must be less real than the other, or that one cannot be real at all. Both, in fact, are real experiences and real feelings, though each is of quite a different order; it is merely the limitation of language that obliges us to apply the same descriptive term in either case. The nature and quality of the feelings are, however – and literally – singular.

After admitting that 'musical inspiration is, in its ultimate profundity, as unexplainable as our capacity of thinking in general', Hindemith has little information to contribute to our existing knowledge of the innermost creative processes of the composer. 'What the genius has', in his opinion, '. . . is vision', the 'flash of a single moment' in which the musical creator 'sees a composition in its absolute entirety, with every pertinent detail in its proper place'. And after the vision, there comes the patient work towards the ideal of 'congruence':

> A tremendous effort is necessary in order to work towards it; not merely a technical effort but a moral effort, too – the effort to subject all considerations of technique, style, and purpose to this one ideal: congruence. Again, it is the aspiration towards the ideal unity of the Augustinian and the Boethian attitude towards music which must ennoble our endeavours and which on the other hand pushes, as we know, the final goal into an utter remoteness close to inaccessibility.

A book, to be sure, that must be taken into account; but Hindemith's music, as distinct from his credo, offers us fewer limitations and wider horizons.

NOTE

1 MC: The belief that a personal response to a work of art can be meaningful only if the beholder perceives something familiar in it may well hold more true in the visual arts than Hindemith claims it does in the more abstract sphere of music. E. H. Gombrich, in *Art and Illusion: A Study in the Psychology of Pictorial Representation* (Phaidon, Oxford, 1960), cites the familiar Rorschach ink-blot test as a case in point, and – like Hindemith – invokes the deductions of ancient philosophy:

> What is important to us in looking at these instruments of psychiatry is that they confirm the intuition of the ancient philosopher. What we read into these accidental shapes depends on our capacity to recognize in them things or images we find stored in our minds. To interpret the blot as, say, a bat or a butterfly means some act of perceptual classification – in the filing system of my mind I pigeon-hole it with butterflies I have seen or dreamed of. [p. 155.]

Interestingly, Picasso criticized one of Braque's cubist still-lives on the grounds that an onlooker might find a certain pattern in it reminiscent of a squirrel:

> Day after day Braque fought that squirrel. He changed the structure, the light, the composition, but the squirrel always came back, because once it was in our minds it was almost impossible to get it out.
>
> (Picasso, as quoted in Françoise Gilot and Carlton Lake, *Life with Picasso* (Virago, London, 1990), p. 69.)

Weill's Mahagonny *and 'Eternal Art'*

In the second act of Kurt Weill's opera *Mahagonny*, which is still in production at Sadler's Wells this month,[1] the scene in Mrs Begbick's tavern opens with a paraphrase for piano of the sentimental ballad known as 'The Maiden's Prayer'.

'That is eternal art,' comments one of the citizens of the City of Mahagonny; and one certainly takes Brecht's and Weill's point. 'The Maiden's Prayer' stands for the oozing sentiment and escapist romanticism of the kind of 'art' that is pleased to seek the protection of inverted commas. They keep damaging reality at a safe distance.

But while one smiles at the swooning, maudlin, cascading phrases of Weill's extraordinarily cunning arrangement, which wonderfully re-creates the lost Lisztian skill of artful decoration, one is also oddly and perhaps rather disturbingly touched by it. It is, we come to realize, almost with a sense of guilt, rather beautiful, in its own right.

'Eternal art'? Well, perhaps not that exactly, but certainly, yes, it *has* a validity. One can't, in fact, simply laugh it off, because Weill's paraphrase very subtly and even painfully reminds us that a whole tradition of romantic music, a glorious tradition, indeed, however debased it may have become, is bound up with what might easily be mistaken for a straightforward parody.

Perhaps it was just that – a frank take-off – that Brecht wanted, against the background of which his 'That is eternal art' could be

---

'World of Music', *Daily Telegraph*, 9 February 1963

thrown like a hand-grenade. But it is the special power of music to add levels of meaning to librettists' texts; and Weill's paraphrase puts a new slant on Brecht's comment. In the light of the music, 'That was the eternal art that was' must also form part of our response to 'The Maiden's Prayer' variations.

I have dwelled on this one event in the opera because it conveniently illustrates the complex feelings and references that lie beneath the surface of an outwardly simple musical style, simple in language, though quite remarkably unconventional in vocabulary, and seemingly simple in dramatic intent. It is our failure to hear what is actually involved in Weill's 'simplicity' that multiplies misunderstandings and wrong assessments of his artistic achievement.

When *Mahagonny* was first performed in 1930, the scandal precipitated by its première obscured the importance of the work as a contribution to the musical theatre of the twentieth century. What we have to guard against in the less frenzied atmosphere of 1963 are basic misapprehensions of the composer's purpose.

In a sense, Weill was his own worst enemy, in that he brought his art of simplicity to a very fine art indeed – so fine, that he demands peculiarly discriminating ears of his audience. This is nowhere more evident than in the justly celebrated and justly popular songs, which one is compelled to describe as 'cabaret' songs because one can't think of another term to apply to them. It is confusingly true, moreover, that they do use, though at far remove, a stock of clichés that is associated with the popular-song style of the 1920s and 1930s. But if one stops short at recognition of the clichés and does not come to grips with Weill's most *un*cabaret-like harmony, with his exquisitely precise and novel instrumentation and the highly personal shapes of his tunes – which, once experienced, one seems to have known all one's life (hence the illusion that there must be precedents: one is reminded of 'models' that in fact don't exist) – then one is almost certain to miss both the dramatic significance and musical independence of the songs; to hear them, in fact, as the opposite of what the composer intended them to be.

The only way to approach these remarkable songs, and to understand them, is by way of their dramatic function in the opera. They are undeniably and brilliantly appealing, but their haunting melodies, we find, carry the weight of unexpected and disconcerting sentiments. A famous example is Jenny's song, with its lethal refrain:

> And if someone's going to kick, it'll be me,
> And if someone's kicked, it'll be you.

Scarcely a typical cabaret-song text; and of course the gap between the anti-social sentiment and the 'trivial', jaunty setting only intensifies, as Brecht and Weill intended it should, the impact of the song, which seduces one with a smile and then kicks one in the teeth.

But there is much more to the songs than a simple and deliberate discrepancy between texts and music. Weill not only succeeds in promoting the special alienation effect at which Brecht aimed but also, miraculously, builds into his music a critical commentary on its own 'triviality' (which is where his singular harmonic invention has an important role to play). At the very moment when Jenny is singing her haunting refrain, Weill's music is itself actively protesting at its inhuman, anti-social implications.

I cannot hope to describe this mysterious achievement in words. The best way to savour it is by studying the vocal score of the opera (Universal Edition). Thumping through the work at the piano very soon convinced me that it is only as *anti*-cabaret songs that Weill's inspirations make musical and dramatic sense.

It is unfortunate, if not surprising, that the songs in *Mahagonny* have claimed so much attention for the wrong reasons; they represent only one dramatic sphere of the opera – a philosophy of life that composer and librettist are anxious to criticize, not commend – and establish only one aspect of the composer's style. Their ironic popularity has meant that the positive pole of the opera, the music associated with the growth of a moral conscience in Jim Mahoney, the tough but innocent lumberjack from Alaska, has been unwarrantably neglected.

Yet it is in Jim's great aria of imprisonment, his love duet with Jenny and his evocation of Alaska ('The seven winters') that one is impressed by the scope of Weill's art. Here is quite another kind of intense musical invention which confirms that he was equal to the challenge of composing first-rate operatic music, stamped as plainly with his 'biological personality' (Stravinsky's words about Prokofiev) as any of the popular songs, and yet free of popular associations.

It is perhaps one of the signs of the born operatic composer that he cannot resist identifying himself with his characters. That Jim's fate ultimately engages our compassion pays tribute to the success of a musical characterization that snatches its victory from the puritanical, moralizing jaws of Brechtian theory.

In short, it is as an opera that we must judge the work; and unorthodox though it may be in theatrical conception and in many of its materials, it is by the integrity and subtlety of Weill's music that the City of Mahagonny stands or falls. He was a uniquely gifted composer who created a unique operatic language. We should do him the honour of examining his score seriously. Then, and only then, as in the case of any other opera, have we the right to cry triumph or failure.

NOTE

1 MC: See David Drew, *Kurt Weill: A Handbook* (Faber and Faber, London, 1987), where he writes:

> [In 1962] I became involved in preparations for the first-ever production of the *Mahagonny* opera by a non-German company. The young English director Michael Geliot and the designer Ralph Koltai had won Lenya's support for a London production early in 1963, to be conducted by Colin Davis and mounted by the Sadler's Wells Opera (now the English National Opera) . . .
>
> The Wells *Mahagonny* was, however, more than a local phenomenon. For the first time for more than thirty years the work was being staged on the understanding that the fate of the production would depend on the strength of its musical convictions, and that there was no hope of doing justice to the libretto on any other basis. Perhaps only in England and only

> at that particular juncture could a truth so obviously fundamental to the nature of the work and yet so heretical in relation to its composer's current reputation have emerged into the light of day, have survived throughout the rehearsal period, and have finally triumphed. With the press and with the public the production was a major success.

In the fascinating Introduction in which Drew unravels the complex story of his proposed critical biography of Weill, he reports,

> Since the early 1960s the music and music books divisions of Faber had been under the wing of the author and scholar Donald Mitchell. In his Notting Hill Gate home in 1956 I had written my first letter to Lenya, together with a specimen chapter that owed much to his and Hans Keller's writings on Mahler and Britten, and to their joint admiration for Weill.

This in turn reminds me that among DM's early published writings was an article on Weill – 'Kurt Weill's *Dreigroschenoper* and German Cabaret-Opera in the 1920s', *Chesterian* 25/163 (July, 1950), p. 1 – though he now no longer wants attention paid to it.

Vaughan Williams

I think one of the main points about Vaughan Williams has to be stated at the outset, that he commanded an extremely strong and immediately recognizable voice as a composer – created a sound of music that was his own and that for many people, and not only for his countrymen, has become identified with English music. Vaughan Williams was not only English by birth, that is, but demonstrably, avowedly, English in his music. No mean achievement this, whatever ultimate judgement may be made of his art. Furthermore, whatever attitude one may care to take to his music, whether one loves it or deplores it or is uncertain quite what to make of it – and up to a point that's my situation – it has to be taken notice of: it just can't be shrugged off. And if one is English, of my generation or an earlier one, then this kind of Vaughan Williams image is more or less a permanent part of one's experience; it's there, so to say, in one's blood, even if rarely listened to, even if consciously rejected.

Perhaps it is not altogether surprising that we are, as it were, so effectively, well, not brainwashed, but impregnated by Vaughan Williams's music. The actual dissemination of his art, in fact, was unusually wide; more than that, the width of it, the scope of it, was also part, and an unusual part, of its character. His popularity and eminence in his own lifetime had something to do with it, of

---

BBC Third Programme, 25 April 1965; originally broadcast under the title 'Vaughan Williams and the English Tradition' with recorded music examples

course; but much more important than this, and again it was a singular feat, above all in a twentieth-century context, was Vaughan Williams's remarkable and quantitatively successful attempt to provide us with music from the cradle to the grave. It is one of the merits of Michael Kennedy's study of Vaughan Williams's works[1] that it presents in the clearest possible way, with every conceivable fact scrupulously recorded, the wide range of Vaughan Williams's music. As one closes the book, one feels, yes, there is something here for more or less everybody in every imaginable situation: a song for the child in the classroom; a hymn for the congregation in church; music for the audience in the concert hall (and in the cinema); for the brass-band enthusiast; the massed choir; ballet; opera; the mouth-organ virtuoso or the amateur string-player. The list is endless and impressive for its scope alone; and one realizes on reading the catalogue through how inevitable it was that Vaughan Williams should have impinged so vitally on so many English ears. His music was indeed a methodically planned cultural force, an instrument of reform, education, edification and of course enjoyment, a peculiarly English conception which had its roots in the great liberal, reforming tradition of the nineteenth century. And I think anyone who reads Mrs Vaughan Williams's extremely well-written and sympathetic account of her husband[2] will recognize that this was the tradition to which the composer belonged. The world and our society changed a good deal during Vaughan Williams's lifetime, and have changed even more radically since his death; but for him, music, the arts, could still be a moral force, a necessary component and manifestation of the good life, and, perhaps most importantly, made accessible to the community as a whole. Vaughan Williams undoubtedly believed in a grass-roots as distinct from an élite culture. He wrote in 1931:

> If we want to find the groundwork of our English culture we must look below the surface – not to the grand events chronicled in the newspapers but to the unobtrusive quartet parties which meet week

> after week to play or sing in their own houses, to the village choral societies whose members trudge miles through rain and snow to work steadily for a concert or competition in some ghastly parish room with a cracked piano and a smelly oil lamp where one week there is no tenor because at the best there are only two, and one has a cold and the other being the village doctor is always called out at the critical moment; and there they sit setting their teeth so as to wrench the heart out of this mysterious piece of music which they are starting to learn for the coming competition.[3]

This conviction of his is surely an extension of the democratic and optimistic liberalism of the nineteenth century, when the artist in some sense could regard himself as a dedicated public servant, again perhaps a peculiarly English phenomenon: certainly a quality of moral concern has always been a distinguishing feature of the English radical. It is no exaggeration to suggest that Vaughan Williams's life and works reflect this great and still-living tradition; after all, though Britten in many ways is Vaughan Williams's absolute musical opposite, he too shows something of the same liberal concern for music as a cultural, social influence; and this too might be thought to be part of Britten's Englishness. I doubt, however, if we shall see again anything like Vaughan Williams's methodical, unceasing efforts to make music, and in particular English music, count for something at every level of society. For us it is not a question of one culture, or even two cultures, but whether a cohesive culture is now possible at all.

The only European composers who perhaps showed something of the same romantic and yet at the same time practical idealism as Vaughan Williams were Hindemith in Germany and Kodály in Hungary. With Hindemith's language, of course, there is not much common ground, though one does sense in Vaughan Williams's music that often-remarked quality of integrity and nobility that is also strong in Hindemith. Vaughan Williams, in his own terms, could often give us a *Nobilissima Visione*, as in his Fifth Symphony. I think one can talk of idealism in the context of that piece, as one can in the case of Hindemith: the idealism one might think is there, in both composers, even in their bad music. And Kodály too, happily still with us,[4] is another idealist. Here indeed the parallel with Vaughan Williams is so close, down to the materials out of which they build their music, that it does not help us on this occasion to pursue it; we should end up, I guess, simply saying how like one another they are in many vital respects. No, if we want to place Vaughan Williams in any kind of perspective, gain a little distance for our judgement, then we must surely look to Bartók as a kind of measuring stick; and it is no surprise to read in Mr Kennedy's book that, among his European contemporaries, it was Bartók who was esteemed most highly by Vaughan Williams.[5]

It would be easy here too, of course, as in the case of Kodály, to discover a seductive and superficially convincing parallel. After all, we have two leading musical figures, both of them anxiously concerned to strip off from their own musical cultures the veneer imposed by a previous cosmopolitan tradition: their rescue operations were designed on the one hand to reveal the English oak that lay beneath, and on the other whatever the equivalent is in Hungarian timber. Both of them vigorously affirmed the conviction that a musical culture must be soundly based on a secure and authentic nationalism, and both found a means of musical renewal and reinvigoration in folksong. And yet if this parallel were taken to its logical conclusion, both Bartók and Vaughan Williams ought to have much more in common than in fact they prove to have, even when due allowance has been made for two artistic personalities of stubborn independence. Moreover, the inescapable fact remains that whereas Bartók is regarded as a modern European master, Vaughan Williams is, I think, not. Well, why not?

It would be a crass error, let me say first, to think of either composer as a folklorist pure and simple; this was a trap into which Stravinsky fell when evaluating Bartók.[6] But there is no doubt that folksong was central to both Bartók's and Vaughan Williams's creativity; and it is precisely in this sphere that we find a radical difference in musical approach.

It is true, of course, that Bartók's ardent exploration and documentation of folk materials was nationally assertive, and meant to be; likewise Vaughan Williams's determined efforts not only to restore to English music an awareness of a neglected heritage but also to give English music an identity. But whereas Bartók's music developed, for all its national assertiveness, in a European context, and came to form part of the mainstream of the new music of the twentieth century, Vaughan Williams's has remained much more an isolated, closed phenomenon, a language turned in on itself and not open, as Bartók's was, to the turbulent but surely very stimulating innovations, above all in the sphere of harmony and rhythm, that were such marked features of the first decades of the century. Bartók may not have relinquished his cultural mission, but it seems clear to me that as he matured he became more interested in his folk sources as building materials and less concerned with their function as a kind of identity card. For example, in this music, so self-evidently of our time, we do not really respond to it in any special folkloristic sense, least of all in any specifically Hungarian sense. How could we? In short, the folksong component is a musical not a national idea, and free, I think, of a particular cultural symbolism or associations. But when we turn to Vaughan Williams we find a rather different situation and certainly a very different kind of music. One could argue, I think, that in many of his works, as in many of Bartók's, the folksong or national element takes second place – and, to do him justice, Vaughan Williams never suggested that folksong could do the composer's composing for him – but the impression remains, for me, of the folk source, however much subdued, remaining for Vaughan Williams an insisted-on birth certificate. This certainly helps to define his character but also decisively limits it and – yet more importantly – his vocabulary of available techniques. The quasi-folk melody that begins and ends the finale of the *Pastoral Symphony* – or rather the impact made by the melody – heavily depends on an act of personal, sympathetic identification by the listener: if one *is* sympathetic, no doubt the music, the atmosphere, can hold one. If one is not, the going is harder, because there is not, as there is in Bartók, the same degree of musical invention brought to bear on, or abstracted from, the basic materials. Musical patriotism, we may think, is not enough; and Vaughan Williams, perhaps more so than most composers, demands of his listener a sympathetic view of his art that is conditioned to some extent by extra-musical considerations: one has to like his ideals, as it were, the premisses of his music, if one is to make much headway with the music itself. Hence, I think, the importance of understanding what he was trying to achieve through his music, a point I made earlier in this talk. Perhaps it is at least understandable that so many Europeans cannot themselves achieve this act of comprehension and thus retreat baffled before Vaughan Williams's music.

I suggested a moment ago that his vocabulary of techniques was limited; and I must confess that on listening to a great quantity of his music, as I have done these past weeks, while one emerges with respect for the wide variety of media, the actual consistency of the music can sometimes be disconcerting. There is a sameness of invention about Vaughan Williams, wherever one turns and whatever the contrasts in, say, occasion or instrumental conception. It is hard to think of a case where his imagination was stimulated to fresh flights by the exploitation of an instrument or performer. His was very much one kind of music, presented in various forms but not, I think, notably rich in technical resource.

For me, indeed, there is something slightly claustrophobic about Vaughan Williams's music, about the combination of an inexorable cultural preoccupation and a strongly personal but restricted style. Perhaps this concentration we find in Vaughan Williams was indeed necessary if he was to achieve his cultural mission; none the less, the consequent limitations are there. Are they not, after all, part of the reason why we find it hard to think of Vaughan Williams, as we do of Bartók, as a European master?

Well, I can hear many people asking, what about the Fourth Symphony, in which, surely, musical nationalism takes a back seat and which has every right, singular though the symphony may be in Vaughan Williams's output, to be regarded as an authentically modern work, in the mainstream of twentieth-century music? This was the symphony, first performed in April 1935 – almost exactly thirty years ago in fact – which, as Mr Kennedy tells us, caused such a stir: 'No one could remain indifferent to this particular violent utterance.' And of course it was about this symphony that Vaughan Williams made one of his most famous remarks: 'I don't know whether I like it, but it's what I meant.' What he meant – was it a personal or public confession? – is open to many interpretations, and I don't intend to add to their number. But what is clear is how, in general, the symphony was received in this country: there were a few reservations, prominent among them an acute notice by Neville Cardus,[7] but in the main the feeling was, first, that here at last was a modern work by an English composer – 'modern' in quotation marks, so to speak – and, secondly, that Vaughan Williams in assuming modernity had renounced his previous national allegiances. The second reaction proved to be unfounded, though the implied judgement, nationalism *or* modernity, is interesting in itself. As to the first: looked at strictly in the context of Vaughan Williams's music up to that date, the Fourth Symphony was indeed a modern piece; and looked at too in the broader scene of English music, the climate of which Vaughan Williams had himself done so much to create, this was indeed a radical, adventurous and 'advanced' work. The general elation was certainly pronounced. As Mrs Vaughan Williams tells us, William Walton, as he then was, spoke of 'the greatest symphony since Beethoven'; and Patrick Hadley declared to Balfour Gardiner, no less, that 'It has knocked Europe sideways.' But all this exuberance now makes very strange reading and only goes to show, it seems to me, the incurable insularity of English music between the wars. This much celebrated 'modernity' of the Fourth Symphony, does it not tend to pale a little when one thinks of works by, say, Bartók or Stravinsky? The *Rite of Spring*, we no doubt remember – but England in the 1930s conveniently forgot – preceded Vaughan Williams's Fourth Symphony by more than twenty years. That, no doubt, is an obvious example to choose, and perhaps an inappropriate one, because Vaughan Williams once confessed that most of Stravinsky bored him.[8] But there are countless others available, not only from Bartók or Stravinsky but from Berg or Schoenberg. One must not blame Vaughan Williams for not writing a kind of music that he did not intend to write; nor is there any reason why any English composer should be expected to study the works of his contemporaries, European or otherwise. None the less, it still strikes me as well worth observation that Vaughan Williams in particular, and English music in general of this period, proved to be so unaware of, so resistant to, musical developments outside this island. This may have been inevitable in the case of Vaughan Williams, who was intent on affirming a style independent of cosmopolitan influences, who succeeded in this aim, and then became a captive, as it were, of the emancipation he had helped bring about. I find it hard to believe, notwithstanding, that his music would not have increased in technical resource and sheer density of musical incident and interest if it had remained open to influence by his great European contemporaries: there is surely everything to be said for a Common Market in music, whatever opinions one may hold of the institution as a political idea. But here history, or rather the history of English music, was against Vaughan Williams, as it was against his contemporary Holst, who, as it happens, reacted in his music to European innovations as Vaughan Williams did not. It is not at all surprising that today it is the more cosmopolitan Holst who is enjoying a revival.

If this abstention, or whatever one may care to call it, of Vaughan Williams's affected his own art, it also, because of his status and pervasive influence, affected the whole climate of musical opinion and ideas in England between the wars; another contributing factor was the curious deification of Sibelius, who almost became an English composer by appointment. But the Sibelius story, in relation to prevailing musical attitudes in between-the-wars England, is another script altogether. One just has to notice for this occasion that, undeniable man of genius though Sibelius was, his music had little to do with the major formations and re-formations of style in the twentieth century.

Michael Kennedy's account of Vaughan Williams's opinions of contemporary music makes depressing reading. They are extraordinarily parochial – I don't think one can avoid using the word. It is not the opinions that matter so much as the seeming absence of interest in musical ideas foreign to his own routine. All the great upheavals in the first decade of our century seem not only to have left him virtually untouched but also to have gone virtually unnoticed. There was, I repeat, absolutely no obligation on Vaughan Williams to show any sympathy for music to which he felt hostile or indifferent. But how odd, and how significant, that it was not until 1956, only two years before his death, that this major figure in our twentieth-century musical life was prompted to *inquire* about the serial principle in music. The rights and wrongs of the note-row are not the issue here: it is surely just remarkable that our senior composer could have lived so long without feeling at least obliged to keep himself informed about an important movement in music that had engaged the significant interest of at least some of his significant contemporaries. Again, one might say, that Vaughan Williams didn't need the information; and one might be right. But it is the sad truth, I think, that this blinkered, even ignorant attitude was characteristic of English musical life as a whole, with a few shining exceptions; that our exclusive, self-regarding musical culture, however necessary the exclusiveness was for building up a tradition, in the end excluded more, much more, than it could afford to do without; that in some sense our musical development as a nation was inhibited by too fervent, too defensive and self-protecting a nationalism.

It would be unjust to load Vaughan Williams with responsibilities for trends in history that were certainly not wholly within his control; it is a measure of his influence and stature that as soon as we start thinking about the English tradition in twentieth-century music we have to spend a great deal of time assessing his contribution to it. I make no apology for having adopted in this talk what I suppose might be called a historical approach, because it seems to me that Vaughan Williams himself, quite knowingly, took history on and attempted to shape it. He was indubitably a great – and good – man, a composer of powerful personality and a major voice in our musical culture. But his *art*, I think, though it made history, was also defeated by it, and will, if I have to hazard a guess, prove to be minor.

NOTES

1 Michael Kennedy, *The Works of Ralph Vaughan Williams* (Oxford University Press, Oxford, 1964).

2 Ursula Vaughan Williams, *RVW: A Biography* (Oxford University Press, London, 1964).

3 MC: Vaughan Williams's remarks are quoted from the preface he provided to Sir Henry Hadow's book *English Music* (Longmans, Green & Co., London, 1931), which Kennedy glosses as

> the most pungent of Vaughan Williams's statements of his beliefs . . . It is in an angry, even slightly embittered, vein, for in 1930 he perhaps realized that the English musical life he had hoped might emerge from the war was still dominated by influences he had himself fought to shed, even though there was no doubt of the existence of a new and talented group of composers. His principal target was artistic snobbery. [p. 233.]

4 MC: Kodály died in 1967, two years after this talk was written.

5 MC: Kennedy's brief assertion that Vaughan Williams thought Bartók 'greatest of all' occurs on p. 294, but is not backed up by any evidence beyond drawing a parallel between the outlook of the two composers on the subject of nationalism. On p. 390 Vaughan Williams is reported as having disliked *Bluebeard's Castle* 'extremely'. For his part, however, Bartók apparently heard Vaughan Williams's 1931 Piano Concerto and 'much admired it' (p. 237).

6 MC: Stravinsky said of Bartók: 'I could never share his lifelong gusto for his native folklore. This devotion was certainly real and touching, but I couldn't help regretting it in the great musician.' (Igor Stravinsky and Robert Craft, *Conversations with Igor Stravinsky* (Faber and Faber, London, 1959), p. 74.) The same comment might equally well have been applied to Stravinsky himself in the period *c.* 1908–18.

7 MC: Cardus's review of the Fourth Symphony appeared in the *Manchester Guardian* on 11 April 1935:

> A man might as well hang himself as look in the work for a great tune or theme. I decline to believe that a symphony can be made out of a method, plus gusto . . . I could not, for all my admiration of its parts, believe that it is

likely to be listened to twenty years from today or that it will take its place in the works that go beyond national boundaries ... The music fails to warm the senses or to enter the mind as an utterance of conviction. The Continental listener this evening would wonder why the composer, having discarded the idioms and general emotional tones of pre-war English music, has stopped short of a post-war freedom of rhythm and a post-war harshness of dissonance ... The content of Vaughan Williams's music – considered in the abstract, apart from the technique – is respectable middle-class English, and the technique, as I have suggested, is old-fashioned, looked at from standards unashamedly modern ... [Quoted in Kennedy, p. 245.]

8 MC: Vaughan Williams expressed his opinion of Stravinsky in a letter to Kennedy dated 26 November 1957 (quoted in Kennedy, p. 390):

Most of Stravinsky bores me. I wish he even shocked me, especially *The Rite of Spring*. I do not think the scoring is masterly at all, he always makes a nasty sour sound with his orchestra, but I do like the *Symphony of Psalms*, *Les Noces* and the Suite for violin and pianoforte ...

Malcolm Arnold I

Although our time is rich in technical achievements in all musical spheres, there are still a few executants and composers whose gifts are of a virtuoso character. Such a composer is Malcolm Arnold, whose ability to tackle most kinds of musical jobs – from film score to symphony – is marked by an unusually brilliant handling of whatever instrumental forces he has at his disposal. The versatility of his invention is matched by a rare capacity for creating transparent textures in the most varied instrumental circumstances. The peculiarly bright, clear, ringing, chiselled sound of his scores, in every medium, is part of both his professional virtuosity and his singular artistic personality.

Arnold is a 'professional' in more ways than one. He was born, in 1921, at Northampton. At the Royal College of Music, to which he won a scholarship at the age of sixteen, he studied composition with Gordon Jacob and the trumpet with Ernest Hall. (The choice of instrument is suggestive. It corresponds, perhaps, to that extrovert exuberance which is so notable an aspect of Arnold's creative make-up.) He remained faithful to the trumpet in later years, as trumpeter in the London Philharmonic Orchestra, before and after the war (as principal trumpet until 1948), and as composer: lavish trumpet solos abound in his music. That he has, as it were, sat inside an orchestra is very evident from the natural feel of his instrumentation; yet throughout his scores it is not only his intimate experience of the potentialities of an orchestra that is

---

Musical Times 96 (August 1955), pp. 410–13

explicit, but also the judgement of an unusually discriminating and original ear.

The pure sound of Arnold's music is, to a degree, an expression of his exceptional musical practicality – practicality raised to the very high level of virtuosity. (Virtuosity might be defined as super-charged practicality.) Two other striking features of his musical personality – his astonishing fertility and his wide-ranging eclecticism – are no less bound up with his special kind of professional competence. His formidable list of works is sufficient evidence of his fertility, often misnamed 'facility', though the latter is quite another talent, sometimes fruitful, sometimes fatal. Facile composers may be barren of the gift of genuine invention, while fertile composers – Beethoven, for instance – may not find composing all that easy. In Arnold's case I suspect that fertility and facility go hand in hand. On the one hand his creativity is fertilized by the challenge of the occasions for which music is demanded, as in his ballet music, for example, or his concertos (where the solo instrument constitutes the germinating challenge); and on the other – 'facile' – hand, his professional competence ensures a ready answer to every problem. This particular combination of fertility and facility depends upon and derives from a background of musical virtuosity. As for Arnold's eclecticism – and it is pretty well all-embracing – it lies in yet another aspect of his thorough-going professionalism. He is, so to speak, musically well read, and does not disdain displaying the knowledge he has digested. Originality is not so much his aim as selection of the right ideas for the job under way – again an expression of the pervasive practicality of his attitude to composing.

There is no doubt that Arnold *enjoys* writing music. The enjoyment he takes in his own skill he communicates to his audiences with a complete lack of inhibition. Arnold, indeed, is probably the least inhibited of all our contemporary composers, both in what he says and how he says it. His refreshing, immodest freedom of spirit – his high spirits – are well known. It is almost impossible to write about his music without using such adjectives as 'gay', 'vital', 'breezy', 'humorous', 'witty' and so on. They are all relevant and apt. Not surprisingly, he excels in scherzos, in brilliantly jovial finales (cf. Ex. 3(b), the main theme of the Second Symphony's last movement) and works of the divertimento type. Examples of the latter are the charming *Divertimento* for flute, oboe and clarinet and the *Three Shanties* for wind quintet, the first of which is an irreverent treatment of 'What shall we do with a drunken sailor?' At one point (Ex. 1), Arnold parades his drunk in the context of a lugubrious tango.

This amusing side to Arnold's music is widely appreciated. Some of it, doubtless, springs from his very real sense of fun and mischief, but much of his good humour, to my mind, reflects his satisfaction at the plenitude of his gifts. We are faced here by a certain type of creative personality. Arnold is not a composer who wants to save the world with every slow movement (the observation is Schoenberg's); nor is he an unrealistic optimist. He merely delights in musical prowess as an athlete may in brawn and muscle. In a sense, his rare equanimity is yet another facet of his basically practical attitude to his art. As I have said already, he enjoys writing music. But since the world deplores a composer who does not toil and sweat in an attempt to save it, Arnold's approach tends to be misunderstood as superficiality or downright frivolity.

His music is, in fact, more varied in mood than his reputation as a robust, merry music-maker would suggest. On one occasion, in the funereal slow movement of the Second Symphony, he touches upon a mood that is almost tragic, though the 'conventional' content ('this is what is to be expected of a *serious* symphonist') is expressed by highly original means. In the concertos, however, the character of the movements emerges rather from the character of the solo instruments than from subjective states of mind on the part of the composer (cf. the dreamy flute song (Ex. 2(b)) of the Flute Concerto's *Andante*).[1] As for Arnold's cheery 'irresponsibility', it has a most positive artistic function. He composes as if composing were still easy, and problems that floor

Ex. 1 *Three Shanties*, No. 1

his contemporaries leave him unruffled. What other composer, aware of the crushing finale problem of our time, would have dared, as Arnold did in his First Symphony, to crown his last movement with a catchy street song? A 'responsible' contemporary might have developed from simplicity to complexity, but would probably have suppressed the thought of the reverse process with a conscientious shudder. Yet Arnold's 'irresponsibility' – his contradiction of conventional expectations – decidedly comes off.

It might be said irresponsibility is essentially naïve. 'Innocent' would be a better term for it. It is, as it were, under the compulsion of this virginal condition that Arnold's most personal music is written – perhaps even his whole idiom is related to it. How else, except in a state of innocent grace, could a composer so versatile and experienced utter music so forthright, so direct, so blandly diatonic, in a manner that takes little account of the harmonic emancipation of the twentieth century? There arc, of course, plenty of diatonic composers about, but few of them possess the gift for melodic invention that distinguishes Arnold's best pieces. It is indeed his capacity for writing memorable tunes that justifies his relatively orthodox style; he can still do something new in what is strictly a past language. Arnold pours out tunes as if he were unaware that much music in our century has had to get along without them. That his tunes are personal despite the echoes of their models, may swiftly be verified by glancing through Exx. 2(a)–(h). It is immediately noticeable how *x*, in the unfolding lyric span of Ex. 2(a), crops up all over the place as a recognizable Arnold fingerprint (cf. Exx. 2(b), (f), (g) and (h)); how the melodic shape *y* in the same example recurs in various guises (cf. Exx. 2(c), (d) and (e)); how naturally Ex. 2(d) extends itself by means of *z*. By a composer's melodic profile, by his melodic fingerprints, you may know him. Arnold, rightly, leans on his tunes. He states them twice, sometimes three times, as in the Second Symphony's first movement where, in the recapitulation, the second subject, with marvellous effect, is introduced between the first and second restatements of the principal tune (Ex. 2(a)), while the bridge passage, thus displaced, goes to form the coda. The third statement of the tune is discarded. We realize that the recapitulation's surprise depends upon the exposition's repetitions. It is round his tunes that Arnold builds whole movements (e.g. the first movement of the *Sinfonietta* (cf. Ex. 2(c)), and subsidiary and principal subjects are often closely related (e.g. Exx. 2(d) and (e) from the Oboe Concerto). The principal tune reigns supreme. It is rare for Arnold's tunes to lapse into slovenly continuations, though this does happen on occasions: cf. *x* in Ex. 3(a), and Ex. 3(c), the latter an astonishingly feeble consequent to the characteristic and invigorating Ex. 3(b); sometimes, it must be admitted, Arnold's uninhibitedness has its defects.

Ex. 2(a) Symphony No. 2

Ex. 2(b) Flute Concerto

Ex. 2(c) *Sinfonietta*

Ex. 2(d) Oboe Concerto

Ex. 2(e) Oboe Concerto

Ex. 2(f) *Homage to the Queen*

Ex. 2(g) *Homage to the Queen*

Ex. 2(h) *Divertimento*

The tunes exposed in Ex. 2, especially (a)–(c), have more than their fingerprints in common. They share a common *cantabile* mood, the mood Arnold most often offers as opposition to his extrovert brilliance: cf., say, Ex. 2(b) with Ex. 3(b). It is in these tunes and the glowing, lambent movements to which they give rise that Arnold demonstrates most perfectly – and now and again most poignantly – what might be called his *unique recovery of innocent lyricism*.

Ex. 3(a) *Homage to the Queen*

Ex. 3(b) Symphony No. 2

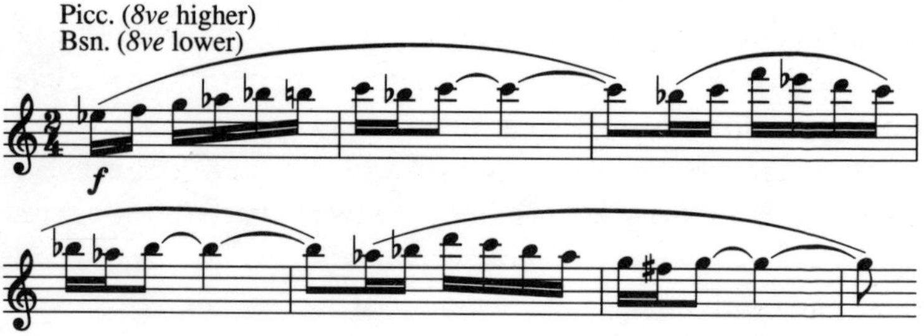

Ex. 3(c) Symphony No. 2

NOTE

1 MC: DM refers to the Flute Concerto No. 1, Op. 45 (1954). In 1972, Arnold wrote a Second Flute Concerto, Op. 111.

Malcolm Arnold II: The Curse of Popularity

I shall be returning to the significance of a particular passage [see Ex. 1, overleaf] from the finale of the Piano Concerto for three hands that Malcolm Arnold wrote in 1969 for Phyllis Sellick and Cyril Smith, music, I think, that will help clarify the title of this talk. Why the *curse* of popularity? After all, isn't that what composers or at any rate many composers aspire to be, popular? But popular, like most words used in connection with music, can mean very different things at very different times; and change its meaning according to the composer one is talking about. I'm not going to attempt anything like a general definition of popular on this occasion, even if such an ambition could be realized. I'm simply going to look at the term in the context of one composer's music – Malcolm Arnold's – and see if I can make it mean something fairly precise in the context of his particular art; and at the same time I'll show, I hope, why the word 'curse' comes into my title. Even in this limited area there's still going to be plenty of complexity. There's certainly no one simple way of answering the question, 'What is the popular component or element in Arnold's music?' As with all composers worth serious study – and Arnold certainly demands and deserves that – blanket labels don't get us very far. For example, one could say that at least part of the aesthetic intent of this next piece by Arnold might properly be described as popular. Its every compositional aspect, that is, is directed towards making an instant, vivid, bold and colourful

---

BBC Radio 3, 23 March 1977

Ex. 1 Concerto for Two Pianos (Three Hands) and Orchestra (finale)

communication in a musical language – the originality of which, by the way, I for one don't underrate – which quite deliberately uses an acknowledged, even familiar vocabulary [Ex. 2].

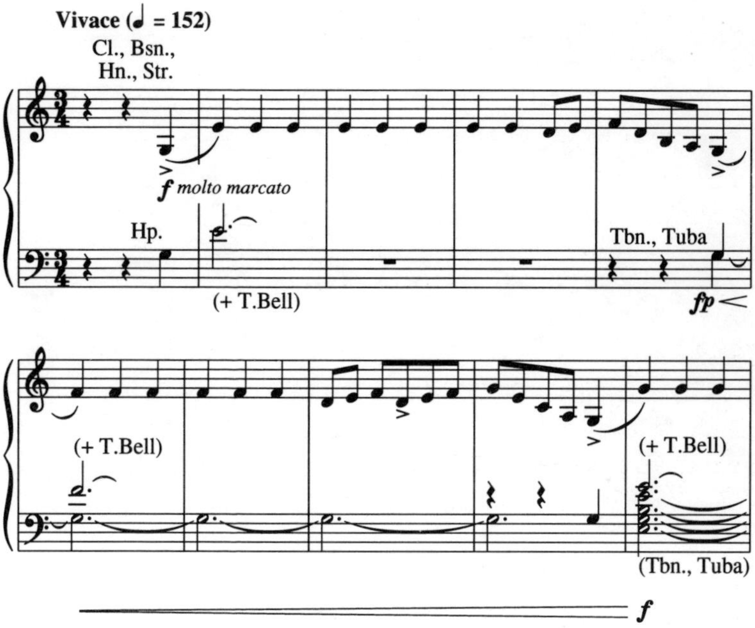

Ex. 2 *Four Cornish Dances*, No. 1

One might well describe *that* sort of music, No. 1 of Arnold's *Four Cornish Dances*, as popular. It's music that exploits quite consciously a popular vein. But here's something slightly different, the long principal melody that opens the first movement of his Third Symphony – a work and a melody I've always very much admired [Ex. 3].

Ex. 3 Symphony No. 3

Pretty direct communication again, I agree, but that was a more complex idea and certainly more elaborately treated than anything in the preceding dance. And if we want to interpret it as part of

Arnold's popular musical character or style, what we are saying is this: that Arnold often speaks to us through his remarkable melodies, in short, his good tunes; and that for complicated historical reasons the very emphasis on the melodic dimension in Arnold's art itself gives rise to suspicions that we're being seduced by something vaguely improper, that we're succumbing to the blandishments of the popular while the composer is somehow abandoning the pedestal of high art and is wanting in seriousness. A complex point this, I know, but there is a real sense in which Arnold's extraordinary melodic gift has, ironically, made things difficult for him rather than easy; and that is because when certain pairs of critical ears hear a tune, a warning light switches on. Can this be so? There must be something wrong! And the often highly sophisticated nature of the tune, and above all its role and function in the work in question, all pass unnoticed. No doubt Arnold was and is aware of the risk he takes in affirming his powerful links with a particular tradition of composition in which the melodic component was of great significance and a prime vehicle of communication; and it is precisely in that historic and profoundly serious sense – and not as a way of playing to the gallery – that Arnold uses melody as part of his compositional resources.

So far, so popular; but popular, please bear in mind, sometimes in the same way and for the same musical reasons that great predecessors might be said to be popular: Schubert for example, Tchaikovsky or Mahler. That, then, is another way of looking at the notion of the popular in Arnold's music: one that is bound up with the development of melody in the history of music, as an instrument of direct communication and means of accessibility. But while that definition may suit one kind of Arnoldian post-Mahlerian melodic type, it doesn't necessarily fit another, scarcely less potent type but one that often crops up in his music.

A passage from the brilliant scherzo of his Fifth Symphony makes the point I want to talk about. It illustrates [Ex. 4, overleaf] another aspect of Arnold's melodic popularity which is undeniably

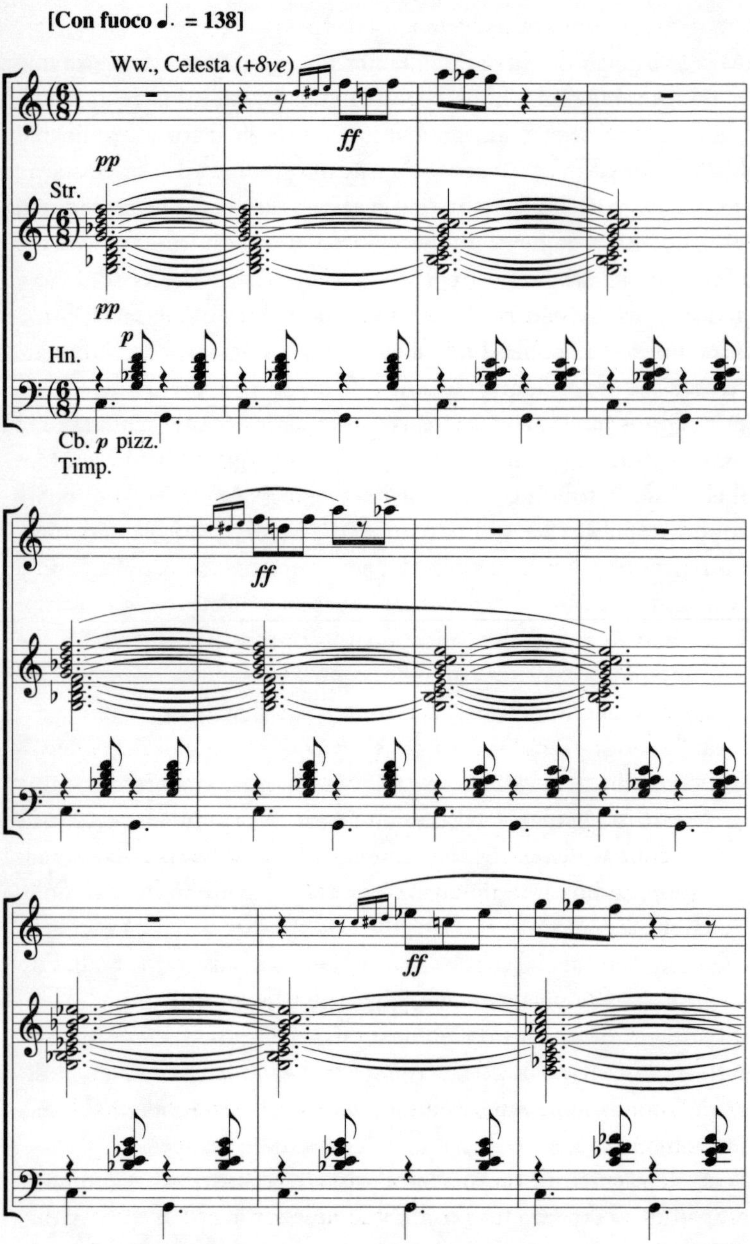

Ex. 4 Symphony No. 5

rooted in gestures derived from the specific genre of popular music: the oompah-bass accompaniment, exuberant syncopation, and vibrant unison of the woodwind: something here of the brilliance one recalls in connection with the jazzy, big-band orchestrations of earlier decades. And there's the rub, of course. What *I* hear is technically brilliant variation and fragmentation of a melody, and references to a popular vein of invention which have particular symbolic or poetic significance in the context of the symphony as a whole. But a lot of people will hear that passage or others like it as examples of Arnold's lapsing – or relapsing rather – into the field of pop, of entertainment music, which is automatically not to be taken seriously. This is where my 'curse of popularity' comes in. Because Arnold has been an extremely successful composer for films; because he has chosen to lend emphatic importance to the idea of direct communication; because of the primary significance he accords memorable tunes; because of all of these, he's criticized for easy indulgence in a popular vein. What people hear in fact is not what he actually writes but what they assume to be an automatic or unavoidable or escapist compulsion to broach the area of entertainment music, which has no place in serious composition and least of all in something as serious and weighty as a symphony. This is part of the unthinking response to the scherzo of Arnold's Fifth Symphony. What, amazingly, one rarely encounters is a listener who has realized that this movement is an outstanding example in the English symphony of close argument, of ingenious motivic transformation, of an altogether exceptional orchestral virtuosity from which we all have much to learn; but of course no one imagines that there is anything to be learned from *this* composer. So worthwhile critical comment is relatively rare. It's part of my argument that we *should* listen and learn. Arnold's popularity, you see, sometimes stands between him and his listeners.

Let me now move on to another aspect of his popular reputation and in so doing return to the example we heard at the beginning of this talk: the barrel-organ tune [Ex. 1] which forms a

Ex. 5 Concerto for Two Pianos (Three Hands) and Orchestra (finale)

prominent part of the Piano Concerto written for Phyllis Sellick and Cyril Smith. There we find Arnold working that vernacular, mundane vein opened up by Mahler, when a popular, vulgar musical invention makes an appearance in an unexpected context and takes on an entirely new significance through its location and treatment, often ironic. Arnold shows himself to be a true disciple of Mahler in this respect. Indeed, in this very finale he makes clear to us that we are not to take the barrel-organ tune at its face value. He builds into the very structure and texture of his music his own commentary on, and key to, the symbolic significance of these extraordinary excursions into the world of the mundane; and as a result what the barrel organ sings to us is not something cheering, but desperate; not something jovial but something empty and mocking, and Arnold comments on it himself accordingly.

For me, this striking passage [Ex. 5, facing] very clearly reveals Arnold's capacity to make the popular bear new meanings which are often the opposite of what they have traditionally been understood to represent. That is why his barrel organ makes me feel not jolly but nervous and despondent: this is the way the world ends, it seems to say, not with a bang but a whimper.[1] It's this technique which, I believe, makes the Fifth Symphony so interesting and complex a work. Here, as is fitting in such a large-scale and profoundly serious composition – and remember Arnold has been writing symphonies since 1946 – his approach to his materials is correspondingly complex; but once again (and I think this is generally true of him as a symphonist) he works symbolically and in order to understand what he is about we have to understand, to read, the significance of the symbols. There is no doubt in my mind that, for Arnold, his popular vein – perhaps it's a particularly innocent bit of melody imagined with a particular radiancy and transparency of orchestration – often represents a lost world of musical innocence, even an unreal world that now can never be regained or re-entered. And in working at this particular symbolic level, by the way, I think Arnold is saying something about the history of twentieth-century music, of which inescapably he is part. Hence I suggest *this* kind of invention [Ex. 6] in the Fifth Symphony's dramatic first movement. It's like a half-remembered, distant experience of peace and serenity, reinforced by its otherworldly instrumentation (glockenspiel, celesta, harp). But as we come later to hear –

as Arnold himself composes it – the momentary calm is false, an illusion: and tension, and with it a high degree of dissonance, returns and banishes the vision.

Ex. 6 Symphony No. 5

Present truth and past truth expressed in musical terms. This seems to me to be at least one of the philosophical ideas that are so brilliantly dramatized in Arnold's symphonies; and it is to serve the representation of past truth that, in his own original way, he conscripts his popular style – not to entertain us but to instruct us, symbolically, poetically. The great drama as I see it in the Fifth Symphony is continued across the whole spread of the work. What I take to be Arnold's preoccupation with a past musical truth and its potentialities: can it still work? Can it be valid for us? What have we lost in abandoning the past? These questions all surface with maximum intensity in the slow movement, an *Andante* which opens with an extraordinary melody [Ex. 7, overleaf]. This is a deliberately, consciously, 'beautiful' and romantic string melody, richly harmonized, which surely attempts to anthologize all the romantic slow movements that have ever been written.

Now, I find that a very beautiful invention in its own living right quite aside from the symbolic function I believe it has as a sign, a reference, to a kind of music that is virtually extinct. But there are others who don't or can't get as far as that, who hear that tune and its romantic harmony, and throw up their hands and shut their ears and say, 'That simply can't be, can't exist, can't work any longer in our day. That's Arnold playing to the gallery again.' Up to a point I see the difficulty, or rather, I agree that the tune is ambiguous – though surely by design, not by accident. Indeed the irony of it all is that Arnold himself proves to be the melody's severest critic. This is partly demonstrated in the slow movement itself, in its restless, unquiet central section; but made absolutely explicit in the finale, where a return of the *Andante*'s opening melody is planned as the movement's, and the symphony's, overwhelming climax. The finale, though it starts relatively unclouded, accumulates a great deal of tension and dissonance, at the height of which erupts, with almost theatrical effect, the *Andante* and the big melody again.

Ex. 7 Symphony No. 5 (*Andante*)

At this stage in the drama one might be forgiven for thinking that such a rhetorical gesture [Ex. 8, facing] is simply an easy way out: a false, romantic end slapped on to bring the symphony to a conclusion. Is sentiment then rather than truth to prevail? With a surprising and ruthless twist of the knife, which to my mind is one of the most original strokes in the work – and also the one that

Ex. 8 Symphony No. 5 (finale)

enables us to comprehend the meaning of the whole exercise – Arnold punctures and deflates his own glorious rhetoric; and the movement ends in a sudden cold and painful collapse, and dies on a low E amid tolling bells [see Ex. 9].

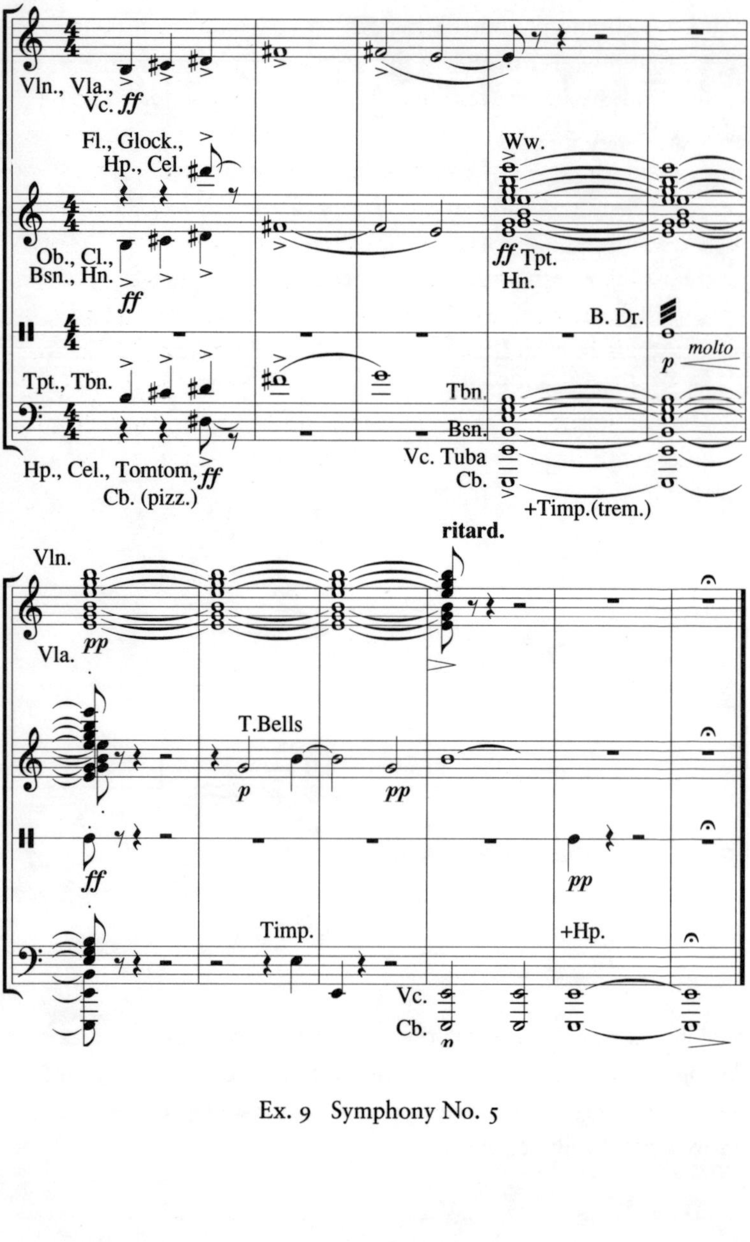

Ex. 9 Symphony No. 5

I don't want to suggest that Arnold doesn't love his big tune, or that we shouldn't, but he is right to conclude thus, to make explicit that however beguiling the simplicities and innocence of a popular vein, however appealing the old concept of the beautiful still may be – and Arnold certainly shows that the old flames can still be made to glow – these have finally to be rejected. It's truth that is the victor in Arnold's Fifth Symphony. Though he once remarked himself that what was wrong with twentieth-century music was that it chose truth rather than beauty, I'm glad he contradicts himself so fruitfully in this work and elsewhere. His best music and his best large-scale forms come out of that basic tension, a conflict that may in a very real sense tear him apart, but offers us a unique musical experience and vision. It should be misunderstood or neglected no longer. It's time for the curse to be lifted.

NOTE

1 MC: A reference to the closing lines from T. S. Eliot's poem 'The Hollow Men' (1925).

Malcolm Arnold III

When I think about Malcolm and his music, it is often Dickens who floats into my mind. It is not that I am confusing music with literature but that I find myself thinking about the two of them in the same sort of way: both of them unequivocally direct communicators; both of them with a healthy respect for and responsibility to the public; and both of them, unashamedly so, *great entertainers*. And yet to say that, which is a lot, is by no means to say enough, either about Dickens, or about Malcolm. For entertain us they may; but at the same time, amid the hilarity, the sentiment, the rollicking exuberance, the side-splitting parodies, there is a profound awareness of man's precarious condition. As with Dickens, so with Arnold: we are pulled up short by an overpowering melancholy, a cry of pain, a glimpse into a Conradian heart of darkness. A moment later, it may be, we are laughing again. Those who recall the Hoffnung days[1] will remember how Malcolm's contributions uniquely combined the irresistibly humorous with the chillingly sinister. A sixty-fifth birthday is an occasion for uninhibited celebration, an activity of which Malcolm is a past master.

But while we raise our glasses, let us look beyond the hubbub of the party and salute too a composer whose unsettling disclosures of the human predicament (so often entrusted to his

---

Programme for Malcolm Arnold's Sixty-fifth Birthday Concert, given by the English Chamber Orchestra at the Queen Elizabeth Hall, London, on 21 October 1986

remarkable series of symphonies) make him the altogether singular creator that he is.

Malcolm's music often sets about qualifying its own happiness, which is why I am fascinated by it. But it is an unqualified happy birthday that I wish him with these few words.

NOTE

1 MC: Gerard Hoffnung (1925–1959), creator of a series of celebrated musical cartoons and founder in 1956 of the Hoffnung Music Festival. Among the humorous works written for this event were Arnold's *Grand, Grand Overture* for three vacuum-cleaners, floor-polisher, four rifles and orchestra, Op. 57 (1957), and his *Grand Concerto Gastronomique* for eater, waiter, food and large orchestra, Op. 76 (1961).

III
Cradles of the New

Gustav Mahler: mezzotint engraving by Emil Orlik, 1902

Mozart: The Truth about Così

The famous court case, in which Lady Chatterley, rather than D. H. Lawrence's novel, was placed on trial,[1] should warn us how deep feelings run when infidelity, real or imaginary, accomplished or desired, is the topic, main or subsidiary, of an artist's work.

It would be surprising, indeed, to place an opera by Mozart in the dock; but, in a very real sense, this is the curious position in which *Così fan tutte* finds itself (herself, perhaps one ought to say). There are still writers on or about Mozart who find the morals of the work a stumbling block, who turn up their noses at the wanton 'frivolity' of the plot.

This is no new attitude, of course. What is frivolity for the censorious of our time was downright licentiousness for the moralists of the nineteenth century, who found even the music hard to swallow, so throttling was their distaste for da Ponte's libretto.

Yet, as Professor E. H. Gombrich has pointed out in an interesting and little-known essay,

> Neither the defenders nor the detractors of the libretto appear to have recognized its venerable ancestry. The motif of the suspicious lover who returns in disguise to test the fidelity of his beloved with presents and blandishments is, of course, prefigured in the myth of

---

First published under the title 'Psychology and Character in *Così fan tutte*' in the *Listener* 64/1656 (22 December 1960), p. 1160; revised and reprinted in Anthony Gishford (ed.), *Tribute to Benjamin Britten on his Fiftieth Birthday* (Faber and Faber, London, 1963), pp. 95–9

> Cephalus and Procris. There is the same fervour of rejection, the same insistence just to the point when fidelity gives way . . . All da Ponte has done is to enrich the plot by the simple device of doubling the pair and replacing Aurora, who, in Ovid, incites Cephalus to this stratagem, by the philosopher Alphonso who makes it the object of a wager . . .What is original in *Così fan tutte* is that here the plot turns round the nature of human passion itself. Da Ponte has perceived that Cephalus' test, whether cynical or not, can be viewed as an experiment about human nature.[2]

Few today would be found who actively deplore the *music* of *Così*; we have grown that much wiser. But it is still not uncommon to run across the opinion that while the music is, of course, 'ravishing', etc., it has nothing to do with the impossible plot, etc.; indeed, this appalling dichotomy goes to show that poor old Mozart really knew how hopeless the whole project was – the very beauty and perfection of the music, etc., makes the point clear, doesn't it?

Does it? Not to me, I fear. On the contrary, the miracle of inspiration and structure that is *Così* tells me the contrary, that Mozart was no less engaged in this opera than in any other – perhaps even more so, if the perfection of the work's proportions and consistency of its inspiration are allowed to appear as evidence for the defence. (It's odd, when one comes to think of it, that they could ever have served, as they have done, as evidence for the *prosecution*.)

But what we are really running up against here is not musical logic but an emotional resistance, the same sort of half-submerged rock upon which Lady C. ran aground, if one may so inelegantly describe her relation to the moral climate of her time.

What shows of these rocks is never very suggestive of what lies beneath the surface; the rational appearance they present to the world is misleading. They are also, if one may continue to personify them a moment longer, impressively productive of rational reasons for their existence, i.e. for sinking *Così* or at least holing the work. Thus what I suspect is the subjective panic (no less) aroused by Mozart's frivolity is transformed into 'objective' lines of critical attack, of which the absence of characterization is perhaps the most frequently encountered.[3] If we can convince ourselves that the characters are just puppets, we are spared the obligation to feel their feelings – which leaves us free to praise the music without a twinge of conscience.

After all, *what* feelings we are being asked to share! Two mean young men set about testing the virtue of their fiancées by means of a particularly cruel trick. Bad enough, even if virtue were triumphant. But not only do the ladies succumb, they even agree to marry their seducers. Virtue is not just crossed, but double-crossed. Worst of all, the whole tangle is presented without moral commentary. Life, composer and librettist seem to say, is very much like this. *Così fan tutti*, in fact.

Our business is music, not morals; none the less, I should be prepared to bet that Mozart's and da Ponte's beautifully organized fable contains a very high proportion of truth, of psychological truth at any rate, compressed into the space of two acts, whose dramatic events, as E. J. Dent was quick to point out, take place 'within a period of twenty-four hours'. The scorching pace of the opera and its inflammable subject-matter combine to raise the blood pressure of even the most phlegmatic of audiences.

Temperatures, however, would not rise if Mozart had not succeeded in making a musical reality of the uncomfortable truth he exposed with such inimitable verve. If the music were just 'beautiful' and nothing else, we may be sure that no one would ever have got so excited about the morals – or lack of them. Characterization is the crucial question: are the characters in *Così* real or not?

I make no apologies for using the word 'real' since it is used so very often – to my mind, quite justifiably so – in relation to Mozart's other operas. We may all agree that *Figaro*, for example, is rich in 'real' characters. *Don Giovanni*, too, despite its strong element of fantasy, is not starved of sharply observed characterizations which owe nothing to the supernatural. But even when judged by these high standards of comparison, *Così* seems to me to survive the test triumphantly. Indeed, I find either one of the two pairs of lovers a good deal more convincing as creatures of flesh and blood than, say, Donna Anna and Don Ottavio.

Let us glance quickly at the six characters who people the world of *Così*. I do not think we can fault the characterizations of the two schemers, Don Alfonso and Despina. Both are rather disagreeable characters: Don Alfonso calculating and a little sinister; Despina bright, hard and money-grubbing, vulgar, even. Can it be denied that each enjoys a quite specific musical personality?

When we come to the quartet of lovers the situation is rather more complex but no less realistically defined in terms of character. It is true, as Gerald Abraham has pointed out,[4] that in his ensembles Mozart often treats the two men and two women as if each pair were one person. But this, surely, is not evidence of an impoverishment of characterization, but, rather, an exact reflection of the true state of dramatic and emotional affairs? Ferrando and Guglielmo are as single-minded in their protestations of belief in their fiancées' fidelity as are the ladies in rejecting the sometimes no less single-minded devotions of their exotic suitors. It is not surprising that identical attitudes should be expressed in identical music. (It would be confusing if they were not.)

But the attitudes, as we know, break up because the barriers break down. As the opera develops away from the expression of unanimities, so too the characters develop greatly in individuality. The more serious the affairs, the more distinctly etched are the outlines of each personality involved. When, for example, at a late stage in Act II, we reach the duet in which Fiordiligi finally yields to Ferrando, we realize that for this pair of 'illicit' lovers, love has become a reality. The sublime music leaves us in no doubt that they are 'in love'. It is precisely at this climax, as Professor Gombrich correctly observes, that 'the interpretation of the opera as an elaborate parody' collapses.

Perhaps we should have guessed that this would be the outcome of their liaison. Fiordiligi's great aria ('Come scoglio', Act I) tells us that she is a woman of altogether unusual character, magnificent, indeed, in the breadth and ambition of her feelings; the immensely wide intervals she encompasses are the very lineaments of her commanding spirit. Ferrando, who grows to be an exceptionally ardent and pressing suitor, has to batter hard to dent Fiordiligi's loyalty. It is remarkable the tension that accumulates: will she, won't she? Finally, she will; and her rapture as she resigns herself is as superb as was her earlier protestation of virtue. I find no inconstancy of characterization here. Each passion is sustained with a fervour peculiar to Fiordiligi. It would have been an unforgivable inconsistency if her eventual embrace of Ferrando had not measured up to her previous rejection of him. One may feel, in fact, that theirs is almost a perfect match.

We can see how clearly Mozart keeps his pairs of lovers distinct by a brief comparison, Guglielmo/Dorabella with Ferrando/Fiordiligi. For a start, the time scale of the affair of the first pair of lovers does not coincide at all with that of the second, nor does the character of their relation. Dorabella is a far less serious person than Fiordiligi. Her great aria ('Smanie implacabili', Act I), like Fiordiligi's, is similarly self-revealing. We need not doubt the genuineness of her sentiments, but her expression of them is relatively shallow; this is a charming girl, a little feather-headed perhaps, who too easily comes to admire the admirable fluency of her feelings. Hence, no doubt, those deliciously repeated and indulgent sobs, with which she rounds off the main arch of her melody.

Dorabella, so to speak, changes sides at the first amorous breath of Guglielmo. One cannot really take her affections very seriously. Mozart makes sure that Guglielmo himself – likewise the lighter of the two suitors – is not wholly convinced, rightly so, that the outcome of the affair is satisfactory. How otherwise explain, in the mock marriage, the twinge of jealous passion that assails him as Ferrando and Fiordiligi, in the A♭ *Larghetto* that preludes Despina's production of the marriage contract, join in a radiant toast? Dorabella, parrot-like, quickly follows suit. But

Guglielmo angrily wishes them dead, in musical terms as distinct from the general texture as those of Don Alfonso in the famous Act I quintet ('Di scrivermi ogni giorno'), where the lovers' farewells are punctured by his cynical laughter.

Guglielmo and Dorabella, in fact, are not possessed by the love that drives Ferrando and Fiordiligi together; and if we glance back through the opera at the character and pattern of their relationship, we find this outcome as logically and consistently prepared, in terms of drama and music, as the eventual rapture of Ferrando and Fiordiligi. An opera that has begun with a symmetrical disposition of relations and emotions ends in comparative disarray.

It does not finally end thus, because the mock marriage is dissolved, and we must assume, I think, that the original relations are restored. But are they? Can they be, indeed?

We stumble here, I believe, on the most uncomfortable aspect of the opera's factuality. What we yearn for is the possibility of a fairy-tale reconciliation. But Mozart was far too truthful an artist to disguise the fact that a healing forgiveness is impossible where the parties are not only equally 'guilty' but share to the full the knowledge of each other's guilt. In *Così*, the best that can be done is to present as brave a front as one may to the facts of life. The coda that succeeds the *dénouement* does exactly that and no more.

But there is no denying, I think, that *Così* leaves one with rather a curious taste in one's mouth. Yes, after all, it *is* a shocking opera, not because of its frivolity but because of its ruthlessly rational exposure of the instinctive irrationality of human behaviour. 'Human kind', we know from T. S. Eliot, 'cannot bear very much reality';[5] which is why *Così* still continues to disconcert us.

NOTES

1 MC: *Lady Chatterley's Lover*, D. H. Lawrence's last novel, was banned in 1928 and Penguin Books was subsequently prosecuted under the 1959 Obscene Publications Act when it attempted to issue a paperback edition in 1960. The famous trial, which resulted in the publisher's acquittal and release of the novel

for sale, took place in the Old Bailey between 20 October and 2 November 1960. The book's treatment of infidelity was, *pace* DM, hardly the principal issue at stake.

2 E. H. Gombrich, '*Così fan tutte* (Procris Included)', *Journal of the Warburg and Courtauld Institutes* 17/3–4 (1954).

3 MC: Gerald Abraham had written in *The Mozart Companion*, edited by DM with H. C. Robbins Landon (Faber and Faber, London, second edition, 1965):

> Dramatic music can – indeed . . . to succeed it *must* – do more than merely dress up characters; it must embody them, no matter what the operatic convention in which the embodiment is framed. If the music is written by a genius such as Mozart, it can give them immortal souls as well . . . He nearly managed to breathe souls into the characters with which da Ponte provided him in *Così*, but *Così* is inferior to *Don Giovanni* just because the plot is so artificial, because the characters are less defined, more puppet-like than those the same librettist had given him in *Don Giovanni*. [p. 287.]

4 MC: Abraham declared that 'The characters are not real enough to present Mozart with the problem of preserving their individuality in a larger ensemble. The artificial symmetry of the plot helps.' (Ibid., pp. 314–15.)

5 MC: A reference to T. S. Eliot's poem 'Burnt Norton' (*Four Quartets*).

To Nobuko and Takashi Funayama

Cradles of the New: Paris and Vienna at the Turn of the Century

I think it is true to say that if one met an inquisitive musical friend on the street and was asked when and where in the twentieth century the New Music was born, one's immediate response, geographically speaking, would be 'Vienna' and, chronologically speaking, 'Vienna at the turn of the century'. I want to suggest here that that is something of an unthinking response, a historical perspective that is altogether too narrow and excluding, one that overlooks the extraordinary and fundamental contribution made to the development of the New in music in quite another location, Paris, by what one might think of, in some major respects, as an alternative and strongly contrasting European culture, and by one of the greatest, as we see now, composers of the century, Claude Debussy, whose dates, may I remind you, were 1862–1918.

Debussy's was a tragically short life – at fifty-five he was dead, killed by a painful and debilitating disease, his last years not only overshadowed by ill-health but by the catastrophe of the First World War. If we turn our eyes to Vienna for a moment, we discern a composer whose life was likewise tragically abbreviated, a life-span, by the way, that was almost identical with that of his great French contemporary – I refer to Gustav Mahler, born just two years earlier, in 1860, who was to die in 1911, seven years before Debussy's death and three years before the outbreak of war. But for the greater part, Debussy's and Mahler's lives ran in parallel.

Now many people, perhaps very many, would argue that a

Lecture, Fourth Tokyo Summer Festival, Quest Hall, 11 July 1988

parallel *chronology* was all that Debussy and Mahler had in common. I want to propose that, on the contrary, there were meaningful links and associations, which were certainly not apparent in their own time but which we, from our historical vantage point at the close of the twentieth century, can perceive; and out of that perception may emerge a view of history that sees Paris and Vienna not as contrasts or opposites but as complementary, which together form the unity out of which the twentieth century was born.

When Mahler was conductor of the New York Philharmonic Society and resident in the United States, he was interviewed by the *New York Daily Tribune* on 3 April 1910, when he was asked for his opinion of the New Music of *his* time, of which he himself was a vital part: 'I am absolutely opposed to dogma in criticism,' he said –

> You cannot limit anything absolutely. The radical of today is the conservative of tomorrow. What really counts is genuine self-expression. It is this that interests me. If a man writes a composition that is sincere, no matter if it breaks the old rules, that man must be admired.

'How can we tell what is decadent?' he said, rather heatedly –

> When a man produces something new, something that surprises the conservatives, it is immediately branded as decadent. I admire Strauss; I admire Debussy. They have done something original. Fifty years from now perhaps we can tell whether or not they are decadent. But we are too near to them to tell now.

'I admire Strauss; I admire Debussy.' In that one, brief statement to a newspaper, made a year before his death in 1911, Mahler encompasses – or, as I think, *integrates* – the Franco-German traditions, acknowledging that both had a vital role to play in the development of the new, the radical, the innovative, at the end of the century, and naming two composers of his own generation, one French, one German, who were both of them rule-breakers and standard-bearers for the New. More than that – and this still remains a little-appreciated cultural fact – Mahler the conductor put his admiration of Debussy into practical effect. He gave the first American performances, not only of the *Prélude à l'après-midi d'un faune*, which he had first heard in Vienna in 1907, in New York in 1910; but even more remarkable still, of two of Debussy's *Images*, *Rondes de printemps* and *Ibéria* – at the time Debussy's most recent orchestral work – which Mahler conducted in New York in November 1910 and January 1911 respectively. It seems scarcely conceivable that in May of the same year the great Austrian composer and conductor was dead.

Remarkable enough that these performances happened at all: they are evidence, certainly, of the openness of Mahler's ears, quite unprejudiced by considerations of nationality. You may recall that he once said: 'Tradition ist Schlamperei' ('Tradition is slovenliness'); and perhaps we should be encouraged by what he said to avoid slovenliness in our own thinking about the past, and cease thinking in so divisive a way about the history or, one might say, the *histories* of twentieth-century music, which so often have been formulated in watertight compartments, each with its own territorial boundary, identity card, date of birth, country of origin, etc., etc. A crippling form of provincialism, in my view. If Mahler, so unpredictably, could think laterally, across frontiers, why can't we?

The truth is, I suggest, that what Mahler heard in Debussy's late music, for all the differences that distinguished his aesthetic from that of his great French contemporary – and much more important than those differences – were certain new ideas and common preoccupations which brought Vienna and Paris at the turn of the century closer together.

Consider, for example, Debussy's *Nocturnes*, the set of three orchestral pieces he composed in the last decade of the nineteenth century, between 1897 and 1899, and which were first performed in the first two years of the new century, *Nuages* and *Fêtes* in 1900, the complete triptych in 1901.

'Three Orchestral Pieces': that, in fact, is what Debussy's

Nocturnes are, and it is a point I want to stress: for the conception of the 'orchestral piece', and flowing from that the *set* of orchestral pieces, whether three, five or six in number, was one of the principal new additive forms to emerge at and after the turn of the century. If we think of the 'orchestral piece', our immediate reaction is to summon up Vienna: Schoenberg and his *Five Orchestral Pieces* of 1909, Berg's *Three Pieces for Orchestra* of 1914, and Webern's *Six Pieces for Orchestra* of 1910, all of which have rightly become celebrated as major documents of the New Music. But preceding them all was Debussy with *his* 'Three Orchestral Pieces', the *Nocturnes*, which we should properly regard as the first work to break the new ground, to establish the new tradition, the new formal possibilities.

Let me be more specific: the middle section of *Fêtes* may have become thoroughly familiar music to our ears since 1900, but is no less extraordinary for that. What has always interested me about that passage (Figs. 10–14) is the constructional principle underpinning it: music – a march – that starts from a very low dynamic level, *pianissimo*, and gradually increases in dynamic intensity until it reaches a powerful climax. It is, so to speak, a large-scale *crescendo*, transformed from a dynamic nuance into a self-contained form in its own right; and the middle part of *Fêtes* is not only that, it is also one of the earliest explorations of acoustic space, which has become such a conspicuous feature of the music of our own time. For Debussy in his processional march introduces music from a great distance which he then manipulates so as to bring it into the foreground of our aural awareness: the music marches up to us and beyond us – it is *mobile* in a peculiarly twentieth-century sense. (Perhaps the only classical composer to precede Debussy in this field was Beethoven, in the finale of the Ninth Symphony, where the processional Turkish march follows the same dynamic contour, though of course it does not aspire to the same formal status.)

After the march, the recapitulation of the opening dance section (Fig. 14 to end) shows how brilliantly faithful Debussy remains to the acoustic and dynamic principles which I believe to be the *raison d'être* of the unique form of *Fêtes*. The coda follows the repeat of the dance fragments and then fades, reversing the dynamic of the dance itself, which in the very *first* bar of *Fêtes* opens *fortissimo* on the basic dance rhythm. Now the dynamic is reduced to a whisper and we have a composed *decrescendo*, the music on the move again, but this time disappearing into silence, with a memory of the march rhythm sustained on the side-drum.

We may guess with some confidence that when Mahler conducted *Fêtes* in New York in 1910 he not only would have given a very striking interpretation but recognized that Debussy was preoccupied with ideas about the relationship between form and dynamics, about the exploration of musical space, ideas with which in his own late music he was himself much preoccupied. We may be sure too that he would have felt thoroughly at home with the emphasis Debussy places on the march: think of all those symphonic movements of Mahler to which the concept of the march is fundamental. And what of the composers of the so-called Second Viennese School, rightly considered to be Mahler's legitimate successors? I have already pointed out that Schoenberg, Berg, Webern all wrote important sets of orchestral pieces. Significantly, the fourth of Webern's *Six Pieces*, Op. 6, composed in 1910, almost exactly a decade later than Debussy's *Nocturnes*, is conceived as a slow march, opening at the lowest dynamic level, *pianissimo*, with the percussion alone, and then gradually increasing in dynamic intensity until it ends in a massive climax. In short, it offers another example of a *crescendo* raised to the status of an independent form. It is, of course, music that is entirely different in atmosphere, style, sound and above all *temperament*, from Debussy's. But that is not the point I am making. What interests me is to emphasize the common ground: that in both Paris and Vienna composers were confronted by the same sort of challenges and were finding their way towards identical solutions. This consideration far transcends questions of *style*. I should be the last person in the world to deny the vivid contrast offered by the Gallic and

Austro-German temperaments; but the temperamental contrast makes the pursuit of common compositional principles all the more illuminating. We are beginning to discover, I suggest, that Paris and Vienna in many ways innovated in precisely the same way, in response to the same problems, and at much the same time. We are not looking at two disparate, irreconcilable European traditions but at one mainstream with a common source. We are right to discern the distinct tributaries into which the main stream was to divide. But the common source dictated – if I may depart from my analogy – a common agenda, which was of equal relevance and urgency, whether the location was Paris or Vienna. The common source, I believe, was Wagner; and the question for composers at the top of the agenda was this: after Wagner, how to go on? And, more specifically, how to go on after *Tristan und Isolde*, that great destabilizing event in European music in the latter half of the nineteenth century which permanently modified the musical landscape, whether it was viewed from Paris or Vienna: composers everywhere had to find a means of responding to Wagner's challenge, which brought into question a system of organized tonality that had governed compositional practice in the West for nearly two hundred years.

The crisis engendered by *Tristan*, in the Gallic tradition quite as much as in the Austro-German tradition, is a whole subject in itself. But Wagner, while creating technical problems for his contemporaries and successors, also offered them solutions, which they were quick to seize and exploit. One of the most famous of Debussy's orchestral works, his *Prélude à l'après-midi d'un faune*, composed in 1892–4 and, as we have seen, again brought to its first American performance under Mahler in New York in March 1910, makes the line of succession absolutely clear: without the precedent created by Wagner, and the techniques along with it, Debussy's *Prélude*, marvellously individual though it is, *could not have begun to exist*. That is what I mean by claiming that Wagner bequeathed his successor solutions along with the puzzles.

It is surely no accident that the music of Wagner that proved to be most *influential* was that which had taken shape – of course in the context of his operas – as purely orchestral preludes or interludes. One might argue, indeed, that these orchestral excerpts, which became familiar in the concert hall and thus widely accessible to a broad public, pioneered the idea of the 'orchestral piece', even before the form itself became fashionable. I have already suggested that the idea of the 'orchestral piece' was to become a preoccupation of a later generation of composers: Debussy's magical *Prélude* was one of Wagner's orchestral offspring.

The new techniques Wagner developed enabled him to create an entirely new musical experience, one in which the old concept of musical time was suspended. The profile of the new language was emphatically harmonic rather than melodic or rhythmic, and made possible the creation of a music that, to my mind, can quite properly be defined as Impressionist. Indeed, I shall be so bold as to claim that the first Impressionist, undeniably, was Richard Wagner; and the *locus classicus*, without doubt, was one of his most influential 'orchestral pieces', 'Forest Murmurs', from Act II of *Siegfried*. There, surely, the world witnessed the birth of Impressionism in music. In that contemplative but momentous interlude in which Siegfried contemplates Nature, and in which the composer contemplates his musical ideas in a context divorced from traditional considerations of harmonic movement, rhythmic animation or extended melody. Wagner invites his audience likewise to contemplate *his* contemplation: in other words, to submit – to surrender – to the primacy of sound, not as a means but as an end. It was the beginning of an aesthetic that is still alive today in the music of contemporary composers all over the world.

Even in *Tristan*, the most interior of Wagner's operas, we can find the same principles at work, allied sometimes, as in the Prelude to Act II, to a vision of Nature, where we encounter the surge of the ocean; and, juxtaposed with that, the void horizon, scanned by the wounded Tristan. Once again this remarkable invention takes the shape of an 'orchestral piece', the *raison d'être* of which is the interplay between two contrasted ideas, the one in

1 *Top*, Family outing, *c.* 1930. DM's father and mother. Seated are DM (second from the left) and his elder brother David (second from the right).

2 Editing *Music Survey*, *c.* 1948.

3 *Top*, The Palermo Festival, October 1962. Left to right, DM (*Daily Telegraph*), Colin Mason (1924–1971, then writing for the *Manchester Guardian*), and Andrew Porter (then writing for the *Financial Times*). Colin Mason was a close friend. DM misses him to this day.

4 At the United Nations, New York, 24 October 1965, for the première of Britten's *Voices for Today*, Op. 75. DM stands with U Thant (1909–1974, then U.N. Secretary-General, centre) and Arpad Darazs, joint conductor of the première (with Hugh Ross).

5 *Top left*, The Faber Music offices at 38 Russell Square, London, 1970. DM with Roderick Biss.

6 *Top right*, DM (1980).

7 *Left*, Peter Pears and DM, Orford Town Square. Aldeburgh Festival 1978.

8 *Right*, Hans Werner Henze and DM, Britten–Pears School at Snape, Henze Study Course, 1982.

9, 10 & 11 Lawn Cottage, Barcombe Mills, Sussex, July 1971, when PP received an honorary degree from the University of Sussex. *Top and bottom*, breakfast in the garden. Lawn Cottage was the Mitchells' Sussex house, where BB and PP occasionally stayed.

12 *Top*, June 1976. The party in the Red House garden to celebrate BB's peerage. DM introduces John Evans (now Head of Music, BBC Radio 3) and Sian Pouncey to Britten. KM with her back to camera.

13 January 1985. PP and DM in PP's study at the Red House during the filming of *The Tenor Man's Story* (Central Television).

14 *Top*, Lutosławski Study Course, Aldeburgh (in what is now the Peter Pears Gallery), 1983. The composer with PP and DM and a backcloth of paintings by John Piper.

15 Aldeburgh Festival 1985. The resident composer, Henri Dutilleux, talks to Sally Groves. DM to Mollie Webster.

16 *Top*, China, March 1983. KM and DM on the Great Wall. DM, on an inter-governmental exchange visit, gave lectures on BB at the Conservatoires in Beijing and Shanghai.

17 With Simon Rattle, in DM's study in London in 1986 during the filming (for BBC2) of the documentary, *The Jade Flute*, on Mahler's *Das Lied von der Erde*.

18 *Top left*, Aldeburgh Festival 1991, when DM was Guest Artistic Director and Thai music and musicians enjoyed a high profile. In the morning room at the Red House DM talks to Somsak Ketukaenchan who was the soloist in a work for *pi nai* and orchestra by Keith Gifford.

19 *Top right*, DM when Chairman of the Performing Right Society (1989–92), in his room in Copyright House, Berners Street, London.

20 Chapel House, Horham, 1988: DM and Philip Reed at work editing Britten's letters and diaries, the first two volumes of which were published in 1991.

the low register of the orchestra, the other in the high. It is the sonorous realization of the void that is so haunting, where Wagner instantaneously creates the most powerful atmosphere by hanging in the air for our contemplation, so to speak, a chain of thirds in the high violins, which is slowly revealed to us – unfolded – and then fades, like a procession, into silence.

There is a compositional principle uncovered here that did not escape Debussy's attention: we need seek no further than *Nuages*, the first of the three *Nocturnes*. The title of the piece may seem to 'explain' the form the music takes. But in fact Debussy is *not* depicting the passage of clouds across the vault of heaven, but isolating a musical idea, in this case an unbroken rhythmic flow combined with a seamless sequence of chords, and exploring and exploiting its constructive potentialities. Debussy treats his ideas like objects, suspended in space and looked at from every point of view, rather as one might walk round and observe a sculpture. The process of observation and assimilation *is* the piece: when the process is completed, the piece too is complete. The delicacy of the imagination in *Nuages*, the subtlety of its dynamics and, above all, the reticence of the composer's voice, must not be allowed to conceal from us its innovatory character.

It is a piece that has almost its whole life concentrated in its changing harmonic textures. These are inimitably Debussian in sound, but the practice, the method, the principle, Debussy owes to Wagner. However, Debussy brought to his aesthetic at the turn of the century something that did not form part of Wagner's. In the wonderful Prelude to the last act of *Tristan*, the music does indeed create a landscape, or at least the bleak *psychological* landscape, which the wounded Tristan inhabits. But Debussy's *Nuages*, I suggest, despite its title, is in reality stripped of all poetic or dramatic or descriptive associations: it is purely functional music, in which certain musical ideas perform (behave) only in accordance with their own inner logic. Debussy brings us, in short, in musical practice, to the verge of yet another aesthetic which was to be predominant in the first decades of the twentieth century, in almost all the arts – the visual (whether painting or architecture), literature and music. It is an aesthetic in which Paris, at and after the turn of the century, had a peculiarly formative and generative role to play. I refer to the rise of one of the great artistic movements of our time: the début of the Abstract.

The idea of abstract art is so familiar to us in the latter half of our century that it is sometimes hard to remember that it was born as the old century, the nineteenth century, expired. Today – and despite the reaction of post-Modernism in so many fields – it still vitally influences how we perceive objects and their design. Music too followed this same path in its own way; and, interestingly enough, it was a path pursued in both Paris and Vienna. There are indeed remarkable parallels to be observed here, but also no less remarkable divergences. In Vienna there was Kandinsky and Abstract Expressionism, an aesthetic that was profoundly influential on Schoenberg and his contemporaries: in Paris, Impressionism – profoundly influential on the culture that surrounded Debussy and his contemporaries – and, later, Cubism. If Impressionism had massively contributed to the dissolution of the object, Cubism, for a brilliant if short-lived period, virtually succeeded in abolishing it altogether.

There are periods in the arts when certain aesthetic strategies and preoccupations seem to be shared among the arts almost without distinction. Such a period was surely the final decade of the nineteenth century and the first decade of the twentieth, when the ideas of painters and musicians, poets and architects, seemed interchangeable; or, to put it another way, a period when creators in whichever medium seemed to have common ambitions which they attempted to achieve by technical means which themselves shared common characteristics. I believe that proposition to hold true of both Paris and Vienna, even while at the same time illuminating profound cultural and temperamental differences. Let me explain these contrasts by returning once more to Wagner, the source of so much of the New in music. The truth is, surely, that Wagner was not only the first Impressionist but also the first Expressionist. I have already mentioned an example of the new ground – no, the new *sound* – explored in the 'orchestral piece' we know as 'Forest Murmurs', one of the very first documents of Impressionism in the history of music. We try to identify the characteristic features of that famous interlude by using words such as 'reflective', 'immobile', and 'contemplative', words that imply a submission to feelings engendered by observation of the *exterior* world, in this case the world of Nature. But there is that *other* world of feeling and feelings which is wholly *interior*, generated by and within the human psyche; and it is that world that Expressionism was to investigate, a world of violent contrasts, of the unpredictable, the irrational, the exaggerated and the threatening, words again that we often use when attempting to define what we mean by describing something as 'Expressionist'. If we turn once more to *Tristan*, and to the third act of that great work, we can find there all the features that we have come to recognize as characteristics of Expressionism. The *locus classicus* here is Tristan's celebrated 'mad' scene, his great monologue at the beginning of Act III where, hallucinating and on the brink of death, he releases a flood of unconstrained, uncontrollable feelings. The phenomenon that Wagner presents to us is inner feeling, a stream of consciousness, heightened and intensified by the fever raging in Tristan's blood, made manifest – exteriorized – as sound. The music does not so much 'depict' the stricken Tristan's delirium as provide us with a graphic map of it: to continue the analogy, the contours of the music – its form – precisely represent the irregular, asymmetrical contours of Tristan's outpourings. Hence, of course, the precipitous vocal writing, the extravagantly wide leaps of which were to become one of the leading features of the style (both vocal and instrumental) of succeeding generations of composers, from Schoenberg and Berg to our own time, to become, indeed, one of the indispensable characteristics of the style we identify as 'Expressionist'. In Tristan's monologue, furthermore, form and content are absolutely indissoluble; one cannot be divorced from the other because outward form is at the same time the unfettered 'expression' of content (Tristan's inmost psyche). Perhaps it was only in the heroic years of Expressionism at the turn of the century that any distinction between form and content in music was finally erased.

I am suggesting, then, that Impressionism and Expressionism, those two great movements in the twentieth-century arts, were not so much contrasted as *complementary*; and that both these tributaries from the main flow of what was New in the arts at the turn of the century had their source in Wagner, that extraordinary Colossus who, during the second half of the nineteenth century, was a dominant and fertilizing force in both Gallic and Austro-German culture. Impressionism has largely become identified with Gallic attitudes, Expressionism with characteristic Austro-German achievements; and it is true that we meet here a genuine difference in *temperament* between the two cultures, between Paris and Vienna. But although the temperamental contrast was – and remains – a real one, and while the interior/exterior comparison tells us something fundamental about both movements, it would be a serious error to judge Debussy to be all *ex*terior, and Mahler, say, or Schoenberg, as all *in*terior. On the contrary, if one thinks of the work of Debussy's that is regarded rightly as quintessentially Debussian, his opera *Pelléas et Mélisande*, composed – *across* the turn of the century! – in 1893–1902, we cannot but be impressed by its almost exclusively *in*terior quality. It is often said that *Pelléas* is the very antithesis of the Wagnerian aesthetic, that it represents Debussy's rejection of Wagner. But this is to think in that divisive, compartmentalized way that I am eager to escape. The truth it seems to me is quite other: that *Pelléas* is not at some opposite or opposing pole to *Tristan* but is, rather, its *obverse*; and one of the meanings of obverse, the dictionary tells us, is a 'statement *complementary* to another'. A statement has to be made first if a complementary statement, a counterpart, is to emerge. It is thus that I assess the relationship of *Pelléas* to *Tristan*, not as contradiction, but as complement. *Tristan*, self-evidently, is an interior drama; but I have always been convinced that dormant in it, despite its gigantic resources and superhuman rhetoric, was a chamber-musical conception of opera, which would allow for the subtlest nuances and inflexions of the psychological action. Within *Tristan* there was, as it were, a *Pelléas* awaiting its release. It was exactly that possibility offered by *Tristan* which Debussy grasped and developed in *Pelléas*, pushing back the frontiers explored by Wagner in his own bold journey into the interior. This is a relationship of altogether profounder significance than the Wagnerian echoes that everyone hears in *Pelléas*, especially in the orchestral interludes which were in any event accretions imposed on Debussy by the exigencies of scene-shifting in the theatre when the opera was first staged in 1902. It is fascinating, none the less, that it was *Parsifal* that must have been at the back of Debussy's mind when putting his interludes together, in particular the interlude between Scenes 1 and 2 of Act I, music that never fails to remind one of that marvellous remark of Debussy's about *Parsifal* which tells us so much about the way Debussy heard music and how he himself imagined it. This was what he wrote to André Caplet, in August 1912, when he had just finished composing his late ballet score, *Jeux*: 'I'm thinking of that orchestral colour which seems to be lit from behind, which there are such wonderful examples of in *Parsifal*!'[1] 'Orchestral colour . . . *lit from behind*' (my emphasis). What a penetrating description, in itself worth a dozen treatises on the art of orchestration! We observe too that, even as late as 1912, Debussy was still referring admiringly to Wagner and *Parsifal* as models! 'Lit from behind': an *interior* conception, we note of the orchestral sound that was Debussy's ideal; and his insight enables us further to refine our definition of Impressionism and the contrast between Impressionism and Expressionism. His remark confirms that Impressionism too was an interior art; yet it was one that had to have a surface, an exterior, for the creation of its quite special effects. If there has been a widespread error in the way we judge Impressionism then it rests perhaps in our recognizing the surface but overlooking the factor that makes the surface magical: that interior light to which Debussy refers. Whereas in the case of Expressionism, as I have already suggested, the surface is at the same time the interior. Nothing stands between us and the expressive feelings: the unmasked expression of them constitutes the totality of the created work. We cannot get *behind* Expressionism. We are already sunk deep in the recesses of the human psyche.

One last word on the inside/outside, interior/exterior juxtaposition. There is another fascinating letter of Debussy's, written in May 1902, in which he laments the absence of André Messager from the conductor's podium at the Opéra-Comique: 'The only thing lacking [in the performance] was you . . . you knew how to bring the music of *Pelléas* to life with a tender delicacy I dare not hope to find elsewhere.' And, he adds, 'Sure as I am that in all music the *interior rhythm* [my emphasis] depends on the interpreter's evocation of it, as a word depends on the lips that pronounce it . . .'[2] 'Interior rhythm': another unforgettable comment which tells us a very great deal about the nature of Debussy's art and again helps define the characteristic techniques of Impressionism.

I have already suggested that both Impressionism and Expressionism led to the rise of a later and major new aesthetic, the Abstract, but as an ideal and as a technique. It was an aesthetic that asserted the absolute autonomy of art, repelled all associations with the representational, the realistic, the narrative or programmatic, and above all affirmed the sovereignty of form, often geometric form.

The history of abstract painting alone would require many lectures, but there are one or two dates and events of crucial importance. First, 1907, when the great commemorative exhibition of Cézanne was held in Paris. It was this art which, in its own inimitable way, dissolved the object and the representational into the geometrical and thus opened up the possibilities of the Abstract and, more specifically, the development of Cubism. In the same year, Picasso painted *Les demoiselles d'Avignon*, the seminal work which initiated his vastly influential Cubist period, in close association with Georges Braque. All this was happening in France and, more particularly, in Paris. It was a period during which Debussy was himself to develop an emphatically 'abstract' manner of his own, exemplified in the remarkable late piano works of his last years: the *Etudes*, for solo piano, of 1915 and, in the same year, *En blanc et noir*, for two pianos.

When discussing Debussy's great set of three orchestral pieces, the *Nocturnes*, I pointed to his ability to suspend a musical idea in space for our inspection and contemplation from many different angles. I used an example from *Nuages* because there, already, Debussy was on the brink of the abstraction that he was to carry through to its logical conclusion in his late *Etudes*. He presents them as if they were exercises in pianistic technique, with their roots in such famous instructional keyboard methods of the past as Clementi's *Gradus ad Parnassum*. In his *Children's Corner* suite of 1906–8, Debussy had written a parody of Clementi; and, in the first of the *Etudes*, he composes a five-finger exercise 'in the style of Czerny' – 'Pour les "cinq doigts" – d'après Monsieur Czerny'. But the title is really as redundant as is the poetic superscription in the case of *Nuages*. No doubt Debussy was having a little quiet amusement at our expense, for what, in fact, the first *Etude* does, like all the remaining numbers, is to choose an abstract musical idea and exhaustively manipulate it within the constraints imposed on it by the chosen 'exercise'. In other words, Debussy asks himself what, compositionally, can be got out of a fragment of the C major scale, its first five notes in their ascending and descending forms? You could hardly have a more basic, less committed, less 'descriptive' musical idea than that! The answer he comes up with – which is the first *Etude* – has about it some of the pleasure we derive from pure mathematics, from a game, a skill, a scheme, a pattern, raised to the *n*th degree. I have to call on an abstract vocabulary, you note, in order to attempt a description of the abstract musical world the first *Etude* inhabits.

Debussy does not leave us long with his unadorned basic idea. For only one bar, indeed; in bar 2, an intruder appears in the shape of an inexplicable, insistently repeated A♭. But in bar 7, all is made clear to us: A♭ is revealed as the point of departure for the elaborate sequence of interruptions and developments of the scale fragment that constitutes the totality of the piece.

In the third *Etude*, although the compositional principle is the same, the music is of a quite different character, most obviously because it is built entirely out of the dissonant interval of the fourth, the interval in which so frequently the spirit of the New Music of the twentieth century was made incarnate. (In this context one recalls above all the famous opening of Schoenberg's *First Chamber Symphony*, Op. 9, composed in 1906, with its chain of ascending fourths in the horn, one of those ideas in the history of music which, for succeeding generations, permanently modify the musical soundscape.) But it is not only Debussy's systematic exploration of fourths in the third *Etude* that should claim our attention, significant though it be. There are two other innovatory aspects of the piece that are scarcely less striking (or seminal). First, its abrupt disruptions and dislocations of tempo, of dynamics, of musical character, all of which contribute to making the impression and effect of an *improvisation*. My second observation is really bound up with my first. For if we ask ourselves what specific kind of improvisation, then we have to conclude that in this late *Etude* Debussy was again responding to the profound impact made on him by the gamelan music from Indonesia that he had heard in Paris in 1889: those extraordinary, unpredictable and loud eruptions of energy in bars 7 and 18, for example – their percussive clamour – have their origins, I am convinced, in the gamelan, just as much as anything in *Pagodes*, which Debussy had composed in 1903.[3] To the topics of improvisation and the gamelan I shall be returning. Meanwhile one leaves the *Etudes* with a sense of the rightness of Charles Rosen's assessment of them as 'one of the monuments of our century'.

As the *Etudes* themselves suggest, the piano piece, like the orchestral piece, was another of the forms dominant in music around and after the turn of the century. Debussy was one of its principal modern creators; and once more there is an illuminating parallel with Vienna, where Schoenberg entrusted some of the most challenging of his new ideas to the piano. I am thinking here in particular of the *Six Little Piano Pieces*, Op. 19, composed in 1911, which bear a specific relationship to an aesthetic that was shared by both painters and musicians. If Debussy's *Etudes* show a preoccupation with abstraction through a deployment of 'neutral' intervals, patterns, rhythms, figuration – ideas innocent of description, narration or poetic content, ideas that are the uncommitted (I almost wrote 'non-committal') materials of music rather than the deliberated composition that later incorporates, subsumes, those materials into a larger and more meaningful entity – then Schoenberg's Op. 19 is even more clearly linked with another, though very different manifestation of the Abstract, this time the Abstract Expressionism of Kandinsky.[4] In Schoenberg's *Six Little Pieces*, it is intuition that produces the musical ideas; and the forms last for just as long as the intuition persists – the kinship with Kandinsky's aesthetic (and consequent technique) is clear. One might think that there was a yawning gulf between Schoenberg's surrender to 'instinct' and Debussy's pre-determined 'calculation', as we encounter it, say, in his first *Etude*, the five-finger exercise; but as the third of Debussy's *Etudes* shows, he, no less than Schoenberg, was interested in discovering what quasi-improvisation might have to offer as one solution of the formal problem: through different aesthetic strategies, each of them evolved techniques that have more in common than one might at first have supposed.

This last point is vividly confirmed by one of Schoenberg's aphoristic piano pieces, the last of the set, Op. 19. It could hardly be more different in character from Debussy's *Etude*, yet – as in the *Etude* – it is the interval of the fourth that is its *fons et origo*. (Likewise, the interval of the third is the 'subject' of the second of Schoenberg's Op. 19, as it is of the second of Debussy's *Etudes*.) In addition, Schoenberg suspends his central idea – an alternation of two sustained chords – in musical space for our observation, a process that I have suggested was part of Debussy's innovative compositional practice. The insistent tolling of the funeral 'bells' (chords) – Schoenberg had attended Mahler's burial in May 1911 – creates a remarkable impression of immobility, of numbed grief. One might claim that the nine bars of the piece make a perfect Impressionist miniature – but one composed in Vienna, not Paris. At the same time the totality of the piece is feeling materialized as sound, and thus too a perfect, concise example of Expressionism.

The history of twentieth-century music, I believe, would have been radically modified but for two events: first, the catastrophic interruption and fragmentation of European culture caused by the First World War of 1914–18; and, second, the untimely death of Debussy in 1918, the last year of the war. The post-war world was an altogether different place, and not yet ready, and particularly, I suggest, not ready in Paris, to recognize what Debussy's legacy might offer the future. It was not until after the end of the *Second* World War that the world became aware of the new options Debussy had revealed at the turn of the century and which had lain uninvestigated and largely unacknowledged in the intervening decades. This was the more ironic when one remembers that one of the dominant figures in Parisian musical culture after the end of the First World War was Stravinsky; and that it was to Debussy that Stravinsky and the musicians of his generation owed an essential part of their liberation, the century's 'first musician' as Stravinsky was later to describe him.

Debussy and Stravinsky: in that relationship we find the source of one of the main tributaries of twentieth-century music, a line of succession based on Paris which parallels that other line of succession based on Vienna, which runs from Mahler, through Schoenberg, Berg and Webern, and on to much later generations of composers, dispersed on a global scale. (In some respects one can think of Mahler and Schoenberg in the same juxtaposition – and sometimes with the same attendant tensions – as Debussy and Stravinsky.)

I have not the space to elucidate all the details of the momentous friendship of the French composer, born in 1862, and his younger Russian colleague, born in 1882. We can read about their association in Stravinsky's memoirs and Debussy's letters, where we also find recorded that unique encounter between two great twentieth-century musical minds: it was on 9 June 1912 that Debussy and Stravinsky together played through *The Rite of Spring* in its piano-duet version, Debussy undertaking the bass part, Stravinsky the treble. A few months later, in November, Debussy wrote of the occasion to Stravinsky: 'It haunts me like a beautiful nightmare . . .' '*Beautiful nightmare*' (my emphasis): one of those elegant, paradoxical summaries of Debussy's which, in two words, seems to tell us all we need to know about what *The Rite* meant to him – something to admire, an experience to cherish, but also, perhaps, something to fear. A certain caustic, *defensive* wit was one way Debussy had of protecting himself against the Stravinskian revolution: '*The Rite of Spring*', he was to write in 1913, 'is extraordinarily wild . . . As you might say, it's primitive music with all modern conveniences!'

It was not only *The Rite* that excited Debussy's admiration and attention, but also *Petrushka*. In 1912, he wrote to Stravinsky,

> I've spent a lovely Easter holiday in the company of Petrushka . . . and I know few things as good as the passage you call 'le tour de passe-passe' [where the showman plays his flute and brings the three puppets to life] . . . There's a sort of sonorous magic about it . . . : it's a spell which, so far, I think you are alone in possessing. And then there are orchestral *certainties* such as I have encountered only in *Parsifal* – I'm sure you'll understand what I mean!

How surprising it is to find Debussy once again referring to Wagner and to *Parsifal*, and this time in such an unusual context. It took a Debussy perhaps to perceive common ground shared by Wagner and Stravinsky.[5] But it is precisely such a cross-cultural, cross-chronological perspective on music that it is my chief purpose to explore. And consider something else: Debussy wrote to Stravinsky in November 1913, 'It is a special satisfaction to tell you how much you have enlarged the boundaries of the permissible in the empire of sound', words that, with equal truth and precision, could have been addressed by Debussy to Wagner. We may guess, indeed, with some confidence, that it was exactly in those terms that Debussy *heard* Wagner, how he experienced his music. Thus there was nothing eccentric about his reference to *Parsifal* in the context of *Petrushka*. On the contrary, it is a telling example of the perception of creative genius overriding the limiting chronology and classification of history.

At the very beginning of these reflections I remarked on the untimely deaths of Mahler and Debussy, the Austrian in 1911, the Frenchman in 1918. If I have suggested that the history of twentieth-century music, had Debussy lived longer, would have been very different, it was for this special reason: that his own late music, radical and innovative in its own right, also unmistakably revealed the impact made on him by the audacious imagination and revolutionary techniques of his younger colleague, Stravinsky.

We can discern this reverse influence clearly enough in the rhythmic gestures and harmonic language of Debussy's late orchestral masterpiece, *Jeux*, a ballet score composed in 1912 and 1913 for Diaghilev and Nijinsky and the Ballets Russes,[6] the proofs of which Debussy sent to Stravinsky, who remembered Debussy's consulting him about problems of orchestration (significantly, it was while completing *Jeux* that Debussy commented to Stravinsky on orchestral colours 'lit from behind', as in *Parsifal*).

In *Jeux*, and again in *La boîte à joujoux* (1913) – another ballet! – we hear Stravinsky as it were through the filter of Debussy's genius, a music that is eloquent of the unique interrelationship between Debussy and Stravinsky, a creative friendship that was to have momentous consequences for the development of twentieth-century music. But they were not *immediate* consequences. They were to be postponed by a succession of extra-musical events: by the outbreak of war in Europe in 1914, by Debussy's death in 1918, even before his last compositions had had the opportunity to establish themselves in the public consciousness and, last but not least, by Stravinsky's own evolution as a composer, when he moved into new aesthetic commitments – neo-classicism above all – which at the time appeared to be a rejection not only of his own past but of the Debussian past too.

Stravinsky, as is common knowledge, was to be one of the dominant figures in Parisian musical life post-1918, and not only the neo-classical Stravinsky but what one might describe as the elegant, witty, iconoclastic and occasionally downright frivolous Stravinsky of the 1920s. It was these characteristics of the great Russian composer – minor rather than major, albeit an authentic part of his personality – that were immensely influential, perhaps especially in Gallic culture and, one may think, out of all proportion to their intrinsic importance or interest. The influential iconoclasm of Jean Cocteau – itself a phenomenon of the period – was a reflection of what Stravinsky in the 1920s was often understood – misunderstood, rather – to be.

As a result of that misunderstanding – and boosted by a strong tide of hostility to German art and music, and to Wagner especially, in which Debussy, with paradoxical vehemence, had participated – one had movements such as Les Six, which in retrospect seem to have fastened on to the trivial and inconsequential and raised them to the status of an independent, self-justifying aesthetic. It was made up of composers who dealt exclusively in the small-change of Stravinsky's currency, and their *chic* attitudes, and smart small-talk and gossip expired along with the decades that gave birth to them. But this excess of the trivial, of the frivolous, was one of the interruptions that undeniably delayed the resumption of the exploration of the principal legacy bequeathed to the new century by Debussy and Stravinsky, which had remained largely unexplored during the inter-war period.

The Gallic frivolities of the 1920s and 1930s were themselves interrupted and finally extinguished by the Second World War; and it was not until after the conclusion of that war, in 1945, that the innovatory paths, the exploration of which Debussy had begun, were once again investigated by the new generation of post-Second World War composers. Prominent among them was the remarkable figure of Pierre Boulez, who was to be one of the principal combatants in the battle to rediscover, re-establish, and reappraise the New Music that had been born at the turn of the century; and a unique feature of Boulez, surely, was his awareness that the New was jointly born of both Paris and Vienna, both of which sources fertilized his own aesthetic and techniques and through *his* prodigious influence was to fertilize succeeding generations of composers, to our own day. To consider in detail his achievement would take me far outside my chronological limits, but let us note that those twin tributaries to which I have often referred were, post-1945, and in the personality of Boulez, reunited, and the mainstream, of which Debussy and Mahler had both been part, resumed. It is no accident that as an interpreter Boulez was to become famous for his performances of both those composers' works; and the wheel turns full circle, and carries us back to my point of departure, when we recall that among his most notable achievements as conductor and interpreter was his performance of the complete *Ring* cycle at Bayreuth [in 1976], an event that succinctly symbolizes the fundamental importance of Wagner as prime source of the New, for Paris no less than for Vienna.

Vienna between the wars was experiencing its own series of interruptions, notably the rise of Fascism in the 1930s, which led to the dispersal and exodus of so many Jewish musicians – Schoenberg among them – and to an assault on the aesthetics of the New Music; in addition, there was the inherent conservatism of Vienna, that city of paradox and contrast, stubbornly rooted in the past and yet at the same time determinedly expanding the frontiers of the future. No one could argue that the New had an easy time of it in Vienna, or for that matter anywhere else in the inter-war period, but there was a sense in which the line of succession – Wagner, Mahler, Schoenberg, Berg, Webern – remained intact, while the alternative tradition – Wagner,

Debussy, Stravinsky – was disrupted, subjected above all to the discontinuities of the diversity of traditions that Stravinsky himself seemed to embody after 1918. But, as I have suggested, after 1945, and largely through the reassessments of Boulez, who brought a cool, analytic and discriminating intelligence to bear on the two seemingly contrasted or opposing traditions, we were shown that they were in fact complementary and, on the broader historical view, integral.

It may seem odd in this context to quote a French composer who in many respects must be regarded as the very antithesis of the New, an arch-conservative, Camille Saint-Saëns; and yet it was he who, in 1879, made one of the clearest analyses of the problems that composers faced at the end of the nineteenth century; and, even more interestingly, indicated the sources to which the New Music would have to look for refreshment and revitalization. This is what he said:

> Tonality, which is the basis of modern harmony, is in a state of crisis. The major and minor scales no longer have exclusive rights . . . The ancient modes are making a comeback, to be hotly pursued by the scales of the East in all their tremendous variety. All this will strengthen melody in her present exhausted state . . . Harmony too is bound to change and we shall see developments in rhythm, which has so far hardly been exploited. From all this will spring a new art.[7]

In retrospect – that is, from the vantage point of the 1980s – very many of Saint-Saëns's technical observations have about them the ring of prophecy. All of them, one may think, were to become of particular relevance as the turn of the century approached, but none more so than 'developments in rhythm', an area Stravinsky was boldly and brilliantly to renovate and occupy, and the hot pursuit of 'the scales of the East in all their tremendous variety'. His encounter with non-Western music and with non-Western culture was to make a profound impact on Debussy, and open up for him new means of musical expression; and by 'new means' I mean new sounds, new techniques, of which once again he was the pioneer.

'The scales of the East', to which Saint-Saëns refers, were precisely what Debussy was to hear when a troupe of Javanese dancers and instrumentalists performed at the Paris World Exhibition held on the Champ de Mars in 1889, in which same year, by the way, Debussy visited Bayreuth and heard *Tristan* for the first time – one of those fascinating conjunctions which history, from time to time, obligingly vouchsafes.

In 1895, when he was working on *Pelléas*, he remembered his experience of the Javanese musicians in these words: it was, he wrote, 'music . . . which contained every nuance, even the ones we no longer have names for. There tonic and dominant had become empty shadows of use only to stupid children.' A description entirely true of Javanese music, but words again that could also serve as a precise comment on Wagner's technique in *Tristan*. The wheel revolves full circle once more.

There was a general interest at the turn of the century in the arts and artefacts of the Orient which amounted to a widespread European cultural phenomenon in its own right. Much of the enthusiasm for *chinoiserie* and *japonaiserie* was a manifestation of fashion, and preoccupied with the decorative, the exotic, the 'mysterious' East, and so forth. But in the visual arts and in music, the influence could and did strike deep. It did not leave Mahler untouched, as *Das Lied von der Erde* shows, not merely in the choice of texts but in specific compositional techniques; Vienna, indeed, no less than Paris, surrendered to the allure of the Orient.[8] This was also a time when the first scientific studies of non-Western musics began to be made, which has led to the flourishing industry of ethnomusicology in our own day. There is no doubt that the impression made on Debussy by the Javanese gamelan was a profound one; and every single writer on Debussy has subscribed to that opinion. But where, when it comes to the point, do we actually hear the gamelan functioning directly as an influence on a specific work by Debussy? This, I think, is a far harder question to answer.

Most commentators will point to *Pagodes*, the first of

Debussy's three *Estampes* for piano, published in 1903: with a title like *Pagodes* there must surely be an 'oriental' dimension? And so there is: the piece is conspicuously pentatonic, it most ingeniously represents in terms of the modern keyboard the characteristic figuration, textures, dynamics and sonorities of the gamelan, and aspires often to the condition of an improvisation. We may be certain that improvisation – the idea of freedom, of a free form, implied thereby – would have been one of the principal impressions that Debussy carried away with him from his encounter with the Javanese group.[9]

The improvised, spontaneous, 'free' form: we have seen already how Schoenberg in Vienna made that particular approach by way of the Kandinskian aesthetic, by relying on intuition, inner fantasy, the subconscious. In Paris, we find Debussy trying to achieve the same goal by way of his experience of the Javanese gamelan; and interestingly enough, in *Images*, the late orchestral pieces that Mahler conducted in New York, in one of them, *Ibéria*, Debussy singled out a passage for special mention in a letter he wrote to André Caplet in February 1910. The transition, he suggested, between 'Les parfums de la nuit' and 'Le matin d'un jour de fête' (Figs. 52^{+6}–56), '*sounds as though it's improvised*';[10] and as if to draw attention to the importance of that achievement, Debussy himself emphasizes those words.

Thus Debussy, once again, in his own inimitable manner and through techniques absorbed from contact with a wholly different musical culture, was operating in an area which we perceive now to have been a widespread preoccupation of composers in the first decades of the twentieth century, when so much of the New Music, whatever its origins, whatever its national identity, or cultural orientation, *aspired to the condition of improvisation.* I give those words of mine their own emphasis, and remind you of those other 'improvisatory' works I have already mentioned: the third of Debussy's *Etudes* and the last of the *Six Little Pieces* by Schoenberg.

And the gamelan presence? Yes, it is certainly there in Debussy, though like all profound influences on a composer of genius it manifests itself as a *technique*, which has been assimilated into, and become almost indistinguishable from, the style, the 'voice', which we identify as the very embodiment of a composer's unique personality. But 'style', 'voice', is none other than a collection of techniques; and it is among Debussy's compositional practices that we must seek to discover what the Javanese gamelan meant to him. In the set of orchestral pieces we know as *La mer*, for example, we find a passage in the first piece, 'De l'aube à midi sur la mer' (Figs. 2^{+9}–6), that, naturally enough, sounds quintessentially Debussian. But when we come to analyse it, to hear it analytically, we find that it is a music, to borrow Debussy's own words and use them in a different context, 'lit from behind' by the gamelan idea and by one of the strongest technical features associated with it: the pursuit by the individual player of his own independent rhythmic version of the main melody. It is the heterophonic totality of rhythmically independent parts that often comprises the unique sound world of much non-Western music and especially the gamelan music of South East Asia. It is precisely this technique which is fundamental to the way in which Debussy around the turn of the century conceived his orchestral textures. The individual players in the gamelan are replaced in Debussy's orchestra by clearly differentiated instrumental groups or units, to each of which is allotted an independent rhythmic role. All the parts are then combined in a continuous texture, a continuous stream of sound, which unfolds not only a polyphony of instrumental groups but an elaborate polyrhythmic texture that clearly anticipates the preoccupation with complex rhythms which was to develop as the new century grew older (and which Saint-Saëns had predicted with such prescience).

Once it had been established as one of Debussy's compositional resources, this polyrhythmic, gamelan-derived orchestral texture was to become a permanent part of his musical landscape. In *Ibéria*, for example, the second of the later set of three orchestral pieces, *Images*, we find an elaborate passage (Figs. 12^{+2}–19^{-3})

which in compositional principle is precisely comparable to the passage I have mentioned above from the first movement of *La mer*. If we do not immediately hear it as such, it is because of its suppressed dynamics, which mask the features it shares with the earlier model.

It was thus that Debussy incorporated into his art compositional processes drawn from a non-Western musical culture; and in doing so opened up a whole area of technical influence and discovery which, once again, was taken up seriously by composers in their music only after the Second World War, in the most diverse ways and in many different countries – by Olivier Messiaen in France, for example, and by Benjamin Britten in England, to name only two famous names. And in our own immediate time we can see the influence persisting in the West Coast minimalist composers of the United States, distant and distinct though their aesthetics (and their achievements) may be from those of Debussy.

When talking and thinking about Paris at the turn of the century and its function as a cradle of the New, I have deliberately tried to see everything – that is, *hear* everything – through the creative personality of Claude Debussy. I realize only too acutely that that has meant the omission of many other important personalities and events and I apologize for all the inevitable injustices done to them. But the truth remains, I think, that it was Debussy who was – and is – fundamental to the history of twentieth-century music as we now understand it; and perhaps we stand a better chance of understanding it in 1988, when the century itself has only a little over a further decade to run. Debussy, as I hope I may have shown, left untouched not a single musical area that was singled out by Saint-Saëns for comment: tonality, the diatonic scales, the ancient modes, the scales of the East, harmony and rhythm. Every single item on his agenda was on Debussy's agenda too; and Debussy subjected every single item, in and through his music, to comprehensive reassessment and often radical innovation, thus initiating revolutionary ways of thinking years before they were assimilated into the mainstream of the New Music. At the same time, and this has been no less significant a part of my purpose, I have tried to show how Debussy's preoccupations were in many respects the same kind of preoccupations of composers elsewhere, and in particular in Vienna; and that in both Paris *and* Vienna the problems and preoccupations of composers were the legacy of Wagner.

Saint-Saëns's searching inventory neatly summarizes many of the areas where answers were found to the problems confronting composers in both Paris and Vienna at the turn of the century; and when we analyse those answers we come to realize that, transcending – though in no way suppressing – cultural differences and contrasts, the answers had much in common. If I have at least succeeded in demonstrating that the tradition of the New had a common source and then a joint birth in two great centres of musical ferment, Paris and Vienna, as the old century gave way to the new, then I believe we shall have made some progress towards establishing a truer account of the New Music in the twentieth century than we have had before. How satisfactory to achieve that understanding before we ourselves are overtaken by a new century which, we may be sure, will bring its own puzzles and, we must hope, the geniuses to solve them.

NOTES

1 MC: See François Lesure and Roger Nichols (eds.), *Debussy Letters* (Faber and Faber, London, 1987), p. 262. For an illuminating investigation of the influence of *Parsifal* on *Pelléas*, see Robin Holloway, *Debussy and Wagner* (Eulenburg, London, 1979).

2 MC: Lesure and Nichols, op. cit., p. 126.

3 MC: For further discussion of Debussy's encounter with the Javanese gamelan, see Neil Sorrell, *A Guide to the Gamelan* (Faber and Faber, London, 1990), pp. 2–8. It should be emphasized, of course, that gamelan music is in no way improvised, although Debussy is likely to have perceived the idiom as 'improvisatory' from his Western viewpoint.

4 MC: See Jelena Hahl-Koch, *Arnold Schoenberg–Wassily Kandinsky: Letters, Pictures and Documents* (Faber and Faber, London, 1984) for an account of the relationship between Kandinsky and Schoenberg and its artistic consequences.

5 MC: For his part, Stravinsky is unlikely to have shared Debussy's enthusiasm. The furthest he went in praising *Parsifal* was to admire the under-stage placing of the orchestra at Bayreuth which made the work 'still a headache, but a headache with aspirin'. See Robert Craft, *Stravinsky: The Chronicle of a Friendship* (Gollancz, London, 1972), p. 56.

6 Dance was often itself a cradle of the New; and in thinking of Stravinsky, of Debussy, of Ravel (and of course of their association with the Ballets Russes), one notes that here at least was one area in which Paris was quite distinct from Vienna. Unquestionably, turn-of-the-century Vienna produced untold riches in terms of orchestral music, much of it breaking new ground. But great twentieth-century ballets? I cannot think of a single Austro-German candidate. Perhaps we uncover here a genuine difference in cultural traditions. All the odder then that the culture that generated the waltz left it to a Frenchman (Ravel) to write an apotheosis of the dance which was both a tribute and ironical epitaph – and also a ballet: *La valse*, his 'poème chorégraphique' of 1919.

7 MC: Quoted in Roger Nichols, *Debussy* (Oxford University Press, Oxford, 1973), p. 7.

8 MC: For an exhaustive study of the oriental dimension of *Das Lied von der Erde*, see DM, *Gustav Mahler III: Songs and Symphonies of Life and Death* (Faber and Faber, London, 1985), *passim.*

9 MC: See note 3 above.

10 MC: Lesure and Nichols, op. cit., p. 217.

Mahler and Nature: Landscape into Music

I am going to speculate about a possible relationship between landscape and music; and about one particular landscape – Toblach, now Dobbiaco, in the Italian Dolomites – and Gustav Mahler. Before the First World War the area was part of the Austro-Hungarian Empire and accessible by train from Vienna. It was there, amid this landscape of forests, lakes and mountains, that Mahler in the last summers of his life, from 1908 until his death in May 1911, wrote his last works, *Das Lied von der Erde*, the Ninth Symphony and the incomplete Tenth.

Why Toblach? To answer that one has to look back to 1907, when Mahler spent his summers composing in a rented house at Maiernigg on the Wörther See. Here, three heavy blows fell on him: it was in this year at Maiernigg that one of his two daughters, Maria, caught diphtheria and cruelly died; at almost the same time, Mahler's doctors diagnosed a heart condition that certainly caused him anxiety, restricted his physical activities, though not his creativity, and contributed to the weakening of his hitherto powerful constitution, which finally succumbed to a viral infection in 1911. In addition, in the same year, 1907, he found himself at loggerheads with the bureaucrats in Vienna; and, frustrated and taxed beyond the tolerable, he resigned as Director of the Hofoper – the Vienna Court Opera – and signed a contract to conduct at the Metropolitan Opera, New York.

Lecture, 'Musikwoche *in memoriam* Gustav Mahler', Toblach, 22 July 1986; originally given with recorded musical illustrations

Maiernigg could no longer offer him the serenity of spirit he needed for composition. He had to find a new place to make a new start. What was found was a farmhouse near Toblach, at Alt-Schluderbach, on the second floor of which Mahler in those last summers lived with his wife and surviving daughter. (It stands today virtually untouched.)

From that farmhouse Mahler continued to explore and absorb the sights and sounds of Nature, something he had done all his life, the impact of which we encounter in his earlier symphonies as much as in his later. But Mahler's enthusiasm for Nature was perhaps of a rather different order from the conventional kind. He was no passive observer of landscape but an active explorer of it, especially on foot. We know of his fondness for walking amid the lakes and mountains, and can guess with some certainty of being right that what attracted him to mountains at least was their *silence* – that unique silence which in fact constitutes an aural experience in itself, a silence that is itself a sound. It is a silence moreover that magically articulates any natural sound that may impinge upon it – the cry of a bird, cowbells from the valleys below, the murmuring of a mountain stream. All these sounds, the individuality of which might be lost when they form part of the larger chorus of noise that surrounds our day-to-day life on earth, are heard sharp and clear, each with its own sonorous physiognomy, in the context of silence.

Now all this may begin to sound like poetic 'rhapsody'; but in fact my purpose is not to rhapsodize but to remind us of something very essential about Mahler, namely that he walked not only on his feet but also *with his ears*: that a walk for this wholly extraordinary man was as much a *sonorous* experience as a matter of physical locomotion. We have to remember that for a walking composer his ears are at least as important as his eyes; while Mahler's eyes performed a much more complex role than drinking in, in a general way, the grand beauty of lake and mountain. His eyes, I think, could be almost as specific as his ears. (This is a point to which I shall return.)

To one form of Nature's music, birdsong, Mahler's ears had always been open. We don't have to wait until his late works, for example, to encounter the incorporation into his music of the song or cry of a bird. (I have often thought that in this respect alone Mahler and Messiaen might have had much to say to each other.) I could quote many examples from the earlier works. But perhaps one is of particular interest and importance, the great cadenza in the finale of the Second Symphony, *Der grosse Appel*, the summons that leads to the final elevation of the dead to paradise. At this critical juncture in the symphony, which is both a *coup de théâtre* and a radical exploration of acoustic space, Mahler, after a great release of orchestral hubbub and activity, creates a moment of silence and then fills it with a huge instrumental cadenza compiled from horn calls and trumpet fanfares, and, no less significantly, birdsong. It is indeed the liquid aria of the bird, the flute and piccolo combined, that surely represents after the travail and tension of life on earth, the promise of hope, light and eternal life. The distant rumble of thunder on the drums also has a role to play in this remarkable passage, the innovatory techniques employed in which continue to surprise one. But what grips the attention especially is the free, quasi-improvisatory character of the cadenza and in particular the free, *un*measured nature of the birdsong, not bound by the tyranny of the barline, any more than the birds themselves in the real world are subject to the rules of composition. I have no doubt, moreover, that while that great cadenza in the finale of the Second is pre-eminently *symbolic* not *naturalistic* in its intention and effect, it none the less had its roots in Mahler's acoustic experience of the universe. The free mix of the sounds, the unmeasured birdsong, all these speak for the response of Mahler's ears to what they heard about them and to his capacity – wherein of course lies his genius – to assimilate them and transform them into music.

The free profile of the flute song in that cadenza reflects, one might think, the *freedom* of Nature, unconstrained by considerations of art, of classical proportion, of a need to discriminate between sounds and events which are proper to art while others are *im*proper and to be excluded. Mahler, as he grew older and as his work developed, moved away more and more from a figurative, decorative or symbolic representation of Nature, and of birdsong in particular, towards a (for him) new kind of naturalism, of realism, in which the barriers between art music (*Kunstmusik*) and the sounds and events of Nature were further and radically lowered. There is a remarkable example of this development in the 'Abschied' of *Das Lied von der Erde* – the passage where Mahler graphically describes the nocturnal stirrings and twitterings of the birds and other noises and creatures of the night at the moment when night and silence descend. 'Description' indeed is entirely the wrong word. Mahler does not so much describe as faithfully *document* the sounds of Nature just before the world surrenders to sleep:

> Die Vögel hocken still in ihren Zweigen.
> Die Welt schläft ein!
>
> ('The birds crouch in silence on their branches;
> the world goes to sleep!')

Here, the music that surrounds the voice is a music taken from Nature, received by Mahler's ears and then transformed by his imagination, but certainly not out of recognition. I have written about that passage elsewhere[1] and suggested that its extraordinary motivic organization and audacious instrumentation amount to a kind of Mahlerian Impressionism, but an Impressionism that does not aspire to a blend, a blur, but comprises a brilliant and incisive articulation of birdsong. Once again Mahler has created a moment of silence, as he did in the finale of the Second Symphony, but this time filled it not with symbolic but as it were with *actual* birdsong and other nocturnal noises. There is a big difference between the two aesthetic approaches.

Mahler of course did not altogether abandon in his last period the figurative, decorative or symbolic use of birdsong. When he needed it as a resource he made use of it. Indeed, in *Das Lied von der Erde* itself, the two modes of incorporating Nature, the two strategies, are juxtaposed in the same work. Take the fifth movement of *Das Lied*, 'Der Trunkene im Frühling'. In the third strophe of the song, it is a bird that brings the pessimistic singer a message of hope and reconciliation, a confirmation of the presence of spring – 'Der Lenz ist da, sei kommen über Nacht!' ('Spring is here, it's arrived overnight!'). And Mahler permits us to hear the tenor overhearing the bird singing in the tree. But this is a very well-trained and musically educated bird which impersonates the solo flute, with a highly developed sense of melody, of symmetrical phrasing and above all with a striking capacity to build its song out of the motifs with which the composer has obligingly provided it [see Figs. 7^{-3}–9^{+5}]. In short, this is principally a symbolic bird, whose song has been conditioned by long-established tradition, a very different concept of sound from the nocturnal passage from the 'Abschied' to which I referred above, or from the free untrammelled birdsong in the cadenza from the Second Symphony.

One might argue that there is nothing exceptional about a composer with an emphatic love of Nature building birdsong into his music. Birds are Nature's musicians, Nature's own singers, and composers have long been in the habit of conscripting birdsong to serve their own purposes. In 'Der Trunkene im Frühling' Mahler had one foot in tradition; in the 'Abschied' he established a *new* tradition, a kind of authenticity of reproduction that formed no part at all of that earlier decorative or symbolic tradition. But Mahler, we may be sure, was not in the business of achieving a faithful, literal replication of birdsong. What was it, then, that we should try to identify as Mahler's particular interest in birdsong, in the sounds of the natural universe? Or, to put it another way, are we able to identify in any meaningful way other than the decorative the influence of Nature on Mahler's musical thinking?

The aspect of the relationship between Mahler's own music and the music of Nature that interests me most is the unmeasured freedom that characterizes the latter and the ever increasing freedom of Mahler's late compositional techniques, especially in the fields of rhythm and melody. I have perhaps talked about birdsong to excess. But I should like to bring forward one final example from this sphere, though in fact it is not a literal representation of birdsong at all. You remember the cadenza from the finale of the Second Symphony, and the marvellously free, quasi-improvised duet for piccolo and flute which unfolds a continuous flow of unmeasured melody. In a famous passage from the 'Abschied' – the first of the recitatives – the flute obbligato that accompanies the voice has an innovatory, improvisatory unmeasuredness [see Figs. 3–4]. Now I am not suggesting that what we hear there is undiluted birdsong – if that were the case, it would be a virtuoso bird indeed! Moreover, it is clear to me that the concept of that recitative has its roots in Bach, in Bach's recitatives from the Passions in particular (Mahler was a great admirer of the *St Matthew Passion*) and in the style of Bach's instrumental obbligatos in his Passions and cantatas. One might think one could not get further away from Nature than the music of Bach. But as so often in Mahler's music, one thing does not exclude another; or, to put it another way, he integrates in and through his music elements and influences that normally would have been thought irreconcilable. In short, while recognizing the predominant Bach influence, at the same time the free shape of that extraordinary flute obbligato has been conditioned, I suggest, if only unconsciously, by the asymmetries, the irregularities, of the music of Nature. And when we take into account the poetic context and content of that first recitative from the 'Abschied', in which the protagonist responds to a nocturnal mountain landscape, it is not altogether far-fetched to hear in it an audacious mix of Bach and the last song of the bird before nightfall.

Let us leave birds for a moment and move on to other features of Nature which might have caught not only Mahler's ears but also his eyes. No doubt you will be asking whether it is really possible for a composer's music to be influenced by what he perceives with and through his eyes. I am reminded of something Mahler himself once said to a friend who was visiting him at Steinbach and admiring the mountain landscape. 'There's no need to look at that,' Mahler said, 'for it's all in my music' – he was working on his Third Symphony at the time.[2] Mahler of course was expressing the thought of the relationship between landscape and music in the form of a joke. But it is my conviction that there is more than an element of truth in it, a truth that became more pronounced as Mahler moved into his late phase. Let me illustrate this point with another example from the 'Abschied' of *Das Lied*, the extraordinary oboe melody that introduces the text describing both the sight and sound of a murmuring stream creating its own melody in the darkness amid flowers fading in the twilight [see Figs. 7–10^{+5}]. It is technically one of the most radical and challenging inspirations in *Das Lied*, and what is particularly striking about it is its rhythmic asymmetry. There is no bar in the melody that repeats a previously established rhythmic pattern: each bar is rhythmically unique. The melody extends itself systematically through bar-by-bar rhythmic variation. Moreover, this melody, which is built out of an additive chain of asymmetries, is itself accompanied by figuration with its own built-in rhythmic asymmetry: at the outset the clarinets' and harp's articulations of the rocking minor third make their irregular effect by alternating within the bar groups of 2s and 3s. There is scant harmonization of the melody in any conventional sense. After the ambiguous tonality of the first two bars of introduction, F is established, but an F – for the ensuing three bars – with a persistently sharpened fourth degree of the scale, B♮ instead of B♭. This Lydian inflexion introduces a diatonic 'irregularity' into the melody that complements the associated irregularities of rhythm and asymmetries of phrase. Small wonder that the melody seems to wander irregularly on, without punctuation or traditional cadencing, until it is abruptly cut off, just before the voice enters with 'Der Bach singt . . .' ('The stream sings . . .') and with three words accounts for the characteristic of the musical process in one simple poetic image drawn from Nature.

This passage is not only a remarkable manifestation of Mahler's late style, of the development of new and surprising features, it is also something else: it is a graphic tone-picture of a mountain stream pursuing its irregular course, singing its song as it flows. It was not only the *sound* of it that worked on Mahler's imagination, but also the *sight* of it. It is a passage in which one might claim sight has been transformed into sound. This takes me back to the point I made earlier: that Mahler was as much a pair of walking eyes as a pair of walking ears.

I do not want to exaggerate the influence of Nature on Mahler to the degree that it loses all sense: I am far from suggesting that Mahler in his music was a kind of gazetteer or Baedeker. I *am* suggesting, however, that when we analyse some of the characteristics of the late style of Mahler and his growing preoccupation with the potentialities of asymmetry and irregularity, we should bear in mind that what was perhaps a development in his music that would have happened anyway, for purely musical reasons, was backed up, intensified, reinforced, by his *absorption* of the irregularities and asymmetries of the sounds and sights of the world of Nature by which he was so often surrounded. And where, as in *Das Lied*, the poetic content of the work is much bound up with observation of and reflections on Nature, then the influence surfaces in a highly original and immediately identifiable manner.

I have been expounding relatively marginal detail in order to support my general proposal that we may perceive a connection between Mahler's response to Nature and the manifestation of asymmetry and irregularity in his music. But while it is true that some of the asymmetries I have commented on and illustrated from *Das Lied* very clearly have their origins in Nature, there are other aspects of his systematic employment of asymmetry which altogether escape the graphic or depictive and assume a profound formal and symbolic significance. Perhaps not altogether surprisingly we find an elaborate example of a symbolic/formal use of asymmetry – the employment of asymmetry as a major musical and poetic resource – in the finale, the 'Abschied' of *Das Lied*. If I am to explain, even in the barest outline, how Mahler's method works, then I must say something very brief about what, I suggest, *Das Lied* is about, the poetic meaning of Mahler's song-cycle, and in particular the content of the 'Abschied'. I think there are various points on which we might reach ready agreement: for a start, that *Das Lied*'s principal preoccupation is with the idea of man's mortality, his struggle against the idea of death, the possibility of his being reconciled to the inescapable fact of his extinction. All this, we may think, was bound up with Mahler's own personal history, the events from 1907, and in particular the diagnosis of the heart condition that was to contribute to his untimely death in 1911.

Das Lied, I suggest, concerns itself both with the fight against oblivion and the transcending of it, an altogether typical Mahlerian conflict and dichotomy. It is a conflict that is played out and finally resolved in and by the 'Abschied' and in terms of the contrast, the opposition – I am now speaking purely musically – between the symmetrical and the asymmetrical, the regular and the irregular, the strict and the free.

We all know how important for Mahler was the concept of the march – marches of all shapes and sizes abound in his symphonies. But has it struck us that the finale of the 'Abschied' is also conceived as a gigantic march? Though with this difference: that it is a march that from the very outset of the movement never succeeds in establishing itself until a very late stage in the movement has been reached. The very opening prelude to the 'Abschied' unfolds the dichotomy: we hear the march, and above all its symmetrical march rhythm, trying to assert itself. But within the space of a few bars, the march breaks up or, rather, breaks down, disintegrating into a fragmenting music that leads us naturally into the first recitative and introduces us for the first time to the remarkable freedom and asymmetries of the flute obbligato. And Mahler, having thus concisely juxtaposed at the beginning of his finale the symmetrical and the asymmetrical, the regular and the irregular, then proceeds with extraordinary logic and consistency, to play off one kind of music against the other. Furthermore, as the movement extends itself, we come to realize that the two types of music, the strict and the free, the symmetrical and asymmetrical, are brilliantly identified with the two poles of experience which the song-cycle as a whole encompasses: the fact of mortality on the one hand, and the possibility of its transcendence – mitigation, reconciliation – on the other. Mortality and death are represented by the constraints of symmetry. The *escape* from mortality and its metrical bonds is represented by asymmetry, a freely conceived music, the irregularity of which is the very opposite of the metrical and the predictable. The contrast is as sharp as that between the fear of annihilation and a positive embracing of it. It is precisely the reconciliation of those seeming irreconcilables that it is the main formal business of the finale of *Das Lied* to achieve.

The march idea, naturally enough, represents the most intensive concentration of symmetry and rhythmic regularity; and when finally the march succeeds in establishing itself unequivocally in that extraordinary interpolation for orchestra alone that precedes the closing stages of the 'Abschied', Mahler leaves us in no possible doubt of the symbolic relationship between the concept of death and its embodiment in music which, of its very nature, is born out of symmetry and metricality. Moreover, it is a grand *funeral* march, a ritual celebration of death, that Mahler releases, has in truth reserved for this moment; could he have spelled out for us more clearly in the context of the finale of *Das Lied* the identification of mortality with metricality? This is the moment when what has been anticipated in – announced by – the prelude is at last fulfilled, at last materializes: a march.

But mortality and the metrical are not to triumph in *Das Lied* and do not, distinctly not, provide the work with its ultimate *dénouement*. Throughout the 'Abschied', as I have already suggested, Mahler, with consummate skill, has played off the free against the strict, the asymmetrical against the symmetrical. Some of those intimations of the escape from mortality through a conspicuously free, unmeasured music I have already mentioned: not only the nocturnal passage, 'Die Welt schläft ein' – and it must have been just such music that Adorno had in mind when referring in his monograph on Mahler to the 'unregimented voices of living things'[3] – but also that amazing passage, the oboe melody, which I have spoken about in connection with Mahler's observation, through his ears and eyes, of a mountain stream. It seems hardly credible that one movement should contain two such radically contrasted musics, one so improvisatory and irregular, and rhythmically amorphous, the other so definedly symmetrical in melody and regular in rhythm. But it is precisely the task of these two contrasted compositional techniques to represent the two poles of experience that I have suggested the 'Abschied' is built around.

It is revealing, I think, that one could argue that the innovating oboe melody – the liberated song of the stream – has its roots, its origins, in Nature. But by no means all the music that I should allot to the 'free' category in the 'Abschied' is bound up quite so unequivocally with Nature, with Mahler's depiction or observation of it. Take the long, seamless string and horn melody, for example, which, in its own way, is quite as free as the oboe melody, 'Der Bach singt' – transferred to the flute on the entry of the voice, which it succeeds and complements. The freely evolving, spontaneous character of that melody, which uncoils itself unpredictably *across* the barlines and is rarely punctuated by them, is typical of the asymmetrical, irregular and often very long string melodies that emerge with increasing frequency in Mahler's late works, though perhaps nowhere is there such a concentration of them as in the finale of *Das Lied*. In the example I have just cited, we may note that the melody is not directly linked with observation of Nature. On the other hand, it without doubt articulates the response of the protagonist in the 'Abschied' to the overwhelming beauties of Nature, of the physical world. I find it altogether fascinating that the protagonist in the finale, who was surely Mahler himself, chose to exploit the resources of asymmetry in expressing his felt response to Nature, just as asymmetry and irregularity were the means by which elsewhere he incorporates into his music the actual sounds (and some of the sights!) of the natural universe. Whatever Mahler's predisposition was towards the asymmetrical in shaping his melodies, we may conclude, I believe, that the influence of Nature was a heightening factor, especially in those works in which Nature is a central preoccupation, of which *Das Lied* is a prime example. Is there not something very magical, as well as logical, about Mahler's unleashing his tumultuous feelings *about* Nature in a melody whose contours are as unregimented as those of Nature herself?

And so amidst the very landscape amidst which *Das Lied* was conceived and created and which, I suggest, exercised a profound influence on the profile the musical materials assumed, we come to the apotheosis with which *Das Lied* ends. As I said earlier, it is not the metrical that finally triumphs in the 'Abschied' but its very opposite. In the ecstatic coda that rounds off the finale, indeed, Mahler achieves an unprecedented beatlessness, a suspension of pulse and beat which virtually erases rhythmic measurement. This, combined with the proliferation and heterophonic combinations of long spans of asymmetrical melodies, provides Mahler with that consummation of the free style, that other pole, in the 'Abschied', which at the same time signifies the *transcendence* of death, the reconciliation and identification with the perpetual renewal of earth's beauties which has been the goal of *Das Lied* from the outset. Through the manipulation of two contrasted compositional techniques, the strict and the free, Mahler plays out the poetic drama which is at the heart of *Das Lied* and brings it to its radiant *dénouement*. I do not doubt myself that landscape and Nature – not pictorially, but at far deeper levels of the creative imagination – were profoundly influential in, as it were, drawing the contours of some of the music we find most remarkable in *Das Lied*. Landscape into music. A unique act of transformation, and like most things about Mahler, without precedent, and unsurpassed.

NOTES

1 MC: See DM, *Gustav Mahler III: Songs and Symphonies of Life and Death* (Faber and Faber, London, 1985), pp. 373–6 and 380–81.
2 Bruno Walter, *Gustav Mahler* (Hamish Hamilton, London, 1958), p. 33.
3 Theodor W. Adorno, *Mahler: Eine musikalische Physiognomik* (Suhrkamp, Frankfurt am Main, 1960), pp. 25–7.

Mahler's Hungarian Glissando

When I was in Budapest at the end of last year I passed by the splendid Vigado, facing the Promenade along which residents and tourists stroll to enjoy a magnificent view of Buda, across the Danube.

The Vigado was built between 1859 and 1864 in what the guidebooks tell us was a 'Hungarian Romantic style'; and it was there, in the concert hall (Redoutensaal) that Mahler's First Symphony was first performed on 20 November 1889, the composer conducting. At the time, Mahler was Director of the Royal Budapest Opera, a post to which he had been appointed a year earlier, in a country which, he exclaimed, 'will probably become my new homeland!'

Naturally enough, as I sauntered along, the symphony began to unroll in my mind like some accompanying soundtrack. More particularly, and perhaps stimulated by the overt attempt at something specifically Hungarian by the architect of the Vigado, Frigyes Feszl, a few bars from the slow movement insistently returned, demanding my attention.

The bars that haunted me were bars 58 and 59 of the slow movement, the famous Funeral March – *A la pompes funèbres*, as it was first described in the 1889 programme. I reproduce the bars

---

Programme note written for a London performance of the First Symphony by the Vienna Philharmonic Orchestra under Claudio Abbado scheduled for 18 February 1991 but cancelled due to the Gulf War; first publication

below, in which it is easy to recognize the brief but arresting event they embody: in particular, a glissando for the strings which the composer clearly intended us not to miss.

The exaggerated dynamics, which accelerate from *pp* to *ff* and back to *p* again – the dynamic high point coinciding with the peak of the glissando – and the very intervention of the strings (reinforced by a pair of flutes) in a primarily wind-and-percussion-band texture indicate the emphatic articulation of these bars that Mahler wanted to secure:

I soon came to realize precisely why it was that it was this glissando that had invaded my inner ear as I dawdled along the Promenade. It was, of course, because like all visitors to Budapest – and at the receiving end of Hungarian hospitality – I had been serenaded by any number of gypsy ensembles, of varying degrees of authenticity, to be sure. But common to all of them when fiddlers were present was the ubiquitous – ascending or descending, but always swooning – glissando. Small wonder that it was Mahler's glissando that came to mind as I sauntered.

It further occurred to me that it was more than probable that this, as I was now beginning to hear it, specifically 'Hungarian' dimension of the Funeral March was part of Mahler's compositional tactics. Here was a reference that the locals, so to say, might have expected to welcome as representing the familiar and entertaining; but it was a reference, an image, that proved to have such a sharp cutting edge that any pleasure of recognition must have given way to the pain of expectations incomprehensibly reversed. This was gypsy music with a vicious bite, an acid tongue.

This contradiction of expectations seems to me to be the *raison d'être* of the Funeral March from its very outset. What, I wonder, had the audience expected of this movement at the Budapest première? Something along the lines of Beethoven, or Wagner, or Chopin in funereal mood? It was a shock for them, then, to encounter two bars of drum-taps and then the strange, strangulated voice of a muted solo double-bass, singing as best it can an old nursery tune, 'Frère Jacques' (or 'Bruder Martin'), in the minor. What sort of funeral march was this? Moreover, this initial shock, the first section, was to be followed by another. As the March dies away, a pair of oboes introduces the popular tune that leads into the section which Mahler himself marks *Mit Parodie* – an injunction to treat this passage in a parodistic manner. It is, I think, the first time this particular command found its way into one of Mahler's scores; and it is certainly the first time, on this sort of scale, that the caustic, sceptical, sarcastic and ironic Mahler emerges, as it were, in top gear.

The more I thought about it that sunny afternoon, the more intrigued I became by the thought that this first substantial manifestation of what we all know now to be a major feature of Mahler's capacity to disturb, to unsettle, his audiences, if not exactly prompted by his temporary residence in Hungary, may well have been powerfully influenced by it. We cannot be absolutely sure of course that the gypsy glissando was not lodged in Mahler's inner ear pre-Budapest. After all, this was the time of the Austro-Hungarian Empire and the cultures of Vienna and Budapest were in some musical respects virtually interchangeable: there was nothing strange about gypsy music to the Viennese (think of Brahms). But Mahler, before Budapest, had been in Kassel, Prague and Leipzig; and it seems more than likely to me that the gypsy element in the First Symphony's Funeral March was part of the furnishing of Mahler's musical mind that can be attributed more specifically to his residence in Hungary, where, I dare say, he had been a recipient of the compulsory gypsy experience that greets all visitors to the country, now as then; and in a typically ironic manner he used this music to criticize itself, placing it in a grotesque context – a Funeral March – that was itself grotesquely conceived.

It is not surprising that it was precisely with this movement that the first audience in Budapest began to lose contact and perhaps its collective temper with the symphony. The first half of the symphony, which in 1889 was in five movements and entitled 'Symphonic Poem', had been moderately well received. The extraordinary slow introduction and ensuing first movement were certainly full of novel sounds; with hindsight we can hear just how many Mahlerian characteristics and formal features were adumbrated there, in profusion. Eyebrows may have been raised here and there but there was nothing to give actual offence or arouse hostility. There followed a sentimental *Andante*, the so-called 'Blumine' movement, later to be discarded (and properly so), and the scherzo (*Ländler*), the most traditionally imagined movement in the whole work.

Everything changed, however, with the onset of the Funeral March, as was Mahler's intention, I have no doubt. The opening 'Frère Jacques' idea was affront enough; but what followed was an insult: the parody of a domestic and 'national' music hit a target that was altogether too close to home. Mahler himself claimed that after the Budapest première, 'My friends avoided me in terror. Not a single one of them dared to speak to me about the work or its performance, and I wandered about like someone sick or outlawed'.[1]

In fact, Mahler had his friends and admirers in Budapest; rightly so, because he had, as Director of the Opera, identified himself with Hungarian national aspirations – 'my new homeland!' – to the serious and significant extent of his requiring that Wagner's operas should be sung no longer in German but in Hungarian. But respect for a nation's language was one thing. Respect for its café society and a café music masquerading as an exotic nationalism was altogether another; it is surely easy to understand why Mahler chose to mock it in his Funeral March. Was he not to turn his sceptical attention to the Viennese waltz in later symphonies?

The most – perhaps the only – intelligent review of the First Symphony's première was contributed to the *Pester Lloyd* on 21 November 1889 by August Beer, who did not fail to note the parodistic tone of the Funeral March, both of its first section, the 'Frère Jacques' canon, and of its second, where the performers, he observed, kept to '*the Hungarian manner*' (my emphasis), with the parodistic intent of the composer revealed 'in the ironic accents of the violins'.[2]

Here, then, was one pair of ears that had received the full import and impact of Mahler's Hungarian glissando and survived the ordeal. The majority of the audience, one may surmise, was not so receptive. (There was even some booing when the finale was over.) Their views were probably summarized by another critic present at the first performance: 'The fourth movement . . . which includes a pitiful theme in canon in a very inadequate manner only to alternate it with one that is *offensively trivial* [my emphasis], is a complete disaster. The music is not humorous, only ridiculous'.[3] A different response to Beer's; but one that again vividly confirmed that Mahler's unsettling parody had achieved its object. It was a weapon, a strategy, that he was to refine and sharpen and use time and time again in the future that awaited him. His Hungarian glissando was a warning of what was to come.

NOTES

1 Henry-Louis de La Grange, *Mahler*, vol. 1 (Doubleday, New York, 1973), p. 207: see also the authoritative French text, *Gustav Mahler: Chronique d'une vie*, vol. 1: *Vers la gloire 1860–1900* (Fayard, Paris, 1979).

2 MC: See DM, *Gustav Mahler II: The 'Wunderhorn' Years* (Faber and Faber, London, 1975), pp. 150–54, for the complete text of this review together with a facsimile of the original publication.

3 La Grange, op. cit., p. 205.

Mahler's Abschied: *A Wrong Note Righted*

Some recent work[1] on which I have been engaged has involved a detailed scrutiny of Mahler's *Das Lied* and some of its principal manuscript sources. One general impression I have been left with is the exceptional care and subtlety of Mahler's approach to word-setting, something I suppose I had been aware of but to which I had never before paid much attention.

I could quote many examples but shall introduce only one into this short essay because it proved to have rich consequences and resonances. The passage in question comes toward the end of 'Der Abschied' at Fig. 57:

Ex. 1

There is nothing world-shaking, I concede, about that phrase. On the other hand, it is an admirable example of Mahler's scrupulous setting of his text. In particular, the repeated Cs clearly embody the level, steady, and serene beat of a heart at peace with itself.

I could quite easily quote a considerable number of like

Musical Quarterly 71/2 (1985), pp. 200–204

examples, some of them a good deal more complex. But it was this one that caught my ear and eye at a time when I was also busy with looking through the source materials of the movement; or, to be more precise, it was these bars and their immediate predecessors, five bars after Fig. 56, that led me to investigate Mahler's composition sketch. For what we find in the published score is this:

Ex. 2

I confess that I had never in any sense questioned this phrase; on the contrary I had always thought of it as a neat example of the kind of integration of which Mahler was a master, that is, the complementary vocal phrase 'Still ist mein Herz' taking over the rhythmic pattern of 'Ich werde niemals' and the identical interval and pitches, but reversing their order and their direction. On this occasion, however, I wondered why, if Mahler were intent on making a point with the repeated notes in his setting of '*Still* ist mein Herz' (my emphasis), he used the same device only a few bars earlier in an entirely different context, where an image of stillness, of calm, was not involved.

It was this consideration I had casually in mind when turning over the pages of Mahler's short score of 'Der Abschied', his original composition sketch, which is owned by the Gemeente Museum of The Hague [see plate 21]. What immediately leapt to my eye was, of course, 'Ich werde niemals . . .', which in the composer's hand quite clearly does *not* follow the repeated-note pattern of Ex. 2 but is laid out thus:

Ex. 3

There is no doubt about the composition sketch: the A (which appears in all published versions) is undeniably a G. How, then, did the repeated As arise?

This can be answered simply: because they appear thus in Mahler's fair manuscript full score of *Das Lied*, now part of the Robert Owen Lehman deposit at the Pierpont Morgan Library in New York City. There is no room for doubt either about what Mahler wrote in this autograph. It is what we are all thoroughly familiar with and reproduced in Ex. 2. One might well conclude, if this were all the evidence that might be assembled, that Mahler had had a change of mind at a very late stage or made a slip of the pen, but that it was impossible to determine which was the more likely explanation of an A replacing the G. For reasons I shall come to now, I think there can be hardly any doubt that it *was* a slip of the pen and that we should without more ado correct the errant A to G. I can outline my arguments as follows:

1 If we adopt G in bar 442, then the repeated-note response to the image of 'Still ist mein Herz' is no longer paradoxically anticipated and its impact thus diminished in bars 446–7.

2 The motif *with* the G appears not only in the composition sketch but also in the draft and probably earliest extant orchestral score in Mahler's hand (currently held by the Gemeente Museum) and in the autograph fair copy of the vocal score (owned by Mr John Kallir, Scarsdale, New York).[2] So there are at least *three* manuscripts in Mahler's own hand in which the motif in its A–G–A form appears; and it is indisputable that it was with the G that Mahler first conceived the phrase.

3 There is one further piece of evidence which I personally find the most convincing of all and which derives from the special character of the counterpoint in *Das Lied* and in 'Der Abschied' in particular. Adorno was among the first to spot this: in his monograph on Mahler he refers to it as the manifestation of an 'unfocused unison' ('unscharfe Unisono') in which 'identical voices differ slightly from one another in rhythm'.[3] This was a brilliant insight of Adorno's, and it is indeed the case that intensive study of 'Der Abschied' will reveal numerous examples of contrapuntal textures, which, in principle, are heterophonic, that is, it is a rhythmically dis-synchronized unison, shared between the parts, which is at the heart of the counterpoint.

It is precisely this relationship we encounter in bars 442–7, where the voice part and the counter-melody of the violins are built out of an identical melody and simultaneously combined, an octave apart, in two different rhythmic versions.[4] At least, that is how the passage was originally conceived by Mahler and how, in my estimation, we should hear it in the future, if my correction is accepted and becomes established performing practice:

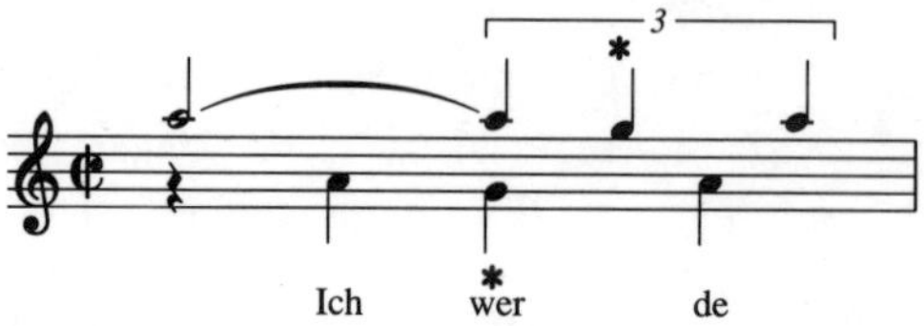

Ex. 4

If we leave the repeated As as they appear, alas, in the so-called critical edition of the score (which makes no mention whatsoever of all this),[5] then of course this tiny but significant feature of Mahler's marvellous finale not only goes unheard but allows its erroneous substitution to blunt the effect of the stillness that is created by the (legitimately) repeated notes a few bars later.

A last point, though one not directly related to the manuscript sources. If there is one thing that I have learned from working closely alongside composers during the last twenty years or so, it is to be sceptical about claims of infallibility made for their autographs, even when those autographs are impressively tidy fair copies, wearing all the signs of finality and authority. It is in making his fair copy, into which, very often, a substantial element of the mechanical enters, that the composer can sometimes nod and commit – and thereby unwittingly perpetuate – an error. Of course, if Mahler had ever heard *Das Lied* in performance, he would doubtless have made the necessary correction. That was not to be. It is my guess that when he started to pen the voice part for 'Ich werde niemals', his mind had already raced ahead to the next vocal entry, 'Still ist mein Herz', and under the influence of those repeated Cs, A–*G*–A became repeated As.

We have become so familiar with 'Ich werde niemals' in its erroneous form that it may take a little while before we hear how natural, convincing, and expressive the correct version is: for instance it brings to life a crucial word, 'werde', which is otherwise locked into an accentless monotone.

The expressive gain was recently noticed by one of the London critics who attended the first performance of the revision. Simon Rattle adopted it for his performance of *Das Lied* at the Royal Festival Hall, London, on 19 April 1984, when he conducted the Philharmonia Orchestra, with the contralto Florence Quivar as soloist in 'Der Abschied'. Meirion Bowen, writing in the *Guardian* on 21 April, made it clear that in prospect the whole thing seemed slightly ridiculous, this recovery of *one* note, and I would be the first to concede that the whole affair might appear, in the abstract, to be grotesquely over-inflated (the same thought occurred to me, especially when, at the morning rehearsal, Mme Quivar quite overlooked the emendation and stuck to what she had always been used to singing). And yet, after Mr Bowen heard the wrong note righted, he declared that for him the phrase would never sound right again if sung in its old form. I would go along with that.

NOTES

1 I acknowledge gratefully the kind co-operation and assistance of the Pierpont Morgan Library, New York (the Robert Owen Lehman deposit), the Willem Mengelberg Stichting and the Gemeente Museum of The Hague, and Dr Edward R. Reilly.

2 MC: Mahler's piano reduction of *Das Lied* was published in 1989: see note 5 below.

3 Theodor W. Adorno, *Mahler: Eine musikalische Physiognomik* (Suhrkamp, Frankfurt am Main, 1960), p. 194.

4 *Three*, actually. For, as David Matthews has pointed out to me, in the composition sketch the third part (system 3, stave 2, bar 4) yet again gives us the A–G–A pattern. (In the fair copied full score this became a second violin part and is delivered at a different pitch.)

5 MC: In the second volume of the *Supplement to the Mahler Critical Edition* (Universal Edition, Vienna, 1989), which published Mahler's own vocal score of *Das Lied von der Erde*, Stephen E. Hefling, in his table of errata (p. xxiv), lists and corrects the error that was originally Mahler's in his autograph fair copy of the full score (blindly followed in the Critical Edition's published full score), without, however, acknowledging DM's thoroughly documented discovery of the mistake four years earlier. See, however, Hefling's contribution 'Perspectives on Sketch Studies' to M. T. Vogt (ed.), *Das Gustav-Mahler-Fest Hamburg 1989* (Bärenreiter, Kassell, 1991), pp. 445–57.

The Character of Lulu: Wedekind's and Berg's Conceptions Compared

I Berg and Wedekind

On the title-page of Berg's opera appears the phrase, '*Lulu* . . . after the tragedies *Erdgeist* [*Earth-Spirit*] and *Büchse der Pandora* [*Pandora's Box*] by Frank Wedekind'.[1] Berg's 'after', however, is more a matter of compression and condensation than of verbal transformation; the transformation occurs in Berg's music, not in his handling of Wedekind's text. This, of course, is what one would expect; but it is, I think, of interest to note how closely Berg followed the dramatist's dialogue and the chronological course of the two dramas; and, lastly, how much of the two plays Berg was able to embrace within a single opera. The relationship between the structure of the plays and the opera may be exposed by means of a simple table (see overleaf).

Thus Berg's *Lulu* included the four acts of *Earth-Spirit*, and (presumably) the three of *Pandora's Box*; the whole action of Wedekind's two dramas is compressed into the structure of a three-act opera, a feat of condensation effected with considerable literary skill. As is, of course, well known, Berg did not live to complete his third act in every detail, although it seems that the music was composed more or less from first note to last. Dika Newlin[2] refers to the act as not being 'in shape for publication', and varied rumours of attempts at (a) publication of Berg's short score (?), and (b) completion by another hand (e.g. by Arnold

---

Music Review 15/4 (November 1954), pp. 268–74

Lulu[3]	*Earth-Spirit*	*Pandora's Box*
Act I		
Prologue	Prologue	–
Scene 1 (Schwarz's studio)	Act I, Scenes 1–9	–
Interlude	–	–
Scene 2 (Schwarz's house)	Act II, Scenes 1–7	–
Interlude	–	–
Scene 3 (Theatre)	Act III, Scenes 1–9	–
Act II		
Scene 1 (Schön's home)	Act IV, Scenes 1–8	–
Interlude (Film)	–	–
Scene 2 (Schön's home)	–	Act I
Act III[4]		
Scene 1 (Lulu's salon?)	–	Act II?
Interlude (Variations)	–	–
Scene 2 (a London attic)	–	Act III

Schoenberg) have remained rumours. As the opera stands at present, if the work is not to cease altogether at the end of Act II, and if the music from the third act which Berg fully prepared for use in the *Lulu* Suite[5] is to be heard in something like its proper dramatic context, the action must run straight on, from the death of Dr Schön (Act II Scene 1) and Lulu's subsequent escape from prison and alliance with Alwa (Act II's Interlude and Scene 2), to the London attic (Act III Scene 2);[6] we miss, thereby, the news of Alwa's financial ruin and the threats of exposure aimed at Lulu by the unscrupulous Marquis Casti-Piani (hence the couple's flight to England). Most important of all, the absence of Act III Scene 1 means a substantial loss in the dramatic development of the character of the Lesbian Countess Geschwitz. If *Earth-Spirit* is more particularly a vehicle for Lulu, it is in *Pandora's Box* that Geschwitz comes into her own. Wedekind's own remarks on the Countess are highly illuminating:

> The tragic central figure of the play [i.e. *Pandora's Box*] is not Lulu . . . but Countess Geschwitz. Apart from an intrigue here and there, Lulu plays an entirely passive role in all three acts; Countess Geschwitz on the other hand in the first act furnishes an example of what one can justifiably describe as superhuman self-sacrifice [i.e. Geschwitz's substitution of herself for Lulu in the prison hospital]. In the second act the progress of the plot forces her to summon all her spiritual resources in the attempt to conquer the terrible destiny of abnormality with which she is burdened; after which in the third act, having borne the most fearful torments of soul with stoical composure, she sacrifices her life in defence of her friend [i.e. is slaughtered by Jack the Ripper while trying to protect Lulu].[7]

In Wedekind's dramas, therefore, there is a change of emphasis in *Pandora's Box*; it is Geschwitz, not Lulu, who is 'the tragic central figure'. Since Berg's libretto so strictly coincides with Wedekind's text, it is not unreasonable, when examining the opera, to look for a corresponding shift in dramatic and musical emphasis from Act II Scene 2 onwards; and, while there is no foreword to *Earth-Spirit* by Wedekind, there is little evidence to suggest that Lulu's role therein is any the less 'passive' than in *Pandora's Box*. Indeed, I do not think it is stretching the bounds of probability too far to see in the fated Dr Schön, whom Lulu almost casually murders, a tragic figure comparable to Geschwitz, although tragic for the opposite reasons. He is ruined by Lulu's love, while Geschwitz is ruined by the lack of it. It should be kept in mind, none the less, that Lulu's statement (after she has shot Dr Schön 'with five consecutive bullets on the ascending chromatics of the violins, C♯, D, E♭, E, F')[8] – 'The only man I ever loved!' – is not so much a conscience-stricken cry, as an 'innocent' announcement of an unemotional fact, in the same category, perhaps, as her remark to Schön's son: 'Isn't that the very sofa on which your father bled to death?'

The only big cut Berg made in either of Wedekind's texts is at the beginning of the first act of *Pandora's Box*, where Geschwitz explains the device by which Lulu was spirited out of prison. The missing narrative dialogue is brilliantly realized both musically and visually in the 'film' interlude which links the scenes of Act II.

II Berg: Librettist and Composer

This very brief scrutiny of the two plays on which *Lulu* is founded permits us to draw a few conclusions about Wedekind's dramatic intentions with a reasonable certainty of their accuracy. Lulu, we may suggest, he conceived as a largely 'passive' figure, in the words of Feuchtwanger, 'the innocent corruptress . . . whose effect on bourgeois society can only be destructive'.[9] Arthur Eloesser writes that 'the earth-spirit is Eve as she was on the first day, Wedekind's ideal woman; he meant this character of Lulu to be played in a spirit of perfect innocence'.[10] The destructive results of Lulu's innocence are largely seen in the respective deaths of Dr Schön in *Earth-Spirit* and Geschwitz in *Pandora's Box*; and, for me, the basic dramatic situation of *Lulu* resides in this triangle – Schön–Lulu–Geschwitz – in which Lulu occupies the apex, and Schön and Geschwitz opposite, but corresponding, angles.[11] How did Berg meet the demands of dramatic development and characterization in his opera? How far did he amend and adapt?

As we have seen from Section I above, Berg did not tamper with, but condensed, Wedekind's text; the essential dialogue, action and chronology remain unaltered. From this we may justifiably conclude that Berg's intentions were, perhaps, not so far removed from Wedekind's, although we must not underestimate the potential transformation that may be effected through an opera's music without a word of the original drama being changed. (Newlin[12] writes that the original inspiration for *Lulu* was the première of *Pandora's Box*, presented in Vienna on 29 May 1905. The performance was preceded by an introductory speech from Karl Kraus (*Die Fackel*) which Berg had never forgotten and in which, Newlin continues, 'the completely amoral Lulu is justified and defended; [Berg] entirely agreed with Kraus's explanation of her character, which would make her a female version of Don Juan'.) Certainly as far as Geschwitz is concerned, Berg exactly carries out Wedekind's thoughts as disclosed in the paragraph from his foreword to *Pandora's Box* quoted in Section I. Throughout the latter half of the opera, Geschwitz's role is increasingly prominent, and there is no doubt whatever that she is the most successfully characterized of the opera's dramatis personae. Although the third act is not available – thus one is defeated in the task of making final assessments and evaluations – the superb and ennobling *Adagio* offers us a distinct hint as to the musical atmosphere of at least the last act's final scene where Geschwitz stands as a 'tragic central figure'. When she sings the opera's last sung notes ('Lulu! – My angel! – Let me see you once more! – I am near you – will stay near you – in eternity!'), one realizes that Berg has not only fulfilled the condition Wedekind specifies in his foreword – 'I was fully aware that I must over and over neutralize and outdo [Rodrigo's (the "clown's")] mockery [of Geschwitz] by my serious treatment of the Countess's fate, and that in the end this tragic seriousness must have emerged as unconditional victor if the work was to have fulfilled its purpose' – but also, in the great *Adagio*, composed a profound meditation upon the tragedy of Geschwitz's abnormal, unrequited and yet essentially selfless love. The *Adagio*, in fact, is a requiem for both Lulu *and* Geschwitz, with the serious treatment of the latter's fate, in strict accordance with Wedekind's desire, emerging (dramatically and spiritually) as 'unconditional victor'.

Geschwitz, in fact, is shaped as Wedekind shaped her, if with far greater intensity and artistic success; and Dr Schön, Geschwitz's symbolic opposite number (or angle), in more ways than one, similarly undergoes a rich musical endowment in both life and death, a highly satisfying characterization which surely would have pleased his creator. When one bears in mind Berg's almost total adherence to Wedekind's texts, there are good grounds for supposing an intimate alliance between his conception of Lulu and Wedekind's. (It is odd that Berg – and presumably

Wedekind – should have agreed with Kraus's depiction of Lulu as 'a female version of Don Juan', which implies a role more active than passive.) There is, of course, a serious objection to approaching the topic of Lulu via the libretto rather than the music, but with so complex a title figure under discussion all approaches are permissible that have as their humble aim the elucidation of the composer's art. As far as the essential character of Lulu is concerned, most commentators would seem to be in agreement on her main features. There is much common ground between the above-quoted comments of Feuchtwanger, Eloesser and Karl Kraus. Hans Hartleb, the Essen company's producer, writes that Lulu is 'a completely natural and unintellectual creature continuously being driven into new entanglements by *sexus*';[13] I suggested, in *Opera*, that

> Lulu . . . is not a person, but . . . one aspect of the human animal magnified to an enormous degree. She is a 'myth', necessarily representing a partial truth as a whole one. Herein lies her fatal attraction and her universal appeal. She is not a Universal Mother, but rather the Universal Mistress we all desire to possess or emulate.[14]

Disagreements arise – which involve an examination of the music – when deciding in what respects Lulu is a character who 'develops', and, above all, how far her feelings are profoundly engaged in the situations and relationships in which she finds herself. Wedekind, I think, has made his position clear; and, in *Earth-Spirit* and *Pandora's Box*, Lulu is a decisively non-developing role, 'passive' throughout; events occur to, round and about Lulu, not because she 'wills' but because she is – irrevocably – what she is. One might say that from the point of view of the coherence of Wedekind's drama, it is vital that Lulu does *not* develop. She is akin to a straight-burning candle flame. The moths clatter their wings, singe themselves and burn themselves to death. The flame burns on, supremely alluring, supremely irresponsible and quite unaware of the litter of corpses. What would happen to the symbolism, however, if the flame developed feelings and a conscience?

This, in effect, seems to me to be the crucial turning point in our survey of Berg's *Lulu*. Faithful to Wedekind in all else, and while still faithful to the text, Berg gives birth to a Lulu, not burdened with a moral conscience, but with many a deep feeling from which, logically, a conscience would have emerged; only the conscience, in fact, does not. We are left, instead, with a host of disengaged and dramatically unjustifiable feelings. His Lulu, indeed, is a most unhappy coalition; half Wedekind's Earth-Spirit, half a suffering woman. There are two obvious reasons why Berg was obliged to make this fundamental alteration to Wedekind's conception of his heroine. First, it is almost impossible for music to preserve a neutral attitude; and it is, in Wedekind's plays, Lulu's neutrality, her utter 'innocence', committed to no morality, which is her most distinguishing feature. Secondly, as Dr Hartleb rightly comments in his communication, Berg was doubtless interested in a 'development', not a static situation; he composed the opera, one might surmise, with both ears on the final *Adagio*, and the deeply felt *Adagio* had to be prepared by previous outbreaks of deep feelings. So far, so sensible. But one cannot avoid wondering why Berg, in these circumstances, did not further amend the text – as it stands stage action and speech are at constant variance with the music – and why he chose in the first place a libretto that, in Hans Keller's words, 'does not allow the composer to fulfil opera's essential purpose, i.e. to *real*ize the emotions of the dramatis personae'.[15] To take Lulu as our main example, it is, paradoxically, where Berg '*real*izes' her emotions that the fatal inconsistency appears which flaws the opera's dramatic structure throughout. That the operatic Lulu has profound and poignant feelings drastically denied to her purely theatrical counterpart is easily ascertained by glancing at two passages in the score. First, compare Lulu's great cry upon her return home from prison – 'Oh, freedom! God in heaven!', perhaps the most moving bars in the whole opera (Act II Scene 2) – with the corresponding passage in *Pandora's Box* (Act I). She speaks the same words, admittedly, but, from her entrance into the room until the end of the act,

Wedekind directs that she is to address her companions 'in the most cheerful tone'. Berg's music tells us most beautifully that she has suffered, and that she knows she has suffered; Wedekind's play tells us she is the same old Lulu, the same old flame, as unaffected by prison as by the deaths of her lovers. In *Earth-Spirit* (Act II Scene 3) Lulu makes a declaration of her attitude to Dr Schön, speaking, according to the stage directions, 'in a decided tone':

> If I belong to anyone in the world, I belong to you. Without you I should be – I wouldn't care to say where. You took me by the hand, gave me food and clothing when I tried to steal your watch. Do you think I can forget a thing like that?

In the opera (Act I Scene 2), a transformation has occurred. No longer is the statement a typically Lulu-ish recital of plain and emotionally detached facts; her words are cast in the form of a short melodrama and projected over a noble theme (one of the work's leading motifs, substantially dwelt upon in the *Adagio*) which symbolizes Lulu's affection for Dr Schön ('Meines Mannes . . .', bars 615–20 [facing]).[16]

The exceptional beauty of this passage leaves us in no doubt as to the depth of Lulu's love. The 'love', however, was not originally part of Wedekind's dramatic intentions – indeed, it is destructive of them – but has been introduced by the composer. It seems ungracious and ungrateful to criticize or 'discredit' a musical moment so moving and so expressive, and yet, if the passage quoted above is 'true' of Berg's Lulu, it somewhat invalidates the actions of (Wedekind's) Lulu in the next act when she casually shoots Dr Schön.

Musically speaking, 'The only man I ever loved!' (see Section I above) does not receive an emotional musical setting comparable to 'Meines Mannes'; often, as here, Berg succeeds in presenting Wedekind's non-emotional Lulu, particularly in his treatment of the exchange between Schwarz and Lulu (Act I Scene 1):

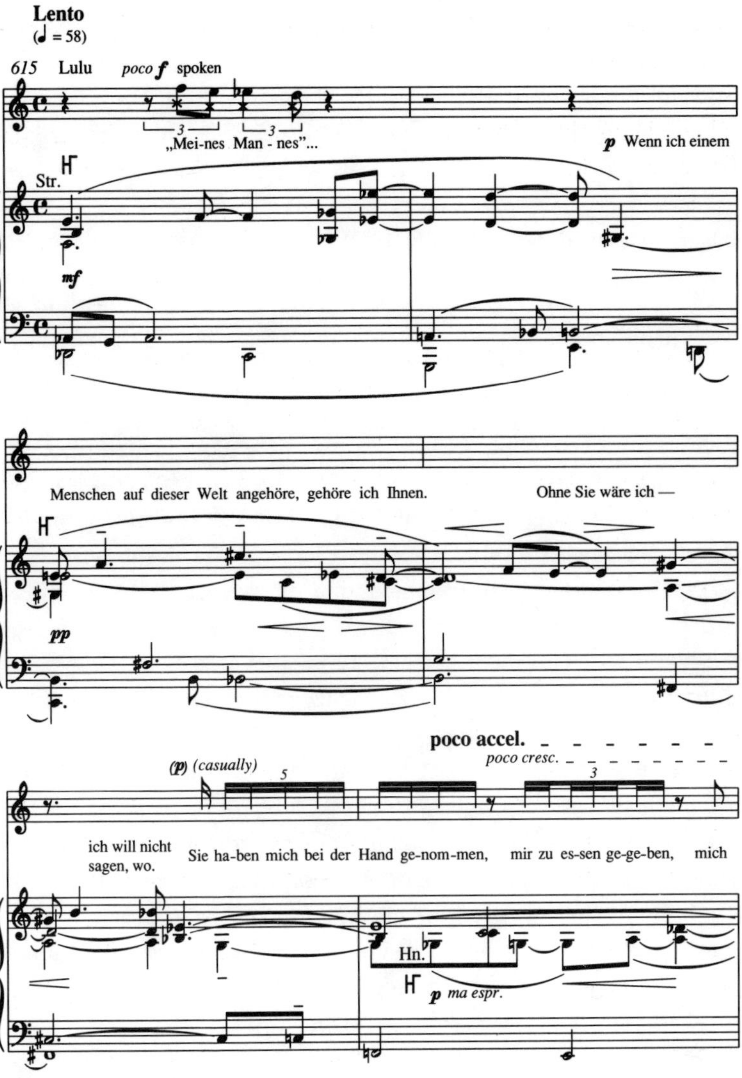
Lento
(♩ = 58)
615 Lulu poco f spoken
„Mei-nes Man - nes"...
p Wenn ich einem
Str.
mf
Menschen auf dieser Welt angehöre, gehöre ich Ihnen.
Ohne Sie wäre ich —
pp
poco accel.
poco cresc.
(p) (casually)
ich will nicht sagen, wo.
Sie ha-ben mich bei der Hand ge-nom-men, mir zu es-sen ge-ge-ben, mich
Hn.
p ma espr.

'Can you speak the truth?'
'I don't know.'
'Do you believe in a creator?'
'I don't know.' [Etc.]

III Conclusions

I believe that I have shown in Sections I and II that Berg himself may have precipitated a large-scale dramatic confusion when basically (either consciously or unconsciously) altering the constitution and character of the opera's Lulu without duly amending the text and dramatic action. While bearing in mind the tantalizingly incomplete last act, which, if finished, might have made many events clearer, I think there is little doubt that *Lulu*, as it stands, is not a convincing musico-dramatic entity; what goes on in the orchestra pit and on the stage fail to match, and one suspects that the third act, however conclusive, would not have succeeded in balancing the two levels. This inconsistency, perhaps, would be an altogether shattering flaw were it not for the fact that the music, unlike the drama, is satisfyingly consistent on its own masterly level; and I suggest that the problem of Lulu's at present ill-integrated and alarmingly erratic characterization could be partially overcome by deriving the true state of dramatic affairs from the music rather than the libretto and its origins. In short, the next production of *Lulu* (and is there any reason why Covent Garden should not take a few practical steps in this direction?)[17] must jettison Wedekind and preconceived notions founded on *Earth-Spirit* and *Pandora's Box*, and concentrate on Berg's transformed and developing Lulu drawn from the opera. It is useless, in my view, to attempt to reproduce Wedekind's static 'innocent corruptress' who plays 'an entirely passive role' when, in musical terms, she is most active and experienced in her feelings (as in 'Meines Mannes' quoted above). Since Berg allows his Lulu to indulge in emotional disclosures that would not disgrace a tragic operatic heroine of a less eccentric disposition, the producer of the opera must respond by creating a stage figure and environment from which these disclosures may naturally proceed. The trouble with Hartleb's Essen production was not that Lulu developed from act to act, but that she developed from impossible beginnings. By permitting Lulu to develop at all, Hartleb was halfway towards the realization of Berg's Lulu, but by too great an insistence on her as a 'completely natural and unintellectual creature' he was still trying to cling to Wedekind's coat-tails; and, as I have suggested, Berg's and Wedekind's Lulus are almost mutually exclusive. Or, more accurately, Berg's music excludes Wedekind.

If nothing else, this rudimentary comparison between Wedekind's text and Berg's opera proves that a large part of the difficulties of producing a convincing *Lulu* is due to Berg's own curious approach and attitude to his heroine (an inconsistency that extends besides to other characters, Alwa especially). One may also reasonably conclude that the course his adaptation eventually pursued was forced upon him by the very nature of the art he practised. Music ceases to be music when it ceases to express feelings, *pace* Stravinsky; and to write an opera about a heroine virtually without any feelings would not only have been beyond Berg's creative powers, but, as a creative musician of genius, beneath his contempt.

NOTES

1 *Lulu*, Oper von Alban Berg nach den Tragödien *Erdgeist* und *Büchse der Pandora* von Frank Wedekind; vocal score by Erwin Stein (Universal Edition, Vienna, 1936).

2 Dika Newlin, *Bruckner, Mahler, Schoenberg* (King's Crown Press, New York, 1947), p. 275.

3 My indications of each scene's setting derive from the Essen company's performance at the Holland Festival, 1953.

MC: DM had attended the first night of the production on 7 July.

4 The disposition of the last act, while I believe it to be correct, is, of course, not based on personal acquaintance with the composer's original draft.

5 Berg's Symphonic Suite from *Lulu* was put together and first performed (1934) while he was still working on the opera; it included (from the music of Act III) the *Variations* which, it seems, were to function as the orchestral interlude between the act's two scenes, and the final *Adagio*, which brings the second scene (and, indeed, the whole opera) to its magnificent conclusion.

6 This was the scheme adopted for the recent production of *Lulu* by the Essen opera company. For further details of the manner in which the producer, Dr Hans Hartleb, ingeniously set the *Variations* and *Adagio* within a skeletal framework of dialogue and dramatic action drawn from *Pandora's Box*, Act III (the London attic), see my reviews in *Musical Times* 94 (September 1953), pp. 422–3, and *Opera*, September 1953, pp. 549–51, *Musical Opinion* 77/913 (October 1953), pp. 23–5, and *Tempo* 29 (autumn 1953), pp. 5–7.

MC: It was in DM's *Tempo* review that he first drew attention to the problem of Lulu's characterization:

> The production, while revealing many of the beauties of Berg's score, also revealed a basic and crippling defect in Hans Hartleb's . . . conception of Lulu's character. It is not a simple task to explain who – or what – Lulu, in fact, is. But reading, as it were, from the score upwards, and bearing in mind the two plays of Wedekind . . . from which Berg drew his libretto, one finds nothing to suggest that she is no more than a highly sexed chorus girl. She is, rather, a spirit, beyond morality, both needing to be loved and compelling all who come within her orbit to love her, incapable of any kind of personal discrimination, or of realizing the fatal consequences, potential or actual, into which her eclectic love plunges her and her lovers. Lulu runs the entire circle of passions, normal and abnormal, and yet what one might describe as her fundamental 'innocence' is unimpaired. She cannot be called to account for her actions because she is responsible for none of them. Her gruesome death in Act III at the hands of Jack the Ripper is just tragically bad luck; it is not the case of a bad lot justly coming to a bad end. Although one could discuss Wedekind's Lulu at length and, perhaps, never reach a decisive conclusion, it is certain, nevertheless, that Essen's Lulu stood in the plainest contradiction to the implications of Berg's music. Carla Spletter, who sang the part in this production with much allure and an often astonishing musical virtuosity, was simply not the sort of Lulu whom Berg would have commemorated in the magnificent *Adagio* which brings the opera to a sublime close. On Spletter's Lulu, one feels, Berg would not have wasted a single note, least of all a masterly symphonic edifice which must rank as one of the greatest slow movements of our time. [p. 6.]

7 This quotation from Wedekind's foreword to *Pandora's Box* is taken from *Five Tragedies of Sex*, translated by Frances Fawcett and Stephen Spender with an Introduction by Lion Feuchtwanger (Vision Press, London, 1952). All subsequent quotations are from this edition of Wedekind's plays.

8 Nicolas Slonimsky, *Music since 1900* (Dent, New York, 3rd edn, 1949), p. 428.

9 Feuchtwanger, op. cit., p. 19.

10 Arthur Eloesser, *Modern German Literature* (Hamish Hamilton, London, 1933), p. 127.

11 MC: For DM's comparable interpretation of a 'triangular' relationship in a Britten opera, see his 'A *Billy Budd* Notebook (1979–91)', in Mervyn Cooke and Philip Reed (eds.), *Benjamin Britten: 'Billy Budd'* (Cambridge University Press (Cambridge Opera Handbook), Cambridge, 1993), pp. 117–19.

12 Newlin, op. cit., pp. 275–6.

13 In a communication that replied to my criticism (published in *Opera*: see note 14 below) of the Essen production of *Lulu*. Dr Hartleb's views have not, so far, achieved print in this country, although *Opera* undertook to give them a hearing.

14 *Opera*, September 1953, pp. 549–51.

15 Hans Keller, '*Lulu*', *Music Review* 14/4 (November 1953), pp. 302–3.

MC: The Wedekind texts were in fact Berg's second choice of libretto source, his negotiations for the use of his preferred material (Gerhart Hauptmann's *Und Pippa tanzt*) having fallen through in April 1928 due to copyright difficulties. See Mosco Carner, *Alban Berg: The Man and the Work* (Duckworth, London, 1975), pp. 71–3.

16 See Willi Reich, *Alban Berg* (Herbert Reichner, Vienna, 1937; rev. edn (trans. Cornelius Cardew), London, Thames and Hudson, 1965, p. 166). In many ways, of course, the great *Adagio* immortalizes not only Lulu and Geschwitz but also Schön; thus the eternal triangle is commemorated nobly in *Lulu* (Act III Scene 2).

17 MC: The complete, three-act *Lulu* reached the Royal Opera House stage on 6 February 1981, two years after the world première of Friedrich Cerha's realization at the Paris Opéra.

IV

Expressionism

The Shriek: woodblock by Edvard Munch, 1895

What is Expressionism?

Expressionism – a particularly puzzling term in some respects. Puzzling because of its clear verbal associations – with expression, with expressiveness – words we're always using about the arts and about artists. Indeed, Expressionism one might think of as something that creative art has always had and must always have, at any rate as a significant component. Yet we know that it has an altogether stricter application, to a defined movement in the arts which developed at the end of the last century and flowered in Europe with an astonishing burst of luxuriance during the years leading up to the First World War. We know that it was a movement influential and active in all the arts – in literature (especially in the Scandinavian and German theatre), in music, in architecture, in painting, in the cinema – and we know the artists involved and their work. An articulate and articulated movement, though short-lived; it's perhaps a singular feature of twentieth-century movements in the arts that they burn with extraordinary intensity and brilliance over relatively brief spans of time and yet echo on down the corridors of history with a persistence that is striking.

I would be prepared to argue that there is much art today, of the immediate present, that is, that has its roots in the Expressionism rampant at the turn of the century, which was written off, all to soon, as a peculiarly *fin-de-siècle* or even degenerate phenomenon. However, *that* relationship – the debt that our post-war arts owe the pre-First World War creators – is really the subject for another lecture altogether. I shall content myself with observing that it may be that the persistence of Expressionism, and the rebirth of it in our day, is bound up with the suggestion I

Professorial Inaugural Lecture, University of Sussex, 13 March 1972

touched on in my very first sentences: that Expressionism in some sense has always been with us in the arts – whether in painting – and I'm thinking of a masterpiece from the early sixteenth century such as Grünewald's *Crucifixion* – or in music; the *dénouement*, say, of Mozart's *Don Giovanni*, when the Statue, the supernatural Stone Guest, comes to supper and seizes his host, an opera first performed in 1787.

Expressionism, in fact, continues to be with us, whenever a critical point of tension is either introduced into a work of art or indeed is the total all-enclosing topic of the work of art. Grünewald's Christ at the moment of crucifixion, Mozart's Don Giovanni at the moment of his descent to hell – two human beings *in extremis*. But having made this point, which I wish to emphasize, because I believe that one of the ways in which we can isolate and identify one significant form of Expressionism is to recognize the likelihood of its manifestation at moments of extreme tension, of high psychological drama, I want to go on to emphasize the wide variety of Expressionism, a factor that contributes to the difficulty of arriving at a tidy definition of the movement.

There are certainly, as I have already suggested, certain *technical* features and predominant sources of inspiration shared among a number of artists who allied themselves to the Expressionist cause. There's very good reason, for example, why, in a study of Kandinsky, the painter, we find Mr Frank Whitford[1] making significant reference to Schoenberg, the composer. Because the painter and the composer, for a brief, heroic period, in the first decade of this century, each developed in his own field a form of Expressionism in which we can distinguish *technical* parallels between the two arts. But the Kandinsky–Schoenberg link[2] was a rare example of two men of genius in different arts pursuing for a time almost common ideals, though we also have to remember that Schoenberg was himself an accomplished Expressionist painter, and that Kandinsky was influenced in some of his ideas about painting by Schoenberg's famous *Harmonielehre*, his treatise on harmony.

If one looks elsewhere, away from Kandinsky and Schoenberg,

and perhaps no further than the two groups of artists, Die Brücke ('The Bridge'), organized in 1905, and Der blaue Reiter ('The Blue Rider'), founded some years later, in 1911, both of which were identified with Expressionism and Expressionist ideals, we find profound contrasts in style and spirit, between the groups and indeed often within the groups. Yet this very diversity also tells us something profoundly important about the nature of Expressionism. It was confessedly and deliberately a movement of the most intense *subjectivity*. Its very *raison d'être* was to bring to the forefront the artist's *intuition* – what Kandinsky often refers to as 'inner necessity' – and permit the work of art, whether it be a painting or a musical composition, to materialize, to find its own characteristic shape and form, as a result of a free, uninhibited, *unrestrained play of feeling*.

It was no longer a question of feeling, of 'inner necessity', if you prefer, *selecting* an appropriate or perhaps inherited form: on the contrary, form was to be created anew, even unconsciously created, out of this pact the artist was to make with his intuition. Small wonder, given the diversity of temperaments and personalities that made up the Expressionist movement, that the range of Expressionist art defeats tidy classification.

But this variety, paradoxically, is proof of the consistency with which so many Expressionist artists applied the principle set forth in the manifesto that accompanied the first exhibition of Der blaue Reiter in 1911: 'We wish to demonstrate by means of a *variety* of forms that the *inner wish* of the artist can be structured in many different ways.' In passing, of course, one must note that this *surrender* to intuition, to inner necessity, to feeling, to the exploitation and exploration of the Unconscious, has very significant parallels in other movements in the arts of about the same period: Surrealism, for example, or Dadaism, where the cultivation of the irrational or the absurd also represented a surrender to intuition and impulse, though in a narrower field. Here again, if we look at the creative world about us, in which the irrational and the absurd, the 'happening', the 'event', play a considerable role, we see an extraordinary revival of ideas that were current in the first decades of the century and that seemed to have died a natural death, but now prove to have been lurking beneath the surface, awaiting resurrection. That, though, is also another and complex story.

I have already said something about the difficulty of defining Expressionism. As so often is the case, the defence of a movement against unjust attack can sometimes provoke the defender into making admirably positive statements about the movement's ideals. In Hitler's Germany, the art of the Expressionists, in whatever medium, was condemned by the Nazis as degenerate and Bolshevist: the artists were forbidden to exhibit; performances of the composers' music were banned. By a fearful stroke of irony, the gifted Expressionist German poet Gottfried Benn (1886–1956) was deluded enough to lend brief support to the 'new' Germany, only to find that the artistic movement of which he had been a prominent member was roundly denounced by his new heroes. To his credit, I think, he sprang to the defence of Expressionism, his old love, in a brilliant paper, first published in 1934. It makes uncomfortable reading, because of the painful friction between his old faith and his new one, but it also offers some striking thoughts on the nature of Expressionism. The basic intention of Expressionism, he says, is

> to shatter reality, to go to the very roots of things ruthlessly until they are no longer individually or sensuously coloured or falsified or displaced in a changed and weakened form in the psychological process; but instead await in the a-causal silence of the absolute ego the rare summons of the creative spirit . . .[3]

That seems to me to say very well, if somewhat exaltedly, what I've been trying to say; and Benn also confirms another point that I've made: that this art of Expressionism – in his Kandinsky-like words, the art of 'inner reality and its direct revelation as form' – was anticipated throughout the nineteenth century.

Indeed, one of the most interesting parts of Benn's document is the long and grand list of eminent Germans (including Goethe, who would surely have been surprised) and other Europeans who anticipated Expressionism in certain features or certain passages of their works. Benn doubtless hoped that by providing a respectable pedigree for Expressionism, the Nazis might be converted. But, this political strategy apart, there was of course a wholly valid point he was making, and with which he sums up his conclusions about Expressionism's illustrious parentage. 'We can truthfully say', he writes, 'that Expressionism is part of all art; but only at a certain time (namely the period which has just passed), when it springs from many men, does it determine a style and an age.' Given the way the arts developed during the nineteenth century, indeed, I would argue that Expressionism was a perfectly logical outcome of that development. This again is an immensely complex subject, but I'll risk none the less one or two generalizations: for example, that the arts during the nineteenth century became more and more highly subjective, more intensely self-conscious and autobiographical. (I use those terms without the usual derogatory associations, simply as factual descriptions.) If the word may be forgiven, art became progressively *interiorized*, in the sense that the work we name Expressionist was intimately and explicitly bound up with the inner nature of an artist's personality in a way that radically redistributed the balance and proportions which, in earlier periods, had been accepted as a kind of working compromise between established forms and conventions on the one hand, and the artist's personality – or his ego – on the other: a compromise, or perhaps reconciliation would be the better word, that has given us some of the greatest art we know.

It seems to me undeniable that it was through an intensification of Romanticism that we moved from an art of persuasion, in which a formal game – the game artists play – was enacted between the artist and his public, with at least some objective rules and conditions understood by all the participants, to an art of direct revelation, of direct confrontation, of form subordinate to feeling, and to a game, if I may continue the analogy, in which, as

Kandinsky himself said 'today' (that was in 1912) 'everything is permitted', though what he had in mind I believe was something very different from the permissiveness of 1972. Another generalization I'm prepared to float is this: that if an extreme expressiveness is a feature of Expressionism, then it was towards a condition of extreme expressiveness that the arts, and especially music, were moving in the nineteenth century; and by the end of the century, and at the turn of it, had arrived at that extreme expressiveness which I would regard as the indispensable precondition for the birth of Expressionism and which induced that birth to take place.

Wagner, inevitably, is one of the precursory names mentioned by Gottfried Benn; in fact there are few artists he doesn't mention. But Wagner, rightly so, remains a remarkable, unique and multiple source of influential modern movements. How much, for example, *Im*pressionism owes to Wagner, and how badly that much used label needs a precise definition, or at least a comprehensive investigation. For *Ex*pressionism, too, Wagner is a central figure. What I shall suggest a little later as a feature of some important Expressionist art – and what I have in mind is a quite explicit exploration, almost a clinical investigation, one might think, of minds at the very end of their tethers – was certainly foreshadowed by Wagner in *Tristan*, Act III, when the mental stability of his hero is undermined by his wound, his fever and his distraught longing for Isolde. A character – the so-called 'mad' Tristan – caught at a moment of extreme tension, which you may remember I earlier put forward as an area in which Expressionism was peculiarly at home.

Isolde, too, celebrating in visionary rhapsody the dead Tristan, is revealed at a moment of epic tension. I think we'd all agree that her *Liebestod* is of an extreme expressiveness; for me, it is a significant example of a musical form almost exclusively conditioned by the discharge of the feeling that has accumulated at this critical stage of the opera, just as the overall shape of the 'mad' Tristan's nightmarish monologue – in itself a brilliant and innovatory kind of Expressionist solo cantata – is minutely articulated by the free, a-formal unfolding of his feverish, hallucinatory dreams. The *Liebestod* is, as it were, paced and measured, and its successive waves of climax articulated, by Isolde–Wagner's vast release of feeling. The moment the feeling that generates the form is exhausted, the form itself expires.

I classify this music, in essence, as an inspired example of the relationship between feeling and form – that is, a surrender to feeling in order to arrive at the appropriate form.

Other aspects of Wagner's *Liebestod* also seem to me to be prophetic of the techniques we identify as Expressionist, the extreme contrasts in dynamics, for instance, and the concept of an all-enveloping sonority which finally engulfs the listener and drowns him in sound and sensation. This handling of sound, and above all the handling of large volumes of sound, is a particularly interesting feature of Expressionist music: and here, as in so many respects, Wagner was the innovator, which makes him a founder member of Expressionism. I shall have more to say about the role dynamics play in Expressionist music, which perhaps can be legitimately compared to the Expressionist painters' dynamic use of colour as a means to secure maximum emotional impact.

I want to return for a moment to Mozart and to *Don Giovanni*, to the last act, and to the entry of the Commendatore's Statue. A moment of high tension, and also a moment when the *sur*real is introduced: thus a moment when one might expect, or at least *I* should expect, a whiff of Expressionism. Well, I think the passage shows more than one Expressionist technique, but let me draw your attention to at least two aspects, the organization of the dynamics, and the character of the Statue's vocal line, the wide, extravagant leaps of which reflect the expanding pressure of supercharged feeling at this moment. As for the dynamics, we have the methodically organized contrasting dynamics of the Statue's accompanying chords, and the ascending and descending scale which repeatedly presents a vivid dynamic contrast in a narrow space and brilliantly suggests the rhythm of breathing – breathing in, then breathing out – under stress. It's the Statue, gigantically breathing down our, or more particularly, Don Giovanni's, neck. If we agree that Expressionism represents an intense form of Romanticism, small wonder that it was in that scene in *Don Giovanni* that the nineteenth century discerned the onset of Romanticism in music.

Wagner demonstrates the condition of extreme expressiveness that developed as the nineteenth century progressed; and if we take a later figure, a crucial figure such as Mahler, then we find music of an expressiveness so extreme that the only remaining step could be to cross the frontier into the territory of Expressionism proper; and this is often what we discover in Mahler, a juxtaposition of extreme expressiveness and Expressionism, an unsurprising juxtaposition of styles in a man of genius whose life and art straddled the critical decades when the nineteenth century was ending and the twentieth beginning.

Can we bear in mind for a moment the wide leaps that characterize the Stone Guest's vocal line in *Don Giovanni*, composed in 1787? We should not be surprised then to find that a feature of late-Romantic melody is the positively vertiginous leaps in pitch, which seem to grow wider and more extreme as the tension increases. Take, for instance, the great, slow first movement of Mahler's Tenth Symphony, the composition of which was left incomplete when he died in 1911: music that is perhaps more than one world away from Mozart. Still, the same principle seems to be at work melodically in either case. True, the tension in Mozart is activated by the drama: we cannot quite call it Mozart's tension, in the way that we might attribute Mahler's tension to Mahler – on the assumption, that is, that we accept as valid my suggestion of the progressive interiorization of much art during the nineteenth century.

I think we would all agree, however, that the movement's principal theme is certainly an example of ultra-expressiveness, beyond which extremity it would have been difficult to go technically unless something different altogether was done. It is just this that Mahler does, still bent, I think, on a release of feeling of an extremeness that demanded a new formulation. Hence the bleak explosion of a piled-up dissonance, a constellation of superimposed thirds, which so shatteringly erupts, and in which, it seems to me, extreme expressiveness clearly topples over the border into Expressionism. But while I would agree that this passage reflects in vertical form a kind of concentrated, even brutal summing-up of the high rate of dissonance that prevails in this movement, for the rest I don't think the gesture can be wholly justified or explained rationally in terms of the movement's form. It happens, it erupts: it *is* a happening, an event. Not I think irrational, but attributable less to the logic of the total form of the movement than to the inner life of the composer. Mahler was compelled, I think, to attempt a final turn, a final intensification, of the emotional screw. How to intensify extreme expressiveness was his problem. This was how he solved it:

(Incidentally, the passage returns, cyclically, in the finale of the symphony, and thus achieves, retrospectively, a perfectly respectable formal status. But my hunch is that the dissonance in the first movement was, so to speak, unscheduled. It just happened, under pressure [see plate 26].)[4]

From what I have already said I think it is clear that Expressionism for me is a perfectly logical outcome of the development of Romanticism. Clear too, I think, that I view an important part of the development of Romanticism as a process by which the artist, the creator, became more and more a topic for, or subject of, his own art.

It is no accident that Berlioz's *Symphonie fantastique*, composed in 1830, is a prime document in the history of Romanticism. The work is not only subtitled 'Episode from the Life of an Artist' but exactly illustrates the process of interiorization to which I have referred; that is, it is explicitly built out of the imagined artist's *inner* life, his dreams. Berlioz was an audacious, early explorer in this field, which was to have such influence in and on the future. I do not question the legitimacy of this striking, inward development, but I think one must concede that in some respects it modified, even quite substantially, the nature of the arts and their techniques.

Although Expressionism was in my view a movement that emerged as a result of this steady, cumulative interiorization, it was, also, a peculiarly and obligatorily *personal* mode of communication. Historically speaking, Expressionism flowered at a time when it seemed to provide at any rate one kind of possible answer to the critical, end-of-tradition problems that beset virtually all the arts as the old century closed. Tradition was not only under attack but seen to be exhausted. Not only had the very language of the arts to be renewed, but above all their forms. There obtained indeed an extraordinary state of dissolution, which had been brought about by the onwards, *inwards*, drive of Romanticism; and was now brought to a climax by the intensification of Romanticism that was Expressionism. This state of flux was to throw up the new visions and the new sounds – and the new techniques that embodied them – which were indelibly to characterize much of the so-called revolutionary art of the early twentieth century, until neo-classicism triumphed – a reaction *outwards* if there ever were one, against the *inwardness* of Expressionism. With neo-classicism, in a sense, tradition returned, reinstated ironically enough by some of the leading figures of the Expressionist movement, Schoenberg among them. We see now, in fact, that the gulf between Stravinsky's music and Schoenberg's in the 1920s and 1930s, which seemed to be unbridgeable, was largely illusory. More united them than divided them. What they had substantially in common was neo-classicism, an aesthetic thought to be exclusively Stravinsky's, but which of course was equally part of an unacknowledged and for a significant time *unheard* part of Schoenberg's conception of serial music. But that again is another story.

What I want to emphasize at this moment is this: that if, as I've just suggested, Expressionism is a highly personal art, and one that often elects to explore moments of high crisis, it was also an art itself born at a historical moment of profound crisis and tension, when the established outward forms and appearances of art were all under threat. The flight to Kandinsky's 'inner necessity' – where 'form is the outer expression of inner content', where 'necessity creates form' (all his own words) – must be viewed simultaneously from two angles: both as a result of a particular historical situation and as a means of circumventing the stylistic and formal impasse which that same historical situation had created.

Since I've touched here on several historical considerations, I must mention the extraordinary parallel development in the study of the mind which was marked in 1900 by the publication of Freud's *Interpretation of Dreams*. It somehow seems all too pat – that what I have described as the growing interiorization of the arts should have been accompanied by a clinical investigation of the mind, which revealed – or at least proposed the existence of – the *Unconscious*, and, more than that, the extent to which the Unconscious influenced our behaviour. This is not the place for a wrangle about the validity of Freud's ideas, about whether or not psychoanalysis has a scientific basis. I am well aware of the scepticism with which it is fashionable to greet a mention of Freud's name. But the point is, not what we think of Freud *now*, but what he was taken to be by his contemporaries at the turn of the century and after. There is no doubt that his theories were not only immensely influential, so that they became virtually a cultural phenomenon, and remained so for a long period, but must also have been regarded by those Expressionist artists who were particularly aware of the role of the Unconscious in their art as scientific confirmation of their creative methods. One has to think of Freud in the context of the Expressionist movement; and that Freud received a mention in Gottfried Benn's majestic roll-call of the sources of Expressionism is surprising only because Benn must have forgotten, in putting up his defence of the movement to the Nazis, that Freud was a Jew. (A Freudian slip that Freud himself would surely have relished.)

One of my preoccupations has been the moment of crisis as a topic for, or subject of, Expressionism. It was, of course, from the intensive study of human beings in crisis that Freud developed his theories of the mind. In this context, it is important to bear in mind the work of the Norwegian painter Edvard Munch (1863–1944). He is commonly, and I think rightly, regarded as one of the forerunners of Expressionism, and certainly exercised a powerful influence on the movement. Many of his paintings select as topics moments of high psychological tension, moments when some formidable interior drama is being played out or is just about to explode. He picks his people at moments when they are being subjected to extreme stress, as in one of his most famous and influential paintings, *The Shriek*.[5] That well-known image, of 1893, shows us how the subject's internal conflict explodes outwards into a shriek, and somehow, by what painter's magic I do not know, Munch actually seems to demonstrate the *sound* of a shriek in visual terms, perhaps, because the contours of the sky, sea and landscape suggest the shape of vibrating soundwaves, a *graph* of the shriek itself. Who would have thought that a scream could, as it were, provide the total topic for a work of art? But perhaps this seems less surprising to us in 1972, when in the theatre, Samuel Beckett, in *Not I*, has taken Munch's concept a stage further in intensity and economy, and made an isolated mouth serve as image of, and vehicle for, a whole interior drama; and once again, one notes, the drama of a personality at a moment of crisis. I do not want to trivialize the great painter, the distinguished playwright, or the founder of psychoanalysis, but is there not a sense in which the creatures of Munch's or Beckett's imagination might be thought of as patients in need of Freud's therapy? I am not making a trite joke here: I think it was very much part of the climate of Munch's period, the awareness that people walked about with, as it were, psychic dynamite inside them; and it seems to me to be an awareness that Beckett has continued ruthlessly to investigate. There were indeed many forerunners of Expressionism in the theatre; Strindberg, some of the late plays of Ibsen, and a whole generation of important German dramatists and film makers. (The plays of Kokoschka, the painter, were among the first manifestations of Expressionism in the German theatre.) Their plays and films were furnished with images, with situations, which reflect the prevailing sense of crisis and inner tension that distinguishes Munch's art. Much Expressionist dramatic art, indeed, introduced characters on the brink of insanity, when the distinction between fantasy and reality is wellnigh obliterated. The interior world of dreams was authentic Expressionist territory, and the border between dream and nightmare, like the border between sanity and insanity, is a thin one. That border was a preoccupation of the most notorious of Expressionist films, *The Cabinet of Dr Caligari*, released in Berlin in 1920. The overall design of the film was close to the Expressionist manner; indeed, three Expressionist artists were finally responsible for the décor. As Siegfried Kracauer remarks in his important history of the German film, 'The settings [in *Caligari*] amounted to a perfect transformation of material objects into emotional ornaments'.[6] The Expressionist style of the film had the function of 'characterizing phenomena on the screen as phenomena of the soul'; the film was 'an outward projection of psychological events'. In the cinema, too, Expressionist ideas and techniques conditioned the shape of the visual imagery; powerful interior landscapes, landscapes of the mind, contours of feeling, rather than the realism we describe as 'photographic'. In the cinema too, the inner vision had its moment of triumph.

It was not only the cinema but the development of opera before and after the turn of the century that registered in explicit terms the clinical investigation of the mind which itself was a feature of the period. The demented Tristan in Act III of Wagner's opera already opened up a new vista – surely this was one of the first examples of a genuine 'stream of consciousness' technique? – and this new, if somewhat sombre, horizon was explored to its limits by Richard Strauss, by Schoenberg, by Berg, in a group of brilliant theatrical works, the protagonists of which were deranged. When talking about Expressionism, one sometimes is tempted to neglect Strauss, simply because great stretches of his later, cosier works seem to contradict or cancel out his earlier radical masterpieces. *Elektra*, it seems to me, is an under-estimated work, as important a twentieth-century document in its way as *Erwartung* or *Wozzeck*, both of which are indebted to it. There is a great deal that might be said about *Elektra*, which, if perhaps not wholly a document *of* Expressionism, is certainly an immensely important document *for* Expressionism. One need hardly emphasize that *Elektra* presents a social group, if it can be described as such, in conditions of extreme tension; and it is surely significant that the music – the opera was first performed in 1909 – behaves as one would expect it to behave in these circumstances; that is, it tends towards identifiable Expressionist gestures; and, what is perhaps even more significant, it topples over into Expressionism at a moment when Clytemnestra is dwelling on her nocturnal fantasies and dreams, bad dreams in this case. Here we step in a flash into the dream world and into the sound world of pure Expressionism; and the remarkable harmonic emancipation of that passage, which so clearly foreshadows the style of Schoenberg's Expressionist works, and of *Erwartung* in particular, reminds one of Strauss's status as a twentieth-century innovator. It is also a passage, the logic and intensity of which depend on the power of the feeling released and on the psychological truth which we in turn feel to be both the aim and the justification of Strauss's radical harmonic exploits.

These, as I have just suggested, hinge in *Elektra*, in these pages at least, on a dream; and when we approach Schoenberg's monodrama, *Erwartung* ('Expectation'), composed in 1909, in a burst of creative energy spread over seventeen days, we find a plunge into the dream, into the fantasy, that is virtually *total*. *Erwartung* strikes me as the most extreme example – the 'mad' Tristan apart – in the history of music of that process of interiorization which I have so frequently mentioned. Because here the dream is not part of the work, but the whole; and the attempted projection of it, turning the inside outwards so to speak, constitutes both the creative act and the actual work itself. Briefly, *Erwartung* is conceived as an interior monologue or fantasy, which develops by 'free association' – in the manner of what came to be known in the arts as the 'stream of consciousness' technique, though, as I have already implied, I think Wagner was an authentically early explorer in this field. These were ideas much in the air at the time Schoenberg was writing *Erwartung*, in which an anonymous Woman awaits her lover, as in a dream or nightmare, seeks him at night in a wood, and finally stumbles on his dead body. When we listen to *Erwartung* we might do worse than keep in our mind's eye Munch's painting *The Shriek* – because in many ways *Erwartung* is the musical realization of a protracted psychological shriek. I suggest too that we bear in mind the precedent set by Strauss's *Elektra* and Wagner's *Tristan*. *Erwartung*, which ends with the great cry of the Woman, over the dead body of her lover, confronts us with the same *dénouement* that we meet at the end of Tristan. Schoenberg's work is yet another example of a character at a point of extreme tension – and if what I suggested about the *Liebestod* was true – that it is an early example of form determined by and subordinate to feeling – then the same truth applies even more precisely to *Erwartung*, the totality of which is governed, obligatorily so, by the ebb and flow of the Woman's fantasy, by the rise and fall in the graph of the interior drama. Schoenberg had nothing else musically to guide him in his form but that. I use the word 'obligatory' advisedly because *Erwartung* is a principal document of that crucial period when Schoenberg had composed himself, as it were, *out* of tonality but had not yet composed himself *into* the serial, twelve-note method. It was this period, following immediately on the suspension of tonality, roughly the years 1908 to 1914, that constituted Schoenberg's Expressionist years. The renunciation of tonality meant the renunciation of the form-building, theme-building properties associated with it. There was freedom; there was, in Schoenberg's phrase, the 'emancipation of the dissonance'; but how in fact was one to compose one's freedom, order one's dissonances, project a viable form? These were the questions Schoenberg had to face. The new freedom meant that everything was possible (though in fact I think *that* state of affairs has come true only in our time). But for creators such as Schoenberg that made everything more difficult, not less. His solution – and here, I think, he stood in a position almost identical with Kandinsky's – was to surrender to intuition, to 'inner necessity', with only his ear to guide him; to believe, as he once wrote, 'in one's own inspiration', to be convinced 'of the infallibility of one's own fantasy'. It was this typical Expressionist aesthetic doctrine, with its stress on intuition, which, as it were, formed the rational basis, if you will pardon the paradox, of Schoenberg's technical innovations in his heroic Expressionist period: the renunciation, or at least suspension, of tonality, the unpremeditated and unpredictable character of his forms, the extreme plasticity of his rhythm and the seeming – I emphasize that word – abandonment of extended or at least articulated melody. If we talk of Expressionism in music, then those are some of the features by which we recognize its characteristic presence; to which must be added those components I've already suggested are distinguishing features – the often wide-gapped instrumental or vocal line, the extremes of dynamics (from the whisper to the scream is, as it were, the normal Expressionist range) and the vivid orchestral colours. *Erwartung* offers us the very language of Expressionism, a language conceived, in Schoenberg's words 'as in a dream', and, in this case, uniquely attempting in sound the materialization of a dream. It is true, of course, that when we hear *Erwartung* today we are more conscious of its own consistent harmonic practice, of certain symmetries, of detailed motivic variation, even of the presence of that time-honoured operatic device, the *Leitmotif*. All this means that there was a high degree of calculation behind Schoenberg's idea of freedom, just as there was behind Kandinsky's, in his abstract, seemingly random, graphic improvisations. None the less, we should not underestimate the unprecedented release of intuition, which remained the mainspring of Expressionism.

To round off this brief survey of *Elektra*'s descendants, let us consider a passage from Berg's *Wozzeck*: from Act III Scene 2 of the opera, the composition of which was completed in 1921, where the deranged, downtrodden soldier, Wozzeck, murders his sweetheart, Marie. Berg's opera, as I've suggested elsewhere,[7] was born out of *Erwartung*; and, in some respects, for all its overtly Expressionist gestures, it is a more calculated work than Schoenberg's monodrama, both in its harmonic style, which represents something of a compromise – incidentally, I would be prepared to argue that there is a strong vein of *Im*pressionism in *Wozzeck* – and in its forms, where Berg tended to go in for a kind of musical life-assurance policy by adopting many neo-classical and other formal devices and announcing the fact as part of his prospectus. This scene, for example, is an invention on one note. What I want to distinguish is the famous crescendo with which the scene ends, on the note B: B for the overwhelming sense of guilt and panic that envelops Wozzeck's mind as the implications of the murder sink in. That simple but still very telling example is a characteristic *dynamic* Expressionist gesture. Expressionists had learned a lesson from Wagner, from Berlioz, too, in the strategic use of the volume and density of sound as a means of dramatically involving or even subduing the listener. The physical effect of a crescendo is direct in its impact: it can provide that sensation of immediate revelation, of unimpeded confrontation, that was part of the Expressionist aesthetic. Further, the crescendo is surely one of the purest examples of a sound event, the shape of which closely corresponds to the violent, overwhelming intensification of a *feeling* that is a common human experience. The crescendo is feeling translated into an elementary, elemental form. It does not surprise me that the extremities of dynamic contrast, and in particular the exploitation of the crescendo, were favoured by Expressionist composers, and hugely exploited by their successors today, with all the resources of technology's decibels to back them up, whether it is pop or the avant garde that we have in mind.

I want to cite one further example of a crescendo, this time from 1909, and again from the mainstream of the musical tradition we are considering. It is the fourth of Webern's *Six Pieces for Orchestra*, Op. 6, written in the same year as Schoenberg's *Erwartung* and the first performance of Strauss's *Elektra*. Webern's piece has the mood and character of a funeral march, but it is built to culminate in a huge crescendo, a crescendo that absorbs and consumes the march and finally occupies all our attention. The crescendo takes over and gradually declares itself to be the total form of the piece – one solution, at least, of the critical formal problem that obtained at the turn of the century. It bears out in its own striking way the Expressionist theory – to quote Kandinsky's words again – that 'form is the outer expression of the inner content'. Feeling, in Webern's singularly immobile march – which does not march in fact, but only grows louder – supplies the form; at the same time, it is historically interesting and enlightening to observe that, in the search for new forms and new means of organization, what was previously a component of music could be isolated and developed in its own right, as an organizing principle. Schoenberg's *Five Orchestral Pieces*, Op. 16, also composed in 1909, are well worth looking at from this point of view.

I am not suggesting, of course, that the manipulation of dynamics, and in particular the manipulation of the crescendo, was something that we owe exclusively to Expressionist composers. That would be an absurd untruth. It is rather a matter of degree, of intensity; dynamics, having always been an immensely important means of musical articulation and characterization, of self-evident importance in the fields of structure and texture, none the less underwent this radical intensification in the period I have under review, when they were used not as an articulating means, but as an end in themselves, finally constituting in themselves the musical work. It is rather as if dynamics and music, if such a thing were possible, had become divorced and the concept of dynamics set up as a kind of music in its own right. This may seem an extreme suggestion, but I believe it to contain a solid element of truth. Support for it, I believe, is to be found by looking at some other related aspects of music, where the same process is discovered at work; that is, what was hitherto a component – or at any rate something significantly less than the whole – is raised to the status of a principle. Take the glissando, for instance, a familiar effect in music that has a long and reputable history: on the one hand as opportunity for a display of virtuosity; on the other, and increasingly so in late-Romantic music and in music of the twentieth century, as a uniquely expressive feature. When we reach the first decade of this century and Schoenberg's *Erwartung*, the glissando, with its accumulated load of expressiveness and growth in status, is ripe for transformation into something other than expressive adornment or splashes of colour. Schoenberg, with a touch of magisterial magic, having deprived himself of the possibility to round off *Erwartung* with a tonal cadence, uses instead for that crucial moment a glissando throughout the whole orchestra, a brilliant innovation that changed the history of the glissando overnight. No sooner was the glissando revealed in this new light than it was seized on, above all by Alban Berg, who, again in *Wozzeck*, and again in the same manner as he had exploited the crescendo, made a glissando serve as the total musical encapsulation of one of the most important dramatic moments in his whole opera: Wozzeck's suicide by drowning, the musical substance of which is none other than a glissando built on an unprecedented scale. Of course, it works too as a peculiarly brilliant pictorial image, of the waters closing over the hapless Wozzeck's head. But the significant point is not the excellence of the image, but that here we have the glissando functioning on this sort of scale in this sort of context, not functioning in a subordinate role, but, as it were, occupying the whole stage.

Schoenberg and Berg, in their revolutionary treatment of the glissando, were behaving, I would say, like the Expressionists that, in these particular works at any rate, they were, creating and deploying techniques, and making advances in technique, that I submit are identifiably Expressionist in character. These have become, as I have mentioned more than once, of immense importance for the music of our own time, after a period when it seemed as if Expressionism was a spent force.

I must resist the temptation to step too far outside my chosen historical period, but I cannot help but look briefly at a work composed as late as 1964, the first of Britten's church parables, *Curlew River*. Britten has certainly not been untouched by Expressionism and, in his theatre pieces, Expressionist techniques are prominent exactly where one would expect to find them: in those operas in which the heroes or heroines are in critical situations – Peter Grimes, for instance, or the Madwoman in *Curlew River*. It is surely significant that these two works are linked across a quarter of a century by the common theme of a social outsider, marked down by his (and her) disarray of mind. But I mention *Curlew River* because that work amazingly promotes the glissando to a prime compositional feature of the music. You will find that the glissando pervades almost every part, whether vocal or instrumental; and, in one scene, where the Ferryman rows the Madwoman across the Curlew river, it comprises an important part of the total substance of the music.

Curlew River belongs to the 1960s and goes to show how in our own day the glissando has become isolated and developed as an invention in its own expressive and formal right; and it is not surprising that composers of a more recent generation than Britten's have seized on the glissando and transformed it into a prominent feature of the vocabulary in which the new language of music speaks. The triumph of the glissando in the last decade or so could be illustrated by a score of possible examples. I choose music from a work by the Australian composer, Peter Sculthorpe, who for a year was Visiting Professor of Composition at Sussex. His *Sun Music I* for orchestra, composed in 1965, makes liberal and original use of what I submit are two classic Expressionist gestures, the crescendo and the glissando. The particular techniques that music employs for me place a composer such as Sculthorpe quite clearly among the latterday Expressionists, at least in that work; and that music surely lends substance to the point that I made earlier, that Expressionism is not only still with us, but has undergone an astonishing and unexpected rebirth in music of very recent origin.

It is not altogether fanciful to suggest that one might be able to comment quite significantly on major developments in twentieth-century music by observing the history of the glissando alone. A study of the device means that we must take account of our century's exotic inclinations above all to Asia, since the glissando belongs, as it were, to East and West. In their very different ways both Britten and Sculthorpe owe their common glissandos not only to Expressionism but also to exotic influence from Asia.[8]

It is not only glissandos and crescendos that I have up my sleeve. Let me shake out one final example of what was originally an expressive adornment or device developing from a relatively subordinate position to a principal role. I refer to the trill. Of course, the trill has a very long expressive history, and Beethoven, to mention only one composer, developed it from the sphere of the merely ornamental and converted it into something elemental in expressiveness at the close of his Piano Sonata, Op. 111. That unprecedented passage certainly set a precedent for the future, and once again one finds the trill, in an Expressionist context – that is to say in a condition of extreme expressiveness – following the same laws of development as the glissando. Skryabin is one of those fascinating late-Romantic creators whose art trembles on the dividing line between intensity of expression and Expressionism. (It was Skryabin, by the way, with his conception of music as a mass ritual, with music accompanied by dancing and by an elaborate light show, who really anticipated the characteristics of the typical mass rite that pop sometimes offers.) For example, in his remarkable Tenth Piano Sonata, completed in 1913, the trill is no longer in a subordinate or decorative role: on the contrary, at the pinnacle of the work's central climax, trills form virtually the total texture and substance of the music – ornament is transformed into essence.

No doubt I have only scratched the surface of this particular subject – the substantial enrichment and expansion of the expressive vocabulary of music through the techniques of Expressionism, which can indeed be isolated and then classified and designated as such. Expressionism, in short, *has* its own musical vocabulary, and as I have suggested it is still being spoken, and the vocabulary added to, today.

And so to my summing-up, my coda. There is a marvellous remark of Kandinsky's about form: 'Form', he said, 'should not become a *uni*form.' Adding, 'Works of art are not soldiers.' That is a supremely witty and elegant expression of one of his fundamental beliefs, and the spirit of it reminds me to make an important qualification – that it would be misleading to deduce from *Elektra*, *Erwartung* and *Wozzeck*, as one might, that Expressionism was exclusively crisis-ridden or preoccupied with pathological states of mind. I think it frequently was; and perhaps music contributed rather more than its fair share of shattered minds and painful dreams. Some of the Expressionist painters, however, and perhaps above all Kandinsky himself, were capable of serenity, even of a playful spirit; and from time to time also in Schoenberg's Expressionist period, one comes across music where the tensions are relaxed and the explosions mute.

I am always impressed by the happy and relaxed inventiveness that marked those works of Kandinsky in which he moved into the world of abstraction. One tends, if one is only an amateur in the field of painting, as I am, to associate the birth of abstract, non-figurative and non-representational art with the development of Cubism, a style more pervasive and certainly more readily imitated than Abstract Expressionism because it presented a codified technique, a vocabulary, that could be widely adopted, and was on an international scale. It *became* indeed an international style. Cubism, moreover, was an analytic style, rather than an intuitive one like Abstract Expressionism. None the less, the first abstract painting was not the work of a Cubist, but a watercolour by Kandinsky, painted in 1910. The title that Kandinsky gives to many of his abstract paintings is *Improvisation*; and undoubtedly the musical analogy was quite deliberate. As Herbert Read puts it:

> The musical analogy is always in the background, and the concepts of time, rhythm, interval and metre hitherto reserved to music are freely introduced into the aesthetics of painting. Kandinsky's aesthetics (a total aesthetics covering all the arts) stands or falls by the justness of this analogy, and from the early days of the blaue Reiter it was based on discussions with composers like Arnold Schoenberg.[9]

This is Kandinsky himself describing his *Improvisations*: 'A largely unconscious, spontaneous expression of inner character, of non-material (i.e. spiritual) nature. This I call an "Improvisation".'[10]

Suppose we slightly reword that description, as if it were written by Schoenberg about his *Six Little Piano Pieces*, Op. 19, written at just about the same time as Kandinsky's *Improvisations* were painted. He might truthfully have said, 'These are largely unconscious, spontaneous expressions of inner character, non-tonal and non-thematic in nature. I call these "improvisations".'

Well, in fact Schoenberg didn't say that, but he could have done. If we listen to these miniatures, and hold in mind the aesthetic doctrine that produced them, we surely discern not only a remarkable coincidence of doctrine but also a remarkable identity of technical approach. The very brief *Six Pieces* were written in 1911, the year of Mahler's death, two years later than *Elektra* and *Erwartung*; and they represent, of course, in an extreme manner, one of the formal difficulties facing the Expressionist composer. Unless his works were tied to a text, which could impose a length and extended structure, then his 'improvisations', based on the release of an extreme expressivity, tended to be short. The style was rich in intensity, short on scale. This was undoubtedly a factor that encouraged Schoenberg to seek for a method that would renew the possibility of large-scale form-building.

I'm afraid my account of Expressionism has been necessarily partial. Because of the variety and contrasts contained within the movement, it has been impossible to encompass every aspect. But I hope to have touched on some important features common to both painting and music and to have left you with an impression of the revolutionary importance of Expressionism. Out of it developed the idea of abstraction in the visual arts; and, in a parallel development in Expressionist music, there was the renunciation of tonality and the development of a non-tonal, non-thematic music. Momentous steps in the history of the arts concerned, which had incalculable consequences for the future.

We do not need reminding that we still have abstraction with us in the arts; and I have suggested that Expressionism is *still* a potent force, if in forms that the originators of the movement would scarcely have conceived as possible or come to sanction. I think a scrutiny of the past masters of Expressionism, an acknowledgement of their brilliant imagination, their boldness, idealism, seriousness and superb technical gifts, can usefully provide us with a perspective in which to place and assess some at least of the clamorous art of the present day, which perhaps relies a little too confidently on a public with short memories.

NOTES

1 Frank Whitford, *Kandinsky* (Hamlyn, London, 1967), pp. 16, 18; see also the same author's *Expressionism* (Hamlyn, London, 1970), p. 164.

2 See Jelena Hahl-Koch, *Arnold Schoenberg–Wassily Kandinsky: Letters, Pictures and Documents* (Faber and Faber, London, 1984).

3 Gottfried Benn, 'Expressionismus' in *Kunst und Macht* (Deutsche-Verlags Anstalt, Stuttgart, 1934), which appears as 'The Confession of an

Expressionist' in Victor H. Miesel (ed. and trans.), *Voices of German Expressionism* (Prentice-Hall, Englewood, 1970).

4 In the published full score of the Tenth, in Deryck Cooke's performing version, the comparable passage is to be found on pp. 20–23, bars 194–212, *Breit*: see *Gustav Mahler: Tenth Symphony*, a performing version by Deryck Cooke in collaboration with Berthold Goldschmidt, Colin Matthews and David Matthews (2nd edn; Faber Music, London, 1989).

5 MC: *The Shriek* is an exact translation of the original Norwegian title *Skrik*, which is pronounced identically to the English word. The more commonly encountered renderings as *The Cry* or *The Scream* are neither as accurate nor as striking. Munch was so absorbed by this image that he reproduced it as a woodblock (see p. 201).

6 Siegfried Kracauer, *From Caligari to Hitler: A Psychological History of the German Film* (Dobson, London, 1946), p. 69.

7 DM, *The Language of Modern Music* (Faber and Faber, London, 1963; rev. edn, 1993), p. 51.

8 MC: Britten's use of vocal glissandos in *Curlew River* was undoubtedly influenced by the vocal techniques of the Japanese Noh theatre which inspired the first church parable. See MC, *Oriental Influences in the Music of Benjamin Britten* (Ph.D. thesis, University of Cambridge, 1989), pp. 284–5, and *Britten and the Far East* (Boydell & Brewer (Aldeburgh Studies in Music), Woodbridge, forthcoming, 1996).

9 Herbert Read, *Kandinsky (1866–1944)* (The Faber Gallery, London, 1959), p. 7.

10 Wassily Kandinsky, *Concerning the Spiritual in Art* (ed. and trans. M. T. H. Sadler) (Dover Publications, New York, 1977).

V

Of Peacocks and Waterfalls

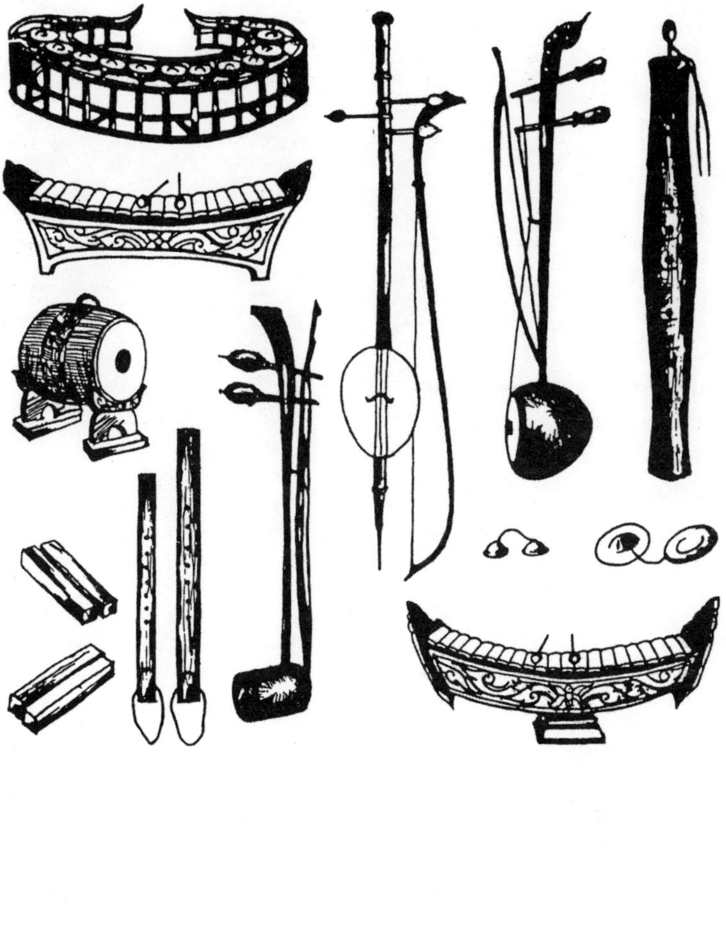

Musical instruments of Thailand

Bangkok Diary I: June 1976

30 June As the plane comes in to land at Don Muang airport[1] I wonder if my friend M. is going to be there to meet me. Before I left London I saw his charming (English) wife who assured me that M.'s reliability in this respect was high. He may forget everything else but he rarely forgot (so she said) to turn up at the airport to meet friends from overseas. He certainly never writes (or answers) letters, and so I don't really know whether he's rented the house for me that he said he would. But L. seemed confident, even though she couldn't remember which house it was in the compound or the telephone number. One should, of course, learn not to worry unnecessarily about these trivial matters; and, like a good Bangkokian, accept whatever it is that destiny has in store for one. (I begin to feel more and more like Gustav von Aschenbach in *Death in Venice*, i.e. 'Was I wrong to come, what is there in store for me here?') Part of my forebodings are removed by the sight of the admirable (and, after all, reliable) M. waiting at the exit from customs examination. It's very early in the morning (07.00) but he looks marvellously spruce and elegant. 'Welcome home,' he says. We're soon in his car, speeding along the highway into the city, and I relish the familiar sights along the way, a bizarre mixture of huge hoardings, temples, factories, lorries, crowded buses, workers' flats, canals, schoolchildren with satchels,

---

Martin Kingsbury (ed.), *Newslink* 12–13 (Faber Music, London, 1976), pp. 9–10; special edition of the Faber in-house staff magazine devoted to Faber Music

in neat white blouses or shirts and blue skirts or trousers – Bangkok getting ready for another day. I also note that the close-cropped head of M.'s driver looks precisely as it did when I last surveyed it from the back of M.'s car, in January. I begin to feel as if I am indeed back home. We drive into the compound and stop at the last Thai-style house on the left, House No. 45. M. says he chose it because it is opposite the swimming pool. The water looks appealing and I determine to have a swim and wash off the long journey. But first of course the house. We enter. It looks remarkably empty and bare. A table and chairs huddled in the corner of the lofty entrance hall and living room (a combined area) but nothing else. We move on into the bedroom. A large double-bed and mattress thrust against the wall. No bedding. A fan turns slowly in the ceiling, but there's no sign of a chair, a lamp to read by, hangers for my clothes . . . I begin to feel slightly less at home and have unworthy thoughts about M. Perhaps his reliability does not extend to the domestic necessities of life? He is undeniably disconcerted and dismayed. 'Where is the servant?' he wonders aloud. Where are the (welcoming) flowers, the tablecloth, the breakfast, the cups and saucers, the knives and forks, the boiled water (to drink), the sheets? Where, indeed? We look in the kitchen, which is again remarkable for its scrupulous lack of any equipment. But M. points with pride and satisfaction to a huge, though very ancient, refrigerator. This, he tells me, has been specially installed for me. On the other hand it is *very* empty; and somehow the yawning fridge further lowers my now somewhat depressed spirits. My resolution to submit myself to my fate seems less attractive than it did half an hour ago, and I determine on action. M. disappears in his car to keep an appointment (I hope with more substance to it than his organization of my domestic affairs). I unpack, push the chairs and table around, put out my books, and take a plunge in the pool, finding tiny frogs as swimming companions: these, the lizards on my ceilings and a variety of miniature land crabs were to be my most numerous neighbours. I can't say House No. 45 looks precisely like home yet; on the other hand the odds and ends I have brought with me do something to clothe its awful nakedness. (How one relies on familiar things about one to sustain a belief in a benevolent universe. Take them away and one feels threatened, disoriented.) I lie on the bed and watch the fan revolving and absurdly have visions, like a cast-away, of a steaming kettle (but there's no kettle) and a welcoming cup of tea (no cup, no tea). But within an hour these melancholy thoughts are dispelled. I had forgotten that time in Thailand is definitely not of the essence of life. No doubt it was intended that flowers, eggcup, fruit, loaf of bread, sheets, pillow case, towel, etc., etc., should all have been ready and waiting at 08.00. No doubt other things intervened, like chatting with the neighbours, getting to and from the market, borrowing necessities from other houses in the compound to meet my needs – all good reasons why my kind servant, Lek, appeared at mid-day rather than 08.00. I was certainly in no mind to complain, so great was my relief when the fridge began to fill up, the bed was made, my clothes put away, a vase of flowers stood on the table, and saucepans and a kettle and plates and a cup and saucer were beckoning in the kitchen. Moreover, at 12.30 there I was actually having lunch – a delicious Thai lunch of fish, rice and fruit, with ample draughts of excellent cold Thai beer (yes, the antique fridge actually worked) – in a house in Bangkok that was at least beginning to look as if I lived in it. But I could not, even on this first day, survive without having a light to read by. For some eccentric reason all the lights in the place were small, dim and placed high up on the wall. Did no one read in bed in Bangkok, I wondered? (And then remembered that the majority of the population wouldn't sleep in beds anyway, but on mats on the floor.) I put the question to M. on his return, who was delighted of course to see that after all everything had turned out as he had meant it to turn out, though on a different time scale. The lamp? Of course, one should be provided. But first one had to be *located*. Phone calls were made. Success. A kind cousin would loan me a bedside lamp. I was grateful, though somewhat embarrassed when M. summoned his driver and car. It seemed we had to cross the city to pick up the lamp. By now it was the end of a long day, for M. too, I thought, who might be wondering whether this particular visitor was not proving to be a fearful burden. But on we drove, finally turning off into a dark, narrow *soi*, the car passing between high garden walls with elegant villas beyond them. In the headlights a small, khaki figure, sitting with his back to an imposing gate. The gardener's boy, said M. Perhaps nothing strange, certainly not in Bangkok, about a small boy sitting on the pavement; but even in that extraordinary city at 11.00 pm or thereabouts one would not often expect to find a sleepy child clutching a large bedside lamp by the side of the road, the flex trailing off into the dust. The lights of the car wake him up and he springs up, salutes M., and hands the lamp through the window. M. smiles, as if to say: that's how things happen in Bangkok! I feel a long way away from London. Go back to bed. Fix up the lamp but fatigue overtakes me and I fall asleep before I have time to use it.

NOTE

1 MC: DM's first extended visit to Thailand: he rented a house in Bangkok (Soi Soonvichai) to begin a preliminary scrutiny of Britten's pocket diaries which the composer had given him (in a shoebox!) along with a request that he should be his authorized biographer. The first draft of DM's 1979 T. S. Eliot Memorial Lectures (University of Kent at Canterbury) also originated on this trip.

Bangkok Diary II: January 1978

9 January As we land at Bombay, *en route* to Bangkok, we fly right across part of the city. A magnificent view of the bay and the ocean, with islands rising out of the mist. All very Mediterranean, I think, until I look down into the streets, packed with people, traffic, markets, stalls, cooking on the pavements, palm trees, white shirts, dazzling light; and I realize I'm back, back East.

10 January Asia Hotel, Bangkok. I determine, my first morning, to start work, knowing only too well that if I don't, it will be that much harder the next day, *ad infinitum*. The open notebook looks peculiarly unpromising, indeed positively unappetizing. Moreover I can't think how to start, and am unconvinced that I have anything to say. As an aid to inspiration I set up my cassette player and insert a tape of *Das Lied von der Erde*.[1] Very fine it sounds. Also, unexpectedly, curiously oriental and certainly more pentatonic than I have ever heard it in England. I'm not quite sure what this proves but am happy that Mahler should strike me as so appropriate, even in the improbable context of Bangkok. Perhaps, I wonder, I shall now find Thai classical music sounding like Mahler.

Not however the Thai national anthem, which sounds like pentatonic Elgar. It is this rousing hymn which greets my ear at 8 o'clock every morning and 6 o'clock every evening. Voices and orchestra are combined and projected at an enormous volume

---

First publication

from loudspeakers in a nearby building. The distortion is massive; but no matter, it's the din that indicates the importance of the event. This is a legacy, so I understand, of the previous government, an attempt to assert national pride and national consciousness. Kwanchai[2] tells me that pedestrians were expected to come to a halt when they heard the anthem booming out – and how could they miss it? – and were given a talking to by a policeman if they kept on walking. This placed me in an awkward dilemma, because at 8 a.m. I was almost always swimming, solitarily, in the hotel pool. What was I supposed to do? The boy watering the garden, I noticed, often stood to attention (perhaps he hadn't realized that there had been a change of government a few months ago). But how can one stand to attention in six (or more) feet of water? I worried about this until I left and never felt I had wholly satisfactorily solved the problem. My compromise was to swim slowly (no splashing or hoots of watery joy) and to look appropriately solemn.

11 January I am delighted to find that it is an old friend, Professor Kamtorn,[3] who comes to pick me up in his car to take me to a lunch organized by the Thai students who visited Aldeburgh last year. He's a remarkable man, very tall, by Thai standards, and with a booming bass voice, again a rare phenomenon in Thailand. This has made him popular as a singer and he tells with relish stories of the unexpected perils attending performances of *Messiah* in Bangkok. One I particularly enjoyed was of the soloist, in full voice and in the middle of an extravagant melisma, who was appalled to observe a mosquito drawn into his mouth by the inhalation that was necessary to keep the second half of his extended vocal ornament aloft. Who won, I inquired, the mosquito or Handel? But Kamtorn was shaking with great gusts of laughter and content to leave the outcome to my imagination.

Kamtorn was sent to England many years ago on a Thai government scholarship and had digs in Brixton. He was very happy there and I am reluctant to spoil his pleasure by telling him that the whole area now is grey and blighted. But it is not just Brixton that he recalls. Other places too. For example, as we are driving down a typical Bangkok *soi* I notice a railway crossing, a station, blocks of long wooden houses on stilts, men playing basketball, a sign that has on it something about the Union of Thai Railwaymen. 'Where are we?' I ask Kamtorn. He considers my question for an appreciable moment, and then the answer booms out: 'You might call this Bangkok's Clapham Junction.' I smile, and clutch at the door as Kamtorn swerves to avoid a cyclist. 'No, no,' he says. 'Not Clapham, *Crewe*.' I nod appreciatively (Crewe, with palm trees?). There's another lurching moment while the Prof. swerves to avoid a huge truck hurtling towards us. 'No, no, not Crewe: *Watford*.' I am much impressed by the wealth of topographical references.

12 January I can see this 'Doctor' business is likely to lead to all kinds of ghastly misunderstandings. I was deep in the midst of writing about the *Kindertotenlieder* – perhaps the work was specially appropriate? – when I was interrupted by a knock on the door. I open it. There stands Yung-Yong, the room boy, rubbing his stomach and rolling his eyes. '*Docteur*, *Docteur*, feeling not so good. Very bad inside, very very bad.' I was moved by his condition but saw no hope of explaining to him that there was more than one kind of 'Docteur' and that I was the wrong kind. I strode purposefully to the bathroom, produced my Enterovioform and handed out two pills together: 'One in the morning and one at night.' I am relieved next day when Yung-Yong reappears, full of smiles and, it seems, fully recovered. I hope he keeps quiet about my medical prowess, otherwise I shall have an unending stream of patients.

13 January I am reminded of this misunderstanding when I take a walk through the maze of little streets that unwind at the back of the hotel. I often walk just before going to bed and never fail to be amazed by the variety and animation of the life that goes on into the early hours of the morning. Among the shops that are among the latest to keep open are the chemists. Bangkok is quite extraordinarily endowed with chemists – I don't think I know another city with so many. Almost every other shop seems to offer every kind of patent medicine and drug (including a lot of dangerous drugs that, in the West, can be obtained only on prescription, hence the importance of reading the manufacturers' small print before you swallow the pills). But it is not only modern medicine that you find in such profusion. In the same shop, rubbing shoulders with, as it were, the latest specifics from Boots, you'll find ancient herbal remedies and strings of dried animal skins and bladders, all of them used by the Thais for centuries and, I have no doubt, just as efficacious as the pills, powders and lotions from the West.

As one walks the streets, almost every kind of human activity presents itself. There are many Thai hotels, half lit and shadowy. 'What goes on there?' I ask. 'Hotels for lovers,' replies Kwanchai solemnly. I move on, past endless small shops and industries and eating houses spilling out on to the pavement. Late at night the shops shut and are converted into bedrooms for the family. People wash on the streets, brush their teeth, put on their minimal night clothes and lie down, some on beds, many more on mattresses and cushions, many on the floor. One shop I walk past is a printing shop. At the front a small boy writes at a table, clearly doing his homework. On a tall pile of paper, against which his school books are propped, is a bowler hat – an unmistakable, authentic English bowler hat. It is the surreal hat that haunts my dreams that night.

28 January In the afternoon I visit the campus of Srinakharinwirot University to watch a classical Thai drama performed by the students. A long affair, it lasts some three hours. My student friends are all playing in the orchestra or acting or singing. There is a great deal of comic action and many, many jokes, to which the large audience responds, familiar though the jokes must be. Somsak[4] kindly offers his services as an interpreter. He gives me the gist of the story but the jokes are beyond him. In any case he's too busy laughing himself to have time to try. It's very, very hot and every now and then trays are passed round with cold drinks on them, including the ubiquitous Coke and the livid green cordial suitably called Green Spot (another case for the 'Docteur', maybe). I have to slip out in the middle of the show to get back to town for another appointment. Somsak says he'll take me to a taxi by a short cut. We walk past the lily pond on the campus and then down a narrow path and to my astonishment find ourselves confronted by a *klong*, a canal. The university is lost behind us; there's a faint roar from the road ahead. We might almost be in the country. At our feet a platform and a narrow wooden boat, punted by a lady – not a ferryman, but a ferrywoman in a broad, circular straw hat. Somsak hands her a few small coins and we glide over the still, black water to the far side. (I began to feel like Aschenbach, crossing the Styx, but relocated in Bangkok.) Another narrow path and then, surprisingly, we suddenly come on Petchburi, one of the city's main arteries. *Klong* and concrete highway: impossible to reconcile, but it is just these paradoxes which are characteristic of Bangkok. Somsak hails a taxi, bargains with the driver, secures a good price. I clamber in the back, slither about on the plastic-covered seat and inwardly groan at the awful little vase of plastic flowers which adorns the driver's dashboard – this in a country where a sheaf of orchids can be bought for a few pence on the street. I turn to wave to Somsak, catch a glimpse of him – that famous Thai smile – through the rear window, and then the taxi carries me off into the no less famous fumes, chaos and congestion of Bangkok's traffic.

NOTES

1 MC: DM's 1978 trip to Bangkok saw him begin work on *Gustav Mahler III: Songs and Symphonies of Life and Death* (Faber and Faber, London, 1985) – hence the inclusion of a tape of *Das Lied von der Erde* in his luggage.

2 MC: Kwanchai Sudsiri, whom DM had known since his first visit to Bangkok.

Mr Kwanchai had helped DM familiarize himself with the topography of the city and the Thai way of life.

3 MC: Professor Kamtorn Snidvongse, the noted musician, scholar, teacher and conspicuous Anglophile, musically at home in two cultures.

4 MC: Dr Somsak Ketukaenchan (b. 1956), then a student, now a prominent teacher and scholar; an outstanding performer on the *pi nai* (see p. 242 below), he gave the first performance of Keith Gifford's *A Scarf of White Stream* with the English Chamber Orchestra under Steuart Bedford at the 44th Aldeburgh Festival on 20 June 1991, the first occasion on which a composer from the West had written a work for a Thai instrument and Western orchestra. Dr Somsak holds a doctorate on Thai music from the University of York, where his MA submission had included an essay on the oriental influences on Britten: see p. 418, n. 10. See also plate 18.

Of Peacocks and Waterfalls: The Traditional Music of Thailand

I

Surely one of the most exciting and innovative ideas we have encountered at the Proms in recent years has been the introduction of music from so-called 'exotic' and far-distant cultures – for example the gamelan from Indonesia that made such a powerful impression at the Proms in 1979. Far be it from me not to salute the BBC for its enterprise and imagination. At the same time, this was clearly a response to what is undeniably a remarkable growth area in musical interest, especially among the younger generation. These days, indeed, some hitherto closed musical books – Balinese music, for example, or Indian music – have become *relatively* open: as the world grows smaller, through the expanding technology of communications, so does our musical curiosity enlarge. I shan't be at all surprised if one of the striking developments in our musical institutions and concert life over the next decade proves to be the exploration of musical traditions and repertoires from the Far East, a marvellous consequence of which will be our getting to know the great virtuosos who sustain the performing traditions of their own lands.

Lest all this should sound too much like special pleading, let's

Part I: programme book for the BBC's 87th season of Henry Wood Promenade Concerts (London, 1981), pp. 27–9; Part II: programme for the performance by the Thai Classical Music Group of Srinakharinwirot University, Bangkok (Prom 35), 22 August 1981

remember that in recent times the excitement and revitalizing freshness of unfamiliar sounds and techniques from the East have been acknowledged not so much in academic circles as in the open-minded, adventurous world of pop. There the best creative minds have not only used the fascinating – if only seemingly free and improvisatory – forms of much oriental music, but also restored the performer-as-creator to the very centre of the musical stage. And if we want to locate a composer of the recent past who was substantially influenced by a musical confrontation with the Orient, we need look no further than Britten, many of whose compositional techniques were actually transformed after his experience of the music of the Far East in the mid-1950s.

All these thoughts and themes will, I believe, be very much in the air on 22 August,[1] when we shall have a very rare opportunity indeed to make the acquaintance of a musical culture which is among the less familiar in the West, but which over the last decade or so has offered me some of my most vivid and memorable musical experiences: the classical music of Thailand. Our Prom visitors are one of the leading ensembles in the country, the Thai Classical Music Group of Srinakharinwirot University, Bangkok. Those who saw the remarkable BBC TV film about the Thai Royal Family, *Soul of a Nation*, will already have heard the group, on the television soundtrack. Many of them are young musicians and/or teachers, whose ancient art has been learned by one generation from another *without* the tradition or practice of written music.

What sounds shall we hear? I can promise you magical and beguiling sonorities and melodies, whether from the *khlui*, the bamboo flute of Thailand, or the *pi nai*, an incredibly wild and pungent double-reed instrument, as penetrating as the oboe and as plaintive as the cor anglais – but much louder! Then there are the wooden-keyed xylophones, the *ranat ek* (high pitch) and *ranat thum* (low pitch), which produce the gentle glitter and liquid tremulousness characteristic of so much Thai music; the extraordinary two- and three-stringed fiddles, played cello-wise, in a sitting position;

the *chakay*, a kind of horizontal zither which shares its shape – and its name – with the crocodile; the *khong wong yai*, a circular rack of tuned gongs, often principal bearer of the melody; an array of drums; and the silvery *ching*, the finger cymbals, whose stroke keeps the ensemble together and marks off the music's formal divisions: enough, I think, to indicate the range of instrumental families and colours.

But that is not all. The group will also be bringing with them some dancers, who will provide the all-important dance dimension which is an indispensable part of so much Thai music. Their bejewelled costumes and headdresses are among the most intricate in the world, reflecting the intricacy of the dancers' movements. The dancers have to be hand-sewn into these costumes before each performance, an operation that may take ten times longer than the duration of the dance itself.

Thai classical music and poetry are replete with images of waterfalls and peacocks, of opulent palaces and luxuriant vegetation; and although I cannot guarantee that all those components will be assembled in the Albert Hall, I can promise that the Thai musicians, singers and dancers will come very close indeed to making them materialize before our astonished eyes and ears.

II

David Morton, the American scholar who is the leading Western authority on Thai music, has written that, historically,

> Thai culture in general has borrowed elements from all the surrounding cultures [e.g. Chinese, Indian, Cambodian, Indonesian, etc.]. These elements have been adapted and combined by the Thai with their own culture to produce a blend that is unique and not to be confused with any of the neighbouring cultures.

Morton further remarks that –

> Few if any Western music influences have penetrated the traditional

> Thai music system, probably because Thai musicians [in early times] were protected within the court and isolated from Western music. The only Western music to have been heard in Thailand . . . was that of an occasional military band.[2]

We shall try here to touch on a few aspects of Thai music that contribute to the uniqueness rightly mentioned by Mr Morton; but at the same time we want to emphasize that what you are going to hear is indeed music, to be experienced, savoured and tasted through the ear, and above all to be enjoyed, like the many other kinds of music with which we may be more familiar. But to an audience that has just absorbed Birtwistle and Messiaen,[3] we cannot believe that Thai music will present any insurmountable hurdles.[4] (Moreover, in some items our ears will be helped by our eyes, as we watch the exquisite Thai dancers who will be taking part with the musicians.)

First, a few notes about what Mr Morton calls 'the traditional Thai music system'. The Thai octave, if it can be so described, is subdivided into seven equidistant pitches. Thus in the Thai diatonic scale there are no tones or semitones, as in ours. The fourth and fifth degrees, however, are quite close to the fourth and fifth of the tempered Western octave. Thai melodies are basically pentatonic, arising from the rare use in Thai music of the seventh degree and avoidance of the fourth degree. 'The effect of such a music', Professor Phra Chen Duriyanga has written,[5] 'is then similar to that composed on the basis of a pentatonic scale.' Incidentally, although Thai music is not harmonic or tonal in any Western sense, there is a complex practice of switching between pitches – with each pitch of the pentatonic scale functioning as the 'tonic' of the new scale or 'mode' – which might be thought of as a form of modulation.

The characteristic texture of Thai ensemble music is heterophonic – an 'imprecise unison', as Adorno memorably remarked in another context altogether[6] – and thus adheres to a central oriental tradition and technique. The main melody in ensemble music is often entrusted to the circular rack of tuned gongs, the *khong wong*, the melodic and sonorous heart of the Thai ensemble. The other instruments, at other speeds, weave varied and sometimes syncopated versions of melody around, about and above the *khong wong*, and the result is often counterpoint of great energy, elaboration and brilliance. The *dynamic* level of Thai music is generally somewhat undifferentiated, or may sound so, to Western ears used to bolder dynamic levels and contrasts. But the dynamic nuances achieved, whether by woodwind, strings, or percussion, can be of the subtlest order, especially in the solo repertoire where a performer's *thang* – best described as the impress of the technical skill and creative imagination that an individual performer brings to bear on the melody in question – is all important. Remember, too, the scale of sound is not that of a Western orchestra or ensemble. As so often, however, small is indeed beautiful.

Thai music is almost invariably in duple metre – so don't expect any lilting three-in-a-bar! And there are three basic tempi: slow, moderate and fast. The basic tempi are established by the all-important player of the *ching*, the small finger-cymbals, whose beat keeps the ensemble together (there are no conductors in Thai classical music!), defines the tempo of the broad sections of the music, and also marks those crucial formal junctures when one tempo gives way to another. In short, form and tempo in Thai music are intimately related.

One of the most important forms in Thai music is the *thao*, a variation form which falls into a sequence of three sections: the *sam chan*, the *song chan* and the *chan dio*. The *thao* is sometimes known as a 'telescopic' variation form because of the proportional relationship between its sections. The *sam chan*, the first and longest variation we hear, is double the length of the succeeding *song chan* variation, which represents the original composition or melody on which the *thao* is based (what we might think of as the 'theme', but in the *thao* placed in the middle of the set). There then follows the *chan dio*, the final variation, which halves the length of the preceding variation, the *song chan*. Thus there is a strict mathematical relation – a constant process of diminution – between the three sections.

The same kind of relationship governs the changes in tempo, i.e. the tempo of the fast and short final variation, the *chan dio*, is twice as fast as the moderato of the preceding *song chan*; and since increases in tempo are registered by increased strokes, the *song chan* doubles the strokes of the opening *sam chan*, while the stroke is quadrupled in the concluding *chan dio*. Hence the importance of the *ching* as formal indicator (as well as quasi-metronome). You can locate your place on the formal map by reference to the number of *ching* strokes to a bar.

There is not space on this occasion to attempt a description of the various types and constitutions of Thai ensembles. But the programme tonight will in fact offer a rich sampling of the textures and sonorities that characterize Thai classical music.

NOTES

1 MC: The concert (Prom 35) was given by the Thai Classical Music Group of Srinakharinwirot University, Bangkok, at the Royal Albert Hall on 22 August 1981. BBC2 also made a film of the occasion (director: Barrie Gavin; broadcast on 6 February 1982) in the closing shots of which DM and his colleague from Bangkok, Dacre Raikes, may be seen reinforcing the group's percussion section. This was undoubtedly DM's Albert Hall début!

2 David Morton, *The Traditional Music of Thailand* (University of California Press, Berkeley, California, 1976), and the 'Thailand' entry in *New Grove* (Macmillan, London, 1980), pp. 712–13.

3 MC: Thai classical music occupied the third part of a tripartite concert: the earlier parts had been devoted to performances of Birtwistle's *For O, for O, the Hobby Horse is Forgot* (UK première) and Messiaen's *L'Ascension* (organ version).

4 MC: DM's optimism was misplaced: the Thai music presented a very real 'insurmountable hurdle' for none other than Hans Keller. Reviewing the concert for the *Listener* on 3 September 1981, Keller declared:

> In view of the Proms' chronic neglect of works from the very centre of our own musical culture, was it right to be introduced to the Thai Classical Music Group of Srinakharinwirot University Bangkok? . . .
>
> I approached the event with maximal humility, as a guilt-laden cultural foreigner who had not grown up with the music's terms of spontaneous

reference, only to discover early on that the unnotated sounds that reached my ears by way of admirable virtuoso performances were primitive music *par excellence* – demonstrably so in both the rhythmic and melodic dimension. Melodically, though we had to cope with a scale of seven equidistant notes whose relation to our own diatonic scale forced us to refocus our attention on unfamiliar intervals, it soon became apparent that the music suffered from a double lack of differentiating development.

For one thing, pitch differentiation was, to put it mildly, crude: pitches which, emerging from different instruments, were treated as identical, weren't really – but to the players' ears, such distonation didn't seem to matter . . .

Rhythmically, elementary simplicity was maintained through a preference for, indeed often the exclusive use of, equal note values – with, again, a proportionately high (sometimes maximal) rate of predictability . . .

Our evaluation of such music (pre-music in my own musical world view) and of its possible role in our lives must needs depend on the importance we attach to the visual component of the total experience. What made the Prom as a whole uncanny . . . was that the Western rest of the evening shared [the] Thais' predilection for equal values, for pulse, metre . . .

DM can no longer trace the letter he must have written to rebuff Keller's extraordinary application of critical criteria quite inappropriate to non-Western music, but on 6 November Keller sent him the following intransigent reply:

I am deeply fascinated by the possibility of 'disagreement' ab't the Thai music: after all, I conscientiously refused to evaluate, & what can one disagree about except one's respective judgements?

Equally conscientiously, I listed facts ab't (a) the material and (b) its creative use on this occasion: are you suggesting that I misheard one or the other factual detail? I doubt that very much, not because I consider myself incapable of a mistake, but because thru'out the performance, I put hasty factual predictions on a piece of paper (in red, whereas observations were in black), every single one of which was duly met.

As I hope I made clear, I am the last to consider myself entitled to judge music which isn't in my bones – with which, so far as its elements are concerned, I wasn't familiar (i.e. which I c'dn't sing) before I c'd speak. I anxiously hope that you didn't perceive judgement where none was intended & none, in my submission, passed.

About there being more music in the Thai part than in the 1st ½ you can't hope to find me disagreeing; I even found more music, within the 1st ½, in the very insubstantial piece of our contemporary (where, however, not much substance was intended: I talked to him) than in the contemporary classic's non-event.

5 Phra Chen Duriyanga, *Thai Music* (Fine Arts Department, Bangkok, 1976), p. 41.

6 MC: Adorno's remark referred to Mahler. See DM's discussion of this quotation on p. 184.

VI

Unwritten Music of the Heart

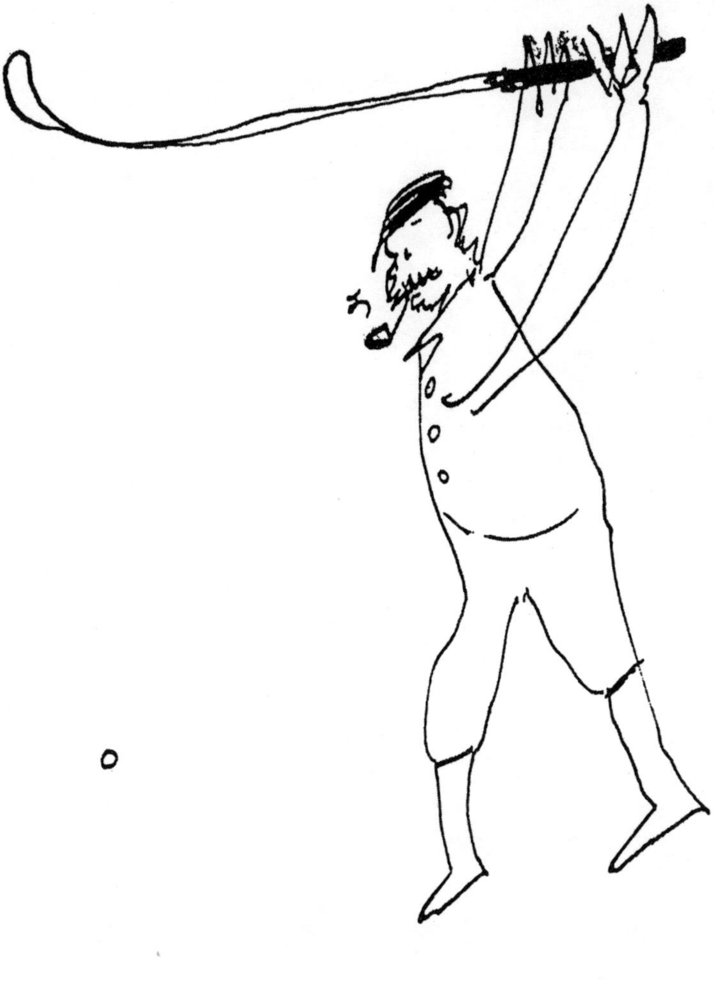

Edward Elgar drawn by Elgar, 1900

Elgar and the English Oratorio

No major injustice is done to Elgar if we view his output as bounded on the one hand by the Cello Concerto (1919) and on the other by the *'Enigma' Variations* (1898) and the *Dream of Gerontius* (1899–1900). It was appropriate that Elgar's maturity should have been ushered in, as it were, on the shoulders of two great works, one instrumental, the other choral – in each category Elgar was to give of his best. And yet there is a paradox at the heart of the apt coincidence. *Gerontius* was, in a limited sense, prepared in a number of earlier choral works, both sacred and secular: it is possible to discern a continuity of intention in Elgar's art that eventually facilitated the birth of a masterpiece. The same may not be said of his instrumental music. Where do we find the precedents in Elgar's immaturity for the accomplishment of the *'Enigma' Variations*, the concertos, the symphonies? These works, in fact, set their own precedents – more than that, they fulfilled those precedents to their limits: the singular nature of Elgar's symphonic achievement resides, in part, in his successful establishment and consummation of a tradition within a tradition-less environment. There was no English tradition to nourish the symphonies. *Gerontius*, at least, was backed up by a lively national choral life, by an appetite for oratorio that often, in more senses than one, devoured the many composers it stimulated.

Odder still, although this oratorio was, unlike the instrumental works, ostensibly attached to a native breeding-ground, *Gerontius*

Listener, 28 February 1957

remained something of a solitary gesture. It was succeeded, of course, by many individual choral works, most of them slight, but two of them, *The Apostles* (1902–3) and *The Kingdom* (1905), substantial; but neither of these oratorios, despite many magnificent passages, kindled the public enthusiasm as *Gerontius* had done and does, nor as the series of instrumental works did and still do.

The third of the oratorios Elgar planned to write – and thus complete his trilogy – was abandoned, and the very fact that *The Last Judgment* (a probable title) was never brought to completion is suggestive of Elgar's curious relation to the English oratorio tradition. One would have thought that in this sphere of all spheres the 'English' composer *par excellence* – or at least one claimed and revered as such by his countrymen – would have plundered the vein more liberally. Yet his great trilogy petered out, and its first two parts, falling short in any case of the achievements of *Gerontius*, are only spasmodically revived; nor have the many secular cantatas and choral *pièces d'occasion* secured a firm grip upon the attention of wider audiences.

It is, ultimately, *Gerontius* that has to bear the weight of Elgar's reputation as a composer of oratorio. Yet more than one instrumental work – to return to my original paradox – will serve as evidence of his symphonic prowess. His musical environment, on the other hand, would have encouraged us to expect the reverse situation – the symphony as the 'sport', the oratorio as the familiar event. The peculiar isolation of Elgar's *Gerontius* should provoke us to review our attitude to the work, in particular to test its status as an 'English' oratorio.

The particular success of *Gerontius* owes, I think, nothing to English tradition – at the most, perhaps, its commission (for the Birmingham Festival of 1900), in which the characteristic English love for the large-scale choral work is explicit; but *Gerontius* had been in Elgar's mind 'simmering' (as Miss McVeagh, a perceptive biographer, puts it)[1] for some eleven years. It was, of course, the power and originality of Elgar's talent that made *Gerontius* the great work it is: that it became the crown of English oratorio was, so to speak, fortuitous, an accident of genius – all the more of an accident when one considers how unexpected and atypical a phenomenon Elgar is in the history of English music. It was not likely, in any event, that *Gerontius* would have grown out of the English oratorio tradition that, as *Grove IV* concisely has it, with Arne's death in 1778 entered 'on a century of artistic darkness': there may have been gleams of light in Parry's oratorios from the 1890s, but it is doubtful whether his debilitating good taste and timid eclecticism served as springboards for Elgar's bold cosmopolitanism and emotional swagger. The English, moreover, are much too prone to treat the oratorio as if it were a peculiarly English form.

The welcome *Gerontius* received in Germany and Strauss's praise[2] make their own comment on the wholesale cosmopolitanism of Elgar's mature style. A derivative composer he was not – on the contrary, the flavour of his personality is strong and pervasive – but it would be perverse to deny his indebtedness to Wagner and many another European master. Would *Gerontius* have been possible without *Parsifal* as a dramatic precedent? The European climate that *Gerontius* inhabits lifts the work out of its English context and places it where it belongs (and where, incidentally, Elgar belongs) – in the great Continental tradition from which, *nota bene*, emerged oratorios as diverse as Berlioz's *L'enfance du Christ*, Franck's *Les béatitudes*, Liszt's *St Elisabeth* and *Christus*, and even Brahms's *Requiem*. It is when seen 'away' rather than 'at home' that Elgar appears in the round as a major European figure.

Englishness is difficult to define in musical terms. I do not believe we shall find anything in *Gerontius* to initiate an attempted analysis. Word-setting is certainly one way in which a composer may publish his birth certificate: his response to a specific turn of speech, to the rhythm of his own language, may result in an idiosyncratic musical equivalent that could not have derived from another tongue. But can one claim that Elgar's treatment of his texts in *Gerontius* is anything more than always adequately sensitive to their contents? Word-painting, that so often leads to characteristically indigenous melodic shapes and rhythms, was not

Elgar's *forte*. He relied on the memorable and repeatable melodic tag or leading motif, active in close partnership with a generous flow of varied harmonic textures, to carry the burden of the message. It is, in a very real sense, the orchestra in *Gerontius* that makes the 'word' explicit.

There is nothing here that bestows an Englishness upon *Gerontius*; and further to intensify what, from the English point of view, is an isolated masterwork, is the oratorio's own isolation in relation to the main body of Elgar's music. This is not the place or the occasion to attempt a musical character-analysis of Elgar's personality, but the foreboding, the feverish nervousness, the intimations of mortality, the morbid shuddering, all so wonderfully expressed in *Gerontius* – more successfully than the consoling affirmations, I think – are conspicuously absent from Elgar's customary mode of utterance, where rhetorical affirmation is, in general, the rigorous order of the day.

It is, I believe, the 'sense of ruin' released in *Gerontius* but suppressed elsewhere – psychologically sanctioned in the oratorio by the doctrinal authority of Newman's text – that constitutes the work's special inspiration and lends it the special status it must assume among Elgar's great works. An overpowering note of agony he sounded once and once only, in *Gerontius*, Part II. The Soul's cry, 'Take me away', is not only profoundly moving but also a profoundly original musical conception. How intelligent Elgar was to register the impact of the blinding 'glance of God' in the searing force of Gerontius' reaction to it. A. J. Jaeger wanted something more ambitious. His arguments were sensible, but Elgar's solution of the problem is eloquent of the sense and sensibility of his genius.

NOTES

1 Diana McVeagh, *Elgar* (Dent, London, 1955), p. 29.
2 MC: See p. 293 below.

Some Thoughts on Elgar

It is a commonplace that Elgar's reputation has suffered a certain decline. His music, to put it crudely, is a little out of fashion. I doubt whether we shall ever again experience the musical atmosphere – perhaps 'social' or 'cultural' would be the better word – in which public enthusiasm for his music will call for performances that stagger one in their sheer numerical extravagance. (I have in mind the reception of the First Symphony: in England alone, 'nearly one hundred performances in its first year'.)[1]

Demand, at this pitch, is unlikely to recur. On the other hand, Elgar remains widely played and widely cherished – hence my cautious choice of adjectives above, 'certain' and 'little'. He may, to a degree, be out of fashion, but he is not out of favour. In the not very long roll of great English composers he continues to wear his greatness without discomfort, without serious challenge. The 'fashion' that has, in a sense, contributed to Elgar's unfashionableness has been this very assumption of his significant calibre, an assumption more in the nature of passive tribute than the result of active acquaintance with the manifestation of his greatness that resides in his music. There is a real danger, I think (at least in my generation), of simply taking Elgar for granted – a polite expression for what elsewhere might be termed indifference or neglect. If I have a wish for this centenary year, it is that we should be prodded into a genuine recognition, rather than a mere admission, of Elgar's genius.

Music and Letters 38/2 (April 1957), pp. 113–23

I have no immodest wish to indulge in autobiography on such an occasion, but a personal event may illustrate how fashion and a hardened habit of mind may combine to Elgar's disadvantage. I was invited, recently, to participate in a series of broadcasts (for consumption in a Commonwealth country) entitled *Twentieth-Century Masterpieces*. Each contributor was asked to offer three works by different composers. It did not take me more than a moment's thought to jot down my three composers' names (the works are of no importance here): Mahler, Stravinsky and Britten. The trinity, I well realize, represents not only personal inclination but fashion – we are all children of our time – besides, of course, what I hope is a measure of good judgement. It was not until long after, when reading through the complete list of chosen 'masterpieces', with its inevitable omissions, that I noted that Elgar was absent; and it was then that I suddenly – and guiltily – realized that I might have promoted Elgar as a candidate had the thought occurred to me – but it hadn't. Since I am a warm-hearted admirer of Elgar's music and since the programmes themselves were liberally conceived – there was none of that inverted parochialism about them that concentrates solely on progressive Continental masters, and a work, to qualify, only required to be composed after 1900 – I am obliged to attribute my forgetfulness not just to fashion but to that slack taking-for-granted turn of mind that can effectively bury a composer while ostensibly keeping his memory green.

Looked at from the 'masterpiece' point of view, it would seem to me that almost any one of Elgar's major works written between 1900 and 1919 – *Gerontius*, either of the two symphonies, *Falstaff*, the Violin or Cello Concerto (the *'Enigma' Variations* just miss the chronological boat) – would have deserved a place amid masterpieces composed after 1900. 'Twentieth-century masterpiece', however, implies something other than something simply written *after* 1900, and here, perhaps, we uncover some excuse for not immediately shouting 'Elgar!' in a twentieth-century context.

If we examine the careers of three of Elgar's leading European contemporaries, Strauss, Mahler and Reger, all of them born long before the turn of the century and creatively active – substantially so – after it, we find that in relation to them, or to their works rather, 'twentieth-century' takes on another colour: their music, in fact, has coloured, in a very real sense, the century. The transition from Reger to Hindemith, for instance, is an obvious one,[2] while Mahler's influence is evident not only in the younger generation of his day – Berg, Schoenberg – but in the younger generation of our own – Copland, Britten, Shostakovich. The question of masterpieces apart, there is no denying the fact that both Reger and Mahler (Strauss, perhaps, to a lesser degree, though one cannot under-estimate the radical character of *Elektra*) not only anticipated certain prominent trends in twentieth-century music proper but actually assisted in the creation of our twentieth-century musical language.

The same can scarcely be said of Elgar, either from a European angle or from an English one. His successors here, in so far as he has had any, have been minor creative figures who have cultivated only very minor aspects of his genius – its secondary characteristics, not its breadth or depth (for example, the whimsicality of the *Serenade* for strings; not the heroic poetry of the symphonies or the human insight of *Falstaff*). Our two composers of weight who have responded to Elgar are Bliss and Walton, both of whom, oddly enough, set out as innovators rather than conservatives, and both of whom, far from being born out of Elgar, have, as it were, regressed *into* him: their Elgarian characteristics represent a dilution of their once specifically 'modern' aspirations. In either case, Elgar's influence has entered the scene as a portent of relaxation.

We must not, of course, measure Elgar's stature by the failings of others; and there is no rule that obliges the great composer to contain within him the seeds that flower in a succeeding generation. None the less, the remoteness, for our century, of Elgar's idiom does stress his singular isolation as a composer. That he had no hand in forming the musical language of our own day, if in no way justifying our tendency to pass him by, memorial-wise, with hat raised, is one more factor that conditions a prevalent neglectful attitude: our present does not forcibly remind us of what Elgar has contributed to our past.

No sooner does one make a generalization than a qualification is entailed, and qualifications are legion when discussing a composer as enigmatic as Elgar. In two respects, without doubt, he foreshadowed a future that *is* our present. His sheer competence – his technical *brio* (a fundamental part of his musical character!) – set a precedent in the orchestral sphere whose value we can begin to appreciate today: the impact may be a distant one, but Elgar's wellnigh single-handed rescue of English music and the English musician from a slough of provincialism and insipid eclecticism echoes on in the highly professional accomplishments of the younger school of English composers. Then again his patent cosmopolitanism – once more a postponed influence – while reflecting his own time (more of this below) no less anticipates the widespread cosmopolitanism that is the distinguishing feature of present-day English music: a postponed influence, because the nationalist revival intervened. (It had to intervene, historically speaking, otherwise we should have had no national tradition from which, as now, to diverge and evolve.) It was the eclectic Holst's misfortune to proffer a cosmopolitanism when it was a suspect practice. It was Elgar's misfortune, too, in so far as his style could provide the basis for no national school, a style, in addition, that was to be partly discredited by the twentieth century's revulsion from a typically nineteenth-century mode of utterance.

Small wonder that from this complex historical situation Elgar's reputation did not emerge altogether unimpaired. Nor, for that matter, did the reputations of his European colleagues, all of whom, especially, perhaps, Mahler and Strauss, found themselves with a foot in either century; but Mahler, in his late symphonies, Strauss intermittently (only at his best) and even Reger in his middle period succeeded, if I may change the metaphor midstream, in making themselves bilingual – at home, as it were, in either century – something that Elgar was never able to do. (It is valid, I think, to stick to comparisons with Austro-German contemporaries: no stretch of the imagination can relate Elgar to the new French school led by Debussy. The influence of the Wagnerian Franck is, of course, altogether another story.)

I do not drag in Mahler, Strauss or Reger to disparage Elgar: indeed, if driven, I would place Elgar as a composer greater than two of these eminent contemporaries, judging him, moreover, as a European rather than an English artist. But a point of substance rests in, say, Mahler's capacity not only to accommodate himself to the twentieth century but to advance its cause. (Elgar's two symphonies, as it happens, coincide chronologically with Mahler's last (complete) three and *Das Lied von der Erde*.) It may well be asked: what is demonstrated by exposing the obvious enough differences between Mahler's style and Elgar's? (I choose Mahler, rather than Strauss, because of the mutual symphonic link.) The answer falls into two main parts that might be entitled 'Convention' and 'Tradition', both of which, I believe, throw light on the nature of Elgar's achievement and the physiognomy of his art, while 'Convention', in addition, raises the question of how English, idiomatically speaking, Elgar really was.

Let me take this last point first. Elgar's public success in Germany, Strauss's famous praise, Hans Richter's well-known judgement of the First Symphony (Richter, at this very time, had been dislodged by Mahler from the Vienna Opera: it is curious how the strands of musical history intertwine) – these eminently *European* appraisals confirm what was, in fact, the case: that Elgar's convention was thoroughly post-Wagnerian in character, English, in any stylistic sense, hardly at all.

It has, I must confess, always astonished me that Elgar has been so strenuously claimed as a representative English figure; he has never struck me as such, and were I, in a state of aural innocence, confronted with, say, the middle pair of movements from either of his symphonies and asked to guess the composer's country of origin, England, I think, would be the last place that I should light upon. I should recognize, I hope, the impress of a most powerful and original personality, evident in no end of unique mannerisms ('Elgarian' could be defined in a dictionary of music by the use of music examples alone), but I doubt whether the Englishness of it would have offered me a clue sufficiently pronounced to solve the question correctly. Is there not something of a paradox here? That the composer who became a spokesman, in music, for a whole national era, was intimately bound up with a convention so wholeheartedly foreign? The paradox is all the more striking when one remembers how suspicious was the succeeding national school, prompted by Vaughan Williams in word and deed, of Continental influences.

Elgar, as we know, aided and abetted by some tiresome friends, did everything possible to play, in life, the part of the Kiplingesque Englishman rather than the artist. The stiff upper lip only rarely quivered, and when it did – as in the extraordinary *folies de doute* that pursued him in connection with the Peyton Professorship – we catch a glimpse of a nervous, feminine, even neurotic sensibility that intermittently – but always very interestingly – breaks out in the music. More so than with most great composers, Elgar the man and musician walked different paths. Perhaps his disinclination to expose his nerves, except under violent creative pressure, may be accounted an English characteristic – certainly this reticence marks him off from his European contemporaries. It also, to a degree, circumscribed the range of his feelings, and thus limited his expressiveness – some regions of feeling were taboo – and the potential versatility of his talent. But that emotional frigidity which is, perhaps, part of the English make-up, inherent or inculcated, was no part of Elgar's musical personality, as distinct from the face he wore in public. He was as frankly emotional as any late nineteenth-century composer in the great Romantic tradition. His 'vulgarity', in part an asset, I might add, speaks for itself as a manifestation of emotional liberation, though, as I shall attempt to show, Elgar was not in some respects liberated enough.

But if, as I believe, Elgar's English character is partly mythical, it is also partly musical, not, to be sure, in the character of his invention, but in its identification with a climate of national belief. There was, indeed, a two-way identification, not only Elgar's convinced committal to what we may generally term 'imperial' topics (the *Coronation Ode*, *Crown of India*, *Spirit of England* and the rest) – to this extent he was English of his period through and through – but the public's immediate and enthusiastic adoption of the music (Elgar in his pomp-and-circumstance guise) as the perfect vehicle for the mass expression of current national sentiment. Thus his not in any sense peculiarly English style was endowed with a fervent Englishness, an assertive patriotism, through what was, basically, the chance association of an eminently serviceable and sympathetic idiom with a dynamic social force. There was nothing, of course, essentially English in the power sentiments of Edwardian imperialism, colonialism, etc.; any like national group, given a similar historical context, would have expressed its power complex in identical terms and, at the same time, laid claim to those terms' uniqueness – hence their 'superiority', which, in turn, confirms and promotes the group's self-confidence. Most group behaviour, moreover, runs along parallel lines. Does not Strauss, for example, in *his* dreadful ceremonial pieces, emerge as Elgar's twin, in more senses than one?

It is Elgar's occasional music that has dated – inevitably so, since the kind of social ideals with which it became inextricably involved have little validity for our own day. I believe, none the less, that the best of his occasional pieces will survive as more than mere historical documents, though the reason for their survival – the quality of their invention and strength of character (the best *Pomp and Circumstance* marches, for example, are profoundly Elgarian, very much of a piece, despite their simplicity, with his major music) – hinders rather than facilitates a genuine revaluation of his status: in hearing (rightly) a precise relation between his major and minor works, we incorporate, to his detriment, the period feelings aroused by the latter into our response to the former. Thus Elgar's most important and complex works, however remote their social connotations, are coloured by – damaged by – a pre-determined attitude of mind on the part of the listener. We tend to hear – and condemn as 'dated' – trends in his music that, by the standards of the convention within which he created, are wholly unexceptionable: it is the extra-musical significance they have been obliged to bear – their national social symbolism – that obscures the issue, that prevents us from hearing the music, as it were, straight; and at the root of this confusion lies the muddling relation between his committed (minor) and non-committed (major) art, with our extra-musical response to the one infecting our approach to the other.

A similar act of transference results in our hearing an explicit voice of England embedded not only in the occasional music but in the symphonies and concertos. *Falstaff*, perhaps, is a special case. But though I would not deny the penetration of Elgar's portrait, its manner of execution is cosmopolitan, or, more exactly, Straussian (more brilliant and original in its parts than a Strauss symphonic poem, I think, but as a big structure less successful than Strauss's best). If penetration of dramatic character were the test of national spirit, would not Verdi's *Falstaff* be the most English of operas? There is not space here to pursue further the beguiling problem of Elgar's Englishness. It remains my view that to find Elgar today specifically English in flavour is to expose oneself as the victim of a type of collective hallucination, an achievement, incidentally, that has had its consequences abroad. After all, Elgar has not always been considered a local genius: witness his early European successes, successes that preceded his popularity at home. Now, he is 'not for export'. Our conviction that he is a home-grown product has not only hoodwinked ourselves but those elsewhere, whose familiarity with this convention in fact had facilitated their early recognition of his outstanding talent.

I hope that my commentary on the very singularity of Elgar's reputation as an English composer will in itself have emphasized the cosmopolitanism of his convention – that despite what he called his 'peremptorily' English name, his idiom evolved from a tradition of which he gave an account in letters dating from his visit to Leipzig in 1883: 'I heard no end of stuff. Schumann principally and Wagner no end. They have a good opera in Leipzig and we went many times'; or, 'I got pretty well dosed with Schumann (my ideal!), Brahms, Rubinstein and Wagner, so had no cause to complain'.[3]

The derivation of a composer's convention is, of course, altogether of less importance than an analysis of what he makes of it. Elgar, there is no doubt, succeeded to a very intense degree in expressing his personality in music that is demonstrably his and his alone. On the other hand, his use of his chosen language, while minutely moulded to the contours of his personality, is not markedly original. (The distinction between originality of style and idiosyncrasy of idiom is a fine one, but I think it can be made.) But not only personal factors shape a composer's style, as important – perhaps overridingly important – as these are (for instance, Elgar's emotional inhibitions, which, one day, must be subjected to full-scale examination [see pp. 269–94]): there are also historical considerations to be taken into account, which, in his case, significantly conditioned the style.

Since Elgar's basic convention, his vocabulary, had so much in common with that of his European contemporaries, there is much to be gained by a brief comparison of his work with theirs. The introduction of Strauss and Mahler clarifies the picture, illuminates Elgar's characteristics – and, I believe, in isolating them, does something to explain why he wrote the kind of music he did. While his idiosyncrasies have been both recognized and analysed, the influence of his historical environment and the nature of the pressures exerted by personal factors have not. A complete understanding of his musical character, however, depends upon some understanding of the formative agents involved in the make-up of his personality.

Let us see where Elgar differs from Mahler or Strauss and attempt to nail down the reasons for the differences. For a start, Elgar's European colleagues were not only idiosyncratic in idiom but also original – original, that is, in the sense (my sense, when I use the word in this article) that each anticipated, practised and furthered the evolution of established twentieth-century procedures of composition: Strauss's and Mahler's inspired harmonic adventures, for instance, or Mahler's late contrapuntal style, a consequence of his tonal emancipation. Has anyone remarked upon the absence of counterpoint in Elgar's music, except on a few set occasions, in the *Introduction and Allegro* or *Gerontius* and particularly *Falstaff*? It was a general feature of music at the turn of the century: counterpoint (Reger!) came in as tonality went out, the logic of independent parts prevailed as harmonic progressions lost their structural functions. That Elgar's music did not develop a genuinely linear contrapuntal character is symptomatic of his relatively low degree of harmonic tension: counterpoint, as it were, was not forced upon him by tonal disintegration. His greatest gift, on the other hand, his rich flow of melody, was promoted by – depended upon – his harmonic stability.

The temptation to pursue stylistic contrasts is acute, but I must resist it. I do not believe it would be difficult to demonstrate with a wealth of convincing detail that, say, Mahler's Ninth Symphony (1908–10) was, in tendency, progressive, whereas Elgar's Second (1910–11) was conservative, despite, let me repeat, a shared basic vocabulary. (I must stress that neither 'progressive' nor 'conservative' is intended as a value judgement.) But I am assuming here the validity of that contention, so far as style alone is concerned; and it is my purpose not to show the how but the why.

Personal factors, of course, play a part. Extensions of style meet the expressive challenge of new feelings; new sounds symbolize the uncovering of hitherto untapped sources of inspiration. There were many new sounds in Strauss, generated by such exploratory pieces as *Elektra* or *Salome*, many in Mahler, in his symphonies, which often present contents not previously encountered in music. It is important, too, to remember that it is often just when a new nerve is exposed that the composer is charged with vulgarity. But every revelation of this kind provokes a like shocked resistance, not only in the field of music; and what is vulgar for one generation is accepted by succeeding generations as a valid enlargement of feeling or knowledge, though doubtless they ride 'vulgar' hobby-horses of their own.

Elgar's conservative personality – self-imposed, as I believe it was in part – did not mean that he felt less deeply, but rather that the range of his feelings was inhibited: he did not plunge into those new regions of feeling that might have forced his style to widen its scope. That there were uncharacteristic elements in Elgar that he sternly suppressed I have no doubt: the volcanic eruption in the Second Symphony's scherzo-rondo has always suggested to me a side to Elgar's character the very opposite of his habitually affirmative self. What he wrote of his First Symphony – 'a *massive* hope in the future' – holds true of much of his assertive music, but here and there, fleetingly, when the hope breaks down, one glimpses a massive if deeply buried anxiety. (I sense it again in that oddly sinister tableau, *The Wagon Passes*, from the *Nursery Suite*.) It is difficult to speculate in this context, but it is my guess that had Elgar liberated himself from a host of protective emotional prohibitions and permitted his tensions to rise to the surface, he might well have responded with some out-of-character music that would have crossed the threshold of the new century in style, not chronology alone. As it was, Elgar lavished a maximum of unleashed feeling only in his most *nobilmente* mood; while his choice of occasion for a total liberation from restraint is revealing, the concentration of feeling released with such violence was all too often disproportionate and damagingly tasteless in effect. Elgar's feelings, in short, were sometimes bigger than the occasion demanded, either in the explicitly occasional music or in the implied drama of the symphonies (e.g. the *grandioso* conclusion of the First Symphony's finale). Hence Elgar's vulgarity is of a kind less functional than Mahler's or Strauss's (when on form); the searching, profoundly motivated feelings were there, but they became almost obsessively diverted into a narrow channel of '*massive* hope': protested so insistently, the security of that hope strikes one as perhaps more slenderly based than the affirmations would have us believe ('over-compensation', the psychologist might call it). Had Elgar's straining after nobility drained off less of his emotional energies, we might have heard more of the note of 'heroic melancholy' that impressed W. B. Yeats in the incidental music to *Grania and Diarmid*, and more, perhaps, of a pessimism that the emphatic optimism, one may think, seeks too often to conceal. But there can be no doubt that in one field – Elgar in his English *musical* context – the aggressively assertive character of his personality, its vulgarity in fact, aided him in the establishment of his unique voice.

It was, indeed, Elgar's vulgarity, the boldness and flashiness of his genius, that enabled him to break with the awful good taste of Parry, Stanford and the rest. Elgar, instead of revering the European classics and at the same time fearing them, instead of turning out page after page of polite but, in a final analysis, anonymous music, grasped the nettle with both hands: he accepted the late-Romantic convention, threw taste to the winds and succeeded in writing great music in established symphonic forms (he was no formal innovator) as full-blooded and pulsing with life as comparable gestures from Germany and Austria. It was a phenomenal achievement, the size of which must compel our continuing admiration. In a handful of big works Elgar challenged and, in some substantial respects, measured up to the accomplishments of Europe's great tradition. The size of his genius, of course, has something to do with the size of his achievement, but it is safe to say that his success would have been endangered had he not swept awe and taste aside and flourished without shame his, to put it crudely, creative 'guts'. Parry and Stanford – whose objectives, in the long run, were not so very different from Elgar's – were paralysed, bled white, by their fastidiousness. Elgar's 'vulgarity' saved him from their fate and facilitated his confident approach to his monumental task. We are indebted to it. Miss McVeagh states the matter concisely: 'Had he been more fastidious, he might well have been less great.'[4]

Most of what I have written above, including my commentary on Elgar's Englishness, has centred upon convention, its derivation and the personal forces that went to mould it. I wrote earlier that tradition, too, must be taken into account. Part of the phenomenon of Elgar rests in the very absence of a native tradition from which he might have evolved (hence his dependence on a European convention): the tradition-less character of his achievement only emphasizes its singularity. The fact, moreover, that he did not emerge from a tradition increases our understanding of the make-up of his convention, especially its relative orthodoxy when compared with Mahler's or Strauss's. For it was not only personal factors that conditioned the latter composers' expansions of their convention, any more than it was personal factors alone that inhibited the development of Elgar's. History, too, exerts influential pressures. Mahler and Strauss lived at the end, the tail end, of a great tradition: they inherited, in part, an exhausted convention. To develop new trends, new forms, new sounds, was an obligation: they had, in a very pressing sense, to originate, and originate hard, if they were to survive as independent voices. Elgar, on the other hand, was encumbered by no tradition. He could handle his more conventional convention with all the enthusiasm of an early starter; the convention simply had not aged for him as it had for his contemporaries in Europe. The oddity of his English situation spared him the necessity of composing, as it were, with history at his elbow. Free of the burden of a tradition; he was able, as an outsider – he owed England this much, at least – to employ a convention that had grown old elsewhere (and thus new!), at an earlier stage in its development; and the power and, indeed, originality of his musical personality charged his – from history's point of view – conventionalities with a conviction and spontaneity that will ride out any fluctuations in fashion.

What is generally accepted as an evil – the composer without a tradition – proved not to be so in Elgar's case; it is only in his chamber music that the absence of tradition is felt as a loss. A composer, I think, needs to be born out of an active chamber-musical tradition if, for example, he is to write a successful string quartet. Chamber music is a craft that has to be lived over a long period: it cannot be learned, as can orchestral technique, of which Elgar, of course, was a master. It is a pity that downright amateurishness of texture mars his String Quartet and Piano Quintet (the Violin Sonata is both more inspired and accomplished); a double pity because, along with the magnificent Cello Concerto, this group of chamber works – the classical challenge it represents is typical of Elgar's spirit – is the nearest we have to a late period. These works flounder badly, I fear, but they are deserving of study for their intermittent inspirations and their hints at the stylistic direction in which Elgar's art might have travelled had it not come to an abrupt stop. Whatever inhibition it was that here stifled Elgar's fertility, it cost us twenty years or so of potential music-making from a great English composer who, none the less, belongs in every best sense of the word to Europe: in that – his! – achievement should rest our pride.

NOTES

1 Diana McVeagh, *Elgar* (Dent, London, 1955), p. 50.
2 MC: See 'The Case of Max Reger II', pp. 63–5.
3 MC: See Jerrold Northrop Moore, *Edward Elgar: A Creative Life* (Oxford University Press, Oxford, 1984), p. 97. According to Moore, Elgar heard Schumann's *Overture, Scherzo and Finale*, First Symphony and Piano Concerto; Rubinstein's *Die Makkabäer* and *Ocean Symphony*; and Wagner's *Parsifal* (Prelude only), *Lohengrin* and *Tannhäuser* – all within the space of ten days in January 1883.
4 McVeagh, op. cit., p. 186.

To Alan Hollinghurst

The Composer Among the Monuments

By far the most interesting enigma of all was Elgar himself. Who was he? I am not by any means convinced that Jerrold Northrop Moore comes up with an answer, despite the length and detail of his biography.[1] Perhaps that would have been to expect too much of a work that assiduously collects the facts and attempts rather little in the way of interpreting them. (Dr Moore's observations on the music, to which I shall return, are conspicuously and blandly descriptive.) None the less his book provides us, for which we must be grateful, with ample material on which to base our own judgements, and he does not fail to include some of the most interesting judgements of others. Some of them are familiar and undeniably prejudiced, but not less interesting for that, like Osbert Sitwell's account of a peculiarly Elgarian occasion in 1927:

> I seem to recall that we saw from the edge of the river . . . and through an hallucinatory mist born of the rain that had now ceased, the plump wraith of Sir Edward Elgar, who with his grey moustache, grey hair, grey top hat and frock-coat looked every inch a personification of Colonel Bogey . . .[2]

And Sitwell ends by turning his attention to the audience:

> Most of them knew, I apprehend, as they listened so intently to the prosperous music of the Master, and looked forward to tea and hot buttered scones . . . and all kinds of little sandwiches and cakes, that this would prove their last outing of this sort. The glossy

---

The Times Literary Supplement, 14 September 1984, pp. 1011–12

motors waited outside to carry them home . . . Some of the motors were large and glossy as a hearse.

All very unfair, no doubt; but at the same time penetrating and (if one allows for the exaggeration) illuminating, in just the same way that I find Arnold Bax's memory of a visit to Elgar (in 1901) illuminating:

Hatless, dressed in rough tweeds and riding boots, his appearance was rather that of a retired army officer turned gentleman farmer than an eminent and almost morbidly highly strung artist. One almost expected him to sling a gun from his back and drop a brace of pheasants on the ground . . . On being told [by George Adler] that I intended to devote myself to composition Elgar had made no comment beyond a grimly muttered, 'God help him!'[3]

We have to remind ourselves that this was an impression of an Elgar twenty-six years younger than Sitwell's 'plump wraith', a pre-First World War model Elgar, a composer just forty-four years old. Moore assists our disbelief in these crusty-squire images of Elgar as representing the total truth about the composer by choosing as frontispiece a photograph which makes sense when read in relation to what remains for me one of the very best and most revealing observations of Elgar ever committed to paper. It was made by Ivor Atkins after a performance of *Froissart* at the Three Choirs Festival of 1890, when Elgar was playing the violin as well as undertaking the conducting of his overture. Atkins wrote:

Sinclair pointed out Elgar to me. There he was, fiddling among the first violins, with his fine intellectual face, his heavy moustache, his dark hair, his nervous eyes, and his beautiful sensitive hands.

And it was Atkins again who left us with a revealing note about Elgar at the piano:

In his home it was always a delight to hear him play the piano, for though he had no considerable technique he had a beautiful touch, delicate and full of personality – ideally suited to ring out the sensitive qualities of his own music. He had a way of giving the chords some fascinating shades of colour which seemed almost impossible to recapture.

Another Elgar altogether, one might think, and one would surely be right. Another Elgar, moreover, who was there, behind the mask of daunting, defensive moustache and tweeds, even on the most improbable occasions. How else does one explain the extraordinary occasion of a rehearsal for the opening ceremony, at Wembley on 23 April 1924, of the British Empire Exhibition:

I was standing alone (criticizing) in the middle of the enormous stadium in the sun: all the ridiculous court programme, soldiers, awnings etc: 17,000 men hammering, loud speakers, amplifiers – four aeroplanes circling over etc etc – all mechanical & horrible – no soul & no romance & no imagination. Here had been played the great football match – even the turf, which is good, was not there as turf but for football – but at my feet I saw a group of real *daisies*. Something wet rolled down my cheek – & I am not ashamed of it: I had recovered my equanimity when the *aides* came to learn my views – Damn everything except the daisy – I was back in something sane, wholesome & *gentlemanly* but only for two minutes.

Undone by daisies amid the monumental jingoism of Empire, King and Country: could one have predicted that of Elgar? The tear, surely, was real enough. But what about '*gentlemanly*'? How does one read that? Moore has nothing to say about it. Was it perhaps Elgar's characteristic recognition in the tiny flowers at his feet of a time past and immemorial, akin to Hardy's 'A time there was . . .', before the blight of feeling had touched the world? A recognition, none the less, which touched him into feeling. I was reminded often of Hardy while reading Moore's biography and especially by Elgar's incurable pessimism. There was surely something intensely Hardy-like about his remark to the consultant who visited him a few months before his death: 'He told me', recalled Arthur Thomson, 'that he had no faith whatever in an afterlife: "I believe there is nothing but complete oblivion."'

All this tells us what in any case the music tells us: that Elgar was a man and artist driven by seemingly irreconcilable and powerfully contrasted passions. It was precisely his fractured nature that made him and his music so interesting. But there can be no doubt that his conflicts made him a peculiarly difficult man to live with. I must confess to finding Lady Elgar a not particularly attractive figure. How on earth, one wonders, did the composer survive the cosiness and baby babble that one encounters in Alice's diary: 'E. dreffuly badly . . . E. raser better on arriving . . . E. still very porsley . . .', and so on, though to be fair, the heavy-handed mock gothic of Elgar's correspondence with Ivor Atkins is not much better (was it the donning of yet another Elgarian mask?). But one has to be sorry for Alice, for whom there seems good reason for believing that her husband's knighthood represented restoration of her former social status, when the wayward Elgar, despite having attended a rehearsal at the Abbey and despite his own recently awarded OM, inexplicably announced 'that he was not going to the Coronation and he refused to allow Alice to go either'. Lady Elgar, wrote a friend, 'whose devotion was proof against almost any humiliation, was really hurt by this prohibition'.

One has a glimpse there of Elgar's own conflict with himself, of one Elgar (perhaps the Elgar who was to be undone by the daisies in 1924) turning on the other (the Elgar too much preoccupied with pomp and circumstance). But there can be little doubt either that there was a great sensitivity in the man. We know that too from the music but perhaps it never found, or was never allowed to find, a wholly satisfying expression in his life. There is nothing I found more delicate or moving in *Edward Elgar: A Creative Life* – it is an incident Moore deals with extremely well – than the account of Elgar's late encounter (1931) with Vera Hockman: 'In Croydon to rehearse *Gerontius*, his eye caught that of a young woman at the second desk of the violins in the orchestra assembled from London Symphony and local players.' It was an extraordinary encounter, and the way Moore tells it brilliantly and painfully illuminates the loneliness of Elgar's old age and reveals a tenderness and gentleness in him that maybe had never shown themselves as they might have done in earlier years.

There was not only the personal isolation of Elgar's last years, especially after the death of Alice – 'You cannot fathom the loneliness & desolation of my life I fear,' he wrote to Atkins in 1920, and again, a year later, 'Everything is dead to me' – but his *musical* isolation. Moore does not spare us (nor should he have done) the details of half-empty halls, of fickle audiences and unsympathetic critics. (The exception in this last category was the remarkable Ernest Newman, and what Moore writes about him and his relationship with Elgar reminds us of a critic whose stature makes most present-day practitioners look puny.) The story of Elgar's being overtaken by the combined events of history (the First World War) and a radical swing in fashion makes uncomfortable reading: small wonder that he was obliged to stick to the image of the gruff, imperial and imperious public figure; more public monument than sentient man. One can only guess at the turmoil and turbulence within.

But what makes one hang one's head in shame, even at this late stage, is the awful tale of Elgar's treatment at the hands of his publisher. The amazing Jaeger, of course, is exempt from these strictures; but he was an editor and not part of the business, which seems to have been conducted with a repellent combination of meanness and timidity. Moore lays out for our inspection much of the correspondence between Elgar and Novello & Co. – it is undeniably one of the most interesting narrative threads running through his book – and thoroughly disagreeable it is to read of the financial humiliations to which the composer was subjected, at a time, incidentally, when the concept of the performing right, and the revenue flowing from it, had not been established. Elgar lived long enough to benefit from the starting up of the Performing Right Society and indeed was an early advocate of the cause. Composers may still have their proper grievances but to see how far we have travelled in recognizing the right of the musical creator to be rewarded – no, *paid* – for performances of his works, we only need to remind ourselves of Elgar's miserable haggling over shillings and pence. His 'God help him!' comment on Bax's ambition, read in this perspective, sounds more like compassion than disgruntlement.

There is no doubt that Elgar was an exceptionally complex and thus interesting man. No doubt too that the complexity can be attributed to specific events in many aspects of his singular life: the fact that he was a late developer; that he was self-made; that he was socially ambitious and yet at the same time sceptical or distrustful of the very society he eventually came to conquer; that he was insecure and a profound pessimist, and perhaps much obsessed by death. The list of singularities and paradoxes might be infinitely extended and debated, and challenged. But no amount of argument or competing interpretations could take Elgar's vivid temperament away from him. Moore certainly does not do that, but perhaps something rather more damaging. He succeeds, I am sure unintentionally, in imposing a kind of blandness on his descriptions of Elgar's music which leaves us not only uninformed about the works in any but the most superficial sense, but also surprised that a man so fascinating could have generated, judged by Moore's words, such unexciting, uneventful music. He is strong and rhapsodical on what he sees as a fundamental relationship between certain of Elgar's compositional methods and 'the patterns of nature in the countryside round Broadheath: gentle undulations of field and hedgerow, copse and dell – fruit trees planted in rows to make an orchard – the linked chain of the Malvern Hills . . .' and so on – and relies heavily, surely too heavily, on Elgar as the supreme embodiment of 'nostalgia', 'which Edward himself would come to prize above all else in his music. Posterity has agreed with him.'

I do not know whether that is entirely true. I am quite sure that I am not alone in finding a lot more in Elgar than the 'sunset quality' singled out by Newman and taken by Moore to excessive lengths: sometimes it appears as if it is the only idea he has in his head about Elgar's music. But if he is short on ideas about the *oeuvre* itself, he is also hardly riveting about the musical context and culture (or lack of it) in which Elgar perforce had to compose, and which were, to my way of thinking, a good deal more influential than the contours of the Malvern Hills.

A sense of that stifling society emerges most powerfully from *The Elgar–Atkins Friendship*.[4] All honour to the memory of Sir Ivor, who was a staunch and warm friend: the letters he wrote to Elgar after Alice's death, trying to encourage him to return to composing, make very touching reading. His son, who has put the massive book together, has created a worthy memorial to his father. But it also memorializes, although he cannot have expected it to, a suffocatingly parochial musical culture which causes one to wonder how Elgar was born out of it and how he managed to survive it as well as he did.

In both the Atkins and Moore volumes, there are accounts of concerts, details of programmes, of the musical experiences and activities that surrounded Elgar, which allow one a chilling glimpse of the prevailing taste. In 1878, at the Worcester Festival, Elgar played in a number of established choral and orchestral masterpieces by Handel, Haydn, Mozart and Mendelssohn, Spohr's *Last Judgment* 'and several modern English works. An oratorio entitled *Hezekiah* had been written by Dr Philip Armes of Durham . . . and there were choral settings by Sir Frederick Gore Ouseley and Sir John Stainer.' Elgar was to recall the works as 'meritorious' but lacking the feeling 'for orchestral effect and elasticity in instrumentation so obvious in the works of French, Italian and German composers'. Things were not much improved in 1911 (the year of Mahler's death), again at Worcester: Parry's Coronation *Te Deum* and Wagner's *Kaisermarsch*, an overture by Granville Bantock, Walford Davies's *Sayings of Christ* and W. H. Reed's *Variations* for string orchestra. Vaughan Williams's *Five Mystical Songs* must have come like a breath of air from another planet (well, almost).

I do not recite these details to scoff but to illustrate the claustrophobic and provincial climate of musical England in the years when Elgar was acquiring his technique and that had not much changed even when he was at the height of his powers before the First World War. I have mentioned Mahler in passing, and one thinks of Vienna and its astonishing and stimulating intellectual life before and after the turn of the century. There is absolutely no sense in any of the Elgar literature I have surveyed here of an intellectual life, of an adventurous life of the mind. What would Mahler's fate have been had he been born at Broadheath?

He might, I concede, have got along without the lively and inquiring intellectual climate that eventually surrounded him (it is significant, incidentally, that Mahler recognized the cultural energy, resource and promise of the United States and went to work there, while Elgar, at his crustiest, loathed the place). But musically? There, I suggest, is the rub – and the nub. Mahler had at the disposal of *his* genius an incredibly rich tradition which still allowed for innovation and evolution. Vienna could be hostile, stuffy and provincial too; but there was always a continuing dialectic between orthodoxy and radical reform (or, come to that, revolution). For Mahler, moreover, to continue the comparison for one moment longer, there was the constant provocation and stimulus of the *formal* riches of the past and the potentialities they had for the present and the future.

At the disposal of Elgar's genius, alas, there were no comparable riches or stimuli: there was the pallid conservatism of Stanford (upon whom history has taken a proper revenge for his spiteful treatment of Elgar: it is the self-made, self-taught composer who has taken up a place in the top class, not his impeccably trained and bred adversary); the 'meritorious' works of mediocrities, and worst of all, an absence of the living, challenging forms to which Elgar's powerful creativity would surely have reacted.

It was perhaps something of a misfortune that Elgar was born where he was and in the midst of a musical community that cherished, cultivated and nourished to excess the idea of the oratorio. The big, sacred choral work was the prevailing musical form; and the pity of it was that of all forms, at least during the later decades of the nineteenth century and beyond, the oratorio was inherently the least interesting and most problematic, and the least productive of and responsive to new formal thinking – to new thought generally, in whatever area of composition. I am aware, naturally, that Elgar himself wrote one of the most powerful exceptions to the rule I am proposing (Schoenberg another). But the success and inspiration of *Gerontius* were the result of its having profound roots in Elgar's personality, and perhaps especially in an imagination for which the idea of death clearly had a quite particular resonance. It was more personal testament than tradition, and remarkably free of dilution by Malvern water. But what a tragic spectacle, when that personal commitment was discharged, to witness Elgar labouring away at two non-starters such as *The Apostles* and *The Kingdom*. Even his great skills could not endow those atrophied enterprises with life. One heaves a sigh of relief when he at last abandons the profitless, pointless struggle.

What distinguished *Gerontius* from an English tradition was its bold absorption of Continental models and influences – of Wagner in particular. It was doubtless this that caught Richard Strauss's ear and prompted his famous tribute to Elgar. In my view, the significance of the salute has been overdone. I do not doubt Strauss's genuine regard but at the same time one must recognize that it was natural for him to acknowledge in his fellow composer from England a manifestation of 'progressivist' tendencies, which were, to Strauss's ears, entirely of Continental origin, and of which Strauss himself was an exponent. In short, it was a back-hander as well as a compliment.

As with *Gerontius*, so with almost all else. Elgar had to seek his models, his forms, and stimulation, elsewhere. There was not much that he could take from the thin, complacent and narrow musical interests of the society that raised him (and later on, it must be said, with an equal, if different, narrowness, toppled him). That Elgar, compositionally, brought off what he did when, on so many occasions, he had virtually to start from scratch, is testament to the size and power of his genius. But it was his tragedy too that there was not more to help him, closer to hand. We might then have had many more major works and certainly far less creative energy devoted to wholly dubious and debatable – and trivial – ends.

Pauline Collett's little book[5] is scarcely essential reading, but it is very nicely done and whole-hogging Elgar fans will surely enjoy it. Moore's *Spirit of England*[6] is a well-illustrated short biography of Elgar, an ingenious reduction of his big book and much to be recommended. Only very occasionally does the inevitable compression seem to have led to a supremely clotted style, for example, 'Out of her husband's employment at the Catholic Church, Ann Elgar had formed a theological focus for her own aspirations.' A somewhat long-winded way, surely, of saying that Ann too, following her husband's example, became a Catholic?[7] As for the title of the book, it has an ironic ring about it for me, believing as I do that the 'Spirit of England' was precisely what made creative life difficult and sometimes impossible for one of our greatest composers.

NOTES

1 Jerrold Northrop Moore, *Edward Elgar: A Creative Life* (Oxford University Press, Oxford, 1984).

MC: All four books on Elgar reviewed by DM in this article had appeared in 1984 as part of the commemoration of the fiftieth anniversary of the composer's death.

2 MC: Osbert Sitwell, *Laughter in the Next Room* (Macmillan, London, 1949), pp. 196–7: quoted in Moore, op. cit., p. 775.

3 MC: Arnold Bax, *Farewell, My Youth* (Longmans, Green & Co., London, 1943), pp. 29–31: quoted in Moore, op. cit., pp. 353–4.

4 E. Wulstan Atkins, *The Elgar–Atkins Friendship* (David & Charles, Newton Abbot, 1984).

5 Pauline Collett, *An Elgar Travelogue* (Thames Publishing, London, 1984).

6 Jerrold Northrop Moore, *Spirit of England: Edward Elgar in his World* (Heinemann, London, 1984).

7 MC: Jerrold Northrop Moore subsequently wrote to the *Times Literary Supplement* and corrected DM on this matter of Catholicism in a letter published on 19 October 1984:

> Mr Mitchell is under the impression that Elgar's father preceded his mother in conversion to Catholicism (penultimate sentence in the review). But as both books clearly show, Elgar's father, despite his organist's job at the Catholic church of Worcester, was never at any time a Catholic. In fact, both of my books make clear that the parents' religious difference was a major factor in the young Edward's early experience.

Moore also took issue with DM's remarks on the subject of royalty payments, noting that, in later years,

> Novello paid Elgar a royalty of no less than 25 per cent on everything he wrote then. The publisher's generosity culminated in Elgar's affectionate friendship with the firm's Chairman.

To A.H.

Unwritten Music of the Heart

A singular confusion of names attended Elgar's friendship with Alice Sophia Caroline Stuart Wortley, daughter of the painter John Everett Millais, and wife of Charles Stuart Wortley, a prominent Conservative MP. Lady Elgar was herself not only another Alice but also another Caroline. When writing to Alice Stuart Wortley she addressed her sometimes as 'My dearest Namesake'.

After their first meeting, in 1902, Elgar wrote to his other Alice as 'Mrs Stuart Wortley' and continued thus until 1909, when he attempted a modulation to 'Carrie', the name by which she was known to her more intimate friends: 'That's what I hear other nice people say,' wrote Elgar, '& so why should not I? – I *may* be nice someday?' But this advance was rebuffed or at least not encouraged – it seems likely that the second Alice would not have welcomed too visible a manifestation, to other eyes, of an acceleration in the relationship – and it was to unadorned 'Alice' that Elgar reverted until, at length, music offered a way out of the tangle of discomfort and embarrassment: the 'Windflower' solution.

That music, finally, was the solvent is not surprising in view of the Wortleys' musical accomplishments. Alice was a gifted pianist, as was her husband, who seems also to have belonged to the great tradition of English eccentrics. His granddaughter recalled that 'He used always to sit down to the Bach *Chromatic Fantasy and Fugue* whenever he was kept waiting for his bath. So invariable was this custom that the music became known in his household as

---

The Times Literary Supplement, 26 May 1989, pp. 587–9

"the bath tune".' Even more spectacularly, there was no question on his return home from the House that he would report on *political* events. On the contrary, he launched at the piano 'into one of the big Wagner scenes . . . the Verwandlungs scene from *Parsifal*, or the Prelude to the third act of *Tristan*'.

If Wortley – later, in 1917, to be raised to the peerage (which may have prompted Elgar's fishing for a similar elevation in the 1920s?) – could dispense Wagner and join his wife at two pianos, accompanying her in the Grieg or Schumann concerto, small wonder that Elgar had the confidence to send him the incomplete piano sketch for the slow movement of a projected violin concerto, the overall shape of which still eluded the composer. Elgar, characteristically depressed and self-doubting, wrote to Mrs Stuart Wortley ('Alice', still):

> I promised to tell you of my London visit – I do not think it has been a success: it is too lonely & I cannot see how we are to 'take' a place big enough for us all: you shall hear of any plans but I think a decent obscurity in the country is all I can attain to – there is really no 'place' for me here as I do not conduct or in fact do anything & I am made to feel in many ways I am not wanted. I suppose I shall still pay an occasional visit to conduct a new thing – if any new things are ever finished.
>
> I am not sure about that Andante & shall put it away for a long time before I decide its fate. I am glad you liked it. I hope your husband will not think I imagine the sketches to be worth having – but people ask me for them sometimes & *don't* get them.

But on the very evening of the day – 7 February 1910 – that Elgar had written that letter in the Athenaeum (from which he was abruptly to resign in 1924 when Ramsay MacDonald, then Prime Minister, was elected to *ex officio* membership), the musical idea came to him that unfroze his creative paralysis and enabled him over the succeeding months to complete the concerto; and it was undoubtedly the other Alice's encouragement ('I am certain that Mother, with the moral support of my father & myself, said to him "Edward, you MUST go on with it"') and personality that had stirred his creativity into life again. Thereafter, 7 February was celebrated, most affectingly, by Elgar and his alternate Alice as an anniversary.

It was that musical idea, and the ensuing hauntingly poignant second subject of the first movement, that gave Alice Stuart Wortley the name by which Elgar was thereafter to address her. Both these ideas, charged with significance and feeling, he had designated 'Windflower' themes, after the white *anemone nemorosa* of early spring. Alice was translated. She became his Windflower.

What was she really like, this transformed Alice? And what did she really mean to Elgar? These are questions that cannot wholly be answered by the volume of correspondence, *Edward Elgar: The Windflower Letters*, which Jerrold Northrop Moore has edited.[1] Few of her letters to Elgar survive; many of his letters to her were mutilated, whole portions excised and words obliterated. Moore conjectures that it was Clare, the Wortleys' daughter, who was the 'most likely destroyer . . . Yet she may not have been the only suppressor'; and he continues,

> The motive for destruction, where there was a motive, was to preserve secrets. The linking text which I have provided does not seek to adjudicate the precise degree of intimacy attained. There is no way to know this.

But the music tells us a great deal, perhaps all we need to know. It must have been an altogether unusual personality that gave rise to the rapt beauty of Elgar's second subject – he often quoted it, in his own hand, in missives to the Windflower. The theme, indeed, offers us the completest portrait we have of the Alice Stuart Wortley Elgar loved, and its existence makes the absence of other documentation, whether lost or destroyed, less critical. But in any event, in the letters of Elgar's that survive untouched, there is ample evidence to suggest that his relationship with the other Alice was a special one. If her presence was a joy, her absences were an affliction. 'It is so dreadful your not coming – I am better & am doing the Ballet – or *think* of doing it – but where are you?' he wrote in an agitated note of February 1917, and concluded, 'I wanted to tell you the theme & *every note* must be approved by you (bless you!) before anything can be done. Oh! why are you so far away & so difficult to get at??' And in an earlier letter, of October 1915 – 'I missed you at Q's [Queen's] Hall, but I thought of you & my eyes wandered to empty Block A' – we find a metaphor for the emptiness that seemed increasingly to characterize Elgar's emotional and creative life. In a fit of despair, intensified by the death of his wife, the first Alice, in April 1920, he was to write to the Windflower in August one of his blackest letters:

> . . . the public have all my best work for nothing & I have not one single friend who cares – except you! My whole past is wiped out & I am quite alone . . . I am glad you played the Cello Concerto – I have forgotten it. Poland [Bolshevik troops were closing in on Warsaw] is too dreadful to think of – I cannot bear it: in fact there is nothing left in the world for me.

This is a case when the loss of the other side of the correspondence is frustrating. But whatever the consolations and encouragement the Windflower was able to offer, she was not able again to work the magic that had persuaded the Violin Concerto from the composer, in 1909 and 1910, although she undoubtedly played the role of an invigorating, enthusing, inspiring Other – not the hypothetical Other whom Stravinsky had in mind when composing, but a flesh-and-blood Other – in relation to the row of works the concerto initiated: the Second Symphony, *Falstaff*, the late chamber works, the Cello Concerto of 1919. But ideas for a piano concerto, with which Elgar was still tinkering in 1925, obstinately refused to materialize.

The outbreak of war caught the Elgars in Scotland, from where Elgar had written to Alice Stuart Wortley, 'Please write as often as you can & tell me news, not only of the war, for which I hunger.' Perhaps his hunger for news from and of her was appeased a little on the difficult journey home: 'It seemed odd being so close as

Leeds to you yesterday & I could not deny myself the pleasure of telephoning to you.' The war, however, was to bring one unexpected consolation to Elgar, whose wartime attitudes and activities (special constable) are documented in a fascinating sequence of letters. This strange, interior man welcomed the black-out as a kind of blessing:

> How beautiful it is in the still quiet streets without the trying brilliant lights: all seems so muffled – a muted life to me and so sweet & pure; I do not like the idea of garishly lit roads & streets again – I love them so much, so much as they are.

Elgar, one might think, was ever a man for the dark.

Speculation, for all Moore's preternatural caution, is inevitable. Would Elgar have been happier if the other Alice had been his partner? More productive? It is the last question that is the more intriguing, especially when one takes into account the shattering event that preceded the establishing of the Windflower relationship by less than a year: the death from tuberculosis in May 1909 of A. J. Jaeger, Elgar's unique publisher, confidant, adviser and above all musical *collaborator* (the first extant Windflower letter belongs to March 1910). Moore records the fact but otherwise leaves it unelaborated. It seems indisputable to me, however, that in rendering Elgar a steady flow of sympathy, loyalty and admiration, the Windflower was functioning in some sense as a proxy Jaeger, though of course what she could not provide was his brilliant musicality and technical equipment, which, as the further two volumes of correspondence under review will show, enabled him to conduct a creative dialogue with the composer of an unparalleled energy and sophistication.

Jaeger was only forty-nine when he died. I confess that it was not until I had read the two marvellous volumes of *Elgar and His Publishers*[2] – I rate them among the most important and revealing of letters by a composer ever to have been published – that I realized to the full the exceptional musicianship that pours out of Jaeger's commentaries and the quality of his creative advice.

Here he is in full spate in 1897, on the subject of *King Olaf*:

> By the way I think the work has one great fault which the audience notice muchly: the absence of a developed broadly melodious lyrical movement with the 'fat' given to the *chorus* where the ear can *rest* & just drink in *quietly* moving strains of a broadly melodious type – à la Evening Hymn, Love Duet & Epilogue in 'Golden Legend'. There is *too much* 'going on' in 'Olaf': as I said in my Crystal Palace notice. The ear is allowed *no rest.* You are *always* 'at it' in splendidly *dramatic* style which would do well to accompany *action*, but which in a *Cantata* is in danger of making one irritable. Even the beautiful Epilogue is too *short* to enable one to quietly sit down to it & close one's eyes & give oneself up to a long spell of pure enjoyment.

This in its own way is first-rate criticism; only a musician could have written it. Jaeger showed an altogether rare gift in being able to combine shrewd criticism with the enthusiasm that would keep going a composer as prone to self-doubt as Elgar was; and as the relationship developed, allowing for greater confidence on both sides, so the criticism became more detailed and specific, as in the case of the *'Enigma' Variations*, where Jaeger, after the première in 1899, suggested to Elgar that the finale ('E.D.U.') required extending if it were to provide a satisfying conclusion to the work. Elgar at first was reluctant; but the technical level on which he replied itself speaks for the kind of dialogue that he was able to have with Jaeger and the seriousness with which he treated his editor's suggestions:

> Now look here – the movement was designed to be concise – here's the difficulty of lengthening it – I *could* go on with those themes for $^{1}/_{2}$ a day. But the *key* G is exhausted – the principal motive (Enigma) comes in grandioso on p. 35 in the tonic & it *won't do* to bring it in again: had I intended to make an extended movement this would have been in some related Key reserving the tonic for the final smash.
>
> In deference to you I made a sketch yesterday – but the thing sounds Schubertian in its sticking to one key.

The end result, however, was, as Jerrold Northrop Moore reminds us, 'a hundred extra bars' added to the finale, 'introducing a new and ultimate tonic statement. When Jaeger saw this in piano score he was overjoyed and said so.' But though Jaeger had succeeded in his submission, he was still not quite satisfied when he heard the extended finale for the first time in November 1899:

> Look here! you won't call me a d— fool & impertinent Hass for making another suggestion re *the* Skore, will you? When I heard the new Finale, *both* at the Worcester Rehearsals & the Richter, I was a little disappointed that the sudden Burst into E flat at 82 did not 'come off' quite as *explosively* & surprisingly as I had anticipated. When I look at the score page 126 I put it down to the fact the 1st Fiddles have *not* the short quaver *rest* that many of the other instruments have. They seemed at the performances to glide up to the B flat instead of *sharply plunging*, *hammering* on it as with stroke of Thor's War Axe! Would it not give you a *stronger* B flat & a stronger E flat chord & a greater *surprise* if ALL instruments had the crochet rest before 82? The Wind could take breath for the fff & not merely use their *last* breath of a *crescendo* for THE effect; & the 1st Fiddles could get a better *grip* of the B flat & give greater *brilliancy* to it?

A letter like this shows strikingly how Jaeger had now moved entirely from the general (as in his comments on *King Olaf*) to the particular, and the minutely particular at that. Of course Elgar did not always accept Jaeger's strictures – as he had written earlier in another context to Littleton of Novello's, 'I am *sure* of my orchl. effects' – but Jaeger's success rate was high. What strikes a modern reader is the absence of the likelihood of any comparable dialogue taking place today between a composer and his publisher. Not only have the skills largely disappeared but so too has the old concept of the composer's taking editorial advice that more nearly approaches creative collaboration. One of the most elaborate examples of this in these letters occurred in connection with *Gerontius* and the moment of climax when the Soul encounters the Almighty. Jaeger was wonderfully rude about

Elgar's first conception of this epic moment in the score:

> Yes, a whine, I called it. You may take it for Gospel that Wagner would have made this the *climax* of *expression* in the work, especially in the ORCHESTRA which HERE should surely shine as a medium for *portraying emotions*! Wagner *always revelled* in seemingly 'IMPOSSIBLE' situations & this one would have brought forth his most splendid powers. He always surmounted the most appalling difficulties like the giant he was, 'rejoicing'. You must not forget, that if Wagner had not been the *poet* musician he was he would never (to mention but one 'Impossible' situation) have given Isolde that *glorious* Death Song (Liebestod) to sing, for no woman that ever was, or ever will be born, would sing or make speeches over the body of her lover at *such* a moment?
>
> No, the poet amongst musicians does *more* than the 'necessary', the 'likely', the 'natural'. He does the UN-likely, the *un*-necessary, IMpossible, BUT the GREAT, the BEAUTIFUL! I *don't* want your 'Soul' to sing a 'dramatic *Song*'. Heavens! But what is your gorgeous orchestra for? & why should you be DULL & sentimental at such a *supremest* moment?
>
> Don't tell me you can't do it in 50 years! Here is your *greatest* chance of proving Yourself *poet*, seer, doer of '*impossible*' things, – and you shirk it. Bah! I see *your* point of view *quite*. It's allright for the despised Brixton Baker & Bayswater Butcher, – *not* for an inspired poet–musician like E.E., though.

Elgar didn't like being told that he had 'shirked it', but attempted a revision. This, however, was not to meet with the irrepressible Jaeger's approval:

> No, PLEASE DON'T alter it as per the M.S. you have sent. It takes away the *surprise*, & the dramatically appropriate 'gliding in' of the new, LOVELY peaceful theme. PLEASE don't alter that if you can't alter it any better way than as per your M.S. I'm truly sorry to worry you like this, but I know *You* don't like the new way better than the old way, do you?

But with the cunning of a Machiavelli, at the same time as he was saying leave well alone (if you can't do better), he was also making the proposal that Elgar was in fact to adopt:

> Do you know, I wanted you to suggest, in a *few* gloriously great & effulgent orchestral chords, given out by the whole force of the Orchestra in its most glorious key, the MOMENTARY *vision* of the Almighty. A few Chords! (remembering those wonderful chords at Brünnhilde's Awakening in Siegfried, Act III) & then for a few bars the Soul's overwhelming agitation with a quasi-choked, suppressed 'Take me away', molto *agitato*, & THEN as miserable a whine as you like. The dejection to come *after* the first agitation. No, it need not have been done 'theatrically' at all, at all! And to suggest the *glory* of the momentary vision need not have been blasphemous either. But I grant you, it wanted a Wagner or R. Strauss to do that, nobody else could dare attempt it. No!, as I know now, not even E.E.

Elgar's response scarcely acknowledged Jaeger's contribution – 'I hope you'll like the emendation,' he wrote, as if he had thought of it himself. No matter. As Moore justly observes, Jaeger's carefully planted suggestion 'made a creative contribution to Elgar's masterpiece without parallel in the history of relations between composer and publisher'.

Novello's were lucky to have Jaeger; Elgar luckier still. But for his illness, Jaeger doubtless felt himself to be lucky too:

> My dear, great Edward, I was allowed to come down today for the first time for a month, and I spent some happy quarter Hours over your Adagio in the Symphony (P.F. arrangement) . . . I wish I were near you that I might press & kiss your hand & say: thank you, my friend, for this great piece of music.

Elgar was Jaeger's luck. But we remain aware that perhaps among this exceptional man's unfulfilled gifts was the capacity to be a critic of altogether unusual distinction and by no means only in relation to the composer whom he loved so selflessly.

He was quick to note (in 1903) that a colleague at Novello's 'never could see anything' in Elgar 'till *Gerontius*': an observation that should perhaps have alerted him to the overwhelming English emphasis on oratorio and obliged him to ask himself if in fact the pressure to succeed *through* oratorio was not exacting too high a price of the composer. Elgar went along with it. But should he have done? My only unrealistic regret is that Jaeger was unable to bring a little scepticism to bear on the post-*Gerontius* oratorios which seem to me to have consumed stocks of creative energy that might have been applied more fruitfully elsewhere. But for that, doubtless, other times, other forms, were required; and Jaeger was as unreservedly enthusiastic about *The Apostles* as he had been about a masterpiece such as *Gerontius*.

Although the friendship of Elgar and Jaeger necessarily consumes much of the reader's attention, there is much else that is of almost equal interest. We learn at first hand, so to say, a good deal more of Elgar's wayward temperament and his constant anxieties about money and the economics of being – or attempting to be – an independent composer. This was a preoccupation that surfaced early in his correspondence with Jaeger: he wrote in 1897,

> Yes! I have some ideas: but am about taking a new house – *very noisy* close to the station where I *can't write* at all – but will be more convenient for pupils (!) to come in – I have no intention of bothering myself with music . . .

and went on to explain that in two years (and with some success) his outgoings exceeded his income. He concludes,

> After paying my own expenses at two festivals I feel a d—d fool! (English expression) for thinking of music at all. No amount of 'kind encouragement' can blot out these simple figures.

The economic theme runs like a scarlet thread through the letters.

It was doubtless Elgar's long and on occasions painful experience of battling for an adequate share of royalties from his publishers that made him a formidable supporter of the principle of a collective of composers and publishers which would secure the creator his and her due. I wonder sometimes if the pop composers who now wield such massive musical and industrial power quite realize what they owe – perhaps rather surprisingly – to a figure such as Elgar. Consider, for example, the speech he made – on the eve of his investiture – to a Great Public Meeting of the Musical Defence League on 4 July 1904:

> My life, ladies and gentlemen, has, as you know, been a self-made one. London called me from my country home, and *you* have made me what I am. But you call other composers from their homes to you, and you allow the law to deprive them of their livelihood. That is all I have to say.

And he was still protesting in 1929, at the proposed Musical Copyright Bill:

> I will record my strong protest against it, adding that the passing of such a measure would mean the extinction of creative musical art in this country and the ruin of the majority of native composers.

Those words have a peculiar resonance to our ears in 1989, when the past year has seen so much debate about new copyright legislation. What would Elgar have had to say to a government that surrendered so shamelessly to the pressure of the blank-tape manufacturers' lobby – on the so-called home-taping issue – and thus deprived composers, native and foreign, of an important right to remuneration?

Elgar and His Publishers will provide, for many years to come, an extraordinarily rich source for the social and economic historians of music. Elgar lived at a time of critical change in the economics of composing and music publishing and his evidence is crucial. Also, it leaves us yet again with an impression of the enigmatic figure he was: not, as it is easy to assume, and was assumed by many, an Establishment totem, but on the contrary, a militant, and sometimes a militantly anti-Establishment man. However, the Windflower letters suggest that in his last years the social circles in which Elgar moved – of which the second Alice was a member – grew ever more constricting and stifling. Jaeger, if he had still been around, might have been able to punch a few holes and let in a little air, perhaps even that 'air from other planets', against which Elgar unyieldingly turned his face – his ears – until he died.

One blunt phrase will not have escaped the scrupulous reader of the copyright missile Elgar released in 1904: 'My life, ladies and gentlemen, has, as you know, been a self-made one.' It was one of the reasons, perhaps, why the Establishment never quite succeeded in assimilating Elgar. He was always sensitive to this question of upbringing, making a point of it in 1904, but in 1900 fussing about an article in the *Musical Times* which seemed about to disclose altogether too much, at least for the comfort of the composer's wife. In any event, it provoked a remarkably revealing reply to the author which shows how sensitive the whole area was:

> Now – as to the whole '*shop*' episode – I don't care a d—n! I know it has ruined me & made life impossible until I what you call made a name – I only know I was kept out of everything decent, 'cos 'his father keeps a shop' – I believe I'm always introduced so now, that is to say – the remark is invariably made in an undertone – but to please my wife do what she wishes . . .

And when, in the light of Elgar's letter, one reads the amendment of the text, the irony of it all is compounded. Elgar, it ran, was 'descended from the fine old *yeoman* stock of Weston, Herefordshire – therefore intensely English'.[3] No '*shop*' in that family tree.

If Elgar grew some sort of carapace, which certainly influenced how he was perceived by the outside world, it must have been because of his hypersensitivity. Time and time again one is struck in these letters by outbursts of pain that could be uttered only by a man with several skins too few. The reactions were intense, one is almost tempted to say, unnaturally so, whether it was the unexpected death of an old friend, Alfred Rodewald –

> I lived on as an automaton – & did everything without thought – then I went to my room & wept for hours – yesterday I came home without seeing anyone & am now a wreck & a broken hearted man

– or one of the setbacks in his musical fortunes, which provoked a response close to a kind of black self-annihilation. One of his severest afflictions was the disastrous première of *Gerontius*:

> I have not seen the papers yet except one or two bits which exuberant friends insisted on my reading & I don't know or care what they say or do. As far as I am concerned music in England is dead – I shall always write what I have in me of course.
>
> I have worked hard for forty years &, at the last, Providence denies me a decent hearing of my work: so I submit – I always said God was against art & I still believe it. Anything obscene or trivial is blessed in this world & has a reward – I ask for no reward – only to live & to hear my work. I still hear it in my heart & in my head so I must be content. Still it is curious to be treated by the old-fashioned people as a criminal because my thoughts & ways are beyond them.
>
> I am very well & what is called 'fit' & had my golf in good style yesterday & am not ill or pessimistic – don't think it: but I have allowed my heart to open once – it is now shut against every religious feeling & every soft, gentle impulse *for ever*.

Elgar's finger was never far removed from the abort button. Of course he was not the only composer to have experienced the depths of despair. The point is, rather, that these indications of a far darker, more complex and fluctuating personality than has generally been recognized, encourage us to listen more attentively to the music.

I've argued before that in certain important respects Elgar's genius was not nourished by English society and musical culture at the turn of the century (the comparison with Paris and Vienna is instructive). It is something on which Elgar himself commented in January 1902, just after returning from Germany: 'The horrible musical atmosphere I plunged into at once in this benighted country nearly suffocated me – I *wish* it had completely.' It was Jaeger to whom Elgar addressed that explosion of frustration, and who himself, a year later and in another context, had spelled out, with his usual acumen, some of the deficiencies of the English musical scene, and ended:

> I pity the young gifted English composer's lot in a country where there are 3 decent orchestras & 3 Conductors with Brains & one Chorus with Brains (somebody else's).

Elgar's feeling of suffocation on return to his 'benighted' homeland had been of course intensified by the triumphs he had just been enjoying in Germany. Among the most stimulating results of the long trawl through the 900 and more pages of this correspondence are the constant reminders they bring us of Elgar's extraordinary successes outside England, especially in Germany but also in Holland and the United States. There was not only the famous toast from Richard Strauss in May 1902, in Düsseldorf – 'who never speechifies if he can help it, made a really noble oration over *Gerontius* . . . & it was worth some years of anguish – now I trust over – to hear him call me Meister!' – but also a gathering momentum of European and American interest in Elgar's music. We can extrapolate from the letters a dazzling roll-call of the names of many of the most celebrated conductors of the day, either performing the works or clamouring to get hold of them: Buths, Damrosch, Nikisch, Richter, Steinbach, Weingartner – and of course Mahler, who does not show up in the letters but who gave some important New York performances of Elgar in his 1910–11 season.

This extraordinary record – perhaps not to be matched by another English composer until Britten arrived on the scene – drives home one of the fundamental Elgarian paradoxes. How, and why, did it happen that the composer, once so widely, generously and enthusiastically received outside England – travelling so to speak on a Community passport, and a fluent linguist – then became identified with a quintessential and narrowing Englishness which with deadly efficacy cut him out of the larger musical landscape to which he naturally belonged, and still belongs? It is a most curious case, in which the parties involved share a common illusion. The effect of it is to stifle Elgar's voice abroad, and falsify our perception of him at home.

I have nothing but praise for Moore's meticulous presentation of all three volumes of letters. It must have been a vast labour. It has been very finely executed. I have a few quibbles. There is a sometimes irritating absence of documentation, sometimes direct, sometimes contextual, which ought to be there for immediate verification of a letter. I dislike the method which attempts to embed the letters in a continuous tissue of explanatory text. It makes hard work for the reader when it comes to identifying works, events, people, places and so forth. The full annotation of individual letters seems to me to be a lot tidier and clearer. But all these reservations pale into insignificance by the side of Mr Moore's achievement, which places us unreservedly in his debt.

In a brief letter to Jaeger in November 1900 Elgar writes:

> It's raining piteously here & all is dull except the heart of E.E. which beats time to most marvellous music – unwritten alas! & ever to be so.

That unwritten music of the heart: we must be grateful for what we have, but when we reflect on Elgar's long life and the silence that, for all the Windflower's ministrations, he came to inhabit, we cannot but ponder, Hardy-like, on what might have been written if some things at least had been otherwise.

NOTES

1 Jerrold Northrop Moore (ed.), *Edward Elgar, The Windflower Letters: Correspondence with Alice Caroline Stuart Wortley and her Family* (Oxford University Press, Oxford, 1989).
2 Jerrold Northrop Moore (ed.), *Elgar and His Publishers: Letters of a Creative Life*; vol. 1: *1885–1903*, and vol. 2: *1904–1934* (Oxford University Press, Oxford, 1989).
3 MC: See the anonymous biographical article on Elgar in *Musical Times* 41 (October 1900), p. 641.

VII
Interlude

Fritz [Frederick] Delius: drawing by Christian Krohg, 1897

The Private World of Frederick Delius

Delius once advised Peter Warlock to write only the music he *felt*. Good advice for a young composer to which, one imagines, Bach, Beethoven, Mozart and Wagner – in fact, all the masters we revere – would have cheerfully subscribed. From such a general comment, indeed, we might think that Delius's reverence for the great 'feelers' in music (i.e. the great composers) could only equal, or exceed, ours. But such, as we know, was not the case at all. Delius had little time for other men's music and, at least towards the end of his life, became increasingly entranced by the sound of his own. Moreover, as Arthur Hutchings has pointed out, 'He had a hatred, unique among composers of large structures, of any planning or manipulating that divorced technique from direct expression of the emotions.'[1] Delius was a classic case of an artist who hopelessly confused 'thinking' and 'feeling'; he was never able to comprehend the feelings that gave rise to thinking – hence his snorts of contempt when, say in a Beethoven sonata, the exposition was over and the development began. 'Padding,' was Delius's impatient reaction. An inveterate improviser himself, it was odd that he was quite unable to appreciate the basically improvisatory character of developments even as highly organized as Beethoven's.

But Delius's improvising, largely harmonic and colouristic, and derived from what Gerald Abraham calls his 'dreamy improvisation at the piano',[2] was very much his own, just as his range of

---

Musical Opinion 907 (April 1953), pp. 405–7

feelings was his own entirely. It was the incredibly *restricted* range of Delius's feelings that prevented him from understanding the musical feelings of other composers. Yet, paradoxically enough, it was just this very restrictedness that made him the unique artist he was. No other composer, before or since, has so assiduously cultivated luxurious nostalgia as a fundamental principle of artistic creation, or raised it to the status of an aesthetic philosophy. Compared with Delius, the tragically inclined Mahler – another composer who developed nostalgia in music as a valid means of expression – was an athletic, hearty optimist.

Nostalgia, it may be claimed, is no new thing in music and no new thing in human nature. The Elizabethans, whom we praise for the exceptional virility of their culture, were streaked with pessimism:

> Golden lads and girls all must,
> As chimney-sweepers, come to dust.

There has always been this 'sad sweetness' present in English art, in our literature and music. Is this, perhaps, Delius's link with the English tradition? Despite the music's essentially cosmopolitan style, a number of sensitive musicians are convinced of the intensely English spirit that lies at the back of *Brigg Fair* or *On Hearing the first Cuckoo in Spring*. Could it be – to continue the English parallel – that Delius's chromaticism is the apotheosis of Purcell's? The proposition (Cecil Gray's) does not stand up to analysis. Purcell's chromaticism was, mostly, the result of free part-writing (in the string fantasias, for instance), while Delius's chromaticism was, mostly, the result not of polyphonic, but purely harmonic procedures. Dowland, rather than Purcell, might initiate a more fruitful comparison; yet there is something far-fetched in promoting Delius as Dowland's successor. It could be as usefully argued that *Tristan* derived from Dowland's plaintive lute.

In addition, an examination of Delius's choral and vocal texts brings little comfort to those who believe a composer may draw powerful inspiration from his native language – even achieving thereby a native musical language; Erwin Stein has dropped the timely and stimulating reminder that '[The] indigenous rhythm and intonation of a nation's language inevitably bear on the character of its music.'[3] Of Delius's forty-eight songs, no fewer than thirty-two are settings of Continental texts, Scandinavian, French and German. His most celebrated opera, *A Village Romeo and Juliet*, is based on a novel by Gottfried Keller, the Swiss novelist. Of his choral works, the vast *Mass of Life* and the subsequent *Requiem* depend for their books on Nietzsche's poetic philosophy, while *Sea Drift* and the *Songs of Farewell* rely on the virile *vers libre* of Walt Whitman, who undeniably wrote English but was, nevertheless, profoundly American; and English and American speech rhythms have (very properly) distinct personalities of their own. It is significant that of the few English poets Delius did set – aside from Shelley and Tennyson – two of the most important of them (Arthur Symons and Ernest Dowson) were, in style, more French than English.

The more one surveys these textual facts the more ironical it seems that Delius should have been born a Yorkshireman (but note the German parentage) and hail from Bradford. His early sojourn in Florida, his periods in Leipzig and Paris, his later residence in France – all indicate a life as eclectic as his music. It is not surprising, then – though not so fully realized as it should be – that Delius's music is far removed from the accepted English tradition. *A Mass of Life* (1904–5), for example, has more in common with Mahler's (choral) Eighth Symphony (1907) and Schoenberg's *Gurrelieder* (1900–1901) than with Elgar's *Gerontius* (1900). Delius, indeed, could hardly have been more bitterly, musically and diametrically opposed to the English oratorio. When Delius jested with Elgar about the latter's 'long-winded oratorios', Elgar replied, 'That is the penalty of my English environment.' It was a penalty Delius never felt any desire to risk having to pay.

It is not at all surprising that it was in Germany that Delius had his first successes, and that it was some of Wagner's music 'that gave young Delius extreme pleasure'.[4] In 1953 it is possible to see that Delius was not only one of the first English Europeans but also one of the very last big European post-Romantics, with all the accent on 'post' that can be mustered to its emphasis. Delius embodied nothing of the future in his music, unlike any of his contemporaries, Schoenberg, Strauss, Mahler or Reger. His influence on other composers has been slight. His style – genuinely inimitable – is intolerable in the hands of his imitators. It has opened up no new technical horizons. His most considerable contribution to the music of our day was his turning of limitless, subjective nostalgia to creative account. This area of the mind Delius conquered for music, but it was one he exhausted and completely assimilated to himself. It was no accident that in debased form Delius's harmonic vocabulary became the current small-talk of the commercial 'nostalgia' parcelled out daily by numberless radios and gramophones. Nostalgia had grown into a widespread social attitude, and what had been Delius's private world was inherited – or invaded – by every Tom, Dick or Harry who had (or thought he ought to have) the blues. Not, to be sure, the real 'blues', but a synthetic, sliding, slithering substitute. If Tin Pan Alley snatched elements of Delius's style, it certainly failed to capture the refinement of his feelings. But as worthy heir to those feelings Delius would have required another Delius and that, by the very nature of his art, was an impossibility. Delius's uniqueness rested – very literally so – on his singularity.

When all is said and done about Delius, it is just this singularity that remains. When we have traced Delius's patent European pedigree, with its echoes of Wagner, Grieg, Debussy, Strauss and Mahler – 'period' echoes, if not straightforward influences – we find ourselves confronted with a naked ego which we either willingly embrace or summarily reject. Historical considerations are of no value here; understanding of Delius is not at all related to recognition of his stature as a composer; it is simply a question of whether we are capable of feeling as he feels. 'For me,' Delius wrote to Warlock, 'music is very simple; it is the expression of a poetic and emotional nature.' '*My* poetic and emotional nature' would, perhaps, be nearer the truth. The ego is arrogant in its demands, and Delius, besides being the last of the post-Romantics, was also the last and most thoroughgoing of the egocentric composers thrown up by the nineteenth century. The musical cult of the ego was a European phenomenon, not an English one; and it would be hard to discover a composer less selfless than Delius. His music *was* himself and himself alone; his acute nostalgia (unlike the 'projected' pathos of a Britten, a Mahler or a Mozart), was the logical consequence of living on a store of personal and mainly poignant memories. In Delius, despite his cosmopolitanism, strictly autobiographical art reached its climax. He was his own exclusive universe.

NOTES

1 Ralph Hill (ed.), *The Concerto* (Penguin Books, Harmondsworth, 1952), p. 261.
2 Gerald Abraham, *A Hundred Years of Music* (Duckworth, London, 2nd edn, 1949), p. 246.
3 Erwin Stein, '*Peter Grimes*' in DM and Hans Keller (eds.), *Benjamin Britten: A Commentary on his Works by a Group of Specialists* (Rockliff, London, 1952), p. 131.
4 Arthur Hutchings, *Delius* (Macmillan, London, 1948), p. 5.

VIII
The Quiet Innovator

Benjamin Britten: drawing by Milein Cosman, *c.* 1949

Benjamin Britten: The Quiet Innovator

What does my title mean? Exactly what it says! On the one hand Britten was an innovator – not the purveyor of orthodoxies that unthinking critics in the past have often thought him to be. On the other, he was – undeniably – quiet; by no means muted in his music but, yes, a quiet personality, with a distinct distaste for committing himself to ideologies or propagandizing on behalf of his own music. Verbalizing was anathema to him. He preferred to let his music speak for itself. If he wanted to speak for other composers' music, then he did so as a *performer*, as an excellent conductor (he was that rare thing, a musician's conductor) and – supremely so – in his collaboration with Peter Pears. Their voice and piano duo represented in its own time an unequalled interpretative achievement. Here, no less, the style was *quiet*. There was certainly nothing overtly theatrical about a typical Pears–Britten performance, of the *Winterreise*, say, and yet how intense and overwhelming was the *drama* they conveyed, from first note to last.

This outward quietness had its drawbacks, naturally. During Britten's lifetime there were many commentators – among them, alas, the most voluble – who could recognize an innovation only when they had read a statement or proclamation about it. They certainly were unable to *hear* it, unaided, for themselves. In this respect, I agree, the habitually silent and word-less Britten landed

---

Programme Book for the 51st Maggio Musicale Fiorentino (Florence, 1988), pp. 31–64; original English text of the Italian translation by Anna Cenni

himself (and his critics) with a difficulty: he issued no statements, no elaborate programme notes, no theoretical position papers or analytic self-examinations, only his – in his eyes – self-sufficient scores. It is my intention in this survey to spell out what has frequently gone unnoticed: the innovations of many different kinds that Britten introduced into his music for the theatre from 1941 to 1973, which, in sum, not only justify the title of this article but also the claim that I make on his behalf: that he made a consistently radical contribution to the development of opera – I use the word as an umbrella, beneath which may congregate all types of music-theatre – in the twentieth century.

It must already be clear, I think, that Britten as man and artist was something of a paradox. How was it, indeed, that someone so conspicuously untheatrical in appearance and manner, born in a provincial town on the east coast of England in 1913, in a country without a native tradition of opera, became the leading composer in the opera house of his day in England and, from 1945 onwards, was catapulted by the success of *Peter Grimes* into the front rank of those few contemporary composers of opera who could command an international audience?

One is tempted to think that everything started with *Grimes*, which for so long was regarded as Britten's first full-length work for the musical theatre. But in fact *Grimes* had a unique predecessor, the full-length operetta *Paul Bunyan*, which had been performed four years earlier in New York, in 1941, a brilliant collaboration with the poet W. H. Auden, which, for a variety of reasons too complex to go into here, was withdrawn soon after its unsuccessful première, and disappeared entirely from view until its revival in 1976, during the very last year of the composer's life.

Even a cursory inspection of *Bunyan* will reveal any number of innovations and – to start with – a paradox: who would guess that Britten's first opera, written in the United States by a youthful and exuberant composer who wanted to catch the ear of his New Found Land, was destined for Broadway before it ended up, for its first production, in May 1941, on the campus of Columbia University, New York?

Britten and – on – Broadway? One cannot quite believe it. But then there are a lot of unbelievable things about Britten that one discovers to be true only by studying his works and not the words of his often purblind critics. *Bunyan*, apart from its unusual origins, goes on to offer a fair share of innovations. For example, its quite astonishing array of orchestrations: throughout the operetta, the constitution of the orchestra changes virtually from number to number. Most remarkable of all, the strings are almost as often banished as they are retained. The norm, rather, is an orchestra predominantly made up of woodwind, brass and percussion (shades of *Billy Budd* to come!). There are rare tuttis, in which the whole band is employed. But the general tendency, to be so typical of future Britten, is in the reverse direction, towards more slender instrumental ensembles. One song, for example, is scored for a combination of piccolo, cymbal, woodblock, piano and double-bass, which looks eccentric but fulfils its function perfectly ['Western Union Boy's Song', Act I No. 6]. In another, the accompaniment is pared down to three solo woodwind, oboe, clarinet and bassoon ['Inkslinger's Regret', Act I No. 16]. Yet another is scored elaborately for woodwind, brass, timpani, xylophone, harp and celesta ['Inkslinger's Song', Act I No. 14]. Already, indeed, in this first full-length stage work we encounter Britten's exceptional instrumental fertility and inventiveness, which led to the freshness and transparency of orchestral sound in his later operas.

Perhaps the ambition to hit Broadway was one of the reasons for a score that was peculiarly rich in popular melody (one should never underrate Britten's ability to write an almost instantly memorable tune: it was a gift he seems to have been born with, and it stayed with him to the end of his life). But the catchy tunes in *Bunyan* speak for themselves and need no elucidation. What might possibly pass unremarked – and certainly went unnoticed in 1941, because both the points I am going to mention proved to have a bearing on stage works as yet unwritten – were first the remarkably bold and original choral writing, which at times directly anticipates the dramatic choruses of *Grimes*, and second, a striking revelation – one of those unbelievable things I referred to above – of an exotic, oriental technique, heterophony, which, almost two decades later, was to dominate the compositional processes of the first church parable, *Curlew River* (1964), and its successors. It is a crucial passage in *Bunyan* – scored, one notes, for an orchestra of woodwind, brass and percussion [Act I Figs. 11–12].

Those extraordinary bars owe their existence to Britten's friendship in New York with the great Balinese scholar and enthusiast, Colin McPhee (1900–1964), himself a highly gifted and original composer. When Britten wrote them, he could not have been aware of how important to him, and how influential *on* him, the principle of heterophony was to become. But it was in *Bunyan* that an innovational technique set out on its long, fertilizing journey until it culminated in the heterophonic textures of Britten's late operas (and not only the operas!). It is perhaps part of the paradox that is Britten that even his innovations often prove to have had their origins in his own past.

The popular vein that Britten so skilfully exploits in *Bunyan* – there's a fine blues quartet, for example, and a cowboy song in the authentic tradition of the American musical – reminds us of the vast quantity of incidental music he wrote for the theatre, radio and film in the 1930s and 1940s, when he was often required to provide – at a moment's notice! – music that adopted the vernacular, popular idiom of the day. It is that huge body of work – to which we have only recently had access and very little of which is published – that gives us the answer to the most important question to which the virtually instantaneous success of *Peter Grimes* gives rise: where – and how – did Britten learn his craft as a musical dramatist? *Paul Bunyan*, yes, offered him valuable experience, perhaps especially the development of a working relationship between a composer and a librettist; there is no doubt, I think, that after *Bunyan*, Britten had a much clearer picture of what he would need from a librettist with whom he might work in the future. But, musically speaking, *Bunyan* was a rather special case, a special, American-oriented kind of musical theatre piece. If one is looking for the precedents that were the guarantors of *Grimes*'s success in 1945, then it is to the scores that Britten wrote as a young composer when working in the 1930s for the experimental theatre and film groups, and for the radio, that we must turn: we tend to forget that for young musicians and writers in the 1930s, radio was itself a new, exciting and innovative dramatic medium which could sometimes approximate to a form of broadcast musical theatre. It was in all of these spheres that Britten learned his trade as a musical dramatist, for example in finding the precise music in which to embody a dramatic event (or situation) or outline the profile of a character. It was here too that he learned that the slender resources dictated by economic necessity could be no less telling dramatically than the employment of lavish forces; and it was in the film and radio studios in particular that he refined and sharpened his already exceptional aural imagination, which allowed him to replicate – mimic – almost any sound of the external world (whether natural or mechanical) by instrumental means, a talent that was to stand him in good stead in the theatre: when 'realism' was required Britten could summon up the sonority to match it – more than that, *evoke* it. Has one ever heard a more convincing concertina than the instrument 'played' by the sinister Leader of the Strolling Players in Britten's last opera, *Death in Venice* (1973)? It is pairs of clarinets, bassoons and horns in the pit that magically do the trick.

Thus *Peter Grimes*, from the point of view of experience and the acquisition of the techniques that a major full-length opera requires, was *many years in preparation*. This does nothing to diminish the extraordinary achievement. It tells us, instead, something very important and true about Britten as a composer: that, contrary to received opinion, he had to work hard and methodically to get the results he wanted. The post-student period, in which his 'incidental' scores were a prominent part of his output, represented his apprenticeship as musical dramatist which was to come to brilliant maturity in *Peter Grimes*.

Grimes took the world by storm. It was a unique event: there is much still to be said, perhaps, about its significance as symbol of the resurgence of the arts, of creativity, in England and beyond, after the catastrophe of 1939–45. It also proved to be, with one possible exception – the special case of *Gloriana* (1953) – the *only* opera of Britten's to fall within the established operatic tradition (and even *Gloriana*, on examination, proves to be not so very traditional after all). After 1945, his works for the music-theatre followed very different and diverse paths. But *Grimes* was still 'traditional', 'grand' opera.

Having said that, one immediately has to contradict it (the Britten paradox again). It is perfectly true, of course, that there is a great deal in the opera that adheres to familiar conventions. I see nothing strange about that. Britten himself would have thought it very odd indeed to attempt in his *first* opera (for so he would have regarded *Grimes*, despite the existence of *Bunyan*) something that iconoclastically departed from the well-tried tradition that admired predecessors had found effective and stimulating. He would first see what he could do with his 'inheritance'. Revolution, if there was to be such, could follow – at a distance.

But as so often with Britten, what he chose to do with 'tradition', with 'convention', turned out to be highly *un*traditional, *un*conventional. For that matter, the illustrious models that one recognizes surfacing here and there in *Grimes* were by no means those that one would have automatically expected to have been plundered by an English composer working in the wartime 1940s. The parallels with Berg's *Wozzeck* (a composer and a work of central importance to Britten throughout his life) have often been drawn; and more recently we have come to recognize the impact of Shostakovich's *Lady Macbeth of the Mtsensk District* which Britten heard in a concert performance in London in 1936. Less frequently cited as a source – and yet it was a surprisingly rich one –

was Gershwin's *Porgy and Bess*: one of the productive consequences of Britten's residence in the States from 1939 to 1942 (he saw *Porgy*, to the best of my knowledge, only once, but clearly the experience went deep: cf., among many other things, the two operas' 'storm' scenes). There was another unexpected, though minor, influence: Strauss's *Rosenkavalier* (cf. the famous Act III trio with the quartet for women's voices in *Grimes* Act II Scene 1), which Britten was studying before he started work on his own opera. As for the past, it was to the Verdian rather than Wagnerian concept of music-drama that Britten remained attached, a passionate loyalty which certainly illumines *Grimes*. But there was also another precedent from the past which, to my mind, was yet more influential: Musorgsky's *Boris Godunov*. As in *Boris*, the chorus in *Grimes* emerges in its own collective right as protagonist of the drama; and it is precisely here, by the way, that *Bunyan*'s predominantly choral profile had provided a lively if relatively rudimentary precedent.

Unusual models for *Grimes*, then, and indeed the more one examines the outwardly 'orthodox' opera, the more unusual the execution of the whole affair becomes. If we agree that the chorus is the opera's protagonist, then who is its hero? Peter Grimes? The answer confirms the paradox, because Grimes is as far removed from everybody's idea of a conventional operatic hero as could be imagined. He is indeed that peculiarly modern thing, an *anti-hero*, one of the first of his kind, along with Wozzeck, in the history of twentieth-century opera, though there was perhaps an earlier precedent in Tchaikovsky's Eugene Onegin, more muted than Wozzeck or Grimes, it is true, but hardly less absolutely lacking in the heroic attributes traditionally encountered in opera. We note that there may be common ground here. But Tchaikovsky and Britten were homosexuals, and in Britten's case it has become fashionable to argue that in *Peter Grimes* he was writing a parable of the homosexual's predicament – his own and Pears's – a minority embattled in a predominantly hostile society. It would fly in the face of reality to suggest that Britten's own life experience and his own sufferings – because suffering there must have been – did not contribute its own profound charge of tension to the opera. It would certainly have added a keen cutting edge to the unequivocal exposure of society's hypocrisy which is such a striking feature of the opera. But it is what an artist makes of his individual predicament that matters; and it imposes an altogether too narrow and doctrinaire interpretation on *Grimes* if we are persuaded to 'read' the opera exclusively in terms of the composer's sexuality. On the contrary, the performing history of *Grimes* shows that like most important works of art it succeeded in far transcending its author's suffering (or joy, or indignation, or any other autobiographical dimension, come to that) and speaks to mankind on human issues that audiences find universally comprehensible. This is not to say that the homosexual condition is incomprehensible or to be reviled or swept under the carpet, but to keep a useful sense of proportion; and, above all, not to attribute to the composer an intent which I think he did not have. He did not, in my view, write *Grimes* as a protest against, or even as a reflection of, the prevailing attitudes to homosexuality in England up to the 1950s and 1960s. Others, whose seriousness I respect, take a different view.[1] I shall much regret it if we succeed in convincing ourselves that Britten's persistent interest in the relationship between non-conformist attitudes and the social antagonism they arouse should be attributed solely to his homosexuality. It is not Britten's sexual constitution that we have dramatized or musicalized before us, but the dramatization in an extraordinary variety of forms of one of the great human topics which is under perpetual debate: the pressure and persuasion to conform on those who assert different values and attitudes from those held by society at large.

It is beyond the limits of the space available to me to dwell on more than one or two of the opera's unique features. What remains one of the most overwhelming and innovative of musical events is Grimes's great solo scene at the end of Act III, his so-called 'mad' scene, which Britten daringly conceived (with

Pears's voice in mind) as a brilliant vocal cadenza. In this extraordinary passage, the unhinged fisherman appears before us deprived of everything, it seems, except dislocated recollections of the past and repetitions of his own name, which ironically echo the vengeful cries – 'Peter Grimes!' – of his pursuers. It is his name that is finally the only bond between Grimes and his persecutors. The town has forgotten, if they ever knew, that Grimes was human: he has become an object of, a target for, communal aggression. Grimes, for his part, no longer knows, if *he* ever knew, what he has been or who he is. His cries of 'Grimes' are more a desperate seeking after identity than a recognition of it. Peter now has nobody to speak for him: all that remains to him is his own voice, talking – singing – to himself, before oblivion – the sea – claims him.

Cadenzas were always much to Britten's liking. In works preceding *Grimes* – the orchestral song-cycle *Our Hunting Fathers* (1936), for example – one of the songs had concluded with a series of prolonged instrumental cadenzas. At this climactic moment in the opera, Britten treats the *voice* as if it were a solo instrument and writes a cadenza for it much as if he had reached the point in a concerto movement where the soloist traditionally intervenes with a final display and sometimes a recapitulation of previous thematic materials. I have no doubt that the concerto model was in Britten's mind when he devised the final (and also recapitulatory) vocal appearance of Grimes. It is a typical example of his particular genius whereby he absorbs all manner of precedents and models and presses them to function in entirely new formal surroundings and serve as fresh means of expression. 'Mad' scenes, mostly frivolous or decorative (or both combined), were nothing new to opera; but there had been nothing before in the history of the genre like this desolating, deranged, virtuoso vocal cadenza, first heard in 1945.

At the end of the opera Grimes has only his own voice left to speak for him. But throughout the opera he has had another vast resource 'speaking' on his behalf: the orchestra, treated with a virtuosity that was certainly new to English music in 1945 and with not that many parallels outside England. It was with orchestral masters such as Tchaikovsky and Mahler, Stravinsky, Berg and Shostakovich that Britten had, so to speak, studied; and the results of his study showed up in the famous orchestral interludes that punctuate the opera, some of which are directly related to Grimes's tormented personality. As Hans Keller once memorably remarked, the brilliant (and Mahlerian!) 'storm' interlude, is not only a manifestation of the wildness of Nature but a representation of the storm in Grimes's own mind.

There were two influential models for the interludes in *Grimes* and indeed for the significant role of the orchestra in the opera: Berg's *Wozzeck* and Shostakovich's *Lady Macbeth*. Britten, if anything, expanded on those models, writing as centrepiece of the opera the great passacaglia which is played between Scenes 1 and 2 of Act II. It is a long and often anguished meditation on Grimes and perhaps above all on his part tender, part brutal, relationship with the apprentice boy. There are two important points to be made about the passacaglia, I think. First, the boy, who is otherwise silent throughout the opera (but for the scream that accompanies his accidental plunge to death) is given a musical profile and a 'voice' (the viola theme) in the passacaglia.[2] This in itself is indicative of the dramatic weight the interludes are required to bear and at the same time set an interesting precedent. It is only in the *orchestral* passacaglia that the composer brings Grimes and the apprentice boy into a musical relationship: for the rest, the relationship goes entirely unsung, has no musical embodiment of its own. It was on this precedent, surely, that Britten was to build further in 1951, when composing *Billy Budd*, where the crucial interview between Captain Vere and Billy was to be entrusted exclusively to a purely *orchestral* passage – the famous series of triads that concludes Act II Scene 2. It is as if there were certain aspects of experience that Britten felt beyond the reach of any form of verbalization, that could be expressed only in terms of instrumental sonorities.

That characteristic process – perhaps also a certain characteristic *ambiguity* – began in *Grimes.*

Second, and no less important than all this, we note that the passacaglia is a monumental set of *variations*, an elaborate instrumental form functioning as the very heart of the opera and repository of its central theme. This is something to keep in mind when we come to consider a later and very different kind of opera, *The Turn of the Screw.*

Britten was not to stay long with the concept of 'traditional' opera. Once he had shown that he could do it – and had learned profoundly from the experience – he dramatically changed direction, the first of two such major changes that we find as the history of his operatic *oeuvre* unfolds. *Grimes* was first heard in June 1945. In the summer of 1946 – for the post-war reopening of Glyndebourne – the première of the first *chamber opera* was launched, *The Rape of Lucretia.* There followed in 1947 – at one year's interval! – *Albert Herring*, and again, in 1948, *The Beggar's Opera.* With the creation of this extraordinary triptych of operas – a sequence of extraordinary contrasts – the idea of chamber opera was not only born but prodigiously, generously established. Let no one think that chamber opera meant diminutive! On the contrary, Britten, in terms of formal proportions and complexity of musical organization, was often working on a scale that equalled – and sometimes exceeded – anything in *Grimes.* Comparative durations tell part of the story. *Albert Herring, in toto* – I rely on the composer's calculations – runs for only one minute less than the whole of *Grimes.* The first act of the chamber opera equals the duration of the first act of *Grimes*; its second act is significantly longer. And *Herring* – an inexhaustibly fertile score – was written between the summers of 1946 and 1947! Such speed and volume of creativity were phenomenal in themselves.

Although it would appear that Britten, after *Grimes*, had turned his back on 'grand' opera – it was certainly a development that no one could have predicted – in fact the *ideal* of chamber opera had already been part of his thinking even before he had started the composition of *Grimes*, after his return from the USA to wartime England in 1942. We find this prophetic passage in a letter he wrote to Ralph Hawkes, his publisher, in London in 1943:

> I have a feeling that I can collaborate with Sadler's Wells opera a bit in the future – it would be grand to have a permanent place to produce one's operas (& I mean to write a few in my time!) It may mean cutting down means a bit (no 4 flutes or 8 horns!) – but that doesn't hurt anyone – look at the Magic Flute or Figaro, with just a tiny orchestra. It's the ideas that count.[3]

There, already adumbrated in essential outline, is the aesthetic of chamber opera. But *Grimes* had to be written first, before the new strategies could be given effect.

What were those strategies and aesthetic considerations? They were numerous and drew upon various sources of creative stimulation. There was, to start with, the social ideal: the smaller, more economical resources of chamber opera would allow for touring, would bring opera within the reach of larger audiences, not only those of the big metropolitan centres. Furthermore, it was to be opera in *English* and, in the main, *contemporary* opera. Chamber opera was designed not only for its potential audiences but also for its potential composers. There was no native tradition of opera in England and Britten's experience of writing *Grimes* had led him to believe that it was impractical and unrealistic to think of his success providing the base for similarly successful ventures by his colleagues. All the odds – economic, organizational, institutional and aesthetic – were against it. Chamber opera, however, afforded new solutions to some of those old problems.

There was yet another important dimension to the new development. The scale of 'grand' opera – the complexity of the organization and number of people involved – often led to a lack of artistic coherence. Chamber opera, so Britten supposed, would offer a reverse situation: a small body of hand-picked singers, defined artistic goals, the *integration* of stage and musical direction and – not least – design.

21 Mahler's composition sketch for 'Ich wandle nach der Heimat . . .', from 'Der Abschied', *Das Lied von der Erde*. (Gemeente Museum, The Hague). See also 'Mahler's *Abschied*: A Wrong Note Righted', p. 181.

22 *Above*, 1985: Portrait of DM by Toby Glanville. This first appeared in *The Sunday Times Magazine*, 17 November, and was later purchased by the National Portrait Gallery for its Picture Library.

23 *Opposite top left*, 1973: Portrait bust (lifesize) of DM by Anna Mahler.

24 *Opposite top right*, October 1993: The press launch of the 1995 *Mahler-Feest* at the Concertgebouw, Amsterdam. DM and Martijn Sanders, the concert hall's General Manager.

25 *Opposite*, March 1973: from the left, DM with Anna Mahler (the composer's surviving daughter), at the University of Southampton, when the Library was presented with a collection (principally) of her father's conducting scores (The Anna Mahler Collection). Looking on, Professor L. C. B. Gower (then Vice-Chancellor) and Peter Evans (then Professor of Music).

26 The famous dissonance in the first movement of the Tenth as it appears in Mahler's draft full score (reproduced from the 1924 facsimile (Paul Zsoinay, Vienna)). In the published full score, in Deryck Cooke's performing version (second edition, London, 1989), the relevant passage is to be found on pp. 20–23, bars 194–212, 'Breit'. See also 'What is Expressionism?', p. 203.

27, 28 & 29 Here, and on the following two pages, is reproduced the complete composition sketch of 'Now sleeps the crimson petal' in Britten's hand, by permission of the Trustees of the Britten–Pears Foundation and Boosey & Hawkes Music Publishers Ltd.

Now lies the Earth all Danae to the stars
Now slides the silent meteor on
legato ed espr.
& leaves a shining furrow
As thy thoughts in me
Now folds the lily all her sweetness up And
slips into the bosom of the lake
molto p
So fold thyself my dearest thou, and

A tempo I°
slip into my bosom and be lost in me.
ppp
pp
BB
March 22nd 1943

30 The first page of the composition sketch of *Nocturne*, Op. 60, reproduced by permission of the Trustees of the Britten–Pears Foundation and Boosey & Hawkes Music Publishers Ltd.

But of course the more profound reasons for the turn to chamber opera were purely musical ones, at least one of which had its roots firmly in Britten's past. He had always shown a preference for selective instrumental ensembles, for slender, transparent (not necessarily thin!) sonorities, for the solo line rather than the tutti. After all, his first published orchestral work, his Op. 1, had been a *Sinfonietta* for chamber orchestra (ten instruments). The constitution of the orchestra for the chamber operas took as its basis the precedent from 1932, while showing a slight increase in numbers from ten to a maximum of thirteen. In occupying so predominantly the chamber orchestral sphere, one might argue that Britten was acting merely as a true child of his time: it was the chamber orchestra and the small, idiosyncratically assembled instrumental ensemble that, rather than the massive apparatus of the modern symphony orchestra, had become the favoured repository of any self-respecting twentieth-century composer's thoughts. But it was Britten's brilliant and innovating idea to perceive what no one had perceived before: that the chamber orchestra could be methodically and consistently imported into opera and provide the basis for a radical rethinking, from top to bottom, of the kind of music that, as a result of developments in the musical theatre in the nineteenth century, everyone had come to assume was the only viable form of authentic 'opera'. Opera, indeed, had come to imply the large orchestra pit, the large chorus, soloists bawling their heads off, with 'dramatic', 'tragic', 'romantic' or supernatural events painted – if one may use the analogy – with very broad strokes.

I exaggerate, naturally. But this was, I think, how 'opera' was generally understood; and it was a mould – a habit of thinking, as much as anything else, that Britten was determined to break.

His introduction of the chamber orchestra – the pre-eminent twentieth-century instrumental ensemble – into the orchestra pit had all kinds of consequences. There are too many to relate here in detail, but I want to mention at least three: (1) audibility of the words, and thus an upgrading of comprehensibility (especially important for comedy, e.g. *Albert Herring* and *A Midsummer*

Night's Dream); (2) the possibility (in which (1) was also an influential factor) of a form of opera that could embrace – or embody – subtle psychological issues and states of mind; indeed to bring *within the scope of opera* areas of the human psyche that had hitherto not been 'musicalized' on the stage. Britten, in this particular respect, was peculiarly modern in his thinking and works as powerfully contrasted as *Albert Herring* and *The Turn of the Screw* show how chamber opera could treat complex psychological themes with particular success; and lastly (3), the facilitating of a highly organized type of formal thinking which in the past had been more often associated with so-called 'abstract' instrumental composition.

It is only for reasons of space that I do not dwell on the individual riches of *Lucretia*, with its topic, central to Britten, of ravished innocence, of an innocence that positively attracts destruction (cf. *Billy Budd*); on the profoundly serious comedy of *Herring*,[4] which is one of the very few operas to touch on issues of social class and the growth of the individual to independence, or the singularity of *The Beggar's Opera*, a special case this, since what chamber opera enables here is not so much a particular form of drama but, rather, an intricate form of *composition*, i.e. the seemingly inexhaustible re-imagining of old and sometimes very familiar tunes in new and surprising instrumental contexts, for which the precedent is to be found in Britten's folksong settings from the 1940s.

There is no thought in my mind that the triptych which spans the years 1946–8 should be considered as mere preparation for later and greater things. But it is not to underrate the significance of the earlier achievements if one acknowledges that it was in 1954, with *The Turn of the Screw*, first performed at Venice as part of the Biennale of that year, that Britten brought the concept of chamber opera to an unsurpassed pitch. It was a work of great psychological complication and intensity on a dramatic theme – this time the corruption of innocence (but whose innocence?) – with which Britten was much preoccupied throughout his life; and the drama was embodied in a form that was not borrowed from the forms associated with dramatic music but on the contrary was itself an established instrumental form: a theme and variations. In fact, the entire opera takes the shape of a huge orchestral variation set, the variations functioning as interludes between the scenes. It was an audacious reversal of a feature of *Grimes* I have already remarked on, where the opera has at – and as – its centre, a passacaglia – Britten's favoured variation format – for orchestra alone. Now, in the *Screw*, *the orchestral variations incorporate the opera.*[5] The work stands, unique, as the wellnigh perfect amalgam of instrumental and dramatic forms and techniques. It is a chamber opera that aspires to and achieves the conditions of elaborate chamber music in the demands it makes of its performers and, no less, of its audiences. (The virtuosity of Britten's scoring for his chamber ensemble is a story of its own. If there is an ensemble of vocal soloists on stage, there is also a team of instrumental soloists in the pit. The combination, whether in *Herring* or the *Screw*, is often electrifying.)

Innovation can be found in almost any dimension of *The Turn of the Screw* one cares to examine. For example, it was this opera that introduced the most elaborate and sophisticated role – the boy, Miles – Britten was ever to write for a treble. But the innovations I wish to emphasize are those connected with the fundamental expansion of Britten's techniques, by which I mean the development of his musical language. I think I have said enough already to suggest that the whole phenomenon of chamber opera was in itself one of the quiet revolutions he effected during his lifetime; and it would have been surprising if it had not been accompanied by the exploitation of fresh techniques to embody the new concepts. In the *Screw*, in particular, this most intensively and rigorously composed of the chamber operas, we encounter – for the first time systematically – techniques of composition and principles of organization based on a conscious manipulation of all twelve chromatic pitches, self-evidently so in the unfolding of the famous 'theme' (the 'screw' itself).

But it is not just in such twelve-note compilations, both vertical and horizontal, that Britten's interest in conscripting all twelve pitches of the chromatic scale to his own purposes manifested itself. The overall tonal scheme of the opera, as laid out scene by scene across two acts, is also systematically ordered by an intention both to mobilize *and* organize the resources of the chromatic scale. Typically, however, Britten's exhaustive exploitation of the spectrum of tonalities and the ingenuity of the symmetries extrapolated from it are entirely bound up with the inmost nature of the drama – the levels on which the action takes place, the remorseless turning of the 'screw'. There is nothing, ultimately, theoretical about the tonal plan: it proves, on scrutiny, to be yet another embodiment of the drama.

In no Schoenbergian sense, of course, was the *Screw* a 'twelve-note' composition, since Britten's rotation of his 'row' had everything to do with the intervallic relationship of his chosen pitches and there was never any question that the construction of the 'row' would influence their vertical disposition. But the opera shows how brilliantly and imaginatively in the 1950s Britten was putting together his own highly personal and idiosyncratic version of 'total chromaticism'. It was increasingly a compositional technique that incorporated principles drawn from serial thinking; but, in making these raids on the serial universe, Britten abandoned none of the riches of tonality. As musical dramatist – and in this respect at least precisely like Wagner – he would not have seen the logic of *reducing* the stock of styles and means of organization available to him.

It is natural, I think, that it was the composition of the *Screw* that required of Britten these new developments in technique. The extraordinary character and complexity of the psychological drama demanded a comparable complexity of musical language and at the same time an over-riding rigour of compositional method. But while there was indeed much that was new about the *Screw*, there were also dimensions of it that brought to fulfilment dramatic and musical preoccupations that had surfaced in earlier stage works. I have already mentioned the 'star' role of Miles – a treble – in the *Screw*. This was not the first time that Britten had used a boy's voice in his operas and indeed there were many precedents for the use of children's voices in his non-theatrical compositions. The *scale* of Miles's role was new, however. But in 1949, in *The Little Sweep*, the miniature opera that formed part of the entertainment *Let's Make an Opera*, Britten had composed a stage work in which children were in the majority as dramatis personae and performers. One might think that the children's opera was worlds away from the *Screw*; and so it was. But its dramatic theme, the plight of chimney-sweeping boys in nineteenth-century England, was yet another form of Britten's preoccupation with 'innocence', this time innocence maltreated; while undoubtedly the experience of writing a perfectly crafted theatre piece which would accommodate children's technical limitations without sacrifice of the composer's technical imperatives, prepared the way for the later incorporation of children's voices into otherwise wholly 'adult' works.

There is one last aspect of the *Screw* that I wish to mention, though not more than that because it really constitutes a topic in its own right. I refer to what might be called its characteristic *ambiguity*, which had already surfaced in *Billy Budd* (1951) and emerged yet more powerfully in the *Screw*. One often writes of Britten's dramatic themes and principal concerns as if they were always straightforward conflicts between Good and Evil, the Individual and Society, Innocence and Experience, War and Peace, and so on and so on. But in fact, while Britten was certainly much taken up with these issues, he was a complicated artist and the positions and attitudes that we find expressed in the particular works of art embodying them, are often – and I believe intendedly – ambiguous. Can we ever leave a performance of *Billy Budd* feeling quite convinced that we have fully understood the morality of Captain Vere's judgement of Billy? Was Vere, like Billy, himself fatally flawed? As Vere himself meditates in the Prologue which opens the opera: 'The good has never been perfect . . . There is always some flaw in it . . . some stammer in the divine speech.'

And likewise when we have heard the *Screw*, can we be quite sure whose innocence has been corrupted? Miles's? The Governess's? The Housekeeper's? And are the Governess and Quint in fact in direct opposition, or perhaps *both* of them instruments of Miles's destruction? The latter surprising conclusion might explain the deliberate ambiguity that Britten creates by allotting in some important respects a common music to the Governess and Quint. I count this fascinating ambiguousness to be one of the new areas of feeling that Britten introduced into twentieth-century opera.

That Britten was able to explore this new territory we certainly owe to the chamber-opera concept which provided him with a dramatic instrument refined enough to deal with such subtle psychological shading. And if someone objects – quite properly – that *Billy Budd* was scarcely *chamber* opera, since the performing apparatus it requires is a large one, and it was written for a big theatre, the answer must be that after *Grimes* and the chamber triptych of 1946–8, all the operas, almost without distinction, were heavily infiltrated by chamber operatic ideals, ideas and techniques; and indeed the very themes and topics of their dramas were much closer to the psychological dramas of the chamber operas than the broad, eventful canvases of conventional opera.

This is in no way to underrate the splendid and imposing set pieces of *Budd*. But in reality this is *not* an opera about life at sea, *not* a successor to *Grimes*, but a *metaphysical* opera, and more a representation of the confusion that attends attempts to define 'eternal truth' than a clarification – or affirmation – of it. This would be singular enough in itself – it is distinctly not the stuff of which grand opera is customarily made – but there are many other singularities to detach *Budd* from tradition: the all-male cast, a score that at times gives greater exposure to woodwind and brass than strings and, at its most extreme, shrinks to a tiny chamber ensemble. Consider, for example, Act I Scene 3, the temptation of Billy by the Novice (Fig. 57 *et seq.*), where the exchange between the two men – in which the *clarity of the words* is critical to the success of the scene [Fig. 117] – is accompanied by the slenderest of instrumental forces: a pair of oboes with cor anglais alternating with lower strings, a pair of muted trumpets added [Fig. 119]. It is a sound world that is rooted in the sonorities of the dramatic chamber music that Britten had devised in the 1940s and the influence of which can be discerned in every single opera he composed in succeeding decades. I chose *Budd* as my example because of the methodical ambiguity that links it to the *Screw* and because outwardly *Budd* seems to belong outside the chamber rather than inside. But the truth is that one could find similar examples of 'interior' dramatic music in any of the operas that succeeded *Budd*, even in *Gloriana* (1953), written to celebrate the Coronation of Queen Elizabeth II.[6] This was a work committed to a big State occasion, but even here Britten eschewed a pomp-and-circumstance manner which almost any other composer might have thought obligatory. Thus there is music in the first scene of Act III, where the Queen is attended by her ladies-in-waiting, the intimacy and lyricism of which evoke memories of *Lucretia*; and there are a dozen other instances of chamber opera textures taking precedence. Once again there is an irresistible logic at work. If Britten was not particularly interested in beating the big orchestral drum that normally accompanies State pageantry, nor was he interested in the romantic or heroic theme as subject of his drama which would have been the predictable choice for such an occasion. He chose instead a topic of some seriousness, as relevant for our own time as it may have been for the Elizabethans: the conflict between personal inclination and public obligation, between passion and duty. And, on top of that, chose to illustrate that theme through the unfolding of the ill-starred love of the Queen for the impetuous (and much younger) Earl of Essex, a relationship pursued throughout the opera with surprising intensity and in no little psychological depth. It was a type of relationship, one might think, for which Britten's chamber operatic thinking had specifically prepared him. An odd kind of Coronation opera, maybe, but a characteristic Britten enterprise and one that was faithful, despite all the ceremonial pressures, to the operatic tradition that he had himself created and within which he continued to create – and innovate – until his untimely death in 1976.

I have already indicated above that a feature of Britten's operatic *oeuvre* across the years was the expansion of his musical language and in particular the incorporation of twelve-note compilations into his armoury of expressive means. As his list of theatrical works inexorably lengthened, so was the methodical exploitation and organization of all twelve pitches of the chromatic scale raised in profile. To both *Owen Wingrave* (1971) and *Death in Venice* (1973), for example, twelve-note 'propositions' (as John Evans, who has done important analytical work in this field, defines them) are fundamental to the compositional techniques – and to the dramatic character – of each opera. It cannot be repeated too often that Britten's twelve-note ideas are never, in the context of his operas, 'theoretical' in practice but always have a specific dramatic association.

A perfect example of this is to be found at the beginning of Act II of Britten's Shakespeare opera, *A Midsummer Night's Dream*, first performed at Aldeburgh in 1960. The magical progression of four chords which opens the act unfolds all twelve pitches without repetition and represents, in its totality, the world of sleep and dreams. It is a world within which all the characters in the opera, for the duration of the act, have their being, the context in which we observe their trials and tribulations, their fortunes and their follies. Sleep closes the act, as it began it: but this time the rotation of the chords underpins the sublime lullaby of the fairies, the promise that

> Jack shall have Jill,
> Naught shall go ill,
> The man shall have his mare again,
> And all shall be well.

Here, surely, the totality of the musical materials has taken on an additional significance and represents not only the healing power of sleep but also in some sense a restoration and reaffirmation of the *natural order of the universe*: at the end of Act II everyone and everything (and therefore all twelve pitches) are in place, and the lovers can wake in Act III to the happiness which has hitherto eluded them in the labyrinth of the magic infested wood.[7]

An entirely different but no less specific form of association is found at the very beginning of *Owen Wingrave* (1971), Britten's penultimate opera, written originally for television. The Britten paradox again: he was not slow to seize the opportunity that television availed him, to address a mass audience, but typically chose as his dramatic theme a minority cause – pacifism – which he had passionately espoused throughout his life. *Wingrave*, indeed, formed a kind of theatrical pendant to *War Requiem* of 1962. The world of violence, to which he was implacably opposed but which he recognized to form a seemingly ineradicable part of human nature, is represented in the opera by a twelve-note idea, another sequence of chords (three this time), and scored, appropriately, for percussion orchestra. This 'pulsation', as I have described it, haunts the opera: it functions both as the basic source of the work's musical materials and as symbol of the source of the drama itself, the overwhelming presence of violence, the world out of which the hero, Owen, is born, against which he valiantly struggles, and by which he is finally overpowered.

A cathartic moment in the opera is Owen's great aria, his celebration of the idea of peace, in Act II, where, for a moment, the hero believes – and his audience in the theatre along with him – that the power of war and violence has been vanquished. The illusion, for that is what is proves to be, is created by a unique orchestral accompaniment which combines two elements: a luminous, otherworldly, gamelan-like percussion texture, heterophonically conceived, which surrounds the aria like a halo; and, supporting Owen's positive proclamations, a series of 'affirmative' triads, the roots of which span all twelve pitches. One's first response to the triads, to be sure, is that they represent a re-formulation of the opening twelve-note idea associated with violence, i.e. violence has been conquered and is now re-expressed in terms of Owen's (and the composer's) passionate pacifism. But in the light of later dramatic events, when Owen is himself struck down by the power of violence and lies dead, we come to realize that the chords can also be differently interpreted: their triadic formation tells us one thing; their roots – rooted, literally so, in a twelve-note series – tell us another. As a result, there is an inexorable and awful logic about the *dénouement*: Owen's confidence in peace was after all based on an illusion: far from being banished, violence was there all the time. Having said that – which represents my view of this celebrated passage – I can see that it would be possible to produce alternative interpretations, e.g. that the majestic series of major and minor triads in fact signifies a real triumph of peace over war, the triad, so to speak, occupying the enemy's positions, all twelve of them. Each listener has to decide for himself how precisely to 'read' the information the music communicates. It is a superb example of the complexity of Britten's dramatic language and at the same time another example of that characteristic and fascinating *ambiguity* that I have already touched on.[8]

My final example comes from Britten's last opera, *Death in Venice* (1973). It is again a twelve-note compilation and again, like the menacing pulsation – the heartbeat of violence – which opens *Wingrave*, is heard at the very start of the opera. There is reason for this, of course. We are *at the start of things*; and the point of departure for the opera is the protagonist's creative paralysis. Gustav von Aschenbach is a celebrated author whose inspiration has left him. He has all the resources of literature effortlessly at his command but can make nothing, create nothing, out of this totality. He is, if I may risk an analogy, the image of a human dictionary, a man of many words who has lost the capacity to put the words together so that they make meaningful and imaginative sense.

It is, I believe, in this perspective that we should understand Britten's use of a twelve-note idea to depict Aschenbach's intellectual frustration and impotence. (One recognizes the paradox, naturally, that in order to get this point over effectively Britten himself had to make the choices with regard to the selection and manipulation of his pitches – for Britten, the equivalent of Aschenbach's words – which were beyond his hero's reach.) The very first bars of the opera lay out the proposition which is not only an image of the source of Aschenbach's dilemma but also the actual source of the materials out of which the opera itself is to be built, materials that incorporate all twelve pitches and thus a summary of the vocabulary of music, of total chromaticism. As the drama develops, so does Aschenbach respond and react to experience, and as he begins to move from restless abstraction to feeling and passion, so too do the musical ideas of the opera cohere and take on identifiable shapes. If, in some sense, the initiating twelve-note idea was intended by Britten to suggest his hero's state of mind *before* experience and imagination had had the opportunity to modify or influence it, it can also be 'read', I believe, as an image of a quasi-precompositional stage in the creating of a work of art, the composer articulating all the materials that are available to him before bringing *his* experience and imagination, i.e. the actual process of creation, to bear upon them. As I have already indicated above, some compositional choices and decisions had to be made even to make manifest Aschenbach's indecisiveness, but that said and taken into account, I am confident that one of the ways that Britten wanted *Death in Venice* to be understood was as a *parable* of the artist's relationship to the work of art that he excavates from the materials available to him. Aschenbach, of course, is a novelist. But substitute notes – pitches – for words and one comes to realize that one of the topics this extraordinary opera is 'about' is in fact the making of it – and indeed the making of works of art in general. And the beauty – or terror – of the basic twelve-note proposition is surely this: that everything that flows from it, every musical idea, however selectively constructed, must in some sense be related to or derived from it. Thus the totality of the proposition creates a kind of all-embracing net, from which Aschenbach cannot escape:

whatever is extrapolated from it, to serve as an image of new feeling, or reflect fresh experience, must none the less be part of it. It is this which allows the opera to achieve its supreme irony, that Aschenbach's pursuit of freedom and liberation from the annihilating paralysis which has him in its grip contains the very seeds of his eventual disintegration and extinction.

We may be conscious here of a parallel with *Owen Wingrave*. There, likewise, the opera's protagonist proves unable to triumph over the destructive influence embodied in the opening twelve-note pulsation. In *Death in Venice*, however, one further irony remains. The act of composing Aschenbach's crucifixion, if one may express it thus, leaves us with the enduring work of art that the opera is. Perhaps this most literary, literate and theoretically minded of Britten's operatic heroes would have thought it a worthy exchange.

In the context of the 'peace' aria in *Owen Wingrave* I mentioned the 'gamelan-like percussion texture' which accompanies Owen's proclamation; and in touching on that dimension of the music, I introduce the topic of what must be considered, I think, the second major phase of innovation in the history of Britten's operas. The first, of course, as I have made clear, was the development, after the launching of *Peter Grimes*, of the chamber-opera concept in the 1940s; and, significantly enough, the second phase, belonging to the 1960s, was also tied up with a yet further intensification of the idea of chamber opera, manifesting itself this time in another remarkable triptych, the so-called church parables, *Curlew River* (1964), *The Burning Fiery Furnace* (1966) and *The Prodigal Son* (1968), all of them, incidentally, composed in Venice and influenced by the acoustics of Venetian churches, which Britten knew so well.

The forces typically required for one of these church parables speak for the innovative economy and idiosyncrasy of the instrumental ensemble. One might have thought the thirteen players of the original chamber operas of the 1940s a minimum beyond which, for theatrical purposes, it was not possible to go. But the

1960s were to prove otherwise, and *Curlew River*, which was to provide the model for its successor, is scored for an even more selective group of just seven players: flute (doubling piccolo), horn, viola, double-bass, harp, percussion and chamber organ.

It was the flute, above all, which was to furnish the characteristic colour of the score of *Curlew River*, providing as it does the opera's protagonist, the Madwoman, with an alternative 'voice', and the opera's successors follow the same principle. The basic ensemble remains, but each work offers a different characterizing instrument: in the *Furnace*, the alto trombone (Nebuchadnezzar), in the *Prodigal Son*, a high D trumpet (the worldly Tempter). There is one hidden aspect of the scoring which goes some way to explaining how it was that Britten could make so much, in terms of sonority, of so little. I mentioned above the influence of Venetian church acoustics, and this explains something fundamental about the parables' sound world. They were imagined, that is, for performance in a resonant acoustic, which on its own account reinforces, multiplies and boosts the volume and mass of sound created by the vocal and instrumental forces. In short, the specific acoustic for which these works were composed plays a role in the scoring – itself constitutes *an invisible but audible resource*.

A further unique feature of the church parables is their all-male casts, for which Britten found the model in Tokyo in February 1956, though there had already been a precedent for that novel departure from convention in *Billy Budd* in 1951. Likewise, if one is seeking for meaningful anticipations, there is no doubt that *Noye's Fludde* (1958), the setting of a Chester miracle play – a form of medieval English religious drama – was a significant step on the road to the later church operas.

Although written primarily for young performers (and with audience participation), *Noye's Fludde* – indubitably the most important and inspired of all Britten's works for children, in which technical constraints prove to be the very *raison d'être* of its arresting musical invention – is both a parable and an investigation of the peculiar properties of a church acoustic. But it is unlikely that in 1957, the year in which *Noye's Fludde* was composed, Britten foresaw the future development of the idea of the church parable. He still had fully to assimilate the impact of the round-the-world trip he had made with Peter Pears between November 1955 and March 1956, a journey that took in, among many other countries, Japan and Bali.[9] In Tokyo, Britten heard the ancient Imperial Court music of Japan, Gagaku, and he visited the Noh theatre, where a performance of *Sumidagawa* ('The Sumida River'), in his own words,

> made a tremendous impression upon me, the simple touching story, the economy of the style, the intense slowness of the action, the marvellous skill and control of the performers, the beautiful costumes, the mixture of the chanting, speech, singing, which with the three instruments made up the strange music – it all offered a totally new 'operatic' experience.
>
> There was no conductor – the instrumentalists sat on the stage, so did the chorus, and the chief characters made their entrance down a long ramp. The lighting was strictly non-theatrical. The cast was all-male, the one female character [the Madwoman] wearing an exquisite mask which made no attempt to hide the male jowl beneath it.
>
> The memory of this play has seldom left my mind in the years since.[10]

These were two musical examples – Gagaku and Noh – which were to have a profound influence on the creation of the church parables, the new form of chamber opera which Britten was to launch in the 1960s, and above all on the first of the parables, based on the very Noh play, *Sumidagawa*, by which he had been so impressed.

A further, fresh source of experience was the visit to the island of Bali (Indonesia). The impact of the Balinese gamelan showed up immediately in the full-length ballet, *The Prince of the Pagodas*, which was first performed on 1 January 1957 at the Royal Opera House, Covent Garden. It was the first major and overt indication of the incorporation of non-Western musical ideas and sonorities into Britten's composing, though now, knowing what we did not know before – of his friendship with the Balinese scholar, Colin McPhee, and the seminal passage from *Paul Bunyan* – we realize that the wheel had in a very real sense turned full circle: it was in 1957, in the *Pagodas* ballet, that the consequences of Britten's first encounter with Balinese music in New York, from 1939 to 1942, unequivocally manifested themselves in one of the most richly imagined – and also the longest – of his purely orchestral scores. We thought at the time of the ballet's first performance, it must be confessed, that the use of the gamelan (i.e. Balinese percussion) orchestra was more 'local colour' than anything else.[11] We had no inkling of Britten's 'Balinese' past and certainly would never have guessed that from this point onwards the gamelan was to play a vital role in certain of the succeeding operas. I have mentioned the gamelan-like halo that surrounds the 'peace' aria in *Owen Wingrave*, but it is in *Death in Venice* that the presence of the gamelan is most vivid: a large, independent percussion orchestra is the means by which Britten characterizes the beautiful Polish boy, Tadzio, and his family. But in fact the influence of Balinese music on the last of the operas is pervasive and fertilizes much music beyond that associated with the Polish family.[12]

If it is through the use of a quasi-gamelan, independent percussion orchestra that the 'oriental' influence in Britten's later works asserts itself most immediately and colourfully, even a cursory examination of his scores from the same period will show how deeply his compositional techniques had been penetrated by a principle that is inseparable from any consideration of how oriental music itself functions compositionally: heterophony.

This technique declares itself unequivocally in the first of the church parables, *Curlew River* (Fig. 5), in the instrumental interlude, the so-called 'robing music', in which the cast of monks assume the costumes of the characters in the drama. In this passage, the tiny, conductor-less ensemble, subjects the plainchant – the basic material out of which the whole opera is built – to 'classical' heterophonic treatment, i.e. different rhythmic forms of the unison are combined at the octave. It is a simple, if arresting, example of the heterophonic practices Britten introduced into his late works and there are many, many others, in all three parables, which are far more complex in texture and construction. It is also *precisely* the technique twenty-two bars of which twenty-three years earlier in New York, Britten had introduced into *Paul Bunyan* to accompany the moon turning blue!

A more complex example of heterophony in *Curlew River* occurs at Fig. 8. At first sight, the first vocal statement of the Ferryman – 'I am the ferryman' – would appear to present a conventional relationship of vocal part and accompaniment. Closer inspection, however, reveals a different state of affairs. This might be described as a continuous unison shared between voice and (principal) horn – the Ferryman's characterizing instrument – the basic motivic shape of which extends itself through the systematic incorporation of hitherto unused pitches, the voice taking over the new pitch from the horn: this, then, is a unison which in certain important and characteristic respects behaves as a 'row'. Moreover, when the texture appears to break down into voice part and 'accompaniment', the accompaniment proves to be none other than a different rhythmic version of the vocal part – the vocal part, as it were, is accompanying itself; and what is true if one looks at the passage horizontally is no less true if one looks at it vertically: the vertical conflations are identical with the horizontal compilation of the unison. It is at this point, when one is uniquely confronted in Britten's music by a systematic regulating of the horizontal and vertical dimensions, that some words of Hans Keller's strike home to the very heart of the matter:

> Biographically and chronologically, Britten's visit to the Far East in 1956 seems 'the cause' of all later heterophonic ventures. A cause, yes, but *causa prima*? On the contrary, it was serial thought that was the *conditio sine qua non* of all later heterophonic development.[13]

It is strange but true that Britten's practice of heterophony brought him closest to the technique of the 'classical' serial method, not through the deployment of all twelve pitches of the chromatic scale but through the vertical and horizontal integration of his musical idea. One recalls that it was precisely this principle, in heterophonic context, that was revealed in 1941 in *Paul Bunyan*.

In the ballet of 1957, *The Prince of the Pagodas*, the influence of Bali was paramount: thus the profile accorded the gamelan was a high one. In the first church parable of 1964, *Curlew River*, the influence of Japan was dominant, not only in the choice of text and performance convention but musically too: the debt owed to Gagaku by *Curlew River* grows the more one studies the score.[14] But while one may perceive a difference in emphasis in the manifestation of the 'oriental' influence as between Britten's ballet and his church operas, after 1964, when the first parable was first performed, there was not a dramatic work of his that did not consistently and comprehensively reflect the new gains in language. *Death in Venice*, the last opera, provides us with generous illustration of the point I am making. We find there not only the gamelan, to identify and embody Tadzio and his companions, but also an invasive heterophony, a technique that can now detach itself from an 'exotic' association and function simply in its own right as a further compositional resource, for example the orchestral prelude to Act II, an exclusively heterophonic texture which assembles itself above E and B pedal notes (a pair of horns). Thus are the diatonic and the heterophonic reconciled! *Death in Venice*, then, brings together all the linguistic innovations I have been dwelling on in these pages – not only heterophony and the gamelan but also the characteristic twelve-note idea – Aschenbach's creative impotence – which opens the opera. By any standards it is a 'major' work, of imposing proportions and incorporating one of the most exacting and elaborate roles for tenor in twentieth-century opera: at the same time it calls upon dance and mime as further means of expression. It is, indubitably, a 'monument'; and yet the roots of its sound world are located in chamber opera, the obligatory medium for Britten if he were to explore a sensibility as complex in its psychology as Aschenbach's.

I put together a few of the opera's distinguishing features – another is its exceptional orchestration – in order to show how in a very real sense the last work for the theatre offered a summation of the continuous process of innovation, expansion, experimentation and remodelling of tradition which was the history of Britten's operatic *oeuvre* during the preceding decades; and all of it accomplished without the composer saying a public word about it. A quiet innovator indeed. But when death silenced the voice of his music in 1976, the world lost a composer who had made one of the most powerful and original contributions to musical theatre in our century. Disdainful of theoretical speculation or dogma, but immensely articulate and audaciously speculative in his music, the Britten paradox was sustained to the end.

NOTES

1 MC: See Philip Brett (ed.), *Benjamin Britten: 'Peter Grimes'* (Cambridge University Press, Cambridge, 1983), pp. 180–96.

2 MC: The identification of the viola theme with Grimes's apprentice was first made by Edward Sackville-West, who described it as 'a desolate, wandering motif depicting the workhouse boy who, accustomed no doubt to a steady lack of kindness, does not know how to deal with Grimes's sudden change of mood': see 'The Musical and Dramatic Structure' in Eric Crozier (ed.), *Benjamin Britten: 'Peter Grimes'* (Sadler's Wells Opera Books No. 3; London, 1945), p. 44. Since Britten himself contributed to this collection of essays on the opera and was close to the author, it seems likely that Sackville-West's interpretation had the composer's tacit endorsement.

3 MC: Letter dated 12 March 1943: see DM and Philip Reed (eds.), *Letters from a Life: Selected Letters and Diaries of Benjamin Britten*, vol. 2 (Faber and Faber, London, 1991), pp. 1128–30.

4 MC: See DM's 'The Serious Comedy of *Albert Herring*', this volume pp. 352–64.

5 In the 1930s Britten had already shown his mastery of variation form, for example in the *Frank Bridge Variations* for string orchestra (1937), a work that helped him secure his early international reputation. It was a form to which he turned again and again throughout his life. Interestingly enough, the

composition of the *Screw* led to a parallel composition in another sphere altogether – vocal chamber music. I refer to Britten's *Canticle III* (1955), the *form* of which is precisely that of the *Screw* – a fascinating instance of a formal relationship between two quite distinct areas of composition. Finally, one must not overlook *The Golden Vanity* (1966), Britten's last theatrical piece for children, and once again an example of his variation technique pressed into the service of a drama, albeit a miniature one.

6 MC: For DM's recent consideration of the musico-dramatic tensions in *Gloriana*, see his essay 'The Paradox of *Gloriana*: Simple and Difficult' in Paul Banks (ed.), *Britten's 'Gloriana'* (Boydell and Brewer (Aldeburgh Studies in Music), Woodbridge, 1993), pp. 67–75.

7 MC: The dramatic symbolism underlying Britten's dodecaphonic manipulations in *A Midsummer Night's Dream* has been further investigated in MC, 'Britten and Shakespeare: Dramatic and Musical Cohesion in *A Midsummer Night's Dream*', *Music and Letters* 74/2 (May 1993), pp. 246–68.

8 MC: DM offered further insight into this remarkable passage during a public forum on *Owen Wingrave* held at the 46th Aldeburgh Festival on 11 June 1993 in the Jubilee Hall with Myfanwy Piper, John Evans and Steuart Bedford. The following is a revised transcript of what he said:

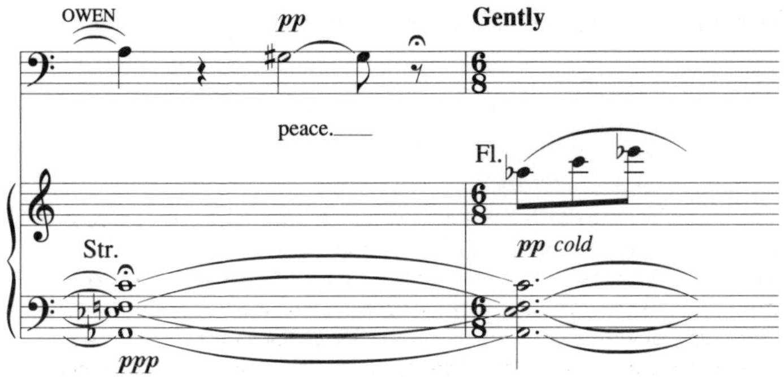

My first example is the so-called 'peace' chord in the second act of the opera (one bar before Fig. 260). The chord itself is identified for us in typical Britten fashion: we hear the chord first in the strings, and then Owen tells us what it means, what it stands for: 'Peace.' (There's a parallel instance in the *Nocturne* (1958), one bar before Fig. 30 in the Keats setting, where precisely the same procedure operates with regard to C major and sleep: the chord first (strings!), and then the identification of it by the singer: 'Sleep.')

I have just suggested that Owen 'tells us' what the chord 'stands for': peace. But does he? Does it? Much depends on whom we decide the chord belongs to. Who is hearing it? Is it Owen's? Is it ours, the audience's? Do *we* know something Owen doesn't know?

Let's take that last point first. Are we to read the chord as a painful illusion, Owen thinking he's achieved peace while we, from the internal composition of the chord, know that in fact at the heart of it – the Ballad (see my second example) – is the old Wingrave history of violence, of which Owen himself, inescapably, is to be a victim, as the *dénouement* of the opera shows? Is the chord telling us that Owen cannot avoid his inheritance as a Wingrave for all his efforts to *dis*inherit himself?

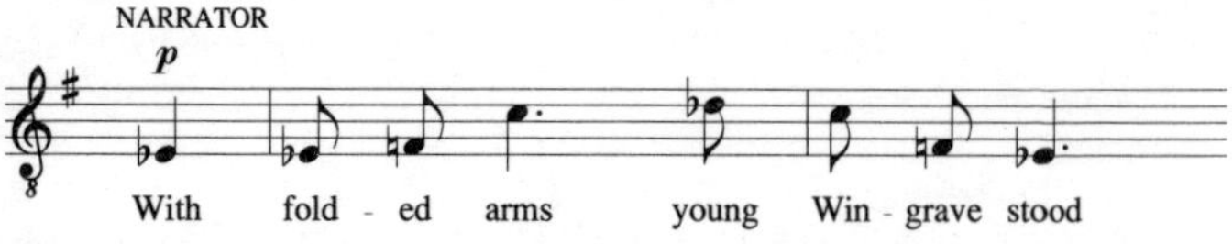

Or is there another way of hearing the chord? That first set of alternatives depends on our hearing the chord as an ironic *commentary* on Owen's illusion, i.e. it represents a predetermined future of which as yet he has no knowledge. But what if the chord belongs to *him* and – because it is undeniably, if briefly, serene and affirmative and prolonged – represents his final *triumph* over his Wingravian ancestry and inheritance? Then the incorporation, the vertical conflation, of the Ballad's opening phrase (my second example above) is not, so to speak, the worm in the bud, but, rather, the ultimate pacification and mitigation, for Owen at least, of the violence, which, he suggests, is locked up in all of us, and locked up in the chord. (In his final encounter with Kate in Act II, Owen locates in the haunted room in which he is to die 'the anger of the world . . . the horrible power that makes men fight' [Fig. 276^{+1}].) We have to decide whether the chord is telling us that for Owen violence at last has been caged, contained; or whether it is waiting there to burst forth and claim its last victim, Owen, the last of the Wingraves.

There's the name too, is there not?, *Win–grave*, a curious conflation, itself juxtaposing the two poles of experience in the opera: triumph and defeat; life and death; war and peace; love and hate; fear and courage. Owen, ultimately, in terms of courage emerges victor; but what he has won is a grave for himself.

The 'peace' chord likewise encapsulates the same enigma, the same ambiguity, one wholly characteristic of the composer, even though there was no uncertainty on his part about *his* commitment to peace. As for Owen – well, the opera closes with a repeat of the Ballad and Owen lies dead on the floor of the haunted room. So from one point of view, yes, the Wingraves get their man; and Owen turns out, after all, to have been a Wingrave. In this perspective, it is tempting to think that the chord *was* an illusion, that the seeds of Owen's destruction are there in it, and that violence prevails. A tempting reading of the chord, but now I think otherwise: that the chord represents Owen at peace with himself. (We must note too that Owen's G♯ (= A♭) supplies the *last* of the twelve pitches of the triadic 'series' that has underpinned the 'peace' aria.) He has brought off the most difficult task of all – conquered the violence, the Wingravian inheritance, within himself. His actual fate is of relatively little importance. He was a hero because he was true to himself. And it is to that truth (close to Britten's heart: 'What we are, we remain', as the three Israelites proclaim in *The Burning Fiery Furnace*) that the 'peace' chord speaks.

DM is a shade embarrassed to recall now that he saluted Britten with the 'peace' chord on the occasion of the composer's sixtieth birthday in 1973, when its potential ambiguities had not fully dawned on him. (See the programme for the London Symphony Orchestra's concert at the Royal Festival Hall, 25 November.) However, the irony of the quotation may have given an ironic composer some unintended satisfaction.

9 MC: See pp. 417–18, n. 10.
10 MC: From the composer's preface to *Curlew River*, Op. 71 (Faber Music, London, 1964).
11 MC: See my account of DM's uncharacteristically dismissive response to the Balinese dimension of *Pagodas* in 1957 (p. XXXIX).
12 MC: See MC, 'Britten and the Gamelan: Balinese Influences in *Death in Venice*' in DM (ed.), *Benjamin Britten: 'Death in Venice'* (Cambridge University Press (Cambridge Opera Handbook), Cambridge, 1987), pp. 115–28.
13 MC: Hans Keller, 'Introduction: Operatic Music and Britten' in David Herbert (ed.), *The Operas of Benjamin Britten* (Hamish Hamilton, London, 1979), pp. XXIX–XXX.
14 MC: See MC, 'Britten and the *Shō*', *Musical Times* 129 (1988), pp. 231–3.

Our Hunting Fathers

Our Hunting Fathers must claim our attention on three counts. First and foremost, because it is one of the most brilliant and original of all Britten's compositions. In my view, it is the work that most excitingly represents the remarkable creative gifts he developed in the 1930s. Second, it is an outstanding example of his close collaboration throughout that period with the poet W. H. Auden (1907–1973); and it could well be argued that *Our Hunting Fathers* was the most considerable work to result from a historic collaboration without parallel in the history of the arts in England between the First and Second World Wars. Third, Britten's first published orchestral song-cycle – its predecessor was the set of orchestral songs for high voice, *Quatre Chansons Françaises*, on texts by Verlaine and Hugo, which he wrote when he was a schoolboy of fourteen, in 1928, but was not brought to first performance until 1980 – very fascinatingly shows the interpenetration of the two compositional worlds that he inhabited with such extraordinary energy and versatility during the 1930s: on the one hand, music that one might think of as in the mainstream tradition of music composed for the concert hall, concert-goers and relatively orthodox ensembles, both large and small, and instrumental and choral; and on the other, music with a precisely spelled-out social message or commentary, and more often than not tied in with one of the media – the experimental theatre (for example, the Group Theatre), the film studio (chiefly the GPO

Sleeve-note to BBC Records REGL 417, 1981

Film Unit), or the radio (the BBC) – in which Britten and his collaborators, and in particular W. H. Auden, were innovatingly at work. This latter category more often than not was a form of engaged, committed music, directly political in content. The politics of Britten and his friends were at this time conspicuously of the Left – a mixed bag of views, no doubt, but certainly united in opposition to the ruling politics of the day, and all of them coloured, indeed haunted, by the common fear of the rise of Fascism in Europe, by the outbreak of the Spanish Civil War (in the summer of 1936), and by the certainty that this was no more than the prelude to a vast conflagration that might altogether sweep away an ailing European civilization.[1]

It was against this menacing backcloth that Britten and his companions moved, worked, loved and lived in the 1930s. *Our Hunting Fathers*, while commissioned in fact by a mainstream English musical festival, the 34th Norwich and Norfolk Triennial Music Festival of 1936, and, in every sense, exploiting conventional resources – the London Philharmonic Orchestra, conducted by the youthful composer, with Sophie Wyss, soprano, with whose voice in mind the work was written – at the same time reflected those political preoccupations which were the concern of so many of the younger generation of painters, dramatists, film-makers, poets and playwrights in the 1930s. *Our Hunting Fathers*, though of course in highly complex, sophisticated and symbolic terms, represented some of the same feelings, anxieties and indignation that were expressed at another level altogether in other and simpler forms of committed music, e.g. the quasi-music-hall songs for *Pageant of Empire*, a satirical *Left Revue*, anti-imperialist, anti-Blimp sketch that Britten wrote with Montagu Slater (the future librettist of *Peter Grimes*!) in 1937.

The backcloth information I give here, though only in the simplest outline, provides us with one essential key to the truth about *Our Hunting Fathers*. For undoubtedly at one level, the work was designed as a commentary on the political events of 1936, the year in which the cycle was composed. Auden and Britten had their first discussion about the project on 2 January. Composition proceeded in fits and starts: Britten had many problems to solve and by no means all the songs came easily. The bulk of the work was committed to paper between May and July, and the song-cycle was finished on 23 July and first performed at Norwich on 25 September. In March 1936, Germany (under Hitler) had occupied the Rhineland; in May, the Italians (under Mussolini) had occupied Abyssinia; on 18 July, the Spanish Civil War had begun. There was much 'hunting' already in evidence, and there was more – and more savage – hunting, to come. *Our Hunting Fathers* was a parable of and for its time, but of a quality that transcended its overt topicality; and the work remains as vivid and sharp for us today as for the scandalized or baffled audience of 1936.

How the threatening turbulence of 1936 impinged on *Our Hunting Fathers* can be assessed by looking at the general shape of the work and at Auden's and Britten's treatment of the texts. (Clearly, it was the poet who put the texts together but I have little doubt that the composer too came up with significant, musical ideas of his own – in the field of emphasis particularly.) The cycle is framed by two texts of Auden's: the first, the 'Prologue' – 'They are our past and our future' – was probably written by the poet in February 1936, and certainly written especially for the work. The second, the 'Epilogue' – 'Our hunting fathers told the story' – was probably written in May 1934, and indeed was published in Auden's 1936 volume of poems, *Look, Stranger!* These two poems are highly complex in their thought and language. Edward Mendelson provides us with the context that illuminates them. Auden, he suggests, found himself at a dividing line, 'on the edge separating two realms':

> On one side was the visible, urgent, public world of nature and social responsibility that promised a future of unity and peace. On the other was the hidden, guilty, private world of thought, desire, and loneliness whose future offered only transience and death. Now, more than at any other time, Auden was divided: between the public summons and the private wish; between 'The liberal appetite

> and power' with their twisted ties to the past; between social or family obligations and erotic impulsive love; between communism and psychology; between the tangible work of the hands and the abstract work of the mind; between the beauty of Alcibiades and the intellect of Socrates . . .[2]

For the musicalization of the frame, Britten provided an elaborate accompanied recitative, which not only shows off his skill in both assimilating and then projecting 'difficult' texts in immensely articulate music, but, no less, in finding the right instrumental textures to support and punctuate – and never cover – the vocal line (shades of the operatic composer to come!). The spacing of the wind and string chords, the transparency of the orchestral colours – these are qualities that arrest our attention from the beginning of the 'Prologue' and they are sustained throughout the cycle. Britten uses a large orchestra, and one may well marvel at the resource with which he handles it at the age of twenty-two. *Our Hunting Fathers* was in fact his first big orchestral work as well as his first (mature) orchestral song-cycle. He was undoubtedly aware of having achieved a particular creative development in the work. We find a diary entry from the period in which he refers to the cycle as 'my Op. 1 alright'. In the light of the achievement, it is all the odder that the first orchestral rehearsal, held in London, broke up in mocking disorder. The orchestra could not believe the young composer actually meant what he had written.

Britten subtitled *Our Hunting Fathers* a 'Symphonic cycle' – probably influenced here by Mahler's *Das Lied von der Erde*, which was so much admired by Britten in the 1930s and after – and the work does indeed reveal intricate forms and inter-movement developmental relationships which speak for the seriousness of the conception and make of the cycle something much more than a sequence of songs. One of the integrating devices Britten uses is a major–minor motto (Mahler!), first heard in the 'Prologue', in the orchestra, as the soloist declaims: 'O pride so hostile to our charity'. It recurs throughout the cycle, sometimes in its basic shape, sometimes varied, but always clearly recognizable.

If the 'Prologue' and 'Epilogue' place the figure of the Artist in an age of anxiety, subject in particular to the tension between the 'public summons and the private wish' (Mendelson) – something both Auden and Britten were acutely conscious of, like so many of their contemporaries – the three poems that form the central part of the cycle directly deal with Animals and their varying relationships to Man. In 'Rats Away!', an anonymous poem 'modernized' by Auden, animals appear as pests; in 'Messalina', another anonymous poem, as pet; in the 'Dance of Death' (a poem by Thomas Ravenscroft: 'Hawking for the Partridge') as prey. But it is precisely in two of these songs, the first and third, that the composer and poet use the texts as symbolic commentary on the terrible political events in Europe that rose to a climax in the summer of 1936.

The opening parody song, 'Rats Away!', should surely be read as a sardonic comment on the vermin – the Fascists – who were assaulting European civilization in the 1930s (and remember, the fear then was that that civilization might be destroyed). A ferociously brilliant orchestral introduction ejects the ascending scale motif which clearly represents the clambering, infesting animals. Scoring of this virtuosity, by the way, was hardly known among English composers of this period, hence no doubt the unpreparedness of the orchestra that gave the première. The voice, in a virtuoso cadenza on 'Rats', converts the motif into a scalic ladder, at the top rung of which we hear the motto (shrill wind). Then follows the appeal to the Saints, to rid the world of rats (notice the pestiferous role of the tuba, a surprising preview of the sonority associated with the plague in *Death in Venice*), and then a brilliant recapitulation in which the rats' scale motif, which has been absent in the middle section, reappears – first in the orchestra, and then in the vocal line, until not only the voice part but the orchestral texture too is infested with ascending scales as the singer's repeated 'Rats! Rats!' becomes ever more frenzied. And there can be no doubt that it is the rats rather than the soloist's prayers that have triumphed. If one makes the topical connection, then 'Rats Away!' is indeed a biting commentary on the threat to civilization, to the old European order, that Fascism represented in the 1930s.

There follows 'Messalina', a slow lament – more than that, an extravagant outpouring of grief on the death of a pet monkey. The song's burden of sorrow explodes in another huge vocal cadenza – *Our Hunting Fathers* is peculiarly rich in cadenzas – on the word 'Fie', and then subsides into a remarkable orchestral passage which is itself a sequence of cadenzas for solo instruments, opening with the flute and ending with the melancholy wail of the alto saxophone.

Yet another cadenza-like invention is what we hear first in the ensuing 'Dance of Death', the third and most elaborate of the songs and the one in which the political parallel is spelled out unmistakably: and once that point is taken we are enabled to 'read' the symbolism of the work as a whole. The song is ostensibly about hawking and opens with an extraordinarily scored passage for the voice alone – a roll-call of the names of the hawks (not, I think, of the hounds) – which leads us into the hunt. It may seem to us at first that the intent of the song is as much to assault the attitudes and *mores* of the hunting fraternity as to press home an argument against man's inhumanity to animals: and indeed there is a passage just before the great development for orchestra alone which is a grotesque parody of traditional tally-ho music. But, immediately thereafter, parody is abandoned and the orchestra embarks on the real 'Dance of Death'. The hunt turns lethal, and it is no longer hawks hunting partridges for man's pleasure, but man hunting man. The 'Dance of Death' is a stunning display of orchestral virtuosity, for which Britten summons up everything he had learned from his predecessors and contemporaries – Mahler, Berg, Shostakovich – and to which he added his own unique ear and imagination, and his passionate denunciation of the 'hunt' itself. The terrifying Dance ends, and in a remarkable vocal coda, just two names drawn from different groups of the roll-call of hawks are juxtaposed: 'German, Jew'. Thus does the European nightmare of the 1930s emerge as the real subject of the 'Dance of Death', and indeed of the cycle as a whole (the elegiac 'Messalina' is the only moment of relief).

The 'Dance of Death' has generated such tension and energy that the work requires an extended postlude in which to wind down. I have already mentioned the 'Epilogue'; but out of this emerges a long, glacial funeral march for orchestra, in which the xylophone takes over as soloist from the singer and repeats again and again, until its final extinction, a hollow version of the theme which was the basis of the 'Dance of Death'. It is with this chilly, despairing requiem, which so clearly reflects the foreboding of Britten and Auden in 1936, that their startling, sometimes savage and often profoundly disturbing song-cycle ends.

NOTES

1 MC: For a full examination of Britten's work in this turbulent period, see DM's 1979 T. S. Eliot Memorial Lectures, published as *Britten and Auden in the Thirties: The Year 1936* (Faber and Faber, London, 1981).
2 Edward Mendelson, *Early Auden* (Faber and Faber, London, 1981), p. 177.

'Now sleeps the crimson petal': *Britten's Other* Serenade

Britten's *Serenade*, Op. 31, for tenor, horn and strings, was first performed at the Wigmore Hall, London on 15 October 1943, with Peter Pears, Dennis Brain and an *ad hoc* orchestra conducted by Walter Goehr. It was dedicated to Edward Sackville-West.

That historic première did not include a setting of a famous poem of Tennyson's, 'Now sleeps the crimson petal, now the white', which Britten had completed in March as one of the pool of songs out of which the *Serenade* was eventually to be fashioned. To understand the complex reasons why the song – both extraordinarily beautiful and extraordinarily passionate, and itself entitled 'Serenade' – came to be excluded, and its remarkable anticipation of the orchestral song-cycle Britten was to compose in 1958, the *Nocturne*, Op. 60, we need to trace in some detail the history of the evolution of the *Serenade* itself.

Commentary on the song-cycle has been extensive. But what did the composer think about it as he was writing it? His letters from this period offer a unique record of the work's composition. For a start, it appears from the first excerpt quoted below that the idea for the song-cycle may have emerged from a discussion with Erwin Stein, then working for Boosey & Hawkes (Britten's publishers at that time), and who, as we shall see, was to have a further important connection with the *Serenade*:

To Erwin Stein [postmarked 8 March 1943]
I am intrigued by the Nocturne idea for Voice & Horn.

Tempo 169 (June 1989), pp. 22–7

There follow two quotations from letters to Peter Pears, as background to which we have to remember that during this period he was often away on tour, giving concerts for CEMA (Council for the Encouragement of Music and the Arts), the forerunner of today's Arts Council:

> *To Peter Pears, 21 March 1943*
> [. . .] what a curse it is that I haven't been able to do these concerts with you – but at least I've been able to write things for you, – better than nothing.

> *1 April 1943*
> Things go on the same here – I work alot, (don't worry, the Nocturne [*sic*] will be worthy of you by the time I've finished!) [. . .]

It was the possibility of Pears's overtaxing himself in the inauspicious circumstances of wartime touring that obviously led to Britten's cautioning him in a later letter:

> *9 May [1943]*
> [. . .] – nurse that heavenly voice of yours – We must do a superb Serenade.

But the fullest comments on the *Serenade* were made by Britten in letters to Elizabeth Mayer, of whose family on Long Island, New York, Britten and Pears were part from 1939 until their return to England in 1942:

> *To Elizabeth Mayer, 6 April 1943*
> [. . .] I've practically completed a new work (6 Nocturnes) for Peter and a lovely new young horn player Dennis Brain, & Strings, which is coming out soon. It is not important stuff, but quite pleasant, I think.

And then after the première:

> *8 December 1943*
> [. . .] I wrote a Serenade (words from Cotton, Tennyson, Blake, Jonson, Keats, etc.) in 6, or 7 pieces for Horn & Tenor & strings. There is a wonderful young horn player called Dennis Brain, who

> plays as flexibly and accurately as most clarinettists, & is a sweet & intelligent person as well. He did the first performance; I leave you to guess who did the singing! – and we had a lovely show, with wonderful enthusiasm and lovely notices.

Britten's mention of '6, or 7 pieces' might tempt us to speculate that even as late as December he was still thinking about including 'Now sleeps . . .' in his cycle. But this seems highly unlikely: the first performance of the *Serenade* had already taken place when the letter was written. More probable that Britten, in dashing off his letter to Mrs Mayer, could not quite remember the quantity of songs finally involved. Six, was it, or seven? Perhaps this momentary bout of numerical dithering shows that the jettisoned song was still a vestigial presence. (The pocket, full and vocal scores were all published, in that order and at different times, in 1944.)

We may be amused, in the light of the place in Britten's *oeuvre* that the *Serenade* soon came to occupy, by his reference to it in April 1943 as 'not important stuff, but quite pleasant, I think'. But most striking of all is his first concept of it as a 'Nocturne' (the letter to Stein), the very title that in 1958 was to be adopted for the fourth and last orchestral song-cycle. This revealing of a common title for *both* works, separated though they were by some fifteen years, points up their common source: the world of sleep and dreams, a world that Britten was as much at home in as the world that we identify as 'reality', the waking world.

The six settings that finally made up the *Serenade* all explore aspects of dusk and/or darker dimensions of the human spirit, e.g. Blake's 'Elegy' and the anonymous 'Dirge'. The solo horn frames the cycle and is integral to all the songs with the exception of the last, an omission of special appropriateness because, although the horn has the last word of all in the concluding 'Epilogue', it is Keats's sonnet that brings the work to the edge of and, we must suppose, *into* sleep. It is surely poetically right that the singer should sing himself to sleep, leaving the work's alternative 'voice', the horn, to make the final comment on the now silent (or silenced) sleeper, whom sleep has overtaken.

The idea of sleep, as we have suggested, was a preoccupation of Britten's; and when he turned to it as a source of inspiration we find the same kind of musical imagery recurring again and again. It was Eric Roseberry who was the first to point out (much to the surprise of the composer) that the sequence of major triads (D, C♯ [= D♭], E♭, C) that magically opens the Keats setting in the *Serenade* – the song dedicated to sleep – offers precisely the same basic chords (or tonalities, rather), minimally re-ordered, that we encounter at the beginning of the nocturnal Act II of *A Midsummer Night's Dream* and over the rotation of which is unfolded the sublime slumber song that rounds off the act, from which dream the lovers will awake to the ensuing dawn. It is in the juxtaposition of two of those tonalities, a characteristic semitonal relationship, C/D♭, that the *Nocturne* too has its basis. As we shall see, consistency of imagery is also a feature of 'Now sleeps . . .'.

Britten's last orchestral song-cycle, the *Nocturne* (first performed at Leeds on 16 October 1958, by Pears with the BBC Symphony Orchestra conducted by Rudolf Schwarz), picks up, as has often been remarked, from the very point where the *Serenade* ends, from the condition of sleep in which the protagonist in the earlier work has been left. This is why the discovery by Marion Thorpe of a hitherto unknown song among her father's – Erwin Stein's – papers was so exciting and illuminating: a setting, in the form of a complete composition sketch, of 'Now sleeps the crimson petal, now the white', dated 'March 22nd 1943'. It is, we note, not only another sleep poem but also a lyric protestation of love, in D♭. However, he never took the song to its final manuscript stage, i.e. a fair-copied full score. What were the reasons for his discarding it? Or, to put it another way, for not including it?

One reason becomes clear if we turn to the *Nocturne* and in particular to the final song in which the work culminates. Whereas all the preceding songs in the 1958 cycle have been concerned with images of night, of the dream world – images both serene and profoundly troubled – the setting of the paradoxical Shakespeare sonnet, 'When most I wink, then do mine eyes best see', lifts the cycle on to an entirely fresh plane of experience: it is the reality offered by a loved one, the work tells us, that is in fact more real than the nocturnal visions of the 'real' world, whether its beauties or its nightmares. The shift in perspective is radical; but in the *Nocturne* it proves to have been elaborately prepared, so that the final avowal of love emerges as an entirely logical and inescapable – though unforeseen – *dénouement*.

In the *Serenade*, however, it is quite difficult to perceive where Britten might have thought of placing 'Now sleeps . . .', which was in fact composed two days *after* he had already composed the setting of the Keats sonnet. Not all the songs are dated, but at least one of them, the setting of Ben Jonson's 'Hymn', was composed even later, on 2 April. The seeming lack of methodical chronology helps us, I believe, to answer the question about the omission of 'Now sleeps . . .'. It was pretty much Britten's compositional habit, when putting together a song-cycle or song set, to write more songs than he proved to need. Moreover, although he must have had in mind some kind of overall shape for a cycle, the precise ordering and selection of songs often belonged to the final stage of composition.

It is my guess that the setting of 'Now sleeps . . .' after the Keats sonnet had already been completed, is less surprising than it may seem at first sight. It probably represented an overflow of the lyric impulse that gave us the Keats. In this context, there may be some significance in the fact that 'Now sleeps . . .' and the Keats sonnet were among the songs specifically inscribed 'PP, Horn, Str'.

The possibility exists of course that Britten may have fleetingly considered 'Now sleeps . . .' as an alternative finale. The hushed sequence of string chords which closes the song might be thought to play something of the same role as the famous 'sleep' chords which bring the Keats setting to an end; and the song's D♭ would have represented a return to and re-affirmation of the D♭ of the *first* song, the Cotton. But it must have soon struck Britten that

'Now sleeps . . .' does not have the weight to round off a sequence that included numbers as dramatic as the 'Dirge' or as intense as the 'Elegy'; and by weight I am thinking not just of duration and character but also a sense of resolution. He must have seen almost at once that it was the already composed Keats that magically completed the exploration of the nocturnal world by bringing the protagonist of the *Serenade* to the very brink of sleep.

It is no easier to find a convincing spot for the song elsewhere. It seems unlikely that Britten would have considered 'Now sleeps . . .' as a candidate for the first place in the sequence: he would surely not have launched the cycle at such a high pitch of lyrical feeling? The song, we must conclude, could not make sense in the scheme – the shape – of the *Serenade* as it was finally and perfectly ordered by the composer.

Ultimately, we can only speculate about Britten's intentions. It might have been even that an adverse influence was exercised by the homophobia current in England in the 1940s: 'Now sleeps . . .' might well have drawn unwelcome attention to itself as expression of a love for which there was little public sympathy or tolerance.[1] But what we can be sure of – because we have all the evidence before us – is that the discarded 'Now sleeps . . .' was the model for the finale, fifteen years on, of the *Nocturne*. What the reclaimed song reveals is its uncanny unveiling of the last orchestral song-cycle that was still to be written, the *Nocturne*. Here, in the discarded song, is the gently rocking string figuration which was to launch the sleeping protagonist of the *Serenade* on his journey through the dreamscape of the *Nocturne*;[2] while the protestation of personal love embodied in 'Now sleeps . . .' has become the very goal – the *dénouement* – of the later cycle, with Shakespeare's Sonnet XLIII replacing Tennyson's lyric.

More than that, the Shakespeare setting not only took over the shift to the personal plane manifest in the Tennyson but also the associated tonal region, which the last song of the *Nocturne* subtly (and sometimes ambivalently) inhabits: D♭. Indeed, it is not too much to say that the discarded forgotten song of 1943 was the source, in all essentials, of the final orchestral song-cycle Britten was to compose. The *Nocturne*, we have long known, evolved poetically and musically out of the *Serenade*; we did not know, however, that the *other* 'Serenade' – 'Now sleeps . . .' – was the crucial compositional link between the two works.

A long history, one might think, to attach to one song. But then it is a history tied into two masterworks, and one that tells us something important not only about their creation, but also about their creator and their principal interpreter. We do not need to spell out, I think, who it was to whom both D♭ affirmations of love were addressed, in 1943 and 1958.

NOTES

1 MC: A more pragmatic explanation for Britten's omission of 'Now sleeps . . .' may be that its inclusion would have given undue prominence to Tennyson as the only poet to have been represented by two settings in the cycle: 'The splendour falls on castle walls' (which Britten subtitled 'Nocturne') was also a Tennyson text.

2 MC: That this 'gently rocking string figuration' remained firmly lodged in Britten's subconscious in the fifteen years between the *Serenade* and the *Nocturne* may explain his unusual decision to compose the latter work straight into a fluent manuscript full score without the need of his customary composition sketch.

For Kathleen

The Serious Comedy of Albert Herring

It is not to insult an audience to offer it ambiguity.
(Howard Barker, *Guardian*, 10 February 1986)

If there is one number from *Albert Herring* that everyone who knows the piece would immediately acknowledge as something quite special, something of an astonishing technical virtuosity and yet at the same time deeply stirring and moving, it is the great elegiac threnody in Act III in which Albert is mourned.

The odd thing is that it was just this climactic ensemble – the richest and most elaborate ensemble in an opera that, as Erwin Stein pointed out many years ago, was positively teeming with ensembles – which some early critics of the opera found hard to take. Neville Cardus was an exception, writing in the *Manchester Guardian* (10 October 1947). But for the most part this massive statement of ritual grief –

> In the midst of life is death,
> Death awaits us one and all.
> Death attends our smallest step,
> Silent, swift and merciful

– left some of our elder statesmen of the day thoroughly confused. This torrent of sorrow, this unseemly raising of the shadow of death, what on earth was something so *serious* doing in the midst of a comedy, and in fact not in the midst of it but at the end of it,

---

Glyndebourne Festival Programme Book 1986, pp. 105–11

when we expect an affirmation, laughter, not an onrush of tears? Difficult enough to make the switch from the comic to the tragic, but there was worse yet to come: Albert, the irrepressible, interrupts his own obituary, as it were, the consequence of which is to show up all that grieving as a charade. We should not have been required, so the argument ran, to participate in an elegy in the first place. But having been drawn into it – and here of course the critics paid unconscious tribute to the power and magic of Britten's threnody – it was insulting to have those feelings mocked. To put it more soberly, there was a widespread view that the composer and his librettist had committed a major aesthetic misjudgement. In short, you could not have a *serious comedy*.

It is strange that those who found *Albert Herring* impossible to swallow in the early days did not give themselves time to think around the subject a little, in which case 'serious comedy' might have seemed less paradoxical and improbable than they supposed. The more one thinks about it indeed the clearer it becomes that most of the best comedies in music are (also) serious – *Rosenkavalier*, for example (which Britten had studied before embarking on *Peter Grimes*),[1] or *The Bartered Bride* (which Britten much admired, whose shy hero, Vašek, was a role Peter Pears was singing at Sadler's Wells between 1943 and 1945 and was one of the models for Albert). But the predecessor of most relevance to Britten was Mozart, and more particularly *Così fan tutte*, not only the 'serious comedy' in music *par excellence* but, I should claim, *deadly* serious. *Albert Herring* undoubtedly discomfited some of its first critics. *Così*, as we know, discomfited a whole century (the nineteenth) and can still – and probably should – leave audiences feeling uncomfortable. *Così* and *Albert Herring* share one feature in common, which has not gone unrecognized: they are both operas in which the ensemble is predominant, a natural formal consequence of the kind of comedies they are, in which the interplay between the dramatis personae is paramount. But there is another feature too, I suggest, which the two operas share: a certain and intended *ambiguity*, which leaves us asking ourselves: How should we respond to this? How should we interpret it? How should we read these signs? How do we make sense of them? It is out of that ambiguity that the discomfort is born and there is surely no intenser challenge in this sphere than the *dénouement* of *Così*, where the four lovers switch back to their original pairs, and which provokes just the kind of questions I have posed above. Not even the threnody in *Albert Herring* is as unsettling as the resolution (if it *is* that) of *Così*. All of this leads me not to blame the composer, whether he be Mozart or Britten, for introducing the irreconcilable, but to believe that the profoundest comedy in music is not only serious but also, from time to time, uncomfortable and disturbing.

It was not only, I suggest, the threnody and its implication that were misunderstood when *Albert Herring* was first performed, but also the true nature of the comedy that is at the heart of the opera. And that the opera *is* a comedy, perhaps is something I ought to emphasize in view of the reflections with which I began and with which I shall continue. There is absolutely no doubt about its comic status and we would all agree, I think, that it succeeds in being very, very funny. (An unexpected aspect of the success of the opera has been its capacity to travel. It may well have entertained audiences in more languages and in more countries of the world than any other opera of Britten's, and to this day there are constant new productions, from workshop to opera house.) But our savouring the work as comedy should not close our ears to that other dimension of the opera that culminates in the threnody and indeed has been very carefully contrived from the outset. The opera, one might claim, grows more serious as it goes along: it is an evolutionary process, not an arbitrary U-turn.

There is, however, a *turning point*; and the point, the hinge, on which the music turns is the turning point in Albert's destiny, the moment when he decides to spend his twenty-five quid, throw caution to the winds, abandon Mum and free himself of his inhibitions – and in so doing, it is important to note, follow the liberating example of Sid and Nancy, the exuberant, lusty young lovers.

The turn is made at the very centre of the musical structure, in the interlude that divides the two scenes of the second act. The hurly-burly of the crowning of Albert in the marquee subsides and a wholly new mood, a new tempo and new range of instrumental colour take over. An instrumental nocturne, a two-part invention for alto flute and bass clarinet, sets the scene for Albert's tipsy return to the empty shop. A crepuscular music this, appropriate to night, to dreams (of freedom), to the pursuit of love. (Night music in this very same format was to recur again in an interlude in *The Turn of the Screw*, Act II.[2] That it could function so successfully in so radically different a context suggests the strength of the engagement of Britten's compositional techniques in the earlier chamber opera: this is a point to which I shall come back.)

The interlude over and the scene set, Albert embarks on his great *scena*. This long solo number for Albert *inside* the shop (and still a captive) is punctuated by the emancipated Sid's and Nancy's courting *outside* the shop and their final departure in pursuit of love's delights: nowhere is the *inside/outside* nature of Albert's predicament spelled out more clearly in this subtle opera. Albert is always on the inside, looking out, and in this instance through a barrier of glass, the shop window. On the other hand this huge solo number which incorporates Sid's and Nancy's love duet is also the means by which Albert discovers himself, his self-respect and his independence; and indeed, by the time the *scena* ends he has screwed up his courage and broken out. Mrs Herring returns to the shop, as empty now as it was when Albert returned, though Mrs Herring is sublimely unaware of the fact that the bird – her 'blinking swan' – has flown.

Albert's voyage of self-discovery is a veritable masterpiece of musical construction. As he recalls his experience of oppression and repression at the hands of Mum, the yearnings stimulated by a glimpse of that other life enjoyed by Sid and Nancy, his recollections bring back with them their appropriate music. This extraordinary recapitulatory survey of his past reminds us that the opera has already provided Albert with a past to reclaim or, to put it another way, the great *scena*, the turning point, does not spring out of the air unannounced but has its roots in the very carefully plotted precedents in earlier scenes. For example, in Act I Scene 2 we encounter for the first time all those components which in one way or another have a bearing on the development of Albert's character: the children, mischievous to a degree, but, as so often in Britten's work, symbols of candour and innocence; Sid and Nancy, the lovers, whose scarcely concealed sensuality – 'Give us a kiss, Nancy!' – arouses Albert's alarm and yet arouses his curiosity; and there is Albert himself, at this moment still very much an insider and yet, in his short solo –

> It seems as clear as clear can be that Sid's ideas
> Are very much too crude for Mother to approve

– already disclosing a pressure of feeling, an irrepressible desire, that will finally surface in his *scena* in Act II Scene 2 (like *Così*, *Albert Herring* makes brilliant use of symmetry as one of its formal strategies) and with perfect dramatic and musical logic leads to his asserting his own rights as a human being, above all the right to be free (even if it means making a mess of one's freedom, as is Albert's experience the first time he exercises it).

I write as if Albert's solo music were the only solos in the opera, which is not quite true. There are of course other celebrated solo set pieces, like Lady Billows's huge and disorganized catalogue of slogans in the marquee, Act II Scene 1, the Vicar's inimitable string of clichés in the same scene, and many others. And yet 'slogans', 'clichés', these descriptions tell their own story. These solos, as diverting and amusing as they are, are not so much disclosures of personality as public statements made for public effect: almost all the other characters in *Albert Herring* – the children, lovers and Albert apart – are playing roles, not themselves. That, one might think, is what's wrong with the Big House and the village worthies magnetized by it and the aura of its formidable mistress.

Here we meet yet another of those formal/dramatic/musical

symmetries that are central to the making of *Albert Herring* what it is and not what it is often taken to be. I have talked about the inside/outside relationship of Albert to his world. That world is itself most brilliantly shown to be dichotomous by Britten and his librettist: on the one hand the stuffy, pompous, repressive and puritanical world of Lady Billows and her circle of conscripts, and on the other the everyday world that impinges on the shop and will ultimately release Albert from its confines: the children with their ball games –

> Bounce me high, bounce me low
> Bounce me up to Jericho!

– the lovers, with music eloquent of their passion; and Albert himself, whose music speaks directly and poignantly of his plight, and at the same time is evidence of the personality that will finally win through. We are aware as soon as we have got to know Albert a little that within the dutiful mother's son is a sentient young man struggling to get out.

The children and Sid and Nancy are all, as it were, on the side of life, the children spontaneously so and the lovers robustly dedicated to opposing stuffiness and hypocrisy: 'Stop prying and poking and probing at him', they cry as Albert is being cross-examined (in a brilliantly composed interrogation at the end of Act III) about his night out, 'With your pious old faces delighting in Sin!' And there is no doubt, because his music tells us so, that it is this group Albert aims to join. This is not a fanciful speculation on my part. On the contrary, Albert and his supporters are united in and by a music that I can only describe as 'vernacular' in character, i.e. it is entirely appropriate to the everyday life in the shop in which Sid and Nancy, Albert (and his awful Mum) and the cheeky kids participate. It is very skilfully done, this; and brings into play the most sophisticated musical skills. For example, it is a style that has easily to accommodate the marvellous informalities and speech rhythms of small-change conversation across the counter. It is a music that is stressedly informal, even anti-formal, though when Britten needs to, he will drop into all this informality a stunning and tightly organized set piece: there are two for the lovers, in Act I Scene 2, 'We'll walk to the spinney', and Act II Scene 2, 'Come along, darling, come . . . follow me quick!', two marvellous duets which carry one along so buoyantly on the sweep of their melodies that one scarcely notices the intricate instrumental counterpoint that, in the first, embellishes the tune. The tunes, indeed, define this 'vernacular' area, simply, in the main, and clear-cut, instantly memorable – and instinct with vitality. It is absolutely no accident that when Albert assumes control at the end of Act III, it is through the means of a tune, 'And I'm more than grateful to you all', his very own, and the first of its kind in his repertoire, that he subdues his Mum and renders her speechless (songless).

All the best tunes in the opera, we may come to conclude, flower in the context of Sid and Nancy, Albert and the children, the group within the community that makes up the whole world of *Albert Herring*: life, love, vitality and a capacity for rebellion are concentrated *here*. By way of contrast, the group comprising the Establishment and Authority, headed by Lady Billows, is furnished with an entirely different kind of music. Nothing 'vernacular' about these important personages. We hear no significant disclosures of personality from these arbiters of public virtue, only public addresses. They all, whether a Chief Constable or Vicar, appear in uniform, and Britten brilliantly provides each of them with a musical uniform to make this very point. Theirs is a music full of Pomp and Circumstance, generating vocal lines quite distinct from the humane contours of the melodies allotted to Albert and his friends. Britten is too great an artist (and in any case too much bound up with his characters) to present us with a gallery of caricatures and he allows an occasional unbuttoning of the uniform which permits us a glimpse of the human being within. But by and large the music associated with Lady B. and her team is rich in admonitory, minatory gestures and finds its consummation in the quasi-Handelian formality of the big ensembles in Act I

Scene 1, 'We've made our own investigations' and 'May King! May King!', in which the Festival Committee first reports to Lady Billows and then unites under her banner. It is wholly fitting that it is through these parody ensembles that the village worthies should express their corporate voice: they represent officialdom and authority, and employ an artificial, formal mode of address. We find nothing comparable in the music emanating, as it were, from the shop floor. In short, there is one ('posh') music for the Big House, another ('vernacular') for the lovers and Albert, Emmie, Cis and Harry.

This very important and carefully worked-out dichotomy gives *Albert Herring* a genuine social dynamic which is sometimes overlooked by those who have not thought about what lies beneath the surface of the 'comedy'. It is an aspect of the opera that could not have existed without Eric Crozier's remarkable libretto, which innovatingly and daringly made the vernacular accessible to Britten in terms of words. Here again, by the way, was yet another source of misunderstanding in earlier days, when it was generally thought that operatic language had to be elevated (posh!) and in another tongue than English (conveniently incomprehensible) and which certainly could never accommodate things like the notorious

> Sorry, Miss Pike!
> Punctured my bike . . .!

or, something rather more complex, this passage from Albert's *scena* in Act II Scene 2:

> Dark in here! – must find match –
> Matches? – Matches! – [*calling*] Swan Vestas! . . .
> Swan Vestas . . .? . . . Ah! . . .
> [*He finds a box of matches on the counter.*]
> That's the chap
> Turn the tap –
> Strike the match
> Like this – oh drat!

[*He drops the box of matches on the floor and grovels for them, leaving the gas-jet on.*]
Butterfingers! . . . Oopsadaisy!
[*He stands up, and with great deliberation and slowness prepares to strike the match.*]
Open your mouth,
Shut your eyes,
Strike the match
For a nice surprise . . .
[*There is a loud and terrifying report and swoosh of flame from the gas-jet.*]
Blast! . . . Dangerous stuff, gas. Smelly, tricky, noisy, dangerous stuff . . .! Leave well alone . . .!

There can be no doubt that the text made a unique contribution to the opera. In particular, it is difficult to envisage how the whole 'vernacular' element and the wonderful, conversational or inquisitorial set pieces could have existed without Crozier's masterly and – I stress again – pioneering libretto. Far from being just another manifestation of the work's comic profile, the text (excellent jokes and all) is profoundly part of the seriousness and originality of the enterprise.

I hope that what I've written up to this point will have done something to suggest that there is rather more to *Albert Herring* than has been popularly supposed. Certainly there is nothing to suggest that Britten's creative gifts were not other than wholly engaged from beginning to end. The extraordinary writing for chamber orchestra, for example, warrants a study in itself: there is something magical about the variety of sonorities Britten can persuade from his thirteen players. One is not surprised by the delicacy of some of it (the so-called 'moonlight' interlude in Act II, for instance); one *is* surprised by the conjuring up of a sonorous power which makes it hard to believe that there is not an orchestra double or triple the size of those players actually sitting in the pit. Another fascinating feature is the versatility of the compositional techniques. *Albert Herring*, although it might not be the first thing that comes to mind along with the opera's reputation, is full of intricate counterpoints of all kinds. It is there in the big public orchestral fugue which forms the first half of the interlude between Scenes 1 and 2 of Act II and subsides into the private (moonlit) two-part counterpoint for alto flute and bass clarinet which introduces Albert's *scena*. There could hardly be a neater example of Britten's counterpoint creating two contrasted worlds. It is counterpoint again that generates the big formal parody ensembles in Act I Scene 1, where counterpoint and officiousness go audibly hand in hand. But it is there too fertilizing the vernacular dimension, quite a different kind of counterpoint but not one bit less sophisticated and cunning. Those marvellous lovers' duets, for example, the first of which is a small masterpiece of canonic art. Here, however, the counterpoint is not in the service of corporate Authority but embodies the idea of two-in-one, the union of individual lovers. Whether it was his 'vernacular' or Top People's hat that he was wearing, it was the same virtuoso compositional skill that Britten deployed.

It is counterpoint again that is at the centre of the great threnody at the end of Act III, the ambiguity of which (to some ears) provided me with the starting point of my discussion. This extraordinary ensemble for the entire cast (except for Albert and the children) ultimately opens out into a gigantic vocal cadenza in which all the principals express their sorrow in their own characteristic melodies, a master stroke of calculation and spontaneity combined. It is literally an *arresting* moment when time stands still – which reminds me that the passage of time is something we are constantly aware of in *Herring* from many points of view. There is the comic eruption of the cuckoo in Act I Scene 1 (time as punctuality); there is experience measured in relation to time, in Albert's case (Act I Scene 2) experience of life still to come:

> And I'd really like
> To try that kind of life . . .
> And golly! It's about time . . .

while Sid and Nancy, in Act II Scene 2, sing of experience threatened by time:

> Time is racing us round the clock.
> Ticking and tocking our evening away.

(Hence the staccato tick-tock of the quick orchestral accompaniment of their duet.)

When we reach the threnody in Act III, the strokes on the bells which introduce it reproduce as it were the strokes of the biggest clock of all, Time itself, the measure of our mortality. The supposed death of Albert shocks the Establishment figures of Loxford into dropping their masks and their uniforms and ceasing their role-playing. It not only shocks them out of their prejudices but momentarily unites them with those (Sid and Nancy in particular) who stand for other values, different attitudes. Interestingly, apart from the corporate celebrations in the marquee in Act II, the threnody is the *only* number in the opera in which virtually everyone, the whole community, sings the same kind of felt music. The social dichotomy is erased. A response to the idea of death has bonded them.

It does not last, of course. Within a moment of Albert's reappearance, the masks are clapped back on and the old hectoring begins all over again. Everything seems as it was, and everybody. But our perception of the participants in this domestic comedy has been subtly altered. The threnody has enabled us to see, to hear, the village worthies momentarily in another light. All the more disconcerting that the moment of illumination, when an imagined experience is so powerful that it breaks through fossilized feelings, petrified postures, is so soon extinguished. It is a revelation of the paradox of the human condition that one carries with one out of the theatre.

But someone – the opera's protagonist – *has* changed! It is Albert who has been transformed by his experience, his taste of freedom – not a wholly agreeable experience, incidentally; and now it is he who takes charge, politely but firmly seeing the Big House off, and for the first time silencing his Mum, all of which leaves him and the stage free to celebrate with Sid and Nancy and the kids, who all along have been representatives of that *other* life, on which at last Albert has embarked.

So *Albert Herring* is about many other things as well as laughter. About growing up – Albert grows across the span of the whole opera – and about the pleasures of love. For Sid and Nancy, Britten wrote some of the freshest and most passionate love music in twentieth-century opera, which effectively rubbishes the idea (which could be clung to only by the deaf) that this was an area outside his scope; and I hope it will have put paid once and for all to an ancient chestnut, overdue for retirement.

And then, yes, the opera, as I have been arguing at some length, has a serious side to it. Let me make just one last point in this sphere. One of the most characteristic numbers in the work is the quartet in Act III in which Mum succumbs to grieving for her lost son and is comforted by the tender-hearted Nancy and the consoling Miss Wordsworth and Mr Gedge, the Vicar, the latter duo putting their best feelings forward. It is an ensemble that is both comically exaggerated and yet deeply stirring (and hence ambiguous and unsettling). Years later (in 1964) Britten was to write the first of his church parables, *Curlew River*, in which we encounter another mother, the Madwoman, lamenting her lost son. Her great spasm of grief [Ex. 2, overleaf] culminates in music which must remind us of the earlier opera [Ex. 1, overleaf].

The intense grief of the Madwoman brings with it precisely the same form of musical expression (the same formula, one might say) as that which characterizes Mum's torrent of sorrow in *Albert Herring*; and that, in turn, in my submission, tells us just how very near to the surface seriousness is in Britten's comedy. I once pointed out this significant relationship and the conclusions I drew from it to the composer. I have to be honest and confess that he did not say he agreed with me; nor, on the other hand, did he say he disagreed. He smiled and said, 'Well, Donald, I've always known *Herring* meant something special to you' – which is exactly why I have written this article.[3]

Ex. 1 *Albert Herring*

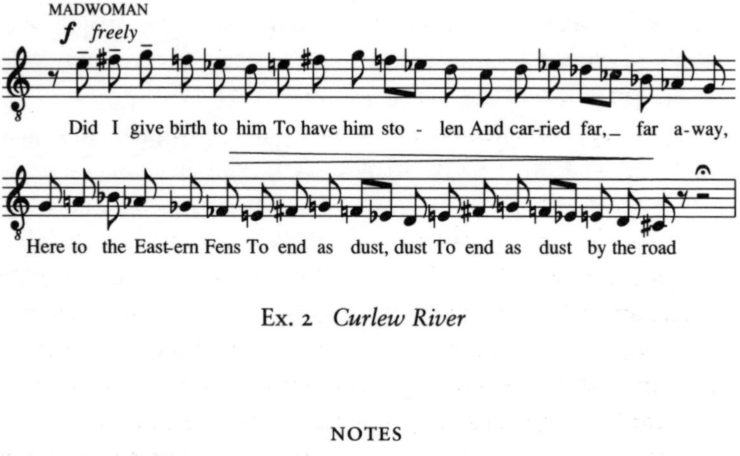

Ex. 2 *Curlew River*

NOTES

1 MC: See DM and Philip Reed (eds.), *Letters from a Life: Selected Letters and Diaries of Benjamin Britten* (Faber and Faber, London, 1991), pp. 50–51, 1121, 1128–9 and 1263.

2 MC: 'Night music in this very same format' was not restricted merely to the scores of *Albert Herring* and *The Turn of the Screw*: Britten had first used it in 1946 in *The Rape of Lucretia* (Act II Scene 1) and returned to it again in the Auden setting 'Out on the lawn I lie in bed' in the *Spring Symphony* (1949).

3 MC: DM had earlier expressed similar views to those contained in this article in his review of the production of *Albert Herring* at the Lyric, Hammersmith, in 1951: see *Music Survey* 3/4 (June 1951), pp. 303–4.

More Off than On Billy Budd

I Preliminaries

One of the opening pre-first-performance shots was fired by Mr Charles Reid in the London *Evening Standard* of 29 November, in a piece entitled 'Britten Makes It Seven . . .' (Mr Reid's mathematics are clear enough when one realizes that he starts counting the operas from the unpublished *Paul Bunyan* (1941) and includes the realization of *The Beggar's Opera*.)

There are three legitimate possibilities open to the critic who writes about a new work prior to its première: (a) he can study the score and make provisional comments which the performance will either prove or disprove (a procedure adopted by Mr Desmond Shawe-Taylor in the *New Statesman and Nation* of 1 December); (b) he can study old works afresh and prophesy likely stylistic characteristics of the new (a method not without its element of danger – witness the unfortunate article by Scott Goddard ('Britten as an Instrumental Composer', *Listener*, 7 July 1949), which, as a preview of the *Spring Symphony*'s first broadcast performance, foresaw everything beside the *Spring Symphony*'s point); (c) he can write about the composer as a figure of popular interest, subjecting him to much the same sort of journalistic analysis as is meted out to politicians, actors, criminals or generals (to take a not-so-mixed bag of notorieties). A fourth possibility is to keep silent altogether until the first

---

Music Survey 4/2 (February 1952), pp. 386–408[1]

performance is over – but that course is rarely an economic possibility.

Mr Reid's article falls into category (c) and far be it from me to suggest that he be blamed for writing a gossip-column piece for an evening paper. After all a genius is a genius, and even an inevitably superficial survey of his character can be of value. Faced with the unenviable task of writing an article that must be read and enjoyed by thousands of non-musicians the only question of conscience that arises is how to be as *harmlessly* entertaining as possible. Not, I should have thought, a very difficult task for Mr Reid who is not only the most expert of journalists but also a music critic of uncommon perception (a judgement recently confirmed by his notice of *Wozzeck*'s first English performance (*Evening Standard*, 23 January)). For a Britten profile I could have imagined no happier combination than the journalist Mr Reid working hand in glove with his music-critical self. Here, in fact, was the chance to prove that the presence of good journalism need not entail the absence of musicality.

But what sort of a profile did Mr Reid's *Evening Standard* article turn out to be? I should be hard put to discover a parallel example of such tasteless fact and factless fancy. Much of Mr Reid's information gives the impression that he was once Mr Britten's bank manager: he specifies the amount left to the composer under his father's will; the composer's initial fees for his joint recitals with Peter Pears (not a mention of the many occasions when both artists have given their services in a good cause); we are even told the price Mr Britten paid for his motor car. Such an extraordinary exposure of any man's private affairs is quite unwarrantable, and, in my experience of musical journalism, the article is without precedent.

Throughout this strange piece crop up emotive phrases such as 'He felt very much at home with the *Bloomsbury Leftists*', or 'Now he has a solid, *bourgeois-looking* house facing the sea at Aldeburgh' (my italics), neither of which is very meaningful on close verbal inspection. There is no necessity for good journalists to borrow their vocabulary from bad politicians; nor should Mr Reid continue to use the time-dishonoured device of false juxtaposition. For instance:

> The man who in 1939 contributed anti-war music (including a satirical Dance of Death) to a Festival of Music for the People at the old Queen's Hall stood eleven years later as godparent with Queen Mary and Princess Elizabeth at the christening of the Earl and Countess of Harewood's baby.

The first half of the paragraph is seemingly invalidated by the second, although a minute's shallow thought exposes the *non sequitur*. Meanwhile the innuendo has cast its shadow. As Mr Reid has it: 'Britten's social life was beginning to glitter.'

Mr Reid winds up his piece with an off-the-mark comment or two on Britten's music, and introduces a group of fanatics (whom I have never remotely met) in order to demolish a ludicrous statement (which I could never imagine being made outside the confines of an asylum): '[Britten] has, I think, too much good sense to credit the extremist clique who say in all seriousness that *he is the most important thing that has hit music since Mozart*.' (My italics.) If Mr Reid can point to any such comment in print, we should be delighted to crown its author as the biggest musical idiot to hit this century.

As for Mr Britten's views on other men's music we are told that 'he has a rather childlike contempt for Puccini' – a remark that is more revealing of Mr Reid's inexact terminology than of Mr Britten's musical judgements. What does 'childlike' mean in this context? According to the *Oxford English Dictionary* the word is defined thus: 'Belonging to or becoming a child; filial. Like a child; (of qualities, etc.) like those of a child. (*Usu. in a good sense, as opp. to childish*).' (My italics.) As far as I am aware a contempt for Puccini is not a characteristic of childhood. It seems that what Mr Reid really meant to write was the opposite of 'childlike' - i.e. 'childish' (*OED*: 'Not befitting mature age; puerile, silly'). But then Mr Reid wouldn't have liked to stigmatize one of Mr Britten's opinions as 'puerile' or 'silly' so he optimistically compromised with 'childlike', which, strictly speaking, makes no sense at all. But, of course, the majority of Mr Reid's readers on this occasion would substitute 'childish' for 'childlike' anyway, so why should Mr Reid have bothered? Could there be any greater satisfaction than writing for an audience that will unconsciously attribute the opposite meaning to the printed word and thus arrive at what was presumably the author's original intention?

So much for Mr Charles Reid's curtain-raiser to *Billy Budd*. In one mouth at least it left a nasty taste.

II Interlude: Which Way to the Sea?

> In the first act the shrill wind, the salt tang and the eternal swell and surge of restless water envelop the listener so that whatever happens aboard the *Indomitable* he can never forget this relentless conditioning of sailors' lives.
>
> *The Times*, 3 December

> But where in the opening act was the tang of salt air and the sound of the sea that we expected of the composer of *Peter Grimes*?
>
> Dyneley Hussey, *Listener*, 6 December

III Resistances Continued

In our most optimistic moments we should never have imagined that one of our leading articles, printed well over a year ago, could have remained so topical. All those who doubted the validity of my colleague's analysis of resistances to Britten's music (this journal, May 1950)[2] should re-read it in the light of immediate criticisms of *Billy Budd*. If further evidence were needed, *Budd*'s first performance has amply supplied it. Indeed with no little frankness it formed the first paragraph of Mr Stephen Williams's review of the opera in the *Evening News* of 3 December:

> One always resents having it dinned into one's ears that a new work is a masterpiece before it has been performed; and Benjamin Britten's *Billy Budd* was trumpeted into the arena by such a deafening roar of advance publicity that many of us entered Covent Garden on Saturday (when the composer conducted the first performance) with a mean, sneaking hope that we might be able to flesh our fangs in it.

In the face of so astonishing a revelation of how some of our critics go about their occupation I find it difficult to make any comment – unnecessary, perhaps, since Mr Williams makes his own. But let me point out without delay that Mr Williams, in spite of this unpromising approach, acknowledged 'with a full heart' before his review was over that '*Billy Budd* is, in its own right, a masterpiece.'

Mr Williams, however, is not only critic for the *Evening News* but also (it appears) London music critic for the *New York Times*; and to that distinguished overseas newspaper he contributed a notice of *Billy Budd* which included a short résumé of other English critics' opinions. (The date I am unable to identify since it is missing from my cutting.)

While Mr Williams had informed his London readers that the opera was 'a masterpiece' it was not upon this theme that he enlarged for the benefit of the Americans. On the contrary, the greater part of his piece is taken up with a discussion of the 'hysterical ballyhoo' that accompanied *Budd*'s first performance. In fact the *New York Times* review is an expansive elucidation of the motives that prompted Mr Williams's first *Evening News* paragraph quoted above. The 'publicity' seems to have got Mr Williams's back up in no uncertain style:

> Mr Britten is in a class by himself. He is the golden boy of British music; 'Hear Britten first' might be the slogan of any English musical tourist agency. He is phenomenally clever and phenomenally lucky . . .[3]

> He has an astute and enterprising publisher who blazes his trail with blinding and deafening advance publicity. He had also fanatical disciples such as those who before the production of *Billy Budd* solemnly assured us that the libretto was to be compared only with Boito's *Otello* and the score only with the last works of Verdi.

At this point Mr Williams must be referring to the very coolly factual preview of *Billy Budd* by Eric Walter White which appeared in the *Listener* of 22 November. The two statements to which Mr Williams seems to take a quite inflated exception run as follows:

> (a) These collaborators [i.e. E. M. Forster and Eric Crozier] have succeeded in offering Benjamin Britten the best opera libretto *adapted from a literary masterpiece* since Boito's version of *Otello*. [My italics: Mr Williams conveniently ignores this highly selective qualification.]
>
> (b) in *Billy Budd* Britten has written his maturest opera to date, one that in skill of construction,[4] psychological subtlety, and theatrical effectiveness can *without exaggeration* be compared with the later works of Verdi. [My italics.]

The second of Mr White's measured opinions is obviously the more important, and no doubt the attentive reader will mark Mr Williams's substitution of 'only' for Mr White's 'without exaggeration' – a slight but vital alteration which affects the whole construction and meaning of Mr White's sentence. In any case I have yet to hear that the comparative method of criticism is a crime, and Mr White's suggestion that *Billy Budd* may be compared to the later works of Verdi is not only legitimate, but helpful to those finding their operatic feet in the history of music.

Oddest of all, as we have seen from the *Evening News* review quoted above, Mr Williams himself considered *Billy Budd* to be a 'masterpiece'; and, ironical as it may be, he was, to the best of my knowledge, the only critic who used the term after the work's first performance. Does then Mr Williams object to one masterpiece being compared to another? And how do we account for the fact that what was a 'masterpiece' in London has been modified for New York into no more than a 'challenging, stimulating work of art'? Is it that Mr Williams's resistances gained the upper hand of his opinions during their transatlantic crossing?

Referring back to his own pronouncements on 'hysterical bally-hoo', 'advance publicity' and so forth, Mr Williams concludes, 'Now all this kind of thing is very damaging' – while it doesn't seem to occur to him that his own efforts (especially in a foreign newspaper) are susceptible of like criticism. If Mr Williams doesn't think *Billy Budd* a masterpiece he shouldn't have written that it was; if he does, then he should be glad of all the publicity the work gets, since great pieces these days are few and far between; and he should certainly cease attacking those amongst his colleagues who voted it a great piece (with rather more musical explicitness) a few days earlier than he did himself.

One final word. My own ears were unembarrassed by the deafening advance publicity to which Mr Williams refers. Surely he can't have been thinking of Mr Reid's *Evening Standard* article? Now if Mr Williams took exception to *that* kind of advance publicity, he would have my active support and sympathy. But, alas, he makes no mention of it. Can the awful din that so distressed Mr Williams have been caused by that elusive 'extremist clique' up to their old tricks again?

IV Interlude: A Critical Tune Which Seems to be Catching

> [Britten] has . . . been daring enough to compose a score without one whistleable tune . . .
>
> Stephen Williams, *New York Times*

> You will find no lovely tunes, but Britten's music is more melodious [*sic*] and warmer than in previous operas . . .
>
> *Sunday Express*, 2 December

> One will go again not only to get a closer grip on the tale but to

hear the music, which has hardly one memorable melody yet is nevertheless insidiously haunting . . .

Scott Goddard, *News Chronicle*, 3 December

There were no arias [*sic*], no pretty tunes, but stern, stormy music, with the tang of the sea, with woodwind, brass and percussion dominating . . .

Reynold's News, 2 December

V Round and About the Libretto

(a) Mr Newman's Comments

As was to be expected, very large tracts of the after-criticisms of *Billy Budd* were taken up with discussions of the libretto and/or short synopses of Melville's tale. The opera's music received less attention and less space. In the present circumstances of newsprint shortage this can hardly be otherwise; every reader wants to know what the opera is about.

On 3 December, the morning after the first performance, the *Observer*, one of the two major Sunday newspapers, carried an article on *Billy Budd* by Mr Eric Blom, while *The Sunday Times* made do with a short news item and a promise: 'Mr Ernest Newman will comment on the opera in *The Sunday Times* next week.'

Was it worth waiting a week for Mr Newman's piece? In an article of some 700 words, as fairly as I can judge, not more than 51 words either relate directly to, or make direct statements about, the music; possibly there are another 50 that imply musical judgements (though this is by no means clear from the text). This quite extraordinary disproportion could have mattered less had it not been for the very weighty *musical* conclusion Mr Newman reached at the end of his first paragraph. Having explained that the 'great emotional impact' Billy's tragic death made on the first-night audience was 'merely a well-deserved tribute to Melville',[5] Mr Newman continues:

> As far as I was concerned the new work was a painful disappointment. This seems to me the least notable of Mr Britten's four operas; I can see no such musical advance in it as I had hoped for.

Now this is very severe criticism (the severest of all the published criticisms of which I have knowledge), and in view of the authority attached to Mr Newman's name and the reputation of the paper for which he writes, the very least the reader might have reasonably looked for was a factual substantiation of so forcefully committed an opinion. But not a bit of it. Mr Newman's next paragraph initiates a lengthy examination of the libretto and he makes no decisive return to the music until the very end of his article.

Is it not a truism that as far as opera is concerned we can evaluate the worth of a libretto only in purely musical terms? That a libretto's virtues and vices are speculative until they are minutely analysed in their musical context? And at that stage may we not find that many of our preconceived literary judgements are reversed? Mr Newman considers that Britten 'has been ill-served by his librettists'. He writes that 'The prime trouble with the opera, as I see it, is that hardly anywhere do the three principal characters come to real musical life.' Mr Newman is, of course, quite entitled to his wrong opinion. But it is symptomatic of the confusion in his mind that he lays the blame for this failure not on the composer, but on the librettists. What Mr Newman considers to be Britten's inability to 'back up' Claggart's 'Credo' in the manner of Beethoven (Pizarro) or Verdi (Iago) seems to be of secondary importance:

> Melville's task was easy; availing himself of the novelist's privilege to speak in his own person, he gives us a searching analysis of each of the three [principal characters]. But to translate these psychological subtleties into operatic terms is a difficult problem, and it is hardly to be wondered at that the librettists have failed to solve it. Claggart's brief soliloquizing shows him only as an ineffectual cross

> between the Iago of the 'Credo' and Pizarro, without a Verdi or a Beethoven to back him up musically in his confession of a natural bent towards evil.

Unlike Mr Newman I don't expect the impossible of librettists; achievement of the impossible belongs strictly to the realms of creative genius. Of course it is difficult to translate psychological subtleties into a libretto; but it is exactly at this juncture that music comes into its own. Indeed, as a means of conveying psychological subtleties of character perhaps there exists no more perfect means of communication than music – to which *Billy Budd* testifies again and again. Mr Newman's virtual obsession with the opera's text prevented him from realizing that the characterization and psychological subtleties he sought were to be found only in one place – in the opera's score.

I, neither, can achieve the impossible, and am unable to refute the charge that in this instance Britten is no Verdi or no Beethoven. Nevertheless certain features of Mr Newman's remarks suggest to me that he has either so misheard or misunderstood the aria that one would be rash in the extreme to show much confidence in his judgement as expressed in its present form. For example his curiously misleading term 'brief soliloquizing'. Why so 'brief'? To follow up one of Mr Newman's own comparisons, Claggart's aria is actually as long as Pizarro's 'Ha! welch' ein Augenblick!' from *Fidelio* (including the chorus even), and there is no doubt to my mind that the Forster–Crozier text is the Beethoven's literary superior.[6] Moreover I am surprised that the Mr Newman who is so conversant with the Melville tale seems to have missed the crucial significance of the aria's line 'But alas, alas! the light shines in the darkness, and the darkness comprehends it and suffers'[7] which is, as it were, a transformation of one of Melville's key observations on Claggart's character: a nature capable of 'apprehending the good, but powerless to be it'. In the libretto the external observation is translated into an internal observation actively made by the character about whom it was originally written. It is with these few bars that we feel for a fleeting moment (possibly for the first and last time) the impact of Claggart's own private tragedy; and the music in fact runs as deep as one of the deepest of Melville's comments: 'Claggart could even have loved Billy but for fate and ban.'

In short the characterization and the subtle psychology is there for those with ears; and the libretto does exactly what is required of it: it provides the verbal clue to the dramatic situation (and very cunningly too). But the solution, the solution, Mr Newman, lies in and with the music. A recognition of the fact that on their own account librettos and librettists can ultimately solve nothing is long overdue.

Mr Newman's nagging insistence on the libretto merely supports my view that his musical understanding of *Billy Budd* was sadly limited; an impression that is strengthened by his own final paragraph, the musical summing-up, so to speak:

> Inexpert as the dramatic handling often is, for it keeps falling between the two stools of conventional 'opera' and modern psychological music-drama,[8] the music, to me, is a greater disappointment still. It has several fine and some great moments, particularly in the third act; but for the most part it indulges too much for my liking in a dry speech-song in the voices and disjointed 'pointings' in the orchestra, and Mr Britten has done all this much better elsewhere.

Mr Newman's downshot is so vague and imprecise that it might apply to any opera composed during the last fifty years. In so far as it makes any ascertainable comment at all, his 'dry speech-song' would seem to be but an intellectual echo of what some of the lower-deck newsmen had written the Sunday previous, quite as wrongly but rather more concisely, i.e.: 'This opera has no tunes.' We had to wait a week for a repeat of that misinformative gem.

(b) Mr Capell's Questions

After Mr Newman's critical vagaries it is almost invigorating to find Mr Capell making a straight-to-the-point inquiry in his column '*Billy Budd* Questions' (*Daily Telegraph*, 7 December). Writing of Act II Scene 1 ('Act I, Scene II' in his text, but this must be a misprint)[9] where the officers 'are discussing the possibility of mutiny on board the frigate' he asks:

> Is there not, by the way, a slip by the librettists here? The Sailing Master makes much of Billy's shout, 'Farewell, *Rights o' Man*!', smelling in it disaffection; but only an hour before he had been informed that *Rights o' Man* was the name of Billy's merchantman, from which he had been pressed, and which must still have been in sight.

Mr Capell may be partially answered by a reference to Melville. In the novella, Billy, as he is leaving by boat for the *Indomitable*, suddenly jumps up and cries to his old ship and shipmates, 'And goodbye to you too, old *Rights-of-Man*!' To continue in Melville's own words:

> 'Down, sir,' roared the Lieutenant, instantly assuming all the rigour of his rank, though with difficulty repressing a smile. To be sure, Billy's action was a terrible breach of Naval decorum. But in that decorum he had never been instructed; in consideration of which the Lieutenant would hardly have been so energetic in reproof but for the concluding farewell to the ship. This he rather took as meant to convey a covert sally on the new recruit's part, a sly slur at impressment in general, and that of himself in especial. And yet, more likely, if satire it was in effect, it was hardly so by intention, for Billy, though happily endowed with the gaiety of high health, youth, and a free heart, was yet by no means of a satirical turn. The will to do it and the sinister dexterity were alike wanting. To deal in double meaning . . . of any sort was quite foreign to his nature.

As in the tale, so in the opera. Billy's farewell from the *Indomitable*'s deck is simply no more than a farewell, and 'The Rights o' Man' is no more than the name of a ship with which he has been lately associated. It is the Sailing Master's and his colleagues' misunderstanding of Billy's adieu that results in the topic being raised once more in the Captain's cabin, not, to be sure, because the Sailing Master has *forgotten* the name of Billy's ship but because he has misconceived the whole incident as an example of potential duplicity on Billy's part (an impression that is all the stronger in the opera when some of the crew, in wordless chorus, pick up the theme of Billy's farewell phrase, previously heard as the working shanty 'O heave! O heave away, heave!' It is at this moment that the shanty, as Mr White correctly observes, 'becomes identified . . . with the idea of mutiny' (*Listener*, 22 November) *but on the crew's and officers' level of misunderstanding*: Billy is unaware of the tragic coincidence which is the very start of his misfortune.) But how is it that this situation is operatically clear to those with no prior (and detailed) knowledge of Melville's story? As I have indicated elsewhere the solution to the problems of librettos must always be heard with the ears, or looked for in the score. When we examine Billy's E major song 'Billy Budd, king of the birds!' we realize (hear) at once that its exultant innocence excludes the possibility of satire emerging as an element in its 'farewell' conclusion. Mr Capell in fact has fallen into exactly the same error as the Sailing Master for exactly the same reason: neither 'understood' Billy's aria. But while it is dramatically essential in many an operatic circumstance that the characters show no signs of comprehending what the music is secretly revealing to the audience, there is really no need for the critics to follow suit.

In Mr Capell's first review of the opera (*Daily Telegraph*, 3 December) he had already complained of one inconsistency – 'The authors' inclination to represent George III's Navy as a hell on earth is not squared with their young hero's perfect satisfaction with all its rough old ways' – and cast doubt on the authenticity of the Novice's flogging in Act I: 'It would be interesting to know whether, in fact, a mere coxswain had authority in those days to inflict, on the spur of the moment, a flogging on a recruit who was guilty of nothing more than stumbling on the deck.' I can do no better than draw Mr Capell's attention to Eric Crozier's authoritatively documented account of the British Navy in 1797 (*Tempo* 21 (autumn 1951), pp. 9–11) which proves that Covent Garden's *Indomitable* is a floating paradise when compared with accounts of contemporary naval conditions. Mr Crozier points out that:

> Men were flogged (and severe flogging crippled or killed) for the most trivial offences, for 'silent contempt', for being last to obey an order. 'Starting' a man – trouncing him with a stick – was common form for officers and petty officers.

It seems likely then that 'a mere coxswain' (Bosun in the libretto) could have had the Novice flogged: that he did so to a recruit 'guilty of nothing more than stumbling on the deck' is factually not quite correct, since the librettists have admirably paved the way for the Bosun's vengeance in a preceding scene where the Novice not only accidentally collides with the officer but omits to call him 'sir' – for the Bosun an obvious case of 'silent impertinence'. It is the accumulated memories of these immediately previous 'insults' that, on the Novice's stumbling, provide the rational (and dramatic) basis for the Bosun's action. In all conscience his action is peremptory enough, but certainly not as peremptory as Mr Capell would have it.

As for Billy, Mr Capell's objection to his singular acceptance of his environment was foreseen by Melville, not merely in relation to his tale but in relation to life itself:

> It is observable that where certain virtues pristine and unadulterate peculiarly characterize anybody in the external uniform of civilization, they will upon scrutiny seem not to be derived from custom or convention *but rather to be out of keeping with these* . . . [My italics.]

The whole dramatic impetus of the opera lies in the 'moral phenomenon' of Billy's character and should any hint of disaffection disturb his otherwise 'uncomplaining acquiescence', the logic of Melville's story and Britten's opera would be seriously impaired, if not utterly destroyed.

(c) *Billy Budd*'s Symbolism

Very many critical evaluations of *Billy Budd* congratulate the librettists on their faithfulness to Melville's original. So far, so good. It is true enough that Messrs Forster and Crozier invent mainly next to nothing but telescope and expand incident and dialogue with great brilliance. Nevertheless, in the one instance where they do radically depart from Melville's text – a departure that introduces an element of the utmost importance to the aesthetic understanding of the opera – none of the critics noticed it. Briefly, *Budd*'s Christian symbolism has gone unrecognized. I apologize in advance for the superficial nature of this contribution to the subject, but neither time nor space allow for anything deeper or more detailed.

I am, of course, aware that there exists already a body of *literary* opinion which views Melville's story in specifically Christian terms. For example Mr Ronald Mason, in an article 'Herman Melville and *Billy Budd*' (*Tempo*, autumn 1951) writes that 'The story of Billy, owing so much to Christian symbolism, dramatizes over again the victory of Innocence over the deadly Experience that had appeared to destroy it.' Mr Raymond Weaver, quoted in Mr Rex Warner's introduction to a selection of Melville's short stories,[10] regards *Budd* as the author's 'last word upon the strange mystery of himself and human destiny' and, according to Mr Warner, 'considered that now finally the author was attempting to justify the ways of God to man'. On the other hand Mr Warner goes on to quote Mr William Plomer's comment on Mr Weaver: 'I do not myself perceive any such attempt at justification; I see the story rather as Melville's final protest against the nature of things'; and Mr Warner himself suggests 'The ways of God are in no obvious sense justified, but . . . the dignity of man is upheld.' These wide differences of opinion confirm my impression that nowhere in *Budd* does Melville commit himself on the Christian issue; his own attitude remains something of an enigma. In fact, the Christian content of Melville's *Budd* is potential rather than actual: for the opera, the librettists, so to speak, have *realized* it.

This Christian realization is plainly ascertainable from the librettists' additions to, and their one striking contradiction of, Melville's text. The revealing contradiction first: in the tale, when Billy is chained beneath deck awaiting execution, he is visited by the ship's chaplain: 'The good man sought to bring Billy Budd to some godly understanding that he must die, and at dawn.' A paragraph later the Melville continues:

> If in vain the good chaplain sought to impress the young barbarian with ideas of death akin to those conveyed in the skull, dial, and cross-bones on old tombstones; *equally futile to all appearance were his efforts to bring home to him the thought of salvation and a Saviour*. Billy listened, but less out of awe or reverence, perhaps, than from a certain natural politeness . . . [My italics.]

This unequivocal statement may now be compared with the libretto, Act IV Scene I, Billy to Dansker: 'Chaplain's been here before you. Kind. And good, his story of the good boy hung and gone to glory, hung for the likes of me, the likes of me . . .' This awareness (however primitively expressed) is, as we have seen, denied him in Melville's original tale, and it finds its ecstatic fulfilment in the libretto in his subsequent and final (B♭) farewell to the world (which, unlike the major part of the libretto, has no germinal verbal equivalent in the story whatsoever):

> But I've sighted a sail in the storm, the far-shining sail that's not Fate, and I'm contented. I've seen where she's bound for. She has a land of her own where she'll anchor for ever . . . Don't matter now being hanged, or being forgotten and caught in the weeds . . . I'm strong, and I know it, and I'll stay strong, and that's all, and that's enough.

The imagery may be nautical but its meaning is apparent enough; indeed it is vitally confirmed when Vere, in the opera's Epilogue, takes up both Billy's words and his music just before the opera's unambiguous B♭ conclusion where *Billy Budd*'s protagonists and conflicting tonalities (derived from the Prologue) are at last reconciled.

In the story, when Vere eventually dies of battle wounds murmuring 'Billy Budd, Billy Budd', Melville permits himself a remark – no more enlightening than that 'These were not the accents of remorse.' But in the opera Vere is explicitness itself, and makes what seems to be a direct biblical reference: 'But he has saved me, and blessed me, and the love which passes understanding[11] has come to me.'

Billy dies 'strong' and the sorely tried Vere is saved by Billy's forgiveness. The opera's resolution on a Christian level should make us view *Billy Budd* more as a Christian parable than as a succession of ironical accidents[12] determined by an implacable and inscrutable Fate. 'But I've sighted a sail in the storm, the far-shining sail that's not Fate,' sings Billy; and is it not significant that we are informed in John Piper's and Basil Coleman's '*Billy Budd* on the Stage' (*Tempo*, autumn 1951) that the composer himself saw the Novice's scene in Act I 'in terms of Stations of the Cross'?

(d) Prologue and Epilogue

The vaguest recognition of *Budd*'s Christian symbolism would have provided a vital clue to the work's relation to Britten's other operas. For the symbolism plus Vere's Prologue and Epilogue would have inevitably guided the listener back to *Lucretia*: and it is *Lucretia* with which *Budd* may be the most fruitfully compared both spiritually and stylistically (not forgetting the all-important and intervening *Spring Symphony*). But it was enough for most critical ears and eyes that *Billy Budd* was a sea story with sea shanties. *Peter Grimes* was taken as *Budd*'s point of departure, and *Lucretia* went altogether unmentioned apart from a bypassing reference of Mr Shawe-Taylor's. (*Herring*, of course, was even more emphatically excluded, except by Mr Stanley Bayliss in the *Daily Mail* of 3 December who wrote that '*Billy Budd* may reassure those who thought that Britten's great talent had been diverted from its true path by trifles [*sic*] like *Albert Herring* . . .')

Had our critics been aware of *Budd*'s link with *Lucretia*, they might have thought a little more deeply about the Prologue's and Epilogue's true purpose and spent less time misunderstanding their dramatic function. Dr Mosco Carner in *Time and Tide*, 8 December:

> In their endeavour to make the significance of the story as clear as possible the librettists had recourse to a prologue and epilogue, *a rather tame and undramatic solution of the problem* . . . [My italics.]

Or Mr Philip Hope-Wallace in *Picture Post*, 22 December: 'Pages of prologue and epilogue (beautifully written *but not dramatically effective*) . . .' (My italics.) And certainly Mr Eric Blom (in the *Observer* of 3 December) would have been spared the trouble of unearthing the most minor and incidental of reasons to justify the reversal of his initial impression that the Prologue and Epilogue, as a device, was 'rather cheap':

> But on studying the music I came to the conclusion that it must have been asked for by the composer, not only because the prologue and epilogue admirably round off his scheme thematically, but also because it enabled him to make a particularly subtle musical point. For when in the prologue Vere says 'The good has never been perfect. There is always some flaw in it . . . some imperfection in the divine image', we first hear the music associated with Billy's stammer, that fatal defect which precipitates the tragedy.

Of course, the primary function of the Prologue and Epilogue (far from introducing Billy's stammer) is to 'frame' – give perspective to – the opera's action, much as the Male and Female Chorus provide a timeless surround to the action in *Lucretia*. This element of timelessness is as important in *Budd* as it is in *Lucretia*. At some point in the opera's structure allowance had to be made for a removal of the action not only from the 'historical present' (i.e. HMS *Indomitable* in 1797) but also from the 'contemporary present' (i.e. Covent Garden in 1951) in order that the action might be freely interpreted in terms that owe nothing to time or place. Relieved of all limitations of either past or present this is, indeed, the Epilogue's special duty. In it both Billy's and Vere's tragedies are transcended and the parable, translated from the sphere of dramatic action, becomes of universal import. The personal Prologue generates the Epilogue as a timeless platform on which this transfiguration can occur. In fact I hear and feel Vere's Epilogue in much the same spirit as *Lucretia*'s final Male Chorus. As for Mr Blom's thematic anticipations (there are more than the one he describes) and his 'round off', no opera composer worth his salt would require a prologue and epilogue for such cyclic devices. (That *Budd*'s Prologue and Epilogue bear the titles they do is, in a sense, misleading: 'Epilogue', especially, severely underrates the piece's climactic importance.)

But the Prologue's and Epilogue's timeless aspect by no means exhausts their significance. The following fragment of conversation between Basil Coleman and John Piper (from their article quoted above) is strictly relevant:

> PRODUCER The main problem seems to me to decide how far we are going to be realistic and how far not. For me the most realistic scene is the Battle, Act III Scene 1, where the crew have very definite things to do . . . Then the mist descends again and they are cut off from the enemy. But the mist is as much a mist of doubt and fear in the mind of Vere when he is about to close with Claggart at the beginning and finally at the end of the scene. And these dual planes of action seem to me to run throughout the opera, as they do in Melville.
>
> DESIGNER Yes, and we must never lose sight of the fact that the whole thing is taking place in Vere's mind, and is being recalled by him.

In spite of the producer's efforts to stress these 'dual planes' with all the theatrical means at his disposal ('I can use the lighting in an unrealistic way . . . with scenes fading in and out to help the illusion of their having been called up by Vere') they don't seem to have been very apparent to the critics. Witness Mr Newman's comment,[13] or Mr Blom's, who liked Mr Piper's stage design but was evidently a little puzzled by its 'detailed realism sitting rather oddly in an unreal frame of outer darkness which suggests the sea no more than anything else'. Most muddles about an opera's libretto or its production proceed from muddles about its music – a dictum that applies above all to opera producers themselves, but not, on this occasion, to Mr Coleman. Had Mr Blom fully understood the Prologue, had he realized the contrast as well as the relations between the thematico-tonal structures of both Prologue and Epilogue on the one hand and of the body of the opera on the other, he would have become alive to the fact that the opera's frame, unlike a picture's, is of central significance: it introduces and solves the tragedy from the spiritualizing level which is the action's artistic *raison d'être*; for without the perspective thus created, Britten's music would never have been interested in the subject.

VI An Interlude on Captain Vere

'The outstanding performance of the evening came from Theodor Uppman as Billy Budd.' So ran a line in almost every post-first-performance review. While I have no desire to lessen Mr Uppman's achievement – as *Budd*'s first Billy he will be long and gratefully remembered – I should have thought it obvious to every ear and eye that it was Peter Pears's Vere that was the supreme musical characterization of the first and subsequent performances; I deliberately include the eye since I am sure that in Mr Pears the singer the stage has lost a great actor. Yet who could have guessed the stature of Mr Pears's performance from the reactions of the press?

> The tenor of the cast was Captain Vere, a stuffed uniform, but . . . Britten and Peter Pears gave him style.
>
> W[illiam]. McN[aught]., *Musical Times*, January 1952

> Theodor Uppman in voice (light baritone) and in person is ideally cast as Budd; Peter Pears and Frederick Dalberg as the Captain and Master-at-Arms rather less so.
>
> Philip Hope-Wallace, *Manchester Guardian*, 3 December

> The part of the victimized Billy is very happily entrusted to a personable young American baritone, Theodor Uppman. If Vere (Peter Pears) and Claggart (. . . Frederick Dalberg), are both rather stiff, there are many lively, well-characterized and well-sung minor performances . . .
>
> Richard Capell, *Daily Telegraph*, 3 December

Wrong about much else, Mr Stephen Williams, to his credit, and in spite of curious agreement with *The Times* on a related matter (see below), was almost alone among critics in his accurate appraisal of Pears's performance:

> Peter Pears played the Captain with such aristocratic poise and musicianship (with what delicate art he passed from the spoken word to the sung word) that the character seemed to belong exclusively to him.
>
> *New York Times*

Dr Mosco Carner, in *Time and Tide*, thought 'Peter Pears as Vere was every inch the noble Captain but seemed a little wooden and not quite at ease in the more intimate scenes in his cabin'; but not satisfied with merely criticizing the performance, he declares elsewhere in the same article that 'The scene in the Captain's cabin which opens the Second Act seems to me wholly superfluous.' Since Dr Carner has just previously complained that one of the opera's 'serious weaknesses' is that 'The richness of psychological detail so striking in Melville's portrayal of his principal protagonists is gone', and since, if anywhere in *Budd*, Vere's character is richly established in the very scene Dr Carner unaccountably wants to be rid of, I may be excused for doubting his logic.

Why is it, I wonder, that moments of extreme culture go uncherished? For it was during this scene that I was struck anew by Pears's marvellous singing and incomparable acting; his every note and gesture added something to Vere's character and contributed to our total understanding of it. The result was superbly beautiful both to listen to and to watch; a rare spectacle and a rare musical experience. Mine, I am aware, is a personal, probably a minority opinion, and does nothing to contradict the opinions of my colleagues; but it certainly needed saying. Some of us are deeply grateful for the little real culture that infrequently comes our way. Most of us seem to have forgotten what culture is and no longer recognize it when either seen or heard.

According to *The Times* critic, however, Captain Vere shouldn't have been a tenor at all: 'The composer has cast his voices upside down: the commander should have been the bass, the recruit the tenor' – an observation approved of by Mr Stephen Williams in the *New York Times*; mysteriously, because Mr Williams admits himself that 'At the première I was not conscious of any disturbing anomaly.' Of course he wasn't. There wasn't – and isn't – any anomaly to be disturbed by. Mr Williams shouldn't allow himself to be bullied by *The Times* into thinking himself wrong when he couldn't have been righter. But for all that he felt himself obliged to bless *The Times*'s heresy: 'Psychologically [*sic*] quite sound. From a slender fair-haired stripling one expects a tenor voice, just as one expects a baritone or bass from a dignified middle-aged commander' – an observation echoed by Mr Philip Hope-Wallace in *Picture Post*: 'The reflective part [of Vere] would more naturally suit a baritone with the tenor role reserved to the young sailor, Budd. Upside-down casting!'

Upside-down thinking, gentlemen! But having recast Britten's opera you might at least have recomposed the music as well. Has it not occurred to you that Captain Vere's music is 'characteristic' to and of the tenor voice for which it is written? Or do you suggest that a simple matter of transposition would enable a 'dignified middle-aged' bass or baritone to take over? What, in any case and in this context, does *The Times*'s 'should have been' mean? What standards of comparison are we expected to use when we don't know what kind of music would have been forthcoming had

Britten chosen such an improbable course? All we *can* know is that a bass Captain Vere would be utterly unlike the Captain Vere of whom we have present, factual and musical knowledge. Meanwhile, acting on *The Times*'s supposition, what happens to Britten's delicately poised balance between his male voices? What happens when, for page after page in Act III, bass meets bass? And in the same act and elsewhere what happens to Vere's conciliatory, characteristic and *characterizing* obbligatos? I don't care if *The Times* thinks that Captain Vere's musical characterization is all wrong – even if the dramatic demands of the role have tenor writ large upon them. What I do care about is the expression of dogmatic judgements, seemingly based on ascertainable evidence, which, on examination, prove to derive from the purest realms of speculation. Speculators should stick to speculating. 'Should have been' merely sticks in my throat.

I have always been suspicious of Gilbert's and Sullivan's influence on English musical taste; a suspicion confirmed by Mr Newman's introduction of *HMS Pinafore* into his notice of *Billy Budd*[14] and by Mr Williams's mention of a 'dignified middle-aged commander'. Is it necessary that operatic naval officers of the future, from admirals downwards, shall be gibbering parodies in reverse? The last thing I should have expected of the commander who seems to have taken hold of Mr Williams's fancy would be quotations from Plutarch. In fact the presence of the classics would have astonished me even more than their delivery by a tenor voice. Perhaps the librettists and composer should have been less faithful to Melville in this respect. After all it was Melville who wrote that 'ashore in the garb of a civilian, scarce anyone would have taken [Vere] for a sailor'; that 'He had a marked leaning toward everything intellectual. He loved books, never going to sea without a newly replenished library, compact but of the best . . .'; that 'He would cite some historical character or incident of antiquity with the same easy air that he would cite from the moderns . . .' How closely does Melville's Vere correspond to Mr Williams's? From such a remarkable, unconventional figure one could have the right to expect only the unexpected; and it is the exception, not the rule, that we have in Britten's opera – tenor voice and all.

Music apart, I should have thought that this was one matter on which there could be no dispute. That for better or for worse the librettists' and the composer's Vere was strictly Melville's.[15] But I was mistaken. Wrote H.S.R., in *Musical Opinion* (January 1952): 'This character, of all the characters in the opera, was the one which was *essentially alien* to that depicted with so masterly an economy of words by Herman Melville.' (My italics.) The inquiring reader may refer to the book itself, or reread the descriptive passages from Melville reproduced above. I myself must attempt to imitate Melville's verbal economy. No comment.

VII A Note on the 'Interview' Chords

Of all passages in *Billy Budd* none was debated with more fire and less fact than the end of Act III Scene 2; the thirty-four chords which, according to the synopsis of the opera in *Tempo*, 'tell of the fatal, invisible interview of the two men'. Mr Blom in the *Observer*, quite apart from giving a bewilderingly wrong reason for the chords' dramatic justification ('I can see that they foreshadow Billy's last resolve to die without weakening')[16] states unambiguously that the triads are 'harmonically disconnected'; while Mr Shawe-Taylor in the *New Statesman* votes for their being 'distantly related but converging towards F major'. Mr Stephen Williams, in the *New York Times*, not only declares the chords once more to be 'harmonically disconnected' (if he's quoting Mr Blom he doesn't make any acknowledgement), but that they are 'certainly monotonous' besides; and he adds a suggestion for their improvement: '[They] could be halved with advantage.' (How would Mr Williams set about this task? By deleting each alternate chord?) While *The Times* holds aloof by classifying the chords as no more than 'antiphonal', Dr Mosco Carner, in

Time and Tide, approaches somewhere nearer the truth with:

> Britten here writes a long series of chorale-like chords, all different harmonizations of the notes F–A–C (which define Budd's key) and scored in different ways.

It is a pity that Dr Carner's imagination fails to keep pace with his perception; for a failure of imagination it is when he writes that the chords are

> effective and suggestive, it is true, but insufficient to serve as a *real* interpretation of that crucial scene [where Vere informs Billy of the court's verdict].

While Dr Carner is quite correct in pointing to the chords' centripetal relation to the F major triad,[17] his definition of the latter as 'Budd's key' is superficial. Throughout the opera keys are not so much attached to persons as to aspects of the drama. More than just Budd, F major represents liberating resignation to the tragic inevitability of F minor. Aside from its descriptive role, the section stands as a highly compressed and formally concentrated survey of the opera's tonal area; and, as so often in Britten, the feeling is intensified by the extreme terseness of expression.

In a reference to the chords' 'wonderful realization . . . of what passed between the two victims of fate's malignancy, from which Melville hedges away', *The Times* does much less than justice to Melville's artistic integrity. Far from hedging, Melville had the honesty to desist from faking; he was aware that any attempt to communicate literally the conversation between Vere and Billy was bound to be inadequate. Such matters run too deep for reported dialogue, and Melville's own moving conjectures on the subject leave the door wide open for music to enter and make explicit what is implicit in the prose:

> Captain Vere in the end may have developed the passion sometimes latent under an exterior stoical or indifferent. He was old enough to have been Billy's father. The austere devotee of military duty, letting himself melt back into what remains primeval in our

> formalized humanity, may in the end have caught Billy to his heart, even as Abraham may have caught young Isaac on the brink of resolutely offering him up in obedience to the exacting behest.

So far, while everyone has either agreed or disagreed on the chords' theatrical effectiveness or their degrees of relatedness or unrelatedness, no one has yet offered an opinion as to why the passage takes the shape it does. Why, in fact, *common chords*?

It seems to me that Melville provides a clue – Vere let himself melt back into 'what remains primeval': so to speak, a verbal rationalization of what most of us felt on hearing the chords for the first time. Melville, of course, is using primeval in the sense of fundamental, of the world's first age; primitive, yes, but not elementary; *elemental*, rather. And it is exactly a disclosure of the elemental that we experience in Britten's succession of slow triads – symbols, in a manner of speaking, of music's first age; bearing in mind our own musical culture, they are perhaps the nearest we can approach to the emotionally musical primeval without becoming self-consciously primitive (in its derogatory application). Our musical primitivity is limited by the history of our culture; and the triad, relative to our culture, represents one of those limits. Britten himself, because of the peripheries imposed by his own culture, could go no further without peril of stylistic anachronism. The triad itself may be a highly cultured concept, the result of long historical development; but in the context of *Budd* it expressed the fundamental, the cosmic even, in the most condensed (if contextually complex) terms. The chords, for me, are the true musical realization of the ultimate passions involved, when, in Melville's words, 'two of great Nature's nobler order embrace'.

NOTES

1 MC: This article did much to secure DM a place on the BBC 'black list' referred to by Christopher Palmer on pp. xix–xxi and xxxii, n. 6. Writing to DM on 13 July 1953 from Broadcasting House, Roger Fiske commented:

> Naturally, when I came into this job, I was told about a large number of people who did not seem up to the mark, and I hasten to say that no special prominence was given to the name of Mitchell on this black list, it was merely one among many, but the words 'rather aggressive' were used, and my mind immediately switched to the most aggressive piece of criticism that I have read for a long time, yours on *Billy Budd* in *Music Survey*. I remember talking to you about this and discovering to my surprise that you had no idea that the people you were attacking might feel any offence; so I thought you could hardly have taken offence yourself at some mild, and believe me, extremely well-intentioned remarks on what seems to me one of your most obvious characteristics. I would hesitate to call it a fault, because it does make for readability. Goodness knows I enjoyed the *Billy Budd* article, but it just was 'aggressive', there is no other word for it – they are all out of step but our Donald!

2 MC: Hans Keller, 'Resistances to Britten's Music: Their Psychology', *Music Survey* 2/4 (spring 1950), pp. 227–36.

3 Mr Williams was going strong on this subject in 1947 and in very much the same words:

> Then there is Britten. Britten is also a cult. He is indisputably the Golden Boy of contemporary music, immensely successful and immensely fashionable. His success is due to two causes: exceptional gifts and exceptional opportunities for putting them over. [*Penguin Music Magazine* 11 (1947), pp. 70–72.]

4 Mr Capell's contention (*Daily Telegraph*, 3 December) that 'Britten's score cannot be called much of a structure' is especially misleading. The highly organic nature of the opera's structure is a topic we shall return to in our future and more musical discussion of *Billy Budd*'s music.

5 This well-deserved tribute to Melville certainly took the wrong turning if a *Daily Mail* report (3 December) is to be believed. It appears that, at the opera's conclusion, 'The musical purists in the gallery pounded the plush-covered rails and shouted, "Bravo, Benjy!"' We must be grateful to Mr Newman for exposing the gallery's misplaced enthusiasm.

6 Nor is there much difference in length between Claggart's aria and Iago's 'Credo'. It occurs to me now, however, that Mr Newman's 'brief' may apply to the text *only*. But if we pursue the Pizarro–Claggart comparison, Claggart passes even this test with flying colours. Deleting all repetitions in both cases, while Pizarro has to make do with some 90 words, Claggart is liberally supplied with over 200. Textually briefer than Pizarro's, Claggart's aria certainly is not. Why Mr Newman should imagine that Claggart's piece is less effectual and revealing than Pizarro's I am quite unable to understand – unless it is that he considers the following lines from the latter to be the very height of psychological penetration:

> And as I stand before him,
> With deadly steel to gore him,

I'll shout into his ear:
'Tis I! 'tis I! 'tis I!
'Tis I who triumph here.
[Trans. E. J. Dent]

7 A line which, I assume, borrows its imagery from St John 1:5: 'And the light shineth in darkness; and the darkness comprehended it not.' The alteration in *sense* between the biblical verse and its version in the libretto is, of course, plain; as is the correspondence between the aria's line and Melville's original comment. The librettists, so to speak, have poetized the moral proposition expounded in Melville's prose and added 'suffering' as a logical consequence of 'apprehension'. For more on *Budd*'s Christian symbolism see sub-section (c), pp. 379–81.
8 That the whole opera takes place on two distinct 'levels' Mr Newman has evidently appreciated; but the real significance of the dual action seems to have escaped him. See pp. 379–84.
9 MC: All act and scene numbering refers to Britten's original four-act version of *Billy Budd*, DM's article having been written nine years before the composer's compression of the opera into two acts in 1960. Ironically, Capell's mislabelling of this scene happens to coincide with unwitting prescience to its correct label in the later two-act version.
10 Herman Melville, *Billy Budd and Other Stories* (Lehmann, London, 1951).
11 Actually a compound of Philippians 4:7 and Ephesians 3:19.
12 'Billy, that happy soul, comes to grief by what is, after all, only a chapter of accidents' – 'R.C.', in the *Monthly Musical Record* (January 1952).
13 See note 8 above.
14 He has since been joined by Mr Winton Dean in *Opera* (January 1952), p. 11.
15 MC: It is by no means incontrovertible to aver, as DM does here, that 'the composer's Vere was strictly Melville's'. Vere's behaviour in the opera's trial scene, for instance, is diametrically opposed to his conduct in Melville's novella: see MC and Philip Reed, *Benjamin Britten: 'Billy Budd'* (Cambridge University Press (Cambridge Opera Handbook), Cambridge, 1993), pp. 28–33, to which DM contributed his later and much revised views of the opera in 'A *Billy Budd* notebook (1979–1991)', pp. 111–34.
16 Mr Blom must have been thinking of the chords' second appearance in Act IV Scene 1, where their dramatic implication is more akin to moral resolution: e.g. Billy's 'I'm strong, and I know it, and I'll stay strong', etc. Two other references are made to the chords: in the orchestral 'execution' interlude between Scenes 1 and 2 of Act IV, and in Vere's Epilogue.
17 The whole section is basically in F major, or to use a term coined by Richard Arnell [in his 'Note on Tonality', *Music Survey* 2/3 (winter 1950), p. 179] 'F chromatic major'.

Britten's Revisionary Practice: Practical and Creative

Composers' revisions really fall into two main groups (though each group itself can be subdivided many times over). The first group I would name 'practical', i.e. revisions or afterthoughts that are designed to make a work more viable; we constantly meet this kind of revising in the opera house, but I should also include under this heading those cases where a composer has written, say, a complete new movement to replace an existing one. More often than not, this is the revision of an early work; his intention is 'practical' – to get rid of the one, perhaps feeble, movement that goes against the chances of the work's success and thus save what is worth preserving in the rest of the work. This is what we might call good husbandry on the part of the composer. He keeps his crops, so to speak, in the best and most marketable condition.

It is into my 'practical' category, for example, that Britten's 1961 revision of *Billy Budd* (1951) belongs. The intention here was to shorten slightly a long (but surely not too long?) opera, in the main by avoiding a somewhat cumbersome division into four acts (with their attendant intervals). In the revised version, the former Acts I and II have been sealed together, to make Act I, and the former Acts III and IV are now rolled together as Act II. So far as the former Acts III and IV are concerned, this means that we lose the preview of Billy's F major lullaby with which Act III originally ended; in the new version, what was the final scene of Act III becomes Scene 2 of Act II and closes on the last – the

---

Tempo 66–7 (autumn/winter 1963), pp. 15–22

C major – chord of the famous series of triads that comprises Captain Vere's fateful interview with the condemned Billy (music that literally goes too deep for words).

I dare say the original version of the opera will always have its champions, and I cheerfully count myself among them. I liked very much, in the original version, the links between Acts I and II and Acts III and IV, which meant that one picked up the music at the beginning of a new act from where one had left it before the interval, and I cannot help regretting the excision of this feature. However, there is no denying the claims practicality makes. One may regret the sacrifice of some fascinating detail (see Exx. 1(a) and 1(b), which give the end and beginning of the original Acts I and II), but there is no doubt at all that the division into two acts is an altogether stronger and more workable proposition, especially from the point of view of the mechanics of the opera house.

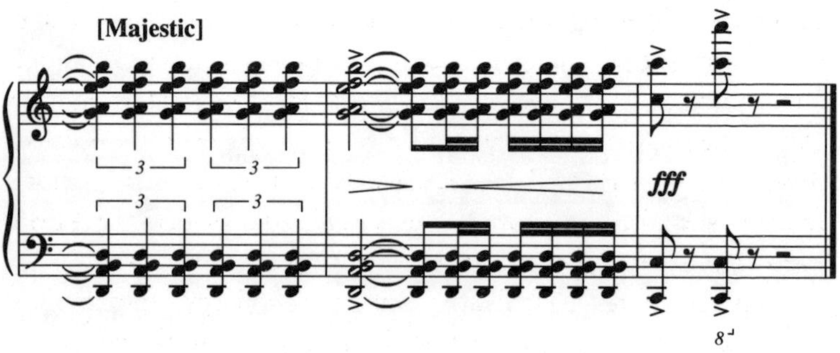

Ex. 1(a)

The major revision in *Billy Budd* occurs, in fact, at the seam between the former Acts I and II (now Act I). The sequence of dramatic events at the end of Act I in the old days (I write, you must remember, as an old *Billy Budd* man, almost a member of Captain Vere's crew) ran as follows (from 9 bars before Fig. 51 in

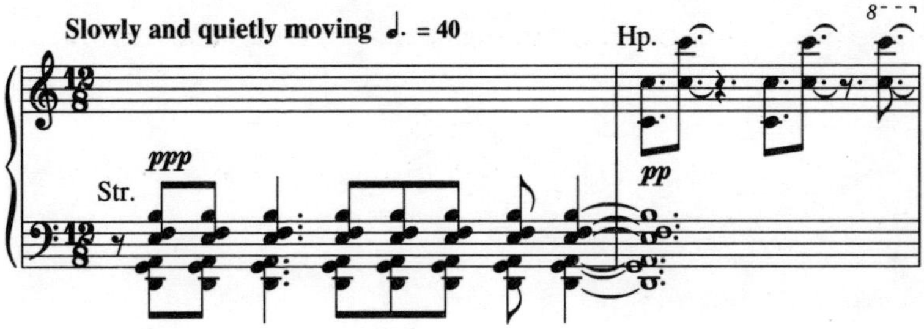

Ex. 1(b)

the original version: it is here that the main revision starts in the 1961 score – at the new Fig. 51):

(1) Captain's muster;
(2) Vere's address to his crew;
(3) Tribute to Vere from the chorus, with appropriately exultant contributions from Billy.

In the revised version, the call for Captain's muster becomes a sign of changing the watch; Vere does not appear (but Billy hears about him and reacts spontaneously to the gossip of his mates), and of course the final chorus – 'Starry Vere!' – no longer exists because there is no longer any dramatic reason for it. In the new version, we run straight on from the deck and quarter-deck of HMS *Indomitable* into the nocturnal scene in Captain Vere's cabin.

I have to confess that I suffer some pangs, despite the obvious good sense of the new disposition. I regret above all the necessary omission in the new version of Vere's long and heroic – C major – address to his crew: 'Officers and men of the *Indomitable*, I greet you!' (see Ex. 2 [overleaf]). (The cut is all the more painful when I remember how brilliantly this was sung by Peter Pears in the original production.) It presented Vere in an immediately forceful, man-of-action guise, whereas in the very beautiful nocturnal cabin scene, in which the Captain now makes his first appearance,[1] it is Vere the thinker, the recluse, the super-civilized commander, that

Ex. 2

we encounter. Still, it is true enough that there is ample opportunity later for Vere to impress us as a man of immense resolution and vigour.

I also freely confess that I have a sentimental reason for sorrowing over the loss of the celebratory chorus that used to round off the original Act I. *Billy Budd* was first performed at a time when Hans Keller and I had much to do with the late Erwin Stein, and for some reason or other – I can't remember now how it happened – 'Starry Vere!' (the chorus) gave rise to 'Starry Stein!'; and for many years it was as 'Starry Stein' that Erwin – always most enthusiastically and affectionately – figured in our conversations (he, of course, was blissfully unaware of his operatic transformation). Thus, in a rather silly but warm-hearted way, the final chorus of the old Act I was very much Erwin's chorus, and I'm sad that I shan't be hearing it again at Covent Garden. ('Starry Vere!', mind you – the musical phrase, that is – still remains in the new version – see Ex. 3: it is simply not elaborated chorally to the degree that it was before.)

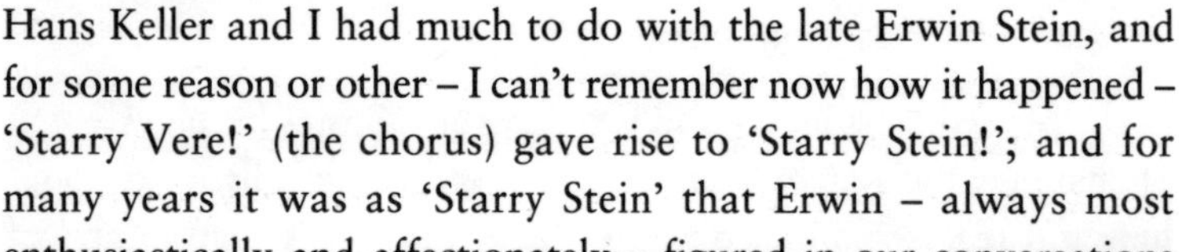

Ex. 3

So much for *Billy Budd*, so much for my doubtless vain regrets, and so much for one instance of the 'practical' aspect of Britten's revisionary practice. The second main group of revisions I would describe as 'creative', a stupid term, no doubt, because practical revisions are creative, too; but I mean it to bear a particular sense in this context, to suggest that there is a whole category of revisions that throw active light on the creative process. In short, we can learn something from them of the approach a composer makes to his materials.

In a quite special sense, indeed, we could really regard a composer's sketches as a kind of revisionary process, in which he refines on his first ideas and gradually unfolds them in their final form. These 'revisions', without doubt, are the most fascinating and the most revealing of all; but, of course, it is just these revisions that we don't see; or only by chance.

It so happens that some while ago I came across a vocal score of *The Turn of the Screw* (not a printed copy but a dyeline copy of the autograph of the vocal score prepared by Imogen Holst) which included a quite substantial passage in the finale of Act II that was radically revised before the vocal score was actually published. Thus we have here an opportunity of comparing what could be taken to be two last thoughts, the final revision, proving to be, as I shall suggest, a major stroke of inspiration.

To appreciate the revision, or indeed the first version (a finished sketch, so to speak), it is important to bear in mind the dramatic context. At the end of Act II of the opera, it will be remembered, the Governess anxiously questions Miles about his tormentor; it is her intention to oblige the boy to speak the dreaded name. The confession once made, peace and sanity may be regained, the spell broken. From every dramatic point of view, then, this is a crucial juncture in the opera, the point of extremest dramatic tension and also the climactic point of the finale's passacaglia; and the composer must have been sensible of the compositional challenge that this passage implied. We may safely surmise that he gave a great deal of thought to it. Ex. 4 [overleaf] shows the first version of

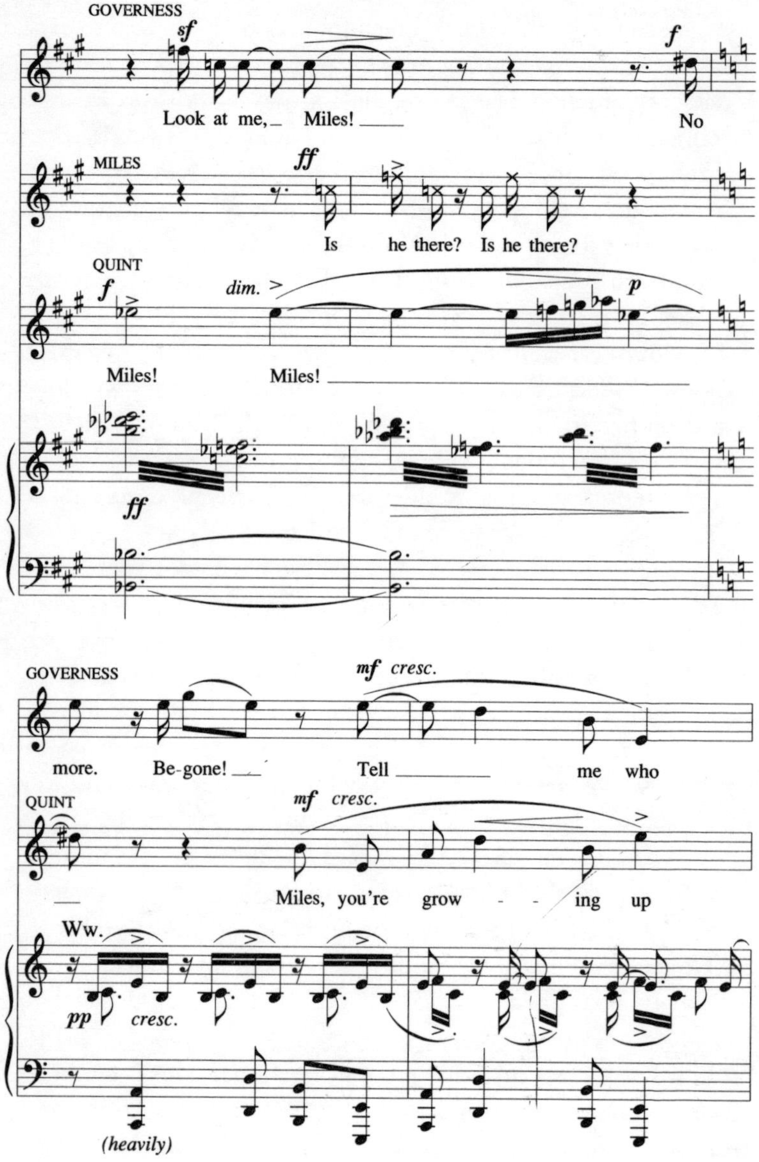
GOVERNESS
sf
f
Look at me, Miles! No
MILES
ff
Is he there? Is he there?
QUINT
f
dim.
p
Miles! Miles!
ff
GOVERNESS
mf cresc.
more. Be-gone! Tell me who
QUINT
mf cresc.
Miles, you're grow - - ing up
Ww.
pp cresc.
(heavily)

Ex. 4

GOVERNESS
Say it, Say it, Who is it? Who?
QUINT
You must be free
GOVERNESS
sf
Who? Tell me. Say it!
MILES
(shrieking)
Pe-ter Quint! You De-vil!
QUINT
It is the last chance!
ffpp

Ex. 4 (cont.)

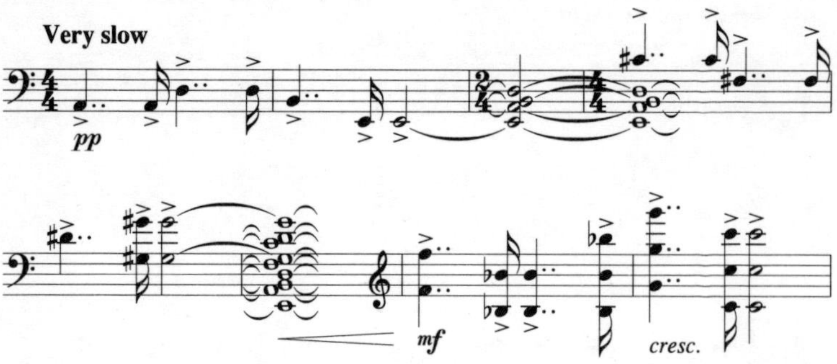

Ex. 5

this all-important climax, which ends with Miles's naming of his pursuer.

What are the basic components that we find in Ex. 4? First and foremost, of course, there is the unfolding in the bass of the 'screw' (Ex. 5, which stands, as it were, for Quint and Miss Jessel, the powers of darkness in the opera) in its entirety; up to this point, the passacaglia has made use only of a segment, though a gradually expanding segment, of the theme. It is appropriate, indeed, that it is at this flash-point of crisis – the Governess insisting, the boy still irresolute, the name trembling on his lips, and Quint pleading – that the 'screw' rotates throughout its total length: the last turn of the screw, with a vengeance. The second component, the agitated, breathless, broken semiquaver figures in the woodwind, is again strictly functional, both dramatically and musically. It derives, in fact, from Act I, the motif (see Ex. 6) associated with Quint's first appearance to the Governess in Scene 4. We might call it the 'Who is it?' motif.

The combination of the turn of the 'screw' and the 'Who is it?' music – in which the bass, ironically, 'answers' the question put by the treble strand and the Governess's own vocal line – provides a texture vivid enough, one would have thought, and charged with sufficient allusiveness, to bear, together with the characteristic vocal parts, the weight of the dramatic moment. If we had not

Ex. 6

known the later revision, should we have found it wanting in any respect? I doubt it. But the composer, it seems, was less easily satisfied, or perhaps suddenly struck at a very late stage by the magnificent inspiration that we know today (Ex. 7 [pp. 402–3]). Here is the 'screw' theme again, but this time we notice a brilliant intensification of its role; and not only intensification, but also an additional statement of it. As it appears in this final version,[2] the rhythmic articulation of the 'screw' (as was not the case in Ex. 4) returns the theme to us as we heard it at the very start of the opera (again, the Prologue excluded). The dotted rhythm plus the sequence of notes (at their original pitch, of course) drives home the theme's memorable presence even more clearly than before. There is no mistaking this as anything but a recapitulatory event. But in advance of this statement, at Fig. 130 (bass), we already have the theme unfolded in its entirety within the space of a single bar, which presents, in condensed form, the same dramatic texture that was the *raison d'être* of Ex. 4: i.e. the bass 'answers' the 'Who is it?' pattern of the Governess's frantic questioning. Ex. 4, in fact, has not been so much abandoned as its essentials compressed into one bar; and, of course, the rapid rotation of the complete 'screw' theme in this bar liberates, at a significant point of climax, and at one blow, the progressive, additive efforts of the theme, throughout the passacaglia, to uncoil itself to its full, i.e. twelve-note, extent.

GOVERNESS
Is
MILES
Is he there? Is he there?
QUINT
Miles! you are mine!
who there Miles? Say_ it! Say it!
No-bo-dy! No-thing!
Don't be-tray us, Miles!
marked

Ex. 7

Ex. 7 (cont.)

This is indeed an example of intensification by means of compression. The rest of the passage, however, is an example of intensification by means of expansion. If Ex. 7 is weightier than Ex. 4, it is due, in part at least, to the length of it (five or six times longer than Ex. 4) and the much increased density of musical incident. There is, as we have already noticed, a majestic, indeed, wellnigh stately, recapitulation of the 'screw' theme which follows this compressed, name-probing statement of it. True, it takes place in combination with flowing semiquaver figuration marked 'Quick and urgent'; but this scarcely applies to the 'screw' theme, which pursues not only its own pitch but also its own pulse. Indeed, there is a metrical complexity in this revised version, and a graphic separation of tonal planes,[3] which we do not find in Ex. 4. The very separation of the musical incident is a phenomenon in itself; and much of it is designed, one may think, to throw into the sharpest possible relief, both rhythmically[4] and tonally, the dramatic return of the 'screw' itself.

But concentration on the 'screw', as important as it is, must not lead us to overlook the nature of the semiquaver figuration and Quint's vocal part. This is a direct quotation of one of the major inspirations in the opera, the duet between Quint and Miss Jessel that forms part of the final scene of Act I, 'On the paths, in the woods, on the banks, by the walls, in the long, lush grass or the winter leaves, fallen leaves, I wait' (Ex. 8).

Ex. 8

It is the return of this marvellous song of seductiveness and temptation – who could resist its insinuating glamour? – that most plainly marks off Ex. 4 from Ex. 7; and it makes us realize how grateful we should be for the revision. The recapitulation of so unforgettable a component from the final scene of Act I fits perfectly, and adds enormously to the impact of the finale of Act II. Here, we have Quint, as it were making his last throw. The prize is Miles's soul and with what better cards – or should it be dice? – to play than the material of the Act I duet? It was a stroke of genius to reintroduce at this point music that presents Quint in the most alluring light (music even more alluring, even more hypnotic, than the musical apostrophizing of Miles's name – in Act I – which, of course, also forms part of both versions of the opera's finale). The tension is stepped up a hundredfold by its electrifying intervention.

Let us note, to conclude, that this revised version of the finale also reinforces the symmetry of a remarkably – intendedly – symmetrical opera. In its new version, the finale makes use of all the principal imagery from the final scene of Act I – the Quint–Jessel duet, Quint's musicalization of the boy's name, the Governess's 'Who is it?' music and the 'screw' theme. If, in the finale of Act II, we feel that the screw has, so to say, turned full circle, it is due in large measure to Britten's final revision of his score. We can see now, presumably as he did at the time (1954), that Ex. 4 did not quite meet the clinching challenge that the ultimate stage of the opera presents. The new version, in its multiform complexity and gathering together of all relevant strands, exactly satisfies it. It only goes to prove that composition for a great composer is an inextricable tangle of inspiration and hard labour, an interplay between the mutual ferocities of creativity and artistic conscience.

NOTES

1 I am, naturally, leaving the opera's Prologue out of my consideration.

2 For reasons of space it is not possible to quote the whole passage. Ex. 7 falls short of completeness by 24 bars, which are rounded off by Miles's shout: 'Peter Quint, you devil!' (see Ex. 4 above, though even this epic bar is slightly different in the final version). Interested readers must, of course, consult the

published vocal score, pp. 191–4. It is clear none the less (I hope) from Ex. 7 that the main statement of the 'screw' theme continues as it is here shown to have begun.

3 We are back where we started as far as the 'screw' is concerned (to the opening of the opera proper), while the recollection of the duet, of course, is in its own key. This means that there is, in effect, a simultaneous recapitulation at this crucial juncture of the opera's two chief tonal centres, A and A♭ (A♭ is reached at the exact mid-point of the opera, and the twin tonal regions reflect the build of the 'screw' theme itself). The relationship of two keys a semitone apart is a favourite Britten device. Think, for example, of the fruitful friction in *Billy Budd* (B♭/B), in the *Nocturne* (C/D♭) and *A Midsummer Night's Dream* (G/F♯).

4 It is for the same reason, surely – to emphasize the contours of the tune in a busy contrapuntal texture – that we have, in the *Spring Symphony*, 'Soomer is icoomen in' sung by the boys in 2/4 against the 3/4 time of the general waltz.

Britten and the Ballet: The Prince of the Pagodas

Why, one wonders, did Britten write so little ballet music? In his maturity, strictly speaking, only one score, the full-length *Prince of the Pagodas*, composed between 1955 and 1956. There were, in fact, in the early years various ballet projects contemplated, scenarios sketched out, and in one case, *Plymouth Town*, a complete orchestral score (now in the Archive at Aldeburgh)[1] was written in 1931 to a scenario by Violet Alford, submitted to the Camargo Society but never brought to performance. Thereafter, apart from occasional ideas that never got beyond the discussion stage – including a Sadler's Wells proposal in the early 1940s in which Robert Helpmann and Montagu Slater (librettist-to-be of *Peter Grimes*) were to have collaborated[2] – Britten was never to become involved in ballet until the *Pagodas* commission.

Choreographers, of course, have made use of certain works of Britten's for ballets, from quite early days onwards. For example, when Britten was in the USA, from 1939 to 1942, a ballet, *Jinx* (choreographed by Lew Christensen), was based on the *Variations on a Theme of Frank Bridge* for string orchestra (Op. 10, 1937), though performed in a two-piano arrangement made by the Canadian-born composer Colin McPhee in 1942;[3] while it was Lincoln Kirstein who commissioned Britten to write a set of additional numbers to the existing set of Rossini arrangements, *Soirées musicales* (1936), which then formed the basis for Kirstein's

---

Royal Opera House Programme Book, December 1989; original title 'Britten and the Ballet: Music and Movement'

Divertimento, first performed by the American Ballet in Buenos Aires in 1941.[4] Those additional Rossini numbers then became known in the concert hall as a complementary suite, *Matinées musicales*. But they had started life as ballet music and so, strictly speaking, it is *Matinées* not *Pagodas* that has to be recognized as the first score of Britten's specifically commissioned by a ballet company and brought to performance.

It was indeed in the USA, and doubtless because of his friendship with Lincoln Kirstein – to whom *Matinées musicales* was to be dedicated – that Britten was most active in the ballet world; and not only through the means of his own music – for example, at Kirstein's request, he also arranged for small orchestra the music of *Les sylphides* (a score that seems to be irretrievably lost). (Odd, when one comes to think of it, that the *first* Rossini suite, the *Soirées*, was itself a spin-off from one of the documentary film scores Britten was busy writing in the 1930s for the GPO Film Unit.)[5]

These works that I have mentioned, whatever their source and origins, proved especially attractive to choreographers. But there is one famous *orchestral* work, *The Young Person's Guide to the Orchestra*, that may have flashed through Britten's mind some years before as an idea for a ballet. In his Royal College of Music days he once mentioned to a friend that he had an idea for a work in which the dancers would represent the individual instruments of the orchestra. It may have been this initially balletic idea that led to the *Young Person's Guide*, though just to confuse matters we have to remember that it was a film project that eventually secured the birth of the *Young Person's Guide* (*The Instruments of the Orchestra*, 1945).

One way and another, *The Prince of the Pagodas* seems to have had more of a pre-history than we have hitherto imagined, and if we think further, this time in purely musical terms, it may come to strike us as distinctly strange that Britten did not write more extensively for dance and dancers. He was, after all, a composer who, from his early experience in the film studio and theatre, was extremely adroit at matching up *movement* and *music* – realizing in the appropriate *musical* gesture a given event or physical action on stage or screen. (He was, moreover, by nature a highly rhythmical composer.) This was an accumulation – a repertoire – of gestural techniques that was to prove of overriding importance and utility when Britten moved out of the film studio and theatre and into the opera house.

His operas reveal a quite exceptional synchronization of music and dramatic action; and by dramatic action I mean not just a narrative sequence of events but precise attention to the detailed movement and gestures of the dramatis personae on – even better, *across* – the stage. I recall Britten telling me once that it was just so that he visualized his operas as he wrote them: in the music is to be found, if we care to look for it, a precise map of how the characters should move. Britten believed that most producers do not bother to look at or cannot read music; for which reason he rarely attended productions of his operas in which he had not played a collaborative role. He found it, he said, simply too painful to witness his carefully planned indication of movements either disregarded or, even worse, contradicted. If nothing else, this anxiety about the correlation of music and movement in Britten's mind shows how much the idea of systematic synchronization mattered to him[6] – interested him – from which, as I have just suggested above, it would not have been unreasonable to expect more than the creation of one ballet, huge score though that turned out to be.

There were reasons for that abstinence which I shall touch on, but it is also vital to recall two fascinating and, in this context, highly significant examples of dance invading opera. We should not forget, for a start, the realistic village dances at the beginning of Act III of *Peter Grimes*; but much more to the point is the high profile dance enjoys in *Gloriana*, the Coronation opera of 1953, in which there is not only a scene that is danced virtually from beginning to end (with choral accompaniment, Act II Scene 1) but, yet more intriguing, a later scene (Act II Scene 3) in which an elaborate series of court dances is integrated into – indeed, forms the eventually explosive substance of – the drama of Elizabeth and Essex. The knot is tied when one recalls that the choreography for *Gloriana* was devised by none other than John Cranko who, a year later, was to invite Britten to write the music for the full-length 'mythological fairy-tale' that he had in mind (which was to become *Pagodas*). In an account he wrote at the time, Cranko recalls that 'one evening I asked Britten if he had any ideas about composers, little dreaming that he would become excited enough with *Pagodas* to undertake it himself'.[7]

There was then already in 1953 a sophisticated interaction between two worlds, dance and opera, which, with the ensuing composition of *Pagodas* – first performed on 1 January 1957 – was finally to be consummated in Britten's last opera, *Death in Venice*. There, dance is not only interpolated into the fabric of the work but also, for large stretches, *services* scenes and episodes (the Polish boy, his mother, his youthful companions) where there are no voices to articulate the action or, even more challenging, the flux and flow of emotion. It is the synchronization of *movement* and *music* that does the work of voices (and words). In *Death in Venice* the composer was putting to use in 1973 some of the technical skills he had refined while working on *Pagodas* in the 1950s. Britten's 'only' ballet, it seems, was not so much a one-off event as part of a continuous evolution that had its roots in the 1930s and its fulfilment at the very end of his life. (We note, incidentally, that the choreographer of *Death in Venice* was Frederick Ashton, which in turn reminds us that it was Ashton whom Britten invited to produce *Albert Herring* when it was first performed at Glyndebourne in 1947. This was perhaps another manifestation of Britten's turning to a specialist in movement even when the work in question was straight opera.)

Given the pre-history of *Pagodas*, and Britten's preoccupation with movement and music, why was it that, having contributed a full-length ballet to the repertoire, he was then so reluctant to return to the score and showed less than overwhelming enthusiasm when approached about its revival? There were, I think, various areas of dissatisfaction and discomfort.

For a start, he seems to have found the sheer extent of the commitment daunting, given even his phenomenal energy and fertility. Something of the scale of the enterprise can be gauged from the dimensions of the full score – 461 pages of it, for an unusually large orchestra that included – in clear anticipation, in this respect, of *Death in Venice* – a virtually independent percussion orchestra. In all, the score offers continuous music, divided into three acts, of 125 minutes, a huge time span. It is not uninteresting to compare the 138 minutes' duration of *Peter Grimes*, say, or the 145 minutes of *Death in Venice*, if only to gain some impression of the scale on which *Pagodas* was conceived. In any event, one statistic is incontrovertible: it is the biggest and longest purely orchestral score Britten was ever to write.

This proved to consume more time and thought than he had envisaged at the outset; and the timetable was further complicated by many other professional engagements and commitments (three Aldeburgh Festivals took place between the announcement of the *Pagodas* project in 1954 and its first performance on 1 January 1957) and above all by the interruption of the ambitious round-the-world tour which Britten and Pears undertook between November 1955 and March 1956, which was succeeded by yet another interruption, and this time an unwelcome one, a bout of ill-health for Britten, after his return home. Small wonder that the première planned for September had to be postponed. During the last months of the work's composition Britten had his back to the wall and no doubt the stress and strain were to leave their mark on him. I very clearly remember Imogen Holst, who was then working for Britten as his music assistant (she was to be a co-dedicatee of *Pagodas*, along with Ninette de Valois), graphically describing the ferocious pace at which he had to work on the final stages of the composition: he scored with such incredible rapidity that she found it hard to keep up with him.

The pace took its toll, not, miraculously, of the music – can anyone point to a sign of haste in the craftsmanship? – but in an altogether more complicated way: it meant that Britten remembered the creating of *Pagodas* as a distinctly disagreeable experience. I am always reminded of this in *Death in Venice* when Aschenbach recollects his frustrating gondola ride: 'A pleasant journey did he say? The whole experience was odd, unreal, out of normal focus.' 'Out of normal focus': that, I believe, precisely describes the bafflement and perhaps bewilderment that overtook Britten when working in the theatre alongside his choreographer and dancers and working against the clock to get the production together on stage and on time. His responsibilities as composer/conductor – Britten conducted the first run of performances – were heavy, and so were his spirits.

It was a case of a tired composer finding himself in a hectic and unfamiliar environment. Britten was by no means the first composer (Stravinsky was another) to find the rites and rituals of choreographic techniques somewhat far removed from the ways in which a musician's mind habitually operates.

To take one very simple example, 'counting' for dancers is not what 'counting' normally conveys to a composer: at the performances of *The Rite of Spring* Stravinsky remembered Nijinsky standing on a chair 'shouting numbers to the dancers. I wondered what on earth those numbers had to do with the music, for there are no "thirteens" and "seventeens" in the metrical scheme of the score.'[8] It was undoubtedly the difficulties of penetrating and comprehending an entirely different system of articulating the relationship between movement and music that, after the punishing labour of trying to complete the score, left Britten with a distinctly jaundiced memory of the whole affair; and ever after, his thoughts about *The Prince of the Pagodas* were irretrievably coloured by his unhappy memories, which had the extraordinary consequence of the score never appearing during his lifetime: thirty-two years after the ballet's first performance it was at last published, in its entirety, by Boosey & Hawkes.

The composer could never bring himself to contemplate

publication, and it was only shortly before his death that he finally authorized publication of a suite, *Prelude and Dances*, in a form suggested by Norman Del Mar, a long-standing admirer of the music. He had, however, been persuaded to record his score for Decca, with the Royal Opera House Orchestra, in February 1957, though only in an abbreviated version. It was not until 1989 that the first recording of the complete score was made, conducted by Oliver Knussen.[9] That *Pagodas* has such a lengthy *post*-history extending to the period of its current revival can be entirely attributed to its curious *pre*-history and the *Sturm und Drang* that attended its first production (though this was not to discourage Britten from inviting Cranko to produce *A Midsummer Night's Dream* at Aldeburgh in 1960 – another opera, by the way, with a significant dance/mime dimension to it).

After a tale of (largely) creative woe, how extraordinary it is to turn to the magnificent score itself, which is wellnigh free of darker shadows of any kind. There is ample, brilliant contrast and plenty of good, old-fashioned suspense, though we all know that fairy-tales end happily. But doubt, scepticism, ambiguity, protest, sorrow at the world's treachery and corrupt ways – none of these normally permanent features of a typical Britten drama was to play a central role in Cranko's ballet. I believe that this release from the high moral ground, to which so much of his energy was dedicated – and which resulted in much of his best work – had at least one entirely refreshing consequence. It was a psychological liberation that meant that he was able to explore to its very limits, with maximum exuberance and winning passion, and not a trace of puritanical conscience, the brilliant colours of the very large orchestra he had at his disposal, which incorporated, as I have said, a big percussion band. Britten was a master of orchestra; but on the whole, when describing that mastery, it is phrases like 'less is more' and 'chamber-musical textures', and words like 'frugality' and 'economy', that fly to the lips. There is nothing at all frugal about the sound of *Pagodas*, which, in its many audacious mixes of timbres, generates colours of a startling freshness. This total immersion in the orchestra, sustained with a dazzling variety for a very long span of musical time, was something new for Britten. It had not happened before on this scale. It was not to happen again. In composing *Pagodas*, however much against the grain, he composed an extraordinary compendium of twentieth-century orchestration, at the very opposite end of the scale occupied by that *other* orchestral compendium – all economy and thrift – that he wrote in his last years, *Death in Venice*.

I have mentioned above the 'interruption' in 1955 when Britten left on his round-the-world tour with Pears. The visit to Bali was to have far-reaching consequences for Britten's music and also an immediate one for *Pagodas*: the Balinese percussion orchestra (gamelan), which Britten had observed with intense curiosity and delight on the island, was an additional resource from which *Pagodas* was to derive a further and spectacular range of colours.[10]

Colin McPhee, who had collaborated in making the two-piano arrangement of the *Bridge Variations* for the ballet *Jinx* while Britten was resident in the USA, had been the first to introduce him to Balinese music. Britten was now to experience for himself that unique synchronization of dance and music that Bali offers. He took notes of rhythms, scales, melodies and textures while listening to performances, and collected recordings, some of which he studied intensively when he returned home and resumed work on the composition of *Pagodas*.

The result was what we hear in the ballet: that is, *not* great splashes of exotic colour or an attempt to pin the façade of a non-Western music on to a Western tradition. On the contrary, in those celebrated passages where the gamelan, so to speak, takes over, Britten gives us the real thing. Of course he had to use the resources of the modern orchestra to re-create what he had heard on the magic island. But with the help of his phenomenal ear, and above all through the fidelity of his transcriptions, we get as close to the characteristic sonorities and textures of the Balinese gamelan as is possible while remaining in our theatre seats. The 'authenticity' was typical of Britten; and at the same time something new. These days we are accustomed to rubbing shoulders with all kinds of non-Western musics and respecting their integrity and independence. It was not like that in 1957; and in his approach to using Balinese music in *Pagodas*, Britten emerges as something of a pioneer of interests and assumptions that are now widely shared. Paradoxically, it was just the authenticity and novelty of the Balinese dimension of *Pagodas* that may have added a level of difficulty to our otherwise unhindered reception of the score. My ears were totally unprepared for anything as uncompromised as this, and they reacted against it.[11] It was some significant while before the light dawned. Little did one realize in 1957 that the Balinese dimension in *Pagodas* was itself the initiating, audible dawn of a whole new development in Britten's music, one that was to continue to the very end of his life.

The 'exotic' element in fact constitutes a relatively small, though highly important, part of the total score, which otherwise adheres to a wholly Western tradition of music for ballet that Britten greatly admired and to which he pays conscious, guilt-free acknowledgement from first number to last. He *meant* us to be aware of these links with his great predecessors in this field, with Stravinsky, with Prokofiev, with Tchaikovsky above all, whose full-length ballets Britten studied before attempting to write one of his own.

Undoubtedly his prodigious feats of orchestration were stimulated by the matchless orchestral imagination of Tchaikovsky and by the sheer untrammelled inventiveness of *Swan Lake* or *The Nutcracker*. One has exactly the same impression of *Pagodas*, where one idea impatiently treads on the heels of another in a ceaseless flow; and each idea, one finds, is formed into a precisely articulated dance, each with its own instrumental constellation and colour. There is something dizzily kaleidoscopic about the flood of colours and brilliant ideas.

But what really makes the bridge between Tchaikovsky and Britten is a common formal preoccupation – and achievement.

What Britten admired more than anything else in his predecessor's great ballets was the perfection of their small forms, a kind of absolute perfection and simplicity which is attained by composers who know what it is to master highly complex forms. The small forms of the *Pagodas* are quite as perfect in their way as those of Tchaikovsky, and stand as unique examples of that effortless simplicity concealing subtle art which was one of Britten's lifelong objectives.

There is, of course, more to *Pagodas* than an accumulation of small forms. Britten, as one would expect of the established musical dramatist he had become by the 1950s, characterizes the principal figures in the fairy-tale by means of powerful themes and particular instruments. As characters and events weave in and out of the small forms, so do their identifying themes tie the myriad forms together across the acts. But there is also another and scarcely less important integrating device: transitional music, often based on previously heard ideas, which carries us from one number to the next. This tissue of transition is a feature of *Pagodas*, in its own right, and involves compositional skills of the highest order.

It is these transitions and the network of themes that provide us with the unfolding of the narrative and profiles of the ballet's dramatis personae, and which together impose a unity on the exceptional diversity of this unique score. In the grandest of the transitions – from the end of Act III Scene 1, to the beginning of Scene 2 and the Pas de Six – Britten effects a union of 'West' and 'East'. He incorporates into this interlude, which is shaped as a crescendo of increasing intensity, both orchestras – the symphony orchestra and satellite percussion band – and materials from the two cultures from which *Pagodas* draws its inspiration. The interlude forms a kind of global, one-world recapitulation in which the participants retain their cultural independence. To the end, Britten remains faithful to the individuality and independence of the very different musics he conscripts to his use, even while seeming to combine them so effortlessly. In a musical fairy-tale of magical transformation and conjuring tricks, this is a last sleight-of-hand before the work is brought to a conclusion. We shall find, as the curtain falls, that we have had an experience unlike any other offered us by Britten's *oeuvre*; and I guess that, as we leave the theatre, we shall not be able to prevent asking ourselves what successors *Pagodas* might have had if his 1957 experience had gone differently, had been in – instead of out of – 'normal focus'?

NOTES

1 MC: See DM and Philip Reed (eds.), *Letters from a Life: Selected Letters and Diaries of Benjamin Britten* (Faber and Faber, London, 1991), vol. 1: *1923–39*, pp. 190, 199, 201, 216, 265. Illustrations from Violet Alford's scenario and Britten's autograph manuscript of *Plymouth Town* appear on pp. 189 and 192–3 respectively.

2 MC: Ibid., vol. 2: *1939–45*, pp. 1122–3.

3 MC: Ibid., vol. 2, p. 646.

4 MC: Ibid., vol. 2, pp. 860, 935.

5 MC: Ibid., vol. 1, p. 488.

6 MC: In this respect, the production of *Pagodas* for which DM wrote this article was often at fault. Kenneth Macmillan ignored many of the original stage directions, and the stage action thus sometimes contradicted the implications of the musical structure. The most glaring example occurred in Act I, where the collage in which Belle Epine dances with each of her four suitors in turn is treated by Britten as a series of recapitulations of the suitors' distinctively contrasting musical material above an ostinato waltz rhythm. Macmillan's princess passed rapidly back and forth between the four men throughout this entire passage, seemingly oblivious to the fact that the music was indicating the correct order of her dancing partners with considerable clarity.

7 MC: John Cranko, 'Making a Ballet', *The Sunday Times* 13/20 January 1957.

8 MC: Igor Stravinsky and Robert Craft, *Conversations with Igor Stravinsky* (Faber and Faber, London, 1959), p. 46.

9 MC: Virgin Classics VCD 759578–2 (1990), with an introduction by MC. Britten's own (shortened) recording with the Orchestra of the Royal Opera House was reissued in 1989 on the Decca London label (421855–2), along with a reprint of the sleeve-notes DM had provided for the original LP release in 1957.

10 MC: DM was the first to discuss the Balinese influence on Britten in depth in two articles: 'Catching on to the Technique in Pagoda-land', *Tempo* 146 (September 1983), pp. 13–24, and 'An Afterword on Britten's *Pagodas*: The Balinese Sources', *Tempo* 152 (March 1985), pp. 7–11. The former was reprinted in Christopher Palmer's *Britten Companion* (Faber and Faber,

London, 1984), pp. 192–210. Further research in this field was carried out by Somsak Ketukaenchan in his MA project for the University of York in 1984 (see also p. 240 note 4 of the present volume), and by MC in his 1985 M.Phil. thesis *Britten and Bali: A Study in Stylistic Synthesis* and 1989 Ph.D. dissertation *Oriental Influences in the Music of Benjamin Britten* (both University of Cambridge). MC's published work on this topic includes the article 'Britten and Bali', *Journal of Musicological Research* 7 (1987), pp. 307–39, the chapter 'Britten and the Gamelan: Balinese Influences in *Death in Venice*' in DM's *Benjamin Britten: 'Death in Venice'* (Cambridge University Press (Cambridge Opera Handbook), Cambridge, 1987), pp. 115–28, and the introductory note to Oliver Knussen's recording of *The Prince of the Pagodas* for Virgin Classics (see note 9 above). His monograph *Britten and the Far East* (Boydell & Brewer (Aldeburgh Studies in Music), Woodbridge) is due to be published in 1996.

11 MC: See pp. xxxix and 331.

Owen Wingrave and the Sense of the Past

I The Past: Prelude and Cadenza

Owen Wingrave is the story, in part at least, of a young man haunted by his ancestral past, a past against which he determines to take a stand and from which he almost escapes (in one sense he does escape, but at the cost of his life). Since his struggle against the past, and more particularly against the bloodily ferocious past of his forebears, the militantly military Wingraves of Paramore, forms the very substance of the drama, it behoves us to pay special attention to the musical images in which Britten establishes 'the sense of the past' (I borrow the title from James) – i.e. the tradition of violence – with which Owen has himself to do battle; and it is indeed with a compact survey of the past that the first act of the opera opens: after a brief Prelude (of which more later), there follows the scrutiny of a sequence of 'official' portraits of the Wingrave family, for each of which Britten writes a characterizing (and wholly characteristic) musical portrait. This brilliantly conceived series of instrumental flourishes, which forms a kind of large-scale cadenza for the orchestra (solo instruments or selected groups), is in no sense impressionistic. On the contrary, this extraordinary opening gesture represents, as it were, the audible archives of the Wingrave family; and in building his opera, Britten returns again and again to his archival musical material. This cadenza of portraits, indeed, is an exposition of the work's basic

---

Sleeve-note for *Owen Wingrave*, Decca Records SET 501–2, 1971 musical invention, a marvellously ingenious formal device, because it presents the Wingraves' powerful and pervasive past in musical terms which are themselves largely to influence and condition future musical events in the opera. Thus we have, as almost always with Britten, a tight formal correspondence between the heart of the drama, i.e. Owen's consciousness of the weight of the past, and the actual organization of the music, which, no less than Owen, reflects the weight of the past in its own way, i.e. out of the archival cadenza (and the Prelude) virtually everything flows and grows.

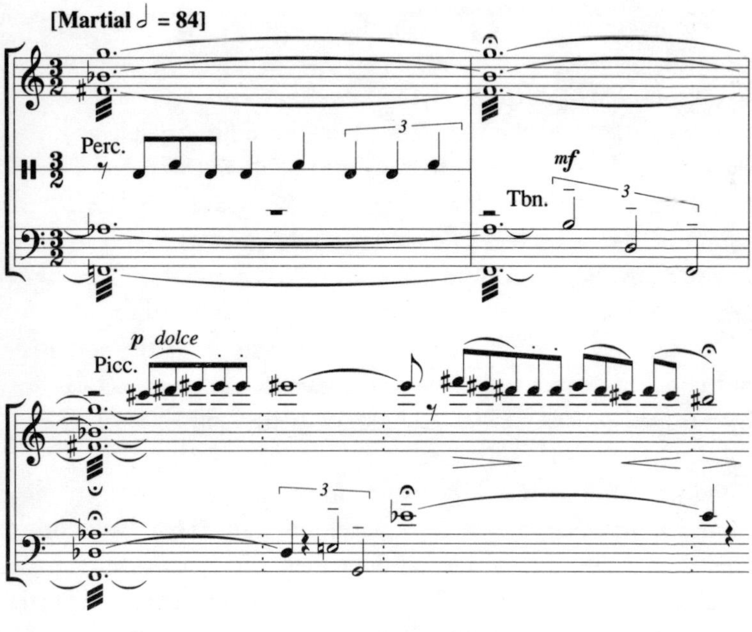

Ex. 1

I have not space here to set out each of Britten's musical portraits or to detail the unifying factors that bind the archives together. There are, however, ten portraits in all, the very important fifth of which is a double portrait, 'a ferocious old Colonel and a young boy', and thus written as a two-part invention at the extremes of the orchestral compass, for trombone (the Colonel) and piccolo (the boy). This fifth portrait (see Ex. 1) depicts the two characters involved in the tragic and horrible family episode that is fully narrated in the Ballad which opens Act II (see Ex. 8), and their

Ex. 2

cadenza echoes on throughout the opera, surfacing in various guises at critical moments in the drama.

The last of the portraits, the tenth,[1] is of Owen's father, a volcanically anguished, disrupted unison line (shades of the explosive unison that rounds off the central scherzo of the *Sinfonia da Requiem*, not to speak of a similar death-rattle in *Our Hunting Fathers*) which seems to sum up at its most intense the unhappy history of the Wingraves. None of the cadenzas has been happy. All, indeed, have been menacing (or menaced), uneasy, or disturbed (or disturbing). But the cadenza for Owen's father, with its grotesquely wide leaps, reaches the summit of violent distortion (see Ex. 2). Thus Owen's *quietly* heroic theme, which steals in to round off the cadenzas in an unambiguous D minor, is all the more striking. We know without being told (see Ex. 3) that this is a Wingrave of an altogether different stamp, because his theme, his musical portrait, shows just the very qualities of balance, symmetry, stability and strength in its interior musical organization that are missing from the chromatic extremes and excesses of the previous cadenzas. (Likewise, the menacing, cumulatively piled-up and sustained chord against which the cadenzas are played clarifies into an octave D, spread throughout the orchestra, as Owen's theme emerges.) Owen, there is no doubt about it, is a

Ex. 3

Wingrave who is *not* going to conform. His theme won't allow it; for in it, the voices of reason and order (musically) prevail.

Owen's theme brings me naturally to the Prelude, because in fact Ex. 3 has already appeared in the midst of this highly important orchestral passage, which of course precedes the portrait cadenzas. The Prelude introduces a leading rhythmic idea – one that has many rhythmic offshoots, too numerous to catalogue – and is always closely associated with the percussion orchestra, which constitutes virtually an independent group within the main orchestra. The sound of this unforgettable pulsation, which is the heartbeat of the opera in more ways than one (one notices, for instance, that the chords successively unfold all twelve notes of the chromatic scale), is not, as were the cadenzas, associated with individual Wingraves, but rather with the idea of their collective military valour, with their power, pride and arrogance; and it is not perhaps accidental that the jingling, jangling sound of this martial pulsation conjures up the vision of a troop of horses and their riders, of cavalry, the very kind of vision that feeds and inflames the imagination of the Wingraves. My Ex. 4 shows the pulsation, which is immediately broken into by a passionate statement of the Owen theme (brass) and then almost as immediately returns to the pulsation; and thereafter the rhythm of the pulsation (and variants of it) is used to link the portrait cadenzas together. Even in this tiny Prelude, which is a veritable powerhouse for all its brevity, we have a precise image of Owen trapped within the pulsation,[2] trapped by the system, by the false glamour of war, on which the family thrives. (We must keep in mind this association of percussion with the military idea. It holds good for most of the opera, but as we shall see later, there is one immensely significant exception.)

If I have spent some time on this opening nest of ideas – the Prelude, the portrait cadenzas – it is not out of some pedantic desire to spell out everything, step by step. It is because if one pays particular attention to this complex exposition in Act I, and again to the Ballad which opens Act II, a great deal of spelling out

Ex. 4

becomes entirely redundant. I have always suggested that the most helpful approach to the Church Parables has been a close acquaintance with the plainsong on which each work is based. Something of the same sort is useful here, where the Prelude and ensuing portrait gallery offer the keys to much that follows. Before turning to other considerations, let me tabulate the order of the opera's opening events:

Prelude
Martial pulsation – (Owen) – pulsation

Portraits (Cadenzas)
No. 1 Bassoon

No. 2 Oboe
No. 3 Horn
No. 4 Clarinet
No. 5 Trombone and Piccolo (Colonel and boy)
No. 6 Trumpet
No. 7 Woodwind
No. 8 Trombones
No. 9 Woodwind
No. 10 All wind (Owen's father)
[No. 11] Horn (Owen)

I have talked a good deal about the past of the Wingraves. What about the opera itself in relation to the composer's past, i.e. in relation to Britten's preceding operas?

II The Use of Parody

It is some eleven years since Britten wrote a full-scale opera: *A Midsummer Night's Dream*, first performed in 1960, was his last venture in this field.[3] Of course we have had in the intervening years the three Church Parables (*Curlew River*, *The Burning Fiery Furnace* and *The Prodigal Son*, 1964–8), the innovations of which fascinatingly leave their mark on *Owen Wingrave*, but to find Britten making a return to large-scale opera is an excitement in itself.

Clearly, Britten has written *Wingrave* with all his experience as an opera composer behind him. Every listener, no doubt, will uncover in the new work reminiscences of, or derivations from, earlier operas – more often than not earlier operas with which the listener happens to be particularly familiar! But the wealth of experience, of creative achievement, behind *Wingrave*, is indeed rich; and there are moments when one is irresistibly reminded of *The Turn of the Screw* (Mrs Julian's music), of *Lucretia* (Owen's aria in the park in Act I), of *Gloriana* or *Albert Herring* or one or other of the church parables. Every listener, no doubt, will compile his own (and a different) list.

Perhaps someone may be surprised by a mention of *Herring* in the Jamesian context of *Wingrave*. But then I have always taken *Herring* very seriously indeed, and always regarded the work as one of the prime sources for our complete understanding of Britten's complex personality.[4] I think in fact that there is nothing particularly surprising if I suggest that the role of the formidable Miss Wingrave, Owen's aunt, combines musical characteristics drawn from both the outrageous Lady Billows and the regal Gloriana: for so forceful and dramatic a soprano role, somewhat larger than life, it is surely only natural that Britten should turn in part to Miss Wingrave's formidable *musical* ancestors. But this is the most superficial of links with *Herring*, with the Coronation piece, and one that every pair of ears will hear. Much more interesting to my mind is a connection that goes altogether deeper and is altogether more subtle. Is it not true, for example, that both Owen and Albert have something in common, i.e. a refusal to conform to the dictates of a social group in which they are each trapped? The relationship between Owen and his family and the relationship between Albert and his Mum (and the worthies of Loxford) are in many respects identical; and surely what is profoundly interesting and illuminating is this: that Britten makes fruitful and extremely effective creative use in *Wingrave* of the brilliant parody techniques that he used in *Herring* to deal with the hectoring busybodies of the village who are determined to shape Albert in their likeness. In *Wingrave*, similarly; and prominently so at the end of Act I, where Owen is instructed by the Wingrave family that he must conform. Here the *tone* often evokes *Herring*; and rightly so, because the inquisitorial Wingraves, like the authoritarian notables in *Herring*, are unconscious victims of their own clichés. In so far as they live by slogans, and suppress their imaginations, they are less than human; and it is just at this stage that Britten puts the parody element most skilfully – and indeed most devastatingly – to use.

We are conscious of it when the Wingraves forgo their humanity and take their stand on mindless tradition, when they also freeze into identical attitudes, e.g. 'How dare you!', or 'Scruples, scruples, scruples', etc. It is through parody, kept (as in *Herring*, too) within bounds – though Britten does permit himself a touch of absolute *grotesquerie* at the end of Act I, as Sir Philip hobbles off after the disastrous dinner party – that the inhuman, *non*-human characteristics of the Wingraves are delineated. At the same time, satire does not decline into caricature, and there is room, as there must be, for substantial flashes of humanity, above all in the case of Kate, who emerges finally in Act II as a fully rounded-out dramatic personality, a creature of passion, not just flesh and blood, but hot-blooded. Indeed all the Wingraves from time to time drop their fearsome masks for a moment and show a human face, even the dreadful old General (Sir Philip), whose tender feeling for Kate is made explicit.

It is, in fact, when the Wingraves are acting corporately, as a cohesive group, all busy conforming, that their humanity, as individuals, as persons, is at its lowest ebb. Hence, in my view, the ironic component of parody peculiarly affects them in their ensembles, when their group solidarity is on show – all of which, one might add, is equally true of *Herring*.

In a real sense, Britten uses parody here, as a style, a convention, to make a moral judgement, a moral discrimination. Morality is often thought to be the death of drama, of the arts in general, though, to my mind, this is no more than a shallow opinion. Britten, in any event, has never been afraid to debate moral issues in his music (on the contrary these have often been the source of his inspiration), and he proves again in *Wingrave* that moral preoccupations – in this case, the idea of public and private violence, of the independent, non-conforming conscience – are not inimical to the creation of the most vivid dramatic art.

III Music and Morality

To survey, even cursorily, so important an aspect of Britten's artistic personality would consume more space than is available to me here. But one point must be made: that in works by Britten where certain of his basic moral or social convictions predominate, we find a specific musical manner – particular images, an identifiable 'tone' (hard to analyse, but there all the same) – which is consistently associated with the area of moral debate.

There is no special reason, at first sight, for astonishment. After all, we shall all immediately recognize in *Wingrave* a link with *War Requiem*; and the link will be established through common images – fanfares of war – aroused by a common theme. (Moreover those images of violence in the *Requiem*'s *Dies Irae*, the opening fanfares, bear the kind of 'archival' relationship to the development of the movement that we meet again in the relationship of the Prelude and portrait cadenzas to the development of *Wingrave*.) We are not, as I say, surprised by the parallel imagery because the two works share a common concern with the idea of war. But it is not quite these images that I have in mind; and if I go on to suggest that there are images in Britten's music that seem to be as concretely associated with issues drawn from the area of moral debate, then perhaps there *is* something to be surprised about. But I believe such to be the case. I confess quite freely that I find it hard to define the tone that fascinates me, but I think I can at least indicate what I am trying to identify when I claim that the operatic predecessor with which *Wingrave* has most to do is not the earlier James essay, *The Turn of the Screw*, but the opera in which perhaps Britten's moral probing, up to *Wingrave*, had been most prominent: *Billy Budd*.

I see *Wingrave*, in fact, in many vital respects as the true successor of *Budd*; and I believe those who know *Budd* well will be continually struck, as I am, by invention in *Wingrave* which is inescapably evocative of the tone of *Budd*. It would be pedantic and superfluous to list all those moments when my experience tells me that *Budd*, as it were, is breaking surface in *Wingrave*; but there are many such, and not of course because Britten has run out of ideas and is plundering an earlier vein but because the areas of feelings and relationships touched on in *Wingrave* are often those that we encounter in *Budd*. It seems clear to me, just to select one area, that Owen's relationship to Coyle is at times very much of a piece with Billy's relationship to Vere; and in the quality of Coyle's characteristic music in *Wingrave*, there is certainly something of the character of Vere's music in *Budd*. Similarly, in Owen's music, there is something of Billy's; and further, in the cut and thrust of the dialogue between Coyle and Owen, there's more than a hint of the memorable Vere–Budd exchanges in the earlier opera. Perhaps what I have just described are more examples of 'tone' than anything else. But the link with *Budd* runs a good deal deeper than that. Consider, for instance, the music that is really the climax of the opera, Owen's 'peace' aria in Act II, a radiant, ecstatic avowal that surely foresees a peace a good deal more profound than the absence of war. This, one feels, is the peace that is the result of inner reconciliation, of one man's victory over himself (see Ex. 5).

That is a great, cathartic moment in *Wingrave*. I return to my adjectives, 'radiant, ecstatic', and I return, too, to *Budd* and to another radiant, ecstatic aria about peace, Billy's in Act II, when he sights 'a sail in the storm, the far-shining sail that's not fate', the substance of which – Billy's inner reconciliation – is taken up again by Vere in the opera's Epilogue [Fig. 143]; and it is at this climactic point in Britten, when Vere too affirms *his* inner peace (see Ex. 6), that the re-creation and expansion of the same image in *Wingrave* becomes apparent. There can be no doubt about it. Britten finds (unconsciously, I am certain) a consistent musical imagery which for him is associated with the idea of pacification, of reconciliation. One senses something almost uncanny about the precision of the imagery for what is so often considered to be an 'abstract' ideal. But for Britten, 'peace', whether public or private, is not an abstraction: for him, it is as real as its opposite –

Ex. 5

violence, war. As a result, he finds invention as powerfully redolent of peace as his fanfares are evocative of war. One can claim, indeed, that Britten has developed a musical language that enables him to engage in the dramatization of moral issues. *Budd* showed the way, revealed the specific tone. *Wingrave* directly extends the tradition.

If one compares the actual sound of Exx. 5 and 6, there is one

Ex. 6

subtle and significant aspect of the sonority of the 'peace' aria in *Wingrave* that immediately strikes one. Whereas the chords in the *Budd* excerpt are dropped like great anchors into and against the quaver flow of piccolo and harp, in *Wingrave* it is the percussion orchestra that sustains the quaver figuration into which the chords of affirmation are injected. Up to this point in the opera, the percussion has been associated, through the opening pulsation, with the idea of war and violence, with the mailed fists of the Wingraves. Now, however, the percussion orchestra (*plus* vibraphone, *minus* drums) functions in quite a different role, as the very opposite of aggression: as a shimmering radiance, no less, surrounding and decorating the chordal affirmations of Owen's resolve. I am reminded, insistently, of the brilliant double-profile which the percussion reveals in Britten's *Children's Crusade*, a complex combination of symbols of innocence (percussion as children's playthings) and horror (percussion as the imitative sounds – the music – of war). This unexpected transfiguration of the percussive image in *Wingrave* is very striking and very typical of Britten's art.

IV Symbols and Images

There is yet another rhythmic pulsation besides Ex. 4, which has a vital part to play in the development of the opera. We first hear it in the orchestral interlude ('Views of the exterior of Paramore'), as Owen approaches the house. What does it stand for? The evil spirit of the house, no doubt, and, more particularly, the image of the haunted room where the tragedy narrated in the Ballad was enacted; and is to be re-enacted. Yet this is to ascribe to this persistent rhythm (see Ex. 7) only the most obvious and superficial levels of imagery.

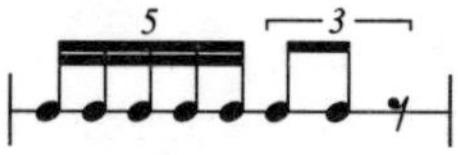

Ex. 7

For Henry James, clearly, the supernatural component in *Wingrave* was no more than a device that permitted him to find immediately comprehensible and vivid images in which to project his own moral debate, to make his own moral discriminations. The same is true, of course, of *The Turn of the Screw*, though there the supernatural apparatus is a good deal more complicated and substantial. In *Wingrave*, the supernatural intervention is confined to the unhappy spirits of the old Colonel and the murdered boy and to the evil infection of the room in which the deed of violence was done. (One remembers, in this context, the crucial images of acts of violence which are so prominent in Britten's operas and in which, so often, the ritual of sacrifice is involved. The Abraham–Isaac relationship is central to Britten's art, appears in many guises, and is reworked afresh in *Wingrave*. One does not forget either the ironic reversal of the image in *War Requiem*, which sets an interesting and relevant precedent.)

It is my view that the supernatural apparatus in *Wingrave* – the apparitions, the room – must ultimately be reinterpreted as complex symbols, along with the idea of the 'family' itself. The Wingraves in fact, are not only themselves, but also representatives, writ large, of the family of man, whose long history of ungovernable violence has massively polluted our planet. But if the Wingraves stand for a tradition of corporate violence, for the cynical brutality of Nation and State against which Owen rails in Act I, using Shelley as his mouthpiece, both James and Britten, again through their images and symbols, break down group aggression into individual deeds of violence, e.g. the Colonel and the boy. And it is not far-fetched in my opinion to understand the idea of the haunted room, not as a device to provide a thrilling climax to a ghost story, but as symbol of that inner chamber in ourselves, in which our own aggression insistently ticks away (Ex. 7), and which we have to conquer if we are to achieve peace within ourselves and for our fellow men.

The distinction I draw above between public and private acts of aggression is actually built into the total architecture of *Wingrave*. The delicately balanced relationship of the proportions of Acts I and II reflects, in my view, the change in emphasis that occurs after Act I, when we move from public to private. The ample first act, with its wealth of detail and continual references to a world larger than the Wingraves' – (incidentally how unequivocal is Britten in his condemnation of the politics of war: would that our politicians were as outspoken) – sets the panoramic, swiftly changing scene[5] against which Owen takes his public stand: 'I can't go through with it, can't go through with it,' he announces to Coyle. In Act II, however, the *private* stand has to be made, and indeed the private act of violence has to be purged and redeemed through the ritual re-enactment of the private murder which is at the heart of public slaughter. This, I believe, is the significance of the Ballad, which prefaces Act II and which surfaces, subsides and surfaces again in the manner that we have met before in the church parables,[6] where the initiating plainsong similarly threads in and out of the texture of the music. The first verse of the Ballad is shown in Ex. 8.

In Act II, we pass from the rich tapestry of Act I to the confined spaces of Paramore, the Wingraves' family seat, and to the innermost chamber of all, the haunted room, which, as I suggest above, stands as symbol of that inner chamber of aggression which is seated in all of us; and it is this room that Owen must enter and in which he must triumph. The dimensions, pace, content and character of Act II – which is substantially shorter than Act I, though one is hardly aware of the fact because it operates on its own time scale, and like Act I, is exactly as long as it needs to be – almost add up to an independent opera. Indeed, one feels as if, in *Wingrave*, one has two operas for the price of one, i.e. the moral debate is first acted out on a public stage (Opera 1), and then on a private one (Opera 2), under the intensest illumination. This, of course, is a gross exaggeration – because ultimately one experiences Act II as a brilliant resolution of Act I – but there is, I think, a point to the distortion. I believe that the listener sensitive to scale and time in musical architecture (and in some respects *Wingrave* introduces a kind of overall architectural relationship new to Britten's operas) must respond to the special relationship between the two acts of this opera, which is not just the conventional sequential one.

It is in this second act that the insistent rhythm I have quoted above (see Ex. 7) – the insistent pulsation which is the heartbeat of

Ex. 8

the house in which a violent private deed was done – attains its apotheosis. Owen has, as it were, to confront violence face to face. He enters the room, Kate turns the key in the lock, and Ex. 9 blazes forth.

The presence of Ex. 7 in Ex. 9 is plain enough; and the combination of the rhythm with the marvellously spaced chord (a particularly remarkable example of Britten's placing a familiar chord in an utterly unexpected context, spreading it through the orchestra and spelling it out in equally unpredictable ways, and thus turning

Ex. 9

the familiar into something strange) makes a wellnigh physical impact.

Do I mean spine-chilling? If *Wingrave* were just a ghost story, an exalted entertainment, then to have our spines chilled at this stage is just what we would expect. But though the tension in Ex. 9 is indeed overwhelming, and possibly our hair stands on end as a result of it, the effect is something quite distinct from spine-chilling in the conventional sense. I keep on returning to those same words – radiant, ecstatic; and surely, if anything, it is these qualities we have already encountered in Owen's 'peace' aria, that again characterize the sonority so powerfully projected in the shape of Ex. 9, a sonority, a sound event (one must notice the affirmative *major* key) that embraces and pacifies – and thus transforms – the aggressive rhythmic pulsation of Ex. 7.[8]

For me, in fact, Ex. 9 constitutes, not Owen's defeat, but Owen's triumph; and I believe the music bears out this interpretation. Through Owen's sacrifice – I have Billy very much in mind as Owen's predecessor – there is a lesson to be learned, at least part of which is a reminder that the battle for peace is not to be won without casualties (or without cost to oneself, if one has the courage to bear witness). So complex and many layered are the levels of symbolism that confront one at the end of the opera,[7] that it may well be that the *dénouement* will be variously interpreted, as triumph or tragedy, victory or defeat. Much depends on the conclusions and significance one draws from the musical symbols and images, of a few of the more important of which I have attempted to give an account in these notes. But whatever view one takes, the exquisite irony of the final scene is not to be qualified or modified: we leave Owen – 'He looked like a young soldier on a battle-field' is the unforgettable last sentence of James's story, which has been so strongly and yet so delicately translated into a libretto by Myfanwy Piper – in the knowledge that, of the fighting Wingraves, he was the bravest of them all.

NOTES

1 My No. 11 in the table that follows is, of course, a portrait of the living Owen.

2 Most of us, to register this point, will have had to wait for at least a second hearing of the work, because the significance of Ex. 3 appearing in the context of the Prelude (Ex. 4) is revealed only retrospectively, when Ex. 3 lets us know that what we heard first embedded in the Prelude was Owen's theme.

3 MC: DM writes in 1971, the year before Britten embarked on what was to prove his final opera: *Death in Venice*.

4 MC: See DM's 'The Serious Comedy of *Albert Herring*', this volume pp. 352–64.

5 Readers of these notes may wonder why I have not touched on the specific characteristics of the opera that one might have thought owed their origin to the television medium. I have not done so for two reasons: first, because I think the subject can best be dealt with by someone who has the required technical knowledge; and second, because it seems to me that the kind of musical techniques we encounter in *Wingrave* – above all the many varieties of transition – which we might imagine to have had their roots in the television medium have in fact been adumbrated elsewhere in Britten's music, far away from the television studio. To choose only one example, the composer of the *Nocturne*, which is quite peculiarly rich in effortless transitional techniques, did not really need to learn this lesson from, or for, television. He came to television with the medium, or at any rate an indispensable part of it, already at his fingertips.

6 The treatment of the Ballad is by no means the only influence of the church parables on *Wingrave*. For example, 'unmeasured' developments of the cadenza idea such as Owen's address to the portraits in Act I ('Is there not one of you to

help me – you? – you?') and the fantastic half-overheard interview in Act II, when Sir Philip disinherits Owen – not to speak of Owen's own 'peace' aria in the same act – all show the impact of the radical freedom of combined independent time, rhythms and melodies which is a feature of the parables, from *Curlew River* onwards.

7 Kate's lament, when she discovers Owen dead, is one of those moments when one is reminded of the *Screw*. One almost expects Kate to sing, like the Governess, 'What have we done between us?'

8 MC: See pp. 335–7, n. 8.

IX

People

To Donald
who's responsible
for it all –

When Cooke roared: 'Mitchell! what about this jazz?'
Don thought, That's just the talent Philip has;
And even if he finds it bad or worse
At least he'll have less time for writing verse . . .

in affectionate gratitude
Philip

The inscription on the flyleaf of DM's copy of
All What Jazz by Philip Larkin, 1970

Down There on a Visit:
A Meeting with Christopher Isherwood

I phoned first from San Francisco.

'This is Christopher Isherwood . . .' Then I realized, of course, that it was an answerphone, because the voice went on to say, 'Wait for the tone, and then please leave your message.' I wasn't absolutely sure whether Isherwood would have received my letter from London, so I embarked on a long explanation, in the middle of which the machine switched itself off. I was somewhat embarrassed by this because I wasn't at all certain that I'd got to the point where I had made it clear who I was and what I wanted. Anyway I left it at that; and then, when I had got to Los Angeles and reached the hotel, I was half expecting to find word from him, a response to my half-message. But there was nothing. So I tried another call. Once again there was that very precise voice inviting me to leave a message. I kept it short this time: 'Here I am now, at the Beverly Wilshire,' I said, 'and it would be very nice indeed if you could call back and we could explore the possibility of meeting.' I unpacked, made a few more phone calls, and then – just before someone was going to come and pick me up for dinner – I thought I'd try the number once more. Again, the clipped voice, 'This is Christopher Isherwood . . .' But this time it was not Isherwood's answerphone, but Isherwood himself. He was actually receiving calls – a distinct step forward. I went through all the routine of saying who I was and so on, and he remembered the

---

Santa Monica, 22 April 1978; *London Magazine* 32/1–2 (April/May 1992), pp. 80–87

letter from London – which had, after all, reached him – and the message from San Francisco, mutilated though it was.

As he spoke, I was forming an impression of the man whose voice, recorded and live, had already made a sharp impression on me. He spoke very fast, very precisely, very clearly. There was a certain nervousness about his speech, however – a nervous energy. From what he was saying – he reminded me that I'd proposed this meeting without any prior consultation (though I had, in fact, sent a letter in advance of my arrival) – it seemed that he had a difficult schedule this weekend, and especially on Saturday, which was the only day possible for me. 'Why don't we start talking now?' he said; and launched without more ado into a lengthy recollection of his long friendship with Britten.

He said by way of a preface that it was all a long time ago and that really he did not remember anything in very great detail of their association in the 1930s. What he did remember very clearly was a return visit to the USA Ben and Peter made after the war – it must have been the first occasion they were back together in the States after their exit in 1942 – when their engagements took them out to the West Coast. Isherwood recalled how terribly tired they got of all the socializing and entertaining, the inevitable accompaniments of a recital tour. There came a moment when Ben or Peter or both of them said, 'For heaven's sake, let's get out of this place for a while, out of the city, away from all this turmoil.' So Isherwood took them off on a trip to the desert, to visit an old friend of his. They ended up at this chap's house, had a meal, and relaxed – relaxed sufficiently, it seems, for them to give, by way of a thank you to their host, an impromptu recital. Isherwood – who claimed that he was not a particularly musical person – said that he had never forgotten the extraordinary quality of the music-making on that occasion.

One further memory of the same evening was this, Britten's patient response to one of those questions that plague composers and was put on this occasion by a nice, earnest American: 'How do you go about composing, Mr Britten?' To which Britten replied, 'Well, I have a certain idea that seems to work well with clarinets, and follow that through and then perhaps another idea surfaces which suggests percussion . . .', and so on and so on. Isherwood was still struck, all these years afterwards, by the sheer down-to-earth character of Britten's answer. Nothing theoretical or inspirational, but purely practical.

I believe that that occasion was pretty much the last contact Isherwood had with Britten until 1976, the last summer of Britten's life, when Isherwood made a visit to Aldeburgh with his companion, Don Bachardy, the artist, and David Hockney. In an interview he gave later to the *Guardian*,[1] Isherwood had described the visit, and he said again to me now, over the phone, what a touching and moving occasion this had been. Everyone withdrew, Isherwood and Britten were left alone in the drawing room at the Red House, and they just sat there, holding hands, saying very little. Not a great deal more came out of this first encounter by phone. It was a case, I suppose, of feeling the way and re-establishing contact. 'Well,' said Isherwood in conclusion, 'if it's possible at all, I'll call you in the morning.'

At ten the next morning or thereabouts my phone rang at the hotel: 'This is Christopher Isherwood . . .' Again the precise voice, and again nervous noises about the difficulties, the logistics, of getting to see him. Boldly, I asked him to name a time, to which he replied – precise as ever – 'I can give you an hour this afternoon, from three to four. I'll be pleased to see you.' He continued, 'I'm terribly sorry, of course I can't get in to Beverly Hills to pick you up. Can you get a car? Can you manage to find your way?' He then embarked on a marvellous bit of Isherwoodiana: a minutely detailed account of how I was to instruct the driver to find his house in Santa Monica. It was amazing, the descriptive precision of it, like a paragraph from one of his novels. I wrote it all down, word for word, an exact verbal map of how to get from the Beverly Wilshire to 145 Adelaide Drive where Isherwood lived.

After lunch, I set off with my driver, Isherwood's directions in my hand; and, of course, it all worked absolutely like clockwork.

We'd been told to find our way on to Adelaide Drive and then locate two palm trees, by the second one of which I was to draw up the car, cross the road, and there would see the mail-box with the number on it, descend the ramp, and so on. Isherwood made a point of saying that these weren't *tall* palm trees, they were *broad* palm trees. And so they turned out to be. At the second one, I got out of the car, crossed the road, and began to walk down the ramp. This was a typical Santa Monica residential area, tropical vegetation, Adelaide Drive running downhill from the top of the cliff, the Pacific glittering away beyond. I came to a white-painted, louvred door – perhaps more of an entrance gate than a front door – pressed the illuminated bell, and waited. From where I was standing I could look down into Isherwood's garden: the path through the garden, from house to gate, seemed to double back under the lip of the cliff.

In a moment or two, I heard an energetic shout, 'Coming!', looked down again, and looked down on to Isherwood, coming along the path, moving very fast, wearing what seemed to be a kind of blue bath-wrap, down to his ankles. It seemed almost impossible to believe that this brisk gait belonged to a man of – what was he? – seventy-four. Another minute or so, and there he was at the gate, Herr Issyvoo himself. I was faced by a short, stocky man, very good complexion, short hair, very, very trim, altogether a very precise shape – just like his voice, in fact. There, before me, were the famous bushy eyebrows and the bluest eyes that I think I'd ever seen, extraordinarily vivid in colour; and the famous wide smile, unmistakably his and instantaneously recognizable from the photographs that John Evans and I had been gathering together for *Pictures from a Life*.[2] He was clutching the wrap round him, he said, because he was just getting dressed, to be ready to go out later in the afternoon to visit friends. He completed the usual conversational preliminaries and then trotted off down the path at a very smart pace, leading me into the house. He took me into the living room, and excused himself for a few minutes while he finished dressing.

I was left in a square room, elegantly furnished. On one side there was a big picture-window, looking on to a piazza. Everything in fact was on quite a modest scale; it was not a monumental, film-star house by any stretch of the imagination. But it had features which of course were peculiarly Californian, and I was conscious above all of the tropical vegetation, tropical flowers, the ground tumbling away, and a marvellous view on to the ocean – Santa Monica Bay, I suppose. The other view looked out on to Santa Monica canyon – where the house is built – this time away from the ocean, but another spectacular view. It was a brilliantly sunny Californian afternoon and I immediately understood at least one of the reasons for Isherwood putting down his roots here: the fascination of the landscape. The room itself was not too cluttered up with furniture. There were sofas and armchairs, a low table, and many books on either side of the fireplace. Everything was infused by the extraordinary Californian light. The whole of the end wall of the room – the wall that faced me as I entered – was a mirror, its glass effectively doubling the size of the room: it reflected back to me the image of the room in which I was sitting, waiting. To the right there was a corridor, which I presume led into the living quarters. The entire house, as far as I could make out, was built on one level.

After a short while, Isherwood returned. He had finished dressing and emerged now wearing a white denim suit, light blue shirt, dark blue tie, chic brown shoes, red socks – an exotic touch, this – and looking very, very smart. He sat down in one of his own armchairs, with his back to the picture-window. He was handsomely outlined against the glittering ocean and the distant beach as I sat on a sofa and talked to him across the intervening space, talked to the face that was so familiar from photographs and so unfamiliar in the flesh. He wore his spectacles and a charming smile, talked quickly, precisely and was very much in command of our conversation.

I kicked off by asking how much he remembered of Ben in the 1930s, to which he replied, not much more than what he'd already recollected in *Christopher and His Kind*;[3] his mention of that title gave me the opportunity to say that I'd read the book. He did remark again on the fact that Ben had always seemed younger in appearance than he actually was – rather pale at that time, Isherwood thought, with curly hair and always very boyish in his demeanour. In fact he remembered Peter saying to him at a later time altogether that this perhaps was one of Ben's difficulties, that he not only looked the youngest of the 1930s circle but also felt himself to be *treated* as the youngest, which gave rise to an occasional friction. Isherwood thought that this was one of the reasons for the problems that Auden, who was older and a dominating character, had. Isherwood himself was the oldest of the group and remembered acting as a pacifier, a mitigator, a conciliator: he described himself as the man who didn't have rows, didn't throw temperaments, who was always willing to mend situations rather than exacerbate them. This was very much the role he played in relation to the unpredictable, volatile Rupert Doone and the Group Theatre. As he talked, Isherwood emphasized that Ben, in the context of the theatre, was ever the fertile, practical musician, sitting there with pencil and paper to hand, ready to provide music at the drop of a hat, to meet the need of the particular moment. He also very much agreed, by the way, with what Robert Medley had told me in London when I visited him with John Evans, that it was often Ben's music that saved the day dramatically speaking in the case of *The Ascent of F6*. He recalled vividly the extraordinary impact made by 'Funeral Blues': it was, he said, a magnificent number. No less, he remembered Hedli Anderson's brilliant performance in *F6* and asked me if she had continued with that kind of work or had given it up. He obviously hadn't kept in contact with her.[4]

He volunteered the information himself that he was of course aware, as were all of Ben's friends, of the rift, the break, with Auden; but added, without my putting a further question to him, that he was unable to throw any light on what was really the cause of the rupture. He was quite certain, however, that it had led in turn to the end of his own friendship with Britten, even though he had been in no way involved in whatever the difficulty was between Britten and Auden: the effect of the end of that relationship had brushed off on him, as if in rejecting Auden – if it was that – Britten was compelled also to reject all the old 1930s associates and associations. Isherwood in later, post-war years, made only infrequent visits to England, and on one of them made an attempt to get in touch with Ben, perhaps at about the time he was working on *War Requiem*. But he didn't get much of a response, and it was his impression that walls were being put up: he did not want to impose himself and did not press the suggestion further. He went on to tell me – and a discernible note of regret coloured his speech – that when he got back to California, and remembering Ben's current interest in Wilfred Owen, he sought out a very remarkable photograph of the poet that had been reproduced in a book (he thought first of all in something by Siegfried Sassoon but then recalled that it wasn't and introduced another author's name, which I have gone on to forget). He took the trouble to send a copy of the photograph to Ben with an explanatory note and was discomfited to receive barely an acknowledgement.[5]

I recognized the incident all too clearly as an example of one of those unhappy actions – an *in*action, rather – on Ben's part, who found it hard to resume an old friendship if it had gone cold, for whatever reason, justified or no. There was little chance of resuscitation; and I think, after this abortive attempt, Isherwood made no further effort to re-establish contact until the last summer of Ben's life, on the occasion I have already related. It was a sad tale, I thought. Though he did not make too much of it, clearly it hadn't been willed by him that this old friendship should have expired, lost somewhere along the way.

He went on a bit to tell me a little about his taking up residence in the States with Auden. I was talking to him again about *Pictures from a Life* and he checked the captions for the photographs in which he appeared with Auden. He told me that the photograph of them both in Central Park, New York, that John and I had thought belonged to 1939, was almost certainly taken in the summer of 1938, when they travelled back to Europe by way of New York. On the occasion of this, their first visit, they were pursued by journalists wanting interviews. Central Park was chosen as a location because its rocks – for the journalists, at least – set up associations with mountains and climbers and thus provided an appropriate background for the authors of *The Ascent of F6*. It was some such nonsense as this, with the thought of the last scene of the play in mind – the ascent to the summit – that the photographers had in mind.

It struck me as I departed, up the ramp, and across the road to the palm tree where my car was waiting, that when Auden and Isherwood wrote *F6* in 1936, or perhaps even in 1938 when they had their first sight of New York, they could hardly have imagined that one of them was soon to become a celebrated inhabitant of Manhattan, the other famously part of the Californian landscape, blue skies, ocean, canyon, *broad* palm trees and all.

NOTES

1 30 March 1977.

2 DM and John Evans (compilers), *Benjamin Britten: Pictures from a Life 1913–1976* (Faber and Faber, London, 1978).

3 Christopher Isherwood, *Christopher and His Kind* (Farrar, Straus and Giroux, New York, 1977; Eyre Methuen, London, 1977).

4 Hedli, who had been married to Louis MacNeice, died in 1990.

5 I have let this stand because this was what Isherwood said, unequivocally. But in fact he was quite wrong in what he remembered. It was not a bare acknowledgement that he received from Britten but a warm note in his own hand from the Red House, Aldeburgh, dated 11 September 1961 and here reproduced for the first time by kind permission of the Trustees of the Britten–Pears Foundation:

My dear Christopher

I ought to have answered your p.c. ages ago, but August was such a difficult month that I had nothing to suggest about our meeting. Now Peter & I are whizzing all over the place, up to Edinburgh, down to Hereford over to Germany & ? to Poland. But we'll be back somewhere around the end of the month & hope very much to see you before you go back across the ocean. May I write & say a time when I know I've got to be in London & hope, so much, that you'll be there too?

I was very touched by your sending the Sitwell book with the [Wilfred] Owen picture. I am delighted to have it – I am so involved with him at the moment, & I wanted to see what he looked like: I might have guessed, it's just what I expected really. It was the nicest and kindest thought of yours to send it to me.

Excuse this scribble. We are only back for 24 hours to pick up clothes & music & there are 1,000,000 things to do.

With much love, & thanks, & hopes we can meet,

Yours ever

BEN

Love from Peter

This important letter not only throws fresh light on the Isherwood–Britten friendship – still alive and well in 1961 – but reminds us of the fallibility of human memory. There is no chance by the way that the letter was not posted or received. Ironically enough it was found among Isherwood's papers and returned to the Britten–Pears Library at Aldeburgh after his death.

Larkin's Music

So life was never better than
In nineteen sixty-three
(Though just too late for me) –
Between the end of the Chatterley ban
And the Beatles' first LP.

In his generous inscription on the fly-leaf of *All What Jazz*[1] Philip wrote: 'To Donald, who's responsible for it all'. I would not care – or dare – to make any such claim.[2] But I can claim to have stimulated Philip to the composition of the quatrain which accompanied the inscription and which hitherto has remained unpublished (and surely it cannot be the good fortune of every contributor to add to the canon?):

When Coote roared: 'Mitchell! what about this jazz?'
Don thought, That's just the talent Philip has;
And even if he finds it bad or worse
At least he'll have less time for writing verse . . .

An annotation or two of that elegant bit of poetic licence – because of course I thought nothing of the kind – will reveal the facts. For a start, the roaring 'Coote' was not some creature of Philip's imagination, in the spirit of Isherwood's and Upward's fantasy world, Mortmere, but none other than the late Sir Colin Coote, the patrician, High Tory Editor of the *Daily Telegraph*

Anthony Thwaite (ed.), *Larkin at Sixty* (Faber and Faber, London, 1982), pp. 75–80

when I was a member – the junior member – of the music staff. (Coote, it was, who reduced me to silence at my interview by asking me in blandest voice 'how *amused*' was I by the thought of joining the paper, a story Philip has always relished.)

Thus it was through my association with the *Telegraph* (certainly an amusing one in view of my political convictions) that Philip came to be appointed the paper's jazz correspondent. Someone in the features department, in bold and innovatory mood, thought it was time that the *Telegraph* accorded jazz official recognition. But whom should we approach, to invite to be our jazz critic? (The *Telegraph*, you will understand, was not rich in connections in this sphere.) By a lucky chance I was in the office that day, took part in the discussion and proposed Philip. (In any case, no other candidates emerged.) Coote – was he amused by the proposal, I wonder? – approved; and the deal was done.

Philip's name flew to my lips that day in Fleet Street, not only because I was aware of his profound knowledge of and sympathy with jazz, but also because I shared his enthusiasm for it. Indeed, some of my earliest memories of Philip, from the days when he first joined the University of Hull (we met through a mutual friend, Peter Coveney), evoke musical memories too: convivial gatherings around the gramophone at Cottingham. All this was a new and stimulating experience for me. For while I had known, as a young man, one other poet – the wild, eccentric but remarkably endowed E. H. W. Meyerstein – his passions were relatively orthodox: Beethoven, Berlioz and Mendelssohn, for example. I found it altogether unusual and surprising that Philip's ears were excited by Louis Armstrong, Duke Ellington and Pee Wee Russell.

Mention of Armstrong reminds me that the publication of Philip's writings on jazz resulted in the creation of more than one new poem: not only the dedicatory quatrain but also the closing paragraph of the long autobiographical Introduction that he wrote to preface the collection. Armstrong is one of the key names to surface in a coda, both comic and elegiac, which is itself a prose poem. It has been widely remarked upon but its quotation here is obligatory, so revealing is it of the power of the feeling that this music released in the jazz correspondent of the *Daily Telegraph*:

> My readers . . . Sometimes I wonder whether they really exist . . . Sometimes I imagine them, sullen fleshy inarticulate men, stockbrokers, sellers of goods, living in thirty-year-old detached houses among the golf courses of Outer London, husbands of ageing and bitter wives they first seduced to Artie Shaw's 'Begin the Beguine' or the Squadronaires' 'The Nearness of You'; fathers of cold-eyed lascivious daughters on the pill, to whom Ramsay MacDonald is coeval with Rameses II, and cannabis-smoking jeans-and-bearded Stuart-haired sons whose oriental contempt for 'bread' is equalled only by their insatiable demand for it; men in whom a pile of scratched coverless 78s in the attic can awaken memories of vomiting blindly from small Tudor windows to Muggsy Spanier's 'Sister Kate', or winding up a gramophone in a punt to play Armstrong's 'Body and Soul'; men whose first coronary is coming like Christmas; who drift, loaded helplessly with commitments and obligations and necessary observances, into the darkening avenues of age and incapacity, deserted by everything that once made life sweet. These I have tried to remind of the excitement of jazz, and tell where it may still be found.

One might think that the whole enterprise finds the justification in that one bit of superb verbal music; but that would do an injustice to the importance of the Introduction as a whole, which contains in fact a classic statement – *the* classic statement – of Larkin's anti-modernist position, which he argues in images as vivid as those on which he floats his final prose-poem:

> My own theory is that [the genesis of modernism] is related to an imbalance between the two tensions from which art springs: these are the tension between the artist and his material, and between the artist and his audience, and that in the last 75 years or so the second of these has slackened or even perished . . . Piqued at being neglected, he has painted portraits with both eyes on the same side of the nose, or smothered a model with paint and rolled her over a blank canvas. He has designed a dwelling-house to be built underground. He has written poems resembling the kind of pictures typists make

> with their machines during the coffee break, or a novel in gibberish, or a play in which the characters sit in dustbins. He has made a six-hour film of someone asleep. He has carved human figures with large holes in them. And parallel to this activity ('every idiom has its idiot', as an American novelist has written) there has grown up a kind of critical journalism designed to put it over. The terms and the arguments vary with circumstances, but basically the message is: Don't trust your eyes, or ears, or understanding. They'll tell you this is ridiculous, or ugly, or meaningless. Don't believe them. You've got to work at this: after all, you don't expect to understand anything as important as art straight off, do you? . . . After all, think what asses people have made of themselves in the past by not understanding art – you don't want to be like that, do you? And so on, and so forth. Keep the suckers spending.

One may agree or disagree. I am not sure that I do not agree in principle while questioning Larkin's actual demonology (Picasso, Pound, etc.: I would adduce a different list of names). But there can be no questioning of the central importance the statement has to any consideration of his aesthetic as a poet. The negative credo, so to speak, represents the obverse of – but perhaps is also responsible for – all the strengths of Larkin's verse: its precision, clarity, formal mastery and above all its marvellous rhythmic organization.

I seem to have lapsed into a kind of musical vocabulary, so it may not be inappropriate to praise Larkin for his *scoring*: he places his words with the same kind of scrupulous care for pitch and timbre that we find in the anti-modernist Britten or modernist (!) Stravinsky. It is surely no accident that we find all these musical qualities in a poem of Larkin's, 'Love Songs in Age', that takes as its topic the very music that means so much to him, music 'each frank submissive chord' of which

> Had ushered in
> Word after sprawling hyphenated word,
> And the unfailing sense of being young
> Spread out like a spring-woken tree, wherein

That hidden freshness sung,
That certainty of time laid up in store
As when she played them first . . .

A lyric, one might think, that in technical organization in some sense deliberately reflects the model 'lyrics' of the love songs which are so poignantly resurrected while at the same time transcending them. The extraordinary way in which 'Love Songs' is virtually through-composed, a continuity that erases the conventional strophic pattern and preserves unbroken the seamless rhythmic flow, is only one feature that distinguishes the poem from the lyrics one supposes the protagonist to be recollecting. It is also a poem that embodies a musical experience that contrasts somewhat with the bleak tone and black imagery – 'vomiting blindly from small Tudor windows' – of the Introduction. Poignant maybe, but not savagely pessimistic.

Our critic, as the Introduction discloses, is a man of powerful convictions and it would have been strange indeed if the modernism he denounces in the high arts (Picasso, *et al.*) were not similarly trounced when it raises its ugly head in jazz. John Coltrane, for example, who found no favour while he was alive, and whose death did nothing at all to diminish Larkin's sense of outrage:

> Virtually the only compliment one can pay Coltrane is one of stature. If he was boring, he was enormously boring. If he was ugly, he was massively ugly. To squeak and gibber for 16 bars is nothing; Coltrane could do it for 16 minutes, stunning the listener into a kind of hypnotic state in which he read and re-read the sleeve-note and believed, not of course that he was enjoying himself, but that he was hearing something significant. Perhaps he was. Time will tell. I regret Coltrane's death, as I regret the death of any man, but I can't conceal the fact that it leaves in jazz a vast, a blessed silence.

Some obituary. Not many of Larkin's denunciations are as lengthy as that or so lethal. His dispatch of the Beatles is perhaps more characteristic. 'What about the Beatles?', he asks himself in 1963; and replies:

> *With the Beatles* (Parlophone) suggests that their jazz content is nil, but that, like certain sweets, they seem wonderful until you are suddenly sick. Up till then it's nice, though.

One trembles a little to think of the obituary John Lennon's bizarre death might have prompted.

But how different the tone is when sympathetic, when Larkin responds to Larkin's music, music, that is, that 'makes me tap my foot, grunt affirmative exhortations, or even get up and caper round the room'. In particular, his assessments of players who have his admiration are no less than miniature portraits – and more than that, *sound* portraits, so precisely coloured is the choice of words. Here for instance is Larkin on James 'Bubber' Miley:

> Miley was a growl trumpeter, and a great user of mutes to give his tone emotional colour. There was nothing new in this: it was at least as old as King Oliver. But Miley's was different: his tone had a snarling, gobbling savagery that stabbed through the coltish orchestrations with primitive authenticity.

Perhaps my favourite Larkin portrait is that of the great clarinet player, Pee Wee Russell:

> No one familiar with the characteristic excitement of his solos, their lurid snuffling, asthmatic voicelessness, notes leant on till they split, and sudden passionate intensities, could deny the uniqueness of his contribution to jazz.

'Snarling, gobbling savagery', 'lurid snuffling, asthmatic voicelessness': not only wonderfully accurate descriptions, but as close to the sound of those unique styles as words can get. What a music critic Philip could have been, had he had more time for it!

NOTES

1 MC: Philip Larkin, *All What Jazz: A Record Diary, 1961–68* (Faber and Faber, London, 1970; revised and expanded as *All What Jazz: A Record Diary, 1961–71*, 1985). The volume was officially dedicated to DM: the 'unofficial'

quatrain Larkin inscribed on the dedicatee's copy is reproduced on p. 439.

2 MC: Larkin wrote to DM on 20 November 1968 from the University of Hull to say:

> As you were responsible for getting me the job of jazz feature writer on the *Daily Telegraph*, I thought it would amuse you to know that I have been contemplating in recent months putting together a book made up of my articles. My idea is to print a small edition privately, just enough to send to the copyright libraries and distribute among friends, with perhaps some minor sales conducted personally.
>
> The first reason I am writing is to ask your permission to dedicate it to you. I do hope you will agree: it is the least I can do to repay your kindness in the first place. This job, despite the peevishness of some of the articles, has brought me a great deal of pleasure, and I hope to go on with it.
>
> Secondly, I thought it might amuse you to read the introduction, which is a *jeu d'esprit* not perhaps to be taken very seriously. In fact, the whole book is not over serious, but I think it might be of interest to people who like jazz and who have heard of me.
>
> Thirdly, it did just cross my mind that it would be interesting to know whether Faber's (for instance) ever *distributed* books they had not actually published, and, if so, what their terms for doing so would be [. . .]

(See Anthony Thwaite (ed.), *Selected Letters of Philip Larkin, 1940–85* (Faber and Faber, London, 1992), pp. 407–8.)

According to Andrew Motion (*Philip Larkin: A Writer's Life* (Faber and Faber, London, 1993), p. 385), Larkin had submitted the manuscript to Hull Printers Ltd; but his worries about private distribution were later to prove inconsequential. DM, by this time editor of the music books list at Faber, wrote a memorandum to his colleagues on 26 November about the project, noting that Larkin's 'distinction between private and public publication seems very odd, particularly when the bulk of the book has already appeared in a mass-circulation newspaper'. Two weeks later Faber agreed to publish the volume and offered Larkin £200 in advance royalties (Motion, p. 386). Larkin said of his newly written Introduction to the collection: 'It's about time jazz had its Enoch Powell.'

Hans Keller (1919–1985)

I apologize for reading from these notes.[1] But in saluting Hans I don't want unduly and inappropriately to fumble or stumble. I'm conscious as I speak of his unique ability to think aloud in perfectly articulated and continuous sentences, something I could not hope to match. And in saluting Hans, I am also saluting Milein,[2] and remembering her fortitude during this last week and recent months.

I should like to talk about Hans, who was a friend for almost forty years, first of all from a professional point of view, and then perhaps more personally; and I shall take Hans as my example and be as brief as I can and make this a *short talk*. Why do I emphasize those words? Because the idea of the short talk was one of the many innovations that Hans introduced while he was working for the BBC in his first appointment there as Music Talks Producer. In tributes I have read since Hans's death, most of them rightly refer to his role in that remarkable institution as a kind of official leader of the opposition, above all as the Corporation's musical conscience. But he was also a marvellous producer and the particular concept of the short five-minute-or-so talk was entirely characteristic of him as a thinker and writer.

For a start one had to have a thought to think, and it had to be a genuinely musical thought, and one's own not somebody else's; and then it had to be expressed with absolute lucidity, or the nearest one could get to it; and one had to be brief. Hans didn't

---

Tempo 156 (March 1986), pp. 2–3

see brevity as the enemy of content but rather as a guarantee of it.

The short talk was a great invention and brought into play so many of the unique qualities that Hans brought to editing; and remember, it was as youthful editors that we first worked together in the 1940s and early 1950s, not only editing *Music Survey*[3] but also, in 1952, putting together the famous old symposium on Benjamin Britten.[4] Hans waged war against sloppy thinking, sloppy writing, received opinions, and above all *wrong* opinions. As an editor he would tolerate none of these things; and where a contributor was unwilling or unable to amend his error, then Hans would add one of those legendary corrective footnotes. This was something that the rather gentlemanly amateur world of writing on music in England had not experienced before, and it came, indubitably, as a bit of a shock.

But of course these footnotes, these attitudes, did not proceed from pedantry but from *passion*, a passion for the truth, or at any rate the best truth that was available, and a passionate commitment to music, to the defence, often, of music and musicians. Was there ever a champion of what one might term *musical rights* as eloquent and courageous and convincing as Hans?

But let me give just one example outside the sphere of music of Hans's passionate commitment to and espousal of a cause. Not one of the public tributes I have read has mentioned the tireless work he did for the Campaign for the Abolition of Capital Punishment in the 1950s. That may seem ancient history now; but I recall Hans's ceaseless persuading, lobbying, petitioning, arguing, attendance at the House of Commons, and triumphant conversions of the unconverted. It was a most remarkable, unforgettable, virtuoso performance and showed him at his best as a proponent of the humane, decent and civilized in our social life.

It must have been of course their sense of Hans's absolute commitment to music and to creativity that made *composers* love and admire him, as they did and do, and enabled him to be such an influence among them – an influence amazingly free of doctrine or ideology, for all the strength of his opinions. And Hans's empathy and sympathy were extended not only to living composers but to their predecessors. For him, surely, a quartet of Haydn's – and for Haydn's string quartets Hans has done what Robbins Landon did for Haydn's symphonies[5] – or an opera of Mozart's was as *immediate* as if it had been composed only yesterday. It was that extraordinary capacity to enter the past and to experience it as the present, that made Hans's insights so fresh and original, so close to the music. He erased history, as a writer, and was never the servant of it. Doubtless it was this same capacity that made him the outstanding teacher he was, whether at Dartington in earlier times or more recently at the Menuhin School.

Hans was one of the most sheerly musical people I have ever met. One of the great bonuses of listening to music with him – a great work perhaps or a great performance – was the absence of the need for words after the event. One didn't need to spell anything out to him in terms of shared experience. His response to music and the musical was instinctive, immediate, and profound – perhaps beyond the reach of words. Small wonder that wordless analysis was one of his achievements.

Hans was not a solemn person and I must not make him sound so. He was a wonderfully amusing and entertaining companion and very often irresistibly funny. He had a very sharp eye and ear for the comedy and confusions of life and nowhere more so than when observing the pretentious or the bogus. He could be magisterial but never pompous. He could shake with laughter, with mischievous glee, as often as with righteous indignation. He was, as I shall always remember, a truly generous friend, one who cared little about the things most people care about, status, wealth, possessions. He shared *himself* without stint.

I am sure that Hans, in the studio, would have long put an end to these words, inadequate words, I fear, judged by his own standards. I have mentioned earlier how he functioned as a musical conscience within and for the BBC. But he played that role in almost every sphere. For composers, for example. Only yesterday I had a note from a composer, expressing his sorrow and adding that whenever he finished a new piece his first thought was of Hans: What will he make of it? What will he think of it? And likewise, I believe, for those of us who still labour on trying to find a way of writing meaningfully about music.

Hans for me has always been, as I told him not so long ago, the identifiably 'hypothetical other' for whom I wrote; and I believe that may be true of many others. I shall continue to write for him, in the light, the intense light, of his illuminating personality and work. In my copy of his book, *1975 (1984 minus 9)*,[6] he wrote a generous inscription which referred to 'a collaboration which we may describe, with due modesty, as historic' – 'with due modesty', a characteristic Kellerian touch, that. The historic dimension was Hans's rather than mine; but I shall always remain proud that there will be occasions when my name is linked with his.

NOTES

1 MC: DM delivered this text as an address at Hans Keller's cremation in London on 13 November 1985.
2 MC: The artist Milein Cosman, Keller's widow.
3 MC: From 1949 until 1952: see pp. XXXVIII–XXXIX and 14–38.
4 MC: *Benjamin Britten: A Commentary on his Works by a Group of Specialists* (Rockliff, London, 1952): see p. 35.
5 MC: See Hans Keller, *The Great Haydn Quartets: Their Interpretation* (Dent, London, 1986): see also pp. 462–5.
6 MC: Hans Keller, *1975 (1984 minus 9)* (Dobson, London, 1977).

Remembering Hans Keller

I need only to hear a few bars from Mozart's G minor Symphony (K. 550) and in a flash Hans is as vivid a presence as he was when he was alive. Not any old bars, mind you: to be precise, bars 125 to 136 of the finale, where in a remarkable unison passage which propels us into the development Mozart exploits (almost) the total resources of the chromatic scale.

Hans thought it to be a presage, a harbinger, of serial organization, as had Heinrich Jalowetz and Luigi Dallapiccola before him: Hans and I had published an article on *Don Giovanni* by Dallapiccola in *Music Survey* in December 1950,[1] which had brought Jalowetz's observation to our attention. One might argue about the prophetic dimension, but what is indisputable is the extraordinary intensity and compression of the music. It was the kind of explosive moment in music that Hans relished, and about which he always found something interesting to say. I can't hear those bars now without thinking of him. I hear them, so to speak, through his ears.

I can think of many other such moments which would similarly excite Hans, when his generous moustache would quiver, his eyes – remarkable eyes – glow, and a smile of pleasurable recognition surface on his lips. There was another Mozartian characteristic – entries on (or from) the dominant minor – which gave rise to just such acknowledgement and was one of the tests by which Hans judged, say, a singer's musicality. I was not at all surprised to find

---

London Review of Books, 3 September 1987, pp. 8–11

that this was one of the points Hans was to make in his 75th birthday tribute to Peter Pears, published in 1985. His salute opened with one of those magisterial rebukes. 'Every musician knows that normally singers are amongst the most unmusicianly, if not indeed unmusical, members of our profession', but went on to praise Pears (as Ferrando in *Così*) for something that Hans had always remembered:

> his deeply moving dominant-minor entries (yes, each of them was different) in the A major duet with Fiordiligi: in my lifetime he has been the only performer with a deep insight into what the dominant minor meant to Mozart.[2]

I continue to look out for dominant-minor entries in Mozart performances and if they are insufficiently felt or badly executed, then I feel a sense of threefold outrage: on behalf of the composer, Hans and myself. It is a reaction that teaches us something about how closely related was Hans's analytical thinking to performances and performing – something, of course, of which one is particularly aware in the study of the Haydn quartets which appeared in 1986.[3]

At the very start of what seems to me to be the most important of Hans's books – at least of those published to date – he makes clear that he is addressing primarily the player – i.e. a string- and quartet-player – who alone can comprehend what, for Hans at any rate, was the 'secret science' of the string quartet. It is impossible, he suggests, 'for any outstanding instrumentalist' who is not a member of the magic string-quartet circle

> to understand a quartet-player's string quartet in all its intended dimensions; likewise, it is impossible for a composer, however great, to write an intrinsic string quartet if he himself is not a quartet player: the quartets of Brahms, Schumann, Debussy, Ravel, and yes, Bartók are more than adequate evidence.

The somewhat daunting (and excluding) exclusivity of this approach – and in any case is the proposition true? – might discourage some readers who are not players from grappling with

Hans's text, which would be the greatest pity because the book offers us the most detailed account available not only of Haydn's quartets but of Hans as incomparable teacher and coach – activities that, after his retirement from the BBC, consumed so much of his energy and brought him untold satisfaction. Here he is, in full flow, on the *Adagio* of Haydn's B♭ major Quartet, Op. 64 No. 3:

> In the *Adagio*, the second violin has to listen to its balance very carefully: it mustn't forget that its solo bars in the principal section proceed under the first's *held* notes, in aural view of which textural relation there is no need whatever to force the dynamics (*mezza voce*) – the less so since the lower two play a purely accompanimental role too, entirely supportive. They as well as the leading second fiddle won't, I trust, fall into what one might describe as the all too frequent first-bar trap: the aim of the first bar's respective phrases is – needless to add by now, one hopes – the second. The antecedent–consequent relationship between the two fiddles is rendered more complex and subtle by the leader not being silent while the second violin speaks, while the second, together with the lower instruments, observes at least partial, respectful silence during the more flowering responses of the first – though carefully considered, the silences don't cover the actual answers, but the ensuing upbeat phrases, which the three lower instruments should be heard to be glad to leave in peace: it is up to the first violin's free phrasing thus to convey the lower instruments' happiness! The silences should not, however, encourage the leader to indulge in unusual liberties; what one hopes are his usual liberties will be quite enough.[4]

Lucky players, lucky pupils! And lucky too even those of us who are not string-quartet players or composers. Everybody, in my view, can learn something from, as it were, overhearing Hans think about music and its performance at this exceptional level. Moreover, as one would expect of a musician for whom interpretation and analysis were virtually indistinguishable, the text continually throws up arresting analytic or historical insights and comments. For example, this on the finale of the C major Quartet, Op. 54 No. 2:

> The work's most shattering and, if I may so put it untimely innovation is, of course, the *adagio* finale, which turns the typical symphonic structure with two *allegros* upside down, throwing up two *adagios* instead. History books credit the nineteenth century with the symphony's slow final movement, whether it came about by accident (Bruckner's unfinished Ninth) or design (Tchaikovsky, Mahler). To my inadequate knowledge, not a single historian has noticed that Haydn was responsible for introducing this new symphonic form.[5]

Or this vintage bit of Kellerian paradox which startles one – performer or not – into a fresh perception of what a composer can get up to and how sophisticated and elaborate both our interpretative and auditory responses have to be. Hans is remarking on a case of 'violent compression' in the first movement of Op. 9 No. 4, a consequence of which is that

> transitional feeling flows over, pointedly has to flow over in performance, into the opening stage of the second subject, which therefore must not be allowed ever to settle down despite its well-established relative major key. For by the time it would have settled down (or has done so in the suppressed background), i.e. after the general pause, thematic definition leaves no doubt about the fact that we are approaching the main cadential stage, the end of the exposition: *we have to be heard to have played the second subject that never happened.*[6]

Hans's italics, not mine, and a penetrating, wholly characteristic observation that combines practical instruction and analytic revelation. There was no one who could match Hans in this particular kind of commentary, which shows so well what he could accomplish with words, distrustful of them though he was when they were applied to music.

There are, needless to say, many oddities in the Haydn book – not only the credentials that one should ideally have in order to understand what Hans is writing about, but yet another bizarre hands-off injunction, this time to persuade players *not* to play, or attempt to play, the F♯ minor Quartet, Op. 50 No. 4: 'Haydn's only supremely difficult quartet', we are told, for which reason Hans has relatively little to say about the work, whose challenging nature, on his own testimony, whets one's appetite to know more. How was it, or why was it, that the supreme quartet composer seems bafflingly to have lost touch with his mastery of the 'secret science' and produced a quartet in which the 'awkward bits' preclude the possibility of adequate performance? Here, the conditions imposed by Hans the player seem frustratingly to get in the way of Hans the analyst.

But these are minor qualifications. The book, as Hans himself might have said, is a towering achievement, and fully justifies the prophetic remark to Hans's teacher made by Franz Schmidt after hearing the youthful Keller participate in the performance – appropriately enough – of Haydn's C major Quartet, Op. 64 No. 1: 'I can't tell you what is going to become of this young musician, but one thing I *can* tell you: the world will know of him.' And the world did. We come face to face with the prophecy on p. 2 of Hans's Preface and it would be a mistake to interpret it as an advertisement for himself. On the contrary, it is Hans laying his credentials on the line, for our inspection.

My quotations from the Haydn book show what a masterly writer on music Hans was – that is to say, how skilfully he conscripted words in the service of musical analysis. Did anyone use them better, more precisely, more meaningfully? And yet – another paradox – he would, I believe, have cheerfully abandoned words altogether if he could have done so. And indeed, in one area, he did: 'Wordless Functional Analysis' 'burst upon the world' in 1957. These are the words of Christopher Wintle, in the Memorial Symposium on Keller in *Music Analysis*,[7] and Wintle shrewdly remarks that 'It was less the matter than the wordless manner of FA that excited greatest musical interest.' I must confess to finding myself in difficulties with FA, though I don't doubt that at least some of them are of my own making. It may well be that I am so hopelessly word-bound that I find myself at sea when these familiar props are knocked away. But there are other considerations: the exclusive concentration of FA on the unity of contrasting themes, for example, which leaves so many of the other parameters of a work untouched and because of its exclusivity endows the one parameter with a primacy that might be open to question. Even more awkward, for me at any rate, is the very musicality of Hans's wordless analyses, their ingenuity and persuasiveness: these, try as I may, begin to assume the status, almost, of independent compositions, and if not to demand, then at least to evoke, a response that is something different from the reception of Hans's communication of analytic information.

Two contributors in the Memorial Symposium touch interestingly on this aspect of FA: Susan Bradshaw, who remarks that Hans's 'greatest original invention' may have been 'his destined compositional outlet', and Alexander Goehr, who claims that

> Behind the form of his Functional Analysis stood a being who really wanted to communicate with the pitches and rhythms that were the subject of his investigation. Like Bernard Williams, who made philosophy by re-composing Descartes, he, I believe, almost thought you could make music by re-composing Mozart.

In FA the medium and the message somehow proved to be not quite the same thing. Whatever our conclusions about or reactions to FA, however, we may be grateful that Hans stayed with words, without which we would not have had the Haydn book, the most single-minded of his major texts: the discursiveness of *Criticism*[8] offers a strong and sometimes exhausting contrast here. Nor would we have had him on his feet talking. Hans had an extraordinary capacity to marshal his thoughts and then deliver them verbally. As the thoughts materialized, so did the perfect, unhurried sentences that embodied them, a measured pace, neither dragging nor hurried, with never a pause for reflection nor a hesitation (only very occasionally was there the indication of a slight stutter).

Not only was there this enviable and singular clarity of thought and articulation: scarcely less striking was an unusual ability to be simultaneously gregarious and isolated (another paradox). Hans was able to sit among friends and conduct a conversation with them, smoke, swim – and at the same time methodically work at a current review or article or script. And what emerged on paper was quite as orderly and smooth-flowing as if he had been concentrating solely on the notebook in front of him. He was a master of this contrapuntal mode of life.

I got to know Hans well before the world did, as a result of encountering his 'analytic' criticism in the late 1940s. I was so stimulated by it that I determined to get in touch with him. I had read somewhere, I think it must have been in *Music Review*, a long notice by Hans, most probably the performance of an opera (Mozart?) at Sadler's Wells or Covent Garden. I was knocked out by it, by its precision, its confidence and all the very specific points it made, whether adverse or positive.

Gone were all those boring generalities and tedious descriptions, stuffed with modifiers and qualifiers – our Sunday-paper review sections are still littered with them – and in their place, detailed observations on rhythm, pitch, tonality, modulation, dynamics, nuances of expression, which left one in no doubt that here was a critic who knew what he was talking about. And even more amazing, knew the work he was talking about, from the inside outwards, as Hans himself might have said. Moreover, I seem to remember that, lest anyone might think that this critic had not done his homework, there were footnotes in which he laid out his sources. It was an astonishing performance – and there were many others of a like kind – which punched a big hole in the façade of English music criticism as it was practised in the 1940s and 1950s. It has never been – or looked – quite the same since.

Very soon after our first meeting, 'H.K.' was among the regular reviewers of *Music Survey*, and in 1949 he contributed a notice of a production of *Figaro* at Covent Garden which was subheaded 'An experiment in concrete criticism'. This incredibly detailed review began, 'And now, dear reader, open your score, and follow me right through the opera, particularly if you are engaged at

Covent Garden', and ended, memorably, some three columns later: 'In sum: The production is not so bad that you cannot enjoy much of it if you shut your eyes.' More often than not at this time in his life, he would have his head in the score on his knees in the darkened theatre, checking out the performers and performance with the aid of a pocket torch and impervious to the indignation of his neighbours. A narrow, searching beam illuminating the score. There is something in this image that symbolizes his early life as a music critic.

The first review I read of Hans's brought us together. We found that we were living near one another, in South London, and arranged to meet – at a concert, I think at the Central Hall. Our first dialogue was on the phone, not only about where we were to meet, but how we should recognize each other. I was rather bewildered by this part of the conversation, which, on Hans's part, not only included sensible references to his prominent moustache but, rather more mysteriously, signals about his 'big' nose. I must have been rather a naïve young man, but it was some time before the penny dropped: this was Hans's coded way of conveying to a stranger that he was a Jew. It pains me still to think of it, pains me above all to think that Hans should have thought it necessary to give me, in some sense, advance 'warning'. If I mention it now, I do so because it shows how profoundly conscious he was of his Jewishness – something he was to make me conscious of, for the first time – and how deeply he had been affected by his fearful experiences in Vienna pre-war. What would he have made of President Waldheim's Austria, I wonder? He would not, alas, have been surprised.

We got on famously at the concert and our next meeting was in Herne Hill, where Hans shared a house with his widowed mother. I had suggested to Hans that he might care, one day, to write a small book on Hans Pfitzner. 'No,' said Hans, 'not Pfitzner, but Franz Schmidt' – the Schmidt of the prophecy (p. 465). I had barely heard of him and not a note of his music, and so had no opinion of my own. But now that I am better informed, it seems to me to have been a revealing choice – very Viennese, traditional and conservative. The paradox of it all was that Hans could be, and I have come to believe was, all those things, and yet at the same time was so plainly sceptical, radical and innovative.

Hans might have scorned my thinking of him as 'Viennese': but he could be conspicuously Viennese when there was a part of that culture with which he could whole-heartedly identify himself. I remember very well when that wonderful old Decca set of *Die Fledermaus* first appeared (1951), with Julius Patzak (one of Hans's heroes), Hilde Gueden, and the rest. The discs were transported to the house next door, where Hans's half-sister lived with her English doctor husband, and were played over and over again with the entire Keller family as audience – and no one enjoyed every inflexion of the performance more than Hans and his mother. I got a sense then of the Vienna in which they had been steeped and which still meant so much to them, despite their brutal ejection.

Johann Strauss, Franz Schmidt, and of course Schoenberg, as powerfully authoritarian and authoritative as he was revolutionary. If one had to choose the twentieth-century composer who might provide the perfect match with Hans, then it would have to be Schoenberg. With Stravinsky, it seems to me, that great contrasting pole, he never quite made his peace, despite the admirable and largely admiring work he did on the old master's later serial pieces.

I can clearly remember a performance of *The Rite of Spring* at a Salzburg Festival, after which 'primitive' was a word that surfaced rather prominently in Hans's response. I was to understand that this was criticism delivered at – or from – a very 'high level' (one of Hans's characteristic phrases): but 'primitive' was his judgement of the piece. I wonder sometimes if he was not influenced here by Adorno's somewhat similar views of Stravinsky.

I remember, too, Hans meeting Stravinsky at a Faber party in the old Russell Square offices in December 1958. Eliot was there, and it was probably an occasion that Hans greatly disliked. He didn't get to speak to Stravinsky until the very end when, on saying goodbye, he half whispered into the astonished composer's ear, 'I think you're a very great genius' – and departed. I'm sure Hans meant it – and also launched it as a missile against all the smart party small-talk he so much detested. On the other hand, it also struck me as an example of a sometimes unnerving habit of his – of wanting to have it both ways, to hold to certain reservations and discriminations and yet at the same time to appear not to hold to them, or at least to have an exchange that on the face of it would seem to preclude holding any such qualifications.

I was not always quite sure how it was that Hans matched up or reconciled his contrasts. Small wonder that the unity of contrasting themes was one of his musical preoccupations. A more trivial instance of the same kind of thing came about in his disputes with Eric Blom, then music critic of the *Observer*, about musical matters that it would now be tedious to spell out. The tone of the correspondence was distinctly acrimonious and unflattering. But it did not stop Hans from telling Blom at the end of one of his letters, 'You must be one of the nicest people I've never met' – a formulation that rooted itself in my memory because it was uniquely Kellerian. But even while I was amused by it, I wondered what compelled Hans to write it? After all, the considerable wrong, without doubt, was on Blom's side. There was something paradoxical in Hans – that word forces itself on one time and time again when writing about him – something that impelled him to the simultaneous delivery of the mailed fist and the generous embrace.

My Stravinsky recollections raise an issue that was central to Hans's writing and to our understanding and evaluation of it. I refer to the positions he took up with regard to contemporary music, and especially to European music of the first half of the century. There can be no doubt of Hans's brilliant work in this field. I am not thinking only of his championing of Schoenberg and Britten – a complementary and paradoxical pair – but of his thinking about what actually constituted 'composition' in the *second* half of the century.

He was the very first, I believe, to point out that the established means of evaluating new music, which had hitherto been able to rely on assumptions about the composer's technical competence, the precision of his ear, his intent to communicate, could not be applied to music composed according to an entirely different set of rules – or rather without any rules at all, neither technically nor as to what in fact was admissible as 'music'. Hans was quick to see that as soon as literally *everything* was possible, a lot of absolute nothingness could acquire a wholly spurious significance. He also cautioned critics, I think again for the first time, in one of his first broadcast talks, made after his return from an International Society for Contemporary Music festival, to be exceptionally wary about falling into the trap of trying to avoid at all costs criticism's miserable record of judgement in relation to the new music of the past. This guilt, particularly evident in England (where one might concede it proper for critics to have felt guilty), led to judgements of contemporary music which had more to do with the fear of yet again missing the critical boat than with any genuine perceptions about what was on offer. Indeed, very often there was nothing to perceive. He writes about this superbly in *Criticism*:

> Impressed . . . by the total failure of their forefathers to catch up with new developments and recognize new major talent, not to speak of the genius of a Schoenberg or Britten (or Gershwin, for that matter), the latest generation of music critics, and to some extent of critics of the other arts, has decided to rush into positive evaluation without the slightest understanding – just to be on the safe side. Pseudo-bridges are being built now, cardboard bridges that give themselves the appearance of concrete – but when you step on them, they and you crash into the abyss. The new method of positive incomprehension has even affected the older critics who, paradoxically, *are now far more tolerant towards the latest non-sense than they were towards the latest sense twenty years ago.*[9]

It was thus that Hans made a powerful contribution to the forming of essential discriminations about the music by which we were besieged in the 1950s and 1960s – random music, chance music, and the rest, so much of which now is as dead as yesterday's *Daily Telegraph*.

One might think that this radical scepticism about many of the manifestations of the 'new' music in the 1950s and 1960s reflected Hans's conservatism, and one would be right – the best side of it, one ought to add. His orthodoxies were founded on the primacy of the ear. This same scepticism led to a famous scandal in 1961, the 'Piotr Zak' affair, a jape perpetrated by Hans with the assistance of Susan Bradshaw, when he was employed by the BBC. Hans, very typically, wanted to prove his point about critics falling headlong into the trap which I have mentioned: the sense of a historically determined duty to be abreast of the times which anaesthetized their ears and prevented them from distinguishing between what was music and what was, in Hans's view, demonstrably not. So, with his accomplice, Hans darted about a studio in which a fair number of percussion instruments were conveniently housed, and recorded what they were randomly, exuberantly and mischievously 'creating' – a bang here, a crash there, *crescendos* and *diminuendos*, strokes, rolls and general clatter: this was the time of liberated percussion, when exclusively percussion pieces were in vogue. The concoction was given a convincing title and a pedigree, attributed to Piotr Zak, and put out on the Third Programme as a first broadcast in a concert of contemporary music.

When the hoax was made known, the consequences were more percussive than anything Zak could have imagined. Hans was accused of double-crossing the critics and abusing his position at the BBC. I don't think he felt the slightest bit guilty on either count. Some day someone ought to research the Zak affair systematically and document the reactions of those who wrote about this significant première in the press the next day.[10] Some were caught out, some wobbled, some were rightly dismissive. Christopher Wintle, in the Memorial Symposium, writes that Zak's *Mobile* was 'not received with much enthusiasm'. On the other hand, Milton Babbitt, who seems to have been offended by the whole enterprise, suggests that the Keller–Bradshaw creation 'apparently was greeted with mainly enthusiastic reviews'. My own impression was that the reviews were, in tone, negative rather than positive. No one, however, realized that it had been a hoax. The whole rumpus proved in the end somewhat inconclusive. In short (as Hans might say), there were too many cards stacked against auditors who *in other circumstances* might have rumbled what was afoot. The 'performance' was put out with the backing and authority of the BBC, its authenticity guaranteed by the billing in the *Radio Times*, the announcer's presentation. There was no excuse for those who took the work seriously, but it is difficult to blame those who wrote about the piece as if it had been composed, was 'real', however bad and empty. How could it have been otherwise? So strong were the factors conditioning the way listeners heard the piece that it was useless, in my view, as an experiment. But it was a characteristic bit of bravura on Hans's part and the intention was serious. It might have been deadly if it had been differently circumstanced – as an anonymous wine-tasting, say, with a bottle of Zak introduced among the respectable beverages. But perhaps less fun.

While one may criticize the format of the Zak affair, the position Hans adopted with regard to this particular and modish eruption of non-music seems to me to have been impregnable and valuably corrective. I think his touch was a shade less certain in regard to earlier – and indeed major – manifestations of the 'new'.

Stravinsky, I have already suggested, was a case in point. His unease about that composer showed up, by the way, in the Symposium we jointly edited on Britten in 1952. Stravinsky received short shrift there – something for which William Glock, in a broadcast review, justly took us to task. This at times thinly veiled hostility gave rise to one of Hans's many *bons mots*: a devastating (and I now think wrong-headed) dismissal of *The Rake's Progress* – the culmination of Stravinsky's neo-classical period – as the result of 'a process less allied to composition than to stamp-collecting'.

If I went along with that at the time, it was because my ignorance of Stravinsky equalled Hans's antipathy. But in later, wiser and more knowledgeable years, I came to comprehend the opera as the masterpiece it is. And when Hans and I were revising our old Symposium for a reprint many years later, I shyly suggested (as Hans might have said) that we should take the opportunity to revise our views, of Stravinsky in particular. But he would have none of it. It was not for the Hans Keller of 1971 to criticize the views of the Hans Keller of 1952 who was no longer around to stand up for himself – which rather neatly left on one side the formulation of what those later views might be.

Identical with those of 1952 would be my guess. His important introduction to Milein Cosman's sketchbook, *Stravinsky at Rehearsal*,[11] significantly concentrates on the psychological motivation of the composer's serial 'conversion' in works written after 1952, though it does include unusual and unqualified praise of the *Symphony of Psalms* – 'a spotless and gigantic masterpiece, where identifications with the past span a wide field'. Just so. But in that case, why not rehabilitate *The Rake's Progress*?

There was on occasion an inflexibility in Hans, as if once having committed himself to an opinion, he was stuck with it for ever. The opinions, the ideas, without question, were extraordinarily powerful and arresting, with an influence out of all proportion to their number. Hans, it seems to me, worked his ideas extremely hard. But they were brilliant, fundamental perceptions which he continually repolished and refined and recapitulated in new contexts, and in their very narrowness was their strength. One may regret that the field was not wider – but it meant that Hans was writing only about what he himself felt he fully understood.

This last point Hans was to make again and again in his writings. Indeed, it was a point he made against other critics, whose adverse criticism he attributed, often rightly, to a lack of basic understanding of what they were reporting on. (I think it was much the same point that Erwin Stein used to make in suggesting that where there was no sympathy there could be no worthwhile criticism.) Hans makes another statement on the subject on the very last page of *Criticism*:

> Every single reader, one or two soft-boiled critics apart, will be able to think of at least one distinguished critic who would have deserved a top salary, and a relaxing pension, for remaining silent all his life. Once again, I speak with the corroboration of personal experience: the noblest critical achievements of my life were the moments when I decided to shut up, temporarily or, as in the case of most of the music of Debussy, Delius and Sibelius, for ever. The amount of nonsense I have thus not committed to print, the violence and posthumous torture which has remained unpractised, would have made me a serious rival of the most highly esteemed members of the profession if all those pseudo-thoughts, those thin rationalizations of incomprehension, had been allowed an outlet.

A characteristic if somewhat tortuous formulation, but I must confess these days to serious misgivings about the adequacy of it as a response to certain composers. It may well not matter too much, or at all, if one does not understand composer A or composer B, and it will certainly be to everyone's gain if one refrains from writing about them. Hans lists Debussy among his exclusions (and Alexander Goehr, in the Memorial Symposium, adds Monteverdi, Musorgsky and Messiaen). But is it good enough, I wonder, when a composer, such as Debussy, is so central to the whole history and evolution of twentieth-century music, simply to respond, in effect: 'no understanding: no comment'? If he were about, I should put it to Hans that there is a handful of composers where one has a positive duty to understand their work and if necessary to write about it, to evaluate it, whatever one's doubts and shortcomings. The Stravinsky of the early decades of the century, and Debussy – these seem to me to be two blank patches at the very centre of the brilliant lens which Hans brought to bear on the music of our century.

Perhaps, too, there is a suspicion – unworthy? – that bound up with Hans's self-denying ordinance was a distinct cultural bias. Gallic music, Gallic culture generally, was not his scene. I have referred earlier to his conservatism, and surely part of the abstention from Debussy had its roots in an Austro-German tradition that found it difficult to recognize any other, or at least feel comfortable with it. One shouldn't hold Hans to things said in front of the TV camera that he might have modified or qualified or edited out if he had been alive when the film was finally assembled. I refer to the Channel 4 obituary, significant stretches of which struck me as being everything that Hans was not: pompous, pretentious, posturing (and occasionally inaccurate). Hans was not a boy wonder who became a prophet or cosmic ombudsman. He was an intensely human human being, often very funny, and on occasion – and like the rest of us – endearingly innocent about himself. This showed up in the film in a memorable flash in which Hans was giving an account of his musical education – an orthodox one, naturally – as a child in Vienna. His mother and family friends made an inspiring contribution: the domestic, chamber-musical experience was undeniably critical to his musical evolution. 'By the age of ten,' he concluded, 'I knew all music.' *All* music? It's not scoring a flippant point if I suggest that that slip of the tongue tells us a good deal about Hans and about the soil from which he sprang.

It was this very innocence that adversaries often misunderstood as arrogance. It enabled him to make those breathtaking claims which, if they fell from other lips, one would react against vehemently. In Hans's case, the impact certainly made one draw breath – but then one was jolted into thinking.

To this same part of his personality I attribute his claim to have conducted a self-analysis. I don't mean for a moment to suggest that this was a false claim, but the result of it was in some ways odd. How was it possible that someone as knowing as Hans, and as knowledgeable about others, could from time to time seem to know so little about himself? And yet one also realizes that if for Hans there were to be any analysis at all, it would have had to be self-analysis. Can anyone imagine him submitting himself to – for – analysis? I can't. He was the most independent person I've ever met, and I cannot see how anyone so resistant to submission could ever have managed a relationship with an analyst, in which some element of submission is inescapable.

As for Hans's own strictly psychoanalytical studies, there was a number of published professional pieces which the Memorial Symposium usefully lists. During the *Music Survey* years Hans talked more than once about projects on which he was collaborating with a psychologist, Margaret Phillips. Did one of them have something to do with prostitution? I remember sitting late at night after a concert in one of those pavement coffee-houses in Mayfair that were popular in London in the 1950s and observing that the business conducted next door was of quite another order. The sight of one of the ladies entering the house prompted Hans to tell me something about the investigation he and his colleague had undertaken. I wish I could claim that the lady who triggered off this conversation had proved to be an interviewee! None the less, the vivid memory I have of an occasion that was peculiarly Viennese in its ingredients – a heady mixture of coffee-house, prostitution and psychological probing (Schnitzler, perhaps?) – was gloriously confirmed by at least one of the unpublished essays from this period based on interviews and found among Hans's papers after his death: 'Prostitutes wear marriage rings.'

Hans would occasionally clasp his head in his hands and give vent to a half-mocking cry of despair: 'Oh God!' The image comes to mind when I think of Hans and football and my inability to say anything about it at all. I feel strongly inclined to shelter behind Hans's own injunction: shut up when you don't know what you're talking about. I can't, of course, and confess to perceiving a gross disproportion between the skilled attention Hans gave soccer and the skills the game brings into play. Why didn't Hans grow out of this surely adolescent enthusiasm?[12]

Hans would have much deplored my saying that, so let me make amends by acknowledging what we owe to his not growing out of certain musical enthusiasms which belonged to his youth and stayed with him for ever. There cannot be a single friend of his who was not, very early on, made aware of his belief that the 'only' violin concerto – I exaggerate, but not much – was Mendelssohn's: and so it is unsurprising from one point of view that a completed monograph on the work was discovered among Hans's papers after his death and awaits publication. Unsurprising, but also mysterious. There is something strange and strangely selfless about Hans bringing these books to completion in manuscript and then abstaining – or so it would appear – from pursuing their publication. Other, more immediate concerns may have intervened – teaching, topical articles and commentaries, his failing health – but even so, how puzzling not to have taken the next step with regard to these major enterprises. It is almost as if he felt that his responsibility was discharged once he had got his thoughts down on paper, and that ours – to attend to the more mundane business of publication – began where his ended. I don't think anyone could deny that Hans's ego was a forceful one, but it seemingly did not impose itself in those very areas of ego-assertion peculiar to authors. Can one think of a like case of a writer detaching himself from the business of disseminating his thoughts? There was something inspiringly unworldly about Hans. Perhaps part of this same extraordinary selfless detachment was also to be found in his indifference to possessions, to money (uncashed cheques surfaced among his papers, along with his unpublished manuscripts), to all the trappings and trivialities of status. He cared for none of them.

In other areas Hans could and did assert his ego to uncomfortable effect. He was not, I think, quarrelsome, but there were occasions when he would pick up a topic on which he knew his audience held a different view and hammer away at it to excess. I was sorry that this seemed to have happened on the only occasion Britten and Pears visited him at home, for dinner – I recall that Deryck Cooke was another guest. It would scarcely be worth mentioning here but for the fact that Hans quite often referred to the incident himself (and does so again in *Criticism*). It appears that Britten and Pears left the dinner party somewhat abruptly. The cause of the trouble, I believe, was Hans's conviction that Britten was too bland in his social relationships, too conventional, too consistently polite, only rarely spoke his mind, would not open up. Hans had very little patience with social graces and rituals and was determined to break through the mask which he assumed Britten habitually wore. The dispute that developed was not a musical one, but focused on Britten's strongly held pacifist attitudes and the 1967 Middle East conflict. Nothing came of it, other than Britten's and Pears's hasty exit. Hans took this to confirm his suspicion of Britten's mannered manners. On Britten's side, there remained a slightly bruised, even bewildered feeling. It seemed not to occur to Hans that guests whom one had invited to dinner might not expect a drubbing for their views. In any event, outwardly conventional or not, Britten discounted his bruises and came to dedicate his third and last string quartet to Hans, which says perhaps everything that needs to be said about a relationship that was always happiest when embodied in notes rather than words.

The Britten incident indicates that a little bending might have eased an awkward social situation. But to bend was not Hans's way. And ultimately, the implacable will had a powerful functional role to play (as Hans himself might have said). Did he not decline to bend – to submit – to death, even to the point of resolutely not acknowledging that he was mortally ill? Death might – and did – take him, but he would not surrender. This made for discomfort and unease. But it was a heroic, epic performance on Hans's part and an entirely characteristic one, though I profoundly wish that he had not had to play it.

I wept when I heard the news of his death. He was so much part of my life, of the way I thought, and think, that I still find it difficult to accept his death. He was by far the most important and original music critic of his day, though he would have disdained the title. I loved him. I shall never forget him.

NOTES

1 MC: Luigi Dallapiccola, 'Notes on the Statue Scene in *Don Giovanni*', *Music Survey* 3/2 (December 1950), pp. 89–97. Dallapiccola's text was translated from the original Italian by Deryck Cooke.
2 MC: Marion Thorpe (ed.), *Peter Pears: A Tribute on his 75th Birthday* (Faber and Faber, London, 1985), pp. 50–51.
3 MC: Hans Keller, *The Great Haydn Quartets: Their Interpretation* (Dent, London, 1986). The volume appeared shortly after Keller's death.
4 MC: Ibid., pp. 157–8.
5 MC: Ibid., p. 123.
6 MC: Ibid., p. 23.
7 MC: *Music Analysis* 5:2–3 (1986).
8 MC: Hans Keller, *Criticism*, edited by Julian Hogg (Faber and Faber, London, 1987).
9 MC: Ibid., p. 36.
10 MC: DM reviewed the 'work' for the *Daily Telegraph*: see p. XXII. See also Christopher Wintle (ed.), *Hans Keller: Essays on Music* (Cambridge University Press, Cambridge, 1994), p. XVII.
11 MC: Milein Cosman and Hans Keller, *Stravinsky at Rehearsal* (Dobson, London, 1962).
12 MC: For Keller's own account of his footballing interests, see *1975 (1984 minus 9)* (Dobson, London, 1977), pp. 270–88.

Britten and Pears: A Double Portrait

Edinburgh, 3 May 1971 I am starting to write this double profile (a daunting task: I wish I were a painter rather than a writer) in a hotel room in Edinburgh where I'm waiting for B.B. and P.P. to arrive, while that peculiarly golden evening sunshine which sometimes engulfs Edinburgh pours in through my window and over the characteristic green and black of the garden and houses beyond. They are driving over this evening, after an afternoon's rehearsal at an old friend's house outside Edinburgh, to spend the night before tomorrow's concert, a lunchtime recital at Edinburgh's National Gallery in memory of Tertia Liebenthal, who died last year. The programme is going to include, besides Purcell and Schubert, an important Britten première, the first complete performance of his most recent song-cycle, *Who are these children?*, settings of poems by William Soutar, the little-known Scottish poet who died in 1943. So tomorrow we shall be seeing B.B. in action in those two roles – as composer, and as Peter's partner, collaborator and co-creator – which for many years now have been the two 'faces' which the public has come to admire in so many outstanding performances.

I sit up on my bed scribbling, and wonder how tomorrow will unfold. Few people have an inkling of the kind of stress and strain to which working artists, however eminent and experienced, are subjected – to which they subject themselves. Of course, that is

---

Ronald Blythe (ed.), *Aldeburgh Anthology* (Snape Maltings Foundation in association with Faber Music, London, 1972), pp. 431–7

what is involved in being totally serious and committed, which is the hallmark of a recital by P.P. and B.B. They themselves may be satisfied or dissatisfied with what they achieve, but the premiss from which they set out is always uncompromisingly the same, as is their aim: to serve the art of music, above all to release the composer's voice – whether it be Schubert's or Percy Grainger's, Purcell's or Schumann's – and let it speak to their audience as if it were indeed the absent composer himself who was transformed into a tenor voice or seated at the piano. This is why I have always thought that recitals by P.P. and B.B. must be any composer's dream: because the performers in fact are *composer*-oriented, not *performer*-oriented. No doubt tomorrow's recital will prove to be just such an event.

Before I rouse myself to go and see if they have arrived I must jot down one memory that always comes to mind when I am thinking of B.B.'s and P.P.'s commitment, their dedication to the notes. We are aloft (in October 1969), somewhere between New York and Boston, amidst the juddering internal plastic splendour of Eastern Airlines (greenery-yallery with a vengeance, if I remember rightly). The 'shuttle' as it's called takes less than an hour, so there's scarcely time to settle down to a good read, though I make some progress with a remarkable short story by Thomas Hardy which Ben has drawn to my attention ('An Imaginative Woman'). *I* read, but B.B. and P.P. are already thinking of tomorrow's recital. One of the songs they performed with great success in New York was that inspired folksong setting of Percy Grainger's, 'Bold William Taylor', but P.P. has found it by no means easy to memorize and is still not sure that he has got it right. The exuberant Grainger makes it difficult for the singer by ingeniously avoiding uniformly regular entries for the voice: there's a beat missing where one expects to count one, and one added when one doesn't expect it.

Up comes B.B.'s briefcase on to his knees, to form an improvised dumb keyboard, and his long, delicately shaped but strong fingers tap out P.G.'s rhythmic patterns on the bulging leather surface. At his side, *sotto sotto voce*, Peter sings the song over. Now and again they stop and patiently go over a tricky entry, then continue. A remarkable and entrancing performance, this! Much finger-tapping and head-wagging from B.B., and semi-soundless, under-the-breath singing from P.P. Heaven knows what the commuting gentlemen returning to their businesses in Boston made of it all, but when, next evening, P.P. sings 'Bold William Taylor', everything is exactly in place – or rather, exactly out of place. The mid-air rehearsal had done the trick.

5 May Yesterday's recital was certainly greatly enjoyed by me and by the audience packed into the rather small gallery, richly hung with splendid paintings. Backstage, conditions somewhat cramped (doors to be locked and unlocked for a visit to the lavatory, which reminds one of the security arrangements that complicate concert-giving in the midst of a substantial national art collection), and the piano a challenge to B.B.'s pacifying, mitigating, modifying fingers, which somehow manage to summon up the substance of a ravishing tone[1] even when, mechanically speaking, or so one imagines, the instrument has long ago given up the ghost. B.B. achieves a minor resurrection, but certainly the piano can't have helped the wear and tear on his nerves.

One almost writes the 'usual' wear and tear, but that would sound callous and also hardly convey the epic nature of the pre-performance tensions to which B.B. is subjected. I don't think many people are aware of this side of his performing life: on the platform it all seems to come marvellously easily to him. It is true, indeed, that on the platform the nerves largely subside and his musical sensibility fills their place, though without displacing the fine nervousness which is a feature of B.B.'s accompanying and of his interpretations in general – something quite distinct from the nerviness that can assail him before he becomes wholly engaged in the business of making music. After the recital or the concert is over, it's a different story. There's the relief that it's done, enjoyment of the music, and praise for P.P.'s performance. To most compliments on his own performance Ben replies, 'Well, it's a glorious *piece*, isn't it?', thus cunningly deflecting the tribute. The tribulations and anxieties that constitute the overture to a recital are real enough, but I believe the compensating factors – the music itself and the insights P.P. brings to his performances – eventually come to outweigh the preparatory attacks of nerves. I believe B.B. himself might agree with this last statement, though only *after* a concert.

This digression has led me away from the concert itself, which opens with a Purcell *Hymn* (an *in memoriam* for Tertia Liebenthal), continues with a group of Schubert, and ends with the Soutar set, Op. 84. I have heard excerpts and sequences of the Soutar songs at the morning rehearsal – not a complete run-through, but rather a look at those songs and those parts of songs that require a warming up. How striking it is at the rehearsal that, despite B.B.'s pre-concert nerves, he is absolutely calm in support of Peter, the singer, only anxious to give him the support he needs and to fulfil his precise musical needs. This is 'accompanying' on an exalted level, professionalism carried to the *n*th degree. Indeed, when one sees these two great artists in rehearsal, neither of them so much conscious of himself as of the composer they are bent on serving, one catches a glimpse of the unique professional understanding that forms the core of their celebrated partnership and which, miraculously, has seen it through decades of ill-tempered claviers, unwanted cocktail parties, inadequate or downright hostile acoustics, exacting audiences, exhausting travel, alarming partners at inescapable formal dinners, and all the other perils associated with a strenuous concert life.

During the actual performance of the Soutar songs I am astonished, not so much by the calibre of the cycle, which I had guessed from the rehearsal and from earlier study of the music, but by P.P.'s projection of this complicated work, which one could never have imagined from the preliminary, partial rehearsal. It was amazing, this sudden opening up of impressive reserves of vocal power and the revealing of a masterly grasp of the total shape of the work. The dramatic span of the cycle was unfolded with complete authority. This taught me anew a lesson that is of profound importance: that the art of the performer lies in just this capacity *to produce a performance* at the right moment, not the day before or in rehearsal some hours before, but at that arbitrary moment which we designate a 'recital', 'concert', or what you will, and during which we expect something eventful to materialize. Magic has to be heard to be done, whether the time for the artists is propitious or not; and it was precisely the magic touch which those of us present at this Edinburgh recital recognized in P.P.'s launching of the Soutar songs.

Needless to add, neither B.B. nor P.P. was as elated by the performance of the cycle as I was. 'We'll get it better' was about Ben's only comment. I think, though, that he was pleased to sense for himself that the cycle did work as a whole (there's been a good deal of shuffling round of the cards that go to make up this particular pack) and felt too that this performance was a useful step towards the ideal performance at which they are aiming. B.B. was full of praise for the way in which Peter had 'brought it off', less full of praise for his own share in the proceedings. Small wonder, when one sees the kind of problem set for B.B. the pianist by B.B. the composer, e.g. the fiendishly difficult canonic accompaniment of 'Slaughter'. I notice, however, that despite the difficulty (the equivalent of tongue-twisting for the fingers, whatever that may be), B.B. the composer shows no sign of intending to help out B.B. the pianist by moderating the passage in question. (If Ben can't play it, I wonder to myself, who on earth can?)

As for P.P., who needless to add has problems enough on his own account in this cycle (the unmeasured freedom of B.B.'s recent vocal writing introduces its own complications), what struck me afresh at Edinburgh was his unique dramatic gift, his capacity to uncover the inner drama of a work and make it tangible, almost. There's no doubt to my mind that this ability to 'act' with his voice has its roots in the fact that P.P. is a conspicuously gifted actor in the conventional sense of the word. Who could forget his noble performance as the old king in Mozart's *Idomeneo* at the rebuilt Maltings? This was not only beautifully sung but also a commanding dramatic impersonation. It was in fact distinguished by the continuous relationship P.P. achieved between his stage actions (whether a glance, gesture or posture) and his vocal 'acting' (whether the articulation of a crucial phrase, the shading of a dynamic or the finding of the appropriate colour of tone). Stage gestures and musical gestures were precisely dovetailed; and it is surely this synthesis which is a major contribution P.P. has made to the musical theatre in our day. (All this reminds me of a fascinating remark of B.B.'s: that a sympathetic and co-operative producer was an absolute necessity for him because, when writing his music for the theatre, he often imagined, even down to the smallest detail, the kind of physical movement or action that should accompany it; and he found it distressing when a producer ignored or contradicted the movement implied by the music.)

I remember as I write this an amusing instance of P.P.'s gift for impersonation. I don't expect I'm alone in recalling in detail his portrayal of Nebuchadnezzar in *The Burning Fiery Furnace*. A memorable impersonation this, which included the splendid miming of P.P. in the Babylonian feast, which the small boys later satirize. He brought to a very fine art indeed his simulated munching and drinking, above all the plucking of the imagined grapes from the imagined bunches, each grape held fastidiously between finger and thumb, appraised and fastidiously gobbled.

This scene was astonishingly evoked one night in New York (an improbable setting), when B.B., P.P., Sue [Phipps], Kathleen and I were taken off to a Japanese restaurant by our generous New York friend, Laton Holmgren, who was not only a kind host but impressed us all by ordering our dinner in immaculate Japanese. The occasion was further distinguished by the unwelcome fact that P.P. was suffering from a catastrophic throat, had lost his voice and had been obliged to postpone his first New York recital. He had been ordered by his doctor to rest his voice, and I have still a vivid picture of him sitting at the opposite side of the alarmingly hot table on which the food was strewn, thence to be cooked under our noses, wrapped almost up to his ears in a long muffler (a bizarre touch, this) and obediently observing his vow of silence.

We had here of course a special combination of circumstances: an explicit link with Japan (shades of the Noh play!), a feast of no less than Babylonian proportions, and a compulsory silence which made mime a convenient substitute for speech. At any rate, the next time I looked across at P.P. I was amazed to find that he had vanished and Nebuchadnezzar sat in his place, going through his Babylonian gobbling routine with inimitable verve, plucking food out of the air, and consuming it with evident satisfaction, much to the mystification of the New Yorkers by whom we were surrounded. It was not a long display but I think we were all transported back to Suffolk and Orford Church in a matter of seconds; and I remember it struck me at the time that this brilliant bit of impromptu stage business only went to show how P.P. carries the art of impersonation around with him at his very fingertips.

That entertaining incident was an example of the attention to detail which is certainly one of the keys to P.P.'s vivid stage presence; and one might think that a passionate concern for detail is characteristic of the approach of P.P. and B.B. to their manifold activities, to the multiple lives they seem to lead.

I think of the kind of attention P.P. pays to Festival exhibitions, not only organizing them in the most basic sense (i.e. tirelessly driving round the country to collect the paintings from obliging owners), but also supervising and directing the hanging (and a good exhibition has to *look* as good as a good performance *sounds*) and preparing the catalogue. It is, in fact, just this pervasive care for detail, bearing the impress of B.B.'s and P.P.'s personalities, that is surely one of the unique qualities of the Aldeburgh Festival and associated events at the Maltings. It seems perfectly logical and consistent to me to discuss all these topics in the context of a performance, because it is just the same care, passion for detail and insistence on 'getting things right' – something wholly different from the merely tidy or pedantically correct – that we experience in P.P.'s and B.B.'s music-making.

B.B., like P.P., has this same inexhaustible energy which extends to whole ranges of details that in my more innocent days I should never have imagined that he would have wanted to bother about. But I think that there can be no partial involvement for B.B., at least in those things that matter to him. It is either total immersion or nothing. I well remember once surveying the Maltings with him when the hall was first being built and was still in a pretty skeletal shape. I was amazed by the account he gave me as we stood overlooking the busy site, an account of the building as it was to be in which his interest extended to the very last detail, even (I recall) to the colour of the external guttering. Yes, it was essential to get it – the colour – right. It was a bit like – no, it was precisely like – a composer talking about a composition, not yet fully sketched out, but all the details of which, even the most minute, were already clear and established in his mind. The Maltings, when it was built, matched up to that detailed account which B.B. had given me; and I realized that this was yet another aspect of his fierce mental energy, a capacity to dream detailed dreams and to make them come true, in detail.

Magic! one might exclaim, and rightly, because there is a magical aspect of B.B.'s personality, that whole area from which his music emerges. Sometimes there's so much emphasis given to one prominent feature of B.B.'s outward image – his practical, no-nonsense, energetic and self-effacing approach to the business of making music (in every sense associated with the phrase) – that it is easy to forget the inner nature of his art. Of course, the moment we hear his music we are reminded of the intense 'other' life that this exceptional man lives, a world profoundly different from the everyday world in which we, as colleagues, or friends, customarily meet him. Those who are close to his art know that at the centre of his music there is an intensely solitary and private spirit, a troubled, sometimes even despairing visionary, an artist much haunted by nocturnal imagery, by sleep, by presentiments of mortality, a creator preternaturally aware of the destructive appetite (the ever hungry beast in the jungle) that feeds on innocence, virtue and grace. All this is, as it were, a B.B. contained *within* the B.B. who is the eminently practical, rational man, the most professional of colleagues and also the kindest and most generous of friends. But that other B.B. is there all the time; and sometimes I think the B.B. one thinks one is talking to or walking beside is actually somewhere else, because for a moment that other world has carried him off. For which reason, however much time I spend with B.B., talking, walking or working, my sense of wonder does not diminish. Though one may know B.B. well on one level, there are other levels where one can in fact only know him through his music. There, of course, one finds B.B.'s own self-portrait, the best likeness one could hope to find; and where Ben's music begins, my words must stop.

NOTE

1 As Peter Pears memorably recalled in *The Tenor Man's Story* (DM and Barrie Gavin, Central Television, 1985):

> Ben somehow had a command over the keyboard with his fingers which came – flashed like lightning – from his very being. But it was amazing what colours he could get. He thought a colour and could do it.

SOURCES

The author, compiler and editor gratefully acknowledge the sources of the original publication of the texts that make up this volume: Aldeburgh Festival (public forum, 11 June 1993); BBC Promenade Concerts Programme Book (1981) and concert programme (22 August 1981); BBC Records (sleeve-note); BBC Script Library; BBC Written Archives Centre; *Chesterian*; *Daily Telegraph*; Decca Records (sleeve-note); Faber and Faber; Glyndebourne Festival Programme Book (1986); *Listener*; *London Magazine*; *London Review of Books*; *Maggio Musicale Fiorentino* Programme Book (1988); *Music & Letters*; *Music Review*; *Music Survey*; *Musical Opinion*; *Musical Quarterly*; *Musical Times*; 'Musikwoche in memoriam Gustav Mahler', Toblach (1986); *Newslink* (Faber); Queen Elizabeth Hall concert programme (21 October 1986); Royal Opera House Covent Garden Programme Book (December 1989); Snape Maltings Foundation/Faber Music; *Tempo*; *The Times Literary Supplement*; Tokyo Summer Festival (1988); University of Sussex.

Further thanks are due for permission to reproduce musical examples from works by Malcolm Arnold, Paterson's Publications Ltd (*Sinfonietta* No. 1; Symphonies Nos. 2, 3 and 5; *Divertimento*, Op. 37; Flute Concerto No. 1; *Homage to the Queen*; Oboe Concerto; *Three Shanties*) and Faber Music Ltd (Concerto for 2 Pianos (3 hands); *Four Cornish Dances*); from *Lulu* by Alban Berg, Universal Edition, Vienna and London; from *Curlew River* and *Owen Wingrave* by Benjamin Britten, Faber Music Ltd, and for examples from 'Now sleeps the crimson petal', *Albert Herring*, *Billy Budd*, *The Turn of the Screw* and *Nocturne*, Boosey & Hawkes (Music Publishers) Ltd.

Every effort has been made to trace and acknowledge the sources of the texts. Should any sources have been overlooked or misattributed, the editor apologizes and asks to be informed, so that amends can be made in any future edition.

D.M., C.P., M.C.

Index

Note: References and sources are indexed only when additional comment is made in the text.